A
TAN AND SANDY
SILENCE
and TWO OTHER
GREAT MYSTERIES

Books by JOHN D. MacDONALD

ALL THESE CONDEMNED · APRIL EVIL
AREA OF SUSPICION · BALLROOM OF THE SKIES
THE BEACH GIRLS · BORDER TOWN GIRL
THE BRASS CUPCAKE · A BULLET FOR CINDERELLA
CANCEL ALL OUR VOWS · CLEMMIE · CONDOMINIUM
CONTRARY PLEASURE · THE CROSSROADS
CRY HARD, CRY FAST · THE DAMNED
DEAD LOW TIDE · DEADLY WELCOME · DEATH TRAP
THE DECEIVERS · THE DROWNER
THE EMPTY TRAP · THE END OF THE NIGHT
END OF THE TIGER AND OTHER STORIES
THE EXECUTIONERS · A FLASH OF GREEN
THE GIRL, THE GOLD WATCH & EVERYTHING
THE HOUSE GUESTS
JUDGE ME NOT · A KEY TO THE SUITE
THE LAST ONE LEFT · A MAN OF AFFAIRS
MURDER FOR THE BRIDE · MURDER IN THE WIND
THE NEON JUNGLE · NO DEADLY DRUG
ONE MONDAY WE KILLED THEM ALL · ON THE RUN
THE ONLY GIRL IN THE GAME
PLEASE WRITE FOR DETAILS
THE PRICE OF MURDER
SEVEN · SLAM THE BIG DOOR
SOFT TOUCH · WHERE IS JANICE GANTRY?
WINE OF THE DREAMERS · YOU LIVE ONCE

The Travis McGee Series

THE DEEP BLUE GOOD-BY · NIGHTMARE IN PINK
A PURPLE PLACE FOR DYING · THE QUICK RED FOX
A DEADLY SHADE OF GOLD
BRIGHT ORANGE FOR THE SHROUD
DARKER THAN AMBER——
ONE FEARFUL YELLOW EYE ——
PALE GRAY FOR GUILT
THE GIRL IN THE PLAIN BROWN WRAPPER
DRESS HER IN INDIGO
THE LONG LAVENDER LOOK
TAN AND SANDY SILENCE · THE SCARLET RUSE
THE TURQUOISE LAMENT
THE DREADFUL LEMON SKY
THE EMPTY COPPER SEA

JOHN D. MacDONALD

A TAN AND SANDY SILENCE

and TWO OTHER GREAT MYSTERIES

J. B. LIPPINCOTT COMPANY
Philadelphia and New York

contents

A Tan and Sandy Silence

To all the faithful readers
at the North Vancouver City Library

In northern Manitoba
a man saw a great bald eagle—
hanging from its neck,
teeth locked in skin and feathers,
the bleached skull of a weasel.

—*Jim Harrison*
"A Year's Changes"

one

On the most beautiful day any April could be asked to come up with, I was kneeling in eight inches of oily water in the cramped bilge of Meyer's squatty little cabin cruiser, the *John Maynard Keynes*, taking his automatic bilge pump apart for the third time in an hour.

The socket wrench slipped, and I skinned yet another knuckle. Meyer stood blocking out a sizable piece of the deep blue sky. He stared down into the bilge and said, "Very inventive and very fluent. Nice mental images, Travis. Imagine one frail little bilge pump performing such an extraordinary act upon itself! But you began to repeat yourself toward the end."

"Would you like to crawl down in here and—"

He backed up a hasty half step. "I couldn't deprive you of the pleasure. You said you could fix it. Go ahead."

I got it apart again. I spun the little impeller blade and suddenly realized that maybe it turned too freely. Found the setscrew would take a full turn. Tightened it back down onto the shaft. Reassembled the crummy little monster, bolted it down underwater, heaved myself up out of the water, sat on the edge of the hatch, and had Meyer flip the switch. It started to make a nice steady *wheeeeeeng*, gouting dirty bilge water into the Bahia Mar yacht basin.

Meyer started to applaud, and I told him to save it until we found out if the adorable thing would turn itself the hell off like it says in the fine print. It took a good ten minutes to pump the water out. Then it went *weeeeeeng-guggle-chud*. Silence.

"Now cheer," I said.

"Hooray," he said mildly. "Thank you very much and hooray." I looked at him with exasperation and affection. My mild and bulky friend with the wise little blue eyes, bright and bemused, and with the bear hair, thatch black, curling out of the throat of his blue knit shirt.

"Another half inch of rain last night," I told him, "and you could have gone down like a stone."

He had stepped out of his bunk in the dark after the rain stopped and into ankle-deep water. He had sloshed over to my houseboat, *The Busted Flush*, and told me he had a small problem. At three in the morning we had toted my auxiliary pump over and set it on the dock and dropped the intake hose into his bilge. His home and refuge was very low in the water, the mooring lines taut enough to hum when plucked. By first light the *Keynes* was floating high again, and we could turn the pump off and carry it back. Now the repaired automatic bilge pump had taken out the last of the water, but he was going to live in dampness for quite a while.

"Perils of the sea," he said.

I stepped up onto the dock and squatted and began to rinse the grease and bilge water off my hands under the hose faucet. Meyer shaded his eyes and looked toward the *Flush*. "You've got a visitor, Travis. Isn't that what's-his-name?"

I stood up and stared. "It sure is. Good old what's-his-name. Harry Broll. Do you think that son of a bitch has come to try me again?"

"After the showing last time . . . was it two years ago?"

"At least."

"I think he's at least bright enough not to try again."

"Not the same way. But he did catch me with one very nice left. True, he broke his hand, but it was one to remember."

"Want company?

"No, thanks."

Harry turned and saw me when I was about fifty feet away. He was big, and he had gotten bigger since I'd seen him last. More gut and more jowls. Not becoming. He wore a pale beige suit, a yellow shirt, and a chocolate-colored neckerchief with an ornate gold slip ring.

He raised his hands in the most primitive gesture of reassurance.

Palms out. Sickly smile to go with it. As I came up to him, he said, "Hi, McGee." He put his hand out. I looked at it until he pulled it back. He tried to laugh. "Jesus, are you still sore?"

"I'm not sore, Harry. Why should we shake hands?"

"Look. I want to talk to you. Are you busy or anything?"

"What about?"

"About Mary. I know you've got no reason in the world to do me any favors. But this concerns . . . Mary's well-being."

"Is something wrong with her?"

"I don't know. I don't really know."

I studied him. He seemed concerned and upset. He had the pallor of desk work. His black hair had receded since I had seen him last. He said, "I couldn't think of anybody else to come to. I can say please if it'll help. Please?"

"Come on aboard."

"Thanks. Thanks a lot."

We went into the lounge. I had on an old pair of denim shorts and nothing else. The air conditioning cooled the sweat on my shoulders and chest. He looked around, nodding and beaming, and said, "Nice. Real nice. A nice way to live, huh?"

"Want a drink?"

"Bourbon, if you've got it."

"Got it."

"On the rocks."

I put out the bottle and the glass and said, glancing down at my soiled hands, "Ice is in the bin there. Help yourself while I clean up, Broll."

"Thanks. You sure keep yourself in shape, McGee. Wish I had the time. I guess I better make sure I have the time one of these days."

I shrugged and went forward, dropped the shorts into the hamper, and stepped into the oversized shower, thinking about Mary and wondering about her as I sudsed and scrubbed away the rest of the grime from the repair job. Miss Mary Dillon when I had known her. Then abruptly—maybe too abruptly—Mrs. Harry Broll. When I put my watch back on, I saw that it was nearly four o'clock. Meyer and I were invited for drinks at six aboard the *Jilly III*. I put on fresh slacks, an oyster-white sailcloth sport shirt, my ancient Mexican sandals. On the way back to the lounge I stopped in the galley and put some Plymouth on the rocks.

He was sitting on the yellow couch, and he had lit a small cigar with a white plastic mouthpiece. "It must really be something, being able to just take off any time you feel like it."

I slouched into a chair facing him, took a swallow of my drink, and put it on the coffee table. "You've got a problem, Harry?"

"About that time I made such a damn fool of myself . . ."

"Forget it."

"No. Please. Let me say something about that. Like they say, the first year of marriage is the hardest, right?"

"So they say."

"Well, I knew you and Mary were old friends. I couldn't help knowing that, right? I mean, you and Meyer came to the wedding and all. I wondered how good friends you had been. I couldn't help wondering, but I didn't want to really know. Do you understand?"

"Sure."

"The way it happened, we got into a hassle. It was the first real one we'd had. People shouldn't drink and fight when they're married. They say things they don't want to say. I started saying some pretty ugly things about her and you. You know Mary. She's got a lot of spirit. She took it and took it, and finally she let me have it right between the eyes. I deserved it. She blazed right up at me. She said she'd been cruising with you alone aboard this houseboat, down through the Keys and up the west coast to Tampa Bay, and she'd lived aboard for a month and cooked your food and washed your clothes and slept in your bed, and you were kind and decent and gentle and twice the man I am. So that Sunday afternoon I slammed out of the house and got in the car and came over here to beat on you. I could always handle myself pretty good. I wasn't drunk enough for that to be any excuse. Jesus, I never hit so many arms and elbows and shoulders in my life."

"And the top of my head."

"That's what popped the knuckles. Look. This knuckle is still sort of sunk in. How many times did you hit me? Do you know?"

"Sure I know. Twice."

"Twice," he said dolefully. "Oh, shit."

"I waited until you ran out of steam, Harry. I waited until you got arm weary."

He looked at me in an appraising way. "I wish I'd done more good."

"I had a pair of sore arms. You bruised me up, Harry. And a three-day headache."

"I guess I had to get it out of my system. Do you understand it's still pretty hard for me to come to you to ask for anything?"

"I suppose it might be."

"Mary kept telling me to grow up. Okay. I'm trying to grow up. I'm trying to be a mature, rational human being. Like they say, I've been examining my priorities and my options."

"Good for you. But where do I fit in?"

"Here's what I want you to tell Mary."

"But I—"

"Give me a chance. Okay? Tell her that as soon as the SeaGate project is all set up, I think we ought to get away, just the two of us. A cruise or fly over to Spain, whatever. And tell her that the Canadian girl didn't mean a damn thing to me, that I didn't bring her back down here or ask her down, that she came on her own. And tell her to please get in touch with me so we can talk."

"Hold it! I don't know where Mary is."

His face turned red. "Don't give me such crap. You willing to let me search this houseboat?"

"She isn't here, you damn fool."

"I'll find something of hers. Clothes, lipstick, something."

"Harry. Jesus. Look around all you want."

He settled back in the chair. "Okay. You and Mary knew I'd come here sooner or later. So you haven't been having your fun aboard this boat."

"That's called paranoia, old buddy. When did she leave you?"

"January fifth."

I stared at him in disbelief. "This is the fourteenth day of April. You have a slow reaction time."

"I've been hoping she'd come back or get in touch. Tell her how much I've been hoping. She caught me dead to rights. She went around the house with a face like a stone for nearly two weeks, then when I got home that Tuesday, she'd packed and left. No note, even. I went down the list of her friends and called them. It was humiliating for me."

"I bet."

"Now just one damn minute—"

"What makes you think she'd come to me?"

"I thought about it. I mean, back in January. It seemed like the most likely thing for her to do. I spent a whole weekend hanging around here. You had . . . another friend. So I decided if Mary had come here, she'd found you were busy, gone someplace else."

"She didn't come here, Harry."

"Not right away."

"What is that supposed to mean?"

He leaned forward. "Okay. Where were you at ten o'clock on Friday morning, April second?"

"I haven't the faintest idea."

"You and Mary came off this houseboat at ten that morning, and you went out to the parking lot and got into a white Ford LTD convertible with rental plates. A friend of mine happened to be here and happened to see the two of you get in and drive off. This friend followed you. You went over to the Parkway and turned south toward Miami, and he came back, and he phoned me about it."

"Are you willing to listen a minute? Are you willing to try to listen?"

"All I know is my wife left me and she's sleeping with you, McGee, and I'd like to see you dead."

"The woman I was with is about Mary's height, and her figure is just as good, at least as good as Mary's used to be. Her hair is dark like Mary's. The woman is an old friend. That's her rental convertible, and it's still out there on the lot. With her hair in a scarf and dark glasses, she was all prepared for a trip in an open car. She's here aboard her boat. Her name is Jillian Brent-Archer. I haven't seen Mary since the wedding. Not once, Broll. And that was better than three years ago."

He looked at me. "You're real cute, McGee. Jesus, you're cute. Most of the damn fools in this world would believe you. Are you going to tell Mary what I told you to tell her, what I've begged you to tell her?"

"How can I, when I don't even know . . . ?"

And the dumb little weapon came out from under his clothes somewhere, maybe from the waist area, wedged between the belt and the flab. A dumb little automatic pistol in blued steel, half-swallowed in his big, pale, meaty fist. His staring eyes were wet with tears, and his mouth was twisted downward at the corners. The muzzle was making a ragged little circle, and a remote part of my mind identified it as .25 or .32 caliber, there not being all that much difference between a quarter of an inch diameter and a third of an inch. There was a sour laugh back in another compartment of my skull. This could very possibly be the end of it, a long-odds chance of a mortal wound at the hand of a jealous husband wielding something just a little bit better than a cap gun. The ragged circle took in my heart, brain, and certain essential viscera. And I was slouched deep in a chair facing him, just a little too far away to try to kick his wrist. He was going to talk or shoot. I saw his finger getting whiter, so I knew it was shoot.

I shoved with my heels and went over backward in the chair. The weapon made a noise like somebody slapping shingles together. My left heel went numb. I rolled to my right, knocked over a small table, fielded the chunky glass ashtray on the first bounce, rolled up onto my knees, and slung it underhand at his head as he came up out of the depths of the yellow couch. I missed him shamefully and was caught there too close to him as he aimed at the middle of my face from five feet away and tried to pull the trigger. But the slide was all the way back, the clip empty.

I got slowly up onto very wobbly knees as Harry Broll lowered the gun to his side, relaxed his hand, let it fall. My heel tingled. A slug had grooved the hard leather on the bottom of the sandal. The lounge smelled like the Fourth of July.

Harry's big face wrinkled like a slapped baby, and he took a half step toward me, arms half reaching out for comfort and forgiveness, and then he plumped back down on the couch and bellowed once, a walrus on a lonely strand.

My drink was gone, spilling when the table went over. I moved cautiously, checking myself for any area that might feel dead and damp. That is the bullet feel, dead, damp, and strange, before the torn nerves and muscles catch up and begin screaming. No such areas. I made tall, careful steps into the galley, made a new drink. I went back in. Harry Broll sat with face in hands, snuffling drearily. The paper had kept me aware of him over the years. Broll plans new condominium complex. Broll given zoning board exception. Broll unveils shopping plaza concept. Chamber lauds Broll.

I sat opposite him again after putting the chair back on its legs. Looking around, I could count five ejected cartridge cases.

"How old are you, Harry?"

He sighed and mumbled it into his hands. "Thirty-five."

"You look fifty."

"Get off my back."

"You're too soft and too heavy. You sweat a lot, and you're short of breath, and your teeth need cleaning."

He lifted his mottled face and stared at me. "Why are you saying these things?"

"Maybe if you hadn't gotten so sloppy, Mary could have given you a second chance. Or maybe it was already a second chance."

"Oh, no. I don't play around. Jesus, I haven't had the time or the energy. This was the first time, I swear."

"You don't play around, and you don't go around killing people."

"You pushed me too far and—"

"You always carry that thing?"

"No, I—"

"You brought it along in case you felt like killing me?"

"Thank God I missed you. I'm not thinking right lately. Everything would have gone down the drain. Everything."

"It would sort of spoil my day, too."

"You know, when a man takes a good look at himself, he begins to wonder why. You know? I've been pushing myself hard. Drinking too much, smoking too much. Late nights. Conferences. For what? Damned if I know. For the sake of winning? How did that get to seem so important? But you shouldn't have tried to lie to me, McGee."

"Your friend is an idiot. Mary never came near me. She hasn't phoned me or written me. I didn't know she'd left you. Look, I knew her a long time ago. She was at one of those crisis points in her life. She'd never met you, Harry. Never seen you, never heard your name, never knew she'd marry you. We were friends. We took a cruise down through the Keys and up the west coast, and she got things sorted out. We made love. Not for the first two weeks of the cruise. That wasn't the purpose of it. Once all the knots and springs began to loosen up, then it seemed like a natural thing to have happen. It made pleasure. It was a way of saying hello. Nobody was a victim. She was a very sweet lady, and what I remember best is that we laughed a lot."

"I . . . I have to talk to her before the thirtieth."

"Why the deadline?"

"It's a business thing. Some things to sign. To protect my interest in SeaGate. Of course, if I'd shot you, what difference would it make whether I kept my share of SeaGate or not?"

"Will it make a lot of difference when I sign the complaint against you?"

"Complaint?"

"Assault with a deadly weapon? Attempted homicide?"

"You wouldn't!"

"What's to stop me? My undying affection for you?"

He pulled himself together visibly. He wrapped up the emotions and put them on a high shelf. I could almost see the nimble brain of the entrepreneur take over. "We'll both have versions of what happened here, McGee. I'm essentially a salesman. I think I can sell my version far easier than you can sell yours."

"What's your version?"

"I'll let that come as a surprise to you."

I could think of several variations that could leave him looking pretty good. And, of course, there was the usual problem of believability. Does one believe Harry Broll, pillar of the business community, or a certain Travis McGee, who seems to have no visible means of support, gentlemen?

"A man as shrewd as you, Harry, should realize that the guy who gave you the bad information made an honest mistake."

"I know Mary. She'd get in touch with you."

"Would that she had."

"What?"

"A troubled friend is a friend in trouble. I'm right here. She could have come around, but she didn't."

"She made you promise not to tell where she is."

I shook my head. "Broll, come with me. I will show you that rental convertible, and I will show you the lady who rented it and who went to Miami with me and came back with me."

"It's a nice try. You've got a lot of friends. They'd all lie for you. Every one. Think it over. Tell her what I said. She has to get in touch with me."

We stood up. I picked up his little automatic, released the catch and eased the slide forward, and handed it to him. He took it and looked at it, bounced it on his big hand, and slipped it into his side pocket. "I better get rid of it," he said.

"If you think you might get any more quaint ideas, you better."

"I was going to scare you. That's all."

I looked him over. "Harry. You did."

"Tell her to call the office. I'm not living at home. It was too empty there."

"If after all these years I should happen to see your wife, I'll tell her."

two

Meyer came aboard *The Busted Flush* at twenty minutes to six, five minutes after Harry Broll left. He was dressed for the small festival at six o'clock aboard Jillian's great big motor-sailer trimaran. He wore pants in a carnival awning pattern and a pink shirt that matched one of the myriad stripes in the awning.

"Goodness gracious," I said.

He put a hand on a bulky hip and made a slow 360-degree turn. "Plumage," he said. "And have you noticed it's spring?"

"If you'd carry a camera around your neck and walk fifty feet ahead of me, nobody would know we were together."

"Faw," he said. "And tush." He went toward the bottle department, saying, "About Mr. Harry Broll . . . ?"

"Who? Oh, yes. Of course. Mr Broll."

"McGee, don't try me, please."

"You are supposed to walk in here, and instead of giving me a fashion show, you are supposed to snuff the air, look about with darting glances. Then you are supposed to find those six cartridge cases in that ashtray and snuff at them. Then you prowl around and find where all six hit, including the one that's hard to find. It hit right smack in the middle of my Model Eighteen Marantz and killed it as dead as Harry tried to kill me."

Meyer backed to the nearest chair and lowered himself into it. "Six shots?"

"Six."

"With serious intent?"

"Damn well told."

I explained the situation. Meyer listened, looking very troubled.

"Don't sit there looking like an old beagle," I told him. "Harry won't be back."

"Maybe somebody else will."

"What is that supposed to mean?"

"Travis, are you just a little slower than you were a few years ago? Half a step, maybe?"

"I don't know. Probably."

"Why should you get slower and get careless at the same time?"

"Careless?"

"Don't try to kid yourself. You would have stumbled against him or spilled something on him and brushed it off. You would have checked him out and located the gun and taken it away from him."

"This was just old Harry Broll."

"And you are just old T. McGee, trying to pretend you don't know what I'm saying. You could be on the floor with a leaking hole in your skull."

"I can't go around acting as if everybody was going to—"

"You used to. And you are alive. What has given you this illusion of immortality of late?"

"Lay off, Meyer."

"Staleness? People are very good at things they are very interested in. If you lose interest, you are dead. If a Harry Broll can damned near kill you, Travis, what about somebody with a more professional attitude and background?"

"Wouldn't I be more alert?"

"Don't some of them look and act as innocuous as Harry Broll?"

"What are you getting at?"

"If you just go through the motions, Travis, maybe it's time to give the whole thing up. What good is a way of life if it turns out to be fatal?"

"Are you going to support me?"

"Not a chance. Anyway, isn't Jillian first in line?"

"Come on!"

"There are worse ways to live."

"Several hundred thousand worse ways, Meyer, but just because Harry Broll . . . consider this. Six shots in a very confined space. What's the matter with my reaction time?"

"The trouble is that they were fired at all. He came here once to try to beat your face flat. So two years later he comes around again, and you invite him in to try his luck with a gun. What are you going to dodge next time? A satchel charge?"

"I have to depend on instinct. I did not sense any kind of murderous intent on his—"

"Then your instincts are stale. Listen. I don't want to lose a friend. Go where I can visit once in a while. Exchange Christmas cards. Better than putting a pebble on your gravestone."

"Just because—"

"Don't talk. Think a little. And we should be going."

I shrugged and sighed. When he gets into one of those moods, there is nothing one can do with him. He smells doom. I buttoned up the *Flush*, making certain my little security devices were in operation. The sun was low enough to make a yellow-orange glow across all the white gleam and brightwork of a vulgar multimillion dollars' worth of seagoing toys. Hundreds of millions, in truth. As we walked over I saw the sixty-plus feet of a big new Bertram, grumbling, bubbling, sliding elegantly into a slip. Six thousand dollars a foot. It doesn't take too many of those, too many Matthews, Burgers, Trumpys, Huckinses, Rybovitches, and Strikers, to make a row of zeros to stun the mind.

I stopped and leaned my crossed arms atop a cement piling and looked down at a rainbow sheen of oil on twilight waters.

"What's the matter now?" asked Meyer.

"Harry is right, you know."

"To try to kill you?"

"Very funny. He's right about Mary getting in touch. I get the feeling she would. Emotional logic. The last time her world ruptured, I helped her walk it off, think it off."

"So maybe she had enough and said the hell with it."

"She is one stubborn lady. Harry is no prize. She married him a little too fast. But she would really bust a gut to make the marriage work. She wouldn't quit. She wouldn't run."

"Unless he did something that she just couldn't take. Maybe it got to her gag reflex. Wouldn't she run then?"

"Yes, I guess so. And maybe she's a stronger person than she was back when I knew her. All Harry said was that he had gotten mixed up with some Canadian girl, a first offense. I know that wouldn't make Mary give any ringing cheers. But I think she's human enough to know it wouldn't be the end of the world or the marriage. Well, he has to locate her before the end of April, or he has big business problems."

"Hmm?"

"Something about signing something so he can keep his interest in SeaGate, whatever the hell that is."

"It's a planned community up in the northeast corner of Martin County, above Hobe Sound where there's no A-1-A running along the beach. It's a syndicate thing, way too big for anybody like Broll to swing by himself."

"How do you know all that stuff?"

"There was a feature story about planned communities in the *Wall Street Journal* a month ago. The local papers have had articles about it for over a year. I believe *Newsweek* had a—"

"Truce. Could a guy like Broll do well in a deal like that?"

"Depends. The ownership structure would be the important consideration."

"Could you find out where he fits and how, and why Mary would have to sign something?"

"I imagine I could. But why?"

"Harry's nerves are bad. He looks bad. He has a money orientation. If he misses out on large money because Mary runs and hides and won't sign, it somehow doesn't sound like Mary. It would be a cheap shot and a dumb shot. She isn't dumb. Whether she stays with him or leaves him, it would be better for him to have money. She's been gone for three months. If he was so certain she'd run to me, where has he been for three months? Time is running out in two weeks. So he comes around with shaking hands and a sweaty shirt and a couple of places he missed while shaving. Time is running out not on the marriage, on the money. It makes me wonder."

"I'll look into it," he said as we walked.

End of discussion. We had arrived at the area where they park the showboats, the ones too big to bring around inside, and thus have to leave them on the river, not far from the fuel pumps, where two out of every three Power Squadron types who cruise by can whap them against the cement with their curling wash. The *Jilly III* is a custom motor-sailer trimaran out of St. Kitts, owned by Jillian, the widow of Sir Henry Brent-Archer. It is seventy feet long with a beam that has to be close to fifty feet. It rides a bad sea with all the stability of a brick church. Minimal superstructure to emphasize an expanse of teak deck as big as a tennis court, with more than half of it shaded by the big colorful awning tarp her crew of three always strings up as soon as they are at dockside.

The bar table was positioned, draped in white damask. A piano tape was playing show tunes with muted discretion over the stereo system I'd helped her buy the last time she was in Lauderdale. There were a dozen guests assembled, three conversational groups of elegant folk sipping the very best booze from the most expensive glasses. Jilly saw us approaching the little gangplank and came a-striding, beaming, to welcome us aboard.

A lady of unguessable years, who made damned well certain she gave you no clues at all. If she turned up as a Jane Doe, DOA, traffic, a hasty coroner could not be blamed for penciling in the apparent age as plus or minus twenty-seven. Tall, slender brunette of such careful and elegant grooming, such exquisitely capped teeth, it seemed safe to assume she was in some area of entertainment. But she had such a much better tan and better physical condition than most show-business people, one might safely guess her to be, perhaps, a model for beachwear? A lead in a commercial water ballet?

But a coroner less hasty, more sophisticated, who searched the scalp and elsewhere for the faintest of traces left by superb Swiss surgeons, who slipped the tinted plastic lenses off and studied the eyes closely, as well as the backs of the hands, base of the throat, ankles, wrists . . . he might add a quotient of years in direct ratio to his quality of observation and his experience.

Jilly had a lively and animated face peering out from the careless spill of black hair, all bright questing eyes, black brows, big nose, broad and generous mouth. Ever since I had known Jilly, her voice had cracked like that of a boy in early adolescence, changing from the piercing, songbird clarity of the Irish upperclass countryside to a burring baritone honk and back again. It was so effective it seemed contrived. But a small sailboat had foundered one night in a bad sea, and she had clung to a channel buoy, permanently spraining her vocal cords shouting at the boat traffic until finally she was heard and she and her injured friend were rescued.

"Meyer!" she cried. "My *word*, darling! You're of a surpassing radiance. Travis dear, what happened to him? Did he molt or something?" She linked her arms through ours and croaked, "Come on, dears. Meet the ones you don't know and get smashed soon as you can because I am gallons ahead of you."

The introductions were made. Jillian slipped away to greet more guests. We drank. The sun went down. The night breeze was gentle but cool, and ladies put their wraps back on. The party lights strung from the rigging were properly dim, flatteringly orange. The buffet materialized, as if the table had risen up out of the teak. The music tape was more lively, the volume louder than before.

I found myself inadvertently paired with a smallish, withered Englishwoman with a shrunken face the color of weak tea and hair dyed the color of raspberry ice. A Mrs. Ogleby. I had seen Meyer talking to her towering and cadaverous husband, pumping him about the latest Common Market difficulties. We carried our buffet plates forward where she could sit on a narrow shelflike bench built out from the bow where the rail was solid. I sat cross-legged on the deck with my plate atop the massive bow cleat.

"I understand that you are one of dear Jillian's very favorite Americans, Mr. McGee."

She managed to load the comment with sweetly venomous insinuation. I beamed up at her. "And she's one of my favorite foreigners."

"Really! How terribly nice for her. Actually, Geoffrey and I were old friends of poor Sir Henry long before he married Jillian."

"Then Jillian isn't one of your favorite people, eh?"

She clinked her fork against the plate and leaned forward and peered down at me. "Whatever gave you such an odd idea? She is *very* dear. Very dear to both of us."

"I knew Sir Henry, too."

"Really! I wouldn't have thought you would have known him."

"I was a houseguest at St. Kitts for a few weeks."

"But that would have been after he was quite ill, I take it." Her smile was thin and knowing in the light of the nearby party lantern. A truly poisonous little woman.

"No. As a matter of fact, Mrs. Ogleby, Henry and I swam our three miles every morning, went riding or sailing every afternoon, and played chess every evening."

She paused and regrouped. "Before he became ill, Sir Henry had really fantastic energies. How strange we all thought it that he would marry someone that young, after being a widower so long. It seemed odd. But, of course, that was so awfully long ago it is rather difficult to think of Jillian as—"

"Just think of me, dears, no matter how difficult it may be," said Jilly. "Hmmm. What is this you have, Lenore? I didn't see it at all. May I? Mmmm. Shrimp, and what a deliciously fiery sauce! Difficult to think of me as what, Lenore darling?"

When Mrs. Ogleby hesitated, I said, "She was about to pinpoint the date when you and Sir Henry were married."

"Were you, dear? It slips my mind, you know. Was it just before or just after that fuss with the Spanish Armada?"

"Don't be absurd! I was only—"

"You were only being Lenore, which is part of the trouble, isn't it? Travis, I was married to Henry long long ago. Matter of fact, I was but three years old at the time, and most of the people in the church thought it was some sort of delayed christening. There was talk that it was an unwholesome relationship, but by the time I was fourteen —eleven years later—I looked twenty, and everyone said that it had probably been all for the best. And it was, of course. Lenore, you seem to be finished. Dear, come with me and show me just where you found the shrimp, will you please?"

"But if there is any left, it should be quite obvi—"

"Lenore!"

"Quite. Of course. I shall be happy to show you, my dear Jillian."

"I knew it would make you happy to have a chance to be nice to me, Lenore."

Off they went. Old friends, smiling and chattering.

Twenty minutes later as I was moving away from the bar with some Wild Turkey straight, instead of brandy, Jilly intercepted me and moved me into relative shadow.

"Travis, if you are a truly thoughtful and understanding man, you have your toothbrush hidden away on your person."

"I had the idea the party girl would need her eight hours."

"Have a little mercy, dear. There's but one way to settle down from this sort of bash. You shall divert me."

"I can leave and then come back. You know. Like a house call."

"Is its tender little romantical pride bruised because the party girl thinks lovemaking is therapeutic? To say nothing of being a hell of a lot of fun. Just stay on, dear. Stay by me. Smile like a tomcat with a little yellow feather caught in his whiskers, and soon now we can smile them off and sing out our merry farewells."

"Giving Lenore more food for thought?"

"Thought? Christ, that poisonous bitch doesn't think. She slanders, because she has her own terrible hunger she can't ease in any way. She burns in fire, my darling, and hates and hates and hates. Poor thing. Brace yourself, pet. I want you horribly."

three

I drifted in and out of a placid and amiable doze. Water slapped the triple hulls, whispering lies about how big the seas could really get. I cocked an eye at an upward angle at the battery digital clock fastened to the bulkhead over Jillian's bed. Watched 4:06 turning magically to 4:07. There was a single light on in her stateroom, a rose-colored globe of frosty glass, big as a cantaloupe, standing next to its twin reflection in the dressing table mirror.

It was warm in her stateroom, not unpleasantly so, just enough to leave a humid dew, rosy highlights on our entangled flesh, sprawled and spent, atop a wrinkled dampness of custom sheets in a pattern of green vines with yellow leaves against white.

Jilly lay oddly positioned, her upper torso diagonally across my chest, face in a pillow, cheek against my right shoulder, her slack right arm hooked around my neck. Her long tanned legs were sprawled down there, off to my left. My right arm was pinned, but my left arm was free, my hand resting on the small of her back.

I traced the velvet geographies of that small concave area of the country of Jilly and then made a coin-sized circle of fingernails and thumbnail and made a slow circling motion against her there, a circle as big as a teacup. In time the pattern of her breathing changed. She shifted. She exhaled through slack rubbery lips, making a sound like a small horse.

"Is someone mentioning my name?" she said in a sleepy voice.

"Pure telepathy."

She raised her head, clawed her hair out of the way, and peered up at the clock. "Gawd! What year is it? Don't tell me."

She heaved herself up, tugging her arm out from under my neck. She sat up and combed her hair back with the fingers of both hands, yawning widely as she did so. She shook and snapped her head back, settled her hair, then curled her limber legs under her and smiled down at me. "Been awake long, Travis?"

"Off and on."

"Thinking? About what?"

I hitched myself higher on the pillows. "Random things. This and that."

"Tell me about them."

"Let me think back. Oh, I was wondering how it's possible to make this bed up. It's shaped to fit perfectly into the curves of this middle hull right up at the bow and—"

"There are little lever things on the legs down there, and when you push them down, then you can roll the bed back and make it up. You certainly think about fascinating things."

"Then I heard a motor go on, and I was wondering if it was a bilge pump or a refrigeration compressor or—"

"You are trying to be tiresome. Didn't you think about what I asked you?"

"Maybe I did. A little bit. Like wondering why it has to be me."

"If one could know why a person settles upon a particular person, one would know one of the mysteries, wouldn't one? I think it was because of four years ago. I think it started then."

A friend of a friend had put Sir Henry Brent-Archer in touch with me. A problem of simple extortion. I had gone down to the British Virgins and spent three weeks at their spacious and lovely home and found exactly the right way to pry the two-legged lamprey loose, file its sharp teeth off, and send it unhappily on its way. And during the three weeks I had become ever more sensuously aware of Sir Henry's handsome and lively wife. She made sure of that awareness.

"Because I kept it from starting?"

"Was I all that distasteful to you, my darling?"

"Not you. The situation. I liked Sir Henry. In spite of the fact I was working for him on a special problem, I was still a guest in his home. In a man's home you live by his code. It does not have to be typed out and glued to the guest suite door. He did not want me to kick his dogs, overwork his horses, bribe his servants, read his diary, filch his silverware, borrow his toothbrush, or lay his wife. I accepted the obligation when I moved in."

She snickered. "Would you believe that was the only time in the years I was his wife that I ever tried to be naughty?"

"There's no reason not to believe it."

"I was very grateful to Sir Henry. He came along at just the right time in my life. My whole dreadful family was sliding into the pit, and through him I could save them, so I snatched him up quickly. I like him well enough for half the marriage, liked him a great deal for the rest of it, and started loving him after he was buried. Anyway, on that stupid night I lay and listened to my heart going *bump, bump, bump*. Then I got up and drenched myself with that lovely scent and put on the little froth of nightgown and crept through the night like a thief and slipped into your bed. And suddenly got lifted out bodily, carried to the door, given a great whack across my bare behind, and shoved out into the hall. I did not know whether to laugh or cry. I did both."

"It was closer than you'll ever know, Jilly."

"So it's you, dear man. The chosen. Relax and enjoy it. Why not? Am I trying to nail you down permanently? Of course, but through your own choice and decision. I give you full disclosure, dear. I have something over eight hundred thousand pounds, carefully managed by nice little Swiss elves. The income is about a hundred and fifty thousand of your dollars a year, and taxes take hardly any. There is the lovely house with the beach, the bay, and the view, and the boats and cars and horses. I am not exactly a junior miss, but I work very hard at myself, and I come from healthy stock. I suspect I shall go on about the same for years and years and years and suddenly one morning wake up as a shriveled, cackling little old witch. All I ask of you is that you come back home with me, darling. Be my houseguest. Be my love. We laugh at the same things. We enjoy the same things. Last trip and this trip we've certainly established . . . physical compatibility. Darling, please! We'll travel when you want to and go where you want to go. We'll be with people when you want to, and they will be the people you want to be with. Please!"

"Jilly, you are a dear and lovely lady—"

"But! I know, dammit. But! Why *not*? Do you even *know*?"

I knew but did not want to tell her. You see many such couples around the yacht clubs and bath clubs and tennis clubs of the Western world. The man, a little younger or a lot younger than the moneyed widow or divorcée he has either married or is traveling with. The man is usually brown and good at games, dresses youthfully, and talks amusingly. But he drinks a little too much. And completely trained and conditioned, he is ever alert for his cues. If his lady unsnaps her purse and frowns down into it, he at once presents his cigarettes, and they are always her brand. If she has her own cigarettes, he can cross twenty feet in a twelfth of a second to snap the unwavering flame to life, properly and conveniently positioned for her. It takes but the smallest sidelong look of query to send him in search of an ashtray to place close to her elbow. If at sundown she raises her elegant shoulders a half inch, he trots into the house or onto the boat or up to the suite to bring back her wrap. He knows just how to apply her suntan oil, knows which of her dresses have to be zipped up and snapped for her. He can draw her bath to the precise depth and temperature which please her. He can give her an acceptable massage, brew a decent pot of coffee, take her phone messages accurately, keep her personal checkbook in balance, and remind her when to take her medications. Her litany is: Thank you, dearest. How nice, darling. You are so thoughtful, sweetheart.

It does not happen quickly, of course. It is an easy life. Other choices, once so numerous, disappear. Time is the random wind that blows down the long corridor, slamming all the doors. And finally, of course, it comes down to a very simple equation. Life is endurable when she is contented and difficult when she is displeased. It is a training process. Conditioned response.

"I'm used to the way I live," I told her.

"The way you live," she said. With brooding face she reached and ran gentle fingertips along the deep, gullied scar in my thigh, then leaned and touched the symmetrical dimple of the entrance wound of a bullet. She hunched closer to me, bent and kissed the white welt of scar tissue that is nearly hidden by the scruffy, sun-faded hair at my temple. "The way you live, Travis. Trying to trick the tricky ones. Trying to make do with bluff and smiles and strange lies. Filching fresh meat right out of the jaws of the sharks. For how long, dear, before finally the odds go bad and the luck goes bad once and for all?"

"I'm sly."

"Not sly enough. Maybe not quick enough any more. I think you've been doing it for too long, darling. Too many years of getting things back for silly, careless people who should not have lost them in the first place. One day some dim little chap will come upon you suddenly and take out a gun and shoot you quite dead."

"Are you a witch? Do you so prophesy?"

She fell upon me, hugged me tight. "Ah, no, dear. No. You had all the years when that was the thing you had to do. Now the years belong to me. Is it such a sickening fate you can't endure the thought of it?"

"No, Jilly. No, honey. It's just that—"

"Give us a month. No. One week. One insignificant little week. Or else."

"Or else?"

She burrowed a bit, gently closed her teeth onto the upper third of my left ear, then released it. "I have splendid teeth and very strong jaw muscles. If you say no, I shall set my teeth into your ear and do my best to tear it right off your head, darling."

"You just might at that."

"You love to bluff people. Try me."

"No, thank you. One week."

She took a deep breath and let it out. "Lovely! Time in transit doesn't count, of course. Can we leave . . . day after tomorrow?"

"I don't know."

"Why don't you know?"

"I just found out that an old friend might be in trouble. It just seems to me that if she was in trouble, she'd come to me."

Jilly wiggled and thrust away from me and sat up. "She?"

"Frowning makes wrinkles."

"So it does. She?"

"A respectable married lady."

"If she's so respectable, how is it she knows you?"

"Before she was married."

"And I suppose you had an affair with her."

"Gee, honey. I'd have to look it up."

I caught her fist about five inches from my eye. "You bahstid," she said.

"Okay. An affair. A mad, wild, glorious liaison which kept us in an absolute frenzy of passion."

Her look was enigmatic. "You are perfectly right, of course, darling. It is none of my business. What's she like? I mean, what physical type?"

"In general, a lot like you, Jilly. Tall, slender brunette. Dark hair, takes a good tan. Long legs, short waisted. She would be . . . twenty-eight or -nine by now. Back when I knew her, she didn't race her motor the way you do. More of a placid, contented person. She really enjoyed cooking and scrubbing and bed-making. She could sleep ten or twelve hours a night."

"You damned well remember every detail, don't you?"

I smiled up into her leaning, earnest face—a small face but strong of feature in the black, bed-snarled dangle of hair. I looked at her limber, brown body in the rose glow of the lamp ten feet away, noting the way the deep tan above and below her breasts decreased in ever more pallid horizontal stripes and shadings down to that final band of pale and pure white which denoted her narrowest bikini top.

"Why are you laughing at me, you dull sod?"

"Not at you, Lady Jillian."

"I am *not* Lady Jillian. That usage is improper. If you are not laughing *at*, then you are laughing *with*. And if you are laughing *with*, why is it that I am not amused?"

"But you are, darling."

She tried to keep her mouth severe but lost the battle, gave a rusty honk of laughter, and flung herself upon me.

"I can't stay angry with you, Travis. You promised me a week. But I'll punish you for that dark-haired lady."

"How?"

"On our way to St. Kitts there will be at least one day or night when we'll spend hour after hour quartering into an ugly, irregular chop."

"I don't get seasick."

"Nor do I, my love. It would spoil it if either of us became ill."

"Spoil what?"

"Dear man, when the chop is effective, one cannot stay on this bed. You are lifted up, and then the bed and the hull drop away from you, and when you are on your way down, the bed comes up and smacks you and boosts you into the air again. It is like trying to post on a very bad horse. When that happens, dear, you and I are going to be right here, making love. We'll see how well you satisfy a lady in midair. I shall have you tottering about, wishing you'd never met Mrs. Whatever."

"Mrs. Broll. Mary Broll. Mary Dillon Broll."

"You think she should have have come to you if she's in trouble? Isn't that a little patronizing and arrogant?"

"Possibly."

"What sort of trouble?"

"Marriage trouble. Her husband cheated, and she caught him at it and left him back in January."

"Good Lord, why should she come galloping to you?"

"It's an emotional problem, and when she had one sort of like it years ago, we got together, and she worked her way out of it."

"And fell in love with you?"

"I think that with Mary there would have to be some affection before there could be anything."

"You poor dumb beast. You're so obvious."

"What do you mean?"

"You can't for the life of you comprehend why she doesn't come scuttling back to Dr. McGee's free and famous clinic. Your pride is hurt, dear. I suspect she's found some other therapist."

"Even if she had, I think she'd have let me know the marriage had soured. I get the feeling something happened to her."

She yawned and stretched. "Let me make one thing abundantly clear, as one of your grubby little political types used to say. Once we have our design for living, if we have any doleful visits from one of your previous patients, my dear, I shall take a broom to her and beat her through the garden gate and down the drive."

"Don't you think you ought to type all these rules up and give me three copies?"

"You're so damned *defensive!* Good Christ, am I some sort of dog's dinner?"

"You are a lively, sexy, lovely, sexy, well-dressed, sexy, amusing, sexy, wealthy, sexy widow lady."

"And some *very* tidy and considerate men come flocking around. Men with all the social graces and very good at games. Not knuckly, scabrous, lazy, knobbly old ruins like you, McGee."

"So grab one of those tidy and considerate ones."

"Oh, sure. They are lovely men, and they are *so* anxious to please me. There's the money, and it makes them very jumpy and nervous. Their hands get cold and damp. If I frown, they look terrified. Couldn't you be more anxious to please me, dear? Just a little bit?"

"Like this, you mean?"

"Well . . . I didn't exactly mean that. . . . I meant in a more general sense . . . but . . . now that you bring it up . . . God, I can't remember now what I did mean. . . . I guess I meant this. Yes, darling. This."

————

The narrow horizontal ports above the custom bed let a cold and milky morning light into the stateroom at the bow of the center hull of the *Jilly III*. As I looked up, 6:31 became 6:32. Jillian's small round rump, her flesh warmer than mine, was thrust with a domestic coziness into my belly. My chin rested against the crown of her head. Her tidy heft had turned my left arm numb. My right hand lay upon the sweet inward curve of her waist.

Worse fates, I thought. A life with Jilly Brent-Archer wouldn't be dull. Maybe it is time for the islands. In spite of all good intentions, all nervous concern, all political bombast, my dirty two-legged species is turning the lovely southeast coast into a sewer. On still days the stinking sky is bourbon brown, and in the sea there are only the dwindling runty fish that can survive in that poisoned brew.

It happens slowly, so you try not to notice it. You tell yourself it happens to be a bad day, that's all. The tides and the winds will scrub it all clean. But not clean enough any more. One life to live, so pop through the escape hatch, McGee. Try the islands. Damned few people can escape the smudge and sludge, the acids and stenches, the choking and weeping. You have to take care of yourself, man. Nobody else is going to. And this deft morsel, curled sleeping against you, is a first-class ticket for all of the voyage you have left. Suppose you *do* have to do some bowing and scraping and fetching. Will it kill you? Think of what most people have to do for a living. You've been taking your retirement in small installments whenever you could afford it. So here's the rest of it in her lovely sleep. The ultimate social security.

I eased my dead arm out from under her and moved away. She made a sleep whine of discontent. I covered her with the big colorful sheet, dressed, turned out the rosy light, and made sure the main hatchway locked behind me when I left.

Back aboard the *Flush*, I put on swim trunks and a robe to keep me warm in the morning chill. The sun was coming up out of the sea when I walked across the pedestrian bridge over the highway and down onto the public beach. Morning birds were running along the wet sand, pecking and fleeing from the wash of the surf. An old man was jogging slowly by, his face in a clench of agony. A fat girl in a brown dress was looking for shells.

I went in, swam hard, and rested, again and again, using short bursts of total energy. I went back to the *Flush* and had a quart of orange juice, four scrambled eggs along with some rat cheese from Vermont, and a mug of black coffee.

I fell asleep seven and a half inches above my oversized bed in the master stateroom, falling toward the bed, long gone before I landed.

four

Thursday, when I got up a little before noon, the remembered scene with Harry Broll and his little gun seemed unreal. Six loud whacks, not loud enough to attract the curious attention of people on the neighboring craft. The *Flush* had been buttoned up, the air conditioning on. No slug had gone through glass.

I found where five had hit. At last I spotted the sixth one in the overhead. It had hit tumbling and sideways and had not punched itself all the way out of sight, so by elimination it was the one that had grooved the leather sole of my sandal and numbed my heel.

I had rolled to my right after going over backward in the chair. It gave me the chance to kick a small table over, creating more distraction and confusion, and it also forced him, being right-handed, to bring his arm across his body to aim at me, which is more difficult than extending the arm out to the side. Two into the deck, one into the chair, one into the table, one into the overhead, and one into my stereo amplifier.

So maybe the clip held six, and he had not jacked one into the chamber until he got to the parking lot at the marina. If he'd put one in the chamber and filled the clip all the way, there would have been one left for the middle of my face.

Dead then or a long time in the institutional bed with the drains in place and the pain moving around under the sedatives like a snake under a blanket.

Don't give yourself any credit, Mr. Travis McGee. The fates could have counted to seven just as easily. You had an easy shot at him with the ashtray, but your hand was sweaty and the fingertips slipped. You missed badly.

Meyer could be right. I had depended on instinct. It had been my instinct that Harry Broll had not come to kill me. Then he had done his best, and I had lucked out. So was instinct becoming stale? When it stopped being a precision tool, when it ceased sending accurate messages up from the atavistic, animal level of the brain, I was as vulnerable as if sight or hearing had begun to fail. If soft, sloppy, nervous Harry Broll could almost do me in with a popgun, my next meeting with professional talent could be mortal.

There was another dimension to it. Once I started doubting my survival instinct, I would lose confidence in my own reactions. A loss of confidence creates hesitations. Hesitation is a fatal disease—for anyone in the salvage business.

There are worse careers than houseguest. Or pet gofer.

Too much solitary introspection started to depress me. I was ready for Geritol and cortisone. I pulled all the plugs and connections on the Marantz and lugged its considerable weight all the way to where I'd parked Miss Agnes, my ancient and amiable old blue Rolls pickup. I drove over to town to Al's Musicade. He is lean, sour, and knowledgeable. He does not say much. He took it out back himself and found bench space in his busy service department. I watched him finger the hole in the front of it. He quickly loosened the twelve Phillips screws that hold the top perforated plate down, lifted it off, found more damage, reached in with two fingers, and lifted out the deformed slug.

"Somebody didn't like the programming?"

"Bad lyrics."

"Week from today?"

"Loaner?"

"Got a Fisher you can use."

We walked out front, and he lifted it off the rack, a used one in apparently good condition. He made a note of the serial number and who was taking it out.

I put the borrowed amplifier on the passenger seat beside me and went looking for Harry Broll's place of business. I had seen it once and had a general idea where to find it. I had to ask at a gas station. It was west of Lauderdale, off Davie Road, over in an industrial park in pine and palmetto country. All of it except the office itself was circled by high hurricane fencing with slanted braces and three strands of barbed wire on top. There was a gate for the rail spur and a truck and equipment gate. I could see a central-mix concrete plant, a block plant, big piles of sand, gravel, and crushed stone. I could see warehouses, stacks of lumber, piles of prestressed concrete beams, and a vehicle park-and-repair area. This was a Thursday at one thirty in the afternoon, and I could count only ten cars. Four of those were in front of the office. The office was a long, low concrete-block building painted white with a flat roof. The landscaped grass was burned brown, and they had lost about half the small palm trees planted near the office.

There were too many trucks and pieces of equipment in the park. It looked neat enough but sleepy. BROLL ENTERPRISES, Inc. But some of the big plastic letters had blown off or fallen off. It said:

ROLL E TERP ISES, Inc.

I cruised slowly by. I was tempted to turn around and go back and go in and see if Harry was there and try once more to tell him I'd had no contact whatsoever with Mary for over three years. But he was going to believe what emotions told him to believe.

I wondered how Meyer was doing, using his friends in the banks, brokerage houses, and investment houses to find out just how sweaty Harry Broll might be. The tight-money times and the overbuilding of condominiums and the pyramiding costs had busted quite a few able fellows lately. Harry probably hadn't come through that bad period without some ugly bruises. I could tell Meyer how idle Broll's place of business looked, if he hadn't found out already.

When I got back to Bahia Mar, Meyer was still missing. I felt restless. I set up the Fisher, hooked up the tape decks, turntables, and the two sets of speakers. It checked out all right. I turned it off and paced. The itch you can't quite reach. Familiar feeling. Like the name you can't quite remember.

I looked up the number for Broll Enterprises and phoned. The girl answered by reciting the number I'd just dialed.

"Maybe you can help me, miss. I'm trying to get a home address for Mrs. Harry Broll."

"In what regard, please?"

"Well, this is the Shoe Mart, and it was way back in November we special-ordered a pair of shoes for Mrs. Broll. It took so long she's under no obligation to take them, but they're more a classic than a high-style item, so I figured she probably wants them, but I been drawing a blank on the home phone number, so I thought maybe they moved or something."

"Will you hold on a moment, please?"

I held. It took her about a minute and a half. "Mr. Broll says that you can deliver them here to the office. Do you know where we are?"

"Sure. Okay. Thanks. It'll probably be tomorrow."

I hung up, and once again, to make sure, I dialed the home phone number for Harry Broll, 21 Blue Heron Lane. "The number you have dialed is not in service at this time."

I scowled at my phone. Come on, McGee. The man is living somewhere. Information has no home number for him. The old home number is on temporary disconnect. The new number of wherever he's living must be unlisted. It probably doesn't matter a damn where he's living. It's the challenge.

Okay. Think a little. Possibly all his mail is directed to the business address. But some things have to be delivered. Booze, medicine, automobiles. Water, electricity . . . cablevision?

The lady had a lovely voice, gentle and musical and intriguingly breathy. "I could track it down more quickly, Mr. Broll, if you could give me your account number."

"I wish I could. I'm sorry, miss. I don't have the bill in front of me. But couldn't you check it by address? The last billing was sent to Twenty-one Blue Heron Lane. If it's too much trouble, I can phone you tomorrow. You see, the bill is at my home, and I'm at the office."

"Just a moment, please. Let me check the cross-index."

It took a good five minutes. "Sorry it took me so long," she said.

"It was my fault, not having my account number, miss."

"Broll. Bee-are-oh-el-el. Harry C.?"

"Correct."

"And you said the bill went where?"

"To Twenty-one Blue Heron Lane. That's where I used to live."

"Gee, Mr. Broll, I don't understand it at all. All billing is supposed to be mailed to Post Office Box Fifty-one fifty."

"I wonder if I've gotten a bill that belongs to someone else. The amount doesn't seem right either."

"You should be paying six twenty-four a month, sir. For the one outlet. You were paying more, of course, for the four outlets at Blue Heron Lane before you ordered the disconnect."

"Excuse me, but does your file show where I am getting the one-outlet service? Do you have the right address?"

"Oh, yes, sir. It's Eighty-five fifty-three Ocean Boulevard, Apartment sixty-one. I've got the installation order number. That *is* right, isn't it?"

"Yes. That's right. But I think the billing is for eleven dollars and something."

"Mr. Broll, please mail the bill back in the regular envelope we send out, but in the left bottom corner would you write *Customer Service, Miss Locklin?*"

"I will do that. I certainly appreciate your kindness and courtesy, Miss Locklin."

"No trouble, really. That's what we're here for."

Four o'clock and still no Meyer, so I went out and coaxed Miss Agnes back to life and went rolling on up Ocean Boulevard. I kept to the far right lane and went slowly because the yearly invasion of Easter bunnies was upon us, was beginning to dwindle, and there was too little time to enjoy them. They had been beaching long enough so that there were very few cases of lobster pink. The tans were nicely established, and the ones who still burned had a brown burn. There are seven lads to every Easter bunny, and the litheness and firmness of the young ladies gamboling on the beach, ambling across the highway, stretching out to take the sun, is something to stupefy the senses. It creates something which is beyond any of the erotic daydreams of traditional lust, even beyond that aesthetic pleasure of looking upon pleasing line and graceful move.

It is possible to stretch a generalized lust, or an aesthetic turn of mind, to encompass a hundred lassies—say five and a half tons of vibrant and youthful and sun-toned flesh clad in about enough fabric to half fill a bushel basket. The erotic imagination or the artistic temperament can assimilate these five and a half tons of flanks and thighs, nates and breasts, laughing mouths and bouncing hair and shining eyes, but neither lust nor art can deal with a few thousand of them. Perceptions go into stasis. You cannot compare one with another. They become a single silken and knowledgeable creature, unknowable, a thousand-legged contemptuous joy, armored by the total ignorance of the very young and by the total wisdom of body and instinct of the female kind. A single cell of the huge creature, a single entity, one girl, can be trapped and baffled, hurt and emptied, broken and abandoned. Or, to flip the coin, she can be isolated and cherished, wanted and needed, taken with contracts and ceremonies. In either case the great creature does not miss the single identity subtracted from the whole any more than the hive misses the single bee. It goes on in its glistening, giggling, leggy immortality, forever replenished from the equation of children plus time, existing every spring, unchangingly and challengingly invulnerable—an exquisite reservoir called Girl, aware of being admired and saying "Drink me!," knowing that no matter how deep the draughts, the level of sweetness in the reservoir remains the same forever.

There are miles of beach, and there were miles of bunnies along the tan Atlantic sand. When the public beach ended, I came to the great white wall of high-rise condominiums which conceal the sea and partition the sky. They are compartmented boxes stacked high in sterile sameness. The balconied ghetto. Soundproof, by the sea. So many conveniences and security measures and safety factors that life at last is reduced to an ultimate boredom, to the great decisions of the day—which channel to watch and whether to swim in the sea or the pool.

I found 8553. It was called Casa de Playa and was spray-creted as wedding-cake white as the rest of them. Twelve stories, in the shape of a shallow C, placed to give a maximum view of the sea to each apartment even though the lot was quite narrow. I had heard that raw land along there was going at four thousand a foot. It makes an architectural challenge to take a 200-foot lot which costs eight hundred thousand dollars and cram 360 apartments onto it, each with a view, and retain some elusive flavor of spaciousness and elegance.

Economics lesson. Pay eight hundred thou for the land. Put up two hundred thousand more for site preparation, improvement, land-scaping, covered parking areas, swimming pool or pools. Put up a twelve-story building with thirty apartments on each of the floors from the second through the eleventh and fifteen penthouse apartments on top. You have 315 apartments. The building and the apartment equipment cost nine million. So you price them and move them on the basis that the higher in the air they are and the bigger they are, the more they cost. All you have to do is come out with about a thirty-three hundred net on each apartment on the average after all construction expenses, overhead expenses, and sales commissions, and you make one million dollars, and you are a sudden millionaire before taxes.

But if the apartments are retailing at an average forty thousand each and you sell off everything in the building except 10 percent of the apartments, then instead of being a million bucks ahead, you are two hundred thousand in the red.

It is deceptively simple and monstrously tricky. Meyer says that they should make a survey and find out how many condominium heart attacks have been admitted to Florida hospitals. A new syndrome. The first symptom is a secret urge to go up to an unsold penthouse and jump off your own building, counting vacancies all the way down.

As I did not care to be remembered because of Miss Agnes, I drove to a small shopping center on the left side of the highway, stashed her in the parking lot, and walked back to the Casa de Playa.

On foot I had time to read all of the sign in front.

Now showing. Model apartments. Casa de Playa. A new adventure in living. From $38,950 to $98,950. Private ocean beach. Pool. Hotel services. Fireproof and soundproof construction. Security guard on premises. No pets. No children under fifteen. Automatic fire and burglar alarm. Community lounge and game area. Another adventure in living by Broll Enterprises, Inc.

The big glass door swung shut behind me and closed out the perpetual sounds of the river of traffic, leaving me in a chilled hush on springy carpeting in a faint smell of fresh paint and antiseptic.

I walked by the elevators and saw a small desk in an alcove. The sign on the desk said: Jeannie Dolan, Sales Executive on Duty. A young lady sat behind the desk, hunched over, biting down on her underlip, scowling down at the heel of her left hand, picking at the flesh with a pin or needle.

"Sliver?" I said.

She jumped about four inches off the desk chair. "Hey! Don't sneak up, huh?"

"I wasn't trying to."

"I know you weren't. I'm sorry. Yes, it's a sliver."

"Want some help?"

She looked up at me. Speculative and noncommittal. She couldn't decide whether I'd come to deliver something, repair something, serve legal papers, or buy all the unsold apartments in a package deal.

"Well . . . every time I take hold of something, it hurts."

I took her over to the daylight, to an upholstered bench near a big window which looked out at a wall made of pierced concrete blocks. I held her thin wrist and looked at her hand. There was red inflammation around the sliver and a drop of blood where she had been picking at it. I could see the dark narrow shape of the splinter under the pink and transparent skin. She had been working with a needle and a pair of tweezers. I sterilized the needle in her lighter flame, pinched up the skin so that I could pick a little edge of the splinter free. She sucked air through clenched teeth. I took the tweezers and got hold of the tiny end and pulled it out.

"Long," I said, holding it up. "Trophy size. You should get it mounted."

"Thank you very very much. It was driving me flippy," she said, standing up.

"Got anything to put on it?"

"Iodine in the first-aid kit."

I followed her back to the desk. She hissed again when the iodine touched the raw tissue. She asked my advice as to whether to put a little round Band-Aid patch on it, and I said I thought a splinter that big deserved a bandage and a sling, too.

She was lean, steamed-up, a quick-moving, fast-talking woman in her late twenties with a mobile face and a flexible, expressive voice. In repose she could have been quite ordinary. There was a vivacity, an air of enjoying life about her that made her attractive. Her hair was red-brown, her eyes a quick gray-green, her teeth too large, and her upper lip too short for her to comfortably pull her mouth shut, so it remained parted, making her look vital and breathless instead of vacuous. She used more eye makeup than I care for.

"Before I ask question one, Miss Dolan—"

"Mrs. Dolan. But Jeannie, please. And you are . . . ?"

"John Q. Public until I find out something."

"John Q. Spy?"

"No. I want to know who you represent, Jeannie."

"Represent? I'm selling these condominium apartments as any fool can plainly—"

"For whom?"

"For Broll Enterprises."

"I happen to know Harry. Do the skies clear now?"

She tilted, frowned, then grinned. "Sure. If a realtor was handling this and you talked to me, then there'd have to be a commission paid, and you couldn't get a better price from Mr. Broll. There used to be a realtor handling it, but they didn't do so well, and I guess Mr. Broll decided this would be a better way. Can I sell you one of our penthouses today, sir? Mr. Public, sir?"

"McGee. Travis McGee. I don't know whether I'm a live one or not. I'm doing some scouting for a friend. I'd like to look at one with two bedrooms and two baths just to get an idea."

She took a sign out of her desk and propped it against the phone. *Back in ten minutes. Please be seated.* She locked her desk and we went up to the eighth floor. She chattered all the way up and all the way down the eighth-floor corridor, telling me what a truly great place it was to live and how well constructed it was and how happy all the new residents were.

She unlocked the door and swung it open with a flourish. She kept on chattering, following a couple of steps behind me as I went from room to room. After quite a while she ran out of chatter. "Well . . . don't you want to ask *anything?*"

"The floor plan is efficient. The equipment looks pretty adequate. But the furniture and the carpeting and the decorating make me feel sort of sick, Jeannie."

"A very expensive decorator did all our display apartments."

"Yeck."

"A lot of people are really turned on by it."

"Yeck."

"We've even sold some with all the decor intact, just as you see it. The buyers insisted."

"Still yeck."

"And I think it is absolutely hideous, and it makes me feel queasy, too. It looks too sweet. Cotton candy and candy cane and ribbon candy. Yeck."

"Got one just like this that hasn't been messed with?"

"Down on five. Come along."

We rode down three floors. The apartment was spotlessly clean and absolutely empty. She unlocked the sliding doors, and we went out onto the balcony and leaned against the railing.

"If the answers to the other questions make sense, Jeannie, my friend might be interested, provided you don't show her that one up on eight."

I asked the right questions. Was it long-term leasehold or actual ownership with undivided interest in the land? How much a year for taxes? How much for the maintenance contract? What were the escalation provisions in the maintenance contract? How much did utilities run? Would the apartment be managed, be rented if you wished when you were not using it?

"How many apartments are there all told?"

"Counting the penthouses—two hundred and ninety-eight."

"How many unsold?"

"Oh, very few, really."

"How many?"

"Well . . . Harry might cut my throat all the way around to the back if I told anybody. But after all, you are my surgeon, and I have the scar to prove it. We've got thirty-six to go. I've been here a month and a half, and I get free rent in one of the models and a fifty-buck-a-week draw against a thousand dollars a sale. Between the two of us, Betsy and me, we've sold two."

"So Harry Broll is hurting?"

"Would your friend live here alone, Travis?"

"It would just be more of a convenience for her than anything. She lives in the British Virgins. St. Kitts. She comes over here often, and she's thinking about getting an apartment. I imagine she'd use it four times a year probably, not over a week or two weeks at a time. She might loan it to friends. She doesn't have to worry about money."

Jeannie Dolan made a small rueful face. "How nice for her. Will you be bringing her around?"

"If I don't find anything she might like better."

"Remember, this floor plan is fifty-five thousand nine hundred and fifty. Complete with a color-coded kitchen with—"

"I know, dear."

"Wind me up and I give my little spiel." She locked up, and we rode down in the elevator. She looked at her watch. "Hmmm. My long, exhausting day has been over for ten minutes. I read half a book, wrote four letters, and got operated on for a splinter."

"There's some medication I want to prescribe, Mrs. Dolan. If there's an aid station nearby, I can take you there and buy the proper dosage and make sure you take it."

She looked at me with the same expression as in the very beginning—speculative, noncommittal. "Well . . . there's Monty's Lounge up at the shopping center, behind the package store."

five

Monty's was no shadowy cave. It was bright, sunny, and noisy. Terrazzo floor, orange tables, a din of laughter and talk, shouts of greeting, clink of ice. Hey, Jeannie. Hi, Jeannie, as we found our way to a table for two against the far wall. I could see that this was the place for a quick one after the business places in the shopping center closed. There were a savings and loan, insurance offices, a beauty parlor, specialty shops all nearby.

The waitress came over and said, "The usual, Jeannie? Okay. And what's for you, friend?" Jeannie's turned out to be vodka tonic, and friend ordered a beer.

In those noisy and familiar surroundings Jeannie relaxed and talked freely. She and her friend Betsy had come down to Florida from Columbus, Ohio, in mid-January to arrange a couple of divorces. Their marriages had both gone sour. She had worked for an advertising agency, doing copy and layout, but couldn't find anything in her line in the Lauderdale area. Betsy Booker had been a dental hygienist in Columbus but hated it because, no matter what kind of shoes she bought, her feet hurt all the time. Betsy's husband was a city fireman, and Jeannie's husband was an accountant.

She seemed miffed at her friend Betsy. There was tension there, and it had something to do with Harry Broll. I tried to pry, but she sidestepped me, asked me what I did. I told her I was in marine salvage, and she said she knew it had to be some kind of outdoor work.

Finally I took a calculated risk and said, "If my friend likes the apartment, then I'll see what I can do with Harry Broll. Hope you don't mind hearing somebody bad-mouth him. Harry is such a pompous, obnoxious, self-important jackass, it will be a pleasure to see how far down he'll come on the price."

"You said you were friends, McGee!"

"I said I knew him. Do I look like a man who needs friends like that?"

"Do I look like a girl who'd work for a man like that?"

We shook hands across the table, agreeing we both had better taste. Then she told me that Betsy Booker's taste was more questionable. Betsy had been having an affair with Harry Broll for two months.

"Betsy and I were in a two-bedroom on the fourth on the highway side, but she has gradually been moving her stuff up onto six into his one-bedroom, Apartment Sixty-one. I guess it hurt her sore feet, all that undressing and dressing and undressing and walking practically the length of the building."

"Bitter about it?"

"I guess I sound bitter. It's more like hating to see her be so damned dumb. She's a real pretty blonde with a cute figure, and she just isn't used to being without a guy, I guess. It isn't a big sex thing going on. Betsy just has to have somebody beside her in the night, somebody she can hear breathing. She makes up these weird stories about how it's all going to work out. She says he's going to make a great big wad of money on some kind of land promotion stock and, because Mrs. Broll deserted her husband, he's going to be able to get a divorce and marry Betsy."

"Couldn't it happen like that?"

"With him? Never!" she said and explained how she hadn't liked Harry's looks and had checked him out. Her best source had been the housekeeper at the apartment building. Last November when the place had been finished, Harry Broll had taken over Apartment 61. He had an unlisted phone installed. He did not get any mail there.

"It's obvious what he was setting up," Jeannie said. "The world is full of Harry Broll-type husbands. The housekeeper said some Canadian broad moved into the apartment a week later. Harry would take long lunch hours. But he must have slipped up somehow, because Mrs. Broll arrived one day about Christmastime and went busting in when Harry was leaving, and there was a lot of screaming going on.

His wife left him, even though Harry had gotten rid of his girl friend. Then Harry moved out of his house and into the apartment. Betsy saw his house once. He took her there and showed it to her. She said it's big and beautiful. She won't ever get to live there. He'll dump her when he gets tired of her."

She said two drinks would be plenty. I paid the check and took her out and introduced her to Miss Agnes. Jeannie was so delighted with my ancient Rolls that I had to drive her up to Pompano Beach and back. I let her out across from the Casa de Playa. I wondered if I should caution her about mentioning my name to Betsy, who might in turn mention it to Harry Broll and turn him more paranoid than ever. But it seemed to be too long a chance to worry about and too little damage from it even if it did happen.

She gave me an oblique, quick, half-shy look that said something about wondering if she would ever see me again. I discovered that I would like to see her again. We said cheerful and conspiratorial good-byes. She walked around the front of Miss Agnes, waited for a gap in traffic, and hastened across the highway. Her legs were not quite too thin, I decided. The brown-red hair had a lively bounce. From the far curb she turned and waved, her smile long-range but very visible.

———

It was dark when I parked Miss Agnes. I walked to F Dock and on out to Slip 18 and made a ritualistic check of the mooring lines and spring lines, then checked to see how the *Muñequita* was riding, tucked in against the flank of *The Busted Flush*, fenders in proper placement to prevent thumps and gouges.

"Don't pretend you can't hear my foot tapping, you rude, tardy son of a bitch," Jilly said with acid sweetness. She was at the sun-deck rail, outlined against the misty stars with a pallor of dock lights against her face.

I went aboard, climbed up, and reached for her, but she ducked away. "What did I forget, woman?"

"The Townsends. I told you I accepted for both of us. Don't you remember at all?"

"What did we accept?"

"Drinks aboard the *Wastrel* and dinner ashore. They're over at Pier 66. Old friends, dear. She was the heavy little woman with the good diamonds."

"Oh."

"You're drawing a blank, aren't you?"

"I seem to be."

"Hurry and change and we can join them at dinner. And, dear, not quite as informal as you were at my little party, please?"

"Is she the woman who kept talking about her servant problem? No matter what anybody else was talking about?"

"Yes. That's Natalie. And Charles is hard of hearing, and he's too vain to admit it or buy one of those little electronic things. *Please* hurry, Travis." She eeled into my arms, pressed herself close to me. She smelled very good, and she felt springy and useful. "The sooner we go, dearest, the sooner we can leave their party and come back and have our own little party."

I gave her a good solid whack on the behind and said, "You go ahead and make excuses."

"Ouch! That was too rough, really. You'll be along soon?"

"Jilly honey, I don't know those people. I can't talk to them, and they can't talk to me. I could use up my life with people like that and never know where it went."

"They're my *friends!* I won't permit you to be rude to my friends. You accepted, you know."

"*You* accepted."

"But I expect you to have some consideration for—"

"Don't expect anything from me, Jillian. Sorry I forgot. Sorry you had to hang around waiting for me. Now go to your party and have a good time."

"Do you mean it?"

"Why shouldn't I want you to have a good time?"

"I have *had* it with you, you bahstid!"

"Sorry, Jilly. I don't go to parties unless I like the people."

She went clicking down the outside ladderway and clacked her way aft and off the *Flush* and down the dock and away into the night. I went below, turned on a few lights, built a drink, ran a thumb down the stack of tapes, picked Eydie, and chunked her into the tape player and fixed volume.

Eydie has comforted me many times in periods of stress. She has the effortlessness of total professionalism. She is just so damned good that people have not been able to believe she is as good as she is. She's been handed a lot of dull material, some of it so bad that even her best hasn't been able to bring it to life. She's been mishandled, booked into the right places at the wrong time, the wrong places at the right time. But she can do every style and do it a little better than the people who can't do any other. Maybe a generation from now those old discs and tapes of Eydie will be the collectors' joy, because she does it all true, does it all with pride, does it all with heart.

So I settled back and listened to her open her throat and let go, backed by the Trio Los Panchos, Mexican love songs in flawless Mexican Spanish. She eased the little itch of remembering just how good my Irish lady had smelled, tasted, and felt.

A lot of the good ones get away. They want to impose structure upon my unstructured habits. It doesn't work. If I wanted structure, I'd live in a house with a Florida room, have 2.7 kids, a dog, a cat, a smiling wife, two cars, a viable retirement and profit-sharing plan, a seven handicap, and shortness of breath.

God only knows how many obligations there would have been once we were living in the British Virgins. Sing to me, Eydie. I just lost a pretty lady.

Through the music I heard the bong of my warning bell. I put on the aft floods and trapped Meyer in the white glare, blinking. I turned them off and let him in. I could not use Eydie for background music, so I ejected the tape and put a nothing tape on and dropped the sound down to the threshold of audibility.

Meyer said, "I was here an hour ago, and there was a beautiful, angry lady here all dressed up, with someplace to go but nobody to go with."

"Fix yourself a knock. She decided to go alone."

"I bet."

"I am a crude, selfish bastard, and she is through with me."

He came back with a drink. He sat and said, "They tell me that a ring in the nose bothers you for the first week or so and then you never notice it again."

"Until somebody yanks on the rope."

"Oh, she wouldn't do that without good cause."

"Who the hell's side are you on?"

"She'll be back."

"Don't put any money on it."

"Speaking of money . . ."

"Harry Broll?"

"Yes, indeed. I had a long, tiring day. I talked to twenty people. I lied a lot. This is what I put together. It is all a fabric of assumption and supposition. Harry Broll is a small- to medium-sized cog in the machine called SeaGate, Inc. It is Canadian money, mostly from a

Quebec financier named Dennis Waterbury, and New York money from a syndicate there which has been involved in other land deals. They needed Broll because of his knowledge of the local scene, the local contacts, legal shortcuts, and so on. It is a privately held corporation. They are going public. The offering price has not been set yet, but it will be about twenty-six or twenty-seven dollars a share. Most of the shares will be offered by the corporation, but about a third of the public offering will be by the present shareholders. Harry will be marketing a hundred thousand shares."

Cause for a long, low whistle. Old Harry with two and a half mil before taxes was a boggling picture for the mind to behold.

"How soon does he get rich?"

"Their fiscal year ends the last day of this month. The national accounting firm doing the audit is Jensen, Baker and Company. They will apparently get a guaranteed underwriting through Fairmont, Noyes. I hear that it is a pretty clean deal and that SEC approval should be pretty much cut and dried after they get the complete audit report, the draft of the red herring."

I stared at him. "Red herring?"

"Do you know what a prospectus is?"

"That thing that tells you more than you care to know about a new issue of stocks or bonds?"

"Yes. The red herring is the prospectus without the per share price of the stock on it or the date of issue. And it is a complete disclosure of *everything* to do with the company, background of executives and directors, how they got their stock, what stock options they may hold, what financial hanky-panky, if any, they've ever been involved in. Very interesting reading sometimes."

"Nice to see an old acquaintance get rich enough to afford a hell of a lot of alimony."

"When a company is in registration, they get very secretive, Travis. Loose lips can sink financial ships."

"What would he want Mary to sign? He said it was to protect his interest in SeaGate."

"I wouldn't have any idea."

"Can you find out?"

"I can try to find out. I suppose the place to go would be West Palm. That's where the administrative offices of SeaGate are. That's where they are doing the audit, starting early so that they can close the books as of April thirtieth. It would be futile to try to pry anything out of the Jensen, Baker people. But maybe somebody in the SeaGate organization might talk. What did you do today?"

I told him. It was complicated and a lot of it was wasted time and effort, so I kept to the things that had worked.

Then I got to my big question. I had been bouncing it off the back of my mind for an hour, and it was going to be a pleasure to share the trauma with someone else.

"Here is this distrait husband, Meyer. He says he doesn't chase women. The Canadian girl was an exception, a big mistake. He wants me to tell Mary he wants her back. They'll go on a nice trip together. He is so rattled and upset he takes out his little gun and tries to kill me. Suppose he had. His two and a half mil would do him no good at all. And Mary could do him no good by coming back. Okay. He stashed his Canadian tail in Apartment Sixty-one at his Casa de Playa, and it was right there that Mary caught him. Harry got rid of the girl friend. Mary gloomed around for a time, and then she left him. He wants her back. He's sending messages through me, he thinks, to get her to come back to him. Let's say she decides to go back. She goes to their house and finds it closed up. She knows he has the apartment. So she'd go there next, and she'd find him all cozied up there with a blonde named Betsy Booker. Draw me some inferences, please."

"Hmmm. We'll assume that the Booker woman is living in Broll's apartment with him, and the signs of her presence are too numerous to eliminate with short warning. Thus, when Broll came to see you, he either was very sure that Mary *would* not come back to him or that Mary *could* not come back to him. Or, possibly, if Mary could come back to him and decided to come back to him, he would have an early warning system to give him ample time to get the Booker woman out of the apartment and maybe even move back to Blue Heron Lane. This would imply that he knows where she is and has some pipeline to her. In either case, there would be considerable insincerity in his visit to you. Yet a man playing games does not pause in the middle of the game to murder someone out of jealousy. So we come to a final postulate which is not particularly satisfying. We assume that he is and was sincere but is too comfortable with his current living arrangement to want to think it through and see how easily it could spoil his second chance with Mary."

"He's not that dumb. Dumb, but not *that* dumb."

"Logic has to take into account all alternatives."

"Would you consider eating Hungarian tonight?" I asked him.

"Considered and approved."

"Poker dollar for the tab?"

"Food and drink, all on one."

six

The way you find Mary is the same way you find anybody. Through friends and neighbors. And patience. Through shopping habits, money habits, doctor, dentist, bureaucratic forms and reports. And more patience.

You reconstruct the events of three and a half and four years ago and try to remember the names and places, the people who could be leads. You find out who Mary used to be, and from that maybe you find out where she is.

To start with, she was Tina Potter's friend. Came down to see Tina and Freddie. Came down from Rochester, New York. It was just a visit, and then she got her own place. Had some money, some kind of income. Didn't have to work. Came down because she had just been through a jolting and ugly divorce action. She'd gotten her maiden name back by court order. Mary Dillon. Dillon and Dolan. I seemed to be working my way through the Ds. D for divorce.

A quiet young woman. We all got to like her. She had been putting the pieces of herself back together very very nicely. Then something happened. What the hell was it?

At last I remembered. Tina Potter had come over to the *Flush* late one afternoon and asked me if I could sort of keep an eye on Mary. Freddie had a special assignment in Bogotá, and Tina would go with him only if she was sure somebody would watch over Mary.

The incident that had racked her up had been the accidental death of her divorced husband a few days before. A one-car accident on a rainy night somewhere near Rochester. Left the road and hit a tree.

I remembered Tina's earnest face as she said, "Two-bit psychology for whatever it's worth, McGee. I think Mary had the idea, hidden so deep she didn't even realize it, that one day her Wally would grow up and come back to her and then they'd have the kind of marriage she thought they were going to have the first time around. So with him dead, it can't ever be. She's trying to hang on, but it's very white-knuckle stuff. Would you mind too much? She trusts you. She can talk to you."

So I had spent a lot of time with Mary. Beach walking, driving around, listening to music. But if she laughed, she couldn't be sure it wouldn't turn into tears. She had no appetite. The weight loss was apparent. A drink would hit her too hard.

I suggested the aimless cruise. Get away. No destination. Mary knew by then it wasn't a shrewd way of hurrying her into the sack, because had that been the target, it would have happened one of the times when her guard was way down. She agreed without much enthusiasm, provided she could pay her share of the expenses and do her share of the chores aboard.

After two weeks she had really begun to come out of it. At first she had slept twelve and fourteen hours a night, as if her exhaustion was of the same kind that happens after an almost mortal wound. Then she had begun to eat. The listlessness had turned to a new energy. She could laugh without its turning to tears.

One day when we were anchored a dozen miles north of Marathon, among some unnamed islands, I took the little Sea Gull outboard apart, cleaned it, lubricated it, reassembled it, while she zipped around out there in the sailing dinghy, skidding and tacking in a brisk bright wind. When she came back aboard the *Flush,* she was windblown, sun glowing, salty, happy, and thirsty. Before she went off to take her very niggardly freshwater shower, she brought me a beer. She told me she hadn't felt so good in a long long time. We clinked bottles in a toast to a happy day. She looked, smiling, into my eyes, and then her eyes changed. Something went click. They widened in small shock and surprise, then looked soft and heavy. Her head was too heavy for her slender neck. Her mouth was softer. Her mouth said my name without making a sound. She got up and left me, her walk slow and swaying, and went below. It had been awareness, invitation, and acceptance all in a few moments, all without warning. I remember hastily fastening the last piece of the housing back onto the small motor and deciding that I could test it and stow it later. The lady was below, and there was a day to celebrate, a cruise to celebrate, a recovery to celebrate.

So try Tina and Freddie Potter. Long gone, of course. Scrabbled around in the locker where I throw cards and letters. Found one a year old. Address in Atlanta. Direct-dialed Atlanta information, then direct-dialed the Potter house. Squeals of delight, then desolation that I wasn't in Atlanta. Freddie had just gone off to work. She had to quiet the kids down, then she came back on the line.

"Mary? Gee, I guess the last I heard was Christmastime, Trav. She wrote kind of a short dreary note on the back of a New Year's card. She sounded pretty depressed, so I wrote her, but I didn't hear from her. What's the matter? Why are you looking for her?"

"She left Harry Broll early in January."

"That doesn't surprise me much. I never could understand why she married him. Or the first one, Wally, either. Some women seem to have to pick losers every time. Like some women pick alcoholics every time. But . . . I'd think she'd get in touch with you or with us. But you know Mary. Doesn't want to be a burden to anyone."

"How about family?"

"Well, there was just her mother up in Rochester, and she died two years ago. That was all she had, Trav. Gee, I can't think of who you could ask. But I'd think she'd have some friend she'd talk to. A neighbor or something."

She couldn't contribute anything more. She wanted me to let her know when I found out where Mary was, and she wanted me to come to Atlanta and stay with them and tell them all the news about everybody around the marina.

I couldn't use the Rolls pickup to visit the neighbors along Blue Heron Lane. There aren't any cover stories to fit that set of wheels. And housewives are very edgy these days. They have little peepholes set into the doors and outdoor intercom speakers and little panic buttons to push if they get too nervous. Respectability is essential. Nothing eccentric, please.

So I borrowed Johnny Dow's Plymouth sedan, and I wore pressed slacks, a sincere jacket, an earnest shirt, and a trustworthy necktie. I carried a black zipper portfolio and a dozen of my business cards. I am Travis McGee, Vice President of CDTA, Inc. It is no lie. Meyer incorporated the company a few years ago, and he keeps it active by paying the tiny annual tax. CDTA means nothing at all. Meyer picked the letters because they sound as if they have to mean something. Commercial Data Transmission Authority. Consolidated Division of Taxes and Audits. Contractors' Departmental Transit Acceptance.

In my sincere, earnest, trustworthy way I was going to hit the neighborhood on this hot Friday morning with a nice check which I had to deliver to Mrs. Harry Broll in settlement of her claim and get her to sign a release. I used one of the checks Meyer had ordered. It was on an actual account. Of course, the account was inactive and had about twelve dollars in it, but the blue checks were impressively imprinted with spaces for his signature and mine. He borrowed a checkwriter from a friend in one of the shops and we debated the amount for some time before settling on a figure of $1,093.88.

"Good morning, ma'am. I hate to bother you like this, but I wonder if you can help me. My name is McGee. Here is my card. I've got out a check payable to Mrs. Harry Broll in full payment of her claim of last year, and I have a release here for her to sign, but the house looks as if they're off on a long trip or moved or something. Could you tell me how I could find Mrs. Broll?"

It was not a long street. Three short, curving blocks. Large lots, some of them vacant, so that the total was not over twenty-five homes right on Blue Heron Lane. The Broll house was in the middle of the middle block on the left. The canal ran behind the houses on the left-hand side, following the curves. Dig a canal and you have instant waterfront.

I made the logical moves. I parked the Plymouth in the Broll driveway, tried the doorbell, then tried the neighbors, the nearest ones first.

"I can't help you at all. We moved in here three weeks ago, all the way from Omaha, and that house has been empty since we moved in, and from any sign of neighborliness from anybody else around here, all the houses might as well be empty, if you ask me."

"Go away. I don't open the door to anyone. Go away."

"Mrs. Broll? Someone said they split up. No, we weren't friendly. I wouldn't have any idea where you could find her."

At the fourth front door—the fifth if you count the place where nobody answered—there was a slight tweak at the baited end of my line.

"I guess the one to ask would be Mrs. Dressner. Holly Dressner. She and Mrs. Broll were all the time visiting back and forth, morning coffee and so forth. That's the next house there, number twenty-nine, if she's home. She probably is. I didn't hear her backing out."

After the second try on the doorbell I was about to give up. I could hear the chimes inside. No answer. Then the intercom speaker fastened to the rough-cut cypress board beside the front door clicked and said, "Who is it? And, for God's sake, just stand there and talk in a normal tone of voice. If you get close to the speaker and yell, I won't understand word one."

I gave my spiel, adding that the lady next door told me she would be the one to ask. She asked me if I had a card, and she had me poke it through the mail slot. I wondered why she sounded so out of breath.

I heard chains and locks, and she pulled the door open and said, "So come in." She wore a floor-length terry robe in wide yellow and white stripes, tightly belted. Her short, blond, water-dark hair was soaked. "I was in the pool. Daily discipline. Come on out onto the terrace. I'm too wet to sit in the living room."

She was a stocky woman with good shoulders and a slender waist. She had a tan, freckled face, broad and good humored, pale lashes and brows, pretty eyes. The terrace was screened, and the big pool took up most of the space. Sliding glass doors opened the terrace up into the living room. The yard beyond the screening and beyond the flower beds sloped down to a small concrete dock where a canopied Whaler was moored.

She invited me to sit across from her at a wrought iron table with a glass top.

"Try that on me again, Mr. McGee. Slowly. Is this the check?"

She picked it up and put it down and listened as I went through it again. "A claim for what?" she asked.

"Mrs. Dressner, it's company policy not to discuss casualty claims and settlements. I'm sure you can understand why."

"Mr. McGee, may I ask you a personal question?"

"Of course."

"How come you are so full of bullshit?"

I stared at her merry face and merry smile. But above the smile the hazel eyes were expressionless as poker chips.

"I . . . I don't quite understand."

"Go back to Harry and tell him that this didn't work, either. What does he think I am? Some kind of idiot, maybe? Good-bye, Mr. McGee."

"This isn't for Harry. This is for me."

"So who the hell are you?"

"How friendly are you with Mary anyway?"

"Very very very. Okay?"

"What happened to her when Wally got killed?"

She frowned at me. "She came apart. She flipped."

"And a man took her on a boat ride?"

"Right. And the way she talked about him, that's the one she should have played house with instead of Harry Broll."

"I almost thought about it seriously."

"You?"

"Travis McGee. *The Busted Flush*. Cruised the Keys and up the west coast to Tampa Bay. Taught her to sail. Taught her to read a chart. Taught her to navigate."

She put her determined chin on her fist and stared at me. "That *was* the name. You, huh? So what's with the funny games, coming here with your funny card and your funny check? If you knew we're close friends, why not start honest?"

"I have not seen her or talked to her in over three years, Holly. And don't jump on my knowing your first name and try to make anything out of it. The woman next door clued me."

"Hitting the whole neighborhood?"

"One at a time. Mary is . . . low-key intense. She hides a lot of herself. She doesn't make friends easily. But she needs people, so I thought she'd have to have a friend in the neighborhood. A friend, not an acquaintance. Right?"

"So right, McGee. Coffee and tears. Most women bug me. Mary doesn't. I . . . still don't feel right about you. About taking you for granted. It *could* be some kind of a trick. I want to ask you things, but I can't think of anything to ask that you couldn't have gotten from Harry."

"He's trying to find her."

"You know it! I thought the silly son of a bitch was going to try to shake it out of me."

"When was this?"

"A couple of weeks ago. He'd had a couple. He got all weepy. He insisted I had to know where Mary is."

"Do you know where she is?"

"McGee, I know why Harry wants to find her. He wants her to come back to him and sign something and live happily ever after."

"It might be an ugly shock if she did come back."

"How?"

"She'd find the house empty, and she'd go look for Harry at the Casa de Playa, where he just so happens to be shacked with a divorcing blonde named Betsy Booker. In Apartment Sixty-one."

I couldn't read her expression. "So?"

"So isn't that where Mary found him with the Canadian?"

"Only two people could have told you that. Or three. Harry, Mary, or Lisa—the Canadian quiff."

"Wrong."

"The hell you say."

"I got it out of Betsy Booker's best friend, Jeannie Dolan, also from Columbus, who got part of it from Betsy and part of it from the housekeeper. Jeannie and Betsy take turns manning the sales desk at the Casa de Playa."

I saw her buy it and give a small nod. "So help me. That rotten Harry. Jesus! The way I read it, Lisa was not the first. Just the first she caught him with. He really is one sorry bastard."

"How did she find out?"

"She thinks it was one of the girls in his office or a girl he'd fired, trying to make things rough for him. She got a phone call. The person on the other end whispered. Mary said it was spooky. Something very much to the point. 'Mrs. Broll, your husband has loaned Apartment Sixty-one in his new building to Lisa Dissat, and he'll be taking another long lunch hour today so he can drive out there and screw her.' So she drove out and hid somewhere until he arrived and went upstairs. Then she went up to the sixth floor and waited until the door opened and he started to come out. She took a quick run at the door and knocked it open and charged past him and found the bare-ass Canadian getting ready to take a nice nap. I take it there was a certain amount of screaming going on for a while."

"Then Harry got rid of the girl friend?"

"She was packed and out of there the next day. Back to Canada, Harry told Mary. He confessed his sad story. He had gone to Quebec for business conferences with his Canadian partners. He had to dictate new agreements. They sent the secretary to the hotel. They worked very late. He was too tired to think clearly. She was pretty and available. It went on for the three days he was up there. He came back. Two days after he was back, she phoned him at his office from Miami. She had quit her job and followed him back to Florida. So he told Mary that while he was trying to talk Lisa into going back, he put her up at the apartment. I guess he was having a hard time convincing her. He talked from the end of November till two days before Christmas. That's a lot of long lunches and a lot of evening conferences."

"But Mary didn't leave him until January fifth."

"Harry told you that?"

I laughed. "I thought the silly son of a bitch was going to try to shake it out of me, too. This was just the other day. And he got weepy."

"So you're finding her for him?"

"May I ask you the same personal question you asked me?"

"Okay. Okay. I'm sorry. Why then?"

"For myself. Pride, I guess. Harry thought if she was really in trouble, she would come running to me. And the more I think about it, the more logical it seems. That she would. Besides—" I stopped suddenly.

"What's the matter?"

"When was Harry here, did you say?"

"Oh, two weeks ago."

"Can you pin it down to a day?"

"Let me go take a look at my kitchen calendar and see."

She came back and said, "Less than two weeks ago. It was a Monday morning. April fifth."

"He told me someone had seen Mary with me on April second. He was wrong, of course. Why would he come after you instead of me if she was seen with me?"

"Maybe he hadn't been told about it before he came to see me," she said.

"And maybe he was trying to get you to admit she'd moved in with me or some damn thing. What difference does it make anyway? He didn't act as if he was thinking very clearly."

"Mary was thinking about getting in touch with you. She was sitting in my kitchen wondering out loud if she should. That was after she'd decided to take off. Then she decided it would be better to have some breathing space in between, some time to herself first. I thought she would have written you long before now. It's over three months."

"She writes you?"

"Don't get too cute, McGee."

"Okay. Do you know where she is?"

"Yes."

"And she is okay?"

"I have no reason to think she isn't. If I was Mary, I would be relishing every damn moment. The farther from Harry, the better."

"That's all I wanted to know, Mrs. Dressner. That she is okay. I had to hear it from somebody I could believe."

"Hey! You're spoiling the fun. You're supposed to worm the whole story out of me. Or try to."

"It's Harry who has to know where she is. Not me."

"Friend McGee, I am not about to get you two men confused, one with the other."

"So she is a long distance from here. And should be relishing every moment. Right?"

"I've gotten some comedy postcards."

"I believe you. There are people you believe and people you don't. I don't need to know any more than I know right now."

She looked rueful. "Everybody believes me. Everything I'm thinking shows. I've got one of those faces. I'd make a rotten spy. Hey, sit down again. I haven't offered you anything. Coffee, tea, beer, booze? Even some lunch?"

"No, thanks."

"Believe me, I'm glad to have anybody show up here. This is one of the days when the house gets empty somehow. David—my husband—has been gone all week. He'll be home tomorrow, probably about noon. He's gone a week or more out of every month. Our two little gals are tennis freaks, so who sees them at all when the weather is like this? I miss hell out of Mary, I really do. You could choke down some terrible coffee at least. Pretend it's delicious, and I'll tell you where Mary is. Even if you don't have to know."

She brought coffee from the kitchen to the glass-top table on the screened terrace. Moving around had loosened the hitch in the terry belt, and when she bent to pour my coffee, the robe suddenly spilled open. She spilled coffee, clutched frantically, put the pot down, and gathered herself together and tied the robe firmly, her face dark red under the freckles. It was obvious she had not contrived it.

"Some people are solitary drinkers. I'm a solitary skinny-dipper."

"It's habit forming," I said.

She got paper towels and mopped up the spilled coffee and filled my cup the rest of the way. She sat and stared at me, lips pursed. Finally she said, "Thank you."

"For?"

"For not jumping to any conclusions, for which I could not exactly blame you. Good God, I tell you my husband is away, my kids are playing tennis, I'm lonesome. I beg you to stay for coffee and then damn near drop my robe on the floor."

"Some days are like that."

"I like the way you can smile without hardly changing your mouth at all. It's kind of all in the eyes. Mary said you're a doll. She said big and brown and sort of beat-up looking. But you're bigger and browner than the idea I had of you. About Mary. That was a sordid scene at the Casa de Playa. It shook her. Friendship is friendship, but you don't tell your friends what to do when it comes to big emotional decisions. Through Christmas and the rest of December she spent a lot of time over here. I let her bounce it all off me. She was thinking aloud, arguing it out. Taking one side and then the other, while all I did was say 'um.' But I could tell which side was winning. Finally she said that if she hadn't already had one divorce, she would definitely decide to leave Harry. It was a lousy reason to stick around, just to avoid being divorced twice, which has a kind of ring of failure to it, failure as a person or as a woman. So she was going to leave him and go away and, to be real fair, think it all through. But the way she felt, she'd probably sue for divorce after the waiting period. I waited for her to really make her mind up, and then I questioned her to make certain she was sure, and finally I told her about a little problem I had once with her husband. There'd been a party down the street and the four of us, the Brolls and the Dressners, had walked back together, a little tight. They came over here for a nightcap. There were supposed to be falling stars. It was in the paper. I wanted to see them. We put out the lights on the terrace, and I stretched out on a sun mattress beside the pool, right over there, to watch up through the screening overhead. David went to the kitchen to fix drinks, and Mary changed her mind about what she wanted and went in the kitchen to tell him. Harry was on a sun mattress near mine. All of a sudden he rolled over and put his big old cigar mouth on mine and pressed me down with his big belly and ran his big paw up under my skirt and started groping me. I froze with shock for about one second, and then I gave a big snap of my back like a huge fishing shrimp and bucked him into the pool in all his clothes. It turned into a big joke. He said he'd gotten up and tripped and fallen in.

"When I told Mary about it, she was furious with me for not telling her sooner. I told her I hadn't told David, because he would have tried to beat Harry to death. I said that now she'd made her mind up, I could tell her about what Harry pulled that time.

Frankly, what I was doing was trying to lock her into her decision to drop that jerk forever. Having her own money made it easy for her to get away. She got it from her trust officer at the Southern National Bank and Trust in Miami. Cash. A lot, I think. She didn't want Harry tracing her through credit cards or personal checks. She told me she didn't want to hear his voice or see his face once she left. Not for a long time anyway. We sat right out here one afternoon, a warm day for early January, and we looked at the travel folders she'd picked up from some little travel agency where she wasn't known. She wanted to go to the islands. Between the two of us we decided that Grenada looked the best, and it was certainly far enough, way down there at the bottom of the West Indies, almost as far as Trindad. So the travel agency sent wires and cables and got her set up at what looked like a very plush place, the Spice Island Inn. She's sent me those joke greetings. Four or five, I guess. Airmail takes eight days! That place is a real hideaway."

"Harry told me she left on January fifth. He said he came home from work and she was gone."

"I think it was an impulse. She wasn't going to leave until Thursday or Friday. I was out most of that afternoon. Maybe she tried to say good-bye. I guess she probably drove down to Miami and stayed in a hotel or motel until her flight left."

"I wonder what she did with her car?"

"I think she was going to leave it at Miami International."

"Which is two fifty a day, no matter how many days, so she is up to a two-hundred-dollar parking charge."

"McGee, the lady had decided to go first class all the way. That is what ladies do when they get mad enough."

"What would Harry be wanting her to sign?"

"I haven't the faintest idea."

"Good coffee."

"Come *on!* It tastes like stewed tire patches."

She walked me to the door. She got ahead of me and leaned back against the door and looked up quizzically. She stood a little taller than my elbow. "McGee, I just wondered. It seems like a hell of a lot of trouble you went to. The business cards and the funny check and the sales talk."

"No big thing, Holly. The cards and the checks were in the cupboard. I have to hunt for people sometimes. You learn to use something that works."

"Why do you hunt for people?"

"I do favors for friends."

"Is that a line of work with you?"

"I really wouldn't know how to answer that question."

She sighed. "Heck, I thought I could solve a problem for Mary. She never *was* able to figure out what it is that you do for a living."

"Salvage consultant."

"Sure. Sure."

When I glanced back, she was standing on her shallow front steps, arms crossed. Her hair was beginning to dry and to curl a little. She smiled and waved. She was a sturdy, healthy woman with a very friendly smile.

seven

I was on the beach by three o'clock that Friday afternoon and that was where Meyer found me at a few minutes to four. He dropped his towel, sat upon it, and sighed more loudly than the surf in front of us or the traffic behind us.

There were nine lithe maidens, miraculously unaccompanied by a flock of boys, playing some game of their own devising on the hard sand in the foamy wash of the waves. It involved an improvised club of driftwood, a small, yellow, inflated beach ball, one team out in the water, and one on the beach. Either you had to whack the ball out over the heads of the swimmers before they . . . or you had to hit it past a beach player who then . . . Anyway, it involved a lot of running, yelping, and team spirit.

"A gaggle of giggles?" Meyer said, trying that one on me.

My turn. "How about a prance of pussycats?"

"Not bad at all. Hmmm. A scramble of scrumptious?"

"Okay. You win. You always win."

He slowly scratched his pelted chest and smiled his brown-bear smile. "We both win. By being right here at this time. All the strain of a long, difficult, and futile day is evaporating quickly. Meyer is at peace. Play on, young ladies, because from here on out life will be a lot less fun for most of you."

"Grow up and be earnest and troubled?" I asked. "Why does it have to be that way?"

"It doesn't. It shouldn't be. Funny, though. They take all those high spirits, all that sense of fun and play, into a commune, and within a year they are doleful wenches indeed. Somber young versions of American Gothic, like young wagon-train mothers waiting for the Indians to ride over the ridge. And their men look like the pictures of the young ones slain at Shiloh. Idealism in our society is pretty damned funereal."

One of the players looked up the beach and gave a quick wave and then went churning into the water to capture the yellow ball.

"One of my constituents," Meyer said comfortably.

"You are a dirty old man."

"You have a dirty mind, McGee. I could not bring myself to ever touch the child. But in all fairness it does enter my mind. Lovely, isn't she?"

"Exquisite."

"Her last name is Kincaid, and I do not know her first name. She is known to everyone as Breadbox. She has an incredible appetite. She's an economics major at Yale. Quite a good mind. Her father grows tobacco in Connecticut. She drove down in a five-year-old Porsche with two other girls. This summer she is going to work in a boutique aboard a cruise ship. She has a dog at home named Rover, which seems to have come full circle and is now an 'in' name for a dog. She is getting over a romance which ended abruptly and does not want to become interested in another man for years and years, she says. Tennis used to be her sport, but now she prefers—"

"So all right already, Meyer. Damn it."

"I think she was waving at someone behind us."

"What?"

"I never saw the child before in my life. I was just putting together into one package some of the things some of the other young ladies have told me."

"Have you been drinking?"

"No. But if you'd like to . . ."

With as little warning as a flock of water birds, the nine maidens dropped the club and went jogging north along the beach, one of them clutching the yellow ball.

Meyer said, "I did not do well today, Travis. Just a few small items. Dennis Waterbury is in his mid-thirties, bland, shrewd, tough, quick, merciless—and completely honest. He gives his word and keeps it."

"Listen. I was able—"

"Let me deliver my few crumbs first. Harry Broll's cost on his one hundred thousand shares was ten dollars a share, and his money and the money the others put in was used to acquire the land, prepare sites, build roads, start the utility construction, water, waste processing, and so forth. A very golden opportunity for a man like Broll to get his foot in the door with people like Waterbury and friends. But in order to make it big, he had to pluck himself pretty clean, I imagine, and borrow to the hilt. Put up one million and drag down two million and a half. The odds are splendid, the risk low enough."

"About Mary, I—"

"I can't seem to find out what she would have to sign. She wouldn't have to sign anything in connection with the stock. It's in his name. She isn't on his business paper."

"Mary is alive and well and living in Grenada."

"In Spain?"

"No. The island."

"Dear chap, the one in Spain is Gran-AH-duh. The island is Gre-NAY-duh. The British corrupted it with their usual mispronunciation of all place names."

"You've been there?"

"No."

"But you know a lot about it?"

"No. I happen to know how to pronounce it. One has to start somewhere."

"Let's swim."

After about ten minutes Meyer intercepted me fifty yards from the beach, to ask, "How come you could find that out and Harry can't?"

"I found the only person who might really know for sure, aside from the travel agent. A neighbor lady, who shows her good taste by disliking the hell out of Harry Broll. She thought for a while Harry sent me. I softened her up. She makes terrible coffee."

"Did Harry try to pry it out of her too?"

"Yes. Nearly two weeks ago. With tears. Without the gun. But rough. She said she thought he was going to try to shake it out of her."

Meyer nodded and went gliding away, head up, in that powerful, slow, and tireless breastroke that somehow makes me think of a seal when I see his head moving by.

When I came out of the water, he was sitting on his towel again, looking petulant, a rare mood for Meyer.

"Something bothering you?"

"Illogical actions and illogical emotions bother hell out of me, Travis. His wife has been gone over three months. How about checking accounts, credit cards?"

I explained about the trust account and her taking cash so that she couldn't be easily traced by her husband. He said he knew one friendly face in the trust department of Southern National, but of course it would be Monday before he could learn anything there.

"Why bother?" I asked him. "I'm satisfied. We know where she is. I don't give a damn how jittery Harry Broll gets."

We walked back across the bridge together, squinting toward the western sun setting into its usual broad band of whisky soup. "I guess it doesn't matter in any case," Meyer said.

"What doesn't matter?"

"What happens to anybody. Look at the cars, McGee. Look at the people in the cars, on the boats, on the beach, in the water. Everybody is heading toward their own obituary notice at precisely the same speed. Fat babies, and old women like lizards, and the beautiful young with long golden hair. And me and thee, McGee. At tick-tock speed moving straight toward the grave, until all now living are as dead as if they had died in Ancient Rome. The only unknown, and that is a minor one, is how long will each individual travel at this unchanging, unchangeable pace?"

"Good God, Meyer! I was going to buy you dinner."

"Not today. This is not one of my good days. I think I'll open a can of something, go walking alone, fold up early. No need to poison somebody else's evening."

Away he trudged, not looking back. It happens sometimes. Not often. A curious gaiety, follwed by bleak, black depression. It was a Meyer I seldom see and do not know at all.

Friday night. I took my time building a drink, showering, dressing, building a refill. Dark night by then, and a wind building up, so that the *Flush* moved uneasily, creaking and sighing against her lines, nudging at her fenders. I felt restless. I was wondering where to go, who to call, when Jillian came aboard.

She clung tightly and said she had been utterly miserable. She looked up at me with two perfect and effective tears caught in her lower lashes, her mouth quivering. The Townsend party had been desperately dull, really. She shouldn't have tried to force me to go. She shouldn't try to force me to do anything. She realized that now.

She would not do it again, ever. Forgive me, Travis darling, please. I've been so lonely and so ashamed of myself, etc., etc., etc.

Once forgiven, all the lights came on behind her eyes, and the tears were flicked away. Mood of holiday. She had been confident of reconciliation; she had brought hairbrush and toothbrush. And all the urgencies a girl could muster.

In the morning a rare April rain was coming down hard, thrashing at the ports beside the half acre of the captain's wrinkled and rumpled bed, bathing us in gray ten-o'clock light.

"Is your friend in trouble?" she asked.

"Who?"

"That respectable married lady friend, of course."

"Oh. No, she's fine. It turns out she's hiding from her husband. She went down to Grenada."

She lifted her head. "Really? Henry and I went down there on the first really long cruise we took in the *Jilly III*. The Grenadines are one of the great sailing areas of the world. And the yacht basin at St. George's is really marvelous. You see people from everywhere, really. Yacht Services is very helpful."

"She's staying at the Spice Island Inn."

"Quite expensive. Is she alone down there?"

"Apparently."

"She can get into all kinds of delicious mischief if she wants. If she's even half attractive, she won't be lonely. The air is full of spice and perfume down there, dear. It's a fabulously erotic island. Always so warm and lazy, with hot hot sun and the hills and jungles and the beaches. Quite near the equator, you know."

"I didn't know."

"Well, it is. Don't you think we should go there one day?"

"I guess so."

"You don't seem exactly overwhelmed with enthusiasm."

"Sorry."

"Are you going back to sleep, you wretch?"

"Not with you doing what you're doing."

"This? Oh, it's just a sort of reflex thing, I guess. Darling, if you're no longer worried about your friend, could we be ready to aim the *Jilly* toward home on Tuesday? I can get her provisioned on Monday."

"What? Oh, Tuesday. I guess so."

"You don't seem to keep track of what I'm saying."

"I guess I'm easily distracted."

"You're easily something else, too."

"What did you expect?"

"I expect, my dear, if we put our minds to it, we might make the *Guinness Book of Records*. Cozy? A nice rain always makes me very randy." After a moment she giggled.

"What's funny?"

"Oh, I was thinking I might decide we should go to Grenada during the rainy season, dear."

"Ho ho ho."

"Well . . . it amused *me*. When I feel this delicious, I laugh at practically anything. Sometimes at nothing at all."

The unusual cold front that had brought the rain ahead of it moved through late on Saturday afternoon. She went back to the *Jilly III*. She said she had a thousand things to do before we sailed on Tuesday. She said to come over on Sunday, sometime in the afternoon. She said I could bring along some of my clothes and toys then if I wanted.

She left and I locked up again, hot-showered, and fell into a deep sleep. I woke at ten on Saturday night, drank a gallon of water, ate half a pound of rat cheese, and dropped right back down into the pit.

I woke with a hell of a start at four on Sunday morning and thought there was somebody coming aboard. Realized it had been something happening in a dream. Made a grab for what was left of the dream, but it was all gone too quickly. Almost a nightmare. It had pumped me so full of adrenaline there was no hope of going back to sleep. Heart bumped and banged. Legs felt shaky. I scrubbed a bad taste off my teeth, put on jeans and boat shoes and an old gray sweatshirt, and went out onto the deck.

A very silent night. No breeze. A fog so thick the nearer dock lights were haloed and the farther ones were a faint and milky pallor, beyond tangible gray. I could hear slow waves curl and thud against the sand. The craft on either side of the *Flush* were shrouded in the fog, half visible.

Meyer's gloomy message had been delivered none too soon. Everybody else had been ticktocked to the grave, leaving one more trip to complete—mine. Then, far away, I heard a long *screeeeee* of tormented rubber and a deep and ugly thud with a small accompanying orchestration of jangles and tinkles. The thud had been mortal, tick-tocking some racing jackass into his satin-lined box, possibly along with the girl beside him or the surprised folk in the other car.

A few minutes later I heard the sirens, heard them stop at what seemed a plausible distance.

So stop thinking about this and that, McGee, and think about what you don't want to think about; namely, the lush future with the rich widow.

I climbed to the sun deck and went forward and slouched behind the wheel and propped my heels atop the instrument panel, ankles crossed.

That old honorary Cuban had simplified the question all to hell when he'd said that a moral act is something you feel good after. Conversely, you feel bad after an immoral act. But what about the act that is neither moral nor immoral, Papa? How are you supposed to feel then?

Look, we are very suited to each other. There is a lot of control either way on both sides, so timing is no problem at all. She pleases me. She knows how to intensify it. I like the textures and juices, spices and rhythms of her, all her tastes and tastings. We truly climb one hell of a hill, Papa, and when we fall off the far side together, it is truly one hell of a long fall, Papa, and we land truly and well and as zonked out as lovers can get. We laugh a lot. We like to hold each other afterward. We make bawdy jokes. She has a lot of body greed and finds me a satisfying stud. In her gratitude she takes a lot of extra effort to keep things varied and interesting. So?

There's this little problem. I go into the head, Papa, and look at this battered and skewed beach-bum countenance of mine, reflected in the mirror, and my eyes look dull, and my mouth looks slack, and I am wearing the remnants of a doggy little smirk. I know she is in there, a-sprawl on the bed, drifting in and out of her little love doze, and I look truly and well at myself in the mirror, and I do not feel good about anything or bad about anything. I just feel as if I had made one of those little diagonal lines you use to keep track. You know—four little vertical lines side by side and then the diagonal that crosses them out and ends the group.

In the mirror my nose looks too big and my skin looks grainy. I wear the doggy little grin. The smells of her cling to my body. There is the feeling of marking something off on a long score sheet. Something well and truly done that will have to be well and truly done for whatever years we both have left, because that is the bargain. Chop that cotton, tote that bale, plow that little acre of God.

What about it when you don't feel good and you don't feel bad? When you just feel that it's done for this time and done reasonably well, and later on the slack dangle of flesh will turn tumescent, and it will and can be done again, just as well as the last time? With proficiency, determination, patience, understanding, power, and skill. Isn't lovemaking as good a way as any to pass the time for the rest of your life? It tones the body, and it's acceptable exercise, and it makes two people feel good.

If I don't grasp the opportunity, somebody will find some quick and dirty way to let the sea air through my skull.

I'm overdue. That's what Meyer says, and that's what my gut says in a slow cold coil of tingling viscera. Overdue, and scared, and not ready for the end of it yet. The old bullfighters who have known the famous rings and famous breeds despise the little country corridas, because they know that if they do not quit, that is where they will die and the bull that hooks their steaming guts out onto the sand will be a poor animal without class or distinction or style.

An animal as ordinary as Harry Broll.

I shifted position, dug the keys out of my pocket, and found the keyholes in the instrument panel. It is one of the tics of the boat-man, turning on the juice without starting up, just to check fuel levels, battery charge. By leaning close, I could read the gauges in the pallid light.

Maybe it isn't just the woman. This woman. Or a passing of time. It is the awareness, perhaps, of the grasshopper years, of always push-ing all the pleasure buttons. The justification was a spavined sense of mission, galumphing out to face the dragon's fiery breath. It had been a focus upon the torment of individuals to my own profit. Along with a disinterest in doing anything at all about all those greater inequities which affect most of us. Oh, I could note them and bitch about them and say somebody ought to do something. I could say it on my way to the beach or to the bed.

Who will know you were ever around, McGee? Or care?

Wait a minute! What am I supposed to be doing? Making up the slogan I shall paint on my placard and tote in the big parade? A pa-rade is a group, and I'm not a group animal. I think a mob, no mat-ter what it happens to be doing, is the lowest form of living thing, al-ways steaming with potential murder. Several things I could write on my placard and then carry it all by myself down empty streets.

UP WITH LIFE. STAMP OUT ALL SMALL AND LARGE INDIGNITIES. LEAVE EVERYONE ALONE TO MAKE IT WITHOUT PRESSURE. DOWN WITH HURTING. LOWER THE STANDARD OF LIVING. DO WITHOUT PLASTICS. SMASH THE SERVOMECHANISMS. STOP GRABBING. SNUFF THE BREEZE AND HUG THE KIDS. LOVE ALL LOVE. HATE ALL HATE.

Carry my placard and whistle between my teeth and wink and smirk at the girls on the sidewalk watching the nut with his sign.

Am I supposed to go out with my brush and yellow soap and scrub clean the wide grimy world?

If you can't change everything, why try to change any part of it, McGee?

The answer lit up in the foggy predawn morning, right over my head. A great big light bulb with glowing filaments, just like those old-timey ones over in Ft. Myers in the Edison place.

Because, you dumb-ass, when you stop scrubbing away at that tiny area you can reach, when you give up the illusion you are doing any good at all, then you start feeling like this. Jillian Brent-Archer is another name for giving up your fatuous, self-serving morality, and when you give it up, you feel grainy, stud-like, secure, and that doggy little smirk becomes ineradicable.

You are never going to like yourself a hell of a lot, T. McGee, so what little liking you have must be conserved. To become Jilly's amiable useful houseguest and bedguest would turn you into something which you are not—yet have an uncomfortable tendency to become.

You retain the fragile self-respect by giving Them the increasingly good chance of ventilating your skull or scragging you through the heart. There have been some rotten little scenes with Jill, but the next one will be the most memorable of all.

So Mary Broll is okay. And there is a good lump of cash money stashed behind the fake hull in the forward bilge of the *Flush*. But it would be a good time, a very good time, to go steaming out and find the plucked pigeon and clean up its little corner of the world by getting its feathers back—half of them, anyway. Get out there on the range and go down to the pits and stand up for a moment and see if they can pot you between the eyes. If they miss, maybe you'll get your nerve back, you tinhorn Gawain.

eight

On Sunday I did not feel up to facing the predictable fury of Lady Jillian. She wanted me aboard for drinks Monday evening. Time enough, I told myself.

Meyer came over to the *Flush* on Monday morning at about ten thirty. I was punishing myself for recent sensual excess by polishing some neglected brightwork on the instrument panel, using some new miracle goop that was no more miraculous than the old miracle goop.

Without preamble he said, "I phoned the trust department of the Southern National Bank and Trust Company and told the girl to put me through to somebody who could give me a trust account number. When another girl answered, I said that my name was Forrester and I was with Merrill Lynch. I said we had received a dividend which apparently should have been sent to Mrs. Harry Broll's trust account. I wanted to advise New York and mail the check along, and to prevent further confusion, I wanted the trust account number and the name of the trust officer handling that account. Mary Dillon Broll or Mrs. Harry Broll, Twenty-one Blue Heron Lane, and so forth. She told me to hold, and in a minute or two she came back and said the number was TA fifty-three ninety-one, and the trust officer was Mr. Woodrow Willow."

"Interesting, but—"

"I asked her to put me through to Mr. Willow. When he came on the line I introduced myself correctly and told him that I was a personal friend of Mrs. Broll, and she had told me before going away on a trip that he handled her account TA fifty-three ninety-one. He said that was correct. He sounded guarded. Properly so. I told him that Mrs. Broll had asked me to give her some advice regarding rephasing ing her accounts to provide a maximum income, as she anticipated some possible change in her personal status."

"You are getting very crafty lately, Meyer."

"Please stop rubbing those damned dials and look at me. Thank you. He sounded huffy then and said they were perfectly competent to give all necessary investment advice. I told him I knew that and that was why I had called him. I certainly didn't want to usurp their authority and responsibility. I said I seldom make portfolio recommendations any more, only for old friends and at no fee, of course. I said that women often become confused about the way a trust account is set up. I said I understood she had discretion over it, that she could determine what she wanted bought and sold and so direct them. He said that was indeed the case. He sounded wistful, as if he wished it weren't true. I said that I had been trying to get in touch with her in order to clear my ideas with her before coming in to discuss them with him. I said her husband had been unable to help me. I said her house was closed, and her neighbors did not know where she had gone. I asked if he could help me. He said she had phoned him early in January and had come in and drawn out all the accumulated interest and dividends, a sizable amount, and told him she was going away for a month or six weeks. She did not know where. He said he wished he could help me."

"A month or six weeks?"

"Yes. Over three months ago."

"She could have decided to stay longer, you know."

"That's what Woodrow Willow said. He said she was quite upset when she came to see him. He said he could guess why she might be thinking in terms of independent income. So I said that, of course, maximizing income would enable her to live comfortably, but with a woman that young, inflation protection was important."

"Did it work?"

Meyer displayed an uncommonly wolflike smile. "He hesitated and I heard a desk calculator rattling and humming, and then he said that with her equities reinvested in income holdings, she'd have a pretax income of from twenty-five to twenty-seven thousand. So I told him that we should probably think in terms of eighteen to twenty or, in case of substantial alimony, consider tax exempts. He said he'd be delighted to talk to me about it, but of course he would have to have clearance from her to discuss her affairs. I said I realized that. He said he expected to hear from her very shortly, before the end of the month. Travis, I couldn't push him any further."

"I can see that. He was all set to snap shut at any moment. You got a hell of a lot out of him. Congratulations."

"I braced myself and took a risk. I said, 'Oh, yes, of course. To sign those things for Mr. Broll.' He hesitated and then said, 'It's inconvenient for her to come here in person. So she told me when she came in what Mr. Broll was asking of her. It's something that they did once before, and it was paid off. I had her sign the note. The loan was later approved by the loan committee and the board. A sizable loan, secured by the assets in her trust, with her signed authorization to me to deposit the loan proceeds in Mr. Broll's personal checking account. The effective date of the loan was to be April fifteenth, last Thursday. He requires the funds before the end of the month. She requested me to get it all set up but not to go ahead with it until she gets in touch with me and tells me to proceed or to destroy the signed documents and forget it. That's why I expect her to be in touch with me soon.' Travis, I remember you telling me to always press the luck when it is running your way. So I told him that I had heard that Broll was getting very agitated about getting the note and the authorization signed, so I imagined that Mr. Broll had been in touch with him. Mr. Willow has a very weary laugh. He said he hears from Mr. Broll almost constantly. He said he saw no reason to tell Mr. Broll everything was signed and ready to go, awaiting only authorization from her. I got the impression Harry tried to bulldoze him, and Mr. Willow got his back up. Then he began to realize he had told me more than he should. I could *feel* him pulling back. So I jumped in and said that actually the documents aren't signed until she says they are signed. Until then it is an approved line of credit, and if she doesn't care to use it, she doesn't have to. I told him he was quite correct, and I could feel him trying to persuade himself I was not working for Harry Broll. I hope he did."

I put the cap on the miracle goop and swabbed up the few white places where it had dribbled on the varnish, miraculously removing the gloss. I spun the helmsman's seat around and looked at Meyer.

I said to him, "You are pretty damned intense about something I don't understand. We don't know whether Mary wants him to have that money or not. We know she's in Grenada, knowing he's sweating it out, and she's probably enjoying it every time she thinks about it. We know that Harry is getting so frantic he's losing control. He isn't thinking clearly. Are you?"

"She's been gone over three months now. Harry is living in a way that means he doesn't expect her to come back. You thought she'd get in touch with you if she was in trouble. She didn't. Who saw her leave? What travel agency did she use?"

I reached into the back of my mind and swatted something down. It had been buzzing in circles back there. I picked it up off the floor and looked at it. "Meyer, once on that cruise years ago we bought provisions and got a lot of green stamps. I think it was in Boca Grande. They got wet and got stuck together. Mary soaked them apart. It soaked all the glue off. She dried them between paper towels. Then she got a green stamp book and some Elmer's, and she glued them into the book. Meyer, she didn't even *save* green stamps. Another thing. We spent a lot of time anchored out, as far from marinas and boat traffic and shore sounds as we could get. So she kept turning off the generator, the air conditioning, even the little battery transistor radio. She made great things out of the leftovers from yesterday's leftovers. She's not stingy. If you asked for her last dime, she'd borrow two bits somewhere and give you thirty-five cents. But she has a waste-not, want-not twitch. I kidded her about it. She didn't mind. But it didn't change a thing. Holly Dressner told me Mary planned to leave her car at the Miami airport. Okay. Would Mary pay two and a half a day indefinitely? Ninety days is two hundred and twenty-five dollars. Not Mary. No matter how upset. She'd find out the rates and turn around, drive a few miles, make a deal with a gas station or parking lot, and take a cab back and catch her flight."

"If she had time."

"Unless she changed a lot, she'd get there two hours ahead when the ticket desk says one hour. She'd have time."

"So we should go look for her car?"

"Holly should be able to tell me what to look for."

"Travis, I don't want to seem efficient, but why don't we phone Mary in Grenada? I would rather go below and drink one of your Tuborgs and listen to you fight with the island operators than drive to Miami."

I struck myself a heavy blow in the forehead with the heel of my hand, said a few one-, seven- and ten-syllable words, and we went below.

I started at eleven thirty, and by the time I got the desk at the Spice Island Inn, I was in a cold rage. It was a radio link, and nobody seemed to give a damn about completing it. I had mentally hung Alex Bell and Don Ameche in effigy several times.

At last I got the faint voice of a girl, saying, "Spice Island Inn. May I help you?" It was the singsong lilt of the West Indies, where the accented syllables seem to fall at random in strange places.

"Do you have a Mrs. Broll registered? A Mrs. Harry Broll?"

"Who? I am sorry. What last name, sir?"

"Broll. Bee-are-oh-el-el. Broll."

"Ah. Broll. There is no Mrs. Harry Broll."

"Was she there? Did she leave?"

"There is a Mrs. Mary Broll. She is here since many weeks."

"From Florida?"

"Yes. She is here from Florida."

"Can you put me through to her, please?"

"I am sorry."

"Do you mean you can't?"

"There is the instruction, sir. Mrs. Broll does not take overseas calls. Not from anyone, sir."

"This is an emergency."

"I am sorry. I can write down for her your name and the number of your telephone. I cannot say if she returns the call. She does not wish to be disturbed by telephone calls from overseas. If you can give me your name?"

"Never mind. Thank you for your help."

"I am sorry." She said something else, but it faded away into an odd, humming silence. There were loud clicks. Somebody else said, "Code eighteen, route through Barbados, over."

I said, "Hey! Somebody."

The humming stopped and the line went dead as marble. I hung up. I stood up and stretched. "Mrs. Mary Broll has been there for a long time, but she doesn't take overseas calls."

"In case one might be from Harry, I suppose."

"That takes care of it. Right, Meyer?"

"I suppose so."

"It was your idea. I phoned. She's there."

"I know. But . . ."

"But?"

"The known facts now seem contradictory."

"Meyer, for God's sake!"

"Now listen to me. She wants to hide from her husband and think things out. She does not want to take any overseas calls. What would it cost her to get the operator and the desk clerk to deny that she's even registered? Ten Biwi dollars each, ten U.S. dollars total? No more, certainly. If she was sure her husband couldn't trace her, then the only call she *could* get would be from her friend Holly Dressner, and she would want to take a call from her, I'd think. If she set it up so that he *can* find out where she is, then the refusal to take calls would mean she wants him to fly down, and the bait would be the loan he needs."

"First you simplify things, Meyer, and then you complicate the hell out of them. I don't know what to think now."

"Neither do I. That's my problem."

"So we drive to Miami anyway?"

Holly was home, and she was very helpful about the car. "It's one of those Volks with the fancy body. Oh, dear. What in the world are they called?"

"Karmann Ghia."

"Right! Two years old. Dark red. Hardtop. Believe it or not, I can give you the license plate number even. We were shopping, and we went to the place you get the plates together, and mine is about the same weight, so we were in the same series. Hers was one digit more than mine, so hers is One D three-one-oh-eight."

We drove down to Miami in Miss Agnes, and I jammed her through the confusions of the cloverleafs and put her in one of the new airport parking buildings, halfway up the long wide ramp leading to the third level, nosing her against the wall between two squatty Detroit products that made her look like a dowager queen at a rock fest. A mediocre hamburger, gobbled too hastily on the way down, lay like a stone on the floor of my stomach.

I pointed out to Meyer how our task was simplified. Apparently there was some kind of stone-crushing plant in operation not too far from the open parking garages. The longer any car had been parked there, sheltered from the rain, the more white powdered stone dust it had all over it. And Mary's would be one of the whitest of all.

There were more than enough ramps and levels and separate structures. Finally, on a top level on the side farthest from the entrance and exit ramp, I saw Karmann Ghia lines, powdery white as a sugar doughnut. Even the plate was powder white, but the bas-relief of the digits made it readable as I neared it: 3108. Three months of sitting and accumulating stone dust and parking charges.

Meyer drew in the dust atop the trunk. It would have been a childish trick except for what he drew. A single large question mark. I wiped the windshield with the edge of my hand and bent and peered in. Nothing to see except a very empty automobile.

A police sedan drifted up and stopped close behind the Ghia. "Got a problem?" the driver asked. His partner got out.

"No problem, officer."

"Your car?"

"No. It belongs to a friend."

The driver got out. "And you can't quite remember the name of your friend, I suppose?"

I gave him my earnest, affable smile. "Now why'd you think that, officer? This belongs to Mrs. Mary Broll, Twenty-one Blue Heron Lane, Lauderdale, for sure."

"Girl friend?"

"Just a friend, officer."

"Doesn't your friend have anything to say?"

Meyer said, "I was not aware that you were addressing me with any of the prior questions, officer. I happen to have here—"

"Easy. Bring it out real real slow."

"I happen to have here a page from a scratch pad which, if you will examine it, gives the name of the owner and the license number and description of the vehicle."

The nearest officer took the note and looked at it and handed it back. "Repo?"

"What?" Meyer asked. "Oh. Repossession. No. We happened to be parked here, and we knew Mrs. Broll has been gone for three months, and we wondered if she'd left her car here."

The other officer had gotten into their car. I heard his low voice as he used the hand mike. He waited, then got out again. "Isn't on the list, Al," he said.

"Parked here, you say. Now both of you, let me see some ID. Slow and easy. Take it out of the wallet. Keep the wallet. Hand me the ID. Okay. Now you. Okay. Now show me your parking ticket. What kind of a car?"

"Officer, it is a very old Rolls-Royce pickup truck. Bright blue. It's over there in that other—"

"I saw that, Al. Remember? That's the one I had you back up and see if it had the inspection sticker."

It stopped being confrontation and began to be conversation. "Nobody," said Al, "but nobody at all is going to arrive here in that freak truck to pull anything cute. Okay. For the hell of it, why were you wondering if this woman left her car here?"

"Not so much if she left it here, but to see if she was back yet. We were just wondering. If we didn't find it, maybe she left it someplace else, or she came back from her trip. But we found it, so that means she's still on her trip."

"She stays away too much longer, she can save money by forgetting the car." They got in and glided away without saying good-bye or looking back. I guessed they cruised the garages from time to time, checking their hot-car lists. It would make a good drop after a stolen car had been used for a felony. Leave it, walk across to the upper or lower level, leave the airport by cab or limousine. Or airplane. Or by private car previously stashed in the parking garage.

Meyer was very quiet, and he did not speak until we were approaching Miss Agnes. He stopped, and I turned and looked back at him and strolled back to where he was standing.

"Are you going to break into tears?"

"Maybe. If you were as axious to find your wife as Harry is, if it's financially important as well as emotionally important, wouldn't you report her missing and give her description and the description of her car with the tag number to the police?"

"I would think so."

"Then the number would be on their list, wouldn't it?"

"Yes. I mean, yes, dammit."

"And because you are thinking what I am thinking and because we happen to be right here, wouldn't it be a good time to find out about airline connections, McGee?"

"For two?"

"I have to finish my paper on the Eurocurrency which replaced the dollar. I promised the conference program chairman."

nine

I should have boarded my early afternoon BWIA flight to Barbados with stops at Kingston and San Juan, thoroughly, if not visibly, bloodied by Jillian. This was Tuesday, and I should have been sailing the sea, not the air.

Cowardice is a very curious ailment. The attacks occur when you do not expect them. Instead of saying the rehearsed words, I heard myself say, "Jilly dear, the matter of the old friend has come up again. I wouldn't want to go cruising down to St. Kitts with that hanging over me. I wouldn't be able to stop thinking about it and wondering. It will take a few days. . . ."

"Darling, I want you to be able to keep your mind on your work. Exclusively. Besides, the five-day forecast is foul. It might work out very nicely."

"No tantrum?"

"What sort of woman do you think I am, dear? That's hardly flattering, you know. All evidence to the contrary, I am not a spoiled little bitch who goes about whining and screaming and drumming her heels. I'm grown up, you know. And more patient than you imagine. I have waited quite a while to have you all to myself."

"This shouldn't take very long."

"I'll be here when you return, dear Travis. Grenada?"

The habit of caution took over. It is an automatic reflex. Never tell anybody anything that they might in turn tell the wrong person. "No. That information is obsolete. San Juan."

"Of course. By this time Grenada must be well emptied out. She could have more fun in Puerto Rico. Are you and she going to have a lot of fun, Travis? Just like old times?"

"I'm not planning to. But you never can tell."

"Really! You are the most—"

"You keep asking the wrong questions. It's a bad habit."

"As bad as giving the wrong answers."

For a moment the tantrum was on the edge of happening, but she forced it back visibly, forgave me, kissed me a lingering farewell.

Now, five miles over Cuba, I wondered if it would have been better for both of us if I had made it clear I was never going to become her tame houseguest. I wondered if it had been cowardice or if I was really, underneath, the kind of miserable son of a bitch who likes to keep something in reserve in case he happens to change his mind.

Our captain, being a pleasantly enthusiastic host, invited us to look down at Cuba. I was following the McGee rule of international travel and was in first class, alone in the window seat, the bulkhead seat on the starboard side. It was British West Indian Airways, BWIA, and the leg room in the bulkhead seats on the 727 is good.

A clear and beautiful day. The tilled-field geometry of Cuba looked like the geometry of any other of the islands from five miles up. We moved across the southern coastline, and the shallow sea was a hundred shades, from the pale pale tan of shallow sand through lime and lavender to cobalt.

"Sir?" the clear young voice said. She was a small, dusky stewardess with a high forehead, a blue-eyed stare of calculated innocence, a dark spill of glossy black hair. Her skin was a matte texture, and it was a half shade lighter than milk chocolate. She was the one with the absolutely great legs I had noticed when I had clambered onto their airplane. "You are going to . . ."

"Barbados."

"Ah, yes. Thank you, sir. Can I get you something to drink?"

"The last time I was on BWIA there was fresh orange juice. Do you still—"

"Oh, yes."

"With vodka then, please?"

"Oh, yes, right away, thank you." She twinkled at me and spun away, the short skirt flirting and snapping. It is changing in the islands, same as everywhere. The conservative island politicians and the white businessmen try to tell you that there is no racism, that black and white are treated alike and live amiably together in happy understanding and compassion.

But if you are observant, you notice that the more desirable the job, particularly the jobs women hold—stewardesses, cashiers in banks, clerks in specialty shops, hostesses in restaurants—the more likely they are to be bleached by past miscegenation. There are some true blacks in those positions, of course, but in a far lower ratio than exists in the general population. Look at the cleaning women, the cane-field workers, the laundry workers, to find the purest blacks in the islands. And the blackest blacks are, of course, probably 75 to 80 percent of the population of the West Indies, the Bahamas, the Windward and Leeward Islands. The other 20 percent is a perceptible lightening of color, shade by shade, all the way to unleavened white. Regardless of all protestations, the whiter you are, the better you live. Blondes have the most fun. One of the thoroughly ignored aspects of the Cuban revolution is how happily the black Cubans embraced the new order. Though the percentage is smaller in Cuba than elsewhere through the Caribbean, the pattern of discrimination was the same. Black Cuba was entirely ready for anything at all that promised equality in education, jobs, and health care. It didn't have to be Khrush or Mao. They would have built statues to a big green Martian if it could have delivered on the promises.

The curious and immediate and personal result of the color prejudice in the islands was that my pale chocolate stewardess with the great legs identified with me. We were both part of the ruling cabal. There could be an earnest friendliness in her unlikely blue eyes, an uninhibited flirtatiousness.

Another little girl of exactly the same color, but a citizen of the U.S. of A. and working, say, for Eastern on a domestic run, would have been working hard on an Afro hairdo, would have given me the precise number of millimeters of smile as prescribed by Eastern, would have been entirely correct, but her eyes would have been as empty as the ice of a long winter, concealing nothing more personal than a propagandized hostility, a prepackaged contempt, an ability to see me only as a symbol of oppression, not as a living creature walking two-legged on the same untidy world, trying to live through the weird years with a little bit of grace and care.

Too bad, somehow. The real guilt is in being a human being. That is the horrible reality which bugs us all. Wolves, as a class, are cleaner, more industrious, far less savage, and kinder to each other and their young.

When she came back with the screwdriver, she leaned one round, delicious knee on the empty seat beside me and reached and put the glass and napkin on the small built-in service area between the seats. I could read her name tag. Mia Cruikshank.

"Mia?" I said.

"Yes, sir?"

"I just meant . . . it's a pretty name."

She made a droll mouth. "Better than what it was, I think. Miriam. Mia is smashing compared to that."

"Smashing indeed."

———

So we went humming down across the blue seas under the blue skies of vacationland at approximately nine hundred feet per second, which is the muzzle velocity of the .45 caliber Colt automatic pistol, an ugly and cumbersome weapon. Our happy captain pointed out this and that. We stopped at Kingston and San Juan and points south. We lost more passengers than we took on. Each island had its quota of red tape, so that the stops were long.

Mia kept me happily supplied with drinks and food, and we found it easy to smile at each other. We stood together when the sun was low, on the little platform at the top of the rolling stairs at the little airport on St. Lucia.

"You are remaining at Barbados, sir, or continuing?"

"To Grenada tomorrow morning."

"Oh, yes. That is so lovely an island. Of course, Barbados is very nice, too. Just one night is a short time to stay."

"I didn't want to stay there at all."

"I know. There is no way. You fly with us or Pan Am to Barbados or Trinidad, from Miami everyone arrives too late for the last flight to Grenada. It has to be by daylight, of course, in the small aircraft. Where will you stay in Barbados?"

"I thought I would check it out after I get there."

"Oh, yes. The season is over. There is room everywhere. But really, there was room in most of the places during the season too this year. We did not carry so many people to Barbados this year."

"Why not?"

She glanced back over her shoulder and moved closer to me, lowered her voice. "I am not a rich, important person who owns a hotel, so perhaps they know what they are doing. But, sir, suppose this was in the season and you are traveling with a lady and you try to make a reservation for the two of you in Barbados, just to stay in a hotel room overnight to continue on in the morning. In your money, in U.S. dollars, to stay at the Barbados Hilton, it will be seventy dollars for one night, and there will be ten percent service charge added to that, so that it will be seventy-seven dollars. Even were you to stay at the Holiday Inn, sir, it will be fifty-five plus ten percent, or sixty dollars and fifty cents."

"Without meals? You have to be kidding."

"Oh, no. You see, sir, they will only make reservations for you on the modified American Plan, which includes breakfast and dinner, even when it is clear you will have dinner aboard this flight and leave so early the next morning there is perhaps time for coffee and rolls. This is happening in all the islands, sir. It is perhaps the worst in Barbados, the worst of all. It is a fantastic greed. It is like some terrible animal out of control, so hungry it feeds upon itself and is killing itself. I should not say so much."

"I won't turn you over to the tourist board, Mia."

"Oh, thank you." She hesitated and scowled. "There is something I am trying to think how to say. It is really what is wrong now with the islands. It is why each year there will be fewer people coming to these lovely places."

"It's a shame."

She turned to face me directly and looked up at me. "Seventy-seven dollars is over a hundred and fifty dollars in our currency. In Biwi dollars. A house servant in Barbados *might* make fifty dollars, Biwi, a month. A waiter or waitress *might* make seventy-five dollars, Biwi, a month. So how does a human person feel serving or cleaning up after another human person who pays two or three months' wages for one single night in a room? Sir, it is like such a terrible arrogance and thoughtlessness. It makes hate, sir. It makes contempt. So the cleaning is done badly, and the serving is done very slowly and badly, and there are no smiles. Then, sir, the person who is paying too much because the hotel owners are so greedy, he becomes very angry because, if he pays so much, the service should be of the very best, and everything should be very clean. When he is angry, then he seems to be more arrogant and rich and thoughtless, sir. Hate and anger back and forth, it is a terrible thing. There is no pleasure in work and no pleasure in vacationing here, and that is why each year, like this year, there will be fewer and fewer tourists, jobs, money. It is wicked. I keep thinking to myself, what can be done—what can be done? It is like the goose, sir."

"The goose?"

"The goose they killed to get at the golden eggs." She looked at her watch. An official was trotting up the stairs. "Now we will be going, sir."

After lift-off she gave me a final drink, and she and the other girls did their desk work and policed their area and changed to their ground uniforms. She had time to give me some advice. She told me that the nearest hotel to the airport was a five-dollar taxi ride. Biwi. The Crane Beach. She said the rooms were very small and primitive, but the beach was beautiful and the food was excellent. She said the management was surly and the waiters were insolent, but it was only for overnight, and it would be almost empty. Besides, the Barbados Hilton and the other hotels were a lot closer to Bridgetown, and so were ten to fifteen Biwi dollars one way from the airport. In most of the islands it appears that committees of taxi drivers determine airport locations.

"Just laugh at whatever they want to charge you at the Crane Beach, sir. The season is over. Put down ten dollars, Yankee, and tell them the service charge percent is included, not extra. They will show you a rate schedule and tell you it is official and they cannot change it. Just laugh. They will take the money and give you a room. It is not so easy to get a taxi in the morning early from there. Just tear a Yankee dollar in two pieces and give half to the taxi driver and tell him when to come in the morning. He will be certain to return. Do not tip anyone at that hotel. They are shameless, and it is all included in the price of everything anyway."

I was genuinely grateful to Mia. I thanked her and said, "I hope I will get a chance to tell you how I made out."

"Perhaps, if you fly BWIA back to Miami, I will serve you again. How long shall you be in Grenada, sir?"

"A few days. Any idea where I should stay?

"Oh, no. I do not know that island so well. This is not a vacation for you. Business, yes?"

"How do you know?"

"I think I can tell if a man is not one who would take a vacation alone, sir. Good luck, sir."

My taximan arrived the next day three minutes before the stipulated hour. He smiled broadly when he saw me standing in the early-morning light outside the hotel gates with my single piece of carryon luggage. He decided that it was a splendid idea, the half of the paper dollar. It left each of us with an investment to protect. He had brought some tape, and he put his dollar back together before we started off. His name was Oswald, and he was a thin old man with several gold teeth. He drove his elderly white Plymouth with that kind of care which is more involved with not breaking anything than not hitting anybody.

I took LIAT, a BWIA subsidiary, to Grenada, a direct flight of about forty minutes. It was an old Avro with the rows shoved closer together to increase capacity, so that the little oval windows did not match the seat positions. Two big propjet Rolls-Royce brutes powered the small aircraft. The stewardess was about the same size and shape as Hubert Humphrey. The pilot had Walter Mitty dreams of being a fighter pilot. It was an interesting takeoff and an even more interesting landing.

At Grenada's grubby little airport I once again had to show my driver's license and turn over that card form which serves as embarkation and debarkation permit, depending on how you fill out the blanks.

And then came a fascinating ride in a taxi. The island is only twenty-one miles long and twelve miles wide. The airport is about as far as it could possibly be from the principal town, St. Georges. The morning ride took one full hour, and I would not have wanted my man to have tried to shave five minutes off the elapsed time. I helped with the brakes so continuously that my right leg was nearly paralyzed when we finally came down out of the mountains to sea level. The driver—he gave me his card—was Albert Owen, and he had a Chevrolet assembled in Australia with a suspension system designed for the Outback of Australia. He had put fifty-three thousand incredible miles on it on that improbable road system, using up God only knows how many sets of brake linings. Drive on the left. Average width of road—one and a quarter lanes. No shoulders. Blind corners. Big lumps, deep potholes, children, dogs, pigs, donkeys, bicycles, trucks, buses, motorcycles. So honk the horn almost continuously, shift up and shift down, swerve, leap, squeal, slide, accelerate—and all the time Albert Owen was hollering back over his shoulder at me, pointing out bah-nah-nah tree, almond tree, sugar cane, sar. Over there mammy apple, coconut plantation, sar, cocoa; also you are seeing nutmeg, sar. Many spices.

Once when a small insane truck came leaping at us on the wrong side around a bend, Albert swerved smartly. It missed us by the thickness of a coat of paint. Albert laughed and laughed. He said, "That is one foolish driver, sar. He nearly mosh us."

But nobody actually did mosh us. It was hard to believe they were not trying. Were the fates to put Albert down on any weekday morning on the Palmetto Turnpike heading into Miami with the in-bound torrent, the terror of it might put him into a dead faint. A Miami cabdriver suddenly transported into Albert's mountains might conceivably run weeping into the jungle.

People certainly did go about moshing people. The dead cars amid the lush vines and wild shrubs were proof enough of that.

Albert asked me where my reservation was as we plummeted down toward the town and blue late-morning sea beyond. I said I had none but would look about a little. He said there were no problems this time of year. There had been trouble with the government water supply. When the hotel cisterns had run out, many people had left. Now the water was on again, but there were not so many tourists as on other Aprils. I found out that the Grenada Beach Hotel was the place most centrally located on Grande Anse, the two miles of cres-cent beach just south of the town, looking westward. I asked him if he would wait there for me. We made certain financial negotiations.

I left my single piece of luggage with him. He parked in the vehicle circle outside the main doors. I walked in and through an open lobby area and found a thatched bar off to the left, open to the outdoors, looking out across a long expanse of green lawn and tall, graceful coconut palms toward the garden of beach umbrellas, to-ward the bright colors of beach chairs and towels on the distant sand.

A bored bartender in a red coat appeared from some unknown hiding place, yawning. He made me a delicious rum punch with grated nutmeg afloat on it. He asked for my room number, and I paid cash for my drink, then gifted him with some of the Biwi I had picked up at the money-changer's booth in the temple of Miami In-ternational. He brightened visibly, and I asked him if he had a phone back there, and he said he did, and he said he would be glad to phone the Spice Island Inn for me. He did so and handed me the phone.

"What number is Mrs. Broll in, please? Mrs. Mary Broll?"

"Ah . . . yes, she is in Cottage Fifty, sir. Shall I ring her for you?"

"No, thank you," I said and hung up.

I finished my drink very very slowly. It is a very strange reluctance, a curious hesitation that can immobilize you at such a time. You are eager to prove to yourself that you've been quite wrong, that you've taken too many small things and built them up into a fantasy structure that cannot be true.

Yet, if by some chance the fantasy proves to be reality, most of the game is still left to play, and an ugly game it can be.

It could be a delicious surprise. I could see the shape of Mary's familiar mouth, the wide and startled eyes, and then the rush of pleasure, the embrace.

"The Spice Island Inn is close by?"

"That direction. Very close. A small walk, sir, Two minutes."

But in the hot tropical blaze of April a man in slacks and sport shirt, socks and shoes would be as conspicuous on that beach, I found, as in a Mother Hubbard at a nudist camp. I went back through the hotel and found Albert dozing in the shade. I woke him, and we got into the broiling taxi and rode south to the entrance to the Spice Island Inn.

Meyer and I had tried to cover all eventualities in the long planning session we'd had before I left. In the islands there appeared to be so little interest in any verification of identity that the risk factor seemed very minor indeed. If we were wrong, I was going to feel a little foolish. But if we were right, there was a chance I could feel something beyond mere foolishness.

And so, in Albert Owen's back seat I switched the cash money, all of it, from the wallet to another and became Gavin Lee. Known as Gav. Known as Mr. Lee. This follows Meyer's theory that when you pick a new name, pick one that has the same basic vowel sounds. Then you will react if you hear somebody behind you say your assumed name.

I was going to carry my own suitcase in. Albert did not think that was appropriate. The desk was very cordial. Nothing creates such a flavor of genuine, heartfelt welcome as a nearly empty hotel. They showed me the rates. They told me I had a choice of plans. They showed me a map of the place with all manner of accommodations. What would please Mr. Lee, the ostensibly vacationing land developer from Miami, Scottsdale, Acapulco, Hawaii, Palm Springs, and Las Vegas? Well, I'm kind of curious about those with the private pool. These here on your map. Just this row of them, eh? How about this one right here on the end? Number . . . I can't read it upside down. Thank you, 50. Full. Are all these full then? Just 50, 57, and 58. Well, in the middle then, as far from the occupied ones as . . .

54? I can see there are two bedrooms, but I don't see any one-bedroom ones with the walled garden and the pool, so . . . now what will it be on . . . a European Plan? After a few days I may change, depending on how the dining room is here. Of course. I'm sure it's marvelous. All right. Quote me on a per day. . . . That's $28, single? That's U.S.? Hmmm. Plus ten percent service charge and five percent tax, which is . . . $32.34 per day. Look, I'm carrying a bit more cash than I intended. Would you mind taking this hundred-dollar bill for three days in advance? And I'll bring you an envelope to put in the safe.

I paid Albert off and told him I would keep his card and I would certainly get him to drive me back to the airport some day. A bellhop led me down a long long path to the newest line of attached bunga-lows, the ones with the pool in the garden. The row was a good 250 yards from the hotel proper. He demonstrated the air conditioning, the button to push for food service, the button to push for drink service.

Then he went away. I was left in silence, in the shadowed coolness of the tourist life.

Drive the clenched fist into palm. *Pock!*

"Be here, baby. Just *be* here!"

ten

The row of tall attached cottages with a double peak on the roof of each one was set at a slight angle to the beach, so that architecturally they could be set back, one from the next, to provide total privacy for the individual walled gardens where the small swimming pools were.

The row of cottages was back a hundred feet and more from the beach. Between the front gates of the cottages and the beach itself was a private expanse of sand, landscaped palms, sea grapes, and almond trees, with sun chaises spotted about at intervals far enough apart for privacy.

I put on swim trunks and took up a position on a chaise fifty feet from my front gate, turning it in such a way that I could watch the gate of number 50. By then it was past noon. The tropic sun had such a hefty sting I knew even my deep and permanent tan would not be immune, not without a little oil and a little limitation on the exposure time.

At twenty minutes to one the gate opened and a young woman came out. She was of medium height, delicately and gracefully built. Her dark hair was quite long, and she had a white band above her forehead clipping it in place. She seemed to be somewhere in her twenties. I could not make a closer guess at that distance. She wore eccentric sunglasses with huge round lenses in dark amber. She wore a don't-swim-in-it bikini fashioned of white elasticized cord and swatches of watermelon-colored terry cloth. She was two shades darker then Mia Cruikshank, a perfect and even tan which could have come only from untold hours of total discipline and constant care.

A man came out with her. Youngish, lithe, laughing, and saying something that made her laugh. Awesomely muscled, moving well so that muscles bulged and slid under the red-bronze tan. A Riviera swimming outfit, little more than a white satin jockstrap. She walked a few steps and then turned in a proprietary way and went back and tested to see if the gate was locked. She looked in her small white Ratsey bag, apparently to make sure that her key was there. Then they walked toward the hotel.

My heart had turned heavy, and there was a taste of sickness in my throat. But you have to be certain, terribly certain. Like a biopsy. Make absolutely sure of the malignancy. Because the surgery is radical.

I gave them five minutes and then followed the same route. I found them in another of the ubiquitous thatched bars, having a drink at a shady table and still laughing. A cheerful pair. I went to the bar and ordered a drink. When I had a chance, I asked the bartender if the woman at the table was a certain Lois Jefferson. He looked troubled. He said he knew them by the numbers. Just a moment, please. He went to the other end of the bar and came back with a signed drink tab. Mary D. Broll. Number 50. He showed it to me. I thanked him, said I was wrong. I winked at him and said, "But that is not Mr. Broll?"

He had a knowing smile. "It is just a friend. He has been a friend for a week, I think. He works, I think, on a private boat. That is what I hear. It is easy to make friends here."

I picked my drink up and moved along the bar to a stool that was about a dozen feet from their table. I turned around on the stool, my back to the bar, and looked at her with obvious and amiable and very thorough appreciation. She was worth appreciating, right from her brown, slender, tidy little ankles right on up—not too quickly— to a ripely cushioned little mouth, dark eyes set at an interesting tilt, a broad, immature, and vulgar little nose.

She put her glasses back on and leaned over and said something to her nautical friend. He put his drink down and turned around and stared back over his shoulder at me. I smiled and nodded at him. He had a Prince Valiant haircut, and his hair was the dark molten shade of some golden retrievers. His face had a tough, pinched, disadvantaged look which did not go with the Valiant hair or the beachboy body. I do not make any judgments about hair length, mine or anyone's. I own some Sears electric clippers with plastic gadgets of various shapes that fit on the clippers to keep you from accidentally peeling your hair off down to the skull. I find that long hair is a damned nuisance on boats, on the beach, and in the water. So when it gets long enough to start to make me aware of it, I clipper it off, doing the sides in the mirror and the back by feel. The sun bleaches my hair and burns it and dries it out. And the salt water makes it feel stiff and look like some kind of Dynel. Were I going to keep it long, I would have to take care of it. That would mean tonics and lotions and special shampoos. That would mean brushing it and combing it a lot more than I do and somehow fastening it out of the way in a stiff breeze. Life is so full of all those damned minor things you have to do anyway, it seems nonproductive to go looking for more. So I go hoe the hair down when it attracts my attention. The length is not an expression of any social, economic, emotional, political, or chronographic opinion. It is on account of being lazy and impatient. No reason why the male can't have long, lovely, dark-golden hair if he wants it. But it is a personal decision now, just as it was during the Crusades and the Civil War.

He kept staring right at me, and I kept smiling at him. So he got up fast and rolled his shoulders as he covered the twelve feet to stand in front of me, bare feet spread and braced.

"Chief, stop the bird-dog routine. You're annoying the lady."

"Me? Come *on* now! Don't let her kid you. Lois and I have known each other for a long time. She knows I like to look at her. Always have. And I know she likes being looked at. Right, dear?"

"You're out of your tree, chief. Knock it off. She isn't Lois."

I stood up. "She's Lois Jefferson. Believe me!" I edged by him as he tried to block me away from the table. "Lois, honey, it's Gav Lee, for God's sake. It was a good joke, but let's not run it into the ground."

She took the glasses off and looked up at me. "Really, I'm not Lois. I'm Mary Broll. Really."

I boggled at her. "Not Lois Jefferson from Scarsdale? Not Tom's wife?"

It sucked in the fellow nicely. He was all alerted for games. When you roam in public with an item like that woman, you keep the guard way up. "Honey," he said, "how about this clown? You get it? Tom Jefferson. Thomas Jefferson. Stop annoying us, chief, or I'll call the—"

I turned on him. "Really. Would it put too much of a strain on you to have a little common courtesy? Her husband has always had the nickname Tom, for quite obvious reasons. His real name is . . ." I turned back to her. "What *is* Tom's real first name, dear?"

She laughed. "But I am really *not* your friend!"

I stared at her. "That can't be possible. It's the most fantastic look-alike. . . . You wouldn't believe . . . Miss Broll, would you—"

"Mrs. Broll."

"I'm sorry. Mrs. Broll, would it be rude of me to ask you to stand up for just a moment?"

"I guess not."

"Now just one goddamn—"

I turned on him again. "What harm can it do, Mr. Broll?"

She stood up beside her chair. I moved closer to her, and I stared into her eyes from close range. "By God, I *am* wrong. I would never have believed it. You are a little bit taller than Lois, and I think your eyes are a darker shade, Mrs. Broll."

"Now go away," the man said.

As she sat down she said, "Oh, shut up, Carl. You get so boring sometimes. The man made a mistake. All right? All right. Please forgive Carl, Mr. . . ."

"Lee. Gavin Lee. Gav to my friends."

"I don't see any friends of yours around here," the man said.

She gave me a very pretty and well-practiced smile. "Gav, this rude animal is Carl Brego. Carl, shake hands nicely with Gav, or you can damned well take off."

I saw the little tightening around his eyes and knew the childish bit he was going to try. So when he put his hand out, I put my hand into his much too quickly for him to close his hand to get my knuckles. I got my hand all the way back, deep into the web between thumb and finger. Then I could just maintain a mild, firm clasp and smile at him as he nearly ruptured his shoulder muscles trying to squeeze my hand to broken pulp.

"Sorry about the little misunderstanding, Carl," I said. "I'd like to buy you two nice people a drink."

He let go of my hand and sat down. "Nobody invited you to join the party, chief."

He had fallen into that one, too. He was scoring very badly. I said, "I don't expect to sit down with you, Carl. Why should I? I was going to go to that table way over there and have my own drink over there and send two to this table. You act as if I'm trying to move in

on you. How far would I get, Carl? As you are not Mr. Broll, then
this lovely lady is a friend of yours. You are having lunch together.
Just the two of you. If I were having lunch with her, I would be very
ugly about anybody trying to move in. I just think you overreact,
Carl. I made a little mistake. You keep getting rude for no reason.
But I'll still buy those drinks. I was thinking of it as an apology, not
a ticket to the party."

So saying, I gave the lady a little bow and marched on over to my
distant table and told the waiter to give them anything they might
want. I sat with my back toward them.

It did not take her long. Four minutes, I think it was, before he
appeared beside my chair, standing almost at attention.

"Excuse me. Mrs. Broll would be very happy if you would join us
for lunch."

I smiled up at him. "Only if you are absolutely certain you don't
mind, Brego."

It hurt his mouth to say it. It hurt his whole face. "Please join us,
Mr. Lee."

All through lunch I knew Brego was waiting and planning. When
I saw that he wasn't at all upset that I was living just a few doors—
or a few gardens—away from his pretty friend, I could almost guess
the kind of routine he had figured out.

And during lunch I had managed to steer the conversation in a direction that gave me a chance to awaken more than a flicker of interest in her eyes and at the same time gave her a chance to shove a little blade into Carl Brego and give it a twist.

I said, "I take little flyers in island property sometimes. Actually,
that's why I'm here. Some associates said I ought to take a look at
this one. Anyway, usually I like to pyramid, but quite a while ago I
got into Freeport up in the Bahamas at the right time and got out at
exactly the right time with much more than I'd expected, so I
thought I'd give myself a little present. So I bought this great big, ri-
diculous brute of a schooner in Nassau and had the yard that sold it
to me hire aboard a crew, and I actually set out for *this* island. But
the guest I invited aboard for the trip became terribly seasick. We
made it as far as Great Inagua and got off, both of us, at Matthew
Town and arranged passage from there back to civilization. I had the
crew take the boat back to Nassau. As I remember, my accountants
told me the net loss was something like thirteen thousand dollars
after I'd had the yard resell the schooner. But it would have been

cruel and unusual punishment to have made the young lady sail one more mile."

Something behind her dark eyes went *ding,* and a cash drawer slid open in her skull. She counted the big bills and shut it again and smiled and said, "Carl knows all about yachts. He sails one around for a very fat rich lady, don't you, darling?"

"That must be very interesting," I said.

"He's waiting on Grenada until she arrives with friends," the woman said. "You know. Like a chauffeur, parked somewhere."

"Knock it off," Carl said in a small humble voice.

"Please?" she said.

"Please."

And that made it even more imperative. I decided I was reading her well enough to see that she knew the direction the tensions would take and would give the ceremony a chance to get under way at the first opportunity. And would want to watch.

When we got to her gate, there was no one in sight. The breeze had stopped. Sweat popped out immediately on all three of us. I felt it run down my back.

"Do come in, Gav," she said. "Do join us."

She was starting to unlock the gate. Carl said, "So it's enough already."

"Enough?" she said blankly. "Enough?"

"Honey, the guy is taking a cheap shot, and I'm going to run him off."

She licked her mouth. "Carl, sweetie, why do you have to be—"

"You can go in out of the heat, or you can stay and watch how it's done, Mary. Either way I run this smartass off."

"Any special direction?" I asked.

"Pick the one you like best, chief," he said with a jolly grin of anticipation. "Start now and save yourself grief."

"Take your best shot, Brego." He took it. I was worried that he might know too much about what he wanted to do. If he did it was going to take a long time in the hot sun, and if he didn't, it could be reasonably quick.

He did a little bounce, a little prance. He pawed with the clumsy, measuring left and then came leaping in, following up on the right hook that he had brought up from about five feet behind him, practically at ground level. He did not know what he was doing. People who know do not go around taking the chance of hitting the solid bone of skull or jaw with the bare fist. A broken hand is incapacitating. It takes a long, tiresome time to heal. He wanted to pop me one and let the momentum carry him into me so he could get his hands and arms on me and put those muscles to work. He gave me lots of time for a decision. If I fell back away from it, he was going to tumble onto me. That way I might get a thumb in my eye before I could unwind and unravel him. The footing in the soft sand was a little uncertain for savate. So I moved forward, a little to my right, to take me inside that long, sweeping hook.

I felt it go around me, and I let his momentum then drive me back. I drove both hands, fingers spread, into his long hair, clenched hard, and went down, pulling him on top of me but getting my knees up against my chest in time. One shoe slipped off his sweaty body, but the sole of the other stayed in place against his belly, and momentum gave me enough leverage to push him up and over. It was a good, high kick, and he spun well. By then I was on my back with my hands straight up over my head.

He hit the soft sand flat on his back with one hell of a *whump*. It exploded the air out of his lungs. I was up first, and I moved into position, waiting for him. He got up slowly, gagging for air. As he pushed up, I cranked his arm around behind him and put my other hand on the nape of his neck and ran him into the weathered boards of the garden fence, quite close to the woman. He splintered a board with the top of his head. She squeaked and chewed her fist. I dragged him back by the ankles, face down. I picked him up and stood him on his noddle legs and slapped him until he started to come around. Then I bent him over and ran him into the fence again. I dragged him back again, and I turned his feet until he rolled over onto his back. I slapped him where he lay, and when he stirred and his eyes came into focus, I levered his mouth open by bracing the heel of my hand against his chin. I packed his mouth full of soft hot sand, from the back of his throat to his pretty white teeth. He came sputtering and gagging onto his hands and knees and coughed himself sick. I grabbed the hair and pulled his head up and back.

"Nod if you can understand me, Brego." He nodded. "Do you want me to break any bones? Do I have to do that?" He shook his head. "She isn't your woman any more. Understand?" He nodded. "Now I am going to start kicking your ass. You better head for the beach. If I ever see you back here, I'll break some bones."

I went around behind and got a pretty good soccer kick into it, using the side of my foot. On the upswing. It slid him onto his face. He came scrambling up with more energy than I expected, but I got him again just as he got his feet under him and his hands free of the sand. Three running steps and he landed on his face again but didn't spend any time resting. He got up and went into a wobbly, scuffling run, fists against his chest, not daring or wanting to look back.

I watched him and then turned and looked at the woman. She gave me a very uncertain smile. There was an unhealthy skin tone under that deep lovely tan. "I . . . I thought you were going to kill him."

"Kill him? What in God's name for?"

"Well . . . it was so quick and so terrible."

"He won't be back, Mary. Are you going to miss him, particularly? You going to be lonesome?"

"That would depend, wouldn't it?"

"Is there any of his stuff in there?"

"Not much. A few things."

"Anything worth his coming back after?"

"I wouldn't think so. No."

"Now you can invite me in again."

Her color was back. "You take a hell of a lot for granted."

I put a knuckle under her chin and tilted her face up and looked at it inch by inch, a long and interested search. "If you want, girl, I can throw you back, like an undersized mackerel. The world is full of Carl Bregos. It's up to you."

She twisted her chin free. "I guess I wouldn't want to be thrown back, Gav. I guess it wouldn't fit my image. Was there really a Lois Jefferson?"

"If you think there was."

"I don't think so."

"Then there never was such a girl."

"Poor Carl. Do you always get what you want?"

"I usually get what I *think* I want."

She tilted her shoulders one way, her hips the other. Her look was challenge. "And sometimes you find out you didn't really want it after all. Me, too. Win a little, lose a little, huh?"

"If you wanted Brego, you'd still have him. I wouldn't have gotten to say more than two words to you."

"Like I was saying when we were so rudely interrupted, you want to come into my house? It's hot out here when the wind quits."

So we went in, and I wondered why I could find no trace of a Canadian accent. She had to be Lisa Dissat.

eleven

Though the plantings were different, the patio furniture of a different style and arrangement, the pool and the cold-water shower head were placed just as in my rented garden. I went to the shower and turned it on and sluiced off the sand that had caked thickly on my sweaty back and on my left side where I had rolled to get up quickly. The woman stood and watched me and then took a big, striped beach towel from a stone bench and brought it to me as I stepped out of the spray and turned the shower off.

As I dried myself, I realized how sexually aware of her I had become. Physical readiness. All her honey-brown curves and cushions were there, appropriate, ready for use.

It is such an old old thing, the pattern of male conflict that wins the female. It is deep in the blood and the secretions, a gut knowledge. We are mammals still caught up in all the midbrain mechanisms of survival. The bison female stood long ago and watched the males thud their brute heads together and tear up the sod with their hooves, watched the loser lope heavily away, and then she waited patiently to be mounted by the victor. The stronger the male, the stronger the calves, and the better protected the calves would be during the long months of helplessness. The victorious male, turning from battle to the prize of battle, would be physiologically ready to mate her and have no question about her readiness.

I knew the musky readiness of the woman. She told me in the way she stood, in the way she looked at me, in the shape of her placid mouth. Maybe 10 percent of what we can say to each other is with words, and words can conceal as easily as they can reveal. The rest of it is body language, our cants, tilts, postures, textures.

And who can prove there is not an actual telepathic signal being transmitted? Tiny electrical discharges occur in the living mind in great and complex profusion. Strong emotion, tautly focused, may send out an impulse so strong it can be read. Hate, fear, anger, joy, lust . . . these seem contagious beyond all objective reason. I knew she was so swollen, so moist, so ready that if I trotted her into the shadowy coolness of the apartment and into her bed, there would be no time or need for foreplay, that she would cling and grind and gasp and within a minute begin to go into a climax.

The violence had caught us up in the first act of the fleshy ceremony, and I wanted to take that quick, primitive jump so badly I felt hollowed out by the ache of it. Bed was her country. That was where, after the first great surge, she would take command. I would become what she was accustomed to and lose any chance of keeping her off balance. I shook myself like a big tired Labrador after a long swim, balled the damp towel, and flipped it at her face. She moved in her slow sensuous dream, getting her hand partway up before it hit her squarely in the face. It fluttered to the floor.

"Hey!" she said, frowning. "What's that for?"

"Pick it up!"

"Sure," she said. She picked the towel up. "What are you sore about? Why are you getting ugly and spoiling the fun?"

"He was supposed to hammer me to bloody ruin out there. That was supposed to be in the fun. Thanks a lot."

She came toward me. "Darling, you've got it all wrong. I was getting *bored* with him! I was so glad you came along."

"Sure, Mary. Only I know the Bregos of this world. They don't start anything they don't think they can win. Their cheap women chouse them into it because they like the blood. You set me up by reacting to me. If you'd cooled it, there'd have been no fight. He was going to smash me around and that was going to turn you on for him, so you'd hustle him into your sack for a quick hump. A little midday entertainment. No, thanks."

She leaned forward from the waist, face contorting, voice turning to a squalling fishwife. "*Goddamn* you! *You* moved in on us with all that crap about me looking like somebody else. *You* thought I was worth the chance of getting your ass whipped. Don't slam the gate on the way out, you son of a—"

Her lips started to say the obvious word, but I had fitted my big right hand to her slender throat, just firmly enough to cut off her wind, not firmly enough to crush any of the tender bones and cartilage. The ball of my thumb reached to the big artery in the side of her throat under the jaw hinge, and my first and middle finger reached to the artery on the left side of her throat.

Her eyes went wide, and she dropped the towel and put her nails into the back of my hand and my wrist. I pinched the arteries gently, drastically reducing the flow of blood to the brain. It gave her a grayout to the edge of fainting. Her eyes went out of focus, and her mouth sagged. When I let up, she tried to kick me, so I pinched again. Her arms fell slack to her sides. When I released the pressure, adjusting my hand enough so that she could breathe, she raised her hands and then hung them upon my wrist.

I smiled at her, pulling her a half step closer, and said, "If you get loud and say nasty things, dear, if you get on my nerves, I can hold you like this, and I can take this free hand and make a big fist like this, and I can give you one little pop right here that will give you a nose three inches wide and a quarter inch high."

"Please," she said in a rusty little voice.

"You can get a job as a clown. Or you can see if you can find a surgeon willing to try to rebuild it."

"Please," she said again.

I let go of her and said, "Pick up the towel, love."

She coughed and bent and picked it up and backed away. I turned away from her and went to the cottage apartment and pulled the door open and went in. I went to the kitchen alcove and checked the bottle supply. I heard her slide the glass door shut again.

I fixed some Booth's with Rose's lime juice and a dash of bitters, humming softly but audibly. I took my glass over to the couch and sat and smiled at her and said, "Did I ever tell you I read minds?"

"You must be some kind of a crazy person." It was not said as an insult. It was said softly, wonderingly.

I pinched the bridge of my nose and closed my eyes. "Many messages are coming through. Ah, yes. You are wondering if you can get the hotel management to throw a net over me and get me out of here. No, dear. I think they would believe me instead of you. If they make life difficult, I could go down to the harbor and find your friend Brego and bounce him up and down until he agrees to write out a personal history of your touching romance and sign it. Then I could go find your husband and peddle it to him. It would cut the heart out of any alimony payments."

"I just want you to—"

"Where and when did you meet Brego?"

"On the beach. Over a week ago. My neck hurts."

"Of *course* it hurts a little! How could I do that without giving you a sore neck? Let me see. What else is in your mind? You're wondering if I'm going to lay you and if I'll be nicer to you afterward. The answer to both questions, dear, is: time will tell."

She went over to the kitchen bar. Ice clinked into a glass. She came back with a drink and sat on a hassock five feet away from me. Her eyes looked better. Her confidence was coming back. She squared her shoulders, tugged the bikini top and bottom into better adjustment, tilted her head, and risked a meager smile. "I guess all that lunch talk about land investments was a lot of crap, huh?"

"What makes you think so? It's what I do."

"You don't act like it's what you do. Like the way you were with Carl and with me, Gavin. I mean . . . well, it's like you enjoyed hurting."

"Well . . . let's suppose there's a man with a good idea where a new interstate is going on a new jetport, and suppose we teamed up, and you had some nice long weekends with him, and he clued you about where to buy the raw land. Mary, I just couldn't stand having you get tricky with me about something like that. I wouldn't want to worry about you selling that information to somebody else. I'd have to have you so trained for the work that if I just stare at your for ten seconds, you start to have the cold sweats and the gags. Hurting is purely business. I guess I enjoy anything that helps make money."

She thought that over, sipping, frowning. "But it's not as if I was going to work with you, Mr. Lee."

"Time will tell."

"You keep saying that. Well, I'm not going to work with you or for you. For that kind of work you're talking about, what you want is some kind of a hooker, it seems to me."

"Does it seem like that to you? Really? I wouldn't say that. You're built for the work. You have just enough cheap invitation in the way you look and the way you handle yourself to keep a man from wasting a lot of time on unnecessary preliminaries."

"Now wait one goddamn minute—"

"Are you still with Brego? No. Then shut up."

"I'm sorry. Don't get sore."

"Fifty bucks makes you a hooker. For five hundred you're a call girl. Five thousand makes you a courtesan."

"What's that?"

"Never mind. But when we move the decimal point one more place, your end of the arrangement is fifty thousand. That makes you a career woman."

The pointed tongue moved slowly across the underlip. She swallowed and said, "I've got my own thing going, thanks."

"Alimony is a cheap hustle."

"It all depends."

"On how much he's got? On the evidence? On the law? It has to be a cheap hustle, because when there's enough money involved, there's more profit from going in some other direction."

I had wanted to test just how deep the hardness went. Her eyes changed. She slopped some of her drink onto her bare knees, wiped it off with her hand. "That's crazy talk."

"Not for careful people who've got the right contacts."

"For me, no thanks. I just wouldn't have the nerve, Gav."

I got up and moved around, carrying my drink. I did not know where to take it from there. I could guess that she had been ordered to keep to herself in Grenada but had finally gotten so bored she had become reckless and picked up Brego. Now the Brego game had mushroomed into something a lot less comfortable for her. If she could live quietly at the inn for the length of time she was supposed to, she could get away with it. She wasn't too much shorter than Mary or too much younger. Dark hair. All American women look alike to the help.

I hadn't wanted to let myself think about Mary. From the physical description the housekeeper had given Jeannie Dolan, this woman was the Canadian, Lisa Dissat. If she was here, Mary was dead. I had the beginnings of an idea. I went back to the conversations at lunch. Neither the first name of her supposed husband nor her stateside residence had come up.

After mental rehearsal and rewrite I sat once again and looked placidly at her and said, "The way you spell that last name is bee-are-oh-el-el?"

"Yes."

"Kind of unusual. It rings a bell someplace. Mary Broll. Mary Broll. It's been bothering me ever since I met you in the bar."

"Why bother with it? Want me to fresh up your drink?"

"Got it!"

"Got what?"

"Where'd you register from? One buck will get you five it's the Fort Lauderdale area. Sure! We had a syndicate set up a couple of years back and we wanted a builder in the Lauderdale area who could put up a hotel and marina complex in a hurry. Heavyset fellow name of Broll. Big. Not old. Frank? Wally? Jerry? . . . Harry! Damn right. Harry Broll."

"Maybe there's more Brolls than you know, Gav."

"Bring me your purse, honey."

"What?"

"Go get your purse. Your pocketbook. Your handbag. Bring it to dear old Gavin Lee so he can look at your ID, dear."

She gave me a broad, bright smile, and her teeth chattered for a moment before she got herself under control. "Okay. My secret is out. You are speaking of the man I used to love."

"How long have you been married to him?"

"Nearly four years."

"Any kids? No? Lucky. Kids seem to get the rough end of the stick. Bring me the purse, honey."

"Why should I? I told you, didn't I?"

"Honey, if we stop getting along, we're going to have to hurt your neck a little until we get squared away."

"Please. It makes me sick to my stom—"

"Get the purse!"

She brought it to me. I found the billfold. I examined the identification. I looked at the signature on the driver's license. I knew my Mary had signed it, and I knew, looking at it, that she was dead.

"Honey, go over to that desk and take a piece of paper and sign your name on it. Mary D. Broll. And bring it back here to me."

"Who *are* you? What do you want?"

"I am the fellow who sat across the table from Mary D. Broll at Le Dome of the Four Seasons in Lauderdale two years ago last month. There were about ten of us at that dinner. Harry was making the big gesture, trying to sucker us into letting him build for us. I spent the evening trying to make his wife. She wouldn't give me a clue. I always have a better memory for the ones who get away. Here's her signature right here. Go over there and forge it for me, honey."

"Who *are* you?" she demanded, close to tears.

I gave her a broad, egg-sucking smile. "Me? I am the fellow who all of a sudden owns himself a whole woman, right from dandruff to bunions and everything in between. Broads like you don't play games like this unless there's money in it. And now it's *our* money, dear. I am the fellow who is going to get it all out of you, and I am going to beat on you until you convince me there's nothing left to tell. Me? Hell, baby, I am your new partner."

"Please. Please. I can't tell you—"

"The little lady in this corner is getting one chance, and one chance only, to go over to the desk and sign her real, true, legal name to a piece of paper and bring it back to the gentleman. And if it turns out that it is not her real true name, it is going to be one of those long afternoons. We're going to have to stuff a towel in the little lady's mouth so the screaming won't spoil anybody's vacation."

She walked to the desk, her back very straight. She wrote on a piece of paper and brought it back and handed it to me and began to weep. She covered her face and ran for the bedroom. Damned few women look well from a rear elevation, running away from you in a bikini. She was not one of them. She had written her name neatly. It was a schoolgirl neatness. Lisa Dissat.

I slowly crumpled the sheet of hotel paper. I felt tired. I got up and walked back to the bedroom, where she lay upon the unchanged sheets she and Brego had stained, sweated, and rumpled. She was on her side, knees hiked up, clenched fists tucked under her chin. She made sucking sounds, whining sounds. Fetal agony.

In the better interrogations there is always a good guy and a bad guy. I had been the bad guy. Time to change roles. I went into the bathroom and took a hand towel and soaked it in cold water. I wrung it out, took it to the bed, sat on the side of the bed, and cupped my hand on her shoulder and pulled her toward me. She resisted and made protest sounds, then let herself roll onto her back.

I hitched closer and gently swabbed her face and forehead. Her eyes went wide with astonishment. The last thing she had expected was gentleness. She snuffled. Her face looked touchingly young. Tears had washed away the challenge and the hardness.

"Have you got anything with you to prove your name is Lisa Dissat?"

"N-no."

"And you're pretending to be Mary Broll?"

"Yes. But I—"

"Does Broll know you're impersonating his wife?"

"Yes."

"Were you having an affair with him?"

"Yes."

"Where's the real Mary Broll?"

". . . I don't know."

"Lisa?"

"I didn't know what he was going to do! I *didn't!*"

"Lisa!"

"I couldn't have changed anything."

"Just say she's dead, Lisa. Go ahead."

"I didn't know he—"

"Lisa! Say it!"

"She's dead. Okay. She's dead."

"Harry killed her?"

She looked startled. "Oh, no!"

"Who killed her?"

"Please, Gavin. If he ever knew I told anybody—"

"You're in a real box, dear. You can worry about what's going to happen in the future, or you can worry about what's going to happen in the next ten minutes."

"I don't even know if he really meant to."

"What's his name?"

". . . Paul. Paul Dissat. He is . . . my first cousin. We worked for the same man. In Quebec. Mr. Dennis Waterbury. Paul got me the job there. I'm a secretary. I was a secretary. Paul is an accountant. He is . . . very trusted. I think he might be crazy. Really crazy. Maybe he really planned to kill Harry's wife. I don't know. I don't even know if he knows."

"How much money is involved?"

"An awful lot. Really, an awful lot of money."

"Stop crying."

"I want to talk about it, and I don't want to talk about it. I've been scared for so long! I *want* you to make me tell you all of it, but I'm afraid to tell you."

twelve

It was a very long afternoon for both of us. But longer for Lisa Dissat, because from time to time she tried to get cute. But the more she tried it, the more conditioned she became, and the more quickly she would correct herself.

At last I was able to bring the complex, wandering fragments of the story into reasonably sharp focus.

Paul Dissat had hungered for a long time to share in some of the large profits Dennis Waterbury made on his varied operations and investments in resort lands, oil and gas drilling programs, new urban office structures, tanker leasing, and so on. Paul Dissat was well paid. There were staff bonuses when things went well. Paul Dissat was shrewd enough to realize that without investment capital he had no chance of participating in the profits and that if he used his skills to tinker with the records of the various corporations and their shifting, changing bank balances, sooner or later an audit would catch him.

He was single, she said, and did not look like anybody's idea of an accountant. Bachelor apartment, sports car. She said he was a superb skier, proficient at down hill racing and slalom. She said that three years ago, when she was working in Montreal, she had run up bills she was unable to pay. She was afraid of losing her job. She had gone up to Quebec to see Paul, whom she had not seen in several years. He had taken her to dinner and back to his apartment and made love to her. He had paid her bills and arranged for her to work for Waterbury. After they had been intimate many times, he had told her of his plan to share in some of the fat profits from Waterbury's operations. He would arrange the necessary leverage through her. He said he would let her know when the right opportunity came along.

He arranged for her to seduce the particularly unattractive minor partner in one of the Waterbury developments and to pretend infatuation. Paul prompted her during the affair, telling her what her lines should be. Eventually, in order to safely end the affair without Lisa's going to his wife, the man deposited a substantial amount of cash in her savings account. Paul told her that the cash was the proceeds from the stock in a Waterbury enterprise that the man had sold to get the money to buy her off. Paul had taken all the cash except a thousand dollars.

They had done it once again prior to her affair with Harry Broll and made a little more than the first time. Paul explained to her that a man who has suddenly made a substantial profit tends to be generous with a mistress who is becoming too demanding and possessive.

I wanted to know why she kept so little of the take and let her first cousin have all the rest. She said it was because she was in love with him. At first.

"The third one was Harry," she said. "I went to the hotel and took dictation. Just like the first two men. Ten minutes after I looked at him in a certain way and told him how real brilliant he was, I was helping him take off my bra, because his hands were shaking so bad. Then after Harry went back to the States, Paul made me quit my job and follow him. I didn't want to. He said this could be the big one, worth a big risk. So . . . I did what he said. Harry got jumpy when I phoned him last November from Miami. He was glad, but he was nervous, too. I told him I had followed him because I was so in love with him I couldn't live without him, and I was putting my future in his hands."

Harry had set her up in the apartment in the Casa de Playa. At about that time Paul Dissat had been transferred to the administrative offices of SeaGate, Inc., in West Palm Beach, just as he had planned and expected. SeaGate was a large, complex situation with very complicated financing and special tax problems. Paul had been involved in it from the beginning.

"I called Paul once, but he got very angry. He told me to keep on following orders. The orders were to make myself just as agreeable as I possibly could, to make Harry as happy as possible, to really work on the sex part of it and do anything and everything to give him so much pleasure he'd never be able to get along without me. That wasn't easy, because Harry worked hard and he didn't keep in shape and didn't have much energy left for bed. But after I learned what turned him on the most, it got better for both of us. I had to pretend to be passionately in love with him. You know, it wasn't such a bad life. Go shopping, go out on the beach, get your hair done, watch your weight, do your nails, take naps. Not a bad life. Then a few days before Christmas, Paul wanted to know when Harry would be with me, definitely. I said I could make sure he'd come in the middle of the day on the twenty-third and spend an hour and a half with me. He told me not to be surprised if Mrs. Broll showed up. I couldn't understand what Paul was trying to do. He told me to shut up and do what I was told. She came barging in as Harry was leaving. Better looking than I'd thought from what Harry had told me about her. She called me some things, and I called her some things, and she went away crying."

Harry Broll had then become very upset. He had told Lisa Dissat that he needed her, that he wanted to get a divorce from Mary and marry her, but he couldn't do that yet. He had to make up with Mary, humble himself, promise never to see Lisa again. He said he had to do that because without Mary's financial backing he was going to miss out on his great opportunity at SeaGate. He said he had to move Lisa out of the apartment and be very careful about seeing her. He said it might last until May, but then he could leave Mary and marry her.

On the night of January 4, shortly before midnight, Harry came to Lisa's motel, where he had moved her after taking her out of the apartment. He was drunk. He said that he and Mary had had a terrible fight, and she was leaving him. As soon as Harry had passed out, Lisa phoned Paul to report, as required, any new development. Paul drove over to the motel, left his rented car there, borrowed Harry's car and house keys, and told Lisa to undress the unconscious Harry and keep him quiet for as long as she could manage.

"He wouldn't tell me what he was going to do. He acted all . . . keyed up, excited, on top of the world. He came back at daylight. He seemed very tired and very relaxed. He helped me get Harry up. Harry was confused. He knew Paul, of course, because of SeaGate and knew he was my cousin. But that was the first he realized that Paul knew about Harry and me. Paul pretended to be very upset about the affair, I guess to keep Harry off balance. The three of us went back in Harry's car to Harry's house on Blue Heron Lane. Paul kept telling Harry he was in trouble. Paul made me wait in the living room. He took Harry into the bedroom. Harry made a terrible sound. A kind of bellowing groan. I heard heavy footsteps running, and then I heard Harry throwing up. When Paul brought him back into the living room, all cleaned up, Harry was like a sleepwalker. Paul kept saying it was an accident, and Harry kept saying anything like that just couldn't be an accident, and Paul kept telling him that everything could be worked out for the best if Harry would just pull himself together. Paul had me make coffee, a lot of it."

Mary had, of course, been interrogated by Paul Dissat and murdered by Paul Dissat when he finally had everything he needed—the air reservations and tickets from the travel agency, the hotel reservation, the complete details of her arrangement with her trust officer, the fact that only one friend knew where she was going and why: Holly Dressner at 29 Blue Heron Lane, a few doors away. And he had the ninety-two hundred dollars in cash she had drawn from the income account of TA 5391. Mary was half packed for the trip. She had bought resort clothes. At Paul's order Lisa finished the packing, hunting through Mary's belongings for what she thought she would need.

"It was weird with her on the bed all covered up. I tried some of the stuff on in her dressing room. She was a little hippier than I am. I mean some of the things were a size ten when I'd be better off in an eight. Harry was like a very sick person. He couldn't seem to get himself out of it. Tears kept rolling down his face. Once he just sort of hung on me. He grabbed me and put so much weight on me he nearly rode me right down onto the floor. He was asking me something, mumbling about how could Paul do that, how could he? They had a terrible argument later on. I couldn't hear most of it. It was about what to do with her body. Harry said he couldn't stand having her buried on the place. There was something about the seawall and a transit-mix truck. Paul told Harry she was going to be buried right on the property; then Harry would not go back on any promises, ever."

She was given her orders, and Paul made her repeat them until there was no chance of her forgetting them. Drive to Miami International. Find accommodations for the night of the fifth and sixth. Stay in the room. Use Mary's ticket on the seventh. Use Mary's driver's license as proof of birthplace when needed. Use her immunization certificate if needed. Use her hairstyle. Wear big dark sunglasses. Travel in her new clothes. Go to Grenada. Register as Mary Broll. Live quietly. Keep to yourself. Send some postcards to Holly Dressner. Pick the kind that do not require a message. Sign with a little drawing of a smiling face.

"I *did* try to keep to myself. But, God, I've been here a long long time, Gav. I really have."

"What do you do next? What are Paul's orders?"

"On Monday, next Monday, I'm supposed to send a cable. Paul dictated it to me." I made her get it. It was to Woodrow Willow at Southern National in Miami.

PROCEED WITH LOAN AS ARRANGED EARLY JANUARY. HAVE AD-VISED HARRY BY PHONE. HOME SOON. MARY BROLL.

Harry's part in it would be to phone Woodrow Willow that same day, Monday, April 26, and tell him that Mary had reached him by overseas phone call from Grenada to tell him she had cabled Willow to go ahead, tell him not to worry, tell him she would be home soon. He would inform Willow that Mary had given him the name of the travel agency she had used and had told him that her neighbor, Mrs. Dressner, had known all along where she was.

Very nice. If Willow felt like double-checking after he got the cable, he could call the travel agency and call Mrs. Dressner.

"Can't they check back on an overseas call?" I asked.

"Sure. That's why I call him at his office next Sunday afternoon. I've got the number. He'll have a secretary there. It will be person-to-person. Mrs. Broll calling Mr. Broll. That's for afterward, in case they do a lot of checking."

"Checking what?"

"I'm reserved to leave here on Monday, the third of May. Paul just didn't have time to work everything out before I left. But the way he wants it to happen, Mary Broll will have some kind of accident. He's going to get a message to me telling me what to do. I just . . . leave everything of hers and arrive back home as myself somehow. Maybe a towel and a beach bag left on the beach, and nothing missing but a swimsuit and a cap."

"Where does the money come from?"

"The way I understand it, Gav, Harry invested seven hundred thousand in SeaGate. The letter of agreement said that on or before April thirtieth, he has to pay in another three hundred thousand to make one million dollars. There is a block of stock escrowed for him and a note escrowed, saying SeaGate owes him seven hundred thousand plus interest. It is an . . . indivisible block. He takes it all and wipes out the money SeaGate owes him and pays three hundred more. If he doesn't, he just gets his seven hundred back with interest, and the hundred thousand shares go to increase the number of shares the corporation is selling to the public and to reduce the number the stockholders will offer. There is no way in the world Harry can get that money except from the bank on a loan on Mary's trust. He can't get an extension, and he can't cut down the number of shares he'll take. And he is borrowed to the hilt everywhere else."

"So he had to keep Mary alive for about four months after she died?"

She shivered. "Or lose a big profit, a million and a half."

"How much to your cousin?"

"He said a million. He didn't say that in front of Harry. I think he could get it all out of Harry." She frowned. "The thing about Paul, he stopped giving a damn *what* he does. It doesn't matter to him any more. It scares me. Once when I was little, a deaf boy took me to the movies, and he laughed when nobody else was laughing. Paul is like that now, sort of."

"And I suppose Harry has been making a big fuss, storming around, shaking up Mary's friends, demanding they tell him where they're hiding her."

"Maybe. I don't know. I guess it would make him look better later on if people could testify to that. I don't know how he is. I keep wondering how he'll sound on the phone."

Her voice dragged. Her face looked puffy with fatigue. Her eyes were irritated because of the many times the tears had come. There wasn't much left of the day. She said, "Can we go for a walk on the beach? Would that be okay, Gavin?"

She got up and got a gaudy print dashiki and pulled it over her head, pushed her hair back into semiorder, put her big glasses on. "Gee, I feel emptied out, as if it's out of my hands somehow. I should be scared, but I'm too beaten down to be scared. You're in charge, Gav. You've taken over. I don't know where we're going, but you're running the ship."

It was so nicely done I had my mouth all set for the bait and the hook. Poor little victim of a sordid conspiracy, clinging to the first man who'd give her the benefit of the doubt.

Sweet little immature face and a busy, nimble little butt and all the conscience and mercy of a leopard shark. Let me be your little pal, mister. Nobody else has ever understood me but you. She had slipped up on one little detail, but it was a bad slip. She let me see how she must have looked trying on Mary's new resort clothes while Mary lay dead. Probably Lisa turned this way and that, looking in the mirror, smoothing her rear with the backs of her hands, wishing the damned dead woman had bought the cute clothes one size smaller. She tried on clothes while the men argued in the next room. "Look at it this way, Broll. You had a look at her an hour and a half ago. They'll want to know why you waited so long before reporting it. What do you tell them?" While Lisa hummed and bit her lip and frowned at herself and wondered if the colors were right for her.

thirteen

We walked up the beach in the orange and gold light of tropic sunset. The tide was moving out and the packed sand was damp and firm under our tread, a coarse, yellow-brown sand. The sun was behind us, setting into the sea just out beyond Long Point. Far ahead, beyond the rocks that marked the end of Grande Anse beach and beyond St. George's harbor, was the toy-town look of the town at evening, spilled up the green slopes, small formal shapes with windows looking toward the sea.

We walked past the Grande Anse Hotel, the Grenada Beach Hotel, the Holiday Inn. Cars had come down to the public areas to park under the sea grapes and the almond trees. People swam in the relative cool of twilight, and people walked the long broad promenade of packed sand. Sloops and ketches and multihull sailboats were anchored off the two-mile crescent of beach. A fast boat was pulling a limber black girl on water skis between the anchored sailboats. Behind us was the blinding dazzle of the sun's path on the quiet sea, and our shadows ahead of us were long in a slanting pattern against the damp sand.

"You were going to talk, I thought?"

"I am. I am." She moved closer, linked her arm through mine, hugged it against her body, and looked up at me. "I have to, I guess. Do you know how things can happen to your life that . . . don't fit it somehow? Then everything else isn't real. When you forget, then everything around you is real again, but what happened doesn't seem as if it could have ever happened. Do you know what I'm talking about?"

"Not yet, girl. Not yet."

"I guess in my own way I was as numb as Harry was. It seems like ten years ago, practically."

"Didn't you think it was pretty damned stupid for Paul to kill Mary Broll? Didn't you tell him it was stupid?"

She had to wait until we had passed a group of people strolling at a slower pace than ours. She indicated a stubby cement pier at the far border of the Holiday Inn property. It projected only to the surf line and seemed to have no purpose other than as some sort of groin to retain the sand. We went up the slope of beach, stepped up onto it, and walked out to sit near the end, our backs to the sunset.

She laced her fingers in mine, tugged at my hand, and rested it palm upward against the smooth, round brown of mid-thigh. She frowned toward the town.

"I've thought about it and thought about it, Gavin. I guess it got to be pretty obvious to Paul that an affair with me wasn't going to be enough leverage on Harry. Harry and his wife weren't getting along so great anyway. There wasn't anything real important to expose, you might say. So why did he tip off Mary Broll so she'd catch me and Harry together? Why did he make sure she *would* catch us? Why did he tell me to yell at Mrs. Broll and make a big scene out of it? Motive, right?"

The point was well taken. Mary would certainly confide her problem to someone. The scene at the apartment had attracted so much attention that even Jeannie Dolan heard about it later. Of late, Harry had been blustering around, threatening people, trying to locate his dead wife.

If the police were tipped, dug for Mary, and found her, even the most inept state's attorney could put together a case F. Lee Bailey couldn't successfully defend.

"So, Lisa, you think Paul had decided to kill her when he made the phone call to her. Does that make sense? He didn't know then she'd decided to go away. He didn't know then what she'd arrange about the loan. She could have left without any warning at all. He'd have to be some kind of warlock, reading the future."

"I know. I think about it until my head starts to hurt, and then I give up."

"Did you think he'd ever kill anybody?"

"You don't go around wondering whether people you know can kill other people, do you? I knew he was mean. I knew how nasty he could get. I knew there was something kinky about him, the way he got something special out of sleeping with me and then making me sleep with those older guys. It was something to do with him never getting married, I think. We look alike, like brother and sister. His eyes are the same as mine, the same dark brown and long black lashes and—see?—the left one set straight and the right one slanty. His mouth is like mine, a lot of natural red to the lips, and the mouth small, and the lower lip heavy and curling out from the upper lip. We both look younger than we are, but that's always been true of the whole family. Aside from that, there isn't the least thing feminine about him. Even my eyes and mouth don't look girlish on Paul, somehow. Except when he's asleep. That's strange, isn't it? I'd watch him sleeping, and then his eyes and lips would look the most like mine and make me feel strange. He is big! He's almost as tall as you are and as big through the chest. But he moves a lot quicker. I guess I mean his normal way of moving is quicker. Nobody is quicker than you were with Carl. Jesus! You looked kind of dumb and sleepy, as if you couldn't believe he was really going to beat on you. Then you were something else."

"I want to know more about Paul. How old is he?"

"He'll be coming up onto thirty-seven, I think in July. Yes. Other companies have tried to hire him away from Mr. Waterbury. So I guess he's a good accountant. He stays in great shape all year. He does competition slalom in the winter and tennis in the summer. His legs are tremendously powerful, like fantastic springs."

"An exercise nut?"

"With weights and springs and pulleys and things. And a sunlamp that travels by itself from one end of you to the other and turns itself off. He's real happy about those legs. One funny thing, he's as dark as I am, and he has to shave twice a day when he goes out in the evening, but on his body, except for those places where everybody has hair, he hasn't any. His legs have a really great shape, and there isn't any hair on them or his chest or his arms. The muscles are long and smooth, not bunchy. When he tenses them, his legs are like marble."

"You called him kinky."

She frowned and thought for a little while. I saw the point of her tongue slowly moisten the curve of underlip. "No. That isn't the right word. The whole sex scene isn't a big thing with him. I mean it's there, all right. It was something we would do. You know, when he couldn't unwind and get to sleep, he'd phone me to come over to his place down in the city. We were five blocks apart. He makes me feel . . . I don't know . . . like one of his damn exercise machines, something with a motor and weights and springs, so that afterward he could put it in his exercise log. Ten minutes on the rowing machine. Eight minutes on the Lisa machine."

"I can't really get the picture of you two."

"What's so difficult, honey?"

"You move to Quebec and change jobs because he tells you to. You come over whenever he phones you. He tells you to seduce Mr. X and then Mr. Y and tells you how to extort money from them, and he takes most of it. He tells you to seduce Harry, quit your job, and follow Harry to Florida, and he tells you to come here and pretend to be Mary. You are awfully goddamn docile, Lisa."

"I know. I know. Yes. It's funny about him. He's just so absolutely positive you're going to do what he tells you to do, it's a lot easier to do it than try to say you won't."

"Did you ever try to say you wouldn't do something he asked you to do?"

"God, yes! In the very beginning, before he even got the job for me. I was at his place, and he asked me to get him something from across the room. I was sitting at the table, and I said something like 'You're not a cripple, are you?' He got up and went behind me and hit me on top of the head with his fist. I blacked out and fell off the chair and cut my chin. It did something funny to my neck, pinched a nerve or something, and I was in bed for three days with it, practically in agony. He was a darling. He waited on me hand and foot. He was so sweet and considerate. I guess . . . it's easier to do what he says, because you have the feeling that neither of you knows what he'll do if you say no. At work he's another person."

"How do you feel about the way you're crossing him?"

"It keeps making me feel as if I'm going to throw up." She looked up at me with a piquant tilt of her dark head. "It's funny," she said. "I never saw you before today. Then you scared me so. You really did. Now you're so nice and understanding. I can really talk to you. About everything."

Her fingers were laced in mine, and she pressed down on my hand, holding the back of my hand against the round, tan thigh, slowly swinging her dangling leg as she did so. I felt the smooth working of the thigh muscles against the back of my hand. It was a sensuous and persuasive feeling. She was a pretty piece, making her constant offer of herself in any way that she could.

"Why trust me?" I asked her.

She shrugged. "I don't know. I guess I'm trying to. I guess I can't go it alone, no matter what it is. I appreciate you didn't mark me up any. I mean I hate to get belted in the face where it shows. It cuts a person's mouth inside, and there's a big puffy bruise, and maybe a mouse comes under a person's eye. It's a bad thing to do to a girl. She goes around ashamed."

"Paul belted you?"

"Sometimes."

"But you trust him?"

"He's a blood relative. Maybe I shouldn't trust him at all. He's strange. He really is. It doesn't show. You have to know him."

"I keep thinking of how boxed in you are."

"How do you mean?"

"Suppose after you go back, Harry is picked up for killing his wife. They have her body. It's certainly no big problem finding the girl friend and proving you were there. With that starting point, Lisa, how long before the state attorney's investigators learn about the impersonation? Would you want to explain on the stand why you took her money, her tickets, her reservations, her clothes, and her car?"

There was a sudden sallowness. "Come *on* now. Don't, honey! Jesus! I don't like jokes like that. We're in this together, aren't we?"

"Are we?"

"What do you *want* of me? What more do you want that I'm not ready and eager and willing to give, dear?"

"Do you think Cousin Paul is going to give you a short count on the money again?"

"If he gets the chance."

I pulled my hand away from her. "Now what would keep him from having the chance? Me?"

"Darling, please don't try to confuse me."

"How am I confusing you?"

"Well . . . you said you own me now, and you said there had to be money in it. So I guess you'll go after the money. I guess you'd have to have my help."

"Doing what?"

"That would be up to you, dear."

"To figure out how you can help me get rich?"

"'That's the name of your game, I thought.'"

"Maybe Paul's game is over."

"How do you mean?"

"Harry Broll is not a complete idiot. Why couldn't he have gone quietly to the police and managed to tell them the truth? So they lay back and wait for you to return and for Paul to make his move, and scoop you both up."

"Damn! I forgot to tell you about the letter I wrote Paul. He was right there when I wrote it. He found Mary Broll's personal stationery for me to use. He told me what to write. I had to do it over because he said it was too neat the first time. I dated it January fifth. It said that Paul had been right and I never should have gotten involved with Harry. It said Harry had done something terrible while drunk and had gotten me to his house afterward to help him but I couldn't. I said I was frightened and I was going away and to wait until I got in touch with him. He held it in front of Harry and made him read it. Then he had me seal it in an envelope and put a stamp on it and address it to Paul's place in West Palm Beach. Paul put it in his pocket to mail as soon as he could."

The sun was gone. The world was darkening. The sky a dying furnace, and the sea was slate. We walked back the way we had come, but more slowly.

"Gavin?"

"Shut up, Lisa. Please."

The beach was almost empty. The outdoor torches had been lighted at the Spice Island Inn. Birds were setting noisily to bed, arguing about the best places. Canned music was coming over all-weather speakers, a steel band playing carnival calypso.

When we reached her gate, she said, "Now can I say something? Like, please come in?"

"I want to sit out in the breeze, thanks. Over there."

"Join you?"

"Sure."

"Bring you a drink, maybe?"

"Thanks. Same as before."

I sat deep in a chaise, legs up, trying to work it out in every possible combination and permutation. With Mary Broll dead, Woodrow Willow was supposed to slam the lid on that trust account. Harry was probably the beneficiary under her will, possibly a coexecutor along with the bank. But had she died in early January, even in a traffic accident, the chances of processing the estate quickly enough for Harry to get his three hundred thousand before April thirtieth were very damned remote. She had to die later on.

So what if Meyer and I had not had all those vague feelings of uneasiness? What if we had accepted my phone call as being proof enough that she was alive and well and living in Grenada?

Then it would have worked like a railroad watch. The timely loan. The news of pending reconciliation. Enough supporting information for Willow to consider the cable legitimate authorization. Then the ironic tragedy. Estranged wife on the point of returning home to her contrite husband, missing in mysterious drowning incident. Search is on for body. However . . .

"Here you go," she said. I thanked her for the drink. She had brought one for herself. She sat on the side of the chaise, facing me. I moved my legs over to make room. The stars were beginning to come out. I could see that she had brushed her hair, freshened her mouth. The bright, block-print dashiki had deep side slits, and she adjusted herself and it, either by accident or design, so that the side slit showed the outside of a bare thigh and hip as high as the waist, a smoothness of flesh in the dying day that was not interrupted by the narrow encirclement of bikini I had seen there before.

"You certainly do an awful lot of thinking," she said.

"And here I am, dear, alive and well."

"But you have been terribly terribly hurt a few times, Gav."

"The times when I wasn't thinking clearly."

"Do I keep you from thinking clearly? I'd sure like a chance to try. Would you mind if I ask you politely to please make love to me?"

"What are we celebrating?"

"You're *such* a bastard! Gavin darling, I feel very very insecure about a lot of things. I've been alone a long time. Now I want somebody to hold me tight and make love to me and tell me I'm delicious. For morale, I guess. Why do you even make me ask? It doesn't have to be any big thing, you know. It doesn't have to take up a hell of a lot of your time. Hitch over just a little bit, darling, and let me . . ."

The way she started to manage it—to lie down beside me and hike her dashiki up and tug my swim trunks down and simultaneously hook one brown leg over me—certainly wasn't going to take up a great deal of anybody's time, the way she was going at it.

I pushed her erect and pulled the trunks back up. "Very flattering. Very generous. But no thanks."

She laughed harshly and picked her drink up off the sand near her feet. "Well, comparing you to Carl, I can say this. You've got a different kind of attitude. If I hadn't uncovered proof, I'd be wondering about you."

"I'm busy pretending I'm Paul, wondering how he has it all worked out."

"Different strokes for different folks."

"I hang back and make sure Harry Broll follows orders. I check with him about the Sunday afternoon phone call from you. On Tuesday morning, the twenty-seventh, I will get in touch with Mr. Willow, in my capacity as an employee of SeaGate, to verify that Mr. Broll will indeed have the funds to pick up his escrowed block of SeaGate shares. I am assured. The money comes through. And I am very very busy right through the thirtieth and through the weekend, because that is the end of the fiscal year for SeaGate. Right?"

"I guess so, dear."

"Then I have to do something about Cousin Lisa. She's expecting a message from me. I'll have to deliver it in person."

"To tell me what to do next?"

"Old Harry is twitchy about his dead wife. And Lisa is twitchy about Harry's dead wife. Harry and Lisa could testify against me if they ever join forces. Lisa is wearing the dead woman's rings. I just have to arrange a nice quick safe way to meet her in the islands and blow her face off and blow her dental work to paste. Then there's no mystery about a body. I can settle down and separate good old Harry from every cent of his gain and every cent he has left over when that's gone. When Harry is empty, it will be time to lay him to rest, too. By accident. Just in case."

I reached an idle hand and patted her on the shoulder. She remained quiveringly still, then was suddenly up and away, to come to rest five feet from the chaise, staring at me.

"No! No, Gavin. He's my first cousin. No."

"He couldn't do that?"

"Absolutely not. Not ever. Not any way."

"Then why are you so upset?"

"Anybody would be upset, hearing something so horrible."

"You know you are supposed to fake Mary Broll's death. There's less chance of a hitch if somebody plays the part of the body. You've been Mary Broll since January. Why switch now?"

"Don't be such a bastard!"

"It's the way I have to read him from everything you've told me. A quirky guy but very logical. A good improviser. If one logical plan doesn't develop the way he wants it to, he thinks up an alternative just as good or better. And . . . Lisa dear, just what the hell good are you to him? The end of usefulness. He knows there's a chance you'll make new friends who'll hear about how you died and get very upset about it and might run into you in an air terminal somewhere a year from now. All you are is a big risk, and an unnecessary risk."

"Shut *up!*"

"Think about it."

"I *am* thinking about it."

"It wouldn't be *my* style, but I have to admire it in a way. It ties up the loose ends. No way out for Harry. Or you."

She found her drink had been kicked over. "Ready for another?"

"Not yet, thanks."

"Want to come in?"

"I'll stay here awhile."

"Be back soon, dear."

fourteen

Though Lisa Dissat was not gone for more than ten minutes, it was full night when she came back, a velvet beach under a brilliance of stars. There were lights behind us from the Spice Island Inn cottages. The lights made a slanting yellow glow against the sand.

She sat beside me again. She had changed to tailored white shorts, a dark blouse with a Chinese collar and long sleeves. She smelled of perfume . . . and Off. The white fabric was snug on the round hip that pressed warm against the side of my knee.

"Took off your instant rape suit, eh?"

She pulled her shoulders up slightly, and her drink made the sounds of ice as she sipped. "I guess you made me lose interest."

"Are you a believer now?"

"Up to a point. I can't see any percentage in taking dumb risks. You are the loose end Paul doesn't know about. I guess I can be the bait in the trap. But we have to be awfully, awfully careful. He's very sensitive to . . . what people are thinking. We can't give him any chance at all."

"How do you mean that?"

"If it's like you say, if that's what he's going to try to do, then he'll have it all worked out so there won't be any risk in it, hardly any at all. So if he really wants to kill me, we have to kill him instead, darling."

"Your very own first cousin?"

"Don't be a stinker, please. What other choice is there?"

"Then what?"

"Then we have to get me back into the States in some safe way. I guess there's no reason why I couldn't go back in as Mary Broll, come to think of it. What harm would it do?"

"None, if you don't try to keep on being Mrs. Broll."

"If he isn't thinking about killing me like you say, then we'll have to play it by ear."

"All goes well, and you and I are back in the States. Then?"

"We just go and see Harry. That's all. I'll tell him that unless he gives us lots and lots of money, he's going to have lots and lots of trouble. And you can beat him up if he tries to bluff us."

"How much money?"

"I don't think we should make him really desperate or anything. I think we should leave him with enough so he'll think he came out of it pretty well. I think we could ask for half a million dollars."

"Each?"

"No, dear. He has to pay taxes on the whole thing, you know. I think with the holding period before the sale to the public, it will be long term. Yes, I know it will. He should get his money next December. Hmmm. His taxes will be a half million. That leaves him two million, and I know he owes four hundred thousand and he will have to pay back the three hundred thousand. So out of his million and three, we'll take five hundred thousand, darling, and he'll have eight hundred thousand left. It would be neater if we took six hundred and fifty and left him six hundred and fifty, don't you think?"

"A lot neater. And you want half?"

"What I want and what you'll let me have aren't the same, are they?"

"They could be with cooperation all the way."

"Moving money like that around without leaving traces that people can find later is very hard. Do you know anything about that kind of problem? I'd think you would."

"If Harry Broll will hold still for the bite, yes."

"There's no problem, Gav honey. None."

"Leaving only Paul."

She finished her drink, bunted me with her hip. "Scrooch over some, honey. Make room. No funny stuff this time, I promise."

She turned, lay back, and fitted her head to my shoulder, swinging her legs aboard.

After a while she said, "Want to order dinner in my place or yours, dear?"

"I don't know yet."

"I'm not hungry, either. Gee, look at all the damned stars. Like when I was a little kid, the night sky looked glittery like this."

"Where was that?"

"Way up in French Canada on the St. Lawrence, north of Rivière du Loup. A little town called Trois Pistoles. Ten thousand saints, ten thousand churches all over that country. Convent school, uniforms, vespers, acts of contrition, the whole scene. I ran away when I was fifteen. With my best friend, Diane Barbet. We got across the border and into the States. Things got kind of messy for us. You survive or you don't, I guess. I don't know what happened to Diane. I think about her sometimes. A guy in Detroit helped me really go to work on my hick Canuck accent. Movies, television, radio, and using a tape recorder. I think in English now, except if something startles the hell out of me or scares me. I get scared in French. Another man sent me to business school to learn to be an executive secretary. That was in Cincinnati. He was a real old guy. He picked me up. I was hitchhiking. He took me home. He lived alone—his wife had been dead two years. He wanted me to stay there with him and pretend I was his grandniece so the neighbors wouldn't turn him in. I wanted somebody to send me to school so I could be a secretary, so it worked out okay. He bought me pretty clothes. I was eighteen by then. He bought me a little car, even. He was retired. He cooked and kept the house clean and did the laundry and made the bed. He even ironed my things that needed it, and he rinsed out stuff. I was really pretty rotten to old Harv. He was forty years older than me. That is a lot of years. When he got on my nerves, I wouldn't let him touch me. I cut off the supply. He didn't really want me too often or give me much trouble. I finished school and got my certificate and got a job. The way I was living, I could put it all in the bank, and I did. I came home one evening, and he was on the floor in the utility room. His whole left side had gone dead. His eye drooped and spit ran out of the left side of his mouth, and he couldn't speak. He just made terrible noises when he tried. I packed all my things into the trunk of my car, and then I called the hospital. I parked in the next block and walked back to make sure they found him and put him in the ambulance. I went to a motel. I finished out the week after I gave notice. I got my money out of the bank. I left and went down to Mobile and sold the car there. You can sell cars easy in Alabama.

Then I flew home to Canada and got a good job in Montreal. I kept missing old Harv. I still miss him, I guess. It was a pretty good way to live, you know? I wasn't very nice to him. If I had it to do over, I'd be a lot nicer. I'd never hold out on him the way I did. It never cost me a thing to make him feel good.

"Anyway, I had a wonderful life in Montreal. There was a great bunch of kids there. And then I fell really *really* in love. When my guy took off with a girl friend of mine, I did what I always do when I hurt. Buy, buy, buy. Shoes, clothes, wigs. I like money. I guess I spend it to hurt myself. You know? I knew I was in real trouble unless somebody bailed me out. So I went up to Quebec and saw Cousin Paul. I think I could have gone the rest of my life without the kind of help *he* gave me. Hey, look!"

"Shooting star."

"I know. But such a big, bright, slow one, huh? It lasted forever."

"Did you make a wish?"

"Was I supposed to? Would it work?"

"The way to make a wish come true is to wish for something you're going to get anyway."

"Is it okay to wish a little late?"

"Go ahead. It wasn't my shooting star."

"Okay. I wished." My arm was around her. She turned in a twisting motion that slipped her breast into my hand. Under the thin fabric of the blouse she wore no bra, and in seconds I felt the nipple growing and hardening. "Does that give you a clue, friend? Something I'm going to get anyway?"

I sat up, raising her with me, slid my hands onto her waist, picked her up, and dropped her onto the sand beside the chaise.

"Ow! That made me bite my tongue, you son of a bitch!"

"Just be a good girl and stop trying to hook me on the product. It's there any time I want it. Stop pushing it."

She stood up. "Don't be too damned sure it's going to be served up on a damn tray when you decide to ask for it, Gav. And I wasn't trying to hook you on anything. I just think it's friendly and nice to get laid. It isn't a big thing, is it? And it got me going, what I was talking about."

"Old Harv, for God's sake?"

"No, you dummy! The money. Big gobs of money. Just thinking about it makes me feel all hollow and crawly inside, and I guess it's so much like the feeling you get when you know you're going to get laid, it works the same way."

"Go take a cold shower."

"You're terribly nice to me. You're oceans of fun. I'm going to walk up and down the beach and think about blizzards and icicles and catheters and having my teeth drilled. That takes me off the edge fast."

"I should think it would."

So she went walking out there, clearly visible, scuffing barefoot through the foamy water that came running up the wet slope after the thud of each slow, small wave. A girl walking slowly, slow tilting swing of hips, legs shapely and dark below the white glow of the shorts.

She had deftly pushed a lot of my buttons. She had worked on proximity, touch, forthright invitation. She had talked in areas that accentuated sexual awareness. She smelled good, felt good, kept her voice furry and intimate. I knew she wasn't being made wanton and reckless by my fabulous magnetism. We were moving toward an association, possibly profitable. For maximum leverage within that association of two, she wanted to put that weapon to work which had profited her in the past, probably in every relationship except the one with her cousin.

I was another version of good old Harv, whom we last saw on the floor with spit running out of his mouth. She'd pushed Harv's buttons and got her secretarial training and a car and a lot of clothes. Her libido certainly wasn't out of control. It was just a useful thing for her to do, a nice little inexpensive favor for her to grant, and if it clouded the recipient's judgment, eventual profit from the relationship might improve.

Were I a great ape, a giant anthropoid, munching stalks torn from the jungle, and able to lead her to forgotten treasure, Lisa would take her best shot at making everything friendlier and nicer. As she said about Harv, it wouldn't cost a thing to make that big monkey feel good.

But knowing how and why the buttons are pushed doesn't diminish the physiological aftereffects of the button pushing. The tumescence is noticeable. The palm of the hand retains the shape of the breast—the precise size, warmth, and rate of erection. The eyes watch the slow walk, creating an increase in the heartbeat and rate of respiration and blood pressure and surface body temperature, as the conditioned mind anticipates the simple progression of events of calling to her, bringing her close, shucking her out of the shorts, pulling her astride, and settling her properly for that sweet, grinding task that would end so quickly the first time.

The buttons tripped certain relays. I had to go back into the mind, into central control, and reset those relays, compensate for the overload, switch the current back to those channels designed for it.

I went searching through the past for the right memory, the one that would most easily turn growing desire to indifference.

I thought a memory of Miss Mary Dillon long ago aboard *The Busted Flush* would do it. There were more than a few, but they would not come through vividly enough to achieve turnoff.

Lisa made it so damned easy, so completely available, there was no importance to it. And with no importance to an act, why did it matter whether or not it happened? Why did McGee need some cachet of importance in this world of wall-to-wall flesh in the weekend living room where the swingers courteously, diligently, skillfully, considerately hump one another to the big acid beat of the hi-fi installation, good from 20 to 20,000 cycles per second?

Is McGee still impaled upon some kind of weird Puritan dilemma, writhing and thrashing around, wrestling with an out-dated, old-time, inhibiting, and artificial sense of sin, guilt, and damnation? Is that why he couldn't accept the lifetime gift Lady Jillian offers? Is that why he has this sickly, sentimental idea that there has to be a productive and meaningful relationship first, or sex degrades? So bang the doxy, because easing the ball pressure is reason enough.

Who needs magic and mystery? Well, maybe it is magic and mystery that an Antarctic penguin will hunt all over hell and gone to find the right pebble to carry in his beak and lay between the funny feet of his intended, hoping for her favor. Maybe sex is a simple bodily function, akin to chewing, sneezing, and defecation. But bald eagles fly as high as they possibly can, up into the thinnest air, making the elegant flight patterns of intended mating all the way up, then cleave to each other and fall, fall, fall, mating as they fall fluttering, pummeting down toward the great rock mountains.

The way it is supposed to work nowadays, if you want to copulate with the lady, you politely suggest it to her, and you are not offended if she says no, and you are mannerly, considerate, and satisfying if she says yes.

But the Tibetan bar-headed goose and her gander have a very strange ceremony they perform *after* they have mated. They rise high in the water, wings spread wide, beaks aimed straight up at the sky, time and time again, making great bugle sounds of honking.

The behaviorists think it is unprofessional to use subjective terms about animal patterns. So they don't call this ceremony joy. They don't know what to call it. These geese live for up to fifty years, and they mate for life. They celebrate the mating this same way year after year. If one dies, the other never mates again.

So penguins, eagles, geese, wolves, and many other creatures of land and sea and air are stuck with all this obsolete magic and mystery because they can't read and they can't listen to lectures. All they have is instinct. Man feels alienated from all feeling, so he sets up encounter groups to sensitize each member to human interrelationships. But the basic group of two, of male and female, is being desensitized as fast as we can manage it. . . .

"What the hell is there about me that turns you off?" Lisa demanded. She had walked up the slope to stand by the chaise, blotting out a Lisa-shaped abundance of stars as she looked down at me with a faint angle of pale yellow light lying across her cheekbone and lips.

"I was wondering what you'd do if I picked up a pebble in my beak and put it between your feet."

"I've heard of a lot of ways guys get kinky, but that is—"

"Why do you want reassurance from me? Take my word for it. You are a fantastic piece of ass. Ask practically anybody."

"I don't know. I haven't checked it."

She stood there for a few seconds in silence. Then she said, "If you ever do want some, friend, you're going to have to take it away from me, because that's the only damned way in this world you're ever going to get any."

"Good night, Lisa."

She walked away from the shoreline, a silhouette moving toward the yellow lights.

fifteen

On Thursday I was up early. Awakening in a new place makes the day of arrival seem unreal. There had been no Carl Brego, no Lisa Dissat trying to be Mary Broll, no Lisa Dissat striding angrily away from me in the hot, buggy night. I went to my cottage after she left, swam in my minipool, two strokes per lap, changed, and went to the open dining room. The food was good, the service indifferent. There were some beautiful people there. A fashion photography team. Some yacht people. Some twosome guests had tried to get as far as possible from wherever they didn't care to be seen together. Some guests were ritualistic sun worshipers who had been there for many many weeks, using the intense tropic sun to add each day's tiny increment of pigmentation at the cost of blinding, suffocating, dazed hours and quarts of whatever oil they happened to believe in: Johnson's or coconut or olive. They were working toward that heady goal of becoming a living legend in Bronxville or Scranton or Des Moines.

"Tan? You think that's a tan? So you didn't see Barbie and Ken when they got back from Grenada that time. Dark? I swear to Christ, in a dark room all you could see were white teeth. And Barbie's diamonds."

I took a cab into town, memorizing landmarks all the way. I negotiated the rental of an Austin Moke. A Moke is a shrunken jeep with a very attractive expression, if you look at the front of it and think of the headlights as eyes. It looks staunch, jaunty, and friendly. It is a simplified piece of machinery. Stick shift which, like the wheel on the right, you work with the left hand. The horn, a single-note, piercing *beeeeep*, is operated by pressing in on the turn indicator with the right hand. A quick whack with the heel of the hand is the approved method. Four speeds forward, small, air-cooled engine, pedals so tiny that if you try to operate one with your bare feet, it hurts like hell. Canvas top nobody ever folds down in the hot season, and all they have in Grenada are two hot seasons, one wet and one dry.

With the tourist season almost over, there were a lot of them in stock. I picked one with a lot of tread, and the rental man and I walked around it and tested lights, horn, directional signals, windshield wiper (singular). He wanted his total rental in advance, which is standard for the area. While we dickered, I practiced getting in and out of the damned thing. I'd learned in Grand Cayman and Jamaica that with the length of my legs there is only one possible way. Stand beside vehicle on right side. Bend over at waist. Reach across body and grasp steering wheel with right hand, while simultaneously lifting left leg and inserting it into vehicle so that foot comes to rest on floor well beyond pedal area. Swoop your behind onto the seat and pick up right leg and lift over high broad sill (which contains gas tank). In driving position both knees are bent sharply, spread wide apart. Steering wheel fits between knees, and lower part of legs must angle in to assure foot contact with pedals. Adjust to inevitability of frequently giving oneself a painful rap on the left leg while shifting.

We arrived at a mutually agreeable fee of five Yankee—ten Biwi —dollars a day for one-week rental or any period of less than a week. I buy the gas. I will phone him when I leave and tell him to pick it up at the Spice Island Inn. I promise not to leave it at the airport. I tell him I would not drive it over that road to the airport for a hundred dollars a mile. Can I drive safely on the left side of the road? I suggest that perhaps no one in Grenada can drive safely on any side of the road. But yes, I have so driven on other islands of this British persuasion.

We accomplish the red tape, and he gives me a free map of St. George's and environs. I note that, as expected, there is at least half a pint of gas in the five-gallon gas tank. I edge carefully into the tourney and immediately am nearly bowled over and over by a small

pale bus with a name across the front of it. The name is: I AM NOTH-
ING.

After I have bought petrol and felt my way back into the center of
town, avoiding too intimate a contact with a large gaudy city bus
called LET IT BE ME, I park my Moke and wait until I am certain my
legs will work. ("You will enjoy browsing in St. George's along the
narrow, quaint streets.")

I changed another wad of Yankee dollars into Biwi at the Bank of
Canada, picking that one from among all the shiny banks downtown, from Chase to Barclay's to the Bank of Nova Scotia, because
there was a faint aroma of irony in the choice. The girl standing
behind the money-changing counter was very dark, very thin, and totally antagonistic—so much so, there was no chance of ever making
any kind of human contact with her unless you were her identical
anthracite color.

I asked some questions and was directed to a big busy supermarket
called EVERYBODY'S FOR EVERYTHING. As long as I had kitchen facilities and could make my own ice cubes, it seemed useful to set up
shop. Gin, rum, fruit juices from Trinidad, mixes, and a couple of
large substantial drink glasses. I am a fussy old party about glassware.
Nothing takes the pleasure out of drinking like the tiny dim glasses
supplied by hotels and motels. I always buy heavy glasses, always
leave them behind. Tiny glasses turn drinking from a pleasure rite to
a quasi-alcoholic twitch.

The final purchase was on impulse at a shop I saw on the
Carenage on the way home: a great big planter's hat of straw with a
batik band. Put a man in a rental Moke with advertising painted on
the side of it and put a funny hat on him, and he is a tourist. All
tourists look alike. Regardless of age, sex, or the number of extra
lenses for their cameras, they all look alike.

I found my way back out to Grande Anse to hotel row, and I
found an overland way to get the Moke close to my cottage. I carried
my box of stuff in. From the moment I had awakened until the moment I finished putting the stuff away and sat down, I had not let
myself think about Mary, Lisa, or the mechanics of impersonation.

It is a useful device. If you keep things in the front of your mind,
you worry at them like a hound chomping a dead rabbit. Throw
problems in the back cupboard and keep them there as long as you
can. The act of stirring around seems to shuffle the elements of a

problem into a new order, and when you take it out again, there are new ways to handle it.

I tossed my sweat-soaked shirt aside. The air conditioning felt good on my back and shoulders. Okay. Mary is dead. I want Paul Dissat. I want him very badly. The money is the bait, and Lisa is the bait in another sense. I want very badly to convince Paul and Lisa and Harry Broll that, if given a choice, they would elect retroactive birth control. I want them so eager to be out of it they'd dig their own graves with a bent spoon and their fingernails.

Secondly, as a professional, as a salvage consultant in areas of considerable difficulty, I want to come out of this with a little salvage for myself. If I walk away without a dime, with only expenses I can't reasonably afford, then I lose all respect for myself as a con artist. I would have kicked the hell out of their little wagon just to avenge one hell of a woman, Mary Dillon. Pure emotionalism is bush league.

So? So I do not advise Mr. Willow not to make the loan on Mary's securities. They go to Harry eventually anyway. That is, if Harry happens to be still around. The money has to be loaned to Harry, and Harry has to pick up his block of stock in time and get himself in position to make a great deal of money when the public issue comes out. But that is a long time for me to wait for my money. I shall use the leverage to extract a reasonable chunk from Paul, maybe from Harry, maybe from both, before I set them to work with those bent spoons.

It may be enough to have Harry and Lisa dig their graves deep with the sides and ends properly squared off and stand in them without the slightest morsel of hope left. Then I walk away and leave them standing there. But Paul is something else.

Program: Lisa must perform exactly as instructed: make her phone call to Harry and send the cable to Mr. Willow at the bank. I want her to be desperately anxious to tell me all the details of any contact by Paul Dissat. Then I will prepare to greet him. Here. There. Somewhere.

I pulled on my salty swim trunks and put on my big tourist hat and went looking for the lady. She was not in Cottage 50. I trudged around, squinting into the hot glare, and found her on a sun cot at the top of the slope that led down to the beach proper. She was face down. The bikini was yellow today. The top was undone, and she had rolled the fabric of the bottom so that it was about as big

around as a yellow lead pencil where it cut across the tanned cheeks
of her behind. She was glossy with oil. Her towel was on the sand. I
sat on it. Her face was turned away.

"You wanna buy nice coconut, Miss lady? Peanuts? Nice spices?"

She slowly turned her heat-stricken, slack-mouthed face toward
me. "I don't want any—" She shaded her eyes, squinted. "Oh. It's
you."

"Me. Absolutely correct. Me, himself."

"Who needs you?"

She lay with her face turned toward me, eyes closed. "You need
me," I told her.

"Not any more. Thanks a lot. But not any more."

"I don't mean that kind of need, honey. I'm talking about financial need. Commercial necessities."

"Thanks loads. I think I'd better take my chances with Paul."

"That should be a lot of laughs for both of you. I wrote an interesting letter last night."

She forgot her top wasn't latched. She sat up fast. "What kind of
a letter? Who to?"

"What's the local policy about the tits on tourists?"

She picked up the top and put it on. "I know what *your* policy is,
friend. You ignore them. What kind of a letter?"

"Double envelope. A sealed letter along, inside the sealed letter.
If he doesn't hear from me on or before May tenth, he opens the
second letter."

"Then what?"

"He takes action."

"*What* action?"

"Oh, he just gets in touch with the right people at the SEC and
says that it looks as if one Mr. Harry Broll bought himself into
SeaGate, Inc., with a final three hundred thou fraudulently obtained
and that this fact might not be uncovered by the accounting firm
preparing the material for the red herring and they should check
with a Mr. Willow regarding evidence as to whether or not Mrs.
Broll was alive at the time he released funds at her earlier request.
My friend is an attorney. He knows all the steps in the new registration folk dance. Delicate, these new issues. They can die of a head
cold."

"Oh, God! Why'd you think you couldn't trust me?"

"Who said anything about that?"

"Isn't that why you did it?"

"Lisa, Lisa, Lisa. What if we miss? Suppose your dear cousin nails us both, lays us to rest in a ceremonial boat, lights the pyre, and sends us out to sea. The last few moments would be a lot more enjoyable knowing Cousin Paul would never make a profit on the deal."

She swallowed hard and looked unhappy. "Don't talk about things like that." I knew that behind her sun squint her brain was ticking away, weighing and measuring advantages. I reached under the sun cot and retrieved her big sunglasses from the magazine on which they lay and handed them to her.

"Thanks, dear," she said, putting them on. "Sure. I see what you mean. And if he catches us sort of off base, it could maybe be handy to tell him about your lawyer friend."

"Yes. I think so. If he gives me a chance."

"Can't you see why I thought you did it on account of me?"

I thought it over. "Well, I suppose I can in a way. If you *did* decide he represents a better chance, you could tip him off about me and he could . . . tidy up the situation."

She turned over and put her feet down on the sand near my legs. Her hairline was sweaty. Trickles of sweat ran down her throat, and a little rivulet ran between her breasts and down across her belly to soak into the narrow yellow bikini. Her knees were apart, and the cot was so short-legged that her knees were on the same level as her breasts. Her eyes were even with the top of my head.

She leaned toward me, forearms on her knees, and said in a cooing voice, "You know, you act so weird about me, about us, that I'm afraid I'm going to keep on misinterpreting the things you say. We're going to keep on having misunderstandings. I waited a long time last night for you to come over to my place to say you were sorry."

I looked at her. Bright sunshine is as cruelly specific as lab lights and microscopes. There was a small double chin, caused by the angle of her head. There was a scar on her lip near the nostril. Her hands and feet were small, square and sturdy, nails carefully tended. Her posture made a narrow tan roll of fat across her trim belly. Her slender waist made a rich line that flowed in a double curve, concave, convex, into the ripe tan hip and thigh. She sat with her plump parts pouched into the yellow fabric, heavy and vital. Stray pubic hairs, longer than the others, curled over the top of the bikini and escaped at the sides of the crotch, hairs the color of dull copper.

Sweat, muscles, flesh, hair, closeness. So close the tightness of the yellow pouch revealed the cleavage of labia. This was the magic and mystery of a locker room, steam room, massage table, or of a coeducational volleyball game in a nudist colony. This was jockstrap sex, unadorned.

"Lisa, I guess we have to say things so carefully we won't have misunderstandings."

"Maybe I got the wrong impression yesterday. You wouldn't be queer, darling?"

"No more than any other true-blue American lad."

"Some kind of trouble? You can tell Lisa. Prostate, maybe? Or some kind of irritation?"

"I'm in glowing health."

"Honey, are you so strung out on some great broad that you just don't want to make it with another girl? I could understand that. I've been through that."

"Nobody I've met lately has gotten to me."

Her mouth firmed, and her throat turned darker. "Am I some kind of pig woman it would turn your stomach to—"

"Whoa! It's just a little rule of mine. Save the dessert until last."

Her mouth softened into a sudden smile. "Dessert? Darling, I am also homemade soup, meat and potatoes, hot rolls and butter, and your choice of beverages. I am mostly meat and potatoes."

"There's another reason for waiting, Lisa."

"Like?"

She was ready again, I decided. Like training a mule. A good solid blow between the eyes, and I should have her total attention.

"It's kind of a sad story, dear."

"I love sad stories. I love to cry and cry."

"Well, once upon a time there was this lovely, delicate little blond lady, and she and I were partners in a complicated little business deal. We took our plans and problems to bed and talked them over during rest periods. I freaked over that little lady. She loved to make love. Then our business deal went sour. It fell apart. That was too damned bad because it was a nice piece of money for both of us. Well, one day a month later we romped all day together, happy as children, and that night I took her out in a boat, a nice runabout, out into the Atlantic. It was calm and beautiful, and I made her sit on the side rail, and I aimed a Colt forty-five with the muzzle an inch from her pretty brow and blew the top of her head off. I wired the spare anchor to her waist and let go in a half mile of water, and the moon was so bright that night I could see her for a long way as she went down. Now you can cry."

Her mouth sagged open. She put a hand to her throat and in a husky whisper said, "Jesus H. Christ!"

"That idiot girl thought that by sleeping with me she was buying insurance, in case I ever found out she had gone behind my back and made her own deal for half again as much as she would have made as my partner. She was so convinced of it, she was starting to smile when I pulled the trigger. You're not crying."

"Jesus H. Christ!"

"You said that before, Lisa. After that I decided it's bad policy. I made the punishment fit the crime, but I hated myself. You know? I used to think of that little blonde a lot. It used to depress me. It seemed like a waste, all those goodies sinking to the bottom of the sea."

"What *are* you?"

"Me? I'm your partner, Lisa. And we trust each other, don't we? Nobody is going to try to be cute. But . . . just in case . . . let's save all the goodies until after we've made the money score?"

"Th-that suits me, Gavin," she said. She clapped her thighs together so smartly they made a damp slapping sound. "L-later. I . . . I got to go for a minute. I'll be back."

"I'll probably be swimming."

She went off toward her place, walking slightly knock-kneed, head bowed and shoulders hunched.

An imaginary letter and an imaginary blond partner. I could imagine that dear imaginary girl sinking down, down through the black water, hair outspread, getting smaller and smaller and more and more indistinct until she was gone out of my imaginary life forever. Poor kid. Gavin Lee was a mean son of a bitch. It made me almost want to cry. Now the Lisa-McGee contest could be declared no contest. The lady wasn't going to come out for the third round. She was cowed. She was going to do as she was told. She was going to have as much sex drive from here on as a harem guard. And at the first word from her cousin she was going to come on the run to tell me all about it.

That evening she was so prim it was as if she had never left the convent school. We walked on the beach and got back to the cottages just after dark. We went to her place. She unlocked the gate. We went in, and she screamed as the two dark shapes jumped me. It got very interesting. They both knew a lot more about it than Carl Brego had. If they had been ready and willing to kill, they had me. But they weren't. And that gave me a better chance than I thought I was going to get.

I took punishment and gave it back. Whistling grunts of effort. Slap and thud of blows. Scuff of feet. I took one on the shoulder, off balance, and fell and rolled hard and came up near a yellow light bulb. A half-familiar voice said, "Hold it! I said *hold* it, Artie! I *know* this joker."

The voice was suddenly very familiar. "Rupe, you dreary bastard, what are you trying to do?"

"A favor for a friend. Lady, if you can get some Kleenex and some rubbing alcohol or some gin, I'd be obliged. And turn on some lights around here."

I told Lisa it was all right. She turned on the garden lights and the inside lights. She had some alcohol and a big roll of paper towels. All three of us were breathing hard. We were all marked, one way and another.

I said, "Mary, this is an old friend of mine. Rupert Darby, a sailing man. Rupe, Mary Broll."

"Pleased to meet you, Mary. And this here, Mary, is Artie Calivan. Artie is mate on the *Dulcinea,* and I'm hired captain. And this big rawboned bastard it's so hard to get a clean shot at, Artie, is an old friend of mine from way back. Trav McGee."

"McGee?" Lisa said blankly.

"It's a kind of joke name, honey," I said. "It comes from an old limerick. Trav rhymes with Gav for Gavin. And McGee rhymes with Lee."

If it had just hung there, I couldn't have brought it off. But Rupe came in very smoothly. "I'd like to recite you the limerick, Miz Mary, but it's just too dirty to repeat in front of a lady. I use that old name on Gav when I'm trying to get his goat. I think I've got one tooth here that isn't going to grow back tight again, dammit."

I looked at his mate. "You brought along a big one."

"Seems he was needed. I needed two like him."

"You were doing fine with just one of him. But *why?*"

"Oh, that damn Brego. What did you think? He whined all day about how us hired captains ought to help each other out, and he said this big fellow, quick and mean as a sneak, had filched his piece —excuse me, Miz Broll, his lady friend. So finally I said to Artie here, let's take the dinghy and run over there to the inn and bounce this tourist around some. Had no idea it was you, Tr—Gav. None at all. Sorry. But not too sorry. First time I haven't been half asleep in two weeks."

I dabbed at a long scratch on my jaw and moved over to Lisa and put my arm around her waist. "Honey, have you got any message you want these fine men to deliver to Mr. Brego?"

"Rupe? Artie? Would you tell him that Mrs. Broll suggests he stop by again and try his luck with Mr. Lee?"

Rupe laughed. "Sure."

"Would you mind taking some of his things back to him?"

"Not at all."

"Let me go gather them up. It won't take a second."

Rupe sent the young man down to keep an eye on the dinghy. Rupe and I sat in a shadowy corner of the garden.

"What happened to the *Marianne?*" I asked him.

"Two bad seasons and the bank finally grabbed her. I don't really mind a hell of a lot. I work for good people. Good wages."

"Thanks for the nice job of covering."

"That? Hell, that's what a good hired captain starts with or learns real fast. When somebody clues you, don't stand around saying 'Huh?' Run with the ball. No point in asking you what's going on. I certainly know something is going on, and that broad in there must be part of it. She looks good enough, but there's better on the island. Any time you have to scruff up a clown like Brego to grab yourself that kind of ass—"

"Like you said. There's more than meets the eye."

"By God, Trav, you know something? That was fun off and on."

"Glad you enjoyed it. How's Sally?"

"Fine, last I heard. She went back to her folks. She married a widower fellow with four kids. Our three plus his four makes a lot of family."

"Sorry to hear about that, Rupe. I really am."

"It hurt some. But I hate the land and everything on it. I hate a tree, and I hate a mountain. The only death worth dying is by drowning. With the licenses I've got I'll stay on the water all the rest of my time. When our oldest girl drowned, that did it for Sally. That finished her, up, down, and sideways. No more oceans. Next time I write the kids I'll put in a note to her saying I saw you. She always liked you, Trav."

Lisa came out with a brown paper bag and gave it to Rupe. "This won't be too much trouble?"

"Not one bit, Miz Mary."

"Thank you so much. Excuse me, but is that mate of yours a mute?"

"Artie just doesn't have very much to say."

We both walked Rupert down to the dingy. He stowed the bag aboard, and they picked the little boat up and walked it out past the gentle surf, scrambled in, and started the little outboard and headed back toward the yacht basin.

"*Imagine* that Carl sending them to beat you up!"

"They gave it a good try."

"Did they hurt you, darling?"

"Hardly at all. A month in bed and I'll feel like new."

"I mean really."

"Honey, the adrenalin is still flowing. So the pain is suppressed. Tomorrow morning when I try to get out of bed I'll know how much damage they did."

"Rupe has really enormous hands, doesn't he?"

"And very hard, too."

"And that gigantic boy is *really* handsome. Did you notice?"

"I wasn't thinkng in those terms. Want to eat in the dining room?"

"Let's order it sent to my place. It's so much nicer, really. We can fix our own drinks and be comfortable. I won't make any passes, Gavin. None at all."

She kept her word. Long after we had dined, when the nightcap was down to the dregs, she came over to me and bent and peered at my face, teeth set into the softness of her underlip.

"You are going to have one great big mouse right on that cheek-bone, friend."

"I can feel it."

She straightened up. "I can't read you, McGee."

"McGee? Who he?"

"Like the limerick. Tell me the limerick, huh?"

"Tell the truth, I can't remember it."

"Was it real dirty?"

"Not very, as I remember. But insulting."

"Funny, you knowing him. I would have thought he would have told Carl you were an old friend. Carl would have told him your name, Gavin Lee, and described you and all."

"Lee is a common name."

"Gavin Lee sure the hell isn't. And how many people are your size anyway?"

"Lisa honey, what are you trying to develop here?"

"I don't know. Is there anything you ought to tell me that you haven't?"

"Can't think of a thing."

"What are we going to do after we get rich, dear?"

"Live rich."

"Like this place?"

"And Las Brisas at Acapulco. And Cala de Volpe on Sardinia. The Reina Cristina in Algeciras."

"In where?"

"Spain, near Gibraltar."

She sat on the couch a couple of feet from me, eyes hooded, mouth pursed. "Will we travel well together when we're rich?"

"Get along?"

"Do you think we will?"

"We'll have to try it."

"Are you terribly dog-in-the-manger about things?"

"Like what?"

"If we had something going for us and I happened to see somebody like Artie Calivan. As long as I didn't overdo."

"Get the guests?"

She shrugged. "When they come in pairs, dear. And both exciting."

"I don't like to set policy. Take each situation on its merits. Okay?" I put my glass down and stood up. Winced. Flexed my leg. It was going to stiffen up very nicely during the night. She walked me out to the garden gate. I kissed her on the forehead and told her to dream about being rich. She said she had dreamed about that ever since she could remember.

sixteen

I came bounding awake in the middle of the night from a dream so horrible I couldn't remember any part of it. I was drenched with icy sweat and trembling badly.

The dream made me recall lying to Lisa about sending a letter. A letter would be a comfort. I couldn't wait until morning. Leonard Sibelius, Esq., attorney-at-law.

The sealed letter inside was about the same, but the cover letter for the sealed letter varied. I asked him to read the sealed letter if he did not hear from me by the last day of May and then give it to some colleague wise in the ways of the SEC and the NASD.

After the lights were out again and the letter tucked away, I thought of how ironic it would be if Harry Broll ended up being defended by Lennie Sibelius on a charge of murder first. Lennie would get him off. He would extract every dime Harry had ever made and put a lock on every dime Harry might make in the future, but he would get him off.

I felt myself drifting off and wondered what the hell there had been in the nightmare that had so thoroughly chilled my blood.

I was up early again on Friday and made another exciting run into town. I stopped at the main post office and sent the letter to Lennie by air, special delivery, registered mail. I drove through the one-way tunnel that leads from the Carenage area under Hospital Hill to the

Esplanade and the main part of downtown. The *Queen Elizabeth II* was in, and it was her last visit of the season. She had spewed about two thousand passengers into the town and onto the beaches. The ones in town were milling around, arguing with each other about the currency and looking for the nonexistent duty-free shops and being constantly importuned to hire a nice taxi and see the sights. The big single-stack ship was anchored out, with fast launches running back and forth like big white water beetles.

I ambled around and admired one out of every forty-three tourist ladies as being worth looking at and did some minor shopping of my own, then tested my skill and reflexes by driving back to the Spice Island Inn.

It was on that twenty-third day of April that I risked two lives instead of merely my own and drove Lisa out toward the Lance aux Epines area and had lunch at the Red Crab—burly sandwiches on long rolls, icy Tuborg beer, green salad—eaten outdoors at a white metal table by a green lawn in the shade of a graceful and gracious tree. After lunch we went exploring. We stopped and looked at the sailboats moored in Prickly Bay. I drove past large, lovely houses, and we got out of the Moke at Prickly Point and walked down the rocky slope and looked over the edge at the blue sea lifting and smashing at the rocks, working away on caves and stone sculpture, biting stubbornly and forever at the land. A curiously ugly species of black crab, big as teacups, foraged the dry sheer stone just above the reach of wave and tide, scrabbling in swift hundreds when we moved too near.

I studied my map and found, on the way back, a turn that led to a stretch of divided highway, probably the only bit of it on the little island. Weeds grew up through cracks. It was the grand entrance to the site of what had been the Grenada Expo of several years ago. I had heard that few visitors came. Many of the Expo buildings were never completed. The ones that had been finished lay under the midafternoon hum of sun's heat, warping plywood shedding thin scabs of bright holiday paint. Some faded, unraveling remnants of festive banners moved in a small sea breeze. We saw a VIP lounge where the doorsill brush grew as high as the unused and corroded doorknobs. Steel rods sprouted from cement foundation slabs where buildings had never stood. We found a huge and elegant motel, totally empty, completely closed, yet with the lawns and gardens still maintained by the owners or the government.

I drove down crooked little dirt roads, creaking and swaying at two miles an hour over log-sized bumps and down into old rain gullies you could hide bodies in. She clung and laughed, and we made it down an angled slope to a pretty and private little stretch of beach where the almond trees and the coconuts and the sea grapes grew closer than usual to the high-tide mark because of the offshore protection of some small islands.

I parked in the shade. We walked on the beach and found one of the heavy local skiffs pulled well up between the trees, with red and blue and green paint peeling off the old weathered wood. She hiked a haunch onto the gunwale, near the hand-whittled tholepin, braced herself there with one knee locked, the other leg a-swing. The breeze moved the leaves overhead, changing the patterns of sun and shade on her face and hair, on her yellow-and-white-checkered sun top, her skimpy little yellow skirt. The big lenses of her sunglasses reflected the seascape behind me. She sucked at her cigarette, looked solemn, then tilted her head and smiled at me.

"I'm trying to figure out why it should be so much fun, just sort of churning around in the heat of the day," she said.

"Glad you're enjoying it."

"I guess it's because it's like a date. Like being a kid again in Trois Pistoles and going out on a date. It's a feeling I haven't had in a long long time. It's sort of sweet, somehow. Do you know what I mean, Gav?"

"Not exactly."

"Ever since I left when I was fifteen, I've been with guys I've either just been in bed with or am just about to get into bed with or both. And if it was a guy I'd already had or one I was going to have, if we were alone in a funny, private place like this, we'd be knocking off a stand-up piece right here. I was thinking I don't want you to try anything, because it would take away that feeling of being on a date. There's something funny and scary about it, like being a virgin again. Or maybe it's you that's scary to me, about that girl sinking in the ocean. I dreamed about her. Jesus! You really did that? Really?"

"It seemed like a good idea at the time."

She slid off the gunwale and snapped her cigarette into the surf line. She bent and picked up a coconut in the husk and threw it with a shot-put motion. She was wiry, and she got surprising distance with it.

"So this is just a little bit of time when nothing happens and we just wait, Gavin."

"For your cousin. After you make the phone call and send the cable."

I leaned on the boat. Some palm fronds had been tossed into it. I lifted them and saw the battered metal fuel tank for the missing outboard motor, and I saw a spade with a short handle, sawed off where it had broken, and decided it was a clumsy improvised paddle. Clumsy but better than none at all. With all that weight and freeboard she would be a bitch to try to paddle against wind or tide.

"Head back?" I asked.

"Can we keep on being tourists, dear? Let's look at that map again."

We went back to the Moke, studied the map, and decided to try the road out to Point Saline and look at the lighthouse. It was a road so wretched that by the time we were halfway I had decided only a jeeplike vehicle such as a Moke could make it. Then around the next hairpin corner I was shouldered into the shrubbery by three taxis coming back from the lighthouse, whamming and leaping over the ruts and broken paving, chock-full of tourists off the QE2

My gratis map had little paragraphs on the back of it about local wonders, so just short of the lighthouse hill we stopped and dutifully got out to walk for a moment on the white sand beach of the Caribbean, then crossed the road and went down a path for about fifty yards to walk on the black sand beach of the Atlantic. Then I roared the Moke up the twenty-degree slope to the lighthouse.

The attendant was there, obviously eager to be a guide, obviously eager for bread. We climbed the several flights to the glass-enclosed top. The treads were very narrow, the steps very steep. Lisa was directly ahead of me, and I was staring at the backs of her knees as we climbed.

It was a view so breathtakingly, impossibly fabulous that it became meaningless. It was like being inserted into a living postcard. It does no good to stand and gawk at something like that. The mind goes blank as soon as you see it. Tourists take pictures and take them home and find out they have postcards. If they put Helen in front of the view, they have a postcard with Helen in it. The only way a person could accommodate himself to a place like that would be to live there until he ceased to see it and then slowly and at his own pace rediscover it for himself. When I found out what the attendant had to do to keep that fifty-mile light operating, I was happy to place some Biwi in his hand.

Lisa was quiet on the way back. When we were nearly back to the deserted Expo site, I glanced over at her and saw the tear running down her quiet cheek, coming out from under the sunglasses. I pulled over in a shady spot and said, "Hey!"

"Oh, God, I don't know, I don't know. Leave me alone."

"Sure."

Glasses off. Dab eyes, snuffle, sigh, blow nose. Fix mouth. Put glasses back on. Light cigarette. Sigh again, huffing smoke plume at windshield.

"Everything is supposed to be so great," she said. "Everything is some kind of a trick. Every time. Some kind of flaky trick, no matter what it is. Fifty-mile lighthouse! Good God! What the hell is a Fresnel lens?"

"A Frenchman invented it long ago. It focuses light into a beam."

"Nothing is ever what you expect. That's what got to me, Gav. A fifty-mile lighthouse and all there is up there is a mantle like off a Coleman lantern and not a hell of a lot bigger, and that poor scrawny black son of a bitch that has to get up every two hours all night long and run up there and pull on some goddamn weights like a big grandfather clock so his fucking light keeps turning around for another two hours. Fresnel! They fake everything in the world."

"What kind of a big deal did They promise you, Lisa?"

She pulled the glasses off and looked at me with reptilian venom and coldness. "They told me, friend, to sing in the choir, love Jesus, do unto others, pray to God, live a Christian life, and then live in heaven in eternal bliss forevermore. They forgot to explain that the choirmaster would give me free private voice lessons when I was fourteen and by the third lesson he'd have his finger up me. They didn't tell me that if I didn't report him, I'd lost out on all that eternal bliss. They didn't tell me that I wouldn't want to report him, because then he wouldn't have a chance to do it again. They didn't explain about it being the temptation of the flesh and how finally you get to the place where you either make a true confession or you run away. They were running their big lighthouse and making it look wonderful, shining its light all over the world to save souls. But it was just a gas mantle and weights and chains and a weird lens. The real thing they teach you without even knowing it is: do unto others before they do it unto you."

"My, my, my," I said in a gentle wonder, and the tears came again. She got them under control at last.

"Will you laugh at me if I tell you what I *really* want to do with the money, Gav?"

"I don't think I will."

"I want to join an order. I want to give the money to the order. I want to take a vow of silence. I want to kneel on stone floors and pray until my knees bleed and I faint. I don't ever want to be screwed again the rest of my life or be even touched by any man. I want to be a bride of Christ. Now laugh yourself sick."

"I don't hear anybody laughing."

"You think I'd go over the wall in a week, don't you?"

"Do you?"

"If I can find the guts to start, I'll never leave. Never. You're doing all this to me by making me feel the way I did a long long time ago. A lot of men ago. A lot of beds ago."

"I don't think people stick with projects they start because they think they should start them. That's image making. People stick to their truest, deepest gratifications, whether it's running banks, building temples out of beer cans, stuffing dead birds, or telling dirty jokes. Somewhere early you get marked."

"I got it early. Stations of the Cross. Easter. Christ is risen. At about twelve I felt so marvelously pure. Jesus loved me, that I know."

"So you fight it all your life or go back to it. Either way, it is a deep involvement."

She found her glasses on the floor, picked them up, and said wearily, "You know so goddamn much, don't you? You know something? You've got a big mouth. A great big mouth. Let's get back on the beach where I belong."

seventeen

That random afternoon had turned Lisa Dissat off in a way she either couldn't explain or didn't care to explain. It amounted to the same thing. We became like neighbors in a new suburb, nodding and smiling when we met walking to or from the main hotel building or up and down the two-mile beach or back and forth from sun cot to cottage.

I saw some of the cruise-ship men, crew and passengers, take their try at her now and then when she walked the long wide beach alone. I saw male guests at our hotel and the other beach hotels make their approach, each one no doubt selecting the overworked line he thought might be most productive. They would fall in step with her, last about a half dozen steps before turning away. I followed her a couple of times and kept count. Prettier young women in bikinis just as revealing walked the beach unaccosted. It was difficult to identify those characteristics which made her such a frequent target. It was something about the tilt and position of her head in relation to the shape in which she held her mouth while walking. It was challenge, somehow. A contempt and an arrogance. Try me, you bastard. Try your luck and see how good you are. Do you think you're man enough to cope, you bastard? There were both invitation and rejection in the roll of her hip. To describe everything that happened to tilt, curve, and musculature in one complete stride from start to finish and into the next stride would have taken a seventeen-syllable word. Provocative, daring, and ineradicably cheap. That was what Rupe had seen so quickly, wondering why I risked even a bruised knuckle to take ass like that away from Carl Brego. It was what I had seen when she sat with Brego for a drink and lunch.

It was a compulsive cheapness. I could not believe that it was deliberate in the sense of being something she had thought out. It had to be something she could not help doing, yet did not do out of some physical warp or out of any flaw in intelligence or awareness.

She had been uncommonly determined to give herself to me. It had been too early an effort. She wanted to be used, not loved. She wanted to be quickly tumbled and plundered. It was what she expected and what she wanted, and it was that need which exuded the musky, murky challenge.

I have a need to try to put people together out of the pieces they show me. The McGee Construct-A-Lady-Kit. For those on a budget we suggest our cheaper, simpler Build-A-Broad Kit.

Once you Build-A-Broad, it pleases you more than it did before you took it apart and examined the components.

She had ripened young. They had drilled virtue into her so mercilessly that, when she was seduced, she believed herself corrupt and evil. Purity could not be regained. So she ran away and had spent a dozen years corrupting because she believed herself corrupt, debauching because she had been debauched, defiling because she was the virgin defiled.

When you cannot like yourself or any part of yourself in mind or body, then you cannot love anyone else at all. If you spend the rest of your life on bleeding knees, maybe Jesus will have the compassion to love you a little bit. She had been destroyed twelve years ago. It was taking her a little while to stop breathing.

I kept in close touch with her. She heard nothing. I killed time restlessly. So on Saturday I got a clear connection and talked to Meyer. I told him to check out Paul Dissat in the SeaGate offices in West Palm. I had to spell the name in my own special kind of alphabet before he was sure of it. Detroit Indiana sugar sugar Alabama teacup.

"Dissat? Paul Dissat?"

"Yes. And be damned careful of him. Please. He bites."

"Is Mary there? Is she all right?"

"She's fine."

After all, what else could I say? Time to talk later.

———

Later on Saturday I drove until I finally found the way to Yacht Services. I parked the Moke and went out onto the long dock and found the *Dulcinea*. She was a custom motor sailer, broad of beam with sturdy, graceless lines. Rupe Darby and Artie kept her sparkling, and she looked competent.

Artie had gone over to the Carenage in the dinghy to do some shopping. Rupe asked me aboard and showed me the below-decks spaces, the brute diesels, all the electronics. He was fretting about the delivery of some highly necessary engine item. It was supposed to come in by air. They couldn't leave without it, and he didn't want to be late meeting his owners at Dominica. He hoped to be out by Wednesday.

I asked about Carl Brego, and he told me that Brego's rich lady had arrived with friends, and they had left early that morning for two weeks sailing the Grenadines.

A sunbrowned and brawny woman in blue denim shorts and a dirty white T-shirt came along the dock and waved and smiled. She had a collie ruff of coppery gold hair, a handsome weathered face. Rupe invited her to come aboard and have some coffee with us. She did, and we sat in the shade of the tarp rigged forward. She was Captain Mickey Laneer, owner and operator of the *Hell's Belle*, a big businesslike charter schooner I could see from where we sat. Mickey had a man's handshake and a State of Maine accent.

"Trav, Mickey here has the best damned charter business in the islands, bar none."

"Sure do," she said, and they both chuckled and chuckled.

"Could be out on charter all the time," Rupe said.

"But that would take all the fun out of it, too much of the same thing," Mickey said.

"She charges high, and she picks and chooses and doesn't have to advertise. Word of mouth," Rupe said, and they kept chuckling.

"Five hundred bucks a day, U.S., and I don't take the *Belle* out for less than five days, and I won't carry less than three or more than five passengers. Price stays the same."

"That's pretty high," I said.

"I keep telling her she ought to raise the rate again."

"Would you two mind telling me why you keep laughing?"

Mickey shoved her hair back, grinning. "Rupe and I just enjoy life, Mr. McGee."

"She does a good trade with business meetings. Three or four or five busy, successful executives, usually fellows in their thirties or early forties, they come down to relax, get some fishing in, get a tan, do a little dickering and planning. You know."

"Why is everybody laughing but me?" I asked.

"She takes male passengers only, Trav."

I finally caught up. "I get it. Your crew is all female, Captain?"

"And," said Rupe, "all nimble and quick and beautiful and strong as little bulls. They range from golden blond—a gal who has a master's in languages from the University of Dublin—to the color of coffee with hardly a dab of cream. Eight of them."

"Seven, Rupe. Darn it. I had to dump Barbie. She was hustling a guest for extra the last time out. I've warned them and warned them. After I provision the *Belle*—the best booze and best food in the Windwards—I cut it down the middle, half for me and the boat, half for the gals. So on a five-day run, they make better than three hundred, Biwi. Everyone from golden Louise all the way to Hester, whose father is a bank official in Jamaica."

"You need eight crew to work that thing, Mick?"

"I know. I know. We're going out Monday for ten days. Four fellows from a television network. Nice guys. It'll be their third cruise. Old friends. That means my gals will be topless before we clear Grand Mal Bay."

"And bottomless before you get opposite Dragon Bay and Happy Hill."

"Could be, dear. Louise flew up to Barbados today. She says she has a cute chum who loves sailing. It's a way for a certain kind of girl to combine her favorite hobbies and make a nice living. I don't take hard-case types. I like polite, happy girls from nice backgrounds. Then we have a happy ship."

She got up and said, "A pleasure to meet any of Rupe's old friends, Travis. Hope you'll sail with us sometime. Rupe has."

"Mickey invited four of us captains to a free five-day cruise last year."

"I had a cancellation," Mickey said, "and we were all wondering what to give the other captains for a Christmas present. Well, nice to meet you."

After she was on the dock, she turned and waved and said, "Tell him our motto, Rupe."

He chuckled. She walked lithely away. He said, "Mickey likes you. In her line of work she gets to tell the men from the boys in a hurry."

"What's the motto?"

"Oh. It's on her letterhead. 'Make a lot of lovely new chums every voyage.'"

"Enjoy the cruise?"

"Oh, hell yes. By God, it is different. There's rules, and Mickey enforces them. None of her gals get slopped. Any and all balling is done in the privacy of your own bunk in your own stateroom, curtains drawn. No pairing off with any special gal, even for a whole day. If a gal is wearing pants, long or short, it means hands off. Otherwise, grab whatever is passing by whenever you feel like it. The gals don't make the approach. The things you remember are like standing aft with a big rum punch in a fresh wind with Mickey at the wheel really *sailing* that thing, putting on all the sail it'll take, and those eight great bare-ass gals scampering around, hauling on those lines, trimming sail. And like being anchored in a cove in the moonlight, the evening meal done, and those gals singing harmony so sweet it would break your heart right in two. Great food and great drinks and good fishing. Everybody laughs a lot aboard the *Belle*. Between all they got to do, those gals put in a day full of work for a day's pay. I can't understand that damned stupid Barbie. Why'd she want to try some private hustling? Her old man must own half the state of South Carolina. Barbie's been a sailboat bum all her life. And she gets this chance to make a good living doing the two things in this world she does best and enjoys most, sailing and screwing, and she blows the whole deal. It's hard to understand. Anyway, we were out five days, and it was like being gone a month, I swear. It's . . . it's something different. If you ever see the *Belle* coming in here or leaving, you wouldn't figure it out. Those gals look like some kind of Olympic people training for a race. Nimble and slender and tough and . . . fresh faced. Scrubbed. You know?"

On Sunday Lisa agreed without much argument to arrange her call so that I could hear both ends of the conversation. She placed it from the cottage. We had to wait a long time before the desk called back and said they had her party on the line. I sat close beside her, and she turned the phone slightly so we could both hear, my right ear and her left.

It was Harry's nervous, lying voice. "Mary, honey? Is that you, Mary darling?"

"Yes, dear. Can you hear me?"

"Talk loud. You sound a million miles away, honey. Where are you? I've about gone out of my head with worry."

I hoped he sounded more convincing to his secretary than he did to me. Lisa followed her prepared script, telling Harry to let Holly Dressner know she was all right and that she had phoned. She said she was afraid he'd find the travel agency she'd used. The Seven Seas. Down in Hallandale. Mrs. DeAngela had been very nice and helpful.

"Are you going to come home? To stay?"

"I think so, Harry. I think that's best, really."

"So do I. When, honey? When will you be home?"

"I've got reservations out of here May third. But don't try to meet me. I don't know when I'll get in. And I'll have my car. By the way, you don't have to worry about the money. Not any more. I'm going to cable Mr. Willow tomorrow to activate the loan and put the money in your account, dear."

"I've been getting pretty nervous."

"I can imagine. I guess I wanted you to sweat a little."

And on and on, and finally it was over, and she hung up. She gave me a strange look and then wiped beads of sweat from her upper lip and throat.

"It spooked me."

"I know."

"If I'd been Mary, I certainly wouldn't arrange a loan for that son of a bitch. I don't see much point in that phone call, really. There's enough without that."

"His secretary will make a good witness. Mary Broll is alive and well and in Grenada. She'll be home May third. She can say she was there when Mrs. Broll called her husband. Probably Harry will have his secretary get Mrs. Dressner on the phone and make sure his secretary hears him give her Mary's message."

"I don't have to send her any more cards. If I was supposed to, Paul would have told me. He thinks everything out."

"It's a good way to be, if you like to kill people."

"It's weird. You know? I've thought and thought about what you said, Gav. The smart thing for him to do would be kill me. Get word for me to meet him on the way back. Some other island. Arrange something. But I just can't believe he would. We're from the same town. We're family. I keep having this dream about him. He's standing watching me sleep, and I sneak my eyes open and find out he isn't really looking at me. He's looking the other way, and he has a mask just like his face that he wears on the back of his head. He's pretending to watch me, but he's looking at something else I can't see. When the dream wakes me up, I'm cold all over."

"We won't have long to wait, Lisa. After you send the cable to Willow tomorrow, you're no use to him."

"Stay close to me, huh?"

I reassured her. I wouldn't let the bad man get her. She'd be safe. Sure.

eighteen

I was up very early on Monday morning when the sun was still behind the green mountains. I swam. The tide was low and getting lower, still running out. I went back to take my shower before dressing for breakfast.

By then, of course, he had talked with Lisa long enough to discover I was one of his priorities. He had immobilized her and come after me. Usually I am pretty good at surprises. Some sense I cannot describe gives me a few micro-seconds of lead time, and when I get that kind of warning, the reaction time seems to be at its best. Perhaps it is hearing or the sense of smell at subliminal levels.

I don't know where he hid. There were good places in the garden. He could have crouched behind the bar in the service area or behind some of the bigger pieces of furniture in the living room. He worked it out well. He saw me go swimming, and he nipped over the wall unobserved. I'd locked the gate but not the sliding door. He could assume I would come inside to take my shower, and I would have no reason to close the bathroom door. Standard procedure is to reach in and turn the handles until you get the roaring water to the right temperature, and then you step in. It is a moment of helplessness, and there is a useful curtain of sound.

I remember that when I got the water temperature the way I wanted it, I straightened to strip the swim trunks off. The whole back of my head blew up, and I went spinning and fluttering down through torrents of white, blinding light.

I know what he probably used. I made things easy for him. I had picked up the piece of driftwood in the surf a few days before. It was iron hard, less than a yard long, a stick an inch and a half in diameter with a sea-polished clump of root structure at the end of it the size of a large clenched fist.

Because he did not give a particular damn whether he killed me or not, he waited for the water roar, then came prowling into the bathroom with the club cocked, poising like a laborer to sledge a stake into hard ground.

The brain is a tender gray jelly wrapped in membrane, threaded and fed with miles of blood tubes down to the diameter of thread. The gray jelly is a few billion cells which build up and discharge very small amounts of electric impulses. The whole wet, complex ball is encased in this bone, covered with rubbery layer of scalp and a hair thatch which performs some small shock-absorbing service. Like the rest of the body, the brain is designed to include its own spare-parts system. Brain cells are always dying at a rate dependent on how you live but are never replaced. There are supposed to be enough to last you. If a stroke should kill all the cells in the right hemisphere involved with communication—hearing and speaking, reading and writing—there is a fair chance of dormant cells in the left hemisphere being awakened and trained and plugged into the other parts of the system. Researchers can run a very thin electrode into an animal brain and hit a pleasure center and offer a chimp two levers—push one, and he gets a little electrical charge that makes him feel intense pleasure; push the other, and he gets a banana. The chimp will happily starve to death, pushing the pleasure lever. They can make a rabbit dangerously savage, a cat afraid of mice. They can put electrodes against your skull and trace pictures of your brain waves. If you have nice big steep alpha waves, you learn quickly and well. People who smoke a lot have stunted alpha waves. People who live in an area with a high index of air pollution—New York, Los Angeles, Birmingham—have rotten little alpha waves that are so tiny they are hard to find. No one knows yet why this is so. It may be a big fat waste of everybody's money, time, and energy sending kids to school in Los Angeles, Chicago, and lately Phoenix.

Anyway, if you take a club to all this miraculous gray tapioca with a good full swing and bash the back of the skull a little to the right of center where a right-hander is likely to hit it, it is not going to function at all for a while, and then it is going to function in some partial manner for a varying period of time, which could be for as long as it lives. If you have any blood leaking in there and building pressure between the bone and the jelly, then it is not going to live very long at all.

Even if there is a perfect, unlikely, one hundred percent recovery, it is going to take a long time to gather up the scattered pieces of memory of the time just prior to the blow and the time just subsequent to the recovery of partial consciousness. The memories will never be complete and perfect. Drop one of those big Seeburg jukes off the back of a pickup truck and you are not going to get any music at all, and even if it can be fixed, the stereo might not ever work too well.

Forget the crap about the television-series hard guy who gets slugged and shoved out of a fast-moving car, wakes up in the ambulance, and immediately deduces that the kidnapper was a left-handed albino because Little Milly left her pill bottle on the second piling from the end of the pier. If hard case happens to wake up in the ambulance, he is going to be busy trying to remember his own name and wondering why he has double vision and what that loud noise is and why he keeps throwing up.

Assembling the bits of memory into some kind of proper order is a good trick, too.

Here's one fragment. On my left side, curled up in a cramped, tilting, bouncing place where things dug into me. Very hot. Some fabric pasted to me with sweat. Head in a small place full of blue light. Something abrasive under my left cheek. Arms immovable, hands dead. Motor grinding. A woman making a keening sound somewhere near, a thin long gassy cry, over and over, not in fear, in pain, in sorrow—but as if she were practicing, trying to imitate something, like a broken valve in a steam plant. Blackout.

Another: being jounced and joggled, hanging head down, bent over something hard digging into my belly. Thighs clasped. By an arm? One brute son of a bitch to carry me that way in a walk, but this one was jogging! Begin shallow coughing that announces imminent vomit. Immediately dropped heavily into sand. Gag, choke, and drift back into the gray void.

There were others, more vague. Some were real and some were dreams. The brain was trying to sort out the world, and it took bits of input and built dreams. On patrol, clenching myself motionless against stony ground while the flare floated down, swinging a little, moving over to burn out against the shoulder of the hill that closed off the end of the valley they were using. A brilliantly vivid fragment of old nightmare of Junior Allen surfacing behind the cruiser, tough jowls wedged into the gap of the Danforth anchor.

Then along came a more detailed one that continued so long the brain was able to go to work on it, sorting out evidences of reality, comparing them to evidences of fantasy. I awoke slowly. I was sitting on sand, leaning back against something that felt like the trunk of a tree. My arms were fastened around behind me, painfully cramped. I tried to move them and could not. I tried to move my hands, wiggle my fingers, and I could feel nothing.

I stared down at familiar swim trunks and down the brown length of my very own legs with the curled hair sun-bleached to pure white against the brown hide. A quarter-inch-in-diameter nylon cord had been tied to both ankles. It had been pulled so tight it bit into the skin. My feet were puffed. There was a two-foot length of cord from ankle to ankle. My legs spraddled. A sea-grape tree grew up out of the sand in the middle of the triangle formed by my spread legs and the ankle-to-ankle cord.

It took time to work it out. It was unlikely I had been there so long the tree had happened to grow there. Do trees grow slowly? Yes. Very slowly. Okay, could I have been fitted over the tree somehow? Long, careful thought. No. Too big. The ankles had been tied after they had been placed on either side of the tree. By me? No, the cord was too tight. My feet were swollen and blood dark. By somebody else then. Untie the cord? Not with arms I couldn't move and hands I couldn't feel. Remove tree? No way. I was supposed to stay there. No choice about it. I turned my head to the left, slowly, slowly. I was in shade. Out there the sand blazed under a high sun. Blue waves, small ones, moved in toward the sand and lifted, crested white, slapped, and ran up the sandslant and back into the next wave. I turned my head the other way as slowly and looked to my right.

A man was sitting there. He was sitting on a small, inflatable blue raft I had seen afloat in Lisa's pool. He had a weathered brown basket made of strips of woven palm frond, and he was pressing it back into shape and working new green strips of frond into it. He sat cross-legged, intent on his task. He had a trim cap of dark curls. He had dark eyes and long lashes. He had a plump red mouth. He wore white boxer shorts. He wore a gold cross on a chain around his neck.

He wore a wristwatch with a stainless steel band and a complicated dial. That was all.

As he tugged and pulled at the stubborn fronds, a lot of useful-looking muscles bulged and writhed and slid around under the smooth skin of arms and shoulders. He rose effortlessly to a standing position and turned the basket this way and that. It was crude. Conical. Half-bushel size. His legs were slender, but the long muscles looked springy and powerful.

A name tugged at the edge of my mind until finally I could fit my sour mouth around it. An articulated croak. "Paul."

He looked at me. There is a way you look at people, and there is a way you look at objects. There is a difference in the way you look at objects. You do not look at your morning coffee cup, at a run-over toad in your driveway, or at a flat tire the same way you look at people. This was the way a man might look at a flat tire that he was going to have to attend to in a little while. Not like the owner of the car but like a service station attendant. Damage appraisal, estimate of time required.

I managed another word. "Untie." I was becoming a chatterbox. He looked back down at his basket repair job. I couldn't understand why he wouldn't talk to me. Then gray mists came rolling in from some swamp in the back of my head, and the world faded away. . . .

I was being shaken awake. I was going to be late for school. I was picked up and placed on my feet. I squinted into a dazzling world and saw Paul looking at me. I was leaning back against a palm bole, weak and dizzy. I looked down and saw the familiar length of cord from ankle to ankle. Where could my sea-grape tree have gone? I could not imagine.

Paul pulled me away from the tree and turned me to face the sea. He walked me carefully, holding on to my upper arm with both hands, helping me with my balance. I had to take short steps. There was very little feeling in my feet. He guided me at an angle down the beach, the trees at my left, the sea at my right. We were out in the hot glare, away from the shade of the trees. He stopped me and said, "Sit." He helped me ease down onto the sea-damp brown sand, facing the basket I had seen him repairing. It was upside down on the sand, like a crude clown's hat. A wave slid up the sand and took a light lick at the edge of the basket and at my right foot.

With the slow grace that accompanies ceremony, Paul reached and plucked the basket away. It was a magic trick. Lisa's head was balanced upright on the sand, facing the sea. Magicians can fool you with things like that. He stood easily in front of her and extended his right foot and put his bare sandy toes against her left temple and slowly and gently turned the head so that it faced me. As he did so, he spoke a rapid, guttural, unmusical French.

Lisa rolled mad and empty eyes toward me, eyes that looked through me at something on the other edge of the world beyond me and creaked her jaw wide and made a thin, gassy, aspirated scream, gagged for air, and screamed again.

He squatted, turned her head back, slid his palm under the chin to uptilt her face, spoke down at her, the French rapid but gentler, almost tender, chiding her.

A wave slid up and under him, and the edge of foam slapped the lower half of her face. She gagged and coughed. He stroked her dark, soaked hair back from her forehead with a tender and affectionate gesture, patted her cheek, said something else to her which ended with one word I understood. *Adieu.*

He moved toward me, and as he did so, I saw a bigger wave coming. She seemed to see it, too. She squeezed her eyes shut and clamped her mouth shut. It slapped against my hip. It washed completely over her head and reached six feet behind her and paused, then came sluicing back, leaving two small divergent ridges in the sand from the nape of her neck toward the sea, shaped like the wake of a boat. The sea had combed her hair forward, left it pasted down over her face.

He lifted me easily onto my feet, turned me to face up the slope of sand, urging me on. By dint of great mental effort I put three words together. "She can't see." Meaning, if she can't see, she can't see the wave coming the next time.

"Never mind," he said. His English was good, but there was a trace of the French-Canadian accent which Lisa had eliminated entirely. As we walked up the beach, I saw the old boat and remembered the day with Lisa. So she had guided Paul to this secluded spot. I saw the spade with the short handle stuck into the dry sand near the trees. Easy to dig a hole big enough for Lisa. With her knees against her chest, her ankles tied to her wrists, it wouldn't take much of a hole at all. I saw the Moke beyond the trees, on that rough little sand road, parked almost where I had parked it on that day of the lighthouse.

He helped me through the thick dry sand and eased me down in the shade with my back against a rough trunk. "Dig her out?" I said. I was getting pretty good with three-word sentences.

He sat on his heels, began picking up handfuls of dry sand and letting it trickle out of the bottom of his fist. "It's too late. Not that it would make any difference. I shouldn't have used the basket. She hated the basket. She begged me not to use the basket. But I had to be sure she told every last thing. But something broke in her head. After she lost all her English. Something gave way. I thought seeing you might put her back together. I guess it was the basket. I'll be more careful with you."

I looked out at Lisa. I saw the biggest wave yet of the incoming tide. It did not curl and smash down at the packed sand until it reached her; then it bounced high off that dark roundness sparkling in the sun, the way a wave will bounce off a small boulder along the shore.

It was hard to believe it was Lisa. From the back only the dark hair showed. Her head looked like some large nut covered with a dark growth that had fallen from a tropical tree and rolled down, coming to rest in the incoming tide.

"If she holds her breath at the right time, she could last a long time, perhaps," he said. "But she is dead. Just as you are dead."

"And . . . Mary?"

There was a slight Gallic shrug. "That was bad luck. I went to her to try to convince her to leave Harry for good. Why should a woman like that have been loyal to a man like that? I wanted her to run because without her Harry would have to find three hundred thousand somewhere else. I have that much. I was going to squeeze Harry for half his stock. Waterbury should have let me buy in. Then nothing would have ever happened."

"Bad luck?"

"She tried to run. The house was dark. I caught her, and we fell badly. Very badly. It was an ugly situation. She knew who I was. I couldn't call an ambulance, could I? She knew how bad it was. I had to find out a lot from her while she could still talk. She was stubborn. I had to . . . amplify the pain to make her speak." He frowned. "I thought it would sicken me to do that. But it was a strange pleasure in a little while. As if we were lovers. So that is bad luck too, I suppose, to learn that about oneself. Gratification is expensive and very dangerous, eh?"

He stood up, clapped his hands to remove the loose sand. "And it was the same pleasure with Lisa, and we will discover if it is the same with a man, too. I should not care to dig a hole big enough for you, Mr. McGee."

"McGee?"

"I am very good about details. Harry described you well enough. Mary is dead. Lisa is dead. McGee is dead. But we must find out who you sent the letter to and what it said. We shall improvise, eh? There is a tire pump and a jack in the tool compartment of that ugly little vehicle. Something will come to mind. There will be enough time to proceed slowly and carefully."

He walked up toward the car, a hundred feet away. The equation was very simple. No unknowns. I could spend the afternoon on this hideaway beach as Paul Dissat whiled away the lazy hours with a question-and-answer game with the penalty for wrong answers and right answers precisely the same. Improvised agony.

Or I could try to stand up. That was the first step. If I couldn't there wasn't any point in wondering about step two. If I could stand up, then I had to see if I could walk down the beach and into the sea. I had to hurry, but with short steps well within the range of my constraining nylon cord, and I had to keep my balance. The third part of it was getting into the water at just the right place. I had seen the place when I had been out there near Lisa's head in the hot sun.

There is no such thing as an undertow. Not anywhere in the world. All you ever find is a rip. To have a rip, you have to have a partial barrier parallel to the beach. It can be a sandbar or a reef. The barrier has to be underwater. There has to be a hole or channel through it. A great volume of water comes in on wind and waves and tide over the barrier, rushing toward the beach with waves marching right along behind each other, hurrying in. Then that big volume of water has to get out to make room for the water coming in. So it goes flowing out through the hole or channel. A big volume and a narrow, deep hole makes one hell of an outgoing current. It is sort of fan-shaped, wide at the beach end, narrowing toward the gap in the barrier, and going faster and stronger as it gets narrower.

You can read a rip on a sandy beach from the way it boils up the sand in a limited area and makes a foam line out toward the gap. If you get caught in one, you swim parallel to the beach until you are out of it, then turn toward the beach. Fight it and you can panic and drown, because they usually go faster than any man can swim.

I got up, scraping some hide off my back on the palm trunk. I went down the beach slope, stamping my feet wide for balance. The beach and the sea kept tilting, misting, merging, flowing. In nightmare slowness I passed the round, black, hairy thing, saw it vividly for just a moment. A wave had come in and covered it entirely. The top of it was a few inches under momentarily motionless water, at rest when a wave had come all the way in and gathered itself to run back out. Her black hair was fanned out, and in that instant of sharpened, memorable vision I saw the spume of sand drifting out of her open mouth, like a strange cartoon balloon, a message without sound. A sandy, tan farewell.

Paul was shouting above the wave noises. I was off balance, leaning forward. A wave slapped my chest and straightened me up. I took a deep breath and lunged forward. I counted on the exceptional buoyancy of the water, the high salinity of the dry season. I had to know if I was in the rip. I managed to roll and float and look back at the beach and saw him and the trees and the raft and the Moke moving into the distance at six or eight miles an hour. It was a good rip, and I hoped it was a long gap in a barrier reef, that the reef was well offshore, and that it would move me out into a current that would take me away from there. Any direction at all. Out to sea and drown while laughing at how Lennie Sibelius was going to nail Paul Dissat, nail him and sweat him and find out how it happened. All of it.

The swell had built nicely, and it was going to play hell on him, trying to find me bobbing around in all that blue-and-white sparkle. If the hands are dead, it is less burdensome to drown, but you try not to drown if you can help it. I could arch my back and float high, my ears full of the drum sounds of the sea, a wave slapping me in the face now and then. Lift my head, pick a direction, and go kicking along. When all the luck has gone bad, do what you can.

nineteen

It was a good rip that carried me way out and put me into a sea current that seemed to be taking me due north at a hell of a pace, increasing speed the farther out I got. The water was warm, and the sky was squinty bright, and I was gently lifted and dropped in the swell. It had been a good way to live, and given a choice of dying, it was as good as any that came to mind. I wanted to stay aware of the act of dying as long as I could. I wanted to touch it and taste it and feel it. When it is the last sensation left, there is a hunger to use all of it up, just to see what it is like at the very end, if it is peace or panic.

I kicked my bound legs slowly and easily. When I lifted up, I could no longer pick out the beach area where Lisa had died. I looked to the southwest and saw the checkerboard pattern of the town of Saint George's to the northeast growing more easterly as I floated farther. Finally, I began to see more and more of Grande Anse beach as I drifted farther out from shore and it came into view beyond Long Point. When all the beach was visible, I estimated that I was two miles from land. I saw the bright sails moving back and forth in the bay when a wave lifted me high. I could not guess how long I had been floating because I kept fading into a semidazed condition very much like sleep. The sun was so high I guess it was past noon.

There was a change in the direction of the current. I believed it had begun to carry me northwesterly, but I was too far from any reference points to be sure. I was opposite the town by then, and as near as I could estimate, I was just as far from the town as I was from Point Saline. When I could no longer see much of the town, see only the green mounded hills, I knew I was at least three miles offshore, possibly four.

I came out of a daze and saw a tall ship bearing down on me about a mile away. There was just enough angle so I could make her out as a three-masted schooner, and she had all the canvas on her, all the fore and aft sails flying, tilting her on a long reach.

I knew it could be reality or fantasy, and the smart money would bet on fantasy. I guessed she had come out of St. George's, and from my estimate of the wind, if she was headed north to the Grenadines, she would stay on that course until she was far enough out to come about and put her on the opposite tack for a single long run that would clear all of Grenada and head her for Carriacou.

I felt remote, as if working out a problem that had nothing to do with me. My arms had no feeling. I moved up and down on big, slow, blue swells. The crests were not breaking. I kept kicking myself back to an angle where I could watch her, see the boil of white water at her bows. My chance of being seen was one in ten thousand, even if she passed by me fifty yards away.

But then I had an idea. I suppressed it because it was going to involve a lot of effort and any effort did not really seem worthwhile. There would be fishermen aboard, people who always scanned the sea even when there is no hope of stopping for a chance at whatever quarry they see. The big fish smash the water, whack it to foam, send the spray flying. Go to work. Make a fuss. Give them something to spot. Hard to do. Double up and snap. Get the bound legs up and whack them down. Get into a spin, writhing and turning the body, kicking. Duck under and come out and kick as high as you can. Dizziness then. Sickness. Vision going. A sound of sails slatting, lines creaking, a thin cry. Sound of an outboard nearby. Hands grasping, lifting me. Fall onto hardness, onto oil stink, fish smell, and vomit up quarts and quarts of seawater. . . .

Then came that burlesque of fantasy, an ironic parody of the seafarer's paradise. I was on a low, broad hatch cover, and I could feel the motion of a ship under me. I squinted up into brightness to see, clustered close around me—all their lovely faces somber, all their girl voices murmuring of concern—the sirens of all the legends, sea wind stirring their tresses, their lovely skin in shades from antique ivory to oiled walnut. They were close around me, a multitude of them, prodding and massaging calves, ankles, and puffy feet—forearms, wrists, and swollen hands.

One lifted my dead left hand, and I stared at it with remote interest. It was a dark purple rubber glove, overinflated, with deep dimples where the knuckles had been.

Suddenly I screamed. It astonished me. I am not the screaming type. There was a pain in my right hand equivalent to having all the fingernails yanked off simultaneously. Pain shoved me far enough into sudden darkness so that the raw scream seemed far away and I could think of it as an angry white bird, clawing and flapping its way out of my open throat.

I came out of blackness in time to get myself braced for the next pain. It was again in the right hand, and as it faded I got a big one in the left hand, which caught me off balance and so I roared. The enchantresses moved back a little, looking down at me in worried specultion. They were all in little sleeveless blouses in bright colors, no two alike, all in little white shorts.

Captain Mickey Laneer came into view and perched a haunch on the hatch cover beside my hip. She wore a khaki shirt and a baseball cap. "What the hell have you been trying to do to yourself, McGee?"

"Hello, Mick. Lost an argument."

"Somebody throw you overboard?"

"Ran away, got into a rip, floated out from shore."

She stared at me. "From shore? Jesus! You could be a little bit hard to kill. Gals, this is an old and good friend of our old and dear friend, Rupert Darby, captain of the *Dulcinea.* Say hello to Travis McGee." They said hello in smiling musical chorus.

"McGee, clockwise around you, starting with Julia in the yellow shirt, meet Teddie, Louise, Hester, Janey, Joyce, Margot, and Valerie. Teddie, get to the helm on the double and tell Mr. Woodleigh he's falling off to port, for chrissake, and bring him back on. Janey, Mr. McGee needs a big mug of black coffee with four ounces of Fernandez rum in it. Margot, you help me get Mr. McGee onto his feet, and we'll put him in my cabin while we run back in."

I started to say something to her, then had to clamp down on the pains. Very savage pain but not as bad as the first ones.

"Speak to you privately, Mickey?"

"Move back, gals."

"Somebody is going to make very damned sure I drowned. It could revise their plans if I didn't. They'll keep a watch on the hospital. They could get to me there, I think. It's a bad risk."

"McGee, I like you. But I can't get involved in anything. The government pretends I don't exist. They like the money I bring in. The black-power types talk about me forcing blacks into prostitution. Bullshit! Hester is the only almost pure black, and there are three less than half. Every girl has freedom of choice, believe me. Any publicity of any kind, any infraction, they hit me with a heavy fine. Enough to hurt without driving me out of business. Don't kill the goose. But don't let her get fat. You need hospital attention for the head and the hands. So I'm going to come about and have a nice run back and turn you over to Rupe to put you in the hospital. I've got four good, regular customers aboard who've paid their money for a ten-day cruise. Sorry."

I started to fade out and couldn't have pulled myself back in time if a sudden pain hadn't hit my right foot, as if an electric icicle were being shoved through it.

"Mick. I'm . . . sorry, too. Rupe heading up to Dominica Wednesday. Take me up to Grenadines, set up a meet, transfer me. Reach him on radio?"

"Yes, but dammit—"

"Take me back, and I blow your tired businessman cruises right out of the water, captain. Sorry as hell. You probably fulfill a pressing need. No pun. Official complaint to your lady governor, if I have to. And the premier. And the *Miami Herald*."

"McGee, I like you less and less. You are a bastard!"

"Only when I have to be."

"But, damn you, you could *die* on me!"

"Sort of a risk for both of us."

"Valerie? V*al!* Get it on over here, girl. This big ugly son of a bitch going to die on me? She was a nurse, McGee."

Valerie was of that distinctive and very special mix you see in Honduras. Mayan, Chinese, and Spanish. She looked at my hands and she had me roll onto my belly while she checked the back of my head. Her touch was firm enough to hurt but gentle enough to let you know the hurt was necessary.

They helped me onto my back again, and she bent close and thumbed my eyelids up and looked gravely into one eye and then the other, back and forth, several times.

"Well?" Mickey said impatiently.

"Eet wass a terrible blow on the head. I don't know. The pupils are just the same size. Probably no fracture because the skull is solid and thick right there. Concussion. Could be bleeding in the brain, captain."

"How do we tell? What do we do?"

"One girl has to be with him every minute, and what she has to do all the time she is with him is count his pulse for one full minute and write it down. Count his respiration for one full minute. Write it down. Over and over. One hour is the most a girl can do that and be accurate. Half hour is better."

"So we set up half-hour shifts."

"Then she must write down a column of figures. Suppose it is like . . . 71, 70, 72, 69, 71, 70, 69. Fine. Then it is 70, 69, 67, 68, 66, 67, 65 . . . right then the girl on duty finds me and finds you, and we get a seaplane alongside to take him to a hospital. They'll have to open his skull and see if the clot is shallow enough so they can take it out and keep him alive."

"My hands?" I asked.

"They'll hurt like hell," Valerie said. "Like living hell. But you'll be fine. No nerve damage. No dead tissue. Good circulation, so that even something that tight couldn't cut it all off."

The pain hit again as I was fading, but it just held me on the edge, and when it stopped I went the rest of the way on down. Blurred memories of being carried, of choking on hot, pungent coffee, of hearing the hiss of water along the side of the hull. Then memories of its being nighttime, feeling that slow swing and turn of an anchored vessel, hearing faint music from topside, of moving in and out of sleep and seeing girls, sometimes the same one, sometimes a different one, solemnly and intently taking my pulse, lips moving, writing on a pad, then staring back and forth from my chest to a watch, counting respirations, writing it down. A Coleman lantern was hung from the overhead with an improvised shade that left the bunk in relative shadow and filled the rest of the small cabin in harsh brightness.

I awoke to a gray morning light in the cabin. The lantern was out. A slender dark-haired girl sat taking my pulse. She had a narrow, pretty face, sallow skin. Her forehead and the end of her nose were sunburned.

"Where are we?"

"I'm counting."

"Sorry. Tell me when you're through."

"You made me get mixed up."

I let her count, write it down. "We're at anchor in a cove by some pretty little islands north of Grenada. They're called the Sisters. Now I have to count your breathing."

"Who are you?"

"Joyce. I'm new. Hush, please."

"From Barbados, eh?"

It startled her. "How'd you know that?"

"I can even remember the words. You are Louise's 'cute little chum.' She flew up and talked to you about the job."

She blushed. "Yes. Let me count, please."

"Dear girl, do your counting, and then I have to get up and use the head."

She wouldn't let me without going and bringing Valerie back to check me over and give permission. I felt shaky and frail. When I came back from the nearby head, clutching at everything handy, Valerie was sitting on the bunk looking at the notebook tabulations, and Joyce was standing near her. They got out of my way, and I sighed as I got in and lay back.

"Now we can take you off the continuous count, I think," Valerie said. "Do you feel dizzy? Do your ears hum?"

"No."

"I think we'll take a count every fifteen minutes. Joyce, your hour will be up in . . . ten minutes. Stay another hour, okay? I'll have Margot take over from you at seven thirty, and you can go help with breakfast then."

"You're a good nurse," I told Valerie. "Isn't there a shortage of nurses around the islands?"

She was so still for a moment that her pretty face looked like a temple carving. Her Indian blood was more apparent. "Oh, yes. A shortage of nurses. And damn lots of patients. And not so many reasons for keeping them living, I think. The children die. The old ones come back, over and over, trying to die."

She spun and left quickly. I tried to smile at Joyce. Maybe I managed it convincingly enough. I think she smiled back as her face tilted and blurred and faded into gray-black. I had to say something to assure Joyce and myself I was not going sour on them.

"What did you do in Barbados, dear?" My voice seemed to come from the bottom of a brass barrel.

"Does it matter?" she said from the far end of a hundred-yard corridor.

"I'm interested. I'm curious. That's all."

She began to emerge out of the humming mists and the metallic distances. I saw her face again, shifting as if underwater, then firming up. "Are you all right?" she asked, frowning. I felt her finger-tips moving on my wrists, seeking the pulse.

"I'm fine."

"You looked different. Your eyes were funny. I work in a boutique in Bridgetown. My husband worked at the desk in a couple of the good hotels. We could live on what we made if we were careful. Maybe he got tired of being careful. He left over a year ago, and I have no idea where he is. What else do you want to know? I'm English and Portuguese mostly with a bit of colored. I make about two hundred and seventy-five to three hundred, Biwi, a month in the season and a lot less when the tourists are gone. I can't quite live on it. I've sold the things Charles and I owned, like the music system we got on hire-purchase and was all paid for, and I let them come and take the things which weren't paid for. The last thing I let go, the last thing worth selling, was my little sailboat my father built for me before he died when I was twelve." Her words were coming faster and faster, and she had stopped searching for the pulse. Her thin fingers were wrapped around my lacerated wrist. "It was the only thing I could use to get away, to be someone else, and I took it out in a gale before I let it go, telling it to drown me, but it would not. . . ."

"Hey, now," I said.

Her eyes had filled. "I mean there is no end to it, Mr. McGee. I've been a decent woman. I have no family at all. A fat political gentle-man wants to give me a cottage in a development he owns. There has been one girl every two years, I understand. He is quite old. They each end up with a cottage and some sort of small pension. I imagine a long street of them with the years marked on little signs in the little yards, with all of us sitting on our little porches. . . ."

"Joyce, honey. There, honey."

Kind words started the flood. She put her forehead down into the bend of my elbow, and the stifled sobs wracked her thin body. I stroked her hair and made soothing sounds. I identified my own feel-ing of guilt. I had not really wanted to know about her life and her problems. I had been talking in an effort to keep the brassy mists from sucking me under. But the words had opened her up, and it had come spilling out.

She pushed herself away, stood with her back to me, blew her nose. "Why should you give a damn?" she said in a choked voice. "Why should anybody?"

"Is this cruise what your friend Louise described?"

She turned, snuffled, sat wearily in the chair. "Oh, yes. Louise didn't lie. She called a spade a spade. It's a ten-day trial, you might say. I will do deck duty, scut work, help with the food, drinks, laundry, scrubbing, and all that. But I don't have to be . . . available unless I decide to be and tell Captain Laneer first. The men really seem quite nice. I can keep my clothes on, thank God. Louise said it took her three days to get used to pottering about the decks and below-decks entirely starko. I think it would take me forever, and even then I couldn't adjust. The girls are so much nicer than I imagined. But an entirely naked woman is not really erotic, do you think? Of course, in a cold wind or offshore insects or one's time of the month or coming into port, clothes are definitely required." She had a brooding look, frowning down at her knuckles. "It's rather difficult for one to imagine being quite ready for it. I mean if one has taken a bucket of scraps aft after cleaning fish, it is so abrupt to be suddenly tweaked, then taken by the hand and led below." She roused herself and looked slightly startled. She had been voicing her internal monologue. "I go on, no?" She forced a wan smile. "At any rate, once the ten days are ended, I shall either go back to the boutique to stay or go back to quit my job and pack. I shall fret about it later, not now. Valerie told me that it would be good for you to get as much sleep as you can now. Can you sleep, dear?"

I could. I slept and slept and slept. The dull ache in hands and feet and head did not inhibit it. In too many of the sleep periods Lisa was way down below the velvet black, waiting for me on the bright beach, the severed head propped on the delicate bones of the jaw, smiling at me.

It was another morning, and Mickey Laneer brought me a stone mug of coffee, nudged me awake, and put the coffee in my hand after I had hitched up, knuckled grainy eyes.

"You are some kind of a sleeper," she said.

"A long swim with your hands and feet tied will do it every time. We moved again, didn't we? Where are we, and what day is it?"

"Anchored in the lee of Frigate Island at eight o'clock on the morning of Thursday, April twenty-ninth."

"Thursday! But couldn't you get in touch with—"

"He'll be off to the west of here about opposite us at fourteen hundred. We'll make a radio check on him an hour beforehand. No sweat. We'll run out and intercept and put you aboard *Dulcinea*."

"I've been a lot of trouble to you and your crew, Mick."

Her smile was sour. "Better this kind than the kind you were going to lay on me if I ran you back in."

"Hard feelings, captain?"

She grinned, punched me on the side of the thigh. "My four passengers haven't made any complaints. Maybe because I run the only game in town. The gals have loved playing nurse. By doing it your way—with you having the grace not to die on me—I've kept my friendship with Rupe. And I put a high value on it. No, McGee. Except for having to give up my own cabin, no hard feelings. How do you feel, anyway? Strong?"

I checked and tested. "Better than I should."

"You look good. If you feel strong enough, I can send you down a little sample of our recreation program here aboard the *Hell's Belle*. Courtesy of the management. Name your favorite nurse, man."

"Joyce?"

The taut smile was gone. "Now you really are a smartass, you know that? I know damned well you know that girl's arrangement aboard, because she told me about talking to you."

"I thought maybe she'd made her decision."

"And you were curious? I wouldn't want you aboard long. You'd make too much mischief. Nobody puts any kind of pressure on that kid. She works it out for herself. She makes her own decisions."

"What will she decide?"

Mickey Laneer stood up, looking weary and cynical. "She'll decide that every other choice she has is worse. I'll send your breakfast."

Teddie brought my breakfast. She was the big, creamy, Minnesota Swede who had learned her sailing on Lake Superior. She was the one who giggled. Her hair was sea-weathered to a harsh spill of pure white hemp. From the bulge of bland forehead down to the clench of prehensible toes, she was tanned to the shade of macaroons. She giggled as she presented the tray with the menu she had devised. Two giant rum sours. A stack of toast. A platter of flying fish, perfectly sautéed and browned, crisp and sweet. A big enameled coffeepot and two of the stone mugs. She latched the door, giggling, and we had breakfast. She took the tray over to the table and came back, giggling. In the moist hollow of her throat, from earlobe to collarbone and across the socket in front, around to the other earlobe, she smelled exactly like fresh cinnamon and Pears' Soap.

The rendezvous was made about fifteen minutes past two, an estimated seven miles due west of Frigate Island. I convinced Mickey that there was no need to use the tender to transfer me. It was a freshening breeze, the sea running sparkling high. I said that though I didn't want to test my skull by diving, I could certainly swim a little. Rupe put the *Dulcinea* dead in the water, rocking in the trough, and hung the boarding ladder over. Mickey at the helm took the *Belle* across the *Dulcinea*'s stern, laying her over so that as I sat on the lee rail and swung my legs around to the outboard side, my feet were but inches from the water.

I dropped and swam the fifty or sixty feet to the *Dulcinea*, bringing from the *Belle* no more than I had brought aboard—the swim trunks, leaving behind somewhere in the sea the scraps of nylon cord they had cut out of my flesh.

There was no hand extended to help me when I clambered aboard the *Dulcinea*. Rupe and Artie stood staring at the *Belle*, jaws slack, leathery paws dangling. Mickey saw no need to change the uniform regulations for an old friend like Rupe. Mickey showed off by taking the *Belle* fifty yards past us, coming about smartly, working hell out of her girls, and then coming back aslant, waving as she angled across our bows on a northeast course not over forty feet away. The girls shouted, grinned, laughed, and waved.

"Fool woman," Rupe said. "All sailor, that fool woman. Artie. Artie? *Artie!*"

"Huh? Me?"

"Bring in that boarding ladder and stow it right this time."

"Boarding ladder?"

"*Artie!*"

"Oh. Sure. Yessir, Rupe. Right away."

Rupe put the diesels back in gear, opened them up to full cruise, checked the chart and gave Artie the compass course, and left him at the wheel. We went below.

"Now what the *hell* is this all about, Trav?"

"It'll take some time."

"Time is what we've got the most of."

twenty

Rupe loaned me the money to get home, and Artie loaned me the clothes, a set of fresh khakis that fit better than I would have guessed from looking at him. I had to buy straw sandals at Kingstown on St. Vincent. Customs and immigration clearance was at San Juan, and I had an interesting time there. People are supposed to have papers and luggage, a wallet and a toothbrush.

They wanted to take my citizenship away from me. I told them it was a little misfortune at sea. I told them we could make some collect phone calls. When I said a magic name they could call collect, they came to attention. They almost smiled. That was on Sunday, the second day of May. I pulled the home number, unlisted, out of the damaged recesses of memory and got his wife, then got him. He talked to the boss immigration fellow, and when they were through, the boss immigration type felt a compulsion to pump my hand and call me sir and ask me if there was any little thing he could do, anything at all.

Before my flight left, I tried Meyer again, and this time he was aboard his boat, and when he heard and recognized my voice, he said in a shaky voice, "Thank God. Thank God." I told him what I needed and what to do and not to be so sentimental, anyway.

It was a bright, clear day to fly across the Bahamas and the incredible tones and shades of the Bahama flats. I wanted to think but not very much. I wasn't very sure about being able to think things through. I wanted to depend on Meyer. The weather across my internal landscape wasn't very good. Patches of gray, like drifting clouds, obscured things I wanted to see. And sometimes in a waking state I would have the same feeling, the same jolt as when you awaken from sleep. For a little while I would not know where I was or where the plane would land.

I got off that flight and walked through the lower level and out to vehicle pickup, and there was Meyer, bless him, standing beside a dark blue rental Ford as ordered. A very anonymous car. I told him he had better do the driving, as I was not entirely sure of the circuitry in my head. He drove. I talked. We selected a ma-and-pa motel on the way into Lauderdale on Route 1, and he got me a room in the back with an air conditioner that sounded like an air hammer breaking up paving. I finished the story in the room.

I unpacked the stuff Meyer had brought from the *Flush*, using that spare key I gave him, which he keeps hidden aboard the *Keynes*. He had packed some Plymouth, which seemed a kindly gesture. He went and got ice from the machine, and we drank from sleazy disposable glasses that looked as though they were about five room guests overdue for disposal.

I sat on the bed, sipping the clean, cool taste of juniper. Meyer paced and paced. He would stop in front of me to ask questions. "I'm not clear on one point. You *did* write the whole thing to Lennie Sibelius, telling him to get moving, open the inner envelope if you hadn't checked in by the end of May?"

"I did. But I told Lisa the tenth of May. I wrote to Lennie later. And I did not tell her who I wrote to, of course."

"She believed you?"

"She very definitely bought it. And she told Cousin Paul everything he wanted to know. Assumption: he believed her the way she believed me. But by the time he found out about the letter, he'd gone too far with both of us to start making deals. His next step was to make me talk to him. And he could have. I'm stubborn, Meyer. Need I mention it? The pain threshold is high, as measured on the dolorimeter. But I could have gotten so anxious to talk I would have fallen all over myself. He scares me. What was your reading on him?"

"Humble beginnings. Very bright, very reliable. Full scholarship to McGill. Went back to his village to work for the man who helped him. Worked for that man about three years, and then one of Waterbury's companies acquired the benefactor's business in a merger situation. Waterbury was impressed by Paul Dissat and took him into the Quebec headquarters. Dissat is thirty-six, single, conservative, devout Catholic. He doesn't drink or smoke. He's apparently managed his own savings very shrewdly. Handsome. Very fit. Superb skier and superior tennis player."

He paced and I sipped, and the air conditioner kept up its whangbang roaring, leaking condensation down the blue concrete-block wall.

He stopped in front of me, using his lectern mannerisms. "He functions very well in a highly pragmatic profession. He is perfectly aware of cause and effect. He can weigh the degree of risk he is willing to take. He will assume that the man who gets your letter will be competent. Can his whole plan stand determined investigation? No. Even without a link as weak as Harry Broll, enough could be learned to bring it before a grand jury. What would this sort of scandal do to the SeaGate stock offering? It would come out that a fraud had been committed to get funds from a bank to pay for a preoffering block of stock. Waterbury could not afford to proceed. Both Jensen, Baker, and Fairmont, Noyes would recommend the applications be withdrawn. This would all happen, if your letter exists, with or without Paul Dissat on stage. See where I'm going?"

"I think so."

"With no public issue to raise money through the sale of stock, SeaGate comes to a shuddering halt. Harry's indivisible block becomes worthless. I can think of a Dissat-like solution."

"Grab the three hundred thousand from Harry?"

"Yes. But don't burn the bridges. Not all the way. Kill Harry because he is the last useful witness left alive. Then take a leave of absence on an emergency basis, somewhere out of touch. Lie back and listen. If there is no letter at all, if it was a bluff, then come back after the deadline and pick up the project again."

I toasted him. "To you, Meyer. If he has left already, I get the letter back from Sibelius, and we wait for him to reappear. If he's still here and working closer to the deadline of the tenth and if he hasn't gotten around to Harry, we pluck Harry away from him and take Harry to a private place and have a long chat about Mary and Lisa."

"If he has left, or is preparing to leave, and wants a door ajar so that he can get back just in case, then he'll have given Waterbury some sort of cover story, I imagine."

"Can we arrange a secret meeting with Waterbury?"

"Travis?"

"Why are you looking at me like that?"

"If we can't find Harry Broll anywhere and if Paul Dissat is still around and if Harry never did buy that block in SeaGate, even if Mary's body is dug up and identified, there's no way you can get Paul indicted. You probably can't even get him fired."

"He's got pretty legs."

"I don't want you to do some damned idiot thing."

"Long black eyelashes, Meyer. Red lips."

"Travis!"

"Maybe I want to dance with him. Maybe I want to whisper in his ear. But I don't want to have him come to me. You see, he's a careful man. He knows I'll come back if I didn't drown. That's why I told you to be careful about being seen going aboard the *Flush*. Am I overreacting?"

"No. You are not overreacting."

"Don't let him get to you, Meyer, when he starts looking for that letter."

"I've never seen you like this."

"He scrambled my brains. We should get away. I know a great cruise we could take."

"A cruise! A cruise?"

"It's different. I'll tell you about it later."

"Do that. There's been no report of Mary Broll's death from Grenada. It's taking a long time."

"A guest is charged for the cottage whether she uses it or not and charged for the food whether she uses it or not. And in the absence of a body it is the kind of island where, if a lady gets invited aboard a yacht for cocktails or up into the hills to an estate for cocktails, a lady could decide to spend a week being entertained. It is, shall we say, an impulsive place. A carefree isle."

"I phoned Mr. Willow last Wednesday. He got the cable from Mrs. Broll on Monday, and he talked with Harry Broll on Monday. On Tuesday morning he activated the loan papers and deposited the funds in Broll's personal account. I thought you'd like to know. That's when I started trying to get you on the phone. Wednesday, Thursday, Friday, Saturday. It was . . . pleasant to hear your voice."

"Paul sent the cable in her name. No problem. I should have realized how easily he could do that." I looked at Meyer's watch after first staring at my empty wrist for the thousandth time. "Five o'clock

on Sunday afternoon. About the only thing we can do is try to find
Harry."

"How?"

"There is a name in the back of this scrambled skull. All the file
cards are spilled on the floor. Let me crawl around back there for a
minute."

I retrieved the red-brown hair, pale green eyes, the vital and
expressive face, the lean, quick-moving body. I let her walk around
and smile, and then I knew her. "Jeannie Dolan of Eighty-five fifty-
three Ocean Boulevard." I hitched along the bed and got her number from information and called her.

"Who?" she asked in a sleepy voice.

"McGee. The guy with the blue Rolls pickup."

"Hey! It's you! I'd about decided I hadn't made any kind of dent
on you at all. And that doesn't help a girl's pride. Where are you?
Ask me out and then sweat out about three minutes of girlish reluctance and then come and get me, huh?"

"I am going to do exactly that later on, but right now I can't do
any stirring around."

"Oh! Are you sick?"

"Not too sick to take you out, Jeannie. But I am trying to give the
impression of being out of town. For good reasons."

"Okay. I'm not even talking to you. I will go around saying,
'Whatever happened to good old whosis?'"

"You are one nice lady."

"Rrrrright!"

"For reasons I may tell you some day, right now I want to know
how goes the course of true love and romance and convenience.
Betsy and Harry."

"It isn't exactly a script Ali McGraw is going to want to star in.
Right now Betsy is teed pretty good. He was real jumpy and mean
last week, and Wednesday morning early, like five, he got a phone
call. It woke her up, but she fell asleep, and then he's shaking her
awake. It's just getting to be daylight, and he's dressed, and he's
packed a suitcase. He tells her he's going away on business. By the
time the front door slams, she has asked him where he's going and
when he'll be back about three times—no answer. I told her I think
she has been handed the personally engraved, natural-bristle brush
and maybe she should move back down here onto four with me.
She's been calling his office and getting brushed off there, too. She
drove out there a couple of times, but there was no sign of his car.

Maybe he is away on business. But it showed no consideration, the way he left."

"Sold any condominiums?"

"Not to that friend of yours. She never showed up. If she really exists."

"You are very suspicious of people."

"If you'd ever met my husband, you'd know why. He could walk into a phone booth and leave by a side door."

"I'm a sneaky type too, Jeannie."

"That's nice. It's what I'm used to."

"I'll be calling you soon."

"You do that, hon. Bye."

———

Meyer and I talked, establishing the new parameters. But it was like the game of guessing which fist contains the chess pawn. Harry had enough animal caution to know that if things went wrong for Paul Dissat, it was runaway time for Harry. So if it was Paul who phoned him, maybe Harry had started to run. Conversely, Paul would know Harry was shrewd enough to know when to run, and so if Paul gave Harry cause to run, he would make certain Harry wouldn't be able to.

"The money will be the clue," Meyer said. "The first thing in the morning, as soon as the bank is open. I don't think it was paid over to SeaGate. And I don't think it's still in the bank."

"How do you manage that?"

Meyer smiled an unexpectedly unkindly smile. "By almost giving Woodrow Willow a coronary. He deserves a jolt. One should not be able to con a trust officer out of any assets held in trust."

"I'm coming along."

"Do you think you—"

"In the disguise you're going to go out and buy me at Happy Sam's Giant Superstore Open Always Practically."

"And on the way back here I buy pizza and beer to go?"

———

The lobby of the Southern National Bank and Trust Company takes up half the ground floor of their new building on Biscayne. It is like three football fields. People at the far end are midgets, scurrying around in the cathedral lighting. The carpeting is soft and thick, dividing the lobby into function areas through the use of colors. Coral, lime, turquoise. The bank colors are pale blue and gold. The girls wear little blue-and-gold bank jackets with the initials SNB on the pocket, curled into a fanciful logo, the same logo that's stitched into the carpet, mosaicked into the walls, embossed on the stationery, and watermarked into the checks. The male employees and officers up to ambassadorial rank wear pale-blue-and-gold blazers. Everybody has been trained to smile at all times. The whole place looks like a huge, walk-in dental advertisement. There is probably also a bank song.

Meyer dropped me a block away, and while he found a parking space, I strolled back to the bank and went in. I wore a Hawaiian shirt, a straw ranch hat with a red band, a drugstore camera around my neck, sunglasses with big pale orange lenses.

A guard moved in from the side and asked if he could help me. I said I was meeting the little woman here because she had to cash a traveler's check, probably to buy some more of those damn silly leather boots, and where would she go to cash traveler's checks. He aimed me across a hundred yards of carpeting, under a forty-foot ceiling. Nobody else looked at me. Tourists are invisible, except to the man trying to sell them something. Otherwise, they are as alike as all the trees in the park. Only a botanist knows there is any difference between trees. Or an apple grower.

I kept moving, because if I stood still, one of the guards would come over and ask me if he could help me. I did not know how long it would take. Meyer said he would come in from the north side corridor after going up to the trust department and coming back down with Mr. Willow. Also, I kept moving because I wanted to make certain that by no ten-thousand-to-one chance was Cousin Paul doing a little banking business this hot, windy Monday morning. Sometimes his face would be completely gone from memory, and that would frighten me. Then it would pop back like a slide coming into automatic focus.

At long last I saw Meyer coming toward me, striding right along, and I guessed that was Mr. Woodrow Willow a half step to the rear. I watched Meyer. He was going to rub his nose if he wanted me to join the act. He looked through me and did not see me at all. Woodrow Willow was not what I expected. This was a young man, tall, fresh-faced, snub-nosed, roundheaded, with the same mouth old Walt used to draw on his chipmunks. I sauntered after them and caught up when they talked to a man who had his own big blond desk in a solitary, private thirty-by-thirty area of coral carpet right out in the midst of everything. The man used a phone. Soon a rangy woman came over walking like one of those heel-and-toe competitors, elbows pointed outward. She listened. She picked up the phone. A far younger girl came, carrying a ledger card. She jogged. Every part of her jogged.

After she left, Meyer shook hands with the man at the desk, and Meyer, Willow, and the rangy woman walked all the way across to a line of teller's stations on the far side of the bank. The rangy woman spoke to a slender girl with brown hair. Then she spoke to a man patrolling behind the cages. The slender girl closed her window and came around and out onto the bank floor. Meyer turned toward me and rubbed his nose. The rangy woman was leaving.

I walked up, and Meyer said, "Mr. Willow, this is my associate, Mr. McGee. McGee, may I present Miss Kathy Marcus."

"Who *is* this person?" Willow said in a voice of despair. "Good God, I had no idea you were going to bring in—"

"A place where we can talk?" Meyer said. "Just to have Kathy tell us in her own words before we get into anything else. Then we won't be taking up so much of her time."

"Take a lot," she said. "I've got a three-dollar short that's driving me up the wall."

"We'd better use one of the small conference rooms upstairs," Willow said.

Upstairs was 1910 banking, as opposed to the 1984 version in the lobby. Oak paneling, green rugs, leather libraries. The computers were hidden offstage. Park your Mercer under the elm trees and come in and talk about buying a block of Postal Telegraph.

There were six chairs around the table in the small conference room. There were two framed prints of clipper ships and a seventeen-pound glass ashtray on the polished walnut. As soon as the door was shut, I shed the ranch hat, shades, and camera.

"Enjoying your stay?" Kathy asked me with a quick wink.

"Little gal, when I come across those Everglades in that big old air-conditioned Greyhound bus, I said to the little woman, I said, Mother, we shoulda—"

Kathy guffawed, stopping me. Willow rang the big glass ashtray with his pipe in authoritarian tempo, silencing everybody. "Please! This is a very serious matter. If I have your attention, Miss Marcus, we would like to find out to what extent you are involved—"

"Whoa, friend," she said sharply, no laughter in her voice or her level stare.

"Now you will *listen* to me, Miss Marcus! I was saying—"

She got up and went to the door and smiled and said, "When you go home to the wife and kiddies tonight, Woodie, tell her that nice Miss Marcus quit the bank and went right down the street to another bank. Some loyalty, huh?"

"Come back and—"

"Woodie dear, the banks are so hard up for anybody who is worth a damn, it's pathetic. They've been hiring people here if they're ambulatory and feel warm to the touch. And I am one very damned good teller, and I have been here four years, and I am not now, nor have I ever been, *involved* in anything hanky or panky."

"Please, come back and—"

"Woodie dear, you just can't have it both ways. You can't call me Kathy and fun around with me when we're alone in an elevator and give me a friendly little grab in the ass and a chummy little arm pressure on the tit and then expect me to sit meek and mild in front of these gentlemen and take some kind of accusatory shit from you. No thanks. I'll tell them downstairs who ran me out of this bank."

"Kathy," he said.

With her hand on the knob she looked at him with narrowed eyes and said, "That's a start at least. Say the rest of it."

"I'm sorry. I didn't mean to imply—"

"Do you want me to come back and sit down, Woodie?"

"Please. I would appreciate it very much."

She came slowly back to the chair, sat, and smiled and said, "If these men had been strangers, Woodie, I would have let you go on being a jackass, and I would have cooked you later. But I'm among friends. Friends who rescued an eerie blonde from the oldest floating house party in the world."

"I remember already," Meyer said.

I looked at her more closely. "Delmonica Pennypacker?"

"Just a little name I made up for my vacation. Anyway, as I understand it, Woodie, you want a play-by-play account of cashing the check for Mr. Harry Broll."

Woodrow Willow was coming out of shock. He cleared his throat and told how a Mr. Winkler, a vice-president of the bank, had received a telephone request last Wednesday at closing time from Harry Broll, stating that he would be in at about eleven on Thursday to cash a check for three hundred thousand on his personal account. He wanted to make certain the bank would have cash available in hundred-dollar bills. This is not an unusual request in an area where large real estate deals are made.

Kathy took over and said, "The way our system works, everything has to go through teller records or we're out of balance. The cashier is Herman Falck, and I suppose Mr. Winkler told Herm to have the cash on hand. Herm told me he would run it through my balance, and he said Mr. Broll would probably bring in a dispatch case for the money. That amount would fit with no trouble. We run a minimum cash balance in the drawer at all times to make the place less appealing to the knockover boys. We signal the vault for more cash or to come make a pickup when we get too fat. They come zipping in a little electric money cart.

"So at ten after eleven Herm brings these two men over to me. I put out my closed sign so that a line won't build behind them. He takes the dispatch case from the man with Mr. Broll and hands it around to me. Mr. Broll gives me the check, and Herm initials it. Then Herm goes back and brings the cash cart behind the cage. It's just a matter of packing the sixty wrapped stacks of hundreds into the case. A black plastic case, imitation lizard. I counted them out as I packed them. Five, ten, fifteen, on up to three hundred. The case was below eye level, looking from the floor of the bank. I snapped the snaps and slid it up onto the counter, and the other man took it, and they walked away."

"Had you ever seen Mr. Broll before?" I asked.

"I think so. He looked sort of familiar. Maybe I waited on him. The name seems familiar."

"How did he act?"

"Well, I guess he's really a pretty sick man. I don't think he could have managed without the other man helping him."

"In what way did he seem to you to be sick?"

"Well, he was very sweaty. His complexion was gray, and his face was wet. He kind of wheezed. Like asthma sometimes. He didn't have much to say. Usually, men joke about lots of money when they put it in or take it out. They joke with me because I'm all girl, I guess. His friend had to kind of support him walking to my window, I noticed. Mr. Broll walked slowly, a little bent over and taking small steps. His friend was very nice to him. Considerate."

"What did his friend look like?"

"Younger. Dark curly hair. Tall. Middle thirties, I'd guess. A very nice voice. Some kind of accent. Marvelous clothes. Conservative mod. But he was too pretty for my taste. Husky pretty. Great eyelashes. He called Mr. Broll 'Harry,' but Mr. Broll didn't call him anything. 'Let me help you, Harry. Here, let me take that, Harry. Come on, there's no hurry, Harry. Take your time, old man.' It took them a long time to walk to the main doors. The fellow helped Mr. Broll and carried the dispatch case. I watched them. They didn't go right out. I guess Mr. Broll felt faint, because they stopped and sat down in that lounge area left of the main doors. It made me uneasy. You like to see three hundred thousand get to where it has to go and get locked up again. They sat side by side on the couch. I could see the fellow leaning toward Mr. Broll and talking quietly and confidentially. I saw Mr. Broll put his hand over his eyes. The other man pulled it away and took his handkerchief and wiped Mr. Broll's face, wiping the sweat away, I guess." She frowned. "Maybe I shouldn't say this, but the whole scene had a funny flavor. It seemed faggoty to me, like a wife with a sick husband. . . . No. The other way around. A youngish husband with kind of a fat, sick old wife he doesn't really love but feels sort of affection and gratitude and . . . a sense of duty to, if I don't sound flippy."

"Not flippy at all."

"I was busy, and when I looked again, they were gone. I would guess it was about twenty minutes before noon when they left the bank together."

Willow said, "Would you say Mr. Broll was drunk or drugged?"

She thought it over. "No. He kept his eyes sort of squinted up. He knew what he was doing. He just seemed . . . fragile. As if he was in terrible pain. As if he had the world's worst bellyache and was wondering if he was going to pass out with it. And . . . he smelled sort of sour. He was wrinkled and he had beard stubble. I wondered if he'd been traveling all night or he'd slept in his clothes. I suppose it *could* have been the world's worst hangover."

"Thank you, Miss Marcus," Willow said. "Uh . . . Kathy."

"That means take off, huh?"

"With our thanks, Kathy," Meyer said. "You are a bright girl and a good observer. And if it ever becomes possible to tell you anything about this whole matter, we will."

"Thank *you*," Kathy said. She paused at the door and said, "McGee, do you still have that wild floating pad?"

"*The Busted Flush*, Slip F-Eighteen."

"I'll come visit. If you haven't gotten married up."

"Come visit, Kathy. Bring your swim pants."

"I'll bring a bowl of Greek salad. I make one hell of a Greek salad."

When the door shut, Willow said, "Good help is so terribly hard to find and hard to keep that one has to . . . uh . . . put up with a degree of impertinence that . . . uh . . ."

"Like she said, Woodie," I told him, "it's a lot easier to get respect from the pretty ones if you don't keep grabbing them by the ass in the elevator. Right, Meyer?"

"Absolutely right. An executive can't have it both ways."

"Keep the pretty ones at a distance," I said. "Grab the dog-faced ones by the ass. Then you have a happy bank."

"A contented bank," Meyer said.

"Goddammit," Willow yelled. "Tell me what this is all about!"

Meyer said, "I'll ask you the same question I asked you before, Woodrow. Could you swear that you were absolutely, positively certain that Mary Broll was alive when you processed that loan?"

"The answer is still the same. But why are you asking the question?"

"I'll ask you another. What was Harry Broll going to use the money for?"

"To buy the SeaGate stock, to pay the balance due of three hundred thousand. Don't look at me like that. It's legal, you know. It is illegal to borrow money to buy *listed* securities."

"He'd lose a great opportunity if he didn't buy the block of stock?"

"Oh, yes! Really great."

"Would he have to have cash to buy that stock, Woodrow?"

"Of course not! A certified check would—"

"Do you think he bought it?"

"I don't know."

"Can you think of any way of finding out?"

"Don't go away."

We were left alone. Meyer sighed. I told him he was pushing Woodie around beautifully. All he did was sigh again. When Meyer gets the silents, he isn't very good company.

twenty-one

As Meyer drove conservatively back toward Lauderdale in fast traffic, he said, "We can summarize what we know, if you think it will help."

"You do it, and I'll tell you if it helps."

"We do not care whether Harry Broll was running from Dissat or hurrying to meet him. Immaterial. Dissat had him from some unknown hour early Wednesday morning until they walked into the bank Thursday at ten after eleven. By three o'clock Wednesday afternoon Harry Broll was forced to make the phone call to Mr. Winkler about the large cash withdrawal. Dissat had to then sustain Broll on that depressed level where he could make his appearance at the bank without creating suspicion, yet would have no interest in appealing for help. Total emotional and physical defeat. A person reduced to Harry Broll's condition is beyond feeling terror. Only despair. The only part left would be the details of disposal or, if he'd already planned how to do it, to go ahead with it. If it required darkness, he would have to have a place to take Broll to wait for night or, better yet, a place to immobilize him safely so Dissat could put in an appearance elsewhere. If we are building the structure of limitation, the parameters of time and space, we need to know if Dissat appeared at the West Palm office on Wednesday and, if he did, the time spent there."

"And where he is right now," I said. "When I wonder where he is right now, I wonder if he's crouched on the floor behind us. That's what he does to me, Meyer. Sorry. He was so *pleased* with himself, so damned *delighted* when he reached out with his bare toes and turned her head so she looked at me with those empty, crazy eyes. It was a funny kind of innocent pleasure, as if he had no idea there was anything really wrong about it. He was like a little kid who'd built a kite that would fly, and he wanted me to tell him how great it was. He tried to talk tough. Movie tough. But it was like something that had to be said. An obligatory part of the ceremony. After that we were going to share something, he and I. Some special personal important relationship. Dammit, I can't say it so that you can understand how it was."

"He fits the pattern of a certain kind of damaged personality I have read about, Travis. He could be called the activated sociopath sadist. Bright, healthy, energetic, competent. Excellent in areas requiring ritual. Mathematics, accounting, engineering. Quite cold inside. Tricky. Unable to concede the humanity of people around them because, having no basis of comparison, they think all of us have their same dry and barren soul. They are loners. They can charm when they choose. Sexually stunted, inhibited, often impotent. When Mary tried to escape from him and he caught her and they fell badly and injured her seriously, that activated him. Now he knows what he wants. He wants inventive episodes like the one with Lisa. The money will be meaningful only in how many such episodes it will buy. He isn't aware of evil. Only of being caught. You have to think of him as a bored child who suddenly discovers that it is wonderful fun to go to the pet store and buy a mouse and bring it home and do things to it until it is dead. Life is no longer boring. It is full of rich and wonderful excitement. The mouse shares the experience, so he feels fond of the mouse for as long as it lasts. You could say that the child loves the mouse to the extent he can feel love."

"Jesus!"

"I know. Stroking Lisa's forehead, drying Harry's sweaty face, are imitations of emotion. We can imagine he spoke tender words to Mary because she was pleasing him, giving him release. He's not a madman in any traditional sense. He cannot feel guilt or shame. If caught, he would feel fury and indignation at the game's ending too soon. He'll go to great lengths to stay free, unsuspected. His career is a lot less important to him than it used to be. My guess is he'll be gone by the deadline, the tenth, a week from today."

We rode in silence for a time. "Meyer? How did you get that Woodie Woodchuck to snap to attention?"

"By reminding him that he had informed me of the approximate value of the assets in one of his trust accounts without any authorization from the trust customer or the senior trust officer. Banks take all confidential relationships very seriously. He soon said he would be very happy to help me find out all about the three hundred thousand."

"How did he find out Harry had forfeited his option?"

"I don't know. Probably phoned a contact at SeaGate and asked what value, as collateral, Harry's hundred-thousand-share block would have. The stuff is too closely held to have an OTC quote."

"Couldn't he have borrowed against the stock he was going to get?"

"Not if he had already done so."

"Sick condominiums and a sick construction business. How about the seven hundred thousand he's supposed to get back from Sea-Gate?"

"If it went into land improvements at the site, then I guess he'd have to wait until the public issue money comes back to SeaGate."

"So that goes to pay off other debts, and then Harry's business quietly fades away and dies?"

"Reasonable guess."

"He had to take Harry somewhere and keep him there. Harry and Harry's car. Transportation problems, Meyer. Logistics and tactics. If he took him to wherever he lives—"

"A cluster apartment complex at West Palm on the bay shore. Rental apartments. Not likely."

"I suppose you have his phone number?"

"You asked me to check him out. Remember?"

"And your overall impression?"

"A very dull fellow, competent and humorless."

"You know the name of the cluster apartments?"

"I'd rather not say it. Palm Vista Gardens. D-Two."

"The first phone booth after we get off the pike, please."

———

He parked at a gas station by a shiny row of vending machines under a roof made of plastic thatch, incredibly green. I phoned from the hotbox provided by Gen Tel out on the cement wasteland. I hoped Palm Vista Gardens was big enough to have a rental and administration office on the premises. It was. The lady's voice came right from the resonant bridge of her Indiana nose.

"Yes, maybe you *can* help me. Have you got any furnished one-bedroom vacancies?"

She was not a well-organized lady. She tended to ramble. She gave information and then with cries of dismay retracted it and called herself names, mostly "old fool."

She finally discovered that one of their renters, "a nice young man" who had been on the special month-to-month basis with one month in advance (an arrangement they made with the "nice young people" from that new SeaGate company) had come in on the last day of April, just last Friday, and given his notice. He said he was vacating in a week. And that would make it . . . the eighth? No. The seventh. Yes. Next Friday. They could start showing it again the following Monday if there wasn't too much to be done. That was number D-2, which meant apartment 2 in cluster D. Just stop at the office. But don't wait too long. They go very quickly to nice young people, providing they don't have any pets. Or any babies, of course. I wondered how they felt about noisy goldfish, the kind that do a lot of leaping and splashing and churning around.

I tried to blot out all rational thought with a lot of peripheral items. Goldfish. Lead-free gasoline. Diminishing aquifer. I walked to the car, realizing I had left the cheap camera on the back seat. An essential part of my tourist costume. Meyer stood beside the rental car, drinking a can of orange pop, and it suddenly seemed insane that Meyer wore no tourist disguise. Paul Dissat knew exactly who I was and where I lived. And if he had gone to Bahia Mar and poked around as such a thorough chap would, he would have learned that Meyer was associated with me in certain obscure but apparently profitable ventures. Though believing me safely drowned off Grenada's lovely beaches, he might conclude that it was a very good chance my letter of self-insurance had been sent to Meyer to stow in a safe place. And so, as a percentage play . . .

It worked on me to the point that Meyer stared at me and said, "What the hell is wrong, Trav?"

My mouth wasn't going to work. Alarm is contagious. He trotted around and got behind the wheel, whipped us out into the traffic flow with a good imitation of teenage technique. At last I managed two words. "No hurry."

I saved the rest of it for my rackety motel unit. I tried to smile at

Meyer. "Pure chicken. Sorry. I just don't know what the hell is . . ."
Then I felt the sudden and humiliating sting of tears in my eyes and
turned quickly to blink them away before Meyer could see them.

I stood with my back to him, staring out between the slats of the
battered tin blinds at the side wall of a restaurant and a row of trash
cans haloed with bluebottled buzzing. I spoke too fast and chuckled
where there was no need, saying, "It's the old bit of the brave and
noble hunter, gliding silently through the jungle, following the track
of the big black panther and slowly beginning to realize that the
panther is also a-hunting and maybe he's flattened out on top of that
thick limb up ahead or behind that bush over there or in the shadow
of that fallen tree, with just the tip of his thick glossy black tail moving and the shoulder muscles rippling and tightening under that
black hide. I'm spooked because I kept telling myself the son of a
bitch would be gone by now, but he isn't going until Friday, and—"

"Travis. Come on. Slow down."

Can't ever really fool ol' Meyer. I sat on the bed. We're all children. We invent the adult façade and don it and try to keep the buttons and the medals polished. We're all trying to give such a good
imitation of being an adult that the real adults in the world won't
catch on. Each of us takes up those shticks that compose the adult
image we seek. I'd gone the route of lazy, ironic bravado, of amiable,
unaffiliated insouciance. Tinhorn knights of a stumbling Rosinante
from Rent-A-Steed, maybe with one little area of the heart so
pinched, so parched, I never dared let anything really lasting happen
to me. Or dared admit the flaw. Maybe in some crazy way Paul Dissat was a fun-house mirror image of me, a warped McGee with
backspin, reverse English.

The adult you pretend to be convinces himself that the risk is
worth the game, the game worth the risk. Tells himself the choice of
life-style could get him killed—on the Daytona track, in the bullring,
falling from the raw steel framework forty stories up, catching a
rodeo hoof in the side of the head.

Adult pretenses are never a perfect fit for the child underneath,
and when there is the presentiment of death, like a hard black light
making panther eyes glow in the back of the cave, the cry is,
"Mommy, mommy, mommy, it's so dark out there, so dark and so
forever."

Cojones are such a cultural imperative, the man who feels suddenly deballed feels shame at reentering the childhood condition.

Papa Hemingway will never take him fishing. George Patton will slap his face.

In all my approximately seventy-six inches of torn and mended flesh and hide, in all approximately fifteen-stone weight of meat, bone, and dismay, I sat on that damned bed and felt degraded. I was unmasked as a grotesque imitation of what I had believed myself to be.

Frowning, I tried to explain it in halting fashion to Meyer. "You talked about . . . the reflexes slowing, the warning system not working, the instincts inaccurate when . . . the only reason Harry Broll didn't kill me was because he lacked one more round in the clip. Then in Grenada I didn't even think of being careful . . . didn't sense his presence, got such a shot in the skull bone my head is still blurred. Meyer, people have been a few steps ahead of me other times. I've played pretty good catch-up. This time I have this feeling that there's no way. He's going to stay out in front, and if I get too close, he'll turn around and take care of the problem. Maybe I've gotten too close already, and I have ten more minutes or ten more hours."

"Travis."

"I know. I'm scared. It's like being very very cold. I can't move well, and I can't think at all."

"So I do the thinking?"

"I wish you would. Don't go back to your boat. I have a very ugly hunch about your boat."

"We have to talk to Dennis Waterbury in absolute privacy, and I have to make contact in such a way that he will trust us to the limited extent that rich and powerful people can trust anyone."

"Can you do it?"

"I don't know. I have to try to reach some people by phone. In Montreal and Toronto and Quebec."

"Start trying."

"If I can get through to someone he knows and trusts, who can tell him I am reputable, not a shakedown artist, then we are going to give him whatever lead time we can spare before I go to the law."

"With what?"

"With enough. Woodrow Willow's contact said Broll didn't buy the stock. So there's a missing three hundred thousand and a missing Harry Broll. If they dig around the seawall at Blue Heron Lane, they'll find Mary's body. Kathy Marcus and the other bank people could pick Paul Dissat out of a lineup. Maybe it will sink the SeaGate public issue without a trace. Even if Dissat never took a penny from the Waterbury enterprises, a breath of scandal can make the accounting firm and the underwriters back off."

"So why don't we go to the law? Why do we screw around with Waterbury if we've got all this?"

"Think about it, Travis. Think about it."

I instinctively fingered the place on the back of my skull where I had been so soundly thumped. Meyer was right. SeaGate was a very large thing, and Dissat was an operating officer in the SeaGate power structure. The lower echelons of the law would never go cantering into battle on the say-so of an apparently unemployed beach bum and a semiretired and eccentric economist. It was a two-county operation with both state and federal implications. Lower echelons would take the eccentric pair into skeptical custody and sweat them both.

Suppose you go to the top level, such as approaching the United States attorney in the area and suggesting he refer the problem to the FBI for investigation because of possible violations of the criminal code insofar as banking regulations are concerned. Then the approach would be made so tentatively—due to the SeaGate clout and the dubious source of the tip—that Dissat would be alerted, and he would disappear into his large countryside or ours.

First, you sell Dennis Waterbury on the idea that his boy, Paul Dissat, has been a very very bad boy lately and any publicity given his activities can founder the SeaGate plans. You convince him and give him some facts he can quietly check. You speak to him in absolute privacy and secrecy. Then, when *he* picks up the phone and relays his unhappy suspicions to the highest level, Dissat will be pounced upon first and investigated later, giving Waterbury additional time to plug up the holes and protect the upcoming public issue from scandal.

I said, "Okay. Do you think I'll ever be able to think things out for myself any more? Or will you have to be on permanent standby?"

"I think they start you on baskets and work up to needlepoint."

"I am supposed to laugh. All right, Meyer. Ha ha ha. Make your phone calls. What if the bastard won't listen even if we can get him alone?"

"Men who are rich have times when they don't listen. Men who are quite bright have times when they don't listen. Men who are both bright and rich *always* listen. That is how they got the money, and that is how they keep it."

"Then do we go to Canada, or does he come here?"

"He's here now. I found that out when I was learning all I could about Paul Dissat. Waterbury is in a guest cottage on a Palm Beach estate. The owners are in Maine now, but they left enough staff to take care of Waterbury. Pool, tennis courts, security system, private beach."

He started making calls. He had to push the thermostat high enough to kill the compressor before he could hear. I lay a-doze, hearing his voice come from metallic distances, sounding like the voices of grown-ups when I had been a child half asleep in a moving car or train.

twenty-two

He found an old friend at last, a Professor Danielson in Toronto, who knew Waterbury well and was willing to try to set it up. Meyer gave Danielson the motel number and unit number and asked to have Waterbury phone him as soon as convenient. If Danielson found that Waterbury was unable or unwilling to phone Meyer for a secret meeting, Danielson would phone back.

Nothing to do but wait and try to digest a roast beef sandwich that lay in my stomach like a dead armadillo. The motel television was on the cable. We turned the sound off and watched the news on the electronic printer, going by at a pace for a retarded fifth grader, white-on-black printing with so many typos the spelling was more like third grade than fifth.

The woes of the world inched up the screen. Droughts and murders. Inflation and balance of payments. Drugs and demonstrations. Body counts and new juntas.

The trouble with the news is that everybody knows everything too fast and too often and too many times. News has always been bad. The tiger that lives in the forest just ate your wife and kids, Joe. There are no fat grubworms under the rotten logs this year, Al. Those sickies in the village on the other side of the mountain are training hairy mammoths to stomp us flat, Pete. They nailed up two thieves and one crackpot, Mary. So devote wire-service people and network people and syndication people to gathering up all the bad news they can possibly dredge and comb and scrape out of a news-tired world and have them spray it back at everybody in constant streams of electrons, and two things happen. First, we all stop listening, so they have to make it ever more horrendous to capture our attention. Second, we all become even more convinced that everything has gone rotten and there is no hope at all, no hope at all. In a world of no hope the motto is *semper fidelis*, which means in translation, "Every week is screw-your-buddy week and his wife too, if he's out of town."

The phone rang, and Meyer sprang up and cut off the compressor and took the call. He made a circle of thumb and finger to tell me we had gotten through the corporate curtain. He listened for several minutes, nodded, and said, "Yes, thank you, we'll be there." Hung up.

"A Miss Caroline Stoddard, Mr. Waterbury's private secretary. We're to meet with him out at the site at SeaGate. We go through the main entrance and follow little orange arrows on sticks that will lead us to the storage and warehouse area. There are two small contracts going on now out there. Earth moving and paving. They stop work at four, and the crews leave. The area is patrolled at night, and the guard shift starts at eight at this time of year. Mr. Waterbury will meet with us at an office out there in the end of one of the warehouses behind the hurricane fencing near the vehicle park and the asphalt plant. We can find the place by looking for his car. If we meet him out there at five, we should have plenty of time for uninterrupted talk."

We got to the area a little early, so we drove down A-1-A for a little way, and when we found a gap in the sour commercial honky-tonk, Meyer pulled over. Down the beach there was a cluster of fat-tire beach buggies, some people swimming. Meyer and I were walking and talking over our plans when a chunky trail bike came growling up behind us, passed us, and cut in and stopped, and a fellow with enough black beard to stuff a small pillow glowered at us and gunned the bike engine. He looked very fit and unfriendly.

"You've got a problem?" I asked.

"You are the guys with problems. How come there are so many of you characters so cramped up you got to come creeping around to stare at naked people?"

"Where, where, where!" Meyer said, smiling. "If it's required, I'll stare. But as a rule, it's dull. If you have some graceful young girls cavorting, that is an aesthetic pleasure for a certain amount of time. Doesn't sand get into the working parts of that thing?"

Meyer is disarming. Maybe a completely frantic flip, stoned blind, could run a knife into him. Otherwise, the belligerent simmer down quickly.

"It's sealed so it doesn't happen too bad. But you can mess it up if you try. I thought you were more guys with binoculars, like the last pair. See, if you walk down this way far enough, then you can see around the end of the buggy and see the girls."

Meyer said, "Excuse me, but I was of the impression that the current belief is that the flaunting of the natural body cures the woes of society by blowing the minds of the repressed."

"A lot of people think that way. But we're opposed to the brazen display of the body and public sexuality. We're here on a pilgrimage mission for the Church of Christ in the Highest. And we have permission to camp on this part of the beach while we're bringing the word of God to the young people in this area."

"Wouldn't it be a lot easier to cover those girls up?" I asked him.

"Four of our sisters have got the crabs, sir, and they are using the salt water and the sunshine to cure them. The drugstore stuff didn't work at all, hardly."

Meyer said, "I have worked and studied in primitive countries, and I have caught about every kind of body louse a bountiful nature provides. And I have yet to contract a case that did not respond immediately to plain old vinegar. Have your girls soak their heads, armpits, and their private parts in vinegar. It kills the crabs and kills the eggs, and the itching stops almost immediately."

"You wouldn't kid me?" the beard asked.

"It is the most useful and generally unknown information in the modern world."

"They've been going up the walls. Hey, thanks. And God bless you guys."

He roared away. I told Meyer he was fantastic. Meyer said that my continual adulation made him uncomfortable, and it was time to see The Man.

We turned around, and where A-1-A curved west, away from the Atlantic beach, Meyer drove straight, down a road that was all crushed shell ruts, and potholes and marked private. Soon we came to the entrance pillars, a huge billboard telling of the fantastic city of the future that would rise upon the eleven square miles of sandy waste, where no child need cross a highway to get to school, where everything would be recycled (presumably vitiating any need for cemetery zoning), where clean industry would employ clean, smiling people, where nothing would rust, rot, or decay, where age would not wither nor custom stale the fixed, maniacal smiles on the plastic faces of the future multitude who here would dwell.

Once past the entrance pillars we were on a black velvet vehicle strip (trucks stay to right, off blacktop) which restored to the rental Ford the youth and ease it had lost during a few months, a few thousand miles of being warped, rocked, and crowded by the dozens of temporary owners.

We followed the small, plastic orange arrows and saw some yellow and green and blue arrows on yard-tall sticks marching in other directions, forming a routing code for workmen, planners, delivery people. A small sign in front of a wilderness of dwarf palmetto said starkly: SHOPPING PLAZA E 400,000 SQ. FT. ENCL. Yes, indeed. A multilevel, automated, air-controlled, musicated selling machine, where—to the violins of Mantovani and the chain-gang shuffle of the housewife sandals—only those processed fools would be offered which the computer approved of as being salable in billion-unit production runs.

We turned away from the sea and against the glare of the high western sun saw the construction headquarters, the belly and stack and hoppers of a portable asphalt plant, saw the trucks and spreaders, piles of aggregate, loader, and loading ramp. That area outside the warehouse and office compound enclosed by hurricane fencing was deserted, as if a flock of Seabees had slapped blacktop on it and been airlifted out. There was a big vehicle gate in the hurricane fencing, and it stood wide open. In the fenced area were some above-ground fuel tanks and pumps for the vehicles outdoor storage of some unidentifiable crated items, a generator building, and six small prefab steel warehouses backed up against a truck loading dock. A dark green Lincoln Continental limousine was parked by the next to the last warehouse.

Meyer parked nearby, and we got out. Meyer said in a low voice, "He'll be tempted to think it's some kind of a shakedown. Give us money, and we'll keep quiet about Dissat and let the public issue go through. But Danielson says Waterbury is honest by choice, not as a matter of necessity or operating policy."

There were three crude steps up to the cross-braced plywood door.

It stood a few inches ajar, the hasp folded back, a thick padlock opened, hanging from the U-bolt in the door frame.

I gave the door a couple of thumps with the underside of my fist. It made a nice booming sound in the metal structure.

"Hello?" said a pleasantly feminine contralto voice, elusively familiar. "Are you the gentlemen who phoned? Come in, please."

It was dim inside. There were no windows at the end where we entered, only at the far end. We were on an elevated area with a floor made of decking with steps leading down to the slab floor of the warehouse proper. The office was at the far end. The air was very thick and still and hot in the warehouse portion, but I could hear the whine of air conditioning in the enclosed office at the far end.

"I'm Caroline Stoddard," she said. "So nice to see you again, Mr. McGee."

I located her off to the left, standing down on the lower level. At first I thought she was one very big secretary in some kind of slacks outfit, and I blinked again, and my eyes adjusted, and it was Paul Dissat. That odd feeling of having heard the voice before was because of the slight residual accent.

"Be very nice," he said in his normal voice, "and be *very* careful. This is a new automatic nailer. They use it to knock the forms together for footings and pilings and so on. That hose goes over there to that pressure tank, and the compressor is automatic, and the generator is on."

It seemed heavy, the way he held it. He turned it to the side and triggered it. It made a hard, explosive, *phutt*ing sound, and nails zinged off the concrete and whanged the metal wall twenty feet away. He turned it toward us again.

"I'm a bad shot," he said. "But these things spray. At more than six inches they begin to turn. They'd make a ghastly hamburger of your legs, I think. I don't know why I've always been a poor shot. I'm well coordinated otherwise. Harry was a fantastic marksman. I guess it must be a natural gift."

"Fantastic marksman?" I asked numbly.

"Didn't you know? You could throw three cans in the air, and with that silly little popgun of his he could hit each one of them twice before they hit the ground without even seeming to aim, just pointing at them by some kind of instinct."

"When he came to see me—"

"He was coming apart. I was having trouble keeping him quiet. He had to make some mock show of being terribly concerned about

Mary so that later people could testify he was almost out of his mind with worry. He said you moved so quickly and startled him so badly, he nearly hit you in the foot."

"Where is Mr. Waterbury?" Meyer asked in a tired and wishful tone.

"Playing tennis, I should imagine. This is his time of day for it. Cool of the evening. When word came this morning of the request for information from Mr. Willow, I called him back and after a little hesitation he told me one McGee and one Meyer had initiated the request. Don't keep edging sideways, McGee! It was really a shock. I thought you dead. From drowning or brain damage. You pranced like a sick, ugly stork, and you went floating out at an incredible speed. You are very lucky and very hard to kill."

"Where is Mr. Waterbury?" Meyer asked.

"You are a bore," Dissat told him. "I went to his eminence and told him I had confidential information that two sharpshooters were going to try to get a private audience with him and try to frighten him into parting with money. I gave him the names. He told me to handle the problem. I handle a lot of problems for the man. When the information came in from Toronto, he had me take the call. Don't you think limousines allay all suspicions? They're so symbolic. Sit on the floor slowly and carefully, Travis. That's very good. Now, Meyer, make a wide circle around behind him and come down the steps. Fine. Walk over to that coil of wire on the floor next to the pliers and stretch out on your face with your head toward me. Very good. Now, Travis, you can come down and go around Meyer and kneel on the other side of him. Hold it. Now I want you to wire your friend's wrists together and then his ankles. The better job you do, the better all three of us will get along."

It was a heavy-gauge iron wire, quite soft and malleable. It was such dim light I felt I could do a fairly sloppy job. Dissat moved back to the wall, and an overhead bank of daylight fluorescent tubes winked on.

"You're doing a lot more talking, Paul," I said. "All keyed up, aren't you? All nerves?"

"Pull that strand tight. There. That's fine. Let's say I'm more talkative because you're more receptive. Would you like to know how the wave action affected Lisa's body?"

"I bet it was fascinating."

"It was. I sat and watched the whole thing. After the waves were breaking way in beyond where she was, the outgoing wash started to scoop the sand out from around her until she was almost uncovered. Finally she toppled over onto her left side. Then the waves began digging the sand out from under her, settling her lower and lower and flowing and forming around her as it began covering her. The very last thing I saw of her was her right shoulder, and it looked like a little, shiny brown bowl upside down on the smooth sand. And then that disappeared, too. I imagine that on all beaches the sea is a scavenger, burying the sad, dead things and the ugly litter every time the tide comes and goes. Now one more turn *under* the other wrist and then twist it and cut it. Good!"

I wished the pliers were heavier. I rehearsed the motions in my mind. Whip the arm up and hurl the pliers at his face, falling forward at the same time to give the throw more velocity and also shield Meyer from the expected hail of nails. I could scramble forward and take the nails in the back and get to his ankles and yank his feet out from under him, provided no nail went head-deep into the spine. And provided he didn't swing the muzzle down fast enough to drive a close pattern into my skull.

I hesitated, thinking how badly I had missed Harry with the ashtray, and while I hesitated, Dissat moved, making plier-throwing a much worse risk.

He shifted the heavy nailer, swinging the pneumatic hose out of the way, much as a singer manipulates the mike cable. In the bright fluorescence he looked almost theatrically handsome. He was like a color still shot for those strange ads Canadian Club used to use. ("I never knew how challenging it would be to hold two men captive with an automatic nailing device until I tried it.")

"Talkative?" he said. "Perhaps. Relief, I suppose. I've made a decision and simplified the future. Harry's money and mine make enough, you know. I've sent it to safe places. You two are the last loose ends. I'm taking sick leave. Actually, I'm retiring. Maintaining two identities compounds the risk factor. I told you in Grenada what I learned about myself from Mary Broll and poor Lisa. Now I shall have a chance to devote all my time to exploring it further. Very thoroughly. Very carefully. Mostly it's a matter of selecting people who might logically disappear of their own accord. I suppose the challenge excites me. So I talk a great deal, don't I? There's nothing I can reveal you can't guess, so it's not a help to you, is it? We shall explore the matter of the letter you sent from Grenada. As a matter of form. It isn't really important whether I learn about it or not, so I don't have to be awfully careful, do I? To keep everything tidy, I might leave with a traveling companion. A certain Mrs. Booker. Betsy. Would you know about her? Never mind. His ankles are finished? Walk backward on your knees. Further. Further. Right there. Sit down there, please, and wire your own ankles together, leaving a length of wire between them, the same length as the nylon cord that day on the little beach."

One uses any small frail idea. From handling the thick, soft wire I guessed that if one bent it back and forth enough times, it would snap. So I took a couple of turns around my ankles, tight enough to keep the wire from turning on my ankle. I made the binding turns, squeezed the wire knots with the plier jaws, nipped away what was left. With luck, management, and timing the wire might part at the squeezed place after enough steps.

He moved to stand over Meyer. He bent over and held the business end of the nailer almost touching the base of Meyer's spine. "I have this on single fire, McGee. Or single nail. If you can wire your own wrists nicely, I'll be so pleased with you, I'll give up the pleasure of finding out just how he'd react to one nail right here. Use ingenuity, McGee. Do a nice job. After Grenada, I take no chances with you."

I did a nice job. I was even able to nip off the extra wire by wedging the pliers between my forearm and the flooring. By holding my wrists together, exerting pressure, I could make it look as if there was no slack at all. Cheap little tricks never do any good at all, except to give the trickster false hope when he needs it.

Dissat came lithely over, bent, inspected, and kicked the pliers away with the edge of his foot. He grunted with satisfaction and walked over and put the nailer down beside the pressure tank, then swung and flexed his arms. "It got much too heavy," he said. He picked up a short, thick piece of metal. I thought it was steel pipe with a dull, gleaming finish, but as he walked toward Meyer, flipping it and catching it, I guessed from the way he handled it that it had to be very light metal, probably aluminum bar stock. It spun and smacked neatly into the palm of his hand each time.

"I don't even know what we use this for," he said. "There's a lot of it in the last warehouse. I've been taking an inventory personally, to check on pilferage of materials, small tools, and so on. That's where I kept Harry, in that warehouse. This piece just happens to have perfect weight and balance. I picked it up by accident the first time. After that, every time I picked it up, old Harry would start rolling his eyes like a horse in the bullring."

He bent suddenly and took a quick swing, very wristy, and hit Meyer on the back of the right leg, just above the knee. It made an impact sound halfway between smack and thud. Meyer bucked his heavy frame completely off the floor and roared.

"See?" Paul said. "Heavier stock would crush bone and tissue, and lighter stuff would merely sting. I experimented with Harry and went a little too far. I whacked him across his big belly once too often and possibly ruptured something in there, God knows what. For a time neither of us thought he could walk into the bank for the money."

"I'll trade Meyer for all you want to know about the letter."

He looked at me owlishly. "*All* of Meyer? Alive and free? That's naïve, you know. Meyer is dead, and you are dead. There's no choice now. I *could* trade you, say, the last fifteen minutes of Meyer's life for information about the letter. He would approve a deal like that when the time comes. But what would be the point? I'm not that interested in your letter, really. I learned a little bit from Mary and more from Lisa and a little more from Harry. Now I can check what I learned and learn a little more. Why should I deprive myself?"

"Why indeed?" Meyer said in a husky voice.

"I like you both," Paul said. "I really do. That's part of it, of course. Remember, Travis, how Lisa became . . . just a thing, an object? It moved and made sounds, but Lisa was gone. I made the same mistake with Harry, but not until the very end. The problem is to keep the person's actual identity and awareness functioning right to the end. Now we have to get Meyer out of here. Get up and bring that hand truck, Travis, please."

I got the truck, and at Paul's request I bent and clumsily wedged and tugged and lifted my old friend onto the bed of the truck. Meyer ended up on his right side. He squinted up at me and said, "I have this terrible pun I can't seem to get out of my head, like one of those songs you can't get rid of. Let's hope his craft is ebbing."

"How is your leg?" I asked him.

"Relatively shapely, I think, but considered too hairy by some."

"Are you trying to be amusing?" Paul asked.

Meyer said in his public-speaking voice, "We often notice in clinical studies that sado-sociopathic faggots have a very limited sense of humor."

Dissat moved to the side of the truck, took aim, and clubbed Meyer right on the point of the shoulder and said, "Make more jokes, please."

Meyer, having exhaled explosively through clenched teeth, said, "I hope I didn't give the wrong impression, Dissat."

"Are you frightened, Meyer?" Paul asked politely.

"I have a lump of ice in my belly you wouldn't believe," Meyer said.

Instructed by Paul, I rolled the hand truck along the warehouse flooring, turned it, and backed laboriously up a ramp, pulling it up. He unlatched a big metal door with overhead wheels and rolled it aside. The white sunlight had turned yellowish outside as the world moved toward evening, but it was still bright enough to sting the eyes. I wheeled the truck along the loading dock and down a steeper ramp where it almost got away from me.

I pushed the truck along the concrete roadway, the steel wheels grating and clinking. I became aware that with each stride I could feel less resistance to bending in the wire joining my ankles, and I was afraid it would snap before I wanted it to. I took shorter steps and changed my stride, feet wider apart to put less strain on the wire. We went through the big gates in the fence and over toward the asphalt plant. Dissat told me to stop. He put a foot against Meyer's back and rolled him off the hand truck. We were in a truck loading area with a big overhead hopper. The concrete was scabbed thick, black, and uneven with dried spills of asphalt tar. Paul motioned me away from the hand truck and pushed it back out of the way. Above us were the hopper and a square, bulky tank that stood high on girder legs.

"Do you see that great big wad of wasted asphalt over there, Travis? Meyer is facing the wrong way to see it. Vandalism is always a problem. Last Thursday night some hippies apparently came over from the beach, and for no reason at all they dropped at least two tons out of the holding tank. That's the big square tank overhead. It's insulated. Just before the shift ends, they run what's left in the plant into the holding tank. It's hot enough to stay liquid all night in this climate, and in the morning while the plant is being fired up and loaded, the trucks draw from the holding tank. But last Friday morning they couldn't drive the trucks under the hopper until they got a small bulldozer over here to blade that solidified hunk of warm asphalt away from where I'm standing. It's all cooled now, of course. And our old friend Harry Broll is curled right in the middle of that black wad, snug as nutmeat in the shell."

I remembered being taken on a hunt when I was a child and how my uncle had packed partridge in clay and put the crude balls into the hot coals until they baked hard. When he had cracked them open, the feathers and skin had stuck to the clay, leaving the steaming meat. Acid came up into my throat and stayed, then went slowly back down.

I swallowed and said, "And the patrol checks here tonight and finds more vandalism?"

"You belabor the obvious, McGee. They'll have to blade your hydrocarbon tomb, big enough for two, over next to Harry's. It's hotter now, of course, in the holding tank than it will be by morning." He moved over to the side. "This is the lever the foreman uses. It's a manual system. If I move it to the side . . ."

He swung the lever over and pulled it back at once. A black glob about the size of your average Thanksgiving turkey came down the chute, banged the hanging baffle plate open, and fell—*swopp*—onto the stained concrete, making an ugly black pancake about four feet across, very thin at the perimeter, humped thick in the middle. A couple of dangling black strings fell into the pancake from overhead. A tendril of blue smoke arose from the pancake. Meyer made a very weary sound. Pain, anger, resignation. The pancake had formed too close to him, splattering a hot black thread across his chin, cheek, and ear. In the silence I heard the faraway flute call of a meadowlark and then the thunder rumble of a jet. I smelled that sweet, thick, childhood scent of hot tar.

When Meyer spoke, his voice was so controlled it revealed how close he was to breaking. "I can certify. It comes out hot."

"Hardly any aggregate in it," Paul said. "It cools and hardens quickly. Travis, please turn Meyer around and put his feet in the middle of that circular spill, will you?"

I do not know what started the changes that were going on inside me. They had started before the meadowlark, but they seemed related somehow to the meadowlark. You used to be able to drive through Texas, and there would be meadowlarks so thick along the way, perched singing on so many fence posts, that at times you could drive through the constant sound of them like sweet and molten silver. Now the land has been silenced. The larks eat bugs, feed bugs to nestlings. The bugs are gone, and the meadowlarks are gone, and the world is strange, becoming more strange, a world spawning Paul Dissats instead of larks.

So somehow there is less risk, because losing such a world means losing less. I knew my head was still bad. It was like a car engine that badly needs tuning. Tromp the gas and it chokes, falters, and dies. It has to be babied up to speed. I had a remote curiosity about how my head would work with enough stress going on. Curiosity was changing to an odd prickling pleasure that seemed to grow high and hot, building and bulging itself up out of the belly into the shoulders and neck and chest.

I knew that feeling. I had almost forgotten it. It had happened before, but only when I had turned the last card and knew the hand was lost, the game was lost, the lights were fading. I had been working my wrists steadily within the small slack I had given myself, bending a tiny piece of connecting wire back and forth, and the bending was suddenly easier as the wire began to part.

The hard, anticipating joy comes not from thinking there is any real chance but from knowing you can use it all without really giving that final damn about winning or losing. By happenstance, he'd made a bad choice of wire. And maybe the twisted child was so eager to squash his mice, he might give one of them a chance to bite him.

The wrist wire broke as I put my hands on Meyer to move him. "Can you roll?" I asked in a voice too low for Paul to hear. Meyer nodded. "Roll on signal to your left, fast and far."

"What are you saying!" Paul Dissat demanded. "Don't you *dare* say things I can't hear!"

"Careful, darling," I told him. "You're going into a towering snit. Let's not have any girlish tantrums."

He quieted immediately. He picked up his chunk of aluminum. "That won't do you any good, and it isn't very bright of you to even try it. You disappoint me when you misjudge me. You take some of the pleasure out of being with you again." I looked beyond him and then looked back at him very quickly. I couldn't be obvious about it.

The instant he turned I broke the ankle wire with the first swinging stride. He heard me and spun back, but by the time he raised the aluminum club I was inside the arc of it. I yelled to Meyer to roll clear.

My head went partly bad. I knew I had turned him back into a kind of corner where the girder legs of the holding tank were crossbraced. I was in gray murk. Expending huge efforts. It was a stage. Somebody was working the strings of the big doll, making it bounce and flap. At times its doll chin bounced on my shoulder. It flailed and flapped its sawdust arms. I stood flat-footed, knees slightly bent, swaying from left to right and back with the cadence of effort, getting calves, thighs, rump, back, and shoulder into each hook, trying to power the fist through the sawdust and into the gristle and membrane beyond.

Pretty doll with the graceful, powerful, hairless legs, with the long lashes, red mouth, and hero profile. Sawdust creaked out of its throat, and Raggedy Andy shoe-button eyes swung loose on the slackening threads.

Soon a blow would burst it, and it would die as only a doll can die, in torn fabric and disrepair. I had never killed a doll-thing with my hands before.

Somebody was shouting my name. There was urgency in the voice. I slowed and stopped, and the gray lifted the way a steamed windshield clears when the defroster is turned on. I backed away and saw Paul Dissat slumped against a cross brace, one arm hooked over it. There was not a mark on his face.

I backed away. I imagine that what happened next happened because he did not realize what punishment to the body will do to the legs. He was conscious. I imagine that from belly to heart he felt as if he had been twisted in half.

The shapely, powerful legs with their long muscle structure had carried him through the slalom gates down the long tricky slopes. They had kept their spring and bounce through the long sets of tennis. So perhaps he believed that all he had to do was force himself up onto those legs and run away on them.

He tried.

When his weight came onto them, they went slack and rubbery. He fought for balance. He was like a drunk in a comedy routine. He flailed with both arms, and his left arm hit the load lever, and he staggered helplessly toward the thick, gouting torrent of asphalt from the overhead hopper. He tried to claw and fight back away from it, screaming as I once heard a horse scream, yet with an upward sliding note that went out of audible range, like a dog whistle. But it entrapped, ensnared those superb and nearly useless legs and brought him down in sticky agony. I ran to try to grab him, yank him out of that black, smoking jelly, but got a steaming smear of it across the back of my hand and forearm. I turned then and did what I should have done in the first place, went for the lever and swung it back to the closed position. The last sight I had before I turned was of Dissat buried halfway up his rig cage, hands braced against the concrete slab, elbows locked, head up, eyes half out of the sockets, mouth agape, cords standing out in his throat, as the black stuff piled higher behind him higher than his head.

I yanked the lever back and spun, and he was gone. A part of the blackness seemed to bulge slightly and sag back. The last strings of it solidified and fell. It was heaped as high as my waist and as big as a grand piano.

I remembered Meyer and looked over and saw him. He had wiggled into a sitting position, his back against a girder. I took a staggering step and caught myself.

"Pliers," Meyer said. "Hang on, Travis. For God's sake, hang on."

Pliers. I knew there wasn't time for pliers. The gray was coming in from every side, misting the windshield as before. I found my way toward him, fell, then crawled and reached his wrists. I bent the wire, turning it, freeing it. I saw a sharp end bite into the ball of my thumb, saw blood run, felt nothing. Just one more turn and then he could . . .

twenty-three

I was not entirely asleep and not yet awake, and I could not remember ever having been so completely, perfectly, deliciously relaxed. The girl voices brought me further across the line into being awake.

Rupe had said how very sweet their voices were, how touching, how heartbreaking, aboard the *Belle*. Their harmony was simple, their voices true and small.

"What a friend we have in Jeeeeee-zusss. All our sins and griefs to baaaaaaaare."

I wondered why the extraordinary crew of the *Hell's Belle* should select a number like that. Yet there was the tidy warmth of Teddie's thigh under the nape of my neck, a sweet, firm fit. Fabric over the thigh. I opened my eyes, and it was night. Light came slanting and touched the girl faces, touching their long, hanging hair. I realized I was on a blanket, and there was the unmistakable feel and consistency of dry sand under the blanket. Teddie's face was in shadow. I lifted a lazy, contented arm and put my hand over the young breast under thin fabric so close above my face. It had a sweet, rubbery firmness.

She took my wrist and pushed my hand down and said, "No, brother." They had stopped singing the words of the song. They were humming the melody. "He has awakened," the girl said. It was not Teddie's voice. They stopped singing.

A man's voice said, "How do you feel, brother?"

I raised my head. There were five or six of them in a glow of firelight. Bearded biblical men wrapped in coarse cloth. I had been hurled out of my historical time and place.

I sat up too quickly. I felt faint and bent forward to lower my head down between my knees.

A hand touched my shoulder. Meyer said, "I was trying to get you to a doctor and ran off into the sand. This one here is their healer, and he—"

"I was a third-year medical student when I heard the call. I'm the healer for the tribe on this pilgrimage mission."

I straightened and looked into a young bearded face. He nodded and took my pulse and nodded again. "We got that tar off your arm and hand with a solvent, brother, and treated your burn and dressed it."

My arm was wrapped with gauze. There was a bandage on my thumb. I turned my head and saw the beach buggies and several campers. A baby was crying in one of the campers.

I lay back very carefully. The thigh was there, cozy as before. The face leaned over me and looked down. "I will comfort you, brother, but no more grabbing me, huh?"

"No more, sister. I thought I was somewhere else with someone else. A . . . different group of girls."

"On a pilgrimage, too?"

"In a certain sense of the world, yes."

"There is only one sense, brother, when you give your heart and your soul and your worldly goods and all the days of your years to the service of almighty God."

"Did your . . . healer put vinegar on my burns?"

She giggled. "That's me you smell, brother. Blessed providence sent you and your friend to us this afternoon before I flipped right out of my tree. If it isn't sacrilege, my sisters and I are enjoying a peace that passeth understanding ever since."

I tried sitting up again, and there was no dizziness. One of the sisters brought me a cup of hot clam broth. She wore a garment like an aba, made out of some kind of homespun. She too smelled of vinegar. There was a crude cross around her neck with green stones worked into it. The automatic slide projector in my head showed me a slide entitled The Last Known Sight of Paul Dissat in This World. A small gold cross hung free around his straining throat.

After I drank the broth, I tried standing, and it worked reasonably well. They were not paying any special attention to me or to Meyer. We were welcome to be with them. Feel free to ignore and be ignored. Listen to the sweet singing, taste the broth, and praise the Lord.

I found the vinegar girl and gave her back her cup with thanks. Meyer and I moved away from the fire and from the lights in the campers.

"I panicked," Meyer said. "I got the rest of the wire off me and threw you in the damned car and drove like a maniac."

"Where is the car?"

"Up there on the shoulder. It was in deep. They pulled it out with a beach buggy."

"What about that limousine?"

"Good question. Joshua and I went back in there on his trail bike. The keys to it were on the desk in the office. We put the trail bike into the trunk. I locked everything in sight, and we were out of there before seven thirty. I took the long way around, and we left it at the West Palm airport, keys in the ashtray. Call it a Dissat solution. By the way, I made a contribution to the pilgrimage mission collection plate in both our names."

"That's nice."

"One of the wrapped stacks of hundreds from the Southern National. Initialed. Unbroken. There were four stacks in a brown paper bag on the desk in the warehouse office."

"What did Joshua say?"

"Thanks."

"No questions about the kind of help you asked of him?"

"Just one. He said that before he took the name of Joshua, he had clouted cars to feed his habit. He said all he wanted to know was whether, if we had committed a sin, we repented of it. I said that even though I didn't think of it as a sin, I was going to pray for forgiveness. That's when he nodded and said thanks and riffled the stack with his thumb and shoved it into the saddlebag on the trail bike. I walked out of the airport parking lot, and he drove the bike out and waited for me down the road from the airport. Long way around coming back here, too. I had the idea you'd be dead when I got here."

"Meyer?"

"Yes?"

"Get me home. Get me back to the *Flush*. Please."

"Let's say good night to the tribe."

I did a lot of sleeping. I was getting to be very good at it. I could get up at noon, shower, work up a big breakfast, and be ready for my nap at three. The gray fog rolled way back into the farthest corners of my mind. People left me alone. Meyer made certain of that. He passed the word McGee has pulled the hole in after him. And he bites.

Meyer would come over during that part of each day when I was likely to be up and about.

We'd walk over and swim. We would come back and play chess. I did not want to be among people. Not yet. So he would cook, or I would cook, or he would go out and bring something back.

The longer we delayed the decision, the easier it was to make. The random parts fell together in a pattern we could find no reason to contradict. Harry Broll had grabbed his three-hundred-thousand loan in case and fled with Lisa, the girl friend he had promised to give up. Except for some irate creditors nobody was looking for him diligently. Harry's wife had been reported missing in the Windward Islands, presumed drowned while swimming alone. Paul Dissat was missing too, possibly by drowning, but in his case it would more likely be suicide, emotional depression, and anxiety over some kind of disease of the blood. He had requested sick leave.

Jillian had been astoundingly sweet and helpful and had even lived up to her promise to ask no questions. She had flown down to Grenada and stayed a few days and with the knowing assistance of an attorney friend had obtained my packet from the hotel safe and my other possessions from their storage room.

The favor was, of course, Jilly's concession to apology, to regret. When she and her new friend got back from Grenada, she came over with him to give me back my belongings. They had a drink with us, and they did not stay long. Meyer arrived before they left.

"I keep forgetting his name," Meyer said later.

"Foster Cramond. Still a close personal friend of both his ex-wives."

"Rich ex-wives."

"Of course."

"Likable," Meyer said judiciously. "Good manners. No harm in him. Good at games, what? Court tennis, polo, sailing. Splendid reflexes. Did you notice the fast draw with that solid gold lighter? Twelfth of a second. Interesting phenomenon when they looked at each other."

"What? Oh, you mean the visible steam that came out of her ears? And the way he went from a sixteen collar to an eighteen? Yes. I noticed."

"Travis, what was your reaction when you met her new friend?"

"Relief at not running into some big fuss about breaking my word to visit her for a week. And . . . some indignation, I guess. In all honesty, some indignation."

"And you wished you could change your mind again?"

I let his question hang in the air for a long time, for three moves, one involving tightening my defense against his queen's bishop. I found a response that created a new problem for him. While he was studying it, I leaned back.

"About changing my mind. No. My instincts hadn't turned bad when Harry came here. He had no intention of shooting me. So let's suppose I'm slower by half a step or a full step. Maybe I'm old enough and wise enough to move into positions where I don't need the speed. The only thing I know is that I am going to run out of luck in the future, just as I have in the past. And when I run out, I am going to have to make myself some luck. I know that what counts is the feeling I get when I make my own luck. The way I feel then is totally alive. In every dimension. In every possible way. It wouldn't have to be Jillian. I could lie back, watch the traffic, select a rich lady, and retire myself to stud. But that would be half-life. I have an addiction. I'm hooked on the smell, taste, and feel of the nearness of death and on the way I feel when I make my move to keep it from happening. If I *knew* I could keep it from happening, there'd be no taste to it all."

Meyer gave that a lot of thought, and then he gave the game a lot of thought. Finally he said, "When in doubt, castle." He moved his king into the short corner, the rook standing guard. "Travis, I am very very glad that you were able to make us some luck. I am glad to be here. But . . ."

"But?"

"Something else is wrong with you."

"I dream some rotten things. I've got my memory almost all straightened out. Picked up nearly all the cards off the floor and put them back in the right order. But I have real rotten dreams. Last night I was buying a shirt. The girl said it was made in the islands, and they weren't sized correctly and I should try it on. When I put it on and came out, I realized that it was exactly the same print that Lisa had worn that first night I knew her. A dashiki. As I started to tell the girl that I didn't want it, she came up to me quickly, and she reached out, and she snapped something onto the front of the shirt. It made a clack. It was a big, round, white thing, too heavy for the front of a shirt. I turned it around, and I saw that the sound had been the lower jaw of a skull being closed with the fabric caught between the teeth. It was a very white, polished, delicate skull, and at first it looked feral, some predator's skull. Then I knew it was Lisa's skull. I tried to get the girl to take it off, but she said it went with that particular shirt. No other shirt. Just that one. And I woke up."

"Good Christ," Meyer whispered softly.

"But usually I don't dream at all."

"Be thankful. Travis. Is something else wrong?"

"Yes."

"Do you have the words for it yet?"

"I think it's getting to the point where there will be words for it. When there are words, I'll try them on you."

"Are you going to check me with that knight? Go ahead. See what happens if you do."

———

On the following Sunday afternoon, a Sunday late in May, Meyer and I were over on the beach. When the wind died, it got uncomfortably hot in the sun, so we moved to a bench in the shade. I watched two lovely ladies approaching along the beach, consciously keeping shoulders back and tummies in as they strode along, laughing and talking. Elegant lassies. Total strangers. They were walking across the edge of my life and right back out of it, and I would never know them or touch them, nor two million nor ten million of their graceful sisters.

"Maybe I can put that problem into words now. But it's just a try. Maybe you can be patient?"

"How often do you see me impatient?"

"This starts with a word Rupe Darby used down in Grenada. A phrase, not a word. It designates a condition. Womaned out. He meant it in the physical sense. Total sexual depletion to the point where you think you never want to see another woman. I think I'm womaned out in a different way. All my love life is pre-Grenada, and that was a lifetime ago."

"So. Womaned out but not in a physical sense."

"God, no. Those two who just went by created the intended reaction. And I keep remembering how neat and warm the thigh of the little Jesus singer felt under the nape of my neck. Physical capacity is just dandy. No, Meyer. I feel foundered and wind broke in some other dimension of myself. I feel sick of myself as if the prospect of me in action would turn me off, way off."

"How?"

"Everything I thought I believed about making love to a woman sounds very stale. I hear myself talking to too many of them. There has to be affection, dear. Respect for each other. We must not hurt each other or anyone else, darling. There has to be giving on both sides and taking on both sides, honeybunch. Oh, Meyer, God help me, it all sounds like a glossy sales talk. I was kidding them, and I was kidding myself. Look. I was holding out a package deal. And on the bottom of the package in small print was the guaran-goddamn-tee. Mary Dillon picked up the package. I didn't force it on her. I just left it around where she'd see it. She picked it up, enjoyed the product, and then married Harry Broll, and now she's buried in a washout behind a seawall under transit-mix concrete. So something is wrong with the small print or the service contact or the damned sales force. Meyer. I just can't . . . I can't stand the thought of ever again hearing my own sincere, manly, loving, crap-eating voice saying those stale words about how I won't ever hurt you, baby, I just want to screw you and make you a more sincere and emotionally healthy woman."

"Travis, Travis, Travis."

"I know. But that's what's wrong."

"Maybe there is some new kind of industrial waste in the air we breathe."

"Fractionated honesty?"

"Don't suffer all over me, McGee. You are a good man. There is no man alive who is not partially jackass. When we detect some area of jackassery within ourselves, we feel discontent. Our image suffers."

"What should I do?"

"How do I know what you should do? Don't make me an uncle. Go get lost in the Out Islands and fish for a couple months. Go hire onto a tug and work yourself into a stupor. Take five thousand of what was in that brown bag and lease the *Hell's Belle* all by yourself for ten days. Take cold showers. Study Hindustani."

"Why are you getting sore?"

He bounded off the bench, whirled, bent over, yelled into my face,

"Who's getting sore? I'm not getting sore!" And he ran down to the water, bouncing hairily along, and plopped in and swam out.

Everyone was not acting like himself. Maybe there *was* some new kind of guck in the air lately.

By the time we had finished our swim, Meyer had gotten over his unusual tizzy. We walked slowly back across the bridge, and as we neared the *Flush* I could see a figure aboard her in the shade of the sun-deck overhang, sitting on the shallow little afterdeck.

I did not recognize her until we were within thirty feet. She lay asleep in the deck chair with the tidy, boneless look of a resting cat. There was a big red suitcase beside the chair and a matching red train case, both well scuffed by travel. She wore a little denim dress with white stitching. Her white sandals were on the deck under the chair. Her sleeping arm clamped her white purse against her.

Suddenly her eyes opened wide. There was no sleep-stunned transition. She leapt back into life and up onto her feet in the same instant, all smiling vitality. "Hey! McGee! It's me. Jeannie. Jeannie Dolan. I should have looked over on the beach, huh?"

I introduced them. Meyer said he had heard nice things about her. He seemed to approve of the lively mop of red-brown hair and the quick glinting of the gray-green eyes.

I unlocked the *Flush*, and we went in. She said, "Leave my stuff right there, unless you've got thieves. Hey, can I look around? Say, this is a great kind of boat, Trav! Look, is the timing bad? Am I in the way or anything? If you guys have something all lined up . . ."

"Nothing," Meyer said. "Nothing at all."

"Wow, what a great kitchen."

"Galley," I said.

She looked at me blankly. "Galley? They row those with big oars. And a man walking around with a whip. Do you row this thing, for God's sake?"

"Okay, Jeannie. It's a kitchen," I said.

"Does it have engines in it? I mean, it will cruise around and so forth?"

"And so forth," Meyer said, looking happier.

"Wow, would I ever like to go someplace on a boat like this."

"Where's your friend?" I asked her.

"Betsy? We got tossed out of that Casa de Playa by the bank that took over. Not we, just me. Because she was gone by then. She went back to cleaning teeth. For a widower dentist in North Miami."

"Vodka tonic for you?" I asked her.

"Exactly right! It's wonderful when people remember things, isn't it? What I'm going to do, I'm on my way back to Columbus. No, not back to Charlie, that creep. But I called my old job, and I can make enough money so I can save enough to fly to the Dominican Republic and get a quickie divorce, instead of beating my brains out down here."

"Won't you sit down, Jeannie?" I asked her.

"I'm too nervous and jumpy, dear. Whenever I impose on people, I get like this. I've got the bus schedule and all, and then I thought, Oh, what the hell, I wanted to see that McGee guy again and never did. A girl sometimes has to be brassy or settle for nothing, right?"

I looked at Meyer. He was wearing a very strange expression. I handed Jeannie her drink and said, "Sometimes a girl gets brassy at just exactly the right time, and she gets invited on a private cruise. What would you say to that?"

"Aboard this wonderful ship? Wow! I'd say yes so fast—"

"*Hold it!*" Meyer roared, startling her. He trotted over to her and with raised finger backed her over to a chair. She sat down on command, staring up at him with her mouth open.

"I am going to ask you some very personal questions, Mrs. Dolan."

"What's the *matter* with you, huh?"

"Have you been in a lot of emotional turmoil lately?"

"Me? Turmoil? Like what?"

"Are you at a crisis point in your life?"

"Crisis? I'm just trying to get myself a plain, ordinary, divorce-type divorce."

"Mrs. Dolan, do you feel like a pathetic little bird with a busted wing who has fluttered aboard, looking for patience, understanding, and gentleness and love which will make you well and whole again?"

She looked at me with wide, round eyes. "Does he get like this a lot, Travis?"

"Pay attention!" Meyer ordered. "How do you relate to your analyst?"

"Analyst? Shrink? What do I need one for? Chee! You need one, maybe."

"Are you in love?" he asked.

"This minute? Hmmm. I guess not. But I sort of usually am. And pretty often, I guess. I'm not a real serious kind of person. I'm just sort of dumb and happy."

"One more question, and I must ask you both this one."

"You answer him, honey," Jeannie said to me.

"Would either of you two happy people mind too much if I spend the next few weeks in Seneca Falls, New York?"

"Speaking for the two of us, Meyer, I can't think of a serious objection, really."

He trotted to the doorway to the rear deck and opened it. He picked up the two pieces of red luggage and set them inside the door, gave us a maniacal smile, and slammed the door and was gone.

Jeannie stood up and sipped frowningly at her drink. Then she looked at me. "McGee?"

"Yes, dear."

"Everybody I know is acting weirder all the time. Have you noticed that too?"

"Yes, I have. Meyer isn't often like that."

"It's pretty weird and pushy for me to barge in on you like this. I'm not like this, really."

"It does have engines."

"That's nice. But do you feel like you've been maneuvered into something you'd just as soon not do, huh?"

"The more I think about it, the better I like it."

She put her drink down and came over and gave me one quick, thorough, and enthusiastic kiss. "There! Now it's just a case of getting acquainted, huh? Want to start by helping me unpack?"

We carried the luggage back to the master stateroom. She asked me what Meyer had meant about her having a broken wing. I said he was one of the last of the great romantics. I said there used to be two. But now there was just the one left. The hairy one.

The Long
Lavender Look

When I play with my cat, who knows but that she regards me more as a plaything than I do her?

—MICHEL EYQUEM DE MONTAIGNE

one

Late April. Ten o'clock at night. Hustling south on Florida 112 through the eastern section of Cypress County, about twenty miles from the intersection of 112 and the Tamiami Trail.

So maybe I was pushing old Miss Agnes along a little too fast. Narrow macadam. Stars above, and some wisps of ground mist below. But not much of it, and not often.

The big tires of the old blue Rolls pickup rumbled along the roughened surface. Big black drainage canal paralleling the road on the left side. Now and then an old wooden bridge arching across the canal to serve one of the shacky little frame houses tucked back in the swamp and skeeter country. No traffic. And it had been a long long day, and I was anxious to get back to Lauderdale, to Bahia Mar, to *The Busted Flush*, to a long hot shower and a long cold drink and a long deep sleep.

I had the special one-mile spots turned on. They are bracketed low on the massive front bumper. Essential for fast running through the balmy Florida nights on the straight narrow back roads, because her own headlights are feeble and set too high.

Meyer, beside me, was in a semidoze. We'd been to the wedding of the daughter of an old friend, at the fish camp he owns on Lake Passkokee. It is a very seldom thing to be able to drink champagne, catch a nine-pound bass, and kiss a bride all within the same hour.

Meyer had been giving me one of his lectures on the marital condition.

So I was whipping along, but alert for the wildlife. I hate to kill a raccoon. Urban Florida is using the rabies myth to justify wiping them out, with guns, traps, and poison. The average raccoon is more affable, intelligent, and tidy than the average meathead who wants them eliminated, and is usually a lot better looking.

It is both sad and ironic that the areas where the raccoon are obliterated are soon overrun with snakes.

I was alert for any reflection of my headlights in animals eyes in the darkness of the shoulders of the road, for any dark shape moving out into the long reach of the beams.

But I wasn't prepared for the creature of the night that suddenly appeared out of the blackness, heading from left to right, at a headlong run. At eighty, you are covering about a hundred and twenty feet per second. She was perhaps sixty feet in front of the car when I first saw her. So half of one second later, when I last saw her, she was maybe ten inches from the flare of my front right fender, and that ten inches was the product of the first effect of my reaction time. Ten inches of living space instead of that bone-crunching, flesh-smashing thud which, once heard, lingers forever in the part of the mind where echoes live.

And I became very busy with Miss Agnes. She put her back end onto the left shoulder, and then onto the right shoulder. The swinging headlights showed me the road once in a while. I could not risk touching the brake. This was the desperate game of steering with the skid each time, and feeding her a morsel of gas for traction whenever she was coming back into alignment with the highway. I knew I had it whipped, and knew that each swing was less extreme.

Then a rear tire went and I lost her for good. The back end came around and there was a shriek of rubber, crashing of brush, a bright cracking explosion inside my skull, and I was vaguely aware of being underwater, disoriented, tangled in strange objects, and aware of the fact that it was not a very good place to be. I did not feel any alarm. Just a mild distaste, an irritation with my situation.

Something started grabbing at me and I tried to make it let go. Then I was up in the world of air again, and being dragged up a slope, coughing and gagging, thinking that it was a lot more comfortable back under the water.

"You all right, Trav? Are you all right?"

I couldn't answer until I could stop retching and coughing. "I don't know yet."

Meyer helped me up. I stood, sopping wet, on the gravelly shoulder and flexed all the more useful parts and muscles. There was a strange glow in the black water. I realized Miss Agnes's lights were still on, and she had to be ten feet under. The light went off abruptly as the water shorted her out.

I found a couple of tender places where I had hit the wheel and the door, and a throbbing lump on my head, dead center, just above the hairline.

"And how are you?" I asked Meyer.

"I'm susceptible to infections of the upper respiratory tract, and I'd like to lose some weight. Otherwise, pretty good."

"In a little while I think I'm going to start being glad you came along for the ride."

"Maybe you'd have gotten out by yourself."

"I don't think so."

"I'd rather think so. Excuse me. Otherwise I have to share the responsibility for all your future acts."

"Do I ever do anything you wouldn't do, Meyer?"

"I could make a list?"

That was when the reaction hit. A nice little case of the yips and shudders. And a pair of macaroni knees. I sat down gently on the shoulder of the road, wrapped my arms around my legs, and rested my forehead on my wet knees.

"Are you all right, Trav?"

"You keep asking me that. I think I will be very fine and very dandy. Maybe five or ten minutes from now."

It seemed very very quiet. The bugs were beginning to find us. A night bird yawped way back in the marshland. Vision had adjusted to the very pale wash of starlight on the road and on the black glass surface of the drainage canal.

Miss Agnes was down there, resting on her side, facing in the direction from which we had come, driver's side down. Sorry, old lady. We gave it a good try, and damned near made it. Except for the tire going, you did your usual best. Staunch, solid, and, in a very dignified way, obedient. Even in extremis, you managed to keep from killing me.

I got up and gagged and tossed up half a cup of swamp water. Before he could ask me again, I told Meyer I felt much improved. But irritable.

"What I would dearly like to do," I said, "is go back and find that moronic female, raise some angry welts on her rear end, and try to teach her to breathe under water."

"Female?"

"You didn't see her?" I asked him.

"I was dreaming that I, personally, Meyer, had solved the gold drain dilemma, and I was addressing all the gnomes of Zurich. Then I woke up and we were going sideways. I found the sensation unpleasant."

"She ran across in front of us. Very close. If I hadn't had time to begin to react, I'd have boosted her with the right front fender, and she would be a piece of dead meat in a treetop back there on the right side of the road."

"Please don't tell me something."

"Don't tell you what?"

"Tell me she was a shrunken old crone. Or tell me she looked exactly like Arnold Palmer. Or even tell me you didn't get a good look at her. Please?"

I closed my eyes and reran the episode on my little home screen inside my head. Replay is always pretty good. It has to be. Lead the kind of life where things happen very quickly and very unexpectedly, and sometimes lethally, and you learn to keep the input wide open. It improves the odds.

"I'd peg her at early to middle twenties. Black or dark brown hair, that would maybe have been shoulder length if she wasn't running like hell. She had some kind of ribbon or one of those plastic bands on her hair. Not chunky, but solid. Impression of good health. Not very tall. Hmm. Barefoot? I don't really know. Maybe not, unless she's got feet like rhino hide. Wearing a short thing, patterned. Flower pattern? Some kind of pattern. Lightweight material. Maybe one of those mini-nightgowns. Open down the front and at the throat, so that it was streaming out behind her, like her dark hair. Naked, I think. Maybe a pair of sheer little briefs, but it could have been just white hide in contrast to the suntanned rest of her. Caught a glint of something on one wrist. Bracelet or watch strap. She was running well, running hard, getting her knees up, getting a good swing of her arms into it. A flavor of being scared, but not in panic. And not winded. Mouth closed. I think she had her jaw clamped. Determination. She was running like hell, but away from something, not after it. If she started a tenth of a second earlier, we'd be rolling east on the Trail by now. A tenth of a second later, and she'd be one dead young lady, and I could have racked Miss Agnes up a little more solidly, and maybe you or I or both of us would be historical figures. Sorry, Meyer. Young and interestingly put together, and perhaps even pretty."

He sighed. "McGee, have you ever wondered if you don't emit some sort of subliminal aroma, a veritable dog whistle among scents? I have read about the role that some scent we cannot even detect plays in the reproductive cycle of the moth. The scientists spread some of it on a tree limb miles from nowhere, and within the hour there were hundreds upon hundreds of . . ."

He stopped as we both saw the faraway, oncoming lights. It seemed a long time before they were close enough for us to hear the drone of the engine. We stepped into the roadway and began waving our arms. The sedan faltered, and then the driver floored it and it slammed on by, accelerating. Ohio license. We did not look like people anybody would want to pick up on a dark night on a very lonely road.

"I was wearing my best smile," Meyer said sadly.

We discussed probabilities and possibilities. Twenty miles of empty road from there to the Tamiami Trail. And, in the other direction, about ten miles back to a crossroads with darkened store, darkened gas station. We walked back and I tried to pinpoint the place where the girl had come busting out into the lights, but it was impossible to read black skid marks on black macadam. No lights from any house on either side. No little wooden bridge. No driveway. Wait for a ride and get chewed bloody. So start the long twenty miles and hit the first place that shows a light. Or maybe get a ride. A remote maybe.

Before we left we marked Miss Agnes's watery resting place by wedging a long heavy broken limb down into the mud and jamming an aluminum beer can onto it. Miracle metal. Indestructible. Some day the rows of glittering cans will be piled so high beside the roads that they will hide the billboards which advertise the drinkables which come in the aluminum cans.

Just before we left I had the final wrench of nausea and tossed up the final cup of ditchwater. We kept to the middle of the road and found a fair pace. By the time our shoes stopped making sloppy noises, we were swinging along in good style.

"Four miles an hour," Meyer said. "If we could do it without taking a break, five hours to the Tamiami Trail. By now it must be quarter to eleven. Quarter to four in the morning. But we'll have to take a few breaks. Add an hour and a half, let's say. Hmm. Five-fifteen."

Scuff and clump of shoes on the blacktop. Keening orchestras of tree toads and peepers. *Gu-roomp* of a bullfrog. Whine song of the hungry mosquito keeping pace, then a *whish* of the fly whisk improvised from a leafy roadside weed. Jet going over, too high to pick out the lights. Startled caw and panic-flapping of a night bird working the canal for his dinner. And once, the eerie, faraway scream of a Florida panther.

The second car barreled by at very high speed, ignoring us completely, as did an old truck heading north a few minutes later.

But a good old Ford pickup truck came clattering and banging along, making the anguished sounds of fifteen years of bad roads, heavy duty, neglect, and a brave start on its second or third trip around the speedometer. One headlight was winking on and off. It slowed down as if to stop a little beyond us. We were over on the left shoulder. I could see a burly figure at the wheel.

When it was even with us, there was a flame-wink at the driver's window, a great flat unechoing bang, and a pluck of wind an inch or less from my right ear. When you've been shot at before, even only once, that distinctive sound which you can hear only when you are right in front of the muzzle is unmistakable. And if you have heard that sound several times, and you are still alive, it means that your reflexes are in good order. I had hooked Meyer around the waist with my left arm and I was charging like a lineman when I heard the second bang. We tumbled down the weedy slope into the muddy shallows of the canal. The truck went creaking and thumping along, picking up laborious speed, leaving a smell of cordite and hot half-burned oil in the night air.

"Glory be!" said Meyer.

We were half in the water. We pulled ourselves up the slope like clumsy alligators.

"They carry guns and they get smashed and they shoot holes in the road signs," I said.

"And they scare hitchhikers and laugh like anything?"

"The slug was within an inch of my ear, old friend."

"How could you know that?"

"They make a little kind of thupping sound, which would come at the same time as the bang, so if it was further away from my car, I wouldn't have heard it. If he'd fired from a hundred yards away, you'd have heard it, too. And if it had been a sniper with a rifle from five hundred yards, we'd have heard a whirr and a thup and then the shot."

"Thank you, Travis, for the information I hope never to need."

He started to clamber the rest of the way up and I grabbed him and pulled him back. "Rest awhile, Meyer."

"Reason?"

"If we assume it is sort of a hobby, like jacking deer, he is rattling on out of our lives, singing old drinking songs. If it was a real and serious intent, for reasons unknown, he will be coming back. We couldn't find where the young lady busted out of the brush, but we didn't have headlights. He does, and he may be able to see where we busted the weeds. So now we move along the slope here about thirty feet to the south and wait some more."

We made our move, found a more gradual slope where we didn't have to keep our feet in the water. Settled down, and heard the truck coming back. Evidently he had to go some distance to find a turnaround place. Heard him slow down. Saw lights against the grasses a couple of feet above our heads. Lights moved on beyond us. the truck slowing down to a walk. Stopped. The engine idled raggedly. I wormed up to where I could part the grasses and look at the rear end of the truck. Feeble light shone on a mudsmeared Florida plate. Couldn't read any of it. Engine and lights were turned off. Right-hand wheels were on the shoulder. Silence.

I eased back down, mouth close to Meyer's ear. "He better not have a flashlight."

Silence. The bugs and frogs gradually resumed their night singing. I held my breath, straining to hear any sound. Jumped at the sudden rusty bang of the truck door.

I reached cautiously down, fingered up a daub of mud, smeared my face, wormed up the slope again. Could make out the truck, an angular shadow in the starlight, twenty feet away.

"Orville! You hear me, Orville?" A husky shout, yet secretive. A man shouting in a whisper. "You all alone now, boy. I kilt me that big Hutch, right? Dead or close to it, boy. Answer me, Orville, damn you to hell!"

I did not like the idea of announcing that there was nobody here named Orville. Or Hutch.

Long silence. "Orville? We can make a deal. I got to figure you can hear me. You wedge that body down good, hear? Stake it into the mud. Tomorrow you call me on the telephone, hear? We can set up a place we can meet and talk it all out, someplace with enough people nearby neither of us has to feel edgy."

I heard a distant, oncoming motor sound. The truck door slammed again. Sick slow whine of the starter under the urging of the fading battery. Sudden rough roar, backfire, lights on, and away he went. Could be two of them, one staying behind and waiting, crouched down on the slope, aching to put a hole in old Orville.

I told Meyer to stay put. Just as the northbound sedan went by, soon to overtake the truck, I used the noise and wind of passage to cover my sounds as I bounded up and ran north along the shoulder. I had kept my eyes squeezed tightly shut to protect my night vision. If anyone were in wait, I hoped they had not done the same. I dived over the slope just where the truck had been parked, caught myself short of the water. Nobody.

Climbed back up onto the road. Got Meyer up onto the road. Made good time southward, made about three hundred yards, stopping three or four times to listen to see if the truck was easing back with the lights out.

Found a reasonably open place on the west side of the road, across from the canal. Worked into the shadows, pushed through a thicket. Found open space under a big Australian pine. Both of us sat on the springy bed of brown needles, backs against the bole of the big tree. Overhead a mockingbird was sweetly, fluently warning all other mockingbirds to stay the hell away from his turf, his nest, his lady, and his kids.

Meyer stopped breathing as audibly as before and said, "It is very unusual to be shot at on a lonely road. It is very unusual to have a girl run across a lonely road late at night. I would say we'd covered close to four miles from the point where Agnes sleeps. The truck came from that direction. Perfectly reasonable to assume some connection."

"Don't upset me with logic."

"A deal has a commercial implication. The marksman was cruising along looking for Orville and Hutch. He did not want to make a deal with both of them. He knew they were on foot, knew they were heading south. Our sizes must be a rough match. And it is not a pedestrian area."

"And Hutch," I added, "was the taller, and the biggest threat, and I moved so fast he thought he'd shot me in the face. And, if he had a good, plausible, logical reason for killing Hutch, he wouldn't have asked Orville to stuff the body into the canal and stake it down."

"And," said Meyer, "were I Orville, I would be a little queasy about making a date with that fellow."

"Ready to go?"

"We should, I guess, before the mosquitoes remove the rest of the blood."

"And when anything comes from any direction, we flatten out in the brush on this side of the road."

"I think I will try to enjoy the walk, McGee."

"But your schedule is way the hell off."

So we walked. And were euphoric and silly in the jungly night. Being alive is like fine wine, when you have damned near drowned and nearly been shot in the face. Perhaps a change of angle of one degree at the muzzle would have put that slug through the bridge of my nose. So we swung along and told fatuous jokes and old lies and sometimes sang awhile.

two

At the first light of oncoming dawn, just when the trees were beginning to assume shape and identity, we came out at the intersection of Florida 112 and the Tamiami Trail. There was a big service station and garage across the main highway. The night lights were on. The sign over the office door said: MGR: AL STOREY.

Traffic was infrequent, and very fast. I was heartened to see a squat, muscular wrecker with big duals on the rear, and a derrick with a power hoist. It was going to take muscle to pluck Miss Agnes out of the canal. The more muscle, the less damage to her.

We looked the place over. Coke machine and a coin dispenser for candy bars and cheese crackers and such. I found a piece of wire and picked the lock on the men's room. We washed up. There was no other building within sight. Management had thoughtfully provided a round cement table and benches off to one side, with a furled beach umbrella stuck down through the hole in the middle of the table.

As half an orange sun appeared over the flat horizon, off in the direction of Miami, we sat at the table and ate our coin-slot breakfast and spread the contents of the wallets on the cement top to dry. Licenses and money. The mosquitoes had welted us abundantly, but I knew the evidence would disappear quickly. There is a kind of semi-immunity you acquire if you live long enough in mosquito country.

The itch is caused by the blood-thinner they inject, so they can suck the mixed fluids up their narrow snouts. But the redbug bites are something else. No immunity there. We both had them from ankles to groin. The itch of the chigger bite lasts so long that the mythology says they lay eggs under the skin. Not so. It is a very savage itch, and the only way to cut the weeks down to a few days is to use any preparation containing a nerve-deadening agent, along with a cortisone spray. The sun warmed us and began to dry the money. More cars and trucks began to barrel through with fading Doppler whine. A flock of ground doves policed the area. I scratched the chigger bites and thought of a big deep bed with clean white sheets.

At twenty of seven an oncoming VW panel delivery slowed and turned in and parked on the other side of the building. Two men in it, both staring at us as they passed out of sight. The money and papers were dry enough. We gathered them up and started toward the front of the place and met one of the men at the corner of the building. A spry wiry fifty. Khakis, baseball cap, with AL embroidered in red over the shirt pocket. I could hear the twanging and banging as the other man was sliding the big overhead doors up.

"You broke down someplace?" Al asked. It was complimentary. We did not look as if we could afford to operate a bicycle.

"We went into the canal last night, a ways up 112."

"Lots of them do," said Al. "Narrer road with a lot of lumps in it. Lots of them don't get out of the car neither. Let me get the place opened up, and when my other man comes on we'll see about getting you out."

"Hope you don't mind," I said. "I slipped the lock on your men's room so we could clean up."

He gave me a quick and narrow look and went quickly to the door to the men's room and inspected the lock. He found the right key in his pocket and tried it. "Long as you didn't bust nothing, okay. How'd you do it?"

"Piece of wire."

"That there's supposed to be a good lock."

"If it was, I couldn't get in. It looks good, but it's builders' junk. If you've got the same junk on your main doors, you better get them changed."

With a certain suspicion and reluctance he thanked me and hurried off to get his station set up. I wandered around. The place was well run. Tidy and clean, tools in the right places, paperwork apparently under control. The other fellow was big and young. It said

TERRY on his pocket. Snug trousers and tapered shirt and big shoulders. Face that could have looked handsome in a rugged way, but the eyes were set too close together, and the chin receded just enough to keep the mouth ajar. So he merely looked tough, coarse, and dumb. They were beginning to get some gas trade and some diesel fuel business.

Then a Highway Patrol sedan stopped at the near island. Al went to take care of it, then called and waved me over. The trooper was older than average, and heavier than average, with a broad red face and very large dark sunglasses.

He asked me if I was the owner and then if I had my license and registration. Then he sighed and dug around for the proper form and we went inside the station and used Al's desk.

After copying the information off my license, he studied the registration. Miss Agnes's age apparently upset him. "A Rolls Royce what?"

"Well, a custom pickup. I mean somebody turned it into a pickup truck a long time back."

"Is it worth all the trouble and the expense to get it out of where it is, McGee?"

"She . . . uh . . . it has a certain sentimental value."

"Pass the inspection? Got the sticker on the windshield?"

"All in order, officer."

He sighed again. "Okay. Any other vehicle involved?"

"No."

"Where and when did it happen?"

"About twenty miles north of here on Route 112. A little after ten o'clock last night. I was heading south."

"How fast?"

"Sixty to sixty-five."

"In a crock that old?"

"She's very able, officer."

"You were driving and your friend there was with you. And you were going sixty-five and no other vehicles were involved and you put it into the canal?"

"Not exactly like that. A woman ran across the road directly in front of me. She came out of nowhere. I had to swerve to keep from hitting her."

"Sure you didn't?"

"Absolutely positive. I nearly lost it right there. I was all over the road trying to bring my car out of it. I finally started to make it.

Then a rear tire blew and that did it. She went in fairly easy. It's in about ten feet of water, aiming back the way we came, resting on the left side. We got out of it. Then we came here and waited until Al showed up to open up."

"Point of departure and destination."

"We were coming from Lake Passkokee and going home to Lauderdale."

"Twenty miles north from here would put you in Cypress County. Here. This copy is yours. Al will probably call them on his radio when he's in range. If Sher'f Norm Hyzer has a car come out to look it over, this is your proof you turned in the accident report. And maybe your insurance will want to take a look at it, too."

He went out to his car. I saw him talk into the hand mike and knew he was checking in to make sure there was nothing out on the car or the driver. It is standard procedure and seldom forgotten, as nothing makes a cop look sillier than finding out later that the plausible stranger is wanted for a bank job.

He talked for a long time, then reached in and hung the mike up, shoved his hat back a little with one paw, and unholstered the Police Positive with the other. "Okay. Both of you. Face down. Spread it out. Grab the back of your neck."

Quick, rough, thorough, and very cautious. Officer Nagle was a competent cop.

"What'd they do, Beef?" Al asked.

"I wouldn't hardly know. All I know is Norm wants 'em, and he'll be coming right along to get them."

"Isn't there something about rights?" I asked humbly.

"If I was the arresting officer, I'd read you what it says on the little card, McGee. But all I'm doing is detaining you, a professional favor for the sher'f of Cypress County. Move back there in the shade, and lean against the wall. Move a little further apart from each other, boys. That's fine."

"You're making a mistake," Meyer said.

He looked owlishly astonished. "Me? How can I be making a mistake doing what the man asks me to do, asks me nice? Any kind of mistake in this is all Norm Hyzer's, and I hear he doesn't make too many. Int that right, Al?"

"They seem to keep on electing him up there," Al said. From the tone I guessed he wasn't a Hyzer fan. He headed out to the island to take care of a dusty Buick with a noisy fan belt. The big young one named Terry stood and stared at us with vacuous, adenoidal intensity.

A blue Rambler came down Route 112, waited at the stop sign, then came across and parked beside the station. A broad brown man with a white grin got out. It said HENRY over the pocket of his coveralls. "Hey there, Beef. What's going on?"

"How come you can't hardly ever get here on time?" Al demanded.

"Now look, honest, I had a bad night, and I clean slept right through that alarm again, and . . ."

"And Hummer was promised the Olds at ten-thirty and you haven't even started on the brake job yet, so don't stand around asking dumb questions. I don't want Hummer so damn mad he starts yelling in my face again. He sprays spit."

Time passed. Traffic was picking up, but visibly and audibly slowing at the sight of the patrol car with the distinctive blue roof lights. Meyer started to say something to me, and Beef Nagle said politely that he'd rather we didn't carry on any conversation.

At last I heard the thin distant scream of an approaching siren. It came down 112, slowed a little at the sign and plunged across, swung and left rubber on the apron in a dramatic smoking stop. Green sedan with a red flasher on the roof. Cypress County Sheriff's Department. Sheriff Norman L. Hyzer. The man who climbed out quickly from behind the wheel wore a khaki uniform that said DEPUTY SHERIFF on the shoulder patch. Long lumpy face, sallow complexion, blond-red hair, and glasses with steel rims that did not give him the slightest look of bookish introspection.

So the other one had to be Hyzer. Late forties. Tall and slender and very erect. Black suit, shiny black shoes, crisp white shirt, dark blue necktie, gold wedding ring, white Stetson. He had dark hair and noble-hero face, expressionless. He kept the mouth pinched shut. The eyes were very blue, and his examination of each of us was long, intensive, unrevealing.

Next he examined the pocket-contents Nagle had taken from us, and the accident report Nagle had filled out. The occupations as listed on the Florida driver's licenses seemed to intrigue him.

"Salvage consultant?" he said in a deep, soft voice, barely audible over traffic sounds. "Economist?"

"Unlikely as it may seem at the moment," said Meyer in his best guest-lecturer delivery. It didn't match the bristled jowls, the mud-stained clothes and the sorry shoes.

"You have the right to remain silent. You have the right to legal counsel. If you cannot employ an attorney, one will be provided for you. If you choose to answer questions, anything you say may be used in evidence against you. Do you understand, McGee? Do you understand, Meyer?"

"We understand," I said. "We'll answer anything you want to ask. But it would be nice to know the charge."

"Suspicion of premeditated murder." His face showed nothing. Nothing at all regional about his voice. Not your stock Florida sheriff by any means. A lot of ice-cold class. Made me wonder why he was content to be sheriff of Cypress County, a lot of swamp and palmetto and maybe, by straining hard, twenty thousand people. "Get into the cruiser." His deputy opened the rear door and stepped back.

"I'd like to make arrangements about getting my car pulled out of the canal, Sheriff."

"We'd arrange that in any case, McGee."

"Can I show this man where it is?"

"We know where it is."

Al said, with a mocking smile, "And no damn need of my asking for the business, is there, Sher'f?"

"I hardly think so, Mr. Storey."

"Who got killed?" big Terry asked.

Hyzer hesitated, then said, "Frank Baither."

"Overdue," said Al Storey.

We got in. Steel mesh between us and the two in front. Safety glass at the sides, with no cranks and no inside door handles. The deputy picked a hole in the traffic and scatted across, and barreled it on up to ninety. Hyzer sat erect, silent, and motionless. A few miles along the road an egret came out of the brush on the canal side, tried for altitude and didn't quite make it. It thudded against the high right corner of roof and windshield. I looked back and saw the white feathers falling to the roadside like strange snow.

We were in a cage that smelled of green disinfectant and last week's vomit, and was going too fast. Meyer rode with his hands loosely clasped in his lap, eyes closed, half smile on his mouth, swaying and bouncing to the hard movements of the sedan.

Far ahead I saw vehicles and activity. The deputy waited a long time, then braked hard and pulled over. They both got out, banged the doors shut, and walked up to where a big blue-and-white wrecker was working. It was backed close to the edge of the canal. Traffic was blocked in both directions. On the side door of the wrecker was painted JOHNNY'S MAIN STREET SERVICE. The cable stretched down into black water, under tension as the big winch wound it up. There were some shouts and arm-waving. Then I saw the gleaming, stately, angular contours of the front of Miss Agnes appear.

"They're doing it just right," I told Meyer. "Stood her up on the back end and the angle brought the wheels right onto the bank."

"Hooray," he muttered.

"They've got the wheels cramped right, so they can bring her up and out in one swing."

"How marvelous."

"Usually you enjoy seeing something done well, Meyer."

"I do not like this, not any part of this."

Neither did I, and maybe not for the same reasons. The wrecker eased forward and brought Miss Agnes out swiftly, gently, and deftly. Made the turn away from us, and pulled over onto the shoulder. The few cars and trucks that had waited were waved on. Hyzer spent a long time checking over old Miss Agnes. The cruiser was getting up to baking temperature inside, sweat popping out and rolling down.

At last they came back and got in. I asked about damage. Nobody answered. On the way to Cypress City we swung out and passed Miss Agnes. She looked a little crumpled around the corners, and there were bright green strings of algae across her windshield and hood. I was happy to see that somebody had been sportsman enough to put the spare on. It would have hurt a little to see her clopping along on the rim.

We couldn't give answers until they came up with the questions. And then it would be apologies, smiles, handshakes.

Maybe.

three

It was a little after noon when a fat elderly deputy brought me a cold and greasy cheeseburger wrapped in waxed paper, and a cardboard container of tepid coffee with too much sugar and cream already in it.

"Why the delay?" I asked. "What's going on?"

"Beats me, friend," he said, and went out and locked the door behind him. It was a small room with a heavy table bolted to the floor, heavy benches bolted to the plaster walls, wire mesh over the ceiling light and over the single window. The window was on the second floor of the Moorish structure. It looked out across a narrow courtyard at another wing of the U-shaped building. The floor of the room was asphalt tile in a mottled tan and green. The walls were yellow tan. I had opened a shallow drawer in the heavy table and found it full of dead cigar stubs and burned matches. Distant sounds of traffic. Radio rock in the distance, on a cheap set. Bird sounds. The room was too warm. I improvised a pillow by rolling my shoes in my shirt, stretched out on the bench, and dozed off.

"Come on," said the deputy with the steel glasses. I stretched and yawned, rolled the stiffness out of my shoulders, worked my way into the shirt and shoes.

"You got a name?" I asked him.

"Billy. Billy Cable."

"From around here?"

"All my life. He's waiting on us. Come on."

He directed me ahead of him to different stairs than I had used coming up. "He said to take you the long way around."

The long way around included a short side trip into the county jail. Billy said this was a brand new part of it, new just three years ago. And these were the maximum security cells. Very bright overhead lights. About five by eight, with a bunk, a sink, a toilet. Meyer sat on the low bunk, hunched forward, head bowed, forearms braced on his knees. The thick, slow, half-clotted blood dripped from his mouth to the cement between his bare feet, into a small puddle as big around as a saucer.

I said his name. He looked up slowly, tilting his head to bring the one slit of one eye to bear. The crushed mouth said, "I still don't like any part of it, McGee."

As I turned on Billy he moved back swiftly, hand on the holster. "Easy now. Easy," he said.

"*Why*, goddammit!"

"You better ask him about that when you see him, McGee."

Hyzer's office was austere. Bare walls, bare desktop, blue carpeting. Efficient air conditioning made it very chilly. I was directed to a straight chair placed about six feet back from the edge of Hyzer's desk, which put me in almost the exact center of the room. A very large deputy sat on another straight chair placed against the wall just inside the door. He looked vaguely familiar to me, but I couldn't come up with the association. Big freckled arms folded. Belly sagging over the belt. Broad, soft, drowsy face.

When I was seated, Sheriff Norman Hyzer said. "This session is being recorded on magnetic tape. When it is transcribed some minor editing will be done to eliminate repetitions. If you have any question regarding the accuracy of the transcription, you will be permitted to listen to the pertinent portion of the recording to satisfy yourself."

"May I make a comment for the record?"

"Go right ahead."

"My friend Meyer is a reputable economist internationally known in his field. He is a gentle person, without malice or enemies, or police record of any kind. We planned to cooperate with you, Sheriff. Get it settled and be on our way. But now you have bought the whole package, Hyzer. I am going to personally nail you to the wall, if it takes five years. From now on I'm coming at you. I'm bringing it to you."

The big deputy sighed and belched. Hyzer opened his pocket notebook. "First interrogation of Travis McGee. Fourteen-forty hours. April 24. Pritchard monitoring tape. Sturnevan witnessing interrogation. Now then. From whom did you hear that Frank Baither had been, or was about to be, released from Raiford State Prison, and, to the best of your recollection, tell me the date on which you received this information?"

"The only previous time in my life I ever heard the name Frank Baither was when you said that name this morning in front of Al's service station, Hyzer."

"Was there a third man with you last night?"

"You're playing your game, Hyzer. The officer of the law. The professional. *If* you were a professional instead of a swamp county ham actor, you'd find out who we are, where we were yesterday, and where we were heading. You'd verify the girl running across the road. You'd make a couple of phone calls. Not you. No, sir. Don't confuse yourself with logic. Net result is you aren't going to play sheriff much longer."

"An unidentified woman ran across the road. We found the place where she crouched in the ditch. Bare footprints in the mud. A place where she braced herself, making an imprint of the knuckles of her right hand. We used the skid marks to locate the area. Sooner or later we'll locate her body."

"She's dead?"

"She almost got across, but you swerved and probably hit her."

"Now why did I do that, Sheriff?"

"Because she was with Baither and saw you and got away from you and you people had to hunt her down."

"With an old Rolls, for God's sake?"

"And you lost control when a tire blew."

"Hyzer, you are having dreams and visions and fantasies. I will tell you who to phone at Lake Passkokee. I will pay for the call. He is an old friend. We went to the wedding of his eldest daughter. He has a fish camp. We went bass fishing. There were rods in that car of mine. And three fresh-cleaned bass on ice."

"Deputy Billy Cable says they were fresh enough."

"Will you phone?"

"This is a small county, McGee. And I am in a small job at small pay. But I am not a fool. Four years ago you people, along with

Frank Baither, planned that job down to the last small detail. And there was just as much at stake now as then. More, because this time you had to kill one you knew of, and one you didn't. First things first. When the time comes to dismantle your alibi, it will fall apart. You know it and I know it. Please stop making speeches. Answer my questions. Was there a third man with you last night?"

"Meyer and I were alone."

"Did Meyer finish him off with the ice pick or did you?"

"Hyzer, the car went into the ditch, and we got out of it by great good fortune, and we walked all the way down to the Tamiami Trail to that station where you found us."

"That is most unlikely, McGee. We had an anonymous call at one in the morning. A man, whispering to disguise his voice. He said Frank Baither phoned him every night at midnight, and if some night there was no call, and no one answered at the Baither place, he was to call the law. He went out there and found Baither still taped to that chair. From that time on I had cars on the road all night. You would have been stopped and questioned."

"There is very damned little traffic on that Route 112 after dark. And when we saw lights coming, we got out of sight."

"Now why would you do that?" He smiled for the first time. I think it was a smile. The corners of his mouth went up about a sixteenth of an inch.

So I told him about the nut in the old truck who'd tried to pot us from the truck window, and thought he'd gotten one of us, thought he'd scragged somebody named Hutch, then tried to dicker with the survivor, somebody named Orville. I said it happened about one hour and four miles south of where I had put Miss Agnes into the canal.

"Describe the truck."

"An old Ford pickup, rough, noisy, and beat. I think it was red. A junker. Not worth licensing."

He slowly turned the pages of his pocket note book. "So, being the innocent law-abiding citizens you people claim to be, you made no attempt to report somebody trying to kill you, either at the time or this morning to either Officer Nagle or to me."

"Sheriff, neither of us saw the man. The plate was too dirty and the light too weak to read the number. You know your own county better than I do. There are probably a lot of fine citizens living back in the boonies off that road. And there are some very rough ones too, nativeborn swamp rats and poachers, and people that came a long way to find a place where they're not likely to be found. A long time ago I spent one weekend here in Cypress City, and after I saw how Saturday night was shaping up, I went back to the motel room and put my cash money in the Gideon and went back out with one ten-dollar bill and had what you could call a memorable evening. I don't really much care if your people kill each other, Hyzer. We were just making certain they didn't kill us and then feel apologetic because the dead bodies didn't turn out to be Hutch and Orville. There wasn't any phone booth handy after that clown drove off in his junk truck. I thought of a way I could attract official attention. We could have walked back four miles and I could have dived down and gotten my tow chain out of the tool compartment and heaved it up over the power lines. Then pretty soon we would have had the use of the CB radio in the Florida Power and Light truck that would show up. I thought of it, and I thought of making a neighborly call at the next house we came to. But I didn't like either of those ideas, Sheriff."

"McGee, you had bad luck, didn't you? When you lost that car in the canal, you went back to Frank Baither's place and tried to use his old Ford truck, but the battery was too far gone and you couldn't get it started. Then, while you were walking, you did some thinking. Somebody was going to spot that car sooner or later, and it could be traced to you, and that was a risk you couldn't accept. So you had to put something together that sounded good, and get Al Storey to hoist it out of the canal and tow it in."

"Hyzer, you are one dumb, blind, stubborn man."

"You have a good act, McGee. So does your partner. Aren't you wondering, a little, why you can't sell it to me?"

"More than a little."

"Then there must be a little more bad luck along with what you already know about. Bad luck or judgment. What could you have forgotten? Think about it."

I thought. "You must have something you like. I don't know what it could be. I will tell you one thing. Don't depend on it. Because whatever it is, it isn't going to prove what you think it proves, no matter how good it looks."

"You never saw or heard of Frank Baither in your life?"

"No."

"You were never inside his house?"

"Never."

"I am going to describe an exhibit to you. It will be a part of the file I am going to turn over to the State's attorney. It is an empty envelope addressed to you, at Bahia Mar, date-stamped a week ago, April 17. On the back of it, possibly in your hand, are some notes about highway numbers and street names. It had been folded twice, and had been immersed in water. Do you recognize it from the description?"

"I think so. Yes. I don't know where you're going with it, though. Jimmy Ames phoned me last Saturday and invited us to Betsy's wedding. He said that the road I'd normally take was closed, that a bridge was out. He gave me directions. I reached down into the wastebasket near the phone and took an envelope out and wrote down the directions. Get hold of him at Jimmy's Fish Camp. He'll verify it."

"When the call came in about the Baither murder, Deputy Cable phoned me at my home. I got dressed and drove to the Baither place. I supervised the investigation. After the county medical examiner had authorized the removal of the body, I posted Deputy Arnstead there to make certain nobody entered the premises before a more thorough daylight search could be made. I was on my way to participate in that search when the call came from Officer Nagle. After he described you and told me about where your car was, and said you had walked all the way to the Trail, I had no choice but to bring you in for questioning. I returned at eleven-fifteen to the Baither place and, with Deputy Arnstead, completed the search of the house and the area. The envelope was found on the floor of the room where Baither died."

So what do you do? The big soft sleepy deputy shifted in his chair, creaking it. One thing you do is stop thrashing and flapping. You back in a couple of steps, tuck the elbows in, get the jaw out of range.

"Question?" I asked.

"Can you change your mind about your rights? Yes. At any time."

"That wasn't what I was going to ask."

"What then?"

"I can tell you exactly what I did with that envelope, where, and when. But I don't know you, Hyzer. It's planted evidence. You had somebody dance Meyer around. I don't like the way you think. I don't like the way you do your job. If I don't want to answer any more questions, and if you have nothing to do with the plant, then you are going to be that much more convinced you've got the right people to make your case. But if I tell you about the envelope, and you are in on building the case against us any way you can, then you can listen to the truth and go plug the holes in your evidence. I don't even know if this *is* going onto tape and, if it is, whether you erase the ones you don't like. I'm boxed because I can't figure out what you are, so I don't know which way to go. You talk about some action four years ago, something we are supposed to have planned with this Baither. Check us out. There's no record of any convictions."

"Which means only that up until now you haven't made any serious mistakes, McGee."

"So *why*, Sheriff, would I go to all the trouble of faking up this wedding story and having the fishing gear and the bass in the car, just to come sneaking into your county after dark to knock off a recent graduate of Raiford? Where's the sense to it?"

"About nine hundred thousand dollars worth of sense, which you are quite aware of. And the chance you might have to go through a roadblock on your way out of the area with it. Misdirection, McGee. A car so conspicous no fool would use it for this kind of purpose. Fresh bass packed in ice. It should have worked, McGee."

So another shaft of light in the murk. That much money is worth a lot of care and attention and it could maybe buy a matched set of Hyzers.

"I think I'd better stop right now, Sheriff. I'd like to phone an attorney."

"A particular attorney?"

"Yes. In Miami. He'll accept a collect call."

"May I have his name?"

"Leonard Sibelius."

I looked for a change of expression. Nothing. He said, "You can make your call at nine o'clock tomorrow morning, McGee."

"Why not now? Isn't that a violation of my civil rights?"

"It would be if you'd been booked, and I'd turned your file over to the State's attorney for indictment by the grand jury. You chose to answer questions. You've been in custody for interrogation since eighty-forty hours this morning."

"Tomorrow is Saturday, Sheriff."

"The twenty-fifth. King, have Priskit put him in a single twelve or fourteen, and move somebody if he has to. I want no contact between McGee and Meyer."

I fitted the two parts of the big deputy's name together. King Sturnevan. I looked at him again and made sure. I'd seen him fight years ago at Miami Beach, at about two hundred then. Maybe sixty pounds heavier now. A spoiler, a mawler. Looked slow, but surprisingly hard to hit. Clever on the ropes and in the clinches, ripping those hooks up into the body, snuffing and grunting with the effort. Would have done better in the division except he had a tendency to cut, which put too many TKO's on his record. So the smart way they took him was to put the little twist of the wrist on the end of he jab, hoping to open up his brows before he bombed their innards to pulp.

"Sheriff, would you please tell this fat, sloppy, old pug not to try to do me the way he did Meyer? Lennie Sibelius can give you enough trouble without that, too."

"There were three witnesses to your partner's accident, McGee. He had taken his shower. He was stepping into the issue coveralls when he lost his balance and fell, striking his face on the wooden bench in the shower room."

"Then I guess if the same thing happened to me, it would look like a strange coincidence."

He didn't answer. He picked up the phone. Sturnevan beckoned to me and held the door open.

As we went along the corridor he said, "Hey, you knew me, huh? You seen me in there, ever?" His voice was soft, husky, high-pitched.

"Miami Beach, just once. Eight or nine years ago."

"That must have been close to the last. Who was I going with?"

"I can't remember the name. A great big Cuban boy."

"Sure! That was a ten-round main. Tigre something. Tigre means 'tiger,' and he had a big long last name, and I knocked him out in the ninth, right? You know what? That *was* the last one. Honest to Christ, that boy was, I mean, conditioned! Like an oak tree, the whole middle of him. He kept moving the wrong way and giving me perfect shots, and I couldn't even take the grin off his face. Then like twenty seconds into the ninth, he cut me. See this one? He popped it just right by dumb luck and opened it up, and I knew it was bad. All I could do, see, was keep turning to keep the ref from getting too good a look at it and hoping before he did, that boy would tangle his feet and move the wrong way again, so when he did I had to put the right hand right on the shelf. I knew it would bust and it did. But he stayed down. All the time I was in there, what I had was bad managers and bad hands. I had to go for the middle because my hands bust too easy. So you saw that one, hey! I was going to go again, all lined up with I forget who, and I bust the hand in the same place on the heavy bag, working out."

As we went down the stairs, I said, "But you didn't chop Meyer bad enough to hurt your hands?"

"He fell on the bench, like Mister Norm said."

"And his head bounced up and down on that bench like a big rubber ball. Must have been interesting to watch."

"What I can tell you is I didn't work him over. Mister Norm got on me about that, and I swore on my baby daughter's grave I never touched him and didn't see anybody else touch him. I told Mister Norm it didn't make sense after all the times I worked a little on some of the people without marking them, all of a sudden I forget how and start hitting a man in the head? Not me. Not the King. Right through here. Hey, Priskie? Fresh fish. Mister Norm says single twelve or fourteen."

"We can give you twelve, sir. A very nice room. I'm sure you'll be very happy with it. Anything you want, just ring." Priskitt was somewhere between fifty and ninety, spry, bald, and shrunken by the heat of time and fortune. He dug into a bin, selected a tagged bundle, put it in a wire gym basket. "All our guests wear costumes," he said. "Gets you in the spirit of the thing."

"Priskie, this here fellow saw my last fight, where I chilled the big Cuban kid and busted my hand. I told you about that one, right?"

"Not over forty times."

I said, "I don't want to spoil your comical routine, Priskitt, but how is Professor Meyer making it?"

"I got him some aspirin and some ice to suck on. I wouldn't say he feels great. But maybe not as bad as he did."

"I got to look in Nat's book and find out what the last name was on that Cuban kid," King said. "I'll get him showered. Come on, McGee. Tote that basket."

The cement shower room smelled of mildew, ammonia, and Lysol. There was a sliver of green soap and a drizzle of tepid water from a corroded shower head, and a thin gray towel.

What you need on the inside of any institution whatsoever are friends. "King, I'm a little ashamed of thinking you busted my friend up. I should have known you've got more class than that."

"Aw, what the hell. I mean I can see why."

"Breaks, sure. They woulda helped. But I coulda stood better the great ones. You know that? A few breaks here and there."

"No, really. I saw you fight. You could have been one of equipment. I cut too easy and my hands were brittle. But I could always move good, and I could take a punch off anybody."

"Where are you from originally?"

"New Jersey. Nutley. Fourteen years old, I was in the Golden Gloves. Fleet champion in the Navy, coming in light heavy. Had fourteen years pro, two in the amateurs. Ninety-one bouts. I win sixty-eight, lose seventeen, draw six. It's all in the record. McGee, what do you go? Maybe around two-o-eight?"

"Very close."

"The clothes on, I would have said one ninety, maybe less. You fooled me. You holding pretty good shape, fella. You ever do any fighting when you were a kid?"

"Nothing serious. Just horsing around."

"You can keep your own underwear. And put the coveralls and these here straw scuffs on and put your other stuff in the basket."

I did as directed. The twill coveralls had been washed threadbare, and they were soft as the finest lightweight wool.

"Come at me a little, McGee. I want to see if you know how to move. Good Christ, don't look at me like that! I'm not making up some kind of way to bust you up."

So I shrugged and went at him, doing my standard imitation of a big puppet badly manipulated from above, jounce and flap, keeping an assortment of elbows and shoulders and wrists in front of the places I don't like to have thumped, keeping a wide-focus stare aimed at his broad gut, because that is the only way you can see what the head and hands and feet are doing, all at the same time.

I don't know how many years older he was. He moved in a slow, skilled, light-footed prance, and the slabbed fat on his body jounced and shook like the pork fat on a circus bear. He held his big paws low and stayed pretty much in the same place. Had it been for real, I would have had as much chance against him as a little kid with a piece of lathe against a member of the Olympic fencing team. Pro is pro. I slapped empty space, sometimes a shoulder. Each effort of mine resulted in a quick little stinging whack of fingertips against jaw, cheekbone, rib cage. Then I decided to try to protect myself. But here is how it is with a pro: You duck under a high left jab, and you see the feet, body, shoulder, head, all moving into the logical right hook, and when you move to defend from that, you are suddenly open for two or more quick jabs. You shift to handle that, and there is the right hook you were going to block earlier, so you rush him to get inside, and he isn't there because he has twisted, tipped you off balance, and stands braced and ready for you to bounce back off the wall. Explosive snort. Grin. Hands raised in signal of peace.

So I gratefully emerged from my ineffective shell and said, "You are real quick, King."

"Hell, I'm slowed down to nothing. Reflexes all shot. Seems quick to you because I know where you're going to be by the time I tap you. Listen to me huff and puff. McGee, you would have made it pretty good if you started soon enough. It would be hard to take a good shot at you. I'd have to bomb you downstairs until you couldn't get your arms up. Then drop you."

He led me to the single cell, telling me, on the way, of the time he had come the closest to top ranking, when Floyd Patterson had nailed him as they came out for the second, and he had faked rubber legs well enough to bring Patterson in, too eager and careless, and he had pivoted and stuffed his big hand and glove deep into Floyd's tough middle, just above the belt, turning him gray and sweaty and very tired. Chased him for seven rounds, while Floyd had slowly regained his strength and health despite all King Sturnevan could do in the way of wearing him down. And then Floyd stabbed and chopped and split his way to the technical knockout.

He dogged the door shut, big face still rueful with the memory of not being able to nail down the disabled Patterson. I said, "What's with this sheriff of yours, King?"

"How do you mean?"

"What kind of an act is it?"

He shifted the wire basket to his other arm. "It's no act. Mister Norm upholds the law, and the County Commission backs him a hundred percent. We got modern stuff here, McGee. We got a teletype tied into FLEX, and one of the first things he did was see if there was any package on you with the F.C.I.C. and then the N.C.I.C., and it puzzled him some, maybe, to come up empty on both of you."

"Real modern methods, King, spoiling Meyer's face."

"All you got is my word, but it isn't like that around here."

"Then why did Deputy Billy Cable bring me through here to admire Meyer before he took me to Hyzer?"

"Billy got gnawed down to the bare bone on that one. He was off in the MP's for a while. Sometimes he forgets Mister Norm doesn't like those little tricks."

"Now how would you know Hyzer came down on Billy Cable?"

"You learn to read that man's face. It isn't easy, but you have to learn. I saw he was upset. And I could guess why. He'd already found out about Meyer, and he was upset about that, too, about it happening at all. By now he's got Billy all peeled raw."

"Who did it?"

"I didn't see a thing."

Priskitt came to the cell. "I thought this man had probably jumped you and made good his daring escape, champ. You want me to lock you there with him so you can keep the dialogue going, or do you want to go back to work? As a special favor to Mister Norm."

"He called for me?"

"He surely did."

And with a single bulge-eyed look of anxiety, King Sturnevan went off, in a light-footed, fat-jouncing trot.

"The department seems to have a plentitude of deputies, Mr. Priskitt."

He looked at me happily. "Plentitude. One rarely hears the good words around here, Mr. McGee. I would say that Mister Norm has an adequacy of deputies. Not a superfluity. Whatever Mister Norm feels is necessary for the pursuit of his sworn responsibility, he asks for. And gets. We must chat later."

He hurried away and I stretched out. . . .

four

Immovable bunk and a thin hard mattress pad. Cement floor with a center drain. Bright bulb countersunk behind heavy wire mesh in the cement ceiling. Iron sink with a single iron faucet and no drainpipe so that water from the sink would run down the pitch of the floor to the drain three feet away. Toilet with no lid or seat. No window. No way to see any other cell through the top half of the door which was of sturdy bars. The lower half was steel plate.

Stretch out on the back, forearm across the eyes. Shove the whole damned mess over into a corner cupboard and kick the door shut. Save it until later, because trying to think about it would only bring the anger back. Angry men do a bad job of thinking.

There had been a lot of waiting-time in my life. Sometimes it was cat-time, watching the mouse hole for all the endless dreary hours. Sometimes it had been mouse-time, waiting all the day through the darkness and the time for running.

So you learn the special resources of both memory and imagination. You let the mind run through the old valleys, the back hills, and pastures of your long-ago years. You take an object. Roller skate. The kind from way back, that fastened to the shoes instead of coming with shoes attached. Look and feel and design of the skate key. With old worn shoes you turn the key too much and you start to buckle the sole of the shoe. Spin one wheel and listen to the ballbearinged whir, and feel the gritty texture of the metal abraded by the sidewalks. Remember how slow and strange and awkward it felt to walk again, after all the long Saturday on skates, after going way to the other end of town. Remember the soreness where the strap bit into the top of your ankle. When it got too sore, you could stop and undo the strap and run it through the top laces of your shoe. Thick dark scab on the abraded knee. The sick-making smack of skull against sidewalk. Something about the other end of the skate key. . . Of course! A hex wrench orifice that fit the nut on the bottom of the skate so you could expand it or contract it to fit the shoe. If you didn't tighten it enough, or if it worked loose, then the skate would stealthily lengthen, the clamps no longer fitting the edge of the shoe sole, and at some startling moment the next thrust would spin the skate around, and you either took one very nasty spill, or ended up coasting on the good skate, holding the other foot with dangling skate up in the air until you came to a place to sit down and get the key out and tighten everything again. Roller skate or sandbox or apple tree or cellar door. Playground swing or lumberyard or blackboard or kite string. Because that was when all the input was vivid. All of it is still there. So you find a little door back there, and like Alice, you walk through it into the magic country, where each bright flash of memory illuminates yet another.

It doesn't work that way for everybody. Once I worked a stakeout for two months with a quiet little man. We were talked out after two days. But he seemed totally patient, totally content. After a month I asked him what he thought about. He said he was a rubber bridge addict. So mentally he would deal himself a random hand, then out of the thirty-nine cards left, deal a random hand to the opponent at his left, then to the one at his right, and give what was left to his partner. Then he would go through the bidding, the play of the cards, and mark the result on the running scorepad in his head. He said that sometimes when he was a little fatigued, he might forget whether the jack of diamonds had been dealt at his left or his right. Then he would have everybody throw their hands in and he would deal again.

When the people we were covering finally made their move, there was a communication problem. We couldn't get through to the vehicle parked six blocks away. So the bridge player handled that problem, at a dead run. He got there in time and they closed that door before the quarry tried it. He sat in the back seat, they said, and gasped and laughed, then squeaked and died. I saw him for a couple of moments, and thought of all the bridge games that died inside his head when all the other things stopped.

"McGee?"

I looked up and got up and went over to the door. "Sheriff?"

"I researched that problem you raised, McGee. I do not want to take any chance of reversal of conviction on a very minor point. I think I am right. If tomorrow were a working day, I would take my chances. But running it over into a Saturday might be questionable. It's a little after four now, but you should be able to reach your Mr. Sibelius, I think."

The operator left the line open on my person-to-person collect call, and I could hear the girl at the other end being professionally indefinite about where and how Lennie could be located.

"Operator, is that Miss Carmichael?"

"Trav? This is Annie, yes."

"Are you accepting the collect call, Miss?"

"Well . . . I guess so. Yes. Travis? Why collect, for goodness' sake?"

"It seemed simpler, on account of I am here in the county jail in Cypress County on suspicion of killing people."

No gasps or cooing or joshing or stupid questions. She went to work. She got the phone number. She said that if we were in luck, she could catch Lennie between the apartment and the marina, on his telephone in his car. If he had already taken off, she wouldn't get him until he monitored the Miami marine broadcast at six o'clock. Then she broke it off.

I told the hero sheriff the call would come back quickly, or not until after six. He looked at his watch. "Wait here for ten minutes. Stand over there against the wall."

No readable inflection, no emotion in the delivery. So you stand against the wall, in your ratty straw slippers, the pant legs of the coveralls ending about five inches above where pants should end, the top buttons unbuttoned because it is too small across chest and shoulders, the sleeves ending midway between elbow and wrist. So you are a large grotesque unmannerly child, standing and watching an adult busy himself with adult things. Man in a dark business suit, crisp white shirt, dark tie, dark gloss of hair, opening folders, making small marginal notes.

The law, in its every dimension of the control of criminals, is geared to limited, stunted people. Regardless of what social, emotional, or economic factor stunted them, the end product is hate, suspicion, fear, violence, and despair. These are weaknesses and the system is geared to exploit weaknesses. Mister Norm was a creature outside my experience. There were no labels I could put on him.

He answered the phone, held it out to me.

"Hello, Lennie," I said.

"From this phone booth, Trav, I can see the *Witchcraft*, all fueled and ready, and my guests carrying the food and booze aboard, and a pair of blond twins slathering oil on each other up on the fly bridge. It was nice to have known you, pal."

"Likewise. Take off, playboy. Cruise the ocean blue in your funny hat. Kiss the twins for me."

"So all right! Bad?"

"And cute. And for once in your brief meteroic career, you'd be representing total innocence."

"Now isn't that nice! And I can't get into a front page with it, because if I make you a star, you are going to have to find useful work or starve. Status right now?"

"Held for questioning. I waived my rights, and then all of a sudden a very bad question came along, and after thinking it over, I took it all back." My mind was racing, trying to figure out some way to clue him into checking out Sheriff Norman Hyzer, because, had I been sure of Hyzer's integrity—and sanity—I would have explained the envelope he had found.

"Innocence can answer any kind of question that comes up."

"If everybody is truly interested in the concept, Lennie."

"Chance of the law there looking for a setup?"

"It's possible."

"Annie said something about killing people."

"At least one, they claim. They haven't said why. Just hinted about some kind of a job long ago netting nine hundred thou."

"So the area swarms with strobes and notebooks and little tape recorders?"

"Not a one."

"So they can put a tight lid on and keep it on. Very rare these days. I know they have a lumpy little patch of grass over there because I had to put down on it a year ago when my oil pressure started to look rotten and the mill started to heat on me. Look, I'll have Wes take this party out and anchor someplace down the bay. I'll make some phone calls here and there, and . . . let me see. I want to hit that grass patch by daylight, so let's say that by six-thirty I'll be holding your hand."

"And Meyer's."

"I always told him evil companions would lead him astray."

Hyzer had me taken back down to my private room. I sat on the bunk and felt very very glad not only about knowing Leonard Sibelius, but about having done him a favor he was not likely to forget. Not a tall man, but notable, conspicuously skinny, with a great big head and a great big expressive and heavy-featured face, and a wild mop of rust-gold hair. A big flexible resonant voice that could range from mountaintop oratory to husky, personal, confidential whisper. Fantastic memory, vast vocabulary, capable of making speeches on any subject at any time. A con artist, a conniver, a charmer, a spellbinder, an eccentric. Italian clothes, fast cars, and fast planes and fast boats. In spite of the emaciation, which made him look like a chronic invalid, he would work at top speed all day and play all night, week after week. Charging through life, leaving a trail of empty bottles and grateful blondes and thankful clients. Huge fees from those who could afford it, and when they couldn't afford it, there was always a market for the life story of any man defended by Lennie Sibelius, after the accused had signed over his rights to the fees and royalties therein. Total defense, in the courtroom, the newspapers, and on the television talk shows. Making it big and spending it big, and running all the way. And, somehow, laughing at himself. Ironic laughter. His black jest was that he had lost only one client. "It took that jury two days to bring back a guilty verdict. There were so many errors by the court, I knew it wouldn't stand up. The route was through the appellate court to the state supreme court to the federal district court to the Supreme Court. And I had just finished a beautiful brief to present to the district court when the silly son of a bitch hung himself in his cell, just two weeks before our book climbed onto the best seller list."

It felt fine to know he was on the way. This whole thing was making me very edgy. It is one of the penalities of not playing one of the roles society wants you to play. No regular hours, no mortgage payments, life insurance, withholding, retirement benefits, savings program. "Okay, where were you, Charlie, at two o'clock on Tuesday afternoon the tenth of April seven years ago?"

"April? Tuesday? Unless I was sick, and that would be on the office records, I was right there at my desk in room fifteen-twenty on the fifteenth floor of the First Prudential Building. I work for

Hutzler, Baskowich, and Troon. Mutual Funds. I'm an analyst. I've been with the firm eleven years now. Ask anybody."

So where was McGee on any April Tuesday you want to name? The best I could do would be a plausible guess. Maybe I should keep a diary. Or have a time card and punch clock. Or is it a punch card and a time clock. Something that goes ding.

So you roam the fringes of the structured society, and it is just fine until they hold you up to the light. Then, somehow, in their eyes and yours, too, you begin to look like a cat burglar.

five

At five-thirty jailer Priskitt came around and said I could take my chances on the American plan dinner, or sign a chit for a take-out meal from a restaurant down the street, said chit to be deducted from my captive funds when they were returned to me. He recommended the special deal. It turned out to be a piece of fried meat, boiled potatoes, overdone turnip greens, battery acid that smelled somewhat like coffee, and a soggy little wedge of apple pie. Four and a quarter plus seventy-five cents for the trusty who had been sent to get it.

Lennie Sibelius did not appear at six-thirty, nor at seven, nor at seven-thirty, nor at eight. I began to wonder if he had tucked his Apache into a swamp.

At almost eight-thirty Priskitt came and got me and took me to a small locker room at the far end of the lower corridor. It smelled like stale laundry. Lennie was sitting on a battered metal table, custom shoes swinging. Lemon-yellow shirt and pale blue slacks.

"Your tailor isn't doing much for you, pal," he said.

"So let's leave and you find me a new one."

"We'll leave. Don't worry about it. But not right now."

I sat on a bench in front of the lockers. "When did you get in?" He said he'd been around more than two hours, having some interesting conversations.

"Anything you want to repeat for the tape recorder?"

—

"My guess would be that this room is clean, Trav. I think he goes by the book. Lawyer and client relationship is confidential stuff. He might stick a shill into a cell with a suspect and bug the conversation to pick up a lead, but I think the rules mean something to him."

"He is something else entire, Lennie."

"He makes better sense when you know the whole pattern. Local boy. Hell of a high-school quarterback. Offers from all over the country. Picked one from Michigan. Did well, but not quick enough for the pros. Married a bright girl up there. Both of them became teachers. She taught speech. She worked on his accent, weeded it out. Both of them worked in the public school system in Rochester, New York. Hyzer's mother became ill, very ill, and Norman and his wife and baby daughter came down here. Hyzer's mother died. He was still here trying to get the house cleared out and put it up for sale when a couple of Miami kids in a stolen car knocked over one of those mini-markets on the edge of town in broad daylight, pistol-whipped the clerk, but suddenly had a cop cruiser riding up on them with the flasher going. They came through town at high speed and lost it on a turn and rode the sidewalk and smashed into a concrete power pole. It killed one of them and crippled the other. But they mashed Hyzer's bride and baby against the front of the post office thirty feet before they got to the pole. Killed them instantly. Hyzer buried them beside his mother and disappeared. Almost a year later he showed up here and announced for sheriff. No party affiliation. Independent. He won big. Sentimental favorite. Two years later he barely squeaked in, because he had done no glad-handing at all. Next time he won big because of his record. Lives for the job. Runs a taut ship. Keeps this county squeaky clean. No outside interests at all. If he is crazy, it is a productive compulsion. The rumor is that he has quietly built up files on every politician in the county, and they would rather not see anybody run against Hyzer. He takes correspondence courses. Law, criminology, ballistics, sociology, crime prevention, rehabilitation, penology."

"And I'm just another of those people who smash wives and babies against the post office wall?"

"Maybe. But buried deeply enough so you won't see any outward effect from it."

"Like Meyer did?"

"That part doesn't fit. It puzzles me. I am going to make it fit, and somebody is going to be sorrier than they can possibly imagine.

But there's more we have to know before that is going to make any sense."

"How much did Hyzer tell you?"

"All the questions and all the answers up to the point where you stopped playing his game."

So I told him about the envelope with the directions I had scribbled on the back. I told him how I could remember clearly what I had done with it. Everything in our wallets had still been sodden by the time we reached Al Storey's gas station in the early morning. "I took everything out. Every time you have to go through your wallet you find junk you don't need. I made a pile of that junk on top of that tin table out in the morning sunlight. I know the envelope and instructions were there because I unfolded it to see what it was. And by then, if what Hyzer says is true, this Frank Baither was already dead. After the station opened up, I picked up Meyer's discards and mine and dropped them into a can by the side of the building, on top of some old newspapers, oil cans, and wiper blades."

"Meaning that somebody took it out and carried it twenty miles north and sneaked past the deputy guarding the Baither place, and planted it inside where it would be found. Meaning that Hyzer has to believe it happened just that way."

"It must have slipped out of my pocket while I was killing Frank Baither."

"Steady as she goes, pal. Now here is something that bothers Hyzer also, I think. You were bound for Lauderdale. You left Lake Passkokee. Did you plan any stops on the way?"

"No."

"Then why come down 112 to the Trail? That's doing it the hard way."

"We *did* it the hard way. I picked a little unmarked road that was supposed to take us right over to the direct route. But with the roads torn up, everything looked different. After about three miles I knew I had the wrong road. So I kept going, hoping that the damned thing would come out on the road we wanted. But it wandered all over hell and gone and finally came out onto 112 about fifteen miles north of the Cypress City cutoff. By then it was obviously shorter and quicker to come down 112 and take the Trail over to Route 27, then cut over to the Parkway on 820."

"And Hyzer keeps thinking about how you and Meyer match the description."

"What description, dammit?"

"Remember four years ago the way some people hit the money truck with all the racetrack cash aboard?"

"Just outside Miami? Vaguely. I've forgotten the gimmick."

"It was beautiful," Lennie said. "Absolutely beautiful. The three clowns who had truck duty stuck to the same routine every time they made the racetrack run. They would get there empty and park in back of a drive-in, and all three would go in, eat, kill some time until the big parking areas emptied and the people in the money room had time to weigh, band, sack, and tally the cash. Then they would go get it, and make a fifty-minute run back to the barn. It was after a very big handle that they were hit. They woke up on a little shell road way back in some undeveloped acreage. The locks had been drilled and the truck and radio disabled. They were too groggy to walk for help right away. They were separated and questioned. And examined. Same story. Each had become very very sleepy about fifteen minutes after they had loaded the money and left the track. Heavy dose of some form of barbiturate. Traces still left in the bloodstream. The driver had pulled over and stopped, thinking he would just take a nice little nap like the guard sitting there beside him, snoring. The police turned up a few people who had seen a big brute of a wrecker put a hook on the armored truck, lift the front end, and trundle it off. They traced it back to the drive-in, a very small place with normally two people working during the daytime, a man in the kitchen and a girl working the counter. At night they'd have a second girl car-hopping. This was the pickup after the big Sunday afternoon race card, with the take including the Friday night and Saturday night meets. The men said the girl on the counter was new. A blonde. They had kidded around with her. By that time they had already had another report which dovetailed. A girl and three men had hit that drive-in a half hour before the money-truck people walked in. They had taped up the waitress and the chef and stashed them in a supply closet. The man had been too frightened and hysterical to pick up anything useful. The girl gave a full report of what she had noticed and remembered. One man was your size, Trav. One description fits Meyer. The third was average height, but very broad and thick in the shoulders and neck. She thought there might be a fourth man on watch outside the rear entrance, but she wasn't certain. She said the girl was young."

"You know a lot about it, Lennie."

"I had a client they were trying to set up for that truck job. And now, all of a sudden, better than three years later, I've got two more."

"This Frank Baither was in on it, then?"

"Sheriff Hyzer didn't exactly break down and tell me all his problems, pal. We established a relationship of mutual respect. There have been generations of Baithers in this county, some very solid and some very unpredictable, but all of them tough and quick, and a few of them tough, quick, and smart. Like Frank. Lived alone in the old family place along that route. He'd be gone for weeks or months. Tax bills and utility bills and so on went to the Cypress Bank and Trust. He kept money in a special account and the bills were paid out of it. No visible means of support. When he'd move back in, he'd usually have a houseguest. Some pretty dolly in tight pants, visiting for a while. Hyzer is concerned about Cypress County, not about what Frank Baither might be doing elsewhere. Then a funny thing happened. Smart Frank Baither, on a Saturday night, got stumbling drunk and held up a gas station right here in town. Went lurching off, spilling the cash out of the till. Got grabbed and put in a cell. Didn't make bail. Pleaded guilty, and got hit by the circuit-court judge with five for armed robbery. Got transported off to Raiford. Did three and a half at Raiford before they let him out twelve days ago."

"So?"

"Item. The blood test on the stumbling drunk, taken under protest, showed that he could have had two small beers, maybe three. Item. Discreet investigation showed he had enough in his special account so that he could have made bail during the three months he had to wait for trial, but he didn't. Item. For a man so involved with the outdoors, the swamps and the glades, Frank made a happy adjustment to this place and also to Raiford. Item. When Hyzer went out and checked Frank Baither's place after arrest, he found that Frank had done all those little chores a man living alone will do when he expects to be away for a long long time. Put up the shutters and drained the pipes, disconnected the pumps and greased them. Drained the aerator."

"Okay. He wanted to be tucked away."

"Hyzer reasoned that if somebody was out to kill Frank Baither, Baither would have ambushed them rather than hide in jail. Hyzer checked out the big scores made anywhere in the county just before Baither set himself up for a felony conviction. He kept coming back to the money truck in Miami. Baither was medium height with a bull neck and a very broad thick shoulders. As a kid he had worked for his uncle who operated a little yard, making cement block, and he carried enough tons of mix and tons of finished block to give him that muscular overdevelopment. Hyzer reasoned that Frank Baither had somehow tricked his partners, eased out with the track money, hid it well, then set himself up for free room and board for a long time, counting on the odds that the partners on the outside would not last long enough to be waiting when he got out. The hard-case operators have very few productive years, Trav. Then they are tucked away, underground or behind the walls. Frank had about two weeks between the money-truck job and landing in the Cypress County jail, assuming he was involved. Hyzer wanted more to go on. He arranged to get word from Raiford on Frank's activities in prison. By the end of the first year he learned that Frank had cultivated a few Latin Americans there. He was diligently studying Spanish. And it looked as if he would become reasonably fluent. The parts fitted together. Get out, pick up the money, and go. And live like a Greek shipowner for the rest of his life, with enough Spanish to learn who to bribe, and enough money to guarantee immunity."

"He told you a lot, Lennie."

"Some of it he told me, some of it he hinted at, and some of it is what I came up with to fill in the blanks. That sheriff went over every inch of the Baither place, and came up empty every time. Now here is another part. Somebody gave Frank a good rap on the head and taped him to a chair, and wound his head with tape, leaving a hole over one ear, and a hole over the mouth. Then they worked on him. They spoiled him. He had to know he was done, and so with nothing left to save except a little more agony, he talked. Then they shoved a rusty ice pick into his heart."

"Assumption?"

"A finality about it. End of interview. From the look of the rest of him, they would have kept going until he died of the special attentions."

"So Hyzer," I said wearily, "buys the idiot idea that we teamed with Frank Baither and took the money truck, and we kept track of him, knew when he got out of Raiford, and set up this complicated cover story, got to him, tortured him and killed him, left an incriminating envelope behind, lost my old car in the canal, and then. . . . For God's sake, Lennie! Can't you straighten him out? Where's the money?"

"Right where Frank Baither hid it. But now you and Meyer know where it is, and you can take your time picking it up."

He made me go over the incident we should have reported and didn't. Lots of questions. Estimates of elapsed time.

He paced in the constricted space, glowering. "The only way to defend a case is to build an alternate possibility up to the stature of reasonable doubt, McGee. There was a girl in the mud beside the canal. Let's say she was the young girl who played waitress. Let's say Frank Baither was prowling after her in the night. Hutch is the big one who fits your description. Orville fits Meyer's description. They came after Frank Baither last night. The girl got away. Baither got in his old truck and went cruising, looking for Orville and Hutch. You went in the canal at ten o'clock. The shots were fired a little after eleven. He thought he hit Hutch in the head. He offered to make a deal with Orville. He drove back to his place, off guard because he thought he knew where Hutch and Orville were. He got back and they jumped him. Maybe they had a car hidden away nearby, and maybe the two of them and the girl are five hundred miles gone by now, laughing and singing, with the trunk packed with money. But that damned envelope, Trav. That is physical evidence. You are *absolutely* positive about what you did with it?"

"Beyond any doubt."

"Then the deputy he posted at the Baither place has to be lying when he told Hyzer nobody entered the place. Can you remember the deputy's name?"

"Arnstead, I think. But why would somebody . . ."

" 'Why' comes way down the list, client. It comes after 'how,' 'when,' 'where,' and 'what.' 'How' is the big word."

He opened the door and whistled. Priskitt took me back after Lennie Sibelius wished me a nice night's sleep, saying he didn't count on getting much himself.

As Priskitt caged me, I asked him about Meyer.

"Feeling much better. Fascinating man. It's guests like you two who make this almost a civilized occupation, McGee. Nighty night."

They had the cell lights on a rheostat. At ten o'clock they faded from white glare to yellow glow.

You can't help wondering what it would feel like to be in such a box for the next dozen years, and wonder if you could handle it, and walk out of it still reasonably sane.

I remembered reading a sentence long ago, I know not where or when, or who wrote it. It said, "The only thing that prisons demonstrably cure is heterosexuality."

Back to the envelope. It had to be an unplanned act on someone's part. An improvisation. A way to muddy the water. Somebody made the decision after Sheriff Hyzer and Deputy Cable had driven off with us. A customer or an employee. Or the boss. Al Storey, or the big young dull-looking one named Terry. Or the older one who had arrived late in the blue Rambler. Henry . . . The one with all the white teeth. Or somebody who came on duty later. Al, Terry, and Henry had all heard Hyzer say that Frank Baither had been killed. His attitude made it evident he thought Meyer and I were involved.

I dug away at my chigger bites. Get me out, Lennie. Get us out of here.

six

Up until eleven o'clock it was a very dull morning. Then Priskitt arrived, humming happily, carrying a hanger with freshly cleaned and pressed slacks and shirt thereon. He had my toilet kit in the other hand.

He unlocked the cell door and said, "Priskitt at your service, sir. You will wish to shower? You are free to go right ahead, by yourself."

"Those clothes were . . ."

"In your suitcase which was in your car, and so was the toilet kit. Still damp, but not at all bad. Compliments of Cypress County, Mr. McGee. I'll be along with shoes and socks and underwear."

"Where is my friend?"

"Under the shower, one might expect."

But Meyer was out of the shower, standing at the sink, and carefully, tenderly, shaving the black stubble from his swollen and discolored face. He turned and said, "Don't make me laugh, please."

"How bad is it?"

"It will add up to a good dental bill. The thing that worries me is the persistent headache, dizziness, some double vision. And something seems to grate in my cheek. Lennie is going to fly me back to Lauderdale and I'll go in for observation."

"Who did it?"

"A large fellow with big cheekbones and small dark eyes and very long sideburns. I wondered why he was putting a leather glove on. You'd mentioned a few useful things one could do under those circumstances. I tried them and they didn't work very well."

"Who was there at the time?"

"Deputy Cable. Objecting."

"Making any physical attempt to stop him?"

"Finally, yes. But at first I would say he was merely whining at the fellow, something about Mister Norm getting upset. He called the sideburned fellow Lew. I discovered the whole name later on. Deputy Lew Arnstead."

"Where was Sturnevan? The big sloppy one."

"He had stepped out. Lew didn't take long. It seemed long. Maybe fifteen or twenty seconds. By then I wasn't aware of whether Sturnevan came back or not, but I think he was one of the two men who helped me to the cell."

"Meyer?"

"Mmmm?"

"I'm sorry about this."

He turned and looked solemnly at me, puffy eyes staring out of the big yellow-blue-green-purple face. "Where is any man's immunity from the unexpected, McGee? I could deny myself the pleasure of your friendship, and decrease the chance of the unexpected. But there is a case on record of a woman in her own bed being struck on the thigh by a bounding chunk of red hot iron, a meteorite that came whistling in from God only knows what corner of the galaxy. I value that night hike, Travis. And the way the dawn looked, and the feeling of being alive after being shot at. I am a grown-up, making choices. And sufficiently grown up to live with the choices I make. My face hurts and my head aches, and I would like to kill that sideburned fellow with anything I could lift. I feel outraged, humiliated, and very very tired. But I'm glad I came along."

"You do go on."

"Do us both a favor and get out of that garment."

He was ready and I was almost ready when Sturnevan came to get us. He clucked and turned Meyer toward the light and gave him a close inspection. "And you weren't very pretty to start with, Professor."

"King," I said, "I might get a chance to strike up an acquaintance with Lew Arnstead when he's off duty."

"Which is now sort of one hundred percent of the time, I hear. You serious, McGee?"

"Serious enough to ask you how to do it."

"He's a strong boy. He likes all the odds his way. With somebody your size, he'd try to fix all the odds fast, like a quick kick in the balls. What you do is, you make it look as if he can get away with it. He's right-handed. He'll kick with his right leg. Watch for the weight shift, sidestep the kick and get his ankle, and swing it on up. Then if you can hurt him fast enough and bad enough, he'll be all through."

"Thanks, King."

"Mister Norm is waiting on you fellows."

No guard just inside the door this time. Just Lennie Sibelius and Sheriff Hyzer, and some exhibits on the bare desk top.

Lennie slouched, smiling, in a wooden armchair. Hyzer sat at attention behind his desk. He asked us to sit. He said to Meyer, "I assure you that what happened to you is against the policy of this department."

"My client accepts that," Lennie said quickly.

"Arnstead was not officially on duty at the time of the . . . incident," Hyzer said. "He had no business being here. His act was without official sanction or official knowledge. He has been dismissed with prejudice, booked for aggravated assault, and released on bond pending trial. Deputy Cable has been fined and reprimanded for permitting it to happen. Please accept my personal apology."

"I accept it," Meyer said.

"Mr. Sibelius has suggested that any dental or medical bills be sent here to my attention. They will be taken care of, if not by the county, then by me personally."

"Do I get one of those, too?" I asked.

Hyzer swiveled slowly and stared at me with those frozen eyes. "One what?"

"An apology?"

"He's making a joke, Sheriff," Lennie said.

"He is? I have very little sense of humor, Mr. McGee. Your rights . . . and your person . . . have been protected. I am releasing you from further questioning because Mr. Sibelius prevailed on me to more carefully investigate your . . . version . . . of what happened Thursday night." There were little hesitations, pauses in which he carefully composed his phrases, making the end product so stilted, so stuffy that it became, in one sense, an armor against the world.

He indicated a .38 automatic pistol, an old one, rust flecked, with the bluing worn away in places. "This handgun was found on the Baither property under a clump of palmetto about fifteen feet from where the pickup truck was parked, and almost in line with the back porch. There were two rounds in the clip. There is a partial print on the side of the clip which matches Baither's left thumb print, and is in the place where a man would logically hold it while loading the weapon. We can assume it was Baither's weapon and was lost in the darkness when Baither was overpowered while walking from his truck to his house. There is no way to tell how many shots were fired, as we do not know how many were loaded into the clip. Examination proved it had been fired recently. A wax test on the right hand of the decedent indicates he had fired a gun not long before death."

He moved along to the next item, three empty brass cartridge cases neatly aligned. "One of these was found on the floor of the truck. The second was found this morning on the shoulder of the highway three and two tenth miles south of the point where your car went into the canal. That area was searched carefully after certain marks and footprints were found in the soft earth beside the canal. This plaster cast of the best footprint matches the left shoe you were wearing, Mr. McGee, when you were taken into custody. This third case is a test round fired from this handgun. Though we have not arranged a ballistics examination with a comparative microscope, examination through a hand magnifying glass indicates the probability that the indentation made by the firing pin is distinctive enough to allow eventual proof that all three rounds were fired from the same pistol."

"This is very reassuring to my clients," Lennie said.

"Taken alone," Hyzer said, "these indications would not be enough to cause me to release these people. There could be too many alternative explanations. And the fact of the envelope seemed conclusive evidence that one of you or both of you were inside the Baither house. However, Mr. Sibelius suggested a method of . . . making Arnstead change his report to me about his assignment to guard the Baither house."

"All Arnstead had to do," Lennie explained, "was leave one little hole in his story, one period of time when that envelope could have been planted. I could drive trucks through any hole like that. Norman, my friend Meyer is looking rocky, and with your permission I'd like to fly him over to Lauderdale. Trav, I'm assuming you'd like to get that old crock truck of yours dried out and running."

Hyzer said, "I would prefer to have Mr. McGee remain in Cypress County until I have completed my—"

"But, Norman, you have my personal guarantee, my personal word that I can produce them right here any time you say."

"I think it would be better if—"

Lennie smiled his best smile. "Hell, Norm, it's all give and take, after all. Famed economist brutally beaten and held, without charges, in Cypress County jail cell."

"I refuse to be—"

"Come on, Norm! I like the way you're thinking. I think you are the first lawman who's got a decent lead on that racetrack money. I don't blame you for keeping a tight lid on it because if word got out, somehow, people would be swarming all over you. I wouldn't want that to happen because I wouldn't want one of those hard-case types the *Miami Herald* would send over here asking you, for the record, if you were so sure Baither was in on the money-truck job, why you didn't have him under twenty-four-hour surveillance. They wouldn't understand your reasoning, and they might use some rude head such as: HICK SHERIFF BLOWS BIG CASE." He shrugged and, turning, managed to wink at me—a combination wink and frown.

I caught on and grabbed my cue. "Lennie, look. It isn't that important I get home. I'm perfectly willing to hang around if Sheriff Hyzer wants me to. But I haven't even got enough cash to take care of the car. If you could . . ."

"Any time at all, pal," Lennie said, and produced the platinum money clip with the emeralds, the one given him in gratitude by the Other Woman after he had secured an acquittal for the heir to a pulp mill and timberlands fortune who had shot and killed what he thought was a prowler, but who turned out to be his insomniac wife.

Counting off money for me would not have been consistent with Lennie Sibelius's life style. He slipped the cash out of the clip, took off a couple of fifties for himself, put them back in the clip, and handed me the rest of it.

"I appreciate your cooperation, Mr. McGee," Hyzer said. "Let me know where you will be staying."

Meyer and I collected the rest of our gear. Laundry and dry cleaning courtesy of Cypress County. A form of apology. We put the small amount of luggage into the white Buick convertible Lennie had rented. I could see them off and bring it back into town from the airstrip, and either turn it in or keep it. I sat in the back. It seemed impossible to talk with the top down and with Lennie pretending he was being challenged for the lead in the Daytona 500. The strip was about five miles east to the city limits. He drove past the hangar and on out onto the hard pan and stopped next to his Apache, all chocked and tied down to eyebolts.

"You can get a very nice room at the White Ibis Motor Inn," Lennie said. "You can go back through town—"

"I saw it when they were taking us in."

"But don't eat there. Eat right in town at Mrs. Teffer's Live Oak Lodge and Dining Room. Exceptional!"

"Now hold it a minute, Lennie. I picked up your cue. But it would be very comforting to know what the hell is going on."

Meyer said, "Nine hundred thousand dollars is going on." His voice was slightly blurred by the mouth damage.

"So don't be in too big a hurry to leave," Lennie said.

"This is one of my stupid days," I told them. "Draw me some pictures."

"I like Norm's thinking. It all seems to fit together. And I think that sooner or later he's going to pick somebody up for it."

"Wouldn't they be long gone?"

Lennie smiled. "By Gad, it is one of your stupid days. If they were long gone, there would be very little point in going to the trouble of planting that envelope. One or more of the people involved have to be right here in the area, tied to it in such a way that the act of leaving would blow the whistle. When Norm grabs somebody, they are going to need the best legal talent they can find. And they should be able to afford me."

"I can have a sandwich sign made and walk back and forth in front of the jail?"

"The Association would frown on that. Hell, they even frown on my little decorations on the airplane and the cruiser."

He pointed and I stepped up and took a closer look. They were small decals, hardly bigger than a postage stamp. A stylized gallows in black on a white background with a black border, and with an X in red canceling out the gallows. The custom decals were on the cowling under the pilot's window. Almost three rows. Twenty-eight of them.

"All this trouble to plant a shill in the area?"

"Trav, pal, I had the idea you might stir around a little. A catalytic agent, bringing the brew to a nice simmer. Then Norm might be able to nail somebody sooner than otherwise."

"He is going to frown on meddling. I will be right back inside his hotel if I try that."

"If you're clumsy, sure. But I have a lot of confidence in your discretion, and if you do slip, I'll be right back to pry you out again. Sibelius never sleeps. Think of it this way. You've agreed to help me out on the pretrial investigation."

"I don't have a license. I don't want a license. I'm tired of Cypress County already."

"Why should you have a license? For what? You've gone on my staff payroll as a researcher."

I took the folded money out of my pants pocket and counted it. "Nine hundred and forty?"

"Let me know when you need more, pal." He clapped me on the shoulder. "Think of it this way. Without Sibelius, you'd still be inside. And so would Meyer. You called and I came over. Am I charging you? Would I charge a friend for a little bit of a favor? What do you think I am? Greedy or something? All you have to do is stir around, talk about Frank Baither, buy a drink here and there, and tell people the truth about me. Don't overdo it. Just tell them I'm the greatest criminal lawyer around. Is that so hard?"

"You are something else, Sibelius. By the way, how did you get Arnstead to change his story?"

Lennie shrugged. "He had to be lying. If he wasn't, you were. Last night I came across the interesting information that Lew Arnstead is the number one stud in Cypress County. It's more obsession than hobby. I straightened out the timetable. You were at the gas station when Storey opened up at twenty to seven. At about seven-thirty you and Meyer left with Hyzer and Cable. Because you stopped while your car was being pulled out, you didn't get to the jail until about eight-fifteen. Arnstead was turning out to have a very long shift. At eight-thirty he went into the Baither place and used the phone to call in and ask if he was going to be relieved. Hyzer told the communications clerk to tell Lew Arnstead to stay right there and that he would be at the Baither place about eleven o'clock, and after it was checked over, he could go off duty. Ask the logical questions, McGee."

"Let me see now. He was expecting Hyzer earlier. Then Hyzer changed his schedule by coming to take a look at us, and take us in. So he had something lined up, and he wanted to be relieved so he could take care of it. But he found out he had another two hours to wait, plus the time it would take for the daylight search. And he had the use of the phone. Sorry, honey, I can't make it, so why don't you come on over here?"

"Inside Baither's house?"

"I . . . I wouldn't think so. Not with Hyzer due to prowl the place."

"How about a narrow old mattress on the slab floor of the pump house about thirty feet from the back porch?"

"Handy."

"So Hyzer took my suggestion and had Lew Arnstead brought in, and asked him to explain why he was in the pump house with a woman at nine o'clock Friday morning instead of keeping an eye on the house as ordered. Arnstead tried a lot of footwork but Hyzer pushed until he broke through. Arnstead got very virtuous about refusing to name the woman. He said he was with her about ten minutes, and he could see the entrance road from the pump house. She arrived and left by car. She was an old friend. So while you are churning around, see if you can come up with an I.D. on the lady, pal. She could have been sent in as a distraction while somebody planted the envelope. A cub scout could unlock that house with a kitchen match."

"While I'm churning around. Anything for a friend."

A redheaded boy in greasy khakis came out and brought the gas ticket for Lennie to sign, then untied the aircraft and pulled the chocks away. I handed Meyer's and Lennie's duffle up. Lennie cranked it up and trundled off to the end of the marl strip. He warmed it up there, and the boy and I stood and watched him make his run and pluck it off and climb over the cabbage palms and live oaks, heading east over the swamps and pasturelands. Good luck, Meyer. No bleeding inside the head, please. It is too valuable and kindly a head.

So I got into my white Buick with the black plastic leather upholstery and the stereo FM radio, and the power brakes, power windows, power steering, air, and supersomething transmission, and took half again as long getting back to town as Lennie had taken coming out.

Smile, McGee. Show your teeth. Honk at the lassies, because here it is nearly one o'clock Saturday afternoon and you don't know where they keep the action. Not the kind you've had so far. The other kind.

seven

The White Ibis Motor Inn had a little symbol on the signs and the registration card indicating it was one of the creatures of a subsection of one of the more ubiquitous conglomerates. So they could afford to operate it at a percentage of occupancy that would hustle an independent owner into bankruptcy.

Some precise fellow in some distant city had used the standard software program for site location, and fed into the program the regional data for population movement and growth, planned and probable highway construction, land cost, *ad-valorem* tax rates, pay scales, and the IBM 360 had said to build one on Alternate 112 west of Cypress City and operate it at a loss until the increased demand for the transient beds would put it back into the black.

Teletype network for instant reservations, approved cards for instant credit, a woman at the desk with instant, trained, formal politeness, who assigned me to Unit 114 and made a little *x* on a map of the layout, and drew a little line to show me where to drive so that I would end up in front of the *x*, in the proper diagonal parking slot. She looked slightly distressed when I said I had no idea how long I would be staying. People should know, so they can keep the records neat.

I closed myself into the silence of Unit 114, unpacked, and took a better shower. Stretched out on the bed. Things to do, but no will to do them. A listlessness. A desire to disassociate, to be uninvolved. The fashion is to call it an identity crisis. I was not doing things very well lately. A juvenile, big-mouth performance for the sheriff, windy threats signifying nothing.

Somebody had made a very cute try to get the two of us involved in a private and violent nastiness, but Lennie's gifts of persuasion and the thoroughness of Norman Hyzer had collapsed the improvised structure.

All cages are frightening. And sometimes a little time spent in a small cage merely gives you the feeling that you have been let out into a bigger cage, the one you have built for yourself over the years. The delusion of total freedom of will is the worst cage of all. And it gets cold in there. As cold, perhaps, as inside Miss Agnes under ten feet of canal water, if Meyer hadn't clumsied me out of there. Or cold as the grave would be had Frank Baither hit me in the face with that first shot.

With enormous effort I forced myself to reach the phone book, look up the Sheriff's Department, and phone in my temporary address to the dispatcher. I got dressed and got into the car and went looking for Johnny's Main Street Service. I found it down by the produce sheds and the truck depots.

There was diesel fuel, and a half dozen big stalls for truck repair work. There was a paint shop and a body shop, and a side lot piled with cars which had quite evidently slain their masters in a crunch of blood, tin, and glass. I saw the big blue-and-white tow truck. There was no shop work going on, the whole area somnolent in the perfect April afternoon. An old man sat in the small office, reading a true-crime magazine. A scrawny girl in jeans and a halter was slowly spreading paste wax on a metallic green MG.

Among a line of cars against a side fence Miss Agnes stood out like a dowager among teenagers. I got out of the Buick and walked over to her. A large young man about nineteen came angling across the hardpan from the shop area. Low-slung jeans and a torn and grease-blackened T-shirt. Thick black glossy hair that fell to his big shoulders.

"You Mr. McGee?" When I nodded, he said, "I'm Ron Hatch. My father is Johnny Hatch. He owns this place. He didn't want me to fool around with that Rolls on account of on an impounded car, we're stuck with it. But I couldn't stand having it just sit. So he said it had to be on my own time. I just finished with it maybe an hour ago. I pulled the tank and the head, got it all kerosened out, blew the fuel lines, got the ignition system all dry, coil and all. The battery took a charge. That tire is done, and I guess you'll have to check around Miami to find a Dunlop that'll go on that rim."

"I'm grateful you didn't let it sit, Ron."

"Hell, it's a great old brute. All that hand-lapping and custom machining and fitting. The bushings are like perfect, Mr. McGee. But there's this problem." He had the big leathery banana-fingered hand of the born artisan. He pulled a complex fitting out of the pocket of the jeans. "See where this is broke off fresh? It maybe happened when you hit the bank, going down. It's the fitting out at the end of the steering arm, front left. I put a clamp on there for temporary, just enough to baby it out here to park, but you couldn't drive it. There's no machine shop I know of can make one on account of right in here, and here, they're not standard threads, so they wouldn't have the taps the right size, and it isn't something you can cast because it takes a lot of strain."

"I've got a mechanic friend in Palm Beach at a place where they stock Rolls parts from the year one."

"Maybe he'll have to have this to match it up right. Meanwhile . . . maybe I could do some body and fender work."

"What do I owe you so far?"

He looked uncomfortable. "The way it works, garages have to bid for the county contract. So it's seventy-five dollars for towing, and ten dollars a day for it while it was impounded. With the tax that's a hundred and nine twenty. Once we got word this morning from the sheriff's office we could release the car to you, then the ten a day stopped."

"And if they'd kept me in there for ninety days?"

"Then . . . if people don't want to pay the storage, like if the car isn't worth it anyway, Dad wholesales them for what he can get. The word around was that you and your friend had surely killed Frank Baither and you got caught, and that's why my father said it didn't make any sense working on your car. But . . . I just couldn't stand seeing it sit the way it was, machinery like that. I mean I did it on my own and if you figure you don't want to pay anything over the towing and storage, that's okay."

I separated two bills from the packet Lennie had handed me. A fifty and a hundred. "Get me a receipted bill on the towing and storage, please. And put the rest against your hours and we'll settle up when you're done."

"Body work?"

"You wouldn't use a filler, would you?"

"You better be kidding." And I knew how he'd do it, banging the dings out with the rubber mallet, sanding, burnishing, smoothing, using a little lead sparingly where it couldn't be helped, sanding down a couple of coats of primer, then using a top-quality body paint, sanding between coats.

"Do you expect to be able to match that paint, Ron?"

"It's a terrible paint job anyway. I'd rather do the whole thing. What I'd like to do it is yellow in a lot of coats of a good gold flake lacquer with a lot of rubbing between coats."

"Sorry, but it has to stay blue. Sentimental reasons."

He shrugged. "That same shade?"

"Not exact."

He smiled for the first time. He looked relieved. "I can get it looking fine. Wait and see. I hope you get that fitting soon. I can't really fine tune it unless I can open it up some on the road. On the lift isn't the same."

The old man in the office came out and bawled, "Ronnie! Come get the phone!"

The boy took off, big lope, long strides. And the immediate image was superimposed on memory. The determined look of the girl, running in the night, the dark hair flying, bare knees lifting. An elusive similarity, like a family resemblance. No more than that, because the girl had been all girl, and this runner was totally male. I find I have one small hang-up regarding young males with masculine features and shoulder-length locks. When they have a mustache or beard or both to go with the hair, they make a fine romantic image, an echo of a distant gallantry, of the old names like Sumter, The wilderness, Sherman's March, Custer. But when, like the Beatles and Ron Hatch, there is no beard or mustache, then I have to get past the mental roadblock of recalling too many Army nurses I have known.

I wondered if Mister Norm had gotten a line on the running girl. It would be too much of a miracle of coincidence for her not to be involved in some way. Involved, possibly, from the beginning. The very young girl playing waitress, in a blond wig, the weekend afternoon when they had mickeyed the money-truck men.

Or maybe she was a decoy, a diversion, setting Frank Baither up so that Orville and Hutch could get at him. Or Baither's woman, local or import, sweet young flesh after over forty months of doing without. The fairly safe guess was that she was woods-wise, and she thought, rightly or wrongly, that somebody was tracking her down in the night, and she used the rush and rumble of my car to cover the sound as she went crashing through the weeds and brush on the far side of the road. Misjudged the distance. Cut it too close. But why the hell not *behind* the car?

I was looking inside the car when Ron came back. It had been cleaned out thoroughly, mud, weeds, water, and everything else.

"Oh, I forgot. All your stuff, the fishing gear and tools and so on, they're locked in a storage room here. I wrote a list of everything. Things disappear. Maybe some stuff is gone already, before I wrote it down. You want to check?"

"Later, I guess."

"Nobody thought you'd get out. That way it isn't so much like stealing."

"People around here think that when Sheriff Hyzer grabs somebody, he's always right? Is that it?"

His gaze was direct for a moment, and then drifted away. "They say he's a good sheriff. They say he's fair."

"Thanks again for going ahead with my car. I'll be around on Monday."

So I drove around and about, getting the feel of the town and the area, had a late lunch in a red plastic national franchise selling the Best Sandwiches Anytime Anywhere, and had a medium bad sandwich and very bad coffee, served in haste by a drab, muttering woman.

On the way in, I had picked up the local morning paper. Eight pages. *The Cypress Call & Journal.* The masthead said it was owned by Jasson Communications. They own a few dozen small-city papers in Florida and South Georgia. Guaranteed circulation of five thousand seven hundred and forty, by the last ABC figures. It had the minimum wire service on national and international, and very exhaustive coverage of service-club and social-club doings. Typical of the Jasson operation. Cut-rate syndicated columnists, ranging from medium right to far right. Lots of city and county legal notices. Detailed coverage of farm produce prices.

I found myself on the bottom right corner of page two.

HELD FOR QUESTIONING

Two Fort Lauderdale men were taken into custody Friday morning by the County Sheriff's Department for questioning in connection with the torture murder of Frank Baither at his residence on State

Road 72 Thursday night after it was learned that the vehicle in which they were riding had gone into the drainage canal sometime Thursday night not far from the Baither house.

And that was it. Local yellow journalism. Sensationalism. Who, what, why, when, where, and how. Exquisite detail.

So after my late and sorry lunch I went around to the *Call & Journal*. It was printed on the ground floor of a cement-block building on Princeton Street. The editorial and business offices occupied the other two floors.

According to the masthead, the managing editor was one Foster Goss. Enclosed in glass in the far corner of the lazy newsroom. A couple of hefty women pecking vintage typewriters. A crickety octogenarian on the copy desk. A couple of slack young men murmuring into phones, heels on the cheap tin desks. Offstage frantic clackety-whack of the broad tape.

Foster Goss was a fat, fading redhead, with thick lenses, saffroned fingers, blue shirt with wet armpits. He waved at a chair and said, "Minute," and hunched over the yellow copy paper once again making his marks with soft black lead. He finished, reached, rapped sharply on the glass with a big gold seal ring. A mini-girl got up and came in and took the yellow sheets, gave me a hooded, speculative glance, and strolled out. Foster Goss watched her rear until the half-glass door swung shut, then creaked back in his chair, picked one cigarette out of the shirtpocket pack, and lit it.

"Meyer or McGee?" he said.

"McGee. I want to complain about all the invasion of privacy, all the intimate details about my life and times."

Half smile. "Sure you do."

"So I came around to give you an exclusive, all about local police brutality and so forth."

"Gee whiz. Golly and wow."

"Mr. Goss, you give me the impression that somewhere, sometime, you really *did* work on a newspaper."

His smile was gentle and reflective. "On some dandies, fella. I even had a Nieman long ago. But you know how it is. Drift of the stormy seas into safe haven."

"Just for the hell of it, Mr. Goss, what would happen if you printed more than Mister Norm would like to have you print?"

"My goodness gracious, man, don't you realize that it has been the irresponsible press which has created community prejudice against defendants in criminal actions? As there is absolutely no chance of anyone running successfully against Sheriff Hyzer, he doesn't have to release any information about how good he is. And very damned good he is indeed. So good that County Judge Stan Bowley has a sort of standing order about pretrial publicity. So the sheriff would read the paper and come over and pick me up and take me to Stan and he would give me a sad smile and say, 'Jesus Christ, Foster, you know better than that,' and he would fine me five hundred bucks for contempt."

"Which wouldn't stand up."

"I *know* that! So I go to the Jasson brothers and I say, look, I've got this crusade I've got to go on, and I know the paper is turning a nice dollar, and I know you nice gentlemen are stashing away Jasson Communications stock in my retirement account every year, but I've got to strike a blow for a free press. Then they want to know who I am striking the blow against, and I tell them it is the sheriff, and they ask me if he is corrupt and inefficient, and I say he might be the best sheriff in the state, who took a very very rough county and tamed it without using any extralegal methods."

"Then what if a hot team comes in here from Miami to do a big feature on this cozy little dictatorship, Mr. Goss?"

He smiled again. "No contempt charges. Maximum cooperation. Guided tours. Official charm. No story."

"But Meyer got badly beaten."

"By a deputy who was immediately fired and booked for assault."

"You keep track, even though you don't print much."

"Old habits. Ancient reflexes. Interested me to find that Lennie Sibelius came on the run when you whistled. That's why we're getting along so well. I wanted to find out what kind of cat you might be, Mr. McGee. Hence the open door, frank revelation policy."

"Learn anything?"

"Hired gladiators like Sibelius, Belli, Foreman, Bailey, and so on seldom waste their talents on low-pay representation unless there is some publicity angle that might be useful. None here. I'd guess it was a favor. Maybe you work for him. Investigator, building defense files, or checking out a jury panel. You handle yourself as if you could give good service along those lines."

"Have you ever thought of going back into journalism?"

"I think about it. And I think about my mortgage, and my seventeen-year-old daughter married to a supermarket bag boy, and I think about my twelve-year-old spastic son. I catch pretty fair bass twelve miles from my house."

"Do you think about Frank Baither?"

"I try not to. Mister Norm will let me know what I need to know."

Then we smiled at each other and I said my polite good-by. He was like King Sturnevan, long-retired from combat, but he still had the moves. No wind left, but he could give you a very bad time for the first two rounds.

I went out into the late April afternoon, into a spring scent of siesta. Head the Buick back toward the White Ibis, where I could make a phone call and find out how Meyer was making it.

eight

I parked exactly where the motel architect had decided the vehicle for Unit 114 should be. Inside the room the red phone light was blinking. I wrote down the numbers the desk-lady gave me. The Lauderdale call was from a very very British female on Lennie's staff, relaying the diagnosis on Meyer: a mild concussion, hairline fracture of the cheekbone, and they were keeping him overnight for routine observation.

The other one was a local number. I let it have ten rings, just like it says to do in the phone book. Hung up. Then I called the sheriff. He was there.

"Yes, Mr. McGee?"

"I don't want to do anything I'm not supposed to do. I was thinking of driving down to Al Storey's station on the Trail. Then I remembered it's outside the county."

"What would be the purpose?"

"I would sort of like to know how somebody set me up."

"That's under investigation. We don't need help."

"Are you getting anywhere with it?"

"I'd rather not comment at this time."

"It's your best approach, isn't it?"

"I'd appreciate it if you'd stay inside my jurisdiction, Mr. McGee."

"So be it, Sheriff."

I glowered at the unspottable, unbreakable rug for a time, then looked up Arnstead in the phone book. No Lew, Lou, Louis, or Lewis. There were three of them. J.A., and Henry T. and Cora.

I tried J.A. "Lew around?"

"Not around *this* house, ever, mister." Bang.

So I tried Henry T. "Lew around?"

"Not very goddam likely, buddy." Bang.

Started to try Cora, then decided I might as well drive out to the address and see for myself. The book said 3880 Cattleman's Road. I found Cattleman's Road a half mile west of the White Ibis, heading north off of Alternate 112. Flat lands, and frame bungalows which were further and further apart as I drove north.

A big rural mailbox on the right-hand side with red stick-on letters spelling Arnstead. Sand driveway leading back to a pink cement-block house, a small place with a lot of unkempt Mexican flame vine climbing its walls. Cattle guard at the entrance to the drive. Outbuildings beyond the house, and some fenced pasture with a big pond. A dozen head of runty Angus grazed the green border of the pond. A small flock of Chinese Whites cruised the blue pond, and after I rumbled over the cattle guard and parked near the house and turned the engine off, I heard their goose-alarm, like a chorus of baritone kazoos. In an acre of marsh across the road, tree toads were beginning to tune up for evening. An inventive mockingbird swayed in the top of a punk tree, working some cardinal song into his repertoire.

A leathery little old woman was yanked out of the front door by a crossbreed dog the size of a bull calf, mottled black and brown, hair all ruffed up around his neck and standing erect down his spine. He made a rumbling in his throat, and showed me some very large white fangs. "Buttercup!" she yelled. "Hold! Hold!"

Buttercup stopped, all aquiver with anxiety to taste me. The old woman wore ancient blue jeans, a dark red pullover sweater, and blue canvas shoes. She clung with both hands to the hefty chain fastened to the studded dog collar. She was thin as one of the stick figures children draw.

"Hoped it was Lew," she said. "Or maybe Jase or Henry coming around finally to see I'm all right. But he's still growling. Who are you? They can't do my eyes till the cataracts get ripe, and I can tell you I'm sick and tired of waiting. Who are you?"

"My name is Travis McGee. I was looking for Lew."

"What for?"

"Just a little talk."

"You stand right still. I got to tell this here dog everything is all right. Buttercup! Okay! Okay! Hush your noise! Down!"

He sat. The rumbling stopped. Tongue lolled. But the amber eyes looked at me with an obvious skepticism.

"Now you come slow right toward him, Mr. McGee, right up to where he can snuff at you. Don't come sudden."

So I made the slow advance. He growled again and she scolded him. He sniffed at a pant leg. She told me to hold my hand out and he sniffed that. Then he stood again and the tail wagged. She said I could scratch behind his ears. He enjoyed it.

"Now he won't bother you. If you come in here and he was loose, he'd come at you running low and fast and quiet, but stand your ground and he'll get a snuff of you and he won't bother you none. I'd get edgy out here alone so much if I didn't have Buttercup."

"He must be a comfort to you. Do you know when Lew . . ."

"Before we get into that, would you kindly do me a favor. I been wondering if I should phone somebody to come help me. That black horse of Lew's has been bawling off and on since early morning, and I can't see enough to take care of whatever's bothering him. It's the near building, and he's in a stall that opens on the far side. Know anything about horses?"

"They're tall, have big teeth, give me a sweat rash, and they all hate me on sight."

"Well, what I think it is, Lew having so much on his mind, he could have forgot feed and water."

I walked out behind the house and found the stall, the top halves of the doors open and hooked back. There was a black horse in there, standing with his head hanging. His coat looked dull. The stall had not been cleaned out for too long. Flies buzzed in the heavy stench. Feed bin and water trough were empty. He snatched his head up and rolled wild eyes and tried to rear up, but his hooves slipped in the slime and he nearly went down. From the dried manure on his flanks, he had already been down a couple of times.

I went back to the house and told Mrs. Arnstead the situation and asked her if there was any reason he couldn't be let out.

"Lew was keeping him in the stall on account of he had a sore on his shoulder he had to put salve on, and it was too much trouble catching him. I guess you best let him out and hope he don't founder himself sucking the pond dry."

When I unlatched the bottom halves and swung the doors open and stepped well back to one side, he came out a lot more slowly than I expected. He walked frail, as if he didn't trust his legs, but slowly quickened his pace all the way across to the pond. He drank for a long time, stopped and drank again, then trudged away from the pond, visibly bigger in the belly, and went slowly down onto his knees and rolled over. I thought he had decided to die. But then he began rolling in the grass, squirming the filth off his black hide.

I looked around, saw rotten sprouting grain in an outdoor bin, saw trash and neglect.

Mrs. Arnstead sat in a cane chair on the shallow screened porch. She invited me in. I sat and Buttercup came over and shoved his big head against my knee, awaiting the scratching.

There was a golden light of dusk, a smell of flowers.

"I just don't know anymore," she said. "Shouldn't heap my burdens on a stranger. Lew is my youngest, the last one left to home. Did just fine in the Army and all. Came back and got took on as a deputy sheriff. Worked this place here and kept it up good, and he was going with the Willoughbee girl. Now being a mother doesn't mean I can't see things the way they are. Jason was my first and Henry was my second, and then it was sixteen long years before I had Lew. Lord God, Jason is forty-three now, married twenty-four years, and their first was a girl, and she married off at sixteen, so I've got a great-grandson near six years old. I know that Lew was always on the mean side. But he always worked hard and worked good, and cared for the stock. It's the last six months he turned into somebody else, somebody I don't hardly know. Broke off with Clara Willoughbee, took up again with a lot of cheap, bright-smelling, loud-voice women. Got meaner. Got so ugly with his brothers, they don't want to ever see him again. Neglects this place and me to go run with trash like them Perrises. Now he's done something, I don't know what, to get himself fired off his job, and he might even have to go to jail. I just don't know what's going to happen. This place is free and clear and it's in my name, but the little bit of money that comes in won't cover food, electric, taxes, and all that. Jase and Henry, they'd help out, but not with me staying out here this way. They got this idea I live six months with one and six with the other like some kind of tourist woman all the rest of my days. What was it my boy did to get Mister Norm so upset he fired him? Do you know?"

"Yes. It isn't very pretty."

"It's like I've run out of pretty lately."

"A very pleasant and gentle and friendly man was picked up for questioning. He knew nothing about the matter under investigation. Your son gave him a very savage beating for no apparent reason. The man is in the hospital in Fort Lauderdale."

She shook her head slowly. In that light, at that angle, I suddenly saw what she had looked like as a young girl. She had been very lovely.

"That's not Lew," she said. "Not at all. He was always some mean, but not that kind of mean. It isn't drinking, because since my eyes have been going bad my nose has got sharp as a hound's. It's something gone bad in his head. Acts funny. Sometimes not a word to me. Set at the table and eat half his supper and shove his chair back and go out and bang the door and drive off into the nighttime. And sometimes he'll get to talking. Lord God, he talks to me a mile a minute, words all tumbling to get out, and he keeps laughing and walking around and about, getting me to laughing, too."

"When was he here last, Mrs. Arnstead?"

"Let me think back. Not since noontime on Thursday. I keep fearing he went off for good. It was yesterday toward evening somebody told me on the phone about him getting fired off his job. I was wishing I could see good enough to . . . well, to look through his stuff and see if I could find something that'd tell me where he'd be. Hate to ask my other sons to come here. What did you say you wanted to talk to him about?"

"I guess I wanted to make sure he was Lew Arnstead, and then I was going to give him the best beating I could manage. That man in the hospital is the best friend I have ever had."

She stared in my direction with those old frosted blue eyes, then laughed well. A husky caw of total amusement. She caught her breath and said, "Mr. McGee, I *like* you. You don't give me sweet lies and gentle talk. And you wouldn't be a man if you didn't come looking for him. But you got to be a lot of man to take my Lew. When I see your shape against the light, you looked sizable enough. But size isn't enough. You got to have some mean, too."

"Probably enough."

"Well, you want to find him and I want to know where he is, so you could maybe come to his room with me and tell me what you can find."

Work clothes and fancy clothes and uniforms. Barbells and hair oil and a gun rack with two rifles, two shotguns, a carbine, all well cared for. Police manuals and ranch journals and comic books. Desk with a file drawer. Farm accounts. Tax papers. She sat on the bed, head tilted, listening to me scuffle through drawers and file folders. Tried the pockets of the clothing in the closet. Found a note in the side pocket of a pair of slacks, wadded small. Penciled in a corner torn off a sheet of yellow paper, a childish, girlish, illiterate backhand. "Lover, he taken off Wesday after work drivin to Tampa seen his moma. I will unhook the same screen windo and please be care you donit bunk into nothing waken the baby. I got the hots so awful I go dizy and sick thinkin on it."

No signature.

"What'd you find?" the old woman asked.

"Just a love note from a woman. No signature. She wants to know why he hasn't come to see her."

"No help to us with no name on it. Keep looking."

I kept looking. There wasn't enough. The man had to have keepsakes of some kind. So he hid them. Probably not with great care. Just enough to keep them out of sight. Easy to get at. But after a dozen bad guesses I was beginning to think that either he had used a lot of care, or threw everything away. Finally I found the hidey-hole. I had previously discovered that the drawer on the bedside stand was a fake. Just a drawer pull and a drawer-shaped rectangle grooved in the wood. But when I reached under, I found there was enough thickness for a good-sized drawer. I took the lamp and alarm clock off the table. The top had concealed hinges.

Plenty of room for dirty books, and for some vividly clinical love notes from female friends. Room for a few envelopes of Polaroid prints. Room for three chunky bottles of capsules. About one hundred per bottle. One was a third empty. All the same. Green and white, and inside the one I pulled open were hundreds of tiny spheres, half of them green and half of them white.

"What did you find now?" she asked.

"The stuff that changed your boy."

"You mean like some kind of drugs? My Lew wouldn't take drugs. Not ever."

"He's got about two hundred and seventy Dexamyl spansules hidden away in here. They're in mix of dexedrine and phenobarb. One of them keeps your motor racing for eight hours. It's what the kids call 'speed.' Super stayawakes. Take two or three for a real good buzz. You can hallucinate on an overdose."

"Speed?" she said. "They said that on the radio way last October.

That was the name of some of the stuff they took out of the lockers at the high school. Mister Norm and my Lew and Billy Cable went in with a warrant and went through all the lockers. And that was . . . about when he started changing."

"At least we know that if he wasn't coming back, he would have taken this along."

"Thank the Lord for that, at least. Anything else in there?"

"A lot of letters."

"From those women of his I expect."

"That's right."

"Well, don't you be shy about reading them. But you don't need to read them to me. Just see if you can find out where he might be."

No need to tell her I was looking for some clue as to who he had entertained in the shed when he was supposed to be guarding the Baither place.

Few of them were dated. But I came across one with a mid-March date that was more literate and less torrid than the others, and interested me mightily.

Dear Lew,

I ran into Frannie in the Suprex yesterday and she was trying to stick the needle in, like always, and she told me she saw you twice with Lilo. Now you can tell me it's none of my business because the thing we had going is over and done, and you know why we had to quit for good. But this is like old times sake, because for a while before it got sour, I really and truly loved you, and I guess you know that. I have never really forgiven you for beating me up for no reason and I guess I never will, but I couldn't stand for you to get in some kind of stupid trouble. LEAVE LILO ALONE!!!! She is bad news for one and all. I know all about her because for a while she and a girl I know well were friends. The reason she went with her mother after the divorce was on account of her father knew he couldn't handle her. He had custody of both kids, but he let Lilo go. Her mother and her stepfather couldn't control her either, and not many people know this, but when she was seventeen, like a year after she dropped high school, she was fooling around with Frank Baither, and he's old enough to be her father, and they say he's getting out soon, and if he wants her back, you better not be in the way. Now I'll tell you something else I happen to know, and I hope it turns your stomach. I'm not making it up because I haven't got the kind of sick mind that can make up something ugly. It happened on a Sunday afternoon last December. Roddy Barramore broke down on Route 112 down by where Shell

282

Ridge Road turns off. A water hose busted, and he decided the best thing to do was walk into Shell Ridge Road to the Perris place, figuring Mr. Perris would have some hose and clamps or at least some tape. It was a warm Sunday and when he got near the house he could hear through the screen in the open windows that Mr. Perris had the football pro game on turned up loud. So he thought instead of ringing the door, he'd go holler in the window, and he had his mouth open to holler and then he saw Lilo and Mr. Perris on the couch, making out like mad, all their clothes in a pile on the floor. Roddy scrunched down quick before they seen him, and walked back and first he told Rhoda there was nobody home, and she said he was quiet for a while and then he told her what really happened. What do you think of a girl who'll make out with her stepfather knowing her own mother is there helpless in the bedroom maybe fifteen feet away, unable to speak or move much since she had the stroke over two years ago which some say was the judgment of God, but I say we aren't to judge because we don't really know what reasons she had for breaking up her own marriage the way she did. Rhoda told me about it. It made me want to throw up. I hope it does the same for you. I don't care that you aren't seeing me anymore, really. I wish the best for you always, Lew, but you won't have anything but heartache and bad trouble if you run around with Lilo.

Always your friend,
Betsy

I went through the Polaroid prints. Amateur nude studies. Thirty-two different poses. Many different girls. A lean blonde with an insipid leer and huge meaty breasts figured in ten of them, prone, supine, standing, reaching, kneeling. Five were of a woman with a superb body, a body good enough to overcome the incompetence of the photographer. In each she kept the lens from seeing her face.

Then there were thirteen different females, which I suppose could be thought of as trophy shots, all head-on naked some taken by flash, some by available light, some indoors, some outdoors. Estimated ages, eighteen to thirty-two. A variety of expression, from timorous uncertain smile to dazed glaze of sexuality, from broad grin to startled glance of herself surprised, to theatrical scowl. The sameness of the pose removed all erotic possibility. They became record shots, and could have been taken in the anteroom of the gas chamber after a short ride in a cattle car.

It was the remaining four shots which gave me a prickling sensation on the backs of hands and neck. Solid, shapely, dark-haired, suntanned chunk of girl. Evenly and deeply tanned everywhere, except for the surprisingly white bikini-band, low slung around the functional swelling of the sturdy hips. One of those pretty, engaging, amusing little toughy faces. An easy-laugher. A face for fun and joy, games and excursions. Not at all complicated unless you looked more closely, carefully. Then you could see something out of focus. A contradiction. There was a harsh sensuality in that face which was at odds with the merry expression. There was a clamp-jawed resolve contradicting that look of amiable readiness for fun and games.

I had seen that face, for a micro-instant, several busy seconds before Miss Agnes squashed into the canal. I felt sure of it. And this chance for a more careful examination confirmed the fleeting feeling that my young volunteer mechanic, Ron Hatch, had to be related to her by blood. Though his face was long instead of round, doleful rather than merry, the curves of the mouth, the set of the eyes, the breadth and slant of forehead were much alike.

"Must be a lot of letters," the old woman said.

I put everything back except the most explicit picture of the dark-haired girl, closed the lid, put the lamp and clock back in position.

"Nothing that helps much. But I want to ask some questions, if you don't mind, Mrs. Arnstead."

"Don't mind a bit. Talked too much already, so I might just as soon keep right on. That's what happens when you're old and alone. Talk the ear off anybody that wants to stop by and listen. But let's go back to the porch. Lew could come roaring in, and he'd get mean about a stranger being in his room."

The sun was down and the porch faced the western sky, faced a band of red so intense it looked as if all the far cities of the world were burning. It will probably look much like that when they do burn.

"Mrs. Arnstead, I remember you said something about your son running around with trash like the Perrises. Is there a Perris girl?"

"There's Lillian, but she's not rightly a Perris. I did hear she's tooken the name, but whether legal in a court, I don't know. Her real name is Hatch. Her daddy is John Hatch, and he had a lot of friends and business interests around Cypress City. He's the kind that's real shrewd about a deal and sort of stupid about women. Anyway he married one that turned out to be trashy for sure. Wanda. He brought her back here from Miami. Must be . . . let me see now . . . oh, many years ago. The first baby was Lillian, and then there was Ronnie, then there was one that died. I'd say there was trouble all along between John Hatch and Wanda. Maybe he worked so hard he left her too much time on her hands, and she was built for trouble. They fought terrible, and the way they tell it, Johnny Hatch finally had enough, and so he set out to get grounds to get rid of that woman. About seven years ago, it happened. He had a good mechanic working at his garage name of Henry Perris, and he had the idea Henry was getting to Wanda every chance that came along. So he brought in a fellow and he got the goods on them for sure, tape recordings and pictures and all. She had no chance of child custody or alimony or anything. Soon as the divorce was final, Henry surprised everybody by marrying her. Lillian was fourteen or fifteen then, and wild as any swamp critter, and when she made up her mind she'd rather be with her mother, John Hatch had the good sense not to fight it. They say Ron is a nice boy. John married again a couple years ago and there's a couple babies now. Let me see. Where was I? Wanda and Henry moved into a place way south of town, down there on the edge of the swamps. She took on a lot of weight they say, and I guess she had the high blood, because she was always highcolored. She had a little stroke about three years ago I guess it was, and then she had a big one and she's been in the bed ever since, helpless as a baby. There's some other Perrises down there, trashy folk, fighting and stealing, running in a pack with the other trash. Lillian is as bad as the worst. Lilo they call her. And my Lew has been messin' with those trashy people."

"You're sure of that?"

"She was calling here, giving me orders, telling me to tell my son Lilo called. I told him to tell her not to call him here. He got ugly about it." She sighed. "He turned from my youngest into a stranger. I guess it was those pills, not really him at all."

"Where does Henry Perris work?"

"He sure doesn't work for Johnny Hatch. He could work anyplace he wants to go, on account of being so good of a mechanic, they say. I heard he works someplace south."

"In a station on the Trail?"

"Could be. I don't rightly know."

"What kind of a car does Lew have?"

"He had a real nice car up till three months back, and then he smashed it all up so bad it was a wonder he wasn't killed. There was something wrong about the insurance, so what he's driving now is the old jeep that was here on the place, fixed up some. It was dirty yellow and he got it painted black, he told me. I've been wondering something."

"Yes?"

"I'm a silly old woman but I'm not foolish. Seems like you have the thought in your mind my Lew might be in some kind of trouble more than from just beating up your best friend."

"He might be. I don't know."

"Then . . . if he is, I hope you find out and I hope you tell Mister Norm. If he is, I want him put away someplace because he's getting so wild he might kill somebody, then he wouldn't have any life left at all. Better he loses a piece of his life and gets over what those pills done to him than lose the whole thing. Unless maybe . . . already he killed somebody?" The dread in her voice was touching and unmistakable.

"Are you thinking about Frank Baither?"

"It was on the radio."

"I think he was on duty when that happened."

"Thank the Lord."

She asked me to phone her if I heard anything about Lew. I told her to let me know if he came home. She said she could use the phone by counting the holes in the dial. I gave her the White Ibis number. I started to repeat it and she said not to bother, that her memory seemed to getting better insead of worse as time went by. But she sure did miss the television. It was just shapes and light that didn't mean anything. She wished the cataracts would hurry and get ripe enough.

As I drove back toward town I was thinking about that ancient and honorable bit of homely psychology, that myth of the ripeness of cataracts. The lens capsule can be removed as soon as it begins to get cloudy. But postoperative vision with corrective lenses is a poor resource at best, compared with normal sight. So the ripeness they speak of is the psychological ripeness of the patient, a time of diminishing vision which lasts long enough, and gets bad enough, so that the postoperative vision is, by comparison, a wonder and a delight. The patient is happy because the basis of comparison has changed.

There are some extraordinarily cruel men in the primitive rural areas of India who travel from village to village curing cataracts for a few rupees. Their surgical tool is a long, very slender, very sharp and hard thorn. They insert it from the side, behind the lens, and puncture the lens capsule. The cloudy fluid leaks into the eye itself and is replaced, or diluted, by the clear fluid within the eye. Sight is restored. It is a miracle. In sixty or ninety days the patient becomes totally and permanently blind, but by then the magician is a dozen villages away, busy with new miracles. Perhaps they do not think of themselves as cruel men. In a country where the big city syndicates purchase children, and carefully maim and disfigure them in vividly memorable ways, and distribute them by truck throughout the city each morning to sit on busy sidewalks with begging bowls, and collect them at dusk, as impersonally as one might empty coin machines, cruelty itself is a philosophical abstraction.

The April night was turning cool, so after I stopped back at the White Ibis and picked up an old blue sailcloth sportcoat, laundered and pressed as a courtesy of the Cypress County taxpayers, I went to a place I had spotted when driving around the town. The Adventurer. A lot of blue neon, tinted glass, an acre of asphalt packed with local cars. Frigid air conditioning, exhaust fans hustling the smoke out, ceiling prisms beaming down narrow areas of glare on the Saturday night faces. Long bar packed deep, and people sitting at small tables, leaning toward each other to shout intimacies over the shattering din of a hundred other people shouting to be heard over the sound of a trio on a high shelf in the corner, three dead-faced whiskery young men boosting by about five hundred watts the sound of an electric guitar, electric bass, and a fellow who stood whapping at a tall snare drum and singing sounds which may or may not have been words into the microphone. The obligatory birdcage girl had her own high shelf. She was meaty and energetic, snapping her hair across her closed eyes, tromping out the big beat with a simple repetitive pattern of bump and grind, belly dance and Tahitian flutter. She was not strictly topless because she had a narrow band of fabric around the busy bouncing boobs. There was a spotlight on her that changed from pink to black to blue to black, and in the black light only her teeth and the two narrow bands of fabric, and her high silver shoes glowed with an eerie luminescence.

As I waited to move in close enough to the bar to get my order in, I looked the crowd over. High-school kids and ranch hands and packing-house workers. Single swingers and young marrieds. Bank clerks and secretaries and young realtors. Carpenters and plumbers, electricians and hard-wall plasterers, along with young dentists and soldiers and sailors home on leave and hospital technicians and nurses and bag boys and store clerks, and a handful of the customary predators, middle-aged men in youthful clothing, watching, appraising, singling out potential prey of either sex, planning their careful reassuring campaigns. It was half beer and half hard. The beer was draft, in chilled heavy glass mugs that hold half what they appear to hold. Waitresses hustled the tables, serving either roast beef sandwiches or bowls of shrimp boiled in beer. So the fun place was a nice money machine, because when the waitress slapped the check on the table you either paid and left, or ordered more. I got hold of a cold mug and got back thirty cents change from my dollar and too much head on the dark beer.

I moved out of the crush and sipped the beer and looked for the controls. When you have a big noisy center-ring act that mixes lions, tigers, bears, sheep, rabbits, weasels, and cobras, you need the men with the whips and kitchen chairs and shiny pistols or you start losing too many animals, and end up with an empty ring and a legal paper nailed to the door.

A disturbance started at a far corner of the long bar and two quiet men appeared out of nowhere and moved in before it had a chance to spread. A good pair, swift and professional, and they picked the right one without hesitation. When they took him by me I saw that his mouth was wrenched apart by pain and his eyes were frightened, his face pallid and sweaty. The two men were smiling, joking with him. A painful come-along of some kind, manual or mechanical, is better for business than a half dozen old-fashioned bouncers. They had hit so quickly, I knew that the place had to be under observation. So by picking the best spot from which one could watch the whole room, I finally picked out the watch station. A mirrored insert was set high over the bar. From there a man could sit at his ease and watch all of the bar, all of the tables, the small dance floor, the cash registers, the entrance, and the doors to the rest rooms. The two men came back in and took up their position to the right of the main entrance. One of them pressed the switch of an intercom box and spoke into it. I could guess the probable message. "He quieted down nice, Charlie. He's driving home, and he won't be back tonight."

So I stood there, in that absolute and lonely privacy that exists only in the middle of a crush of strangers and a deafening din of festive voices and festive rock, staring at the hefty fleshy pumping of the tireless blonde, and wondering why I should feel that too many important parts were missing from my equation.

I had been luckier than I deserved, first in finding that lonely, troubled, talkative old woman, secondly in having her relate to me quickly and trustingly, and thirdly in getting my good look at the private hidden life of Lew Arnstead.

A lot of pieces fit beautifully together, but in some way the fit was too good to be true.

I wished Meyer was standing beside me, so I could try it on him. "Frank Baither planned the money-truck job. He used Hutch, Orville, Henry Perris, and Lilo, Perris's stepdaughter. We saw Henry, Meyer. He was the broad brown guy with the white teeth who arrived late for work at Al Storey's station that morning. Driving . . . a blue Rambler. So Henry was in on the Baither killing. It was Lilo Perris (or Hatch) who ran across our bows. Henry set up a little smoke screen. It was too cute because maybe he was too nervous. Grab that envelope and somehow get it to Lilo. Then she went to the Baither place and faked Lew Arnstead into giving her a chance to plant it in Baither's house. Arnstead is on speed and it has turned him erratic and dangerous. All Mister Norm has to do is trace the envelope, from Henry to Lilo to the Baither house, and bring them in and open them up—Henry and Lew and Lilo. In a hurry, before Lew and Lilo run for it with the money off the truck."

And suddenly I knew Meyer's reaction. I could almost hear his voice. "If our sheriff Norman Hyzer knows as much about this county as I think he knows, then he certainly knows that Frank Baither's little girl friend, before the money-truck operation, was Lilo Perris. He knows a young girl was involved. He might suspect that Henry Perris was in on it, too, and he would check back and find out where Henry was that weekend. He seemed absolutely convinced we were involved. As if he *had* to believe we were. Why?"

"A blind spot, maybe. Maybe he's too close to it to see it. Maybe he's involved in some way. The pieces fit so well, Meyer."

"Do they always?"

"Hardly ever."

"So why do you keep asking these dumb questions?"

Meyer disappeared when big King Sternevan appeared in front of me, Coke bottle dwarfed by his big malformed fist.

nine

"McGee, you didn't come across our buddy Lew yet, huh?"

"How do you know?"

"I'd put my money on you, like I said, but he'd mark you some. You wouldn't be able to help that. I been asking around. Nobody's seen that sucker."

King's civilian garb was a big red sport shirt with white palm trees on it, and a tent-sized pair of wrinkled khaki slacks. He had a small straw hat with a narrow brim perched on the back of his head, and a row of cigars in the sport-shirt pocket.

We had to roar at each other to be heard, and I didn't want to roar what I wanted to say to him. So he willingly followed me out into the abrupt silence of the night, and we went and sat in the top-down Buick.

"Would you say that like six months ago Arnstead started to go bad?"

"Maybe that long ago. I wasn't paying attention."

"Before that, he was okay?"

"He was pretty good. He was maybe as good as Billy Cable, and Cable is one hell of a cop, and you can believe it. But . . . I don't know. The broads, I guess. A few months back he beat up one of his broads. She filed a complaint and then pulled it. There was something maybe I should have reported. I was in my own car. Six, seven weeks ago. He come the other way, alone in our number four cruiser, on 112 and he had it wound right up to the top. We use Fords with heavy suspension and the Cobra 428 mill with a three-point-five-o rear end, so you got an honest hunner twenny-five, and he comes by with that needle laying right on the pin. Hell, I turned around and went in, thinking maybe somebody had hit the bank. Nothing going on. I ast him, what the hell, Lew. You could kill yourself on that kind of road. He told me to shove it. Take fighters now. There have been some greats who went right down the chute when the wrong kind of broad started pecking away at them."

"Ever think he might be on anything, King?"

He took his time, glowered at a long cigar ash, tapped it over the side onto the parking lot asphalt. "Now that you bring it up, pally."

"Suppose I say he is? Definitely."

"Then I say two things. I say you shouldn't ought to be poking around enough to find out, because it will make Mister Norm a little on the soreass side. And I say the more I think, the more it fits. Speed, maybe? You take fighters, there isn't maybe one these days doesn't go into a main bout without being stepped up with superpill. It's no good, pal. They go like hell and they don't get tired and they get a little more quick, but they can get hurt bad and not know it and get up and get killed. You spend more than you got, and you sack out for two, three days to get back to normal. Staying on it is something else. Come to think of it, he hasn't been sleeping much lately, and he's dropped weight. What would get him on it?"

"Like the preacher says. Evil companions."

"Pally, we all got a few of those. All it means is you better not try to find Lew. You better stay the hell away from him."

"And it means his judgment has gone bad. That's why he pounded on Meyer. He could have killed him."

"I stepped out at the wrong time."

"Why didn't Billy Cable stop him?"

"Because Billy and him haven't been getting along so good, and when you see a man bitching himself, why stop him? Anyway, Billy finally did stop him or Lew would have killed your friend. Then when it was your turn with Mister Norm, Billy took the chance of giving you a look at your friend so Mister Norm would get the picture on Lew loud and clear and soon. Poor bastard."

"King, the woman who signed the complaint and withdrew it against Arnstead, was her first name Betsy?"

"Jesus Q. Christ! You're supposed to be a stranger in town,

McGee. Betsy Kapp. Mrs. Betsy Kapp. She's a divorced lady, works hostess in the dining room down at the Live Oak Lodge. Mrs. Teffer's place. Best food in the county."

Nice to have King confirm Lennie Sibelius's appraisal of the local cuisine. I went back inside with King, and twenty minutes later drove into the middle of the city. It was a little after nine when I walked into the dining room. There was a family celebration at a long table near the far wall, champagne and toasts by middle-aged males to a fresh-faced girl and her blushing husband-to-be. Two quiet couples at small tables, with coffee and dessert by candlelight. Three burly businessmen drawing plot plans on the tablecloth.

As the hostess approached me, menus in the crook of her arm, I knew she had to be Betsy Kapp. She was the lean-bodied blonde who had starred in ten of Lew's Polaroid shots, the one with the attempt at a sexy leer which didn't quite come off. She wore a dark blue shift with a little starched white collar, and that mixed look of query and disapproval which told me that it was a little late for dinner.

Before she could turn me away, I said, "My attorney, Mr. Sibelius, said that I'd be a fool to eat anywhere else, Mrs. Kapp."

"Oh?" she said. And then "Oh." She turned and looked at the foyer clock. "Well, it *is* a little late, but if you . . . didn't want anything too terribly elaborate . . ."

"Sirloin, baked potato, tossed salad with oil and vinegar, and coffee?"

"I think that would . . . Sit wherever you want, while I . . ."

She took off for the kitchen in a slightly knock-kneed jog and I picked a table by the wall as far from the other four parties as I could get. She came back smiling. "They hadn't turned the broiler off, thank goodness. But no baked. Home fries?"

"Fine."

"And the steak?"

"Medium rare."

"I can get you a cocktail from the bar."

"Plymouth gin, if they have it, on the rocks, straight, with a twist. A double. Booth's if they don't."

She gave the order, came back with my drink, then went to the register and took care of the departing family party and then the businessmen. I watched her move around. She looked a little younger and prettier than in the amateur nude studies, probably because there was a lively animation in her face and because she moved quickly and stood well. Had I not seen the pictures, I would have wondered if the imposing thrust of bosom might not be a pneumatic artifice, a fabricated symbol of the culture's obsession with mammary bounty. But I knew they were real, imposingly, awesomely real.

When she brought my salad she said. "I have to be the waitress, too. Another drink?"

She brought the dinner. It was a splendid piece of meat indeed. When I was half finished, the last of the two couples paid and left, and I had the dining room to myself.

Betsy Kapp said, "Would you like your coffee now?"

I waved at the empty chair across from me. "With two cups?"

She hesitated. "Why not? Thank you. I've been on my feet since eleven-thirty this morning."

She brought the coffee and sat across from me, leaned to the candle flame to light her cigarette. "It was a real pleasure serving Mr. Sibelius. He's a very charming man."

And, I thought, he tips very big and tips everybody in sight. I held my hand out. "Travis McGee," I said. She shook hands, pulled her long-fingered hand away quickly.

"I heard that you . . . you were in some trouble."

"*Am* in some trouble. Had the very bad luck to be in the wrong place at the wrong time. But I think it's getting straightened out. I never heard of Mr. Frank Baither until we were picked up for killing him. I guess if the sheriff still thought so, I'd be back inside."

Somebody rattled the foyer door, then apparently gave up and went away.

"I keep wondering about something," she said.

"What is it?"

"Mr. Sibelius didn't know my name. I'm sure of that. But you did."

I shrugged. "Some people were standing outside talking. I asked if it was too late to eat here, and they said to come in and ask Betsy Kapp. So when you came at me with the menus, it seemed logical to call you Mrs. Kapp. Maybe that was a mistake. Maybe I made a mistake. Miss Kapp?"

She grimaced. "No. It's Mrs. But I'm not working at it."

"Is this your hometown, Betsy?"

"No. I'm from Winter Haven, originally. But they sent me here to stay with my aunt when I was twelve. She died when I was seventeen and I went back home, but things were terrible there and so I came back here and married the boy I was going with. Then he was killed in a terrible automobile accident, and after I got the insurance settlement I went to Miami and then Atlanta, but I didn't like it in either place. Then I came back here and married a fellow named Greg Kapp, and we fought like some kind of animals until I couldn't stand it anymore and divorced him. I don't know where he went and I don't care. So here I am, and pretty soon it will be four years I've been working here. I get sort of restless, but you know how it is. It's hard to break loose. I sort of like the work, and you get treated pretty good here. Why should I be telling you my whole life story?"

"Because I'm interested. Good reason?"

"I guess you are. God knows why you should be. Are you married, Travis McGee?"

"No. Never have been."

"You must have some kind of work that keeps you outdoors and all. You look like you're in great shape."

"Salvage work, out of Fort Lauderdale."

"Like on a ship?"

"No. I'm an independent contractor. I take whatever comes along. I live alone on a houseboat at a marina."

"Gee, that must be a great way to live. Well, I live alone too, but not on any houseboat. It's a little cottage that my aunt had, that she left me. The bank had it and rented it until I was twenty-one. Greg was after me all the time to sell it. I'm glad now I didn't. I moved in after the divorce, when the lease ran out on the people I had renting it."

"I guess you know Cypress City pretty well then."

"Well enough."

"I'd like to be able to ask somebody about it, about the people. Sheriff Hyzer and Frank Baither and so on. But you've probably got things to do."

"Because it's Saturday night? Hah! The only thing I've got to do is total the tape and count the money and give Frank, the bartender, the cash and checks."

"So I can wait."

"It doesn't take me long, really." Her smile, as she stood up, was the distillation of several hundred motion pictures, refined in the loneliness of the bathroom mirror, born of a hunger for romance, for magic, for tremulous, yearning love. This was the meet-cute episode, immortalized by all the Doris Days, unexpected treasure for a thirty-summers blonde with something childish-girlish about her mouth, something that would never tighten into maturity. It would always yearn, always hope, always pretend—and it would always be used.

She took one of Lennie's twenties and brought me my change and went back to the register. It made a delicate little problem. To tip or not to tip. A tip would put a strain on the relationship she was trying, with concealed nervousness, to establish. So I went over to her and put a five on the counter by the register and said, "Save this for the waitress who was in such a rush to leave, Betsy."

She giggled. "Like turning the other cheek, huh? Helen is a good waitress, but she's always in a terrible rush to get home to her kids. I'll see she gets it, and I'll see you get one of her tables next time."

We walked out together. I asked her suggestion as to where we could go for a drink. She said that first she ought to take her car home. I followed her. She had one of those little pale tan Volkswagens with the fenders slightly chewed up, some trim missing, some rust streaks. I followed her. She drove head-long, yanking it around the corners. She was silhouetted erect in the oncoming lights. We sped through old residential areas where the people sat in their dimly lighted rooms, watching all the frantic imitations of festivity on the small home screens, watching the hosts and the hostesses who were old, dear and familiar friends. Long ago their parents had old familiar friends named Alexander Botts and Scattergood Baines and Tugboat Annie. But reading was a lot harder. You had to make up the pictures in your head. Easier to sit and watch the pictures somebody else planned. And it had a comforting sameness, using up that portion of your head which would start fretting and worrying if it wasn't kept busy.

"Your mission, Mr. Phelps, if you care to accept it, is to discredit the half brother of the dictator of Kataynzia, recover the nine billion in gold, and give it to the leader of the free democratic underground, and disarm the ICBMs now being installed in the Stammerhorn Mountains. If you or any of your I.M. Force are killed or captured . . ."

"Wait one cotton-pickin' minute! Accept it! Accept a dumb-dumb mission like that? Are you some kind of ding-a-ling? We'd never get out of that rotten little country alive."

"Mr. Phelps!"

"Barney won't try it. Paris won't try it. And I won't try it. Go get somebody else. Go get Cinnamon, even. Come back next week, boss, with something that makes sense."

And the screens go dark, from the oil-bound coasts of Maine to the oily shores of Southern California. Chief Ironsides retires to a chicken farm. Marshal Dillon shoots himself in the leg, trying to outdraw the hard case from Tombstone. The hatchet bounces back off the tree and cuts down tall Dan'l Boone. The American living room becomes silent. The people look at each other, puzzled, coming out of the sweet, long, hazy years of automated imagination.

Where'd all the heroes go, Andy?

Maybe, honey, they went where all the others went, a long time ago. Way off someplace. Tarzan and Sir Galahad and Robin Hood. Ben Casey and Cap'n Ahab and The Shadow and Peter Rabbit. Went off and joined them.

But what are we going to do, Andy? What are we going to do?

Maybe . . . talk some. Think about things.

Talk about *what*? Think about *what*? I'm scared, Andy.

But there's no problem, really, because after the screens go dark and silent, all the tapes of the watchers self-destruct in five seconds.

Little mental games often compromise my attention. She braked so hard and unexpectedly I nearly climbed the back slope of the bug. She swung left into a narrow drive between tall thick hedges. I followed, and she drove into a small carport, cut the lights, got out, grinned and squinted back into my headlight glare, turned on a carport light and pulled the edge of her hand across her throat. So I turned off my lights and engine and got out. April bugs were shrilling in the hedges, under a murky half moon.

"A lot of the meat is broiled," she said. "They have those exhaust fans and all, but I'm in and out of there enough so when I get home I smell like meat grease. It gets in my hair and my clothes. It won't take me long to get rid of it, Travis. Come and look at my little nest."

It was to be admired, even though she had enough furniture and lamps and department store art objects for a cottage twice the size. One careless move, and I felt as if I would welt my leg on a table and spill $19.95 worth of pseudo-Mexican ceramics. I had to admire the cat, which was easier. A big male neuter, part alley and part Persian, patterned in gray and black, a wise, tolerant, secure cat who mentioned, politely enough, that he would like to hear the sound of the electric can opener. She opened a can of something that looked horrid, dumped it onto a paper saucer and put it in his corner. He approached it slowly, making electric motor sounds, then hunched into the serious ceremony of eating.

"He can say his name," she said. "Raoul. Raoul?"

The cat looked up at her, chop-licking, and said, "Raoul," and bent again to his gluey feast.

"Come see his yard," she said. "Raoul's personal piece of outdoors."

We went through another door off the kitchen into a fenced grassy rectangle about twenty feet by thirty. She clicked on the outdoor floods as we went out. They were amber-colored. The grapestake fence was about eight feet high, affording total privacy. There were flagstones, planting areas, vines against the grape stake, a little recycling electric fountain in the middle, which she turned on. There was some redwood furniture and a sun cot.

I had the feeling I had been there before, and then I recognized areas of it which had formed the background for the Polaroid poses.

"Raoul and I both love this place," she said. "Neighborhood dogs roam in packs, and he knows they can't get at him. And I can stretch out in the sun absolutely stark and just bake myself into a stupor. It's sort of pointless, really, because I can't ever get a decent tan. My skin resists it. I go pink and then it turns sort of yellow-sallow and then back to white. But I just love the feel of the sun."

I made admiring sounds and she led me back in and back into the living room. "Sit in that chair, dear," she said. "When you put your legs up, it's fabulously comfortable, really. Do you like Brazilian music? I have this thing about the samba. See, I've got it all on these cassettes."

"I like it."

"Good!" As she picked out a couple of cassettes, she said, "A gentleman friend got me a wonderful discount on this stereo cassette player. He makes his own tapes off records and off the air and then he makes duplicates and leaves them with me when he comes through town. Travis, while you're waiting for me, would you like a drink? I've got practically anything. Gin, vodka, rum, Scotch, and so on. I don't drink gin, actually. So I don't know anything about it. There's almost a full bottle somebody left of something called Bengal gin. Is that any good?"

"It's excellent."

"I thought it might be pretty good. I've been meaning to ask Frank, the bartender, but I keep forgetting. I could fix you a drink like you had at the Lodge. Me, I like to come home and make myself a tall tall Scotch and water with lots of ice, and then take a long hot hot sudsy bath and take a sip of the icy drink every little while. It tastes fantastically marvelous then. I'm going to have the drink, dear, but don't worry about waiting for me to take a long bath. I'll make it a quick shower. Can I fix you what you . . ."

"That would be just fine, Betsy."

So she started the cassette and adjusted the volume. She came smiling back with a gin and ice for me in a giant crystal glass tinted green, with grapes and grapevines etched into it, placed it on a cork coaster on the table beside the tilt chair. The cork coaster had small bright fish painted on it. The paper napkin was pink, imprinted with BETSY in red diagonally across a scalloped corner. Beside the drink she put a little blue pottery rowboat full of salted mixed nuts.

"There!" she said above the music of Mr. Bonfa, and went off to get rid of the occupational odor of burning meat, leaving me in my fabulously comfortable chair, next to a drink that would tranquilize a musk ox, semirecumbent in a static forest of bric-a-brac, listening to Maria Toledo breathe Portuguese love words at me in reasonably good stereo.

A compulsive strangler would have damned few tactical problems. She had taken my word that Lennie Sibelius was my attorney. She took my word that my semiarrest was due to bad luck rather than guilt. She went on instinct, and trusted the stranger. But a strangler can look like me. Or thee. The guest could tiptoe in and clamp the sick hand on the soapy throat, and in the moments left to her she could remember an entirely different sequence of motion pictures. Death itself would not be real because it would look like Alfred Hitchcock.

In fifteen minutes she reappeared in the doorway. "*Look* at me!" she wailed. "Will you just *look* at me!"

She wore a floor-length terry robe dyed in a big bold psychedelic pattern of red, orange, pink, and lemon. She held it closed, one hand at her throat, the other at her waist. Her hair was sopping wet, pasted flat to the delicate shape of the skull.

"I am *so* dang stupid about mechanical things," she complained.

"What happened?"

"I got out of the shower and bent over and turned it so the water comes out of the faucets, and then I was going to close the drain for a minute, to sort of rinse the tub, and I hit the shower thing, dammit. I didn't want to get my hair wet. It's very dense and very fine and it takes like forever to dry. I'm terribly sorry, dear. But I can't go out like this, really. Would you mind terribly? We could talk here, couldn't we? And there really aren't that many nice places to go at this time of night. What time is it? My goodness, it's after eleven-thirty already! I had no idea."

"I was going to suggest a rain check. Maybe that isn't the right expression."

"Is your drink all right? Goodness you've hardly touched the surface. Are you sure you don't mind if we just stay in? At least it isn't going to give me any big decisions about what to wear. Back in a jiffy, dear."

She went away. The music stopped. I went over and flipped the cassette and cut the volume back by half, and threaded my way back to the leathery refuge.

She was not, I decided, devious enough to shove her hair under the water and go into an act. Nor, having been asked out, could she step out of her own obligatory role and say it would be cozier if we stayed in. Doubtless it had happened just as she described it. But the mistake, though deliberate, was on a subconscious and inaccessible level. It was all part and parcel of the meet-cute. The entry in the locked diary—and it would be inconceivable for her not to keep one —would say, "Actually, probably nothing at all would ever have happened between us if I hadn't been so stupid and soaked my hair that way. Then again, maybe it would have happened anyway, but not so soon, not on the very first night I met him. There was something inevitable about Travis and me, and I guess somehow I sensed it from the very first minute."

She came out in about a jiffy and a half. She had wound a coral-colored towel around her wet hair and tucked it in place. Instead of the mini-brief, leggedy outfit I anticipated, she wore an ivory white corduroy jump suit, with a kitchy arrangement of wide gold zippers and small gold padlocks on the four pockets, a gold chain around the waist, and a concealed zipper from larynx to crotch. After she had moved through the room a couple of times, straightening and patting, I found myself reacting to the outfit, and decided that, given her figure, it was more provocative than had she worn what I expected.

She took my drink away and "freshened" it, and made herself another tall pale Scotch. She sat on a blue nubbly couch a yard from my leather lair, pulled her long legs up, and said, "I guess I'm a terrible party pooper, Travis, but I'm just as happy not to go out. I guess my little nest is really why I don't leave this town. When I'm here, I'm not really in Cypress City. I could be anywhere, I guess. Because if I were anyplace else, I'd build another nest like this one, with all my own things around me. I'm kind of . . . of . . . an inward sort of person. I don't *really* pay a lot of attention to what goes on . . . out there. So I don't know if I can tell you the sort of things you want to know, actually."

I started her off by telling her I thought Sheriff Norman Hyzer a strange one. So she told me his tragic life story, and how everybody understands why he is so withdrawn and cold and precise. But a fair man, really. Very fair. And they say he is real up-to-date with all the gadgets and advances in police work. He lives for his work, and they say he's got it now so that the job pays so little money, really, that nobody else tries to get elected. He puts all the money into the department, into pay for the deputies, and patrol cars and radios and all that.

"Well, I know some Baithers, because there are a lot of them around the south county, dear. There was one rotten Baither boy in junior high with me. He got killed in Vietnam years ago. His name was Forney Baither. I don't know what relation he was to Frank Baither. But they were the same kind, I guess. Forney got a choice of going to state prison or enlisting. I'd say that a dead Baither isn't much of a loss to anybody, and I guess nearly everybody would agree with that."

I could feel a little Bengal buzz. She wasn't going to give me anything useful unless I found the right door and blew the hinges off. I looked at her blurred image through green glass.

"Penny for your thoughts?" she said.

"I guess I was thinking about the Great Sheriff, the tragic figure, the miracle of efficiency and public service. Why would he keep an animal on his payroll?"

"What do you mean?"

"A brutal, sadistic, degenerate stud animal like Lew Arnstead?"

She put her fingers to her throat. Her mouth worked and her eyes went wide. "Lew? But he's just . . ."

"Just the kindly officer of the law who put my gentle friend of many years in the hospital for no reason at all, and would have killed him with his hands if Billy Cable hadn't stopped him."

"That doesn't sound like . . ."

"He's suspended and facing charges, and I hope Hyzer makes sure he's sent away for a long long time. I'd like to get to him first, for about one full minute."

"But he isn't . . ."

"Isn't such a rotten kid after all? Come on, Betsy! I've been checking him out . . . while I was looking for him. He's been running up a big score in the Cypress County female population. Romping them and roughing them up, and entertaining his buddies with his bare-ass Polaroid souvenirs."

Her eyes went wide-blind, looking at me and through me as she added it up, her long throat working as she swallowed again and again. The cassette had come to the end. There was no automatic turnoff. There was a small humming, grinding sound as the tape drive kept working. This was her sweet nest, all bric-a-brac and make-believe. A talented lady once defined poetry as a make-believe garden containing a real toad. So I had put the toad in Betsy's garden.

She made a lost, hollow, plaintive cry, sprang to her feet, and ran for shelter. Miraculously, in her pell-mell dash for her bathroom, she did not smash a thing. The door banged. I heard distant kitten-sounds. I got up and ejected the tape and put a new one on.

You are a dandy fellow, T. McGee. All the lonely, wasted, wistful ones of the world have some set of illusions which sustains them, which builds a warm shelter in the wasteland of the heart. It does them no good to see themselves as they really are, once you kick the shelter down. This one was easy bed-game for any traveling man who wanted to indulge her fantasies by playing the role of sentimental romanticism, with a little spice of soap-opera drama.

So, while you are digging up whatever might be useful out of the little ruin you have created, at least have the grace to try to put the make-believe garden back in order. If you get the chance.

First step. Go to bathroom door. Knock. "Betsy? Betsy, dear? Are you all right?"

Blurred and miserable answer. Something about being out in a minute. Fix a drink.

Fixed two. They looked the same as before. But hers was real and mine was tap water.

She came out at last, walking sad, shoulders slumping and face puffy, saying something about being sorry, terribly sorry.

Moved over to the couch. Sat beside her. Took her hand. She tried to pull it away, then let it rest in mine. Her eyes met mine, then slid away.

"Betsy, may I make some very personal remarks?" Shrugged, and nodded. "I think you are a fine, generous, warm-hearted woman. People are going to take advantage of those qualities sometimes. But you shouldn't feel bad, really. When . . . . a human being never takes any emotional risks, then she never gets hurt. But she isn't really alive, either, is she?"

"I . . . don't know. I wish I was dead."

"When I opened my big mouth, honey, I had no idea that you could have been involved with Lew Arnstead."

"I wouldn't have been. But he . . . but he was in trouble and he felt so lost and miserable."

"Why don't you tell me about it? That might help."

"I don't want to."

"I think it would be the best thing to do."

"Well . . . the background of it . . . and it took him a long time to trust me enough to tell me . . . he'd always had girls, before he went in the service and while he was away and after he came back. And he fell in love with Clara Willoughbee. Really in love. And I told him the trouble was probably some kind of guilt about all the other girls, and feeling unworthy or something. But after they had plans to get married and everything, he couldn't do it with her. He'd want her terribly, and then it would just get . . . he couldn't do anything."

She became more animated and dramatic as she got into the story. He and the Willoughbee girl had broken up. He had tried going back to prior girl friends, but he was still impotent. And one night, off duty, he had gotten drunk at the Lodge, too drunk to drive. She drove him around in the cold night air in her little car. He had cried and cried and said he was going to kill himself. He passed out and he was too heavy for her to manage, so she had to leave him in her carport asleep in her car. In the morning he was gone. He came back to find out what he had told her. Then he would stop by, just to talk to her. Finally he told her what was wrong. That was in October of last year.

"I have . . . a kind of condition," she said. "It's a sluggish thyroid gland, and that gives me low blood pressure, and makes me feel kind of listless and depressed. I used to have to take thyroid extract, but it made me too jittery sometimes, and made my hands ice cold and sweaty. So a couple of years ago Doctor Grinner gave me a renewable prescription for something called an energizer. I take one every morning of my life. I noticed that sometimes if I get mixed up and take a second one on account of forgetting I took the first one, it makes me feel . . . well, terribly sexy. I might as well say it right out. Anyway . . . I told Lew how they made me feel, and he came over one Sunday afternoon and I gave him two of them, and about an hour later he thought he could. And so. . . . You understand I was helping him. He was so terribly depressed. Well, it worked. He was so happy and laughing and all. And so grateful to me. And we kept making love after that, and fell in love with each other."

"He kept taking your pills?"

"Oh no. He didn't have to, not after the very first time. It was all in his mind, actually. You know. Guilt and fear."

"Then you broke up? Why?"

Her eyes narrowed. "We were having a little bit of a quarrel. It wasn't serious at all. Then he slapped me, *much* too hard. And then he kept right on slapping and hitting me until he knocked me unconscious. I woke up right over there on that little white rug, and he was gone. I was all cut inside my mouth and my face was terrible. The next morning I was sore in a hundred places, and I could hardly get out of bed. I was off work for four days. I reported him, then withdrew the complaint. I told them I fell off a ladder, hanging a picture. And I had to wear dark glasses for a week until my black eyes didn't show anymore."

"How did he act when he was beating you up?"

"He didn't seem mad at me or anything. I was screaming and begging and trying to get away from him, but he didn't hear me, sort of. He looked . . . calm. Sometimes I have bad dreams about it."

"And you've never seen him since?"

"On the street and in the dining room. But not like before. Not that way. I *wouldn't!* He could come begging and I wouldn't ever let him touch me. I wrote him never to come here."

"Are you in his Polaroid collection?"

"Of *course* not!" Too emphatic. Quick sidelong glance to see if I believed her.

"He could have tricked you somehow."

"Well . . . one Sunday afternoon, we had a lot of bloody Marys and we got kind of wild and silly and he had that camera and got it out of his car. They use it for accident investigations, and I sort of remember him taking pictures of me out in the back, in Raoul's yard. But I tore them up." She was frowningly thoughtful. "At least I *think* I tore them all up. He took lots and lots. I certainly wouldn't willingly let Lew or anybody walk away with . . . pictures of me like that in his pocket, would I?"

"Of *course* not!"

She looked grateful for my indignant emphasis. She took her tall drink down several inches. She smiled sadly. "Why anybody should want nude pictures of me is something else again. I'm built kind of weird, practically enormous up here and skinny everywhere else, like I'm thirty-nine-twenty-four-thirty-two. Well, now you know what kind of an idiot I can be, dear."

"I think you ran into a crazy, Betsy." There was no point in telling her that she had, by curing Arnstead's temporary impotence with a strong stimulant, put him well on the road to hooking himself or, more accurately, habituating himself. He matched the classic pattern of the amphetamine user. Mercurial moods, hilarity and depression, little sleep, weight loss, enhanced sexuality, inability to consistently carry out responsibilities, recklessness, increasing tendency toward violence and brutality.

"Lew didn't *seem* like a crazy person."

"The world would be a safer place if you could pick them out at first glance, Betsy."

"Like he could be . . . put away?"

"The odds are better that he'll kill somebody, and get put away for that."

"You've been looking for him?"

"Yes. I talked to his mother. He hasn't been home since Thursday noon. Got any ideas?"

"I suppose he could be with some woman someplace."

"Who has he been running with lately? Got any idea?"

She turned and held my hand with both of hers. "Oh God, Travis, he could be out there in the night right now! We don't know what could be going on in his mind. He might even blame me for all his trouble. He could be . . . waiting for you to go. Please don't leave me. Please!"

Mousetrapped. A device just as real-unreal as the soaked hair episode. Contrived, yet not contrived. Sincere, yet insincere on some level of mind and emotion she had no access to. We were trapped in her garden of make-believe. I told her she would be all right, that there was no cause to worry, but tears stood in her tragic eyes, and she said I could not leave her.

ten

When I awakened the first time on Sunday morning, I was able to give myself a long period of ironic amusement by reviewing the long chain of coincidence, episode, mousetraps, or delusions which had levered me into Betsy's bed at about two-fifteen in the morning. She had Doris-Dayed our coupling far out of the range of any casual accessibility. She had woven such a fabric of myth that I could have torn myself loose only by tearing away her illusions about herself. Sometimes there is an obligation to play the role that is forced upon you. She indulged in a considerable drama. Tears and protestations. Retreats which made the reactive approaches obligatory.

She wrapped us in her compensatory aromas of fate, tragic romance, inevitable loneliness of human beings. She wept real tears for a variety of reasons. She made us both special people in a world of clods, because otherwise she would have been merely a dining room hostess who had brought the tall stranger back home for what the British sometimes call a bit of slap and tickle. I had, in short, so won her reluctant heart that she could not help herself. And we had to live forever with our sense of guilt and human weakness. It happened, of course, because it was written in the stars that it had to happen.

And, all dramatics aside, when it had begun, when it was an un-

mistakable reality superimposed on all the devices of any daytime serial, blanking out those devices in sensual energies, she was a steady,
hearty workman, strong and limber and so readable that she was easily predicted and easily paced, so obviously relishing it, that I was fatuously gratified by the implied compliment, the implied flattery. So
for me, too, it was charade, but I was far more conscious of it as charade than was she. Role playing, under an inevitable canopy over the
double bed, by the small night light of a dressing-table lamp with a
rose-colored shade. The he-she game amid yellow sheets with blue
flowers printed on them, after a welter of stuffed animals had been
exiled to a white wicker divan with cantaloupe cushions which
matched the overhead gauze.

Morning irony, flat on my back, feeling the roundness of her forehead against the corner of my shoulder, her deep, regular, warm ex-
halations against my arm. Could feel the thin slack weight of her left
arm across my lower chest, sleeping pressure of a round knee against
the outside of left thigh. Turned my head slowly and looked slanting
downward, saw disorderly mop of the fine blond hair hiding the face.
Could see tip of one ear, half of the open mouth, edge of a pink
tongue, two lower teeth. Fanciful sheet down to her waist. The arm
across me cut off the vision of one half of the great round whiteness
of the left breast. Small veins blue against the white. Slow, perceptible lift and fall as she breathed.

She sighed audibly and the breathing changed. Then there was a
little sound in her throat as she caught and held her breath. Left
arm moved, and the hair was thumbed back. Blue-gray eyes looked
solemnly up at me as the face turned pink.

"Darling, darling, darling," she whispered, then lunged and
hugged herself into my throat, arms winding tight. "Don't look at
me. I must look like a witch."

"You look lovely." The lines are effortless, because the role has
been played a thousand times in daytime soap.

"I don't know what you must think of me," she whispers. "I'm
not like this at all. I don't know what got into me."

An effort to stop the crude and obvious answer. But easy to read
the words of the shopworn script. "We just couldn't help ourselves,
honey."

"I love you so," she sighs.

Turn the page. Read the next line. "And I love you, too." How
reprehensible is it? To love something is, in some simple sense, to be
unwilling to hurt it needlessly. And it was not said to induce the

lady to spread her satin thighs, because it had been said the first time after the deed was done, to make her fantasy more real to her.

Stroke the slow length of the white back, down to the uptilt of the buttocks. Slowly, slowly, following the instructions in the script, the part in brackets. Until her breath shallows and quickens, her body softens, opens, and she makes a small gritty groaning sound, brings her mouth up to mine, and the engine in her hips begins a small, almost imperceptible pulsation.

When I awakened the second time on that Sunday morning, it was when she stood beside the bed and gave me a quick little pat on the shoulder. Hair tied back with yellow yarn. Little white sunsuit. Eye makeup and lipstick most carefully applied.

"Darling, you can have the bath now. I laid out some things for you. Be careful of the shower. The knob for hot turns the wrong way."

Tiny bathroom. Narrow shower stall. Kept whacking my elbows against the tile. Big bar of sweet pink soap. Big soft tiger towel in black and yellow stripes. Tufted yellow bath mat. Mingled pungent odors of perfumes, salves, lotions, sprays, and of natural girl. Yellow curtains across steamed window. Yellow terry cover on the cover to the toilet seat. Glimpsed my tanned, hairy, scarred body in the full-length mirror. Great, knuckly, fibrous hulk, offensively masculine in all this soapy-sweet daintiness. New toothbrush. Mint toothpaste. Scraped beard off using bar soap and a miniature white-and-gold safety razor with a toy blade. Stopped and looked self in the eye in the mirror over the lavatory. Said severely, "Just what the *hell* are you doing here, McGee?"

Don't get churlish with me, fella. I got caught up in one of the games Betsy Kapp plays. This one was called the bigger-than-both-of-us game. All right. Sure. I could have walked out at any time. Big man. Sorry, honey, I like brighter, funnier, better-looking women. Sorry. You don't match up. Don't call us; we'll call you. Leave your name and address with the receptionist.

"McGee, don't try to kid me and don't try to kid yourself. I'm not interested in your rationalizations. It was handy and you jumped it. Right?"

If you want to be crude. But what you are leaving out is that I had every expectation that she would be a very tiresome item in the sack. Once I was committed, I was going to go manfully ahead with it. I expected a lot of elfin fluttering, and maybe a little bit of clumsy earnest effort, right out of the happy-marriage textbook, and some dialogue out of every bad play I can remember.

"But? But?"

All *right*! So call it an unexpected pleasure.

"McGee you kill me. You really do. You go around suffering so much. All this bedroom therapy you dole out must put a hell of a strain on you. How come, boy, you always seem to find broken birds with all these hidden talents? Just lucky?"

I couldn't answer him. I told him to go away. I got dressed and went looking for her. She had breakfast all ready on the redwood table in a shady corner of Raoul's private garden. Iced juice, a tureen of scrambled eggs, buttered toast stacked under a white napkin, crisp bacon, and a giant pot of steaming black coffee.

She was pleasured to watch a large man eat like a timber wolf. Ah, she was saucy. She was flirty and fancy, chortly and giggly, cooing up and down a two-octave range. She was busting with joy and jollity and high spirits, slanting her eyes at me, blushing now and again, guffawing at the mildest quip, hovering over my needs and my comforts. I was aware of an old and familiar phenomenon. I was no longer able to see her objectively, see her on any comparative basis, rate her on any kind of scale regarding face and figure. The act of complete knowing turns the lass into a familiarity, and she had become Betsy, a person entirely herself. I could see detail that I had not seen before, the extreme slenderness of her long-fingered hands, and the plumpness of the pads at the base of her fingers, a discolored eye tooth—dead perhaps. Two small pock marks on her left cheek, the little squint-lines of the mildly myopic, a puckered line of scar tissue on the side of her throat, less than an inch long. Detail that I could not evaluate as good or bad, tasteful or distasteful, could only observe as being part of this Betsy woman. She pranced and posed, patted and beamed, sighed and chuckled, and I was the great old fatuous toad-king in her garden of celebration, served and feted and extravagantly admired. It was all part of the script, obligatory sauciness of the Doris-Dayism the bright morning after the reluctant-eager surrender of the Most Precious Possession.

I found that she had to work alternate Sundays, and this was her Sunday off. Without any direct dialogue about what we would do with the day, she had begun indirectly to establish the shape of it, some sun-time in the garden, and a marvelous nap, and later on some bloody Marys and the marvelous steaks she had been hoarding

in the freezer for a special occasion, along with some wine a friend
had given her, and he said it was a marvelous wine, Château something or other, but she didn't really know very much about wine.
There were these outdoor speakers a friend had given her and they
were still in the shipping carton in the carport, and maybe I could
help put them up out here because some of her favorite tapes would
sound marvelous in the garden, and there was speaker wire and everything, but she didn't know what gizmo plugged into where. And
we wouldn't think or talk about ugly things all day, not even once.

So I said that it seemed like good planning, but I would like to go
back to the White Ibis and check for any messages and change into
fresh clothes. So she said that made sense, and she leaned into me at
the doorway for a kiss so long and intense it dizzied her into a little
sagging lurch to one side.

I went out and stared at the empty driveway and thought for a
moment somebody had stolen the white Buick, then remembered
her asking me, after it had become evident I would stay the night, if
I would go out and drive it back and over to the side of the carport.
That way the neighbors couldn't see it, and it couldn't be seen from
the street. No point in letting idle tongues wag, she had said.

So I walked toward the carport. I glanced up at blue sky and saw a
large black Florida buzzard sitting in dusty, silent patience on top of
a power pole at the rear of the lot line. Symbol of a Sunday funeral
of some small creature. I glanced back at the house as I neared the
car and saw the buzzard's brother standing on the ridge line of the
cottage, at the rear corner.

And the next step brought me into view of what had engaged
their hungry interest.

I had left the top down. He had been tumbled casually into the
shallow rear seat of the convertible. One foot on the floor, the other
caught on the seat, bending the knee at a sharp angle. A large tough
muscular young man with black hair, high hard cheekbones. Long
sideburns. Meyer had said that Lew Arnstead had small dark eyes.
These were small dark eyes, one open wider than the other. He wore
a stained ranch jacket and dirty white jeans. His head was cocked at
an angle, exposing the crushed temple area, above and forward of his
right ear. It was smashed inward in a pattern that looked as if it
could have been done with a length of pipe about an inch in diameter. There was a little blood, and a dozen shiny flies were pacing the
area.

In all such moments you do absolutely nothing. You stand and concentrate on breathing deeply and fast. Hyperventilation improves the thinking. You start looking at your options.

"Sheriff, I just spent the night here with Mrs. Betsy Kapp and when I went out to get in my car a couple of minutes ago, I found a dead man in there who might be your ex-deputy. Come over any time. I'll be right here."

So the old lady knows you came looking for her son. King Sturnevan gave you a little course in how to whip Arnstead when you caught up with him. Arnstead broke the face of your old and true friend. Hmmm. Betsy Kapp would be questioned. Her relationship with Lew was probably known. "Mr. McGee was with me. He couldn't possibly have killed that rotten crazy person who beat me up."

Somebody had gone to a lot of trouble to leave me this little token. Somebody had taken some risk. Reasonable to assume they had added a few other little touches to sew me more tightly into the bag. Such as a weapon. The piece of pipe under the front seat, or in the glove compartment or in the nearby shrubbery.

I don't call Hyzer, then. I have to take the calculated risk of not calling Hyzer, which might make things a lot worse later on. Maybe Hyzer is already on his way, with Billy Cable at the wheel.

Option. I put the top up and drive away and put him somewhere. They could know it already, and be staked out waiting for me to drive out with the package. That would be a very unhappy scene indeed. The ultimate version of egg-on-the-face.

Or . . . go back in and say I'd changed my mind, and there was no point in going to the motel. Play Betsy's game for a day and another night, and hope they would come and knock on the door, and then convince them with the totality of our horrid surprise.

Or . . . bring Betsy into it right now. Look at this little inconvenience, sweetie. Gibbering hysteria, with a lot of flapping and squalling and running around in small circles.

Fact: I *had* gone out sometime between one-thirty and two and moved the car. Fact: I had stayed, in part, because Betsy had been terrified by the thought of Arnstead skulking about in the night. Fact: I had sought out Betsy because of the letter hidden in Lew's room, and in the course of events Mister Norm would gather up that letter as evidence. And King would remember he had identified Betsy for me.

Supposition: Had I not been roped into the Baither killing and released with a certain obvious reluctance by Mister Norm, I might be able to carry this situation off and make useful explanations. But it was a little bit too much to expect Mister Norm to swallow.

Uneasy suspicion: Dropping the package on me was just a potentially handy byproduct of the primary necessity to turn off the mouth and the memory of a link between Frank Baither and his executioners.

Forlorn option: Hide the package right here, and fast.

I did not like any of my options.

"Trav?" Betsy said, walking toward me. "Trav, honey, I didn't hear you drive out and I wondered . . ."

"Go back in the house!"

"Darling, you're practically *barking* at me! I only—"

I moved to stop her, but she had taken that one step that brought her close enough to the convertible to see the dead face, the dried and dusty eyes.

She swayed, eyes going out of focus. She made a gagging sound. I got to her then, caught her by the upper arms. Her color was ghastly. Her teeth chattered, and there were goosebumps on her long pale arms and legs. She looked at him again, and I turned her away and led her over into the sunshine. She turned into my arms. I held her. She hiccuped, sighed, then pushed herself out of my arms and stared up into my face, frowning.

"I'm all right now. But *why?* My God, how did he get *here?*"

"Is it Arnstead?"

She tilted her head. "Of course! Didn't you ever see him before?"

"No."

She tried to smile, a valiant effort. "For one second I thought that maybe he *was* around here in the night like I thought, and when you went out to move your car. . . . Forgive me, darling. You couldn't have come back into my house, into my bed, and . . . it couldn't have been the way it was for us. But what a filthy thing to do to us, to put his body here."

"Somebody had to know I was here."

She walked around me and went into the carport and came out with a ragged bedsheet which had been used as a drop cloth. She marched to the car, snapped the sheet open, floated it down over the body.

"Why don't you put the top up? You shouldn't have left it down anyway, dear. It's all soppy with dew inside."

I reached in and pushed the toggle. The top ground up out of the well and swung forward and whacked down. The buzzards winged away.

It was comforting to be unable to see him. I said, "You are coming on very staunch, woman."

She looked mildly surprised. "I feel like screaming my head off. But that wouldn't do much good, would it? Should we phone now?"

"Let's see if there's enough coffee left for two cups, and have a little talk and see whether we should phone."

She listened, with all the girlish games turned off. I had to start back at the beginning and cover everything that had happened. Not quite everything. I left out her letter and the pictures of her. I went through my options.

When it had all been said, she frowned at me and said, "But suppose Sheriff Hyzer did jump to the wrong conclusion, and he put you back in jail. Wouldn't that be a lot safer than trying to . . . do something that might not turn out so good? I mean you would certainly be cleared, because, after all, you are not some kind of a criminal, and you have friends and you are in business."

"Add one more murder, Betsy, and the *Cypress City Call & Journal* is going to have to stop covering it like a zoning violation. And there will be Miami papers and television coming in here. And it would not matter one damn if I got cleared and released later. I can't afford that kind of coverage, that much exposure."

"Why not? Are you . . . are you wanted for something else?"

"No. And I am in the salvage business, but not like you think. Personal salvage. Suppose some cutie clips an innocent pigeon for a very big score, and the pigeon exhausts all the possible legal ways of getting it back. Somebody might steer him to me, and if I think there's a fair chance, I'll gamble my time and expenses against a deal whereby I keep half of any recovery I make. Last resort salvage specialist. A small and useful reputation for recovery. And the methods used aren't particularly legal. If Hyzer checks me out carefully, he's going to come up with a life style he's going to label unsavory. I am a lot more conspicuous and memorable than I would like to be. It's a handicap in my line of work. If they ever make me on the front pages, with picture and with colorful account of how I make a living, that is the end of the living, honey. I would never get a chance to get in close enough to make a recovery, and I would have the law keeping a beady eye on me from that point on. So no thanks."

"But you could find some other way to make money, couldn't you?"

"Wouldn't that be just a different kind of prison?"

She stared into space, then nodded. "I guess having the kind of life you want is worth taking a big chance for."

"But now you're taking part of the risk. It isn't fair to ask you to do that. The smart thing for you to do is make the phone call."

"Pooh. If I was any good at doing smart things, I'd have started a long time back. Darling, that houseboat you live on, does it have engines and everything, or does it just sit there?"

"It cruises. Very very slowly but very very comfortably."

"They're shutting down the Lodge in June and remodeling the whole main part, the kitchen and dining room and bar. If a person takes a risk, a person ought to make a profit, don't you think?"

"Okay, honey. The month of June is yours aboard *The Busted Flush*."

"I'll do the cooking and laundry and all that."

No phone call. And considering the various areas of unknown risk, she came up with the best idea. So she changed to a blouse and skirt and went tooling out in her Volks, with a rather shaky wave and a set smile. And I used the time in a careful search for any extra bonus which might have been left with the special gift. I saved the worst until last. He had stiffened up, and it was difficult to go through his pockets. The sun had moved and it heated the inside of the car. The dead deputy was beginning to smell.

Western wallet, cowhide with the hair still on, and L.A. burn-branded into it. Thirty-eight dollars. Scruffy cards of identity and credit. Cracked Kodacolor shot of his black horse. Two snapshots of commercial origin and vivid clinical obscenity.

Plastic vial containing eight of the bi-colored spansules. Dull pocket knife full of lint and tobacco crumbs. Squashed pack containing three Viceroy cigarettes. Zippo lighter. Several keys on a worn chain. Twenty-six cents in change.

The jackpot was in the top right-hand breast pocket of the worn ranch jacket. Half a sheet of blue stationery, carelessly torn off. Hasty scrawl. "Lew if you ever come to my place again I swear to almighty God I've got a gun and I'll kill you dead on sight." Signed with a big B in ballpoint so firmly the downstroke had gouged a little hole in the paper.

Everything back as before, except for the note. No weapon in the car or shrubbery. Body covered with the drop cloth. I was careful how I had handled anything that would take a print.

I had seen Betsy's handwriting before, on the same blue paper, but in a much longer letter, with the words more carefully formed.

What the hell was keeping the woman?

I went in. Raoul wound around my ankles, making little ingratiating mews. I wondered if the lady did indeed have a gun. There is a pattern to hiding places, you always save time by starting with the places most frequently used. Suitcases and hat boxes. Then covered bowls and cooking pots in the kitchen cabinets. Next you try the bedroom drawers. So it took perhaps twelve minutes to find the gun. Bottom drawer on the left side of her dressing table. In the front of the drawer was a plastic bag with a drawstring, containing the diaphragm in its pink plastic case, along with the accessory tube. The gun was in the back, under a batch of bright scarves, each carefully folded. It, too, was in a plastic drawstring bag, the bag wrapped in a fragrant silk scarf. No obscure little small-caliber ladygun this, no European purse-pistol with mickeymouse action and engraved floral pattern. A deadly fourteen-ounce Colt .38 Special, trade name "Agent," drop-forged aluminum frame, full checkered walnut stocks, Colt bluing, equipped with hammer shroud. Six rounds in the cylinder, and a full box of ammo in the plastic bag, with just the six rounds missing therefrom. Almost mint condition. A very hard and heavy close-range punch for a lady to own. If you had an earnest and honest desire to kill somebody, this item would simplify the task and shorten the process.

I put it back exactly as before.

Five minutes later I heard the lawn-mower engine of the VW come chattering along the driveway and into the carport. She came hurrying into the house and into my arms, clung for a little while then gave me a tired unslanted smile, quick peck on the corner of the mouth. She wandered over and dropped onto the couch, kicked her sandals off, leaned her head back, forearm across her eyes.

"Gone a long time, Betsy."

"Well . . . I wanted to find out anything worth finding out. For what's it's worth, there is absolutely no one watching this place. I went around and around and came up on it from all the directions there are. Nothing."

"That's comforting."

"I went to the White Ibis and went to the desk and asked for you. They tried the phone and said you weren't in. I located the box for 114, and I couldn't see any message slips in it."

"You shouldn't have gone there."

"It was the quickest way to find out if anybody was trying to find you, dear. And if they were, and if I came there looking for you, the last place they'd look would be here. What are we going to do?"

"I found this on him," I said, and handed her the note.

She read it and it brought her bolt upright, astonishment on her face. "But I wrote this last year! Why would he be carrying it around? It isn't even all here."

"What was on the top half?"

"Let me think. The date, I guess. And something about how bad he'd hurt me, about how my face looked."

"You wrote it right after he beat you?"

"The second day. I was too sick to write anything the first day."

"Did you think he might come back here?"

She leaned back again. "I don't know. You see . . . I wanted him to come back. That was the sick part. I wanted him to come back, no matter what. I was afraid that . . . if he did come back, I'd go to bed with him if that's what he wanted. I hated him for beating me, but the wanting was stronger than the hate. So I don't know whether I was trying to keep him away from me until I could stop wanting him, or whether I was trying to . . . to challenge him so he would come back."

"Do you even have a gun?"

"Sure. Stay right there. I'll get it." She brought it into the living room, took it out of the plastic bag and handed it to me. "It scares me to look at it. Lew gave it to me. He took it away from somebody and didn't turn it in like he was supposed to. He bought the ammunition for it and loaded it for me and showed me how it works. But I never fired it. Is it a good gun?"

"Very reliable up to thirty feet or so."

"He said if I ever had to use it, not to try to aim. Just point it like pointing my finger and keep pulling the trigger. I don't think I could fire a gun right at anybody, no matter what."

I gave it back to her and she stowed it away. She sat as before and said, "It was just half the note in his pocket so that if somebody found it on his body they'd think he came here."

"Somebody put the note in a handy pocket after he was dead. They brought the body here. They saw the Buick and dumped him into it. They thought you would be alone."

"Then they changed their mind. What do you think they were going to do, if I'd been alone?"

"To set it up to look as if you killed him, there's the little problem of a weapon, something you could reasonably kill him with."

"I . . . I didn't look at him very long. I saw that terrible mushed-in place. What shape would it have to be?"

I demonstrated with my hands. "A piece of pipe about this long and about this big around would do it. You could do that much damage with one full swing."

She shuddered. "I couldn't do anything like that."

"Let's think this out. He's too heavy for you to carry. So the encounter had to happen outside the house. You wouldn't have come out into the night, so it had to look as if it happened earlier. You come home and drive into the carport and get out of the car and go to that side door, right?"

"Yes. It's a delay switch on the carport light. It gives me time to get inside before it goes out."

"So he could have been waiting for you in the carport, or in the bushes near the body. Handy places to drop the body. Now then, in one place or the other, there has to be something that you could pick up and swing."

She sat with elbows on knees, chin on fists, lips pursed. "I can't think of a dang thing around here that . . . Oh!"

"Oh what?"

"Maybe it could be the handle for the doohickey for the corner of the house. The estimate was two hundred dollars to put in a new pillar. The old one sort of started sinking into the ground for some reason and Mr. Kaufman down the street said why didn't I mail-order that thing from Sears for under nine dollars and it would work just as well, and just leave it there."

"You've lost me. You better show me."

We went out, and she sat on her heels by the rear corner of the house and pointed out the construction jack that was bracing it up. It was the type that uses a pipe handle.

The handle, about thirty inches long, was on the ground under the house, beside the jack. I saw that it was too rusty to take a print. I reached under and picked it up and pulled it out. The far end was clotted with dark-dried blood, some short black hairs, some bits of tissue.

She spun, ran three steps, bent over and threw up. When she was finished she trotted into the house, keeping her face turned away from me. I put the jack handle in the Buick, on the floor in back.

I was sitting on the couch when she finally came out of the bathroom. She was wan and subdued. She apologized.

"We have to keep going with it, Betsy. Okay, so they leave him near the corner of the house. You find him in the morning and phone the law. Hyzer is a thorough man. You certainly wouldn't have looked through Arnstead's pockets and found that old note."

"Never!"

"So they reconstruct. Certainly some people know about the affair you had with him."

"Too many."

"You can't explain the note away, and you can't prove it wasn't written yesterday or Friday, or prove he hadn't come here recently. Hyzer gets a warrant. Your story about how you happen to have that gun is a little frail, without Lew around to back it up. So he was waiting when you came back from work alone last night.

"Thank God I didn't!"

"You had a quarrel. You edged over to the corner of the house. The delay light went out. You felt around and found that handle and lifted it and hit him in the skull and knocked him down. You didn't know you'd killed him. You went into the house. When you found the body this morning, you tried to lie your way out of it, bluff your way out of the jam."

"But nobody would really believe that I could ever . . ."

"There's something missing. How did he get here?"

So she went on a casual stroll in the quiet neighborhood. The jeep was four doors away, parked behind the overgrown masses of Cuban laurel in the side yard of a boarded-up house. The guard chain across the drive had been unhooked and rehooked. So I had to go into the dead pocket again, holding my breath, and finger the keys out. She took another stroll and came back and said that one of them fit the ignition, and she had left the keys right there.

The jeep was proof he had arrived alone to visit a woman who had threatened to kill him if he ever came around again. He did. And she did.

"Now what, Travis? Now what do we do? Wait until dark and then take—"

"Dark is too long to wait. Somebody can get impatient. And nervous."

So we had to take the gamble. Plan it first and then take it. A sickening gamble, because moving the body was prime meat for any prosecuting attorney. No jury would ever understand why we did it.

eleven

I drove her VW out of the driveway and parked on the far side of the street. The big banyans made dark shade. A fat lady in red pants knelt three front yards away, troweling her weeds. A household gas truck on special Sunday delivery went by and turned at the next corner. By then she had time to move the Buick to the mouth of her narrow sheltered driveway, so I beeped the horn twice as prearranged, meaning that there was no pedestrian or vehicular traffic.

I drove east, and looked in the rearview mirror and saw her come out and turn west. She had won the argument about the cars. She reminded me that I had told her I was conspicuous, all by myself. And in the white convertible I was doubly memorable, and too many people had seen me in it. Certainly, a lot more people knew her by sight, but not in the big floppy broad-brimmed hat she took from the back of her closet, or in the huge mirrored sunglasses she had bought long ago and seldom worn. In the very ordinary-looking VW and with the tweed cap which her second husband had left behind and never came after, I was not likely to be either recognized or remembered. I had asked her three times if she was sure she could handle the constant awareness of the body directly behind her, and she finally said she planned not to think about it.

The place she had described to me was perfect. She had drawn a map, and I had repeated the directions after her until I knew just how to find it. As she was taking the more direct route, she would be there first. Neither of us would make the last turn unless the highway was empty in both directions.

Out Alternate 112 to where it joined 112 proper. North about four miles, and then turn left and go west on County Line Road. You can tell the turn by the deserted gas station on the corner. Grass is growing up through the cracks in the cement near where the pumps were. It was there, as promised, and I made the turn.

Go about five miles, maybe more, and there is a gradual curve to the left. After the road straightens out again, you'll see a place on the left where there was a house. Now there's just a chimney and foundation.

There was no traffic in either direction when I got there, so I turned into the overgrown drive and around behind the house site and then, as she had described, I drove on sand tracks through palmetto and scrub pine, past a marsh, and saw, ahead of me, the pond she had described and caught a glimpse of the white car beyond the saw grass at the far end of the pond.

She was fifty feet from the car sitting on the trunk of a fallen pine, looking at the pond.

"Any trouble at all?" I asked her.

"None. You?"

"Nothing. You better show me the place first."

She seemed slack and dispirited. "Sure," she said, getting to her feet. "It's over here."

The place was a hundred feet further. It was an old sinkhole. All this land was once the bottom of the sea. Marl and fossils and limestone. Fresh water runs down through the limestone in great underground rivers. Sometimes the underground chambers will collapse after dry cycles, and the land will sink. This was an old sinkhole, the fractures concealed by coarse brush and sizable trees.

She took me to the place she had described, a marl slope, a sun-pale sculpturing of eroded limestone, a brushy pit five feet deep with a dark irregular hole at the bottom of it, at one end of the pit. The hole was about a yard across. I went down into the pit and knelt and looked down into the hole. There was a smell of coolness and dampness. I picked up a piece of limestone bigger than my fist and dropped it into the hole. I heard it hit the side, and in a second or two heard a smaller sound as it hit again. There was an almost inaudible thud a long time later.

"Donny timed it with a stopwatch once."

"Donny?"

"My husband. The young one that got killed. He used a stop-watch and figured out that per second per second thing. I remembered the figure he told me. Three hundred and six feet. He figured in the time for the sound to come back up. He was a real nut about math. It is . . . a good place for what you want?"

"Do many people come here?"

"Nobody, as far as I know. I started going with Donny when we were both sixteen. We wanted a place where we could get away from people. We'd come out here on our bikes and bring picnics. Donny found this hole one time. I came here a lot after he died, before I got married again. I never brought Greg here, or anybody else. I still come here when . . . when I feel down. It's so quiet. I don't think about anything. I just walk around and listen to the quiet, and sit and listen. And I feel better then."

"Why don't you go for a walk right now, Betsy. I'll take care of it."

"Can't I help somehow?"

"No. No thanks."

I had to put the top down on the convertible to get him out. I couldn't move the car any closer. I wrapped the old sheet around him and stood him against the rear fender, on his crooked legs. I squatted and let him tip forward onto my shoulder, and as I stood up with him, the pressure forced gas through his voice box, a ragged croak that chilled me. Though he folded slightly, there was enough rigor to make him feel like a clumsy log.

The weight made me take short jolting steps, and the effort and the heat of the early afternoon brought out the sweat. It seemed a very long way to the pit. I dropped him on the edge, stood on the end of the sheet and rolled him into the small pit. In the unlikely event he was found, a police lab could make a spectroscopic analysis of the paint on the old sheet and compare it to the paint used somewhere in Betsy's cottage, and prove it identical.

I went into the pit, straddled him, picked him up by the waist and slid him headfirst into the hole. Listened. Heard the remote, softened thud. Same impact as going off the roof of a thirty-storied building, if the young husband's math had been accurate.

"I'll never be able to come back here again," she said. I looked up and saw her standing up on the rim of the small pit, outlined against blue sky and small white clouds. The big brim of the hat shaded her face, and the big mirrors of the sunglasses were like the eyes of some giant insect.

"You shouldn't have watched."

"It wouldn't be fair not to, somehow. Like not sharing bad things along with the good parts."

We went back to the cars and the pond. I gathered twigs and dry grass and small dead branches and built a small hot fire. I burned the sheet and the map she had drawn and the fragment of the old letter to Arnstead. I took the jack handle out of the Buick, scrubbed it in the wet muck at the edge of the pond, then held the end that had been stained in the fire for a while. I put it in the VW, and told her to remember to put it back under the house, just as before.

"Can we stay here for a few minutes, Trav? Can you stay with me for a little while?"

"If you want. I have to clean that back seat off anyway."

"I forgot. I'll do it."

I protested, but she insisted. She got the bottle of strong cleaner she had brought along, and the stiff brush and the roll of paper towels. She scrubbed the few small stains away, scrubbed all of the back-seat area and the rug on the floor, making a mingled smell of ammonia and kerosene. There were enough embers left to catch the paper towels ablaze. She put the hat and glasses in the VW and roamed back to the log and sat looking at the pond. I sat near her, in front of the log, leaning back against it. A kingfisher hovered, wings blurred like an oversized hummingbird, then dropped and splashed and lifted away with a small silver fish in his bill.

"There's bream in the pond. Donny used to catch them. Travis, it's like we killed Lew."

"I know." And I did know exactly how she felt. Plan and execution. Terror and disposal of the body and a slack, sick relief.

"We fixed it so whoever killed him won't ever get caught."

"Maybe not for him. They'll be nailed for killing Baither."

"Does it have to be the same people? Or same person?"

"The odds favor it."

She was quiet for a long time. I tilted my head back and looked up at her, saw for an instant a look of a private anguish which changed at once to a small forced smile.

"Betsy, I think he had gone too far down whatever road he . . ."

"Not Lew. I . . . was remembering Donny. I was working waitress when they told me. He was driving back from the construction job he was working on that summer when he got killed. We were saving money. He was going to go to Florida State. They hadn't wanted him to get married so young, and we ran up to Georgia. We had ten months married, only. I dropped the whole tray of dishes. They had to give me a shot finally. I went sort of crazy, I guess."

"It can happen."

"We were such dumb crazy kids, coming out here all the way on the bikes, fooling around and getting each other all worked up, saying we wouldn't really do it, and getting closer all the time. There's a song or saying or something. 'She lost It at the Astor.' I lost it over there on a blanket under that pine tree, on the bed of soft needles, hanging onto him and crying, not because it hurt but on account of feeling sweet and sad and strange. Getting all over mosquito bites. There was a woodpecker way up the tree over us, and I watched him hopping around and turning his head this way and that way and then rapping and knocking that tree. Going home I felt so weak and sick and dizzy I nearly fell off that dumb blue bike. Then I turned seventeen and my aunt died and I had to go up home, but I wanted Donny so bad I thought I could die of it. And I came back and we got married."

Her eyes filled, and then she gave herself a little shake, tossed her hair, smiled brilliantly and said, "Well, I guess we shouldn't be taking the chance of being seen out here, huh?"

We walked toward the cars. She was being someone else, and it took me a few minutes to identify the role. Another one of the games Betsy played. Heroine in a movie of intrigue, suspicion, sudden death. Brave and pert in the face of danger. Ready to help with the schemes and plans.

"I guess we have to worry about that black jeep now, Travis."

"Not by daylight. It isn't a clear and present danger, the way it was before."

"You want me to go right home in my own car."

"I saw some stores open in that shopping center."

"Woodsgate."

"Stop there and do some shopping. Have you got money with you?" She had. She looked puzzled.

I said, "Mrs. Kapp, you left your house at noon or a little before on that Sunday. Please tell the court where you went."

"Oh. Sure. I see. And I should look around for somebody I know and make sure I say hello and say something they'll remember, and be . . . kind of happy and normal and all."

"Exactly. And I'll go back to the motel."

"Travis, darling. Please don't leave me alone in the house too long. I'll be okay for a while, but I think I'll start imagining I hear things. Somebody brought Lew there and killed him there while we were in bed. Somebody knew what they were going to kill him with. It has to be crazy people who hate me for some reason."

I took hold of her hands. "Listen. Nobody hates you. It's a part of a pattern. Somebody is hooked on misdirection. They're blowing smoke, laying false trails. They had that note Lew got from you. So they could quietly take a look around your place while you were working, to see the best way to set it up. I don't think he was killed there. It would be too clumsy and difficult. I think they took that jack handle away, killed him with it and brought the body and the weapon back. Then they saw my car there. Knew it was the car I was driving. Knew I was mixed up in the whole thing, and I think they were a little nervous about my being with you."

"Why?"

"Because of things you might be able to tell me that would make the pattern clearer?"

"What things?"

"We don't know yet. Maybe you've already told me, but it didn't mean anything to either of us. At least not yet."

"But . . . why didn't they just find someplace to put the body where it wouldn't be found? Like we did."

"All I can do is make a guess. I think that if Arnstead disappeared suddenly and for good, the pattern might look a little more distinct to Sheriff Hyzer, and he might go after somebody a hell of a lot more logically suspect than you."

Her eyebrows went up. "Then what we've done will make that happen!"

"It might help, if my guessing is any good lately. And some person or persons unknown are going to wonder just what the hell happened."

"And come around and try to find out? I don't want to go back there alone. Please!"

She needed time. There would be a series of delayed reactions, little tremors on the psychic seismograph. Reality was an uncomfortable intruder in her garden of makebelieve, and she needed time to transmute death-stink, rigor mortis, and the dusty eyes of the onetime beloved into the product of the special-effects man in a suspense cinema. So I told her to do her shopping and then come to the motel, to drive around to the side, park by the Buick and come to Unit 114. Her relief was evident.

She drove out first. There was a place you could stop and see the road in both directions. From time to time I had heard the distant drone of infrequent traffic. I heard her accelerate, heard the rackety little engine fade into the afternoon silence.

Kingfisher came back. The small fire was dead. I kicked the larger charred pieces into the pond, kicked sand over the ashes. I broke a pine branch off and retraced my steps to the sinkhole and the pit, brushing out those footprints so deep they were obviously those of a man carrying a heavy burden. I checked the edge of the hole and found some tan threads from his jacket caught on the limestone. I balled the threads and dropped them into darkness.

They used you, Lew, baby. And if Lennie Sibelius hadn't persisted, hadn't tricked you into revealing the way that envelope of mine could have been planted in the Baither house when you were otherwise occupied in the shed, you might still be one of Hyzer's faithful. But once you'd been opened up, it was only a question of time until Hyzer would get under your guard and find out the name of a woman who decoyed you. And a man hooked on uppers is too erratic. The original idea of planting that envelope was too fancy, Lew, baby. A spur-of-the-moment idea that made more problems than it solved. It turned you into a problem, and now I've turned you into another kind of problem for somebody. For Henry Perris, perhaps. And Lilo, and Hutch and Orville, maybe. Patterns emerging.

So you've got a nice deep black hole for the long long sleep, down there with your hairy wallet and your dirty pictures, and your fond photo of your neglected horse.

I stopped beside my rented car and decided that there was a reasonable possibility I might get picked up again. So I went through the pockets, just in case. Found what I had forgotten, the Polaroid print of my night-running girl, Lillian Hatch alias Lilo Perris. All that merry sensuality and that tough little jaw. Hair askew, and the hard little mouth recently bed-softened. A flash shot. She stood facing the camera, weight on the right leg. Left knee bent, right fist on the right hip, muscular belly sucked in. Hard high conical breasts, the nipples fully erect. Spreading curly black pubic thatch, glossy and vital in the wink of the camera light, with the big pale weight of pudenda faintly visible through the whiskery thicket. I examined the background of the interior shot. It did not reveal much, as it was too shadowed. I could make out a corner of a bed, the edge of a table with a thin line of smoke rising from an ashtray improvised from a Planters Peanuts can. An object on the wall behind her which I couldn't identify. It was partially obscured by her head. A round thing with radiating spikes, like a child's drawing of the sun.

I did not want to destroy the picture, and I felt uncomfortable keeping it on me. I finally put the convertible top up and knelt on the rear seat and partially unzipped the rear window. There was a deep enough fold in the dacron canvas to slip the photograph in and zip it back up.

I drove out to the mouth of the sandy curving tracks and after making certain County Line Road was empty, I gunned it out and headed for Cypress City. There are a lot of places I never want to go back to.

twelve

I parked in my motel slot and went into the room. The phone light was blinking. I went out the other door and up the interior walkway past the pool and the small careful rock gardens to the rear entrance to the lobby.

There were two slips in my box. One was the message Betsy had left. The other said to phone Deputy Sheriff Cable. I took the slips back to the room. Some fat children were wallowing and whooping in the pool. Every year there seem to be more fat children, and they seem to be noisier.

I phoned the sheriff's office. Cable wasn't in. The dispatcher said he'd relay my message to Cable and he would probably get in touch with me. I said to tell him McGee was at the motel.

I saw the cruiser arrive a few minutes later, so I went to the door and said howdy to him as he got out of the car.

"Care to come in, Billy?"

"Don't mind if I do."

I had turned the color set on. A golf match had appeared. The players had green faces. Billy Cable went over and fixed the color, turned the sound down.

"Put the little round ball in the little round hole and they give you forty thousand dollars. Jee-*zuss!* Got me into the wrong line of work, I guess."

He sat on the bed and leaned back, propping himself on his elbows. A very competent, tough, unreadable, watchful face. He had sunlenses clipped onto his steelrimmed spectacles, and he reached and tilted them up.

"To what do I owe the honor and all the routine, Billy?"

"Mister Norm got edgy about you when he found out this morning you didn't sleep here. He wondered if maybe he made some kind of bad mistake about you, McGee."

"You better ease his mind."

"I already did, on my way over here. I wasn't as nervous as he was, though."

"That's nice."

"I did some backtrailing, and I found out from King you were looking for somebody named Betsy that had been close to Lew, and he told you probably Betsy Kapp. So Frank, the bartender, told me you ate at the Lodge and you and Betsy took off in your cars at the same time. Well then I went to her place but there was nobody there at all. But I went around and looked in the kitchen window and there were two of everything drying on the sideboard. Cups, saucers, and so on. Very cozy. I hear those tits are genuine. Hardly seems possible."

"You do good police work, Billy, but we can skip the editorial comment. Okay?"

"All right, you had to come up with that name someplace in order to ask King. And Mister Norm has had me looking all over for that damn fool Lew Arnstead. When I went out there his momma said he hadn't been home for three days and nights, and when I asked her if anybody had been looking for him she said that it was none of my damned business. So I asked if a big fellow named McGee had been looking for him, and she told me that if I knew already, why was I wasting my breath asking. You know, I like that old lady."

"So do I."

"Aside from Betsy, how many other names did you come up with? There'd be a pretty long list."

"I could tell you it's none of your damned business. But let's be friends. Clara Willoughbee. That's all. Maybe his mother didn't keep a running score."

"Clara is a nice girl. About to get herself married. To a rich kid from Fort Myers."

"I didn't look her up. Betsy came after Clara."

"But that was over quite awhile back, toward the end of last year, I think."

"I thought she might steer me to somebody more up-to-date."

"Why would you want that?"

"He's not an officer of the law at the moment. I thought I might locate him and see how much workout I could give him."

"King thinks maybe you could take him."

"I thought it might be worth a try. Incidentally, thanks for pulling him off Meyer."

"I should have moved faster. That last one came up from the floor. That's the one that did the big damage. One more like that and he could have killed the man."

"What was the point?"

Billy Cable sat up and took a half cigar out of the shirt pocket of his uniform and lit it, spat out a wet crumb of tobacco. "At that time it looked to us like you and Meyer gave it to Frank Baither. Frank was a rotten fellow, but nobody should have to die that hard. Both me and Lew saw the body. Lew knew Meyer hadn't given Mister Norm a thing to go on. Sometimes, in this business, you get to where you want to hit somebody."

"Do you obey the urge, Billy?"

"Me? Hell, no. But Lew is something else. Especially lately. Like his gears were slipping."

"Okay, why did you give me the guided tour before you took me to Hyzer?"

"Why not? The damage had been done. I didn't approve of it, and I knew Hyzer'd be scalded. But you use whatever's handy. Anything that might make you think twice, and sit up straight and say yes, sir to the sher'f couldn't hurt anything. But it didn't work that way."

"Because we didn't have anything to do with Baither."

"It's begun to look that way."

"When can I leave this garden spot?"

"That'd be up to Mister Norm. One thing I want to know. Did you find Lew?"

"Not yet."

"I suppose that if Betsy phoned around and finally found him last night and asked him to come over, he might have come over to her place. That would give you a crack at him."

"Good idea. I didn't think to ask her. What made you think of it?"

"A crank call came in about eleven-thirty this morning. I just now put two and two together. No name given. Said he lives on Haydon Street. That's the street behind Seminole, where Betsy lives. Said that three in the morning there was a big fuss, men yelling and cursing and a woman screaming, and if we couldn't keep order in a nice neighborhood, maybe the people ought to elect a sheriff who could."

"A little Saturday night festivity. Sorry, but I wasn't at that particular party."

"Any idea where Betsy is?"

"I'm expecting her to drop by pretty soon. I think she went shopping."

He got up slowly, stretched, flicked ashes on the motel rug. "So now I got to chase my ass over the countryside today locating crazy Lew. Glad you didn't cut out, McGee."

I went to the doorway with him and let him get about three strides toward his sedan and said, "Billy, I don't know if it would clue you on where to look for him, but his mother told me she didn't think he'd have gotten in trouble if he hadn't started hanging around with trashy people named Perris."

He had turned and he looked at me for too long a time. Too many thoughts tumbling around in his head. His expression revealed nothing. Then, too casually, he said, "Might as well check that one out, too. Thanks."

Betsy Kapp arrived ten minutes later, with a big brown paper bag hugged against her. She was pallid and edgy, and eager to get inside and get the door closed.

"I saw the police car, darling, and I went right on by. I went by twice. Who was it? What did they want?"

I gave her the full story, including my final line, and told her how silent Billy Cable became. "Does the name mean anything to you, Betsy? Perris?"

"Somebody told me he was running around with Lilo Perris. She lives down in the south county. She's young, and she's pretty, I guess, in a cheap obvious way. But she's been in trouble with the law over and over. She's loud and mean and hard as nails."

"Sounds like a rare jewel. Sounds like somebody who would know something about how Lew got killed."

"I don't think so, really. She hasn't been in that kind of trouble. Mostly fighting and disturbing the peace and public obscenity. She's just wild and tough, and she doesn't give a damn what she does or who she does it with."

"Not the kind an officer of the law should run with."

"Heavens, no! But she wouldn't be exactly exclusive property. He'd be more like a dog in a pack trotting after a bitch. Men say she's so sexy. I just can't see it. Maybe he's been down in the south county, back there in one of those shacky places along Shell Ridge Road, down there with the poachers and moonshiners. Travis, what did that phone call mean?"

"If you and I were in the county jail at the time, trying to tell them we didn't know where Lew's body came from, how would it sound?"

"Terrible!"

"And what if an autopsy established the time of death at about three in the morning?"

"We've been lucky, haven't we?"

"So far."

"Are you starving too, dear? Look! Good rye bread and lettuce and Black Diamond cheese and sardines and baloney and cold beer. Do you want me to make your sandwich, or do you want to?"

I told her to go ahead. She used the white formica countertop next to the almost inaudible golf match. I had taken the first bite of my sandwich, not waiting for her to make her own, when Billy Cable knocked at the door.

I let him in. She gave him a bright smile of welcome. "Hi, Billy. Make you a sandwich?"

"Just now ate, Betsy. Thanks. Guess I might go for one of those kosher dills though." He bit it, nodded approval, and while chomping away at it, "Saw a car that looked like yours, and McGee said you were going to come by, so I stopped to make sure."

"Make sure of what?"

He sat on the bed. "My life is a lot easier if I can do what I know Mister Norm is going to ask me if I did already. So he is going to ask me if I asked you if maybe you give McGee here a line on how to find Lew."

"I wouldn't have the faintest idea how to find Lew Arnstead, and I can't imagine ever wanting to."

"But Mister McGee here seemed anxious to find him?"

"Well . . . sort of. And I can understand that, can't you? After all, that man Lew hurt was a very good friend of Travis's. Wouldn't you look for somebody who beat up a friend of yours? Of course, maybe you don't have any friend in particular, Billy."

I saw the momentary narrowing of his eyes. And then he smiled blandly. "Then McGee was only half anxious to locate Lew?"

"That's about it."

"Speaking of my having a friend, Betsy, you've got a real talent for friendship, believe you me."

She turned and leaned her hips on the countertop and bit into her sardine sandwich. "Why, thank you, Billy!"

"I think old Homer ought to write you up in that new brochure he's doing for the Chamber of Commerce."

"How do you mean?"

"I don't rightly know. Maybe like sort of a natural resource of Cypress County. It isn't every little city back here in the swamp country that's got a nice dining room with good food and a hostess with the biggest set of knockers south of Waycross."

Her lips tightened and she held her sandwich out of the way and looked down at herself. "Now Billy. They's not so much of a much." Her accent was turning swampy. "Must be forty, fifty women around these parts wear a D-cup, too. Looks like a lot to you on account of the rest of me is on the skimpy side."

"Well, I guess there's enough men around here and there who'd testify they're real enough, Betsy."

This was a strong sexual antagonism coming out into the open. She colored, then smiled. "Oh, Billy Cable, I know you're only funnin' me, but when you try to kid around, honey, it comes out like dirty talk. You just don't have the touch. I *know* you don't mean anything wrong."

"It's nice the way you throw everything into your work, Miz Kapp. Obligin'."

She made a plausible attempt at merry laughter, and looked over at me and said, "Darlin', ol' Billy here could testify how real they are. Must have been a year and a half ago—"

"Watch it!" Billy said sharply.

"Now you started this, Billy, and Mr. McGee might be amused. I thought some sex maniac had got me. Like to scared me to death. I was walking from the Lodge over to my car on a dark night and got grabbed from behind. A girl friend told me one time the thing to do is go all limp and fall down, never try to fight. Well, I sat down on the parking lot and he let go, and I got a look at him, and what do you know, there was ol' Billy weaving and smiling down at me, just couldn't stop hisself from reaching around me and grabbing away like he was trying to honk those old-timey automobile horns. A girl could get a cancer that way. Well, sir, I was so scared and mad I hopped up and swang my pocketbook and knocked poor Billy's glasses right off and they busted. And that made *him* so mad, he took a swing like to slap my head loose, but I ducked back and Billy fell down. Then what was it you were going to do to me, Billy?"

"Knock it off, Betsy."

"Something about I should take him home with me or I was going to get arrested for every kind of thing he could think of. What did I say, Billy?"

"Shut up, Betsy. I forget."

"I said I'd rather spend five years in a prison laundry than five minutes in bed with you. Billy?"

He looked at her and did not answer. She took two steps toward him, thrust her jaw toward him and said in a low voice, "And it's still exactly the same way, Deputy. There's nothing you could ever do or say that'd make me change my mind."

He stared at her and then at me. Expressionless masklike face, but the eyes behind the lenses held a cold reptilian venom. He spun and left, slamming the room door, slamming the cruiser door, shrieking rubber halfway to the front exit onto the highway.

She ran to me and I held her in my arms. She was trembling and panting. Aftermath of another of the games Betsy played. But this game was obligatory. And, in its own way, valiant. Nothing but a cap pistol and a cheap whip between her and the tiger.

"I . . . I'm sorry it had to be in front of you, Travis."

"I understand."

"Do you? I can't ever let him get away with any part of it, any- where, no matter what. If I ever do . . . then he'll take me, and I don't think I could stand it. It wouldn't be . . . nice."

That was the inevitable stipulation. Nice.

"Go eat your sandwich, woman."

She walked over and took it from the countertop and said, "He's going to hate you now because you heard it all."

"So I'm about to faint with pure terror."

She hoisted herself up and sat on the countertop, thin legs swing- ing, holding the sandwich in both hands, munching.

"What a crazy day," she said. "What a weird kind of day."

"Just wondering something. How did Billy Cable take it when you and Lew Arnstead got together?"

"Not so good. I told Lew about how Billy kept circling me. He thought it was funny. I told him he better not make any smart remarks to Billy about the whole thing. Billy is chief deputy, and there are ways he could make things bad for Lew. They had it out, finally. Lew whipped him, but he didn't tell me any details."

Thick sandwiches and cold beer. She yawned deeply, her face softening, and her eyes suddenly heavy, an abrupt change like that of a sleepy child. She slumped onto the bed and slipped her shoes off and yawned again. "Honest, I've got to have a nap."

"You have permission."

She pulled the pillow out from under the spread and lay back. "We can go home later. I wish I could think. What you said about my knowing something and not knowing what I know. There *is* something, but I can't find it in my head."

"Try again when you wake up."

"Dear?"

"What?"

"Don't try to make love to me, huh? I haven't got anything with me. And . . . I might be too willing. That's sort of nasty, isn't it? After . . . what we had to do."

"It happens that way. The body wants to celebrate being alive when somebody else is dead. Anyway I'm going to leave you alone here for a while, Betsy."

Sleepy eyes opened wide. "No!"

"I'll hang the DO-NOT-DISTURB signs on both doors, and I'll lock you in. You'll be fine. I ought to be back by five-thirty or six."

"Where do you have to go?"

"Just an errand. Nothing crucial."

"Okay, so be careful, lover," she murmured. She was on her side, fists under her chin, knees pulled up. In moments she was making a small buzzing sound, with slow deep lift and fall of the narrow, overburdened rib cage. I closed the draperies to darken the room, and floated a blanket over her.

The phone made half a ring before I caught it. It did not disturb her.

It was Meyer. "I am free," he said. "Marked fit for duty. I am an object of awe and curiosity. My once-handsome face looks like a psychedelic beach ball. There are two gentle maidens here aboard my humble vessel, taking turns holding my hand and applying cold compresses and fixing me little taste treats. They say to say howdy. Shall I return?"

"Stay where you are. Enjoy."

"And how are things on the frontier?"

"Confusing. A fine young man had the taste to give Miss Agnes a lot of tender loving care, but I have to get a part for her out of Palm Beach before she can move."

"Would the man let you move?"

"No point in asking him until I get the part installed."

"What are you doing for excitement?"

"Mighty interesting golf match on television today."

"McGee, do not make childish attempts to mislead me. My brain was not damaged. When we left, you were down. You wanted no part of that brouhaha over there. Your voice dragged. Now there is a lift, a hint of a pleasurable urgency. You have become involved."

"Now that you mention it, I guess I have."

"Have you been able to pay my respects to Deputy Arnstead?"

"Not yet. He seems to be absent. Or shy. But I still have hopes."

"If the car was roadable, and Sheriff Hyzer said you could leave, would you?"

"Probably not."

"Have you come across an opportunity for some small salvage contract, perhaps?"

"One might turn up. Meyer, I'm glad you're okay."

"I share your gladness."

After the conversation ended, I looked at the screen. A very somber young man in orange garments was hunched over a putt. A knot of muscle bulged at the corner of his jaw. He stabbed at it, and the ball went by the hole on the high side and stopped inches away. The young man looked at the heavens with an expression of agonized desolation, of classic despair. I punched the set off while he was still on camera. I hung the signs, locked her in, and left.

thirteen

Buttercup came at me, running low and rumbling in anticipation of the clamp of his teeth in the flesh of the stranger. I squatted and held my hand out and said, "Easy, Buttercup. Easy, boy."

He braked to a stop, leaned, and took a delicate sniff, compared it with the memory banks, and looked dejected. Cora Arnstead came out onto the porch and said, "Who is it now? You home, Lew?"

"Sorry. It's Travis McGee again, Mrs. Arnstead."

"You got anything to tell me about my boy?"

"Sorry. I wish I could tell you something."

"That Billy Cable was here today looking for him, too. They fired my boy. No reason why I should fall all over myself helping them. If they want him, they can find him."

"How is the stock making out? Anything I can do?"

"That's nice of you to offer. But I've got the Silverstaff boy from up the road taking care. He was here most of the morning getting caught up. Come on the porch and set."

A haze had moved across the sun. She leaned back in the cane chair and widened her nostrils. "Smell that stink, do you?"

"Afraid not."

"Acidy smell. We get it now most times the breeze comes out of the northwest. Phosphate plants up that way. Wind from the south, and you get the county incinerator smell. Nobody gives a damn, Mr.

McGee. They talk about it, but they don't really care enough to do anything. So one day people are going to grab their throats and fall down dead all over the state of Florida, and I hope I'm safe dead and gone before it happens. What do you want with me?"

"Sheriff Hyzer is trying to locate Lew. Now if he doesn't find him pretty soon, he might come out here or send somebody out here to go through his room, looking for a clue."

"And?"

"He'll find that hiding place just the way I did. I didn't exactly give you an inventory of what's in there."

"Figured you didn't. Filthy stuff?"

"Some standard under-the-counter dirt, and some pretty vivid love notes from some of his women. And a collection of Polaroid pictures he took of a batch of his girl friends, all naked. They could cause some trouble in the wrong hands."

"Like if Billy Cable got ahold of them?"

"That's right, Mrs. Arnstead."

"You said he had a lot of those speed pills in there. Would there be maybe enough so he could get into trouble on that account, too?"

"More than enough. They came under the narcotics legislation."

She glowered into space for a long ten seconds. "I don't hold with lying, Mr. McGee. I wouldn't want anybody to come here and find that place of his and find it empty and ask me if I'd let anybody into that room to take stuff away. And if they asked me if I emptied it out and asked me what was in there, I'd have to tell what I took out. No, sir I can't let you go in my boy's room and take away his personal private stuff and get rid of it any way you see fit. I can't give you permission. Maybe you'd be so kind, Mr. McGee, as to go on in the house and back to the kitchen and get me a glass of water. Best let it run a long time for coolness."

While the water was running, I emptied the cache. Pictures and letters inside one of the books. Books and pamphlets tucked into the front of my shirt. Pills in the trousers pocket.

I took her the glass of water. She sipped and thanked me.

"You come back and visit with me sometime, hear? Sorry I couldn't give you the right to tote off Lew's things."

"I understand."

"Somehow I have this feeling my youngest isn't going to come back not ever. I don't know why. An old woman's notion. He was a good little boy. He really was. He always liked to play by himself. Not much for running with the pack. It was the Army changed him. He wasn't the same after that."

It was uncomfortable booty to carry around. If Hyzer had me picked up for some idiot reason, the list of charges would be fascinating. In the milky fading light of late afternoon I drove north, further out Cattleman's Road into an area of bigger ranches and grove lands. It had been a sentimental mission. After seeing the scene between Billy and Betsy, there was no mistaking the use he would make of Lew's artwork, or the amount of leverage possession would give him. There was the second objective of sparing the old lady any additional pain. The final chick was dead. Whether she ever learned that or not, never seeing him again was enough of a hurt.

I came up on an unpaved road, braked and turned right, and found an adequate place a mile from the highway, a small grove of live oaks heavily fringed with Spanish moss, and a place to drive in where fencing had rotted away. I gouged a deep hole in the soft dirt with a stick, dumped the pills in, covered them, and stomped the earth flat.

His meager and unusual little library would not be easy to burn. I crackled my shoulder muscles rolling a log over, scooped a shallow hole and laid the books therein and rolled the log back into the earth-groove it had made when it fell.

I sat on it and the correspondence and the picture gallery. I remembered my previous impression of the many pictures of Betsy Kapp. Lean, anemic blonde with an insipid leer and comedy breasts. So the leer became a troubled and uncertain smile, and the breasts were oddly wistful, vulnerable. I decided that in some eerie way it was like those ubiquitous photographs of small boys holding up big fish they have caught. Too much camera direction makes them look uncertain. They ache to look like heroes and do not know how to manage it. And the long dead fish has become a dead weight of reality, and there is no way to hold him to make him look alive.

I used one to light the next until all the shots of Betsy were charred. All ten of them. Then the five of the woman who had been so careful to hide her face. Then the extra three of the night-runner who had to be Lilo. I saved the thirteen trophy shots, the head-on singles. I went through the correspondence and burned it all—except Betsy's long letter of warning about Lilo.

All the photographs and the letter fit nicely into the same pocket of the double thickness of canvas by the rear window. I spread them out so that there was no bulge when I zipped it shut. The thought of how Billy Cable might use the pictures of Betsy gave me the idea of possible leverage, for quite different objectives. I had studied the faces. Lilo and the Unknown Thirteen. The odds were that most or all were in Cypress County on this final Sunday in April. Clerking, waitressing, dating, tending babies, fixing dinner, ironing shirts, dancing, watching television. Lew's little garden of ladies. There might be a certain amount of gratitude involved were a lady to get her trophy shot back, and be scratched off Lew's local scorecard. So keep looking at the ladies, McGee. A fellow blundering around in the murk needs the loan of any thirty-nine-cent flashlight available.

The last thread of daylight was about gone as I turned into the parking area of the White Ibis. The little tan VW was gone, and my throat turned sour, and my neck-nape and hands prickled with that million-year-old reflex which tries to lift the coarse animal hair, to make the animal look bigger, more awesome, more difficult to chew. It was sick premonition. Too many old memories of mistake and remorse.

Unlocked the door, flicked the switch, saw the blanket shoved aside, the depression in the bedspread, the shape of the length of her in heavy sleep, the dented pillow.

Her note on the motel paper was on the carpeting, with an ashtray paperweight, in a conspicuous spot.

Lover darling,

I woke up and got thinking about that you-know-what in my car, and getting nervous about it and then not feeding poor Raoul and leaving him alone so long what I decided was put that thing back where it was like you said and feed Raoul and then go find out about that thing I couldn't remember before, which maybe hasn't got a thing to do with anything. And I decided while it is still light I can take a quick sneaky look and see if the jeep is still there in that yard behind the bushes but I hope it is gone and we don't have to think about it at all only about us alone together in my little house with all the world shut out, so what you can do is change your clothes like you never got a chance to and bring your shaving things and all and if you get there before I get back the extra key to the side door is where you go into the carport and reach around in back of the first can of paint on the top shelf the one to your left when you walk in but if my car is in there then you can just knock and if you are lucky I may even decide to let you in and feed you and all that.

Love ya!
Yr Betsy

Very sweet and innocent and diligent, and very stupid, leaving a note with too many things in it to interest, for example, Billy Cable, if he should have taken a turn by the place, seen both cars gone, and decided to take a look. Motels have master keys, and local law has a conspicuous talent for collecting copies of same, because it is a lot less fuss than court orders and warrants and negotiations with management.

So I confettied it and flushed it down, took my fast shower and changed, whipped out of there with toilet kit and sweaty hands, and drove to her place on Seminole Street, making one wrong turn before I found it, because the only other time I had driven to it had been at night, following her.

When I turned into the narrow, high-hedged drive, I felt a sense of relief at seeing lights on inside the cottage, but the feeling clicked off when my lights swung to the empty carport. I put the white Buick at the side of the carport, this time with the top up, in the same spot as it had been when someone had tumbled the big ugly souvenir into it.

I stood in the night, listening, and felt my nostrils widen. Another atavistic reflex, snuff the air for the drifting taint of the stalking carnivore, long after the noses have lost their sensitivity and cunning. Heart bumping under the stimulus of adrenalin, readying the muscles, blood, brain, for that explosive effort necessary for survival in a jungle of predators.

But it was just a side yard of a very small residential plot in a peaceful neighborhood of a small southern city. A neighborhood of postal clerks, retired military, food-store managers, bank tellers, watching the fare that came into their living rooms over the cable, checking the *TV Guide* during the rerun season to see if there was a "Bonanza" they had missed, or a "Mission Impossible."

The blood slowed, and I found the carport light switch, found the key in the place she'd described, and had time to get to the house corner and get a glimpse of the handle laying next to the supporting jack before the delay switch clicked the light off. In the darkness I squatted and reached under the house, felt and hefted the pipe handle to make certain. And in the darkness I went out to the sidewalk and kept to the shadows, went to the yard she had described, ducked under the chain and saw the dark, insectile angularity of the jeep parked there, nuzzling into the untended plantings.

I went back and let myself in. One lamp lighted in the living room, lacy shade on a brass post that impaled a shiny black merry-go-round horse. I trod a narrow route between fragilities and knick-knacks to the kitchen where the fluorescent light over the stove was on. Some crumbs of cat food in the dish in Raoul's corner. I bent and touched one. It was moist instead of being dried to the dish, so she had fed Raoul.

Next I went to her bedroom, found the wall switch. The blouse and skirt she had been wearing were on the foot of the bed. Raoul, curled up on the skirt, lifted his head and looked at me with the benign satisfaction of the full stomach and the comfortable place to sleep. There were water droplets on the inside of her shower curtain and the tiled walls. There was the scent of sweet soap and perfume and deodorant and hair spray, a damp towel spread on the rack, one misted corner at the top of the full-length mirror on the inside of the door.

I sat on the bed and rubbed Raoul's sleepy head and got his gritty, audible engine going. A puzzlement that she should be so full of nervous alarm, so anxious not to be alone, and then go out alone to find out God knows what. I finally realized that it had to be another one of the games that Betsy could play. A new script patterned on the late late movies, suspense, perhaps, with elegant quips and handsome sets, and she was maybe Myrna Loy tracing down one of those fragments of female intuition which would clear up the case which had William Powell baffled. And that, of course, made it all perfectly safe, because if somebody started to really hurt anybody, the Great Director would yell "Cut!" and we would go back to our dressing rooms and wait for the next call.

Eight o'clock. Nine o'clock. Ten o'clock, and that was all I could manage to endure. Locked up and left there and drove down to the complex of county buildings and services and went into the Sheriff's Department. A pair of strangers behind the high desk, cool, disinterested young men in fitted uniforms, busy with forms and routines, busy with the paperwork of booking Sunday drunks, brawlers, DWI's, a couple of fourteen-year-old burglars. The communications clerk finally sent word that I might find the sheriff over at the Emergency Room at City Memorial, and one of the busy young men told me how to find it.

I parked in the hospital lot and walked back to Emergency. Some bloody, broken, moaning teen-agers were being offloaded from a white ambulance with blue dome lights, and wheeled through the double doors into a corridor glare of fluorescence so strong and white it make the blood look black.

I saw a county cruiser parked over at the side, interior lights on, a shadowed figure behind the wheel. So I walked over to ask him if Hyzer was inside the building. But from ten feet I saw that it was Hyzer himself. He looked up from his clipboard and said, "Good evening, Mr. McGee."

"Sheriff. They told me I might catch you over here."

"What can I do for you?"

"I'd like to have a chance to talk to you. Maybe ask some questions. Can you give me fifteen minutes or so?"

"If you come to my office before nine tomorrow . . ."

"It would be better right now, I think."

"What's it about?"

"Baither, Arnstead, Perris."

"You were very insistent about not being involved in the Baither matter in any way. Do you want to change your story?"

"No. But things come up which puzzle me, Sheriff. If we talked them out, it might be of some help to you, and you might let me leave that much sooner."

"I can't see how you could be of any help to me."

"When you find Lew Arnstead, if you haven't already, get him checked for stimulants. He's a speed freak. When they go over the edge, the condition is called paranoid psychosis, and it would be more comfortable to be around a kid playing with dynamite caps."

"Result of an amateur investigation, McGee?"

"I wanted to find him and scuff him up, and I turned up a few things while I was looking for him, and I decided there was no point in being emotional about what he did to Meyer—who, incidentally, is all right."

"I know. I made inquiry."

"Then I keep wondering how Henry Perris fits into the Baither killing, and what the association was between Perris and Arnstead. And right now Mrs. Betsy Kapp seems to be missing, and my amateur investigator guess says that she's gotten herself into the middle somehow, where it wouldn't seem to be a healthy climate."

The stern hero face looked up at me from under the pale brim of the expensive hat. "Come around the car and get in, Mr. McGee."

"When I was in, he put the clipboard on the seat between us, unhooked his mike, and told his people he was leaving the hospital and would call in from his next stop.

"There'll be too many interruptions if we go in," he said. "How about your motel room?"

I drove over in the Buick. He was waiting and as I unlocked the door to 114, he said he had told them where to reach him.

He sat in the armchair, put his hat carefully on the floor beside the chair. I moved over and sat on the countertop where Betsy had sat, eating her sardine sandwich.

"I had a report from Deputy Cable," he said. "So I know you went and talked to Cora Arnstead. I had a report of your conversation with Deputy Sturnevan. I know you spent the night with Mrs. Kapp at her home on Seminole. I was glad to hear you had not left the county. If you had, you would have regretted it. My responsibility is to enforce the enforceable laws and ordinances. Deputy Cable suggested to me that Mrs. Kapp be picked up and charged with public fornication. There is an old ordinance on the books. I have not been able to understand why Billy would want to waste department time on that sort of thing. He is usually a more reasonable officer. I do not wish to make any moral judgments about Mrs. Kapp. She has always seemed to me to be a pleasant enough woman, and she seems to run that dining room well. She would seem to be . . . selective and circumspect in her private life."

"Billy Cable went after her a year and a half ago. He'd had a few drinks. She turned him down flat. Last fall she had an affair with Lew Arnstead."

"I knew about the Arnstead affair. How could you know about Billy? How do you know it's true? He has a wife and three children."

"They had a very rough little scene right here in this room this afternoon. Billy asked for bad news, and she gave it to him.

"So at five o'clock he makes that stupid suggestion about arresting her. I'll check it out. I don't like it. An officer should not use his position for personal vendettas. I'm disappointed in Billy Cable. You say Mrs. Kapp is missing. Tell me about it."

"She was here most of the afternoon. Then she went in her car back to her house. I was supposed to meet her there. She knew I'd be over about seven. I went over and she wasn't there. She'd told me where the key was. I let myself in. She left a note telling me she was going out to find out something about this . . . whole problem which got me into one of your cells, Sheriff."

"Find out what?"

"She didn't say. I waited until ten o'clock and then I came looking for you."

He went over and sat on the bed and looked up her phone number and dialed it. While it was ringing at the other end, I had a closer look at him under the light of the bedside lamp. His dark suit was wrinkled, his shoes unshined. His knuckles and wrists were soiled, and there was an edge of grime around his white cuffs and around the white collar of his shirt. The light slanted on a dark stubble on his chin. It did not match my prior observations of the fastidious officer of the law.

"No answer," he said as he stood up. He went back to the chair and looked at his watch. "Ten past eleven. Maybe, Mr. McGee, she decided not to see you again. Maybe she went to stay with friends, waiting for you to give up and go away."

"Not a chance."

"Where is the note?"

"I threw it away. I assure you it was . . . affectionate."

"You told Mrs. Kapp all about the reason why you and your friend were suspected of being in on the Baither murder?"

"Sheriff, she lives here and she works here. She knows a lot of people. I told her everything I know, including your theory about the money truck, and Baither using Raiford State Prison as a hideout. And I built a little structure of supposition, based on little hints, guesses, inferences. I haven't tested it on Betsy yet. I planned to. One way to go at these things is to build a plausible structure, then find facts that won't fit and tear it down and try again."

He looked at me through a steeple of soiled fingers. "Let me hear it."

"Baither put it together. He used two outsiders, pickup talent, possibly from out of state, he had the contacts, apparently. The fourth man was local, and without a record, gainfully employed. Henry Perris, now working as a mechanic down at Al Storey's station on the Trail. The other two men we know only as Hutch and Orville. Baither needed Henry Perris because Henry had access to a wrecker and knew how to operate it. They also used Perris's stepdaughter, Lillian. She was the young waitress in the blond wig at the drive-in across from the track."

"Pure fantasy!"

"May I go ahead? Thanks. After a big score, the people involved watch each other very carefully. I don't think Frank could have slipped away with the money unless Henry and the girl helped him somehow. This would be the deal. Frank would hide the money and take a fall at Raiford. Henry and the girl would sit tight and wait it out. Frank wouldn't let Henry know where the money was because he would be afraid of another doublecross. A three-way split, if you count the girl, would be a lot better than five ways."

"Why Perris?"

"Because Lilo Perris and Lew Arnstead were or are paired off. It started several months back, and with Baither up for release, it would be good sense to have a pipeline into your department, Sheriff. She's apparently a very rough kid. Then you have Henry Perris in a position to pick my envelope out of the trash at the station, and you have Lilo ready and willing to decoy Arnstead into that shack in back of the place. But it was a bad impulse. People get bad, tricky ideas when something has gone wrong. They get nervous and they don't think things out. Manufactured evidence backfires. So Perris and company was suddenly up against the very dangerous situation of having vital and damaging information lodged in the mind of a speed freak. If you went after the name of the woman who decoyed Arnstead into Baither's shed, you could probably shake it loose. And to have it be the stepdaughter of the mechanic at the station where I swear I discarded that envelope makes everything a little too tight. Have you located Lew?"

"Not yet."

"There's a chance, a reasonable chance, that they had brought Lew all the way into the picture. Maybe they needed the kind of help he could give them. Nine hundred thousand is a lot of persuasion. The girl could make certain he wouldn't be thinking clearly. The girl and the amphetamine, and something a little warped in his mind before he even started downhill. If they did, what's your chance of finding him alive?"

"Facts will tear down your structure, McGee."

"If you have them."

"There were three men working at that station all day Friday. Albert Storey, Henry Perris, and Terrance Moon. They submitted to interrogation willingly. There was a period of about two hours and fifteen minutes, starting at the time we drove away with you and your friend, when their actions are important. None of them left the station at that time. No phone calls were made. They were interrogated separately. The customers who stopped during that period were strangers—tourists and commercial traffic on the Tamiami Trail. The men talked about Frank Baither being killed to each other, but not to anyone else. I am left with the remarkable coincidence of someone unknown to those men stopping for gas, seeing that envelope in the trash barrel, picking it out and taking it up to Baither's house to leave it where we found it later."

"And you can't buy that and neither can I."

"Then you dropped it in Baither's place."

"You know I didn't."

"What choice do I have, McGee? And, of course, your evaluation of Lillian Perris is total nonsense." There was a force in his voice, an animation in his face which surprised me. "The girl has a lot of spirit. She should have had a lot more discipline. She's been in scrapes, but nothing serious. Considering the environmental and social factors, I think she has done remarkably well."

"I was only—"

"Forget any idea of her having any part of it."

"Okay. And Henry Perris is a pillar of the community and a lay preacher?"

"All I know is that he has no record."

"Let's concentrate on Henry for a minute, Sheriff. Just for the hell of it. Let's say he was in on the Baither murder, and it went wrong and he was shaky. He comes to work late. He gets our names and the reason we're being picked up from Al Storey. He goes to put something in the barrel and sees the envelope with my name on it and he picks it out when nobody is looking and puts it in his pocket."

"But I told you that—"

"I *know* what you told me. He had to leave that station soon after we left."

"But he didn't."

The message on his face was clear: Don't pursue further.

"What could Betsy Kapp have remembered that got her into trouble?" I asked.

"*If* she's in trouble."

"Are you going to look for her?"

"Missing persons reports have to be filed by the next of kin."

"I don't think you always go by the book, Sheriff."

He smiled for the first time. "If I did, I would have you back inside, McGee."

He phoned Betsy's house again, with no results. He looked troubled. "I'll put the word out."

"Thanks, Sheriff." I walked him out to the car and asked him if he minded if I looked around.

"Inside the county, Mr. McGee."

"Of course, Sheriff."

So I began my blind quest, because anything was better than going back to her empty house to sit and wait.

fourteen

Cruise the after-midnight streets of the sleepy city, checking the lots, and driveways, the on-street parking for the distinctive shape of the VW bug. Hard to tell gray from tan under the street lamps. Then remembered the thing she had affixed to her radio antenna, handy way to find the car in the jammed-tin wasteland of the shopping-center parking rows—a plastic sunflower, big as a saucer. Easier to eliminate the look-alike VWs.

Stopped once in a while at the bright upright coffin of a pay phone, listened to ten rings, got the same dime back every time. Aware finally of hunger pangs, and I turned back to a place where I had seen the all-night drive in. No car service after eleven. Very bright inside. Big table of teen-agers, whispering and haw-hawing at delicious private nonsense, making a point of excluding the square grown-up world from all of it. A few night-people spaced along the counter. Plastic radio with a burr in the speaker playing muted rock.

The waitress was a plump, pretty girl, hair bleached to a coarse pure white and hanging lifelessly straight. Blue nylon uniform. DORI embossed on the name tag. A smudge of tiredness around her eyes. Mechanical smile, presentation of the grease-spotted bill of fare.

Here they called them a MaxiBurger, and they came on a toasted bun with caraway seeds. Very little taste to the hot meat. Bits of gristle. Much better coffee than I expected. Munched the meat, sipped the coffee, wondered why the girl looked so familiar.

Had paid, left, started the motor before I realized why she might look familiar. Got out the Polaroid shots, sorted them under the interior lights, located Dori. Different hair style. Same face. Same plumpness. Startled expression, one hand blurred by movement.

I replaced the other pictures, put hers in my pocket and went back inside. She came over with the mechanical smile and the menu and then realized I looked too familiar.

"Oh, you were just in, werncha?"

"Decided on another cup of coffee."

"Well, I'll forget you went out and come back, so you get the seconds free anyways."

She brought it and I said, "Thank you, Dori. When you've got a minute, I want to ask you something."

"I got a minute right now. Like what?"

I slipped the picture out and held it low so that only she could see it. I watched her face. She swallowed and bit her underlip and looked warily toward the other girl. She leaned toward me and said, "Look, this is some kind of a mixup. Put that away, huh? He must have got confused or something, honest. He was supposed to have tore those up, mister. Go find him and tell him Dori said he should ought to be more careful."

"He didn't seem to be confused."

"What kind of a car you got?"

"White Buick convertible."

"Look, you drink your coffee and go sit in it and wait, and I got a break coming, I'll come out and explain. Okay?"

In a little while Dori came walking quickly across the blacktop, the white lights strong behind her, yellow cardigan around her shoulders. Yellow straw purse in her hand. I leaned and swung the door open for her. She tugged it shut, pushed the dash lighter in and got her cigarettes out of her purse.

"It would have to be some kind of foulup, because it was always part of the deal he checks with me first, for obvious reasons. And he wouldn't let go of a picture. That's kind of rotten. And what he always did was tell me where to be and when, instead of sending somebody to where I'm working. Way back we made the deal, and I told him then that okay, so I was in a box, I'd go along with it, but only any kind of chance like that. So Fred got back seven months ago and I was nervous about if the deal would stand. But it did. Look, mister. Six weeks ago, maybe two months ago, a guy came in by accident and I'd had a date with him over a year ago, and he is a little bit smashed and thinks he can get fixed up right now. He started to get loud and so I got hold of Lew and he came by and took the fella out into the parking lot and bounced him up and down some and he went away. So it looks to me like something is going on I don't like. Now you tell me how you got that picture and what it is you've got in mind."

"Did you know he was fired?"

"I heard about it. For beating up a prisoner and for goofing off when he was supposed to be watching the house where Frank Baither got killed. I thought maybe he'd come in, but he hasn't."

"Nobody has seen him, Dori. There's a pretty good chance he's dead."

She sucked the final half inch of cigarette down to the long filter, the red glow illuminating her small frown, her hollowed cheek. "Something was going bad for him. He was getting so jumpy he looked flippy almost. I cry no single tear, baby. That was the meanest son of a bitch I ever knew or ever want to know. When I know Lew is surely dead, I'll sleep a little better. Anyway . . . who *are* you? Some kind of a cop?"

There was new anxiety in her voice. "Not exactly. I was picked up with a good friend of mine, the one Lew pounded. It looked like we knew something about the Baither murder but we didn't and they let us go, but I have to stay in the county. I let it be known I wanted to find Arnstead and beat on him. Now I'm worried about how I'm going to make out if they find him in a field or behind a warehouse tomorrow, beaten to death."

"They could make out a long list, mister."

"You don't blame me for trying to protect myself?"

"Not if you don't get me involved."

"I happen to have a little picture gallery that belonged to Lew. Never mind how or where I got hold of it. You looked familiar so I came out and looked at the pretty pictures and found yours."

"Just don't get me involved."

"Dori, put yourself in my shoes. Suppose he is dead and Hyzer tries to make me for it. The only thing I *can* do is spread out my picture collection and tell him to check it out. He'll find out that Lew had this sideline going, and probably as long as he was an officer of the law, nobody wanted to take the chance of putting him out of business. But he lost his immunity with his job. So check out all the husbands and all the boyfriends. Why should I leave you off the list?"

"I swear to God, cross my heart and hope to die, Fred hasn't any idea at all what went on. I love the guy. It would kill him, it really would. And he might kill me. He's got a terrible temper. Give me the picture, please. Don't you have enough without me? How many have you got? I always wondered how many there were of us."

"Fourteen, counting you."

"Jesus! I was thinking six or seven. Don't you have enough to make your point without me in there? I swear he hasn't tried to set me up one time since Fred got back, and that's been seven months. What's your name, anyway?"

"Travis McGee."

"Trav, be nice. Please!" She looked toward the restaurant. "I've got to get back before Carolyn gets really scalded."

"When do you get off?"

"I've been on since five. I get off at two."

"Does your husband pick you up?"

"That's my wheels over there on the back corner."

"Can you come over to the White Ibis when you get off?"

A snort of disgusted laughter. "Oh, boy. The same old crap. Be nice to me, baby, and I'll be nice to you. I must lead some kind of charmed life. Every time old Dori gets boxed in."

"Just talk. I want to get an I.D. on as many of the pictures as I can. I want to know how it operated. Can you do it?"

She looked at me, skepticism in the tilt of the silhouetted head. "I guess. Fred will be asleep on account of he has to get up at six to go to work. I hate this shift every time I pull it. I try to sneak in without waking him up, and he tries to sneak out in the morning without waking me up. Then when he gets off work he comes and eats here and leaves me the wheels and walks home. What's your room number?" I told her and started to explain where it was. She stopped me. "I know the layout. I've been there before. I just didn't expect to have to go back again."

She trotted back and went inside. Through the expanse of glass I saw her, sweater off, standing talking to the other girl, shrugging and gesticulating.

I had something better than forty-five minutes to continue the dogged search for the plastic sunflower. I tried her number again. Nobody heard the ringing except Raoul.

As I drove I thought of what I had said to Hyzer, about facts toppling structures built of supposition. You want facts to simplify and clarify. But this one I had stumbled on merely deepened the murk. What I had thought were trophy shots were in truth a salesman's sample case. Pick your pleasure, sir.

It is a useful and profitable sideline practiced by venal, underpaid, crooked police officers in every urban area of the nation and the world where police administration leaves enough room for improvisation. A certain number of females are always going to get into trouble with the law. A certain percentage of them are always going to be physically attractive. The investigating officer can make a deal that is mutually advantageous. Play ball or face a conviction, honey. The procurer cop has advantages denied the free-lance pimp. He can more safely strong-arm the unruly customer. He can protect his string from arrest, and at the same time keep them in line with the threat of arrest. If he is careful in his selection, they will never fink on him because they, in turn, have too much to lose by any public exposure of the relationship. And he was a handy source of special favors for politicians and administrators. Tonight, sweetie, you got a date with Judge O'Harran. Here's the address. He'll be looking for you about eight o'clock. This one is a freebie.

It was a big-city sickness I had not expected to come across in a small city in the central flatlands of Florida. And it puzzled me that Deputy Arnstead could operate his string right under the cool nose of a man as diligent and professional and subtle as Norman Hyzer. And it bothered me that Betsy Kapp had been in the sample kit. Maybe a very useful talent was fading, my ability to sense what people were after—what made them struggle and what made them give up. That talent had kept me alive a few times when the odds were against it. And I could think of no game Betsy could play which would enable her to turn a little hustling into some kind of romantic dramatics, into a sentimental eccentricity.

I was waiting when Dori parked. When I opened the door for her, she came scuttling in, furtive until the door was closed and she had tugged the center gap in the opaque draperies shut. Then she was at her ease. Saw that all I had was gin and Scotch, said gin and Coke would be fine if I could get some Coke, so I got a bottle out of the machine when I went to get more ice.

She wanted to talk. She was all full of her plump and pretty animation, bouncing around in the chair, gulping at her drink, sucking her cigarettes, brief skirt of the waitress uniform at midthigh, exposing the fine skin texture of her pretty legs. Lots of gestures and animation. She had been aching for a chance to tell somebody about the enormous, heartbreaking tragedy which had befallen poor Mrs. Fred Severiss, and had no idea that it was a drab, tiresome and ordinary little story, because she knew it had happened to her, and she could not feel commonplace, nor can anyone in their unique little time around the track.

She had always been "fantastically stupid" about money, and she had been a salesgirl at Garnor's Boutique at the Woodsgate Shopping Center, and Fred was far away and she missed him and she had this thing about buying clothes and shoes to cheer herself up, and she had charge cards, and besides she had this "wonderful crazy girl friend" and they would go whipping over to the east coast and go to the dog tracks, and she was absolutely true to her Fred, etc., etc. So she got in a terrible money jam, and the credit people started getting very ugly, and she missed car payments and she didn't know what she would do if she lost the car, because how would she explain it to Freddie? So she had eighty dollars and she and her girl friend had gone over to the dog track and she thought that if she could build it into three or four hundred she could get out of the jam, but she lost it all and fifteen dollars more she borrowed from her girl friend. Then she started clipping the cash sales at the Boutique, saving the halves of the inventory tickets, thinking of it as "just sort of a loan, actually, on account of I was going to live quiet as mice and pay it back before Mrs. Garnor took inventory May first. That was the season before last." Then Arnstead had showed up at night at her little studio apartment, and it was the first she knew that the thieving had been detected, and Mrs. Garnor had asked the law to find out which of the five clerks was doing it. She had tried to deny it and Arnstead had broken her in about five minutes, and she had, at his direction, written her confession about it being a little over six hundred dollars taken over the seven weeks. Then he said he would take her in and bail would probably be about five hundred, and the least she could expect for grand larceny would be eighteen months in the state prison for women. Blubbering and begging and pleading for mercy had done no good. And when she was in total despair, he had given her the little hint that she was so pretty that maybe he could delay it, see what he could do, and she had lunged at that like a starving bass, taken him into the narrow Bahama bed, telling herself it wasn't like cheating on Fred actually, because what she was really doing was saving their lives and their marriage from absolute wreckage, and she had vowed "to just be a thing, and go through the motions with my mind a thousand miles away." But the deputy had kept seeing her and he was persistent and she had been alone for months and months, and couldn't help herself really, and got so she responded to him, and got to "needing him in a crazy way even though I didn't like him." Then he wanted her to be nice to a friend, and they had a terrible battle about it, and by then, of course, he had taken some pictures of her, and had the confession which he said was good for seven years, and he could mail a picture with a Xerox of her confession to dear Freddie if that was the way she wanted it. So she had slept with his friend in a motel over in Everglades City a couple of times, and then there had been others, and Lew would bring her fifty dollars, or twenty, or seventy-five, depending. And once, a year ago last July, he'd sent three of them to Naples and they'd gone cruising for four days on a big company boat with a hired captain and three sort of vice-president-type people, and that time it had been a hundred twenty-five from Lew and fifty that the man she was with had put in her purse like a bonus or something. She knew there were other girls, and she had only run into three of them altogether, the two others on the cruise, and one on a kind of double date right here in this motel.

She counted, frowning, on her fingers and said that it had all lasted maybe fifteen months, and she could not remember the number of affairs, or the amount of money. Maybe twenty or twenty-five dates. Lew promised it would end when Fred came home. She had finally realized that Lew knew he could control her, but Fred was something else. Fred would try to kill him and would surely kill her. She'd been terrified that Lew wouldn't keep his promise, and she'd been terrified that Fred would somehow be able to tell what she'd been up to, but it had worked out all right.

By then she had worked her way through the second gin and Coke. She was flushed and her articulation was not quite as distinct.

"I'm just damn lucky I got out of it, Trav. I'm just lucky it's over. I keep telling myself that. But it's funny . . . I don't know. I'm different somehow. I mean I'm sort of faking the happy little wife bit. One time I got to fussing at Lew until he got sore and grabbed my neck and shoved me over to a mirror and hurt my arm and made me look into my eyes and say dirty things about myself. Things like:

'I'm a whore. I peddle my ass. I bang for a living.' Things aren't like what you always think they're like, I guess. It's not real different from dates, where if the guy is sweet and fun you have a good time, and if it's some old fat guy, you just get it over with. I don't know. Sometimes I think of standing on my feet in that place and how long it takes to make fifty, and how long it took to make fifty on my back. Fred is a great guy, really. I think that maybe somebody will come in and look at me and say let's go, baby, and I'll get in his car and never come back."

She lifted her wrist and peered at her little watch. She shifted in the chair, ran her tongue along her lips, took a deep shuddering breath. In a huskier tone she said, "Like now. If you should want it, honey. Like on the house."

"Let's look at the pictures."

She came out of her sensual glaze. "Oh, sure. Jesus! I don't know what's wrong with me lately, I really don't. Yeh, let's look at them and then I got to get going because Fred could wake up and get worried and wonder what the hell and phone and place and find out I've been gone forever."

I laid the pictures out on the countertop under the lamp, one at a time. She came and stood beside me. Thirteen of them.

"That's Donna Lee something. She was on that cruise. She's a real fun kid, real lively, and she's got a real cute body as any fool can plainly see. She works in a real estate office. Up over the bank. Associated Realtors, Inc. No, I don't know *this* one at all. I don't remember ever seeing her around town anyplace. I *have* seen this girl somewhere. Let me think. I think she works in the courthouse. I'm pretty sure. *This* one I know. Sort of. Her name is Brenda Dennis? Dennison? Denderson? A name like that. She was on the double date with me. She's sort of quiet and hard to know, and she isn't built very good, is she? She works at Elian's Stationery, but I haven't been in there in so long I don't know if she's still there. I've seen *this* girl someplace I think, but I don't know where. This one is older, huh? I never saw her before as far as I know."

When I turned the seventh picture she gasped and said, "Holy Maloney! It *can't* be! This is Miss Kimmey, for God's sake. She teaches third grade and sings in the choir at our church. She's got a real nice soprano voice. The kind of clothes she wears, you'd never guess what a great body she's got. Now how in the world did Lew ever nail her? Boy, would I like to find out."

She drew another blank on number eight. But she knew number

nine. "That's Linda Featherman. I nearly dropped my teeth when she turned out to be number three on that cruise. I mean there's lot of money there. Big ranchlands and grovelands in the northeast part of the county. At first I thought she was going to spoil that cruise by acting as if she was so much better than Donna Lee and me. It was her car we went to Naples in, and she drove and hardly said a word all the way. She took darling cruise clothes along, worth like a fortune. But then she was okay after the first day, a lot more human. Poor gal, I couldn't believe it when I read about it."

"About what?"

"She got killed a little while ago. Let me count back. Two weekends ago, I think. The state police said she had to be going at least a hundred miles an hour, heading back out to the ranch at three or four in the morning, about fifteen miles north of here, and they said she probably fell asleep because there weren't any skid marks. She just went right off a curve in a straight line and right into an enormous pine tree and broke it right off and hit the next one sideways. They say it took hours to identify her for sure."

Number ten was one Jeanie Dahl, and on seeing the picture she remembered Lew saying that Jeanie was in the club. She and Jeanie had both been in the Miss Cypress City contest when they were in high school, and Jeanie had been second runner-up and Dori had been third runner-up. Jeanie had been married and divorced, and lived with her mother who took care of her little kid while Jeanie worked in the office at Kramer Building Supply.

Eleven was an unknown. Twelve was somebody she thought she had seen often around town, but had no idea where.

I had adjusted them to leave leave Lillian (Lilo) Hatch (Perris) until last. She actually recoiled from the picture, and made a little coughing, gagging sound and turned away.

"What's the matter?"

"Her name is Lilo Perris. I don't want to talk about her."

"Why not?"

"Give me a minute. Fix me a drink. That made me go cold all over. That girl is crazy. I mean for real crazy. That girl is a maniac."

I made her the third drink. She was back in the chair. When she settled down she told me.

"It was about the fourth time Lew sent me to meet somebody. He was a spook. He wanted things I didn't want to do. So I wouldn't. He got mad and I got mad and it broke up fast and I went home. I was waiting for Lew to come around so I could tell him not to send me to spooks like that. He sent Lilo to see me. That girl is crazy! She hurt me so bad I fainted, I don't know how many times. After she went away I kept throwing up. I was so weak I stayed in bed two days. Then Lew came around and said the spook was a very important man in Tallahassee, and I was going to have another date with him. He said if I didn't want to make the spook happy, he'd have Lilo come to visit me again. I think I would really rather die than have her start doing things to me again, smiling at me and giggling and calling me love names and saying how much fun it would be to really kill me. She's as strong as a man, and she knows every way there is to hurt a girl. She's absolutely insane, Trav."

"How long ago was this?"

"Maybe . . . a year ago last June. Look at me. Look at the goose bumps on my arms and legs just thinking about her. I used to get nightmares about her and wake up bellering and twitching around."

"Do you know of anybody else who was in on it, where I don't have a picture here?"

"Gee, I don't think so. I can't think of anybody."

"Possibly Mrs. Betsy Kapp?"

"In the dining room at the Lodge. The old blonde with the huge boobs. No, and I can tell you why I'm so sure, even." She started to say something, then closed her mouth and looked guilty.

"What's the matter."

"Well . . . I guess I lied a little. But only about one of the gals."

The truth came out. She had lied about Jeanie Dahl, about only remembering Lew mentioning Jeanie when she saw the picture. She saw quite a bit of Jeanie, as a matter of fact. Why shouldn't old friends see each other? As a matter of fact, Jeanie was the crazy friend who'd go with her to the dog tracks, and Jeanie had gotten in as bad a jam about money as she had. And as a matter of fact once she'd started having affairs that Lew lined up, she had some drinks with Jeanie and told her all about it, and how it was, and what the payoff was, and found out Jeanie had been clipping a little bit now and then from petty cash at Kramer Building Supply and was scared of getting caught. So she had asked Jeanie if it was okay if she told Lew that Jeanie might be interested, and at first Jeanie said no, and then she changed her mind. And it was nice to have a friend who knew the whole score, and was in it with you, and you could talk to them the way you couldn't talk to anybody else in the whole world, and compare notes, and tell about the weird things that happened. So because of Jeanie's mother and the kid, they had set it up for Lew and Jeanie to meet at Dori's apartment while Dori was working, and when she got off work Jeanie was still there, alone and asleep, and said she and Lew had made the deal, and sealed it with a lot more than a handshake.

"I kinda sluffed over Jeanie's picture because . . . maybe I felt a little weird about getting her into it all, too. But when you're in a bind, you wish somebody you knew was in it, too. At least I warned her about that Lilo and told her she better not ever get choosy about anything if she got set up with a spook. Since Freddie came home seven months ago, I go have lunch with Jeanie whenever my shift works out right. It's like . . . resigning from something and you want gossip about what's going on since you left. She took a whole week off from work last January and flew to Jamaica free, and her date was there waiting, and it turned out to be . . . well, never mind who. Anyway an important businessman in this town. She came back with a marvelous tan and brought me some fantastic perfume, and she made five hundred dollars!"

"What about Betsy Kapp?"

"Oh. Lew came by when Jeanie was getting off work one day, last November, I think, and he drove her out into the country someplace and parked and he came all apart. She said he cried like a little boy. She said he cried on her shoulder and she held him, and she said it was funny to feel kind of warm-mother toward him, knowing all the time what a mean son of a bitch he is. He finally told her he had beaten up a woman who'd done him the greatest favor any woman could ever do a man. It was all some kind of crazy thing about how he fell in love and he all of a sudden couldn't get it up, and the doctor he went to told him it was a common thing, a guilt thing, feeling unworthy and all that, and gave him shots but they didn't help. And the same thing happened with other girls then, and then the wonderful woman had helped him and he could again, and then he had beaten her up and he didn't know why. Jeanie finally found out it was Mrs. Kapp, and so she just naturally asked him if Mrs. Kapp was taking on customers for him, too. Jeanie didn't mean anything by it at all. But he reared back and gave her such a clout on the side of the head her ear rang day and night for a week, practically. He said Mrs. Kapp was a fine woman, not some cheap little piece of ass like Jeanie. So I guess Mrs. Kapp never had any part of the action. Jeanie said he acted strange, and he had been acting strange, and after that he got more weird. Jumpy acting."

"When did you see her last?"

"This is Sunday. I mean it's Monday morning. Let me see. We had lunch a week ago Friday. We talked about Linda Featherman, mostly. And she said she hadn't heard anything from Lew in three weeks and she was wondering if he was sort of easing off. She said she was getting nervous about keeping up payments on things because she'd figured on the extra money. She said, just joking, that maybe the two of us ought to go over to Miami Beach and see if there was any action. But she was joking. Lew made it awful plain to me and to her, too, that if we did any hustling on the side, he'd find out and we'd be the sickest, sorriest gals in Florida. Anyway, it would be stupid to try to work a place you don't have any protection. The cops pull in the free-lance gals, because that's part of the deal they get paid for by the people who have the action all sewed up. If Lew happens to be really dead, like you think, it's going to be rough for Jeanie to make out. It comes to maybe a thousand or twelve hundred a year, according to what I was making and what she was making, without any tax on it. Part time, like moonlighting, but there has to be somebody like Lew to set you up and do the collecting ahead so no bastard can afford to try to cheat you. We used to figure out what Lew was making, guessing how many of us were working for him. So it had to be what? Fourteen to sixteen thousand a year? But I guess he had to split that somehow, to keep himself out of trouble."

She stood up, yawning. "Do I get my picture back?"

I handed it to her. She looked at it and said, "I can just look at a piece of pie and gain a pound." She tore it into small pieces and took it into the bathroom and closed the door. She came out after a while and said, "You've got any of the other pictures of me?"

"No."

"I wish I knew where they were. I'd feel better. It was some sort of game, I thought, the camera on the table and he'd set a little thing that started buzzing and hop back in with me and then the flash would go off. It was one of those he was going to mail to Fred. He cut it so it was him from the chest down, but there I was, clear as a bell, laughing my fool head off. If you come across those?"

"I'll destroy them and let you know."

"The wrong clown gets those and he can put me right back in action. I wouldn't have a choice. Poor Freddie."

"Can I talk to Jeanie?"

She looked secretly amused. "How could I stop you? Why ask? You are a nice guy, Trav. You really are. I'd like to do you a nice favor for being a nice guy, but if you wanna know the truth, seeing the picture of that Lilo really blew out my fire. Going to be around awhile?"

"I guess so."

"Maybe we can working something out. You know where to find me. You wouldn't have to worry about anything. I mean I'm a healthy girl from head to toe. 'Night now. Take care."

fifteen

Yes, indeed. Take care. I finished the notations on the backs of the thirteen photographs. Six names.

Courthouse, third grade, building supply, real estate firm, stationery store.

Arnstead's Irregulars. Sorry little part-time hookers, each one thinking herself such a very special person, able to play the dark and nimble role, yet remain essentially her own true beautiful self.

There are no hookers with hearts of gold. Just lazy, greedy, dullminded girls whose greatest joys are the clothing rack and the mirror and the makeup table. Such a simple little task, to take that everfamiliar tumescent rigidity into the slippery muscular depths, and brace tight, and hip-smack it into its brief leapings and sagging flaccidity. Simple task, sometimes pleasurable enough to incite an inner matching clenching, hidden explosion, and sighing release. Then say it was beautiful, tell him he's special, tell him it hardly ever happens like that for you. Give him the mirror-practiced expressions, and use the familiar ways to ready him again, because the better you work him, the more chance of a tip, and the thirty-dollar blue sandals are on layaway, and they are darling.

So simple a task it soon has no meaning, and then there is no meaning in being a woman, in that sense of being a woman. The only meaning left is in the ever-changing adornment of the body, that thing they buy. It is like the mercenary who sits alone, smiling, and with oil and stone, puts an ever finer edge on the combat knife, hoping that the next sentry will die so quickly there will be that little feeling in the belly of professional satisfaction, and a feeling almost of fondness for the unknown sentry because it had worked so well.

No evil in either hooker or mercenary. Just laziness, a small familiar greed, a mild anticipation of unimportant sensation, and the ever-challenging problem of what kind of pretty to buy with the fee.

Poor Freddie. Why did she leave and where did she go? She's going, soldier. One day soon. She'll leave because, no matter what the uniform, the mercenary blade always pierces exactly the same heart, stopping it over and over again. Only the angle changes. Until all hearts become the same target. And the hooker receives from all customers exactly the same plum-taut glans, slaying it in the same rocking lubricious clench of inner muscle ring, clasp of outer labia, pumping it to its small jolting death, welcoming it ever again, affixed to the loins of another stranger, but always the same in its greed for death. Only the duration changes. Until all erection is the same, including the husband one, all equally meaningless except for the chance of pleasure-feeling, and the money.

I thought of Betsy and her silly, touching, romantic conviction that each episode was unique and meaningful and full of glory. Faith and conviction made it so, and a stereo at cost and free tapes were gestures of friendship, and a hard man could understand a little of this, and weep for having beaten her.

It was nearly four-thirty in the morning, and again her phone did not answer. I tried the sheriff. He was not available. I stretched out to think of what to do next, how to fit the parts together, and suddenly it was bright morning outside, the room lights still on, my mouth stale, and my eyes grainy.

The phone rang just as I was reaching to turn on the shower. It was Sheriff Hyzer to tell me they had not located Mrs. Kapp or her car yet, but that they had found Lew Arnstead's black jeep hidden in the yard of an empty house four doors down Seminole from Mrs. Kapp's cottage. Maybe I'd like to stop by.

I didn't ask any questions. I hurried the shower, and it was twenty after eight when I got there. Hyzer's cruiser was in Betsy's driveway. He seemed to be alone. Fresh suit, shirt, tie, shoes. He'd nicked himself twice shaving.

We walked up the street. The chain was unhooked. A deputy was dusting it with professional care and deftness, lifting fragments and sections of prints, making notations of location.

"It made me wonder, Mr. McGee, if Arnstead had hidden this here yesterday evening, gone to Mrs. Kapp's house and taken her away with him in her car."

"I suppose that could have happened."

"Not when you see this. Come here." He took me around to the front, pointed to a brown object fastened to a protected place under the headlamp. "Mud dauber," he said. "Fresh. They turn pale when they dry. They don't work at night. This nest is nearly done. You wait a minute you'll see her come flying in with another mud ball. She had to start yesterday morning to get this far. She had to build it up to a certain point then go find the right kind of spider and paralyze it with her stinger and shove it in there. Soon now she'll have just a little hole left. She'll lay her eggs in it and then seal it up, and when the young hatch they'll have the spider meat to live on before they break out."

"Very interesting."

"So it was left here Saturday night, probably. You spent the night with her. Hear anything?"

"Not a thing."

"We had a telephone report of an altercation at three in the morning in this neighborhood."

"I didn't hear that, either."

"It doesn't make sense, at least not yet, for him to hide his jeep here and walk away from it and not come back."

"Meaning he couldn't come back."

"Or somebody abandoned it here to leave a false trail. Tom, don't forget to dust that Dr. Pepper bottle on the floor."

"No sir, Sheriff."

"Getting anything usable?"

"Too many smudges. A few pretty good partials and right here at the top of the windshield, one real good one of the whole heel of a hand. Could be a woman's or a child's from the size."

"Call Johnny's to come tow it in when you're finished, and get those vacuum bags to the Bureau as fast as you can."

As we walked back to Betsy's drive I said, "You're a very thorough man, Sheriff."

"We try."

"I imagine you must be aware of everything that goes on in Cypress County."

"All I need to know, I hope. We put through a consolidation a couple of years back, absorbed the city police into the county and put all the law enforcement under the Sheriff's Department. Cuts duplication and expense."

"Excuse me, Sheriff. You seem more amiable toward me today."

"I like to be fair. You said Perris had to leave that station Friday morning. I tried it once more. I phoned Al Storey this morning and asked him if Henry Perris had left the station for any reason whatsoever, business or personal. First he said no, just as he did before, and then he remembered that Perris had finished a brake job on an Oldsmobile and had taken it down the road to the customer, a man named Hummer. It was a combination road test and delivery. Hummer had then driven Perris back to the station. To get to Hummer's road, Perris had to pass a little roadside park with a public phone booth. Can you fill in the rest of it, Mr. McGee?"

"Make a phone call to someone to pick up the envelope he hid in the phone book."

"Perhaps. Storey did not think of that in the same sense as actually leaving the station. Leaving involves personal business. A delivery is work time. I told Storey not to talk if Perris was nearby. He said Perris was late again, as usual. I told him not to mention the conversation to Perris."

"Are you going to pick Perris up?"

"Not yet. I want him to feel safe. I want to have more to go on."

"Now will you admit the girl is implicated, too?"

His stare was like stone. "If evidence should show at some future date that she is involved, knowingly, in any criminal activity, then she will be arrested and charged."

End of amiability. End of conversation.

I drove down to Johnny's Main Street Service. Miss Agnes had been taken off the line. I found her on blocks in the body shop, with a big sweaty Ron Hatch wielding a rubber mallet and some curved templates with comforting skill.

He came out and said, "Hi, Mr. McGee. Some of it isn't as bad as I thought. But, Jesus, they used some kind of gauge metal in her." I borrowed the broken fitting from him and made a call from the office to my mechanic friend in Palm Beach. I told him what it looked like and where it went. He had me measure it, and had me hold the phone. He came back on the line in about two minutes and said he had it and where and how should he send it. I had him ship fastest means direct to Ron Hatch at the garage. The operator came back with the report of charges, and I gave the exact change to the office girl and she put it in the petty cash box just as a man in his late forties came in. He was trim and held himself well, and his hair was a little too thick and dark to be entirely unaided. He had a golfing tan, and an elegant sport shirt, and a gold-and-black wristwatch with three or four dials and a lot of gold buttons to push.

"McGee?" he said. When I said I was, he said he was Johnny Hatch, and invited me back into his office. Small, paneled, cool, windowless, and private. Golfing trophies and trap-shooting trophies, and framed testimonials about his civic services. A color portrait in a silver frame, showing a very lovely young woman smiling out, her arms around a little boy and a girl. She looked young enough to account for his trimness and his hairpiece and dye job.

"Thanks for treating the kid right on the work he did on the old Rolls truck of yours. It set him up pretty good."

"He's a nice kid."

"Not much you can do with them these days. That Liz Taylor haircut of his makes me want to throw up every time I see it. He won't go back to school. He's a car nut. I'll say this. He'll do the job right for you. Now I got a second litter coming along, and it makes you wonder what kind of problems they're going to be."

"I wasn't exactly eager to put any more money into your operation, Mr. Hatch. It seemed to me like you took me pretty good."

He shrugged. "I could show you the books. We don't get rich on county business. We have to bid it. We lose on some and make out on the others, and hope to end up the year ahead. Don't tell me a fella who can afford Lennie Sibelius is hurting for a little garage bill."

"Word gets around."

"Small town. You know how it is. Everybody hears everything. Trouble is that when they pass it along, they add a little to make it more interesting."

"Then you know Arnstead is missing?"

"I heard about it."

"And Betsy Kapp is missing, too."

He was startled. "The *hell* you say."

"She had a seven o'clock date last night and didn't keep it and hasn't been seen since."

"That's a weird one. That isn't like old Betsy. I tell you, it would take a lot of pleasure out of having lunch at the Lodge if anything happened to her."

"I understand she and Arnstead were pretty close. Maybe they took off together."

"Hell, I can't buy that. They had something going, I guess. But that was months ago. Funny, she'd fool around with Lew."

"Maybe it was a business relationship, Johnny."

He leaned back, watchful. "What's that supposed to mean?"

"I knew the name was familiar, but I didn't connect it up right away. I remembered that a year, year and a half ago, somebody told me that if I ever got stuck in this neck of the woods, I should look up a Deputy Lew Arnstead, and he could fix me up with something real choice, that it would cost, but it would be worth it."

"Do tell."

"You're the one who told me it's a small town. I guess if it was true, you'd have heard about it."

"I think I heard somewhere that Lew had an extra girl friend or two he'd hire out."

"I guess he'd have to be pretty careful about it, working under a man like Hyzer."

"Mister Norm sees what he wants to see and believes what he wants to believe, just like everybody else."

"He doesn't impress you?"

He shrugged. "I vote for him."

"So it's a nice quiet place, with a very quiet little newspaper."

"There's no point in scaring up trouble by printing a lot of things that agitate people."

"Was the car Linda Featherman was driving brought in here?"

"What the *hell* have you got on your mind, McGee! I asked you in here to thank you for the way you played fair with my boy. I didn't know I was going to get some kind of third degree."

I smiled, stood up. "I'm just curious about your nice little town, Johnny. No offense. I admit I am a little curious about your first litter. I like Ron. He's a good one. But from all reports his sister is as rotten a little tramp as you can find anywhere."

His face turned to a brown mask, and he did not move his lips when he spoke. He spoke so quietly I could barely hear him. "Understand this. Nobody mentions her in my presence. She is absolutely nothing to me, and the sick sow that bred her is nothing to me. I don't care if they are alive or dead. I don't care if they roast in hell or find eternal bliss. Now get out of here."

I got. That much hate is impressive, no matter where you find it.

It makes you want to walk on tiptoe and breathe quietly as you get out of range.

I found breakfast and then flipped a coin. Heads was Deputy King Sturnevan. Tails was Mrs. Jeanie Dahl. Had it landed on edge I was going to try Miss Kimmey, in the third grade. It was heads.

King had some reports to finish. He said to wait around. Twenty minutes later he came out and walked over to the Buick. He leaned in and shook his head sadly. "You gotta talent, man. Billy Cable catches you jaywalking, he'll club your head down between your knees."

"Get in, and I'll tell you about it." I told him. I was at the wrong place at the wrong time, and witnessed Betsy chop him down.

King nodded. "I knew he wanted to get into that. But I didn't know he was damn fool enough to go after it that way. If Mister Norm heard he tried to use his badge to get her onto her back, he could be out in the street. Seems like she didn't fight you off much, McGee. That's the way she is. She will, but not often, and she has to do the picking."

"She picked Lew Arnstead."

"I know. Surprised folks. The Betsy-watchers. Not her type. But you can't tell."

"King, how much can we trust each other, you and I?"

He shifted his big belly around and beamed at me and winked a scarred eye. "You can't trust me one damn bit if it's something the man ought to know."

"I have a crazy question which has been growing and growing, and I have to ask. Make it hypothetical. Could and did Lew Arnstead get away with things that Hyzer would have fired anyone else for?"

I watched him make his slow decision. "It bothered me a long time, pal. Tell you the truth, it surprised hell out of me when Hyzer did boot him out and file charges. And I saw Lew's face when it happened, and I think Lew was as surprised as me."

"Do you think Hyzer knew Lew was pimping?"

"You get around good. That wouldn't be easy to come by. I guess Lew started four years back, about then. I think maybe Hyzer decided that if a broad was going to peddle it, it's better to have somebody keep it under control. He had to hear about it, but as far as I know, he never looked into it. And Lew never turned up rich enough to ask for an investigation of where and how he got it."

"Could he have been handling it for Hyzer?"

"I am going to forget you said that, pally. Because if I remember it one minute from now, I am going to pull you out of this pretty car and see if I can rupture your spleen with a left."

"Sorry I asked. I apologize."

"It just couldn't be, believe me."

"Now you know and I know that a cop builds his own string. He doesn't start off with old hustlers. He starts with girls who've gotten out of line and he scares them into making a choice his way. He's usually smart enough to try it on the ones who will take to it without much fuss, or he isn't in business long. He breaks them in himself, then puts them to work."

His broad face was unhappy. "I guess if Mister Norm looked into it and found that was the way it was being done, he would have had to get rid of Lew. So he didn't look into it. I know the score, pally. I remember there was an immigration officer in Miami who put the heat on for whether girls got a renewal or got shipped back to the crummy villages they came from. Then one of them, as I remember it, wrote her kid sister not to come to the States and told her why, and the kid sister gave it to the old man, and he flew up on the money his daughter had been sending back to Peru, and put a knife into that civil servant. He put it in about forty times, starting just above the knees and working his way up. Somebody could have known about Lew and didn't make the move until Lew was no longer a law man."

"I just happened to tell Hyzer about how Billy went after Betsy Kapp a year and a half ago."

"How can one man make himself so popular so fast? You going to run for mayor?"

"I don't know. I think of lots of questions and look for answers. Question: Would somebody kill Arnstead in order to take Hyzer off whatever hook he was on?"

King thought it over. "He doesn't act like anybody with the pressure off. He's pushing harder than ever. I thought over what you said the other night about Lew. He had to be way out on speed. It fits. So how and why does a speed freak get clobbered? Who knows?"

"King, what was the verdict on Linda Featherman?"

He snapped his head around, completely puzzled. "Verdict? What do you mean? Accidental death. One-car accident. Excessive speed. Fell asleep, maybe."

"Insurance company pay off?"

"What the hell are you talking about? Murder? Suicide? What?"

"What if you were absolutely positive she'd been hustling for Lew Arnstead for at least two years?"

"Aw . . . come *on!* The Featherman girl? You're out of your tree, buddy boy. If anybody tried to muscle her, she'd go to Dale Featherman and say, 'Daddy, somebody is bothering me.' And daddy would go skin Arnstead and salt down the hide after he scraped it clean, and tack it on one of the stables out there at the ranch. He might saw off the top of Lew's skull and use it for an ashtray. No, sir. That's four generations of Florida money, and senators from Washington and bankers from New York come down in a Featherman jet and land on that private strip. You're way off, my friend. She was a very pretty girl and she drove too damned fast."

"Brothers or sisters?"

"Three of each, I think. She was somewhere in the middle. Got back from college three years ago, I think. There were plans for a wedding, but it got canceled for some reason. There's no lever to use on a girl like that. She could buy her way out of trouble, or have the muscle put out of business."

"Unless the leverage was on somebody else, and that was the only way she could protect them."

He studied me. "Okay. We're trusting each other. I just might take your word for it. Are *you* positive?"

They have a badge and they swear an oath. So whether or not something is off the record depends on how much they value that oath. So when you see the cop-glint way back in the eyes you back off, just a little.

"King, let's say it's a pretty fair assumption."

"Then you're wandering around out in left field, McGee. Let's say Lew wasn't all too bright, and let's say he was running women. He wouldn't be so dumb he'd try to muscle Miss Linda Featherman into it, pretty as she was."

"Can you come up with any names?"

"I wouldn't want to try, because I might name some it would turn out they were only close friends of Lew's. If he was setting up every woman he'd been out with in the past four years, he'd have to run the operation with IBM cards, and take home the money in a wheelbarrer."

"Wonder what he was doing with what he was making?"

"Salting it away. Slowest man you ever seen when it came to reaching into his pocket to pay for a beer or a cup of coffee. He bought himself some good guns, and one good horse, but that was about it. Had a pretty fair automobile that he bought half wrecked and had Henry Perris put in good shape, then he was too cheap to pay collision, so it was a total loss when he racked it up. He kept his business affairs, and just about everything else to himself. Close mouth and a close pocket. It isn't smart for any cop to have a safety deposit box. I'd guess Lew'd pack it in fruit jars and bury it in the ground."

"Think he dug it up and left?"

"Not if he could still make more than enough to live on around here. I think he's dead."

"Do you think he had guilty knowledge of the Baither killing?"

"Let's you and me stay friends, pally." He opened the door, slowly pulled his bulk out, flipped the door shut, mopped his forehead. "It's going to get way up there before this day is over. See you around, I suppose. Glad to hear your friend is doing fine."

I arrived at the Kramer Home Building Supply headquarters at eleven-fifteen. It was a mile and a half out of town on the airport road. Big lumber warehouse with truck loading docks, a cement-block operation with about two acres of decorative block stacked gleaming in the sun, a retail store with everything for the do-it-your-selfer, and a clerical office at the end of the building which housed the retail outlet. It was a bright brisk operation with that neatness of floor displays which reflects a comforting operating net. Old men were browsing through the hand tools and cupboard latches, spray cans and wallboard just as, in the world of long ago, they had prowled the candy store to find out how best to spend the hoarded dime.

There were two middle-aged women and one young one behind the waist-high fence. The young one was the Jeanie of the picture, looking slimmer in a short fuzzy pink skirt, a white blouse with a fine vertical red stripe, dark auburn hair chopped to urchin length. One of the other women started toward me, but I smiled and pointed at Jeanie, who was running invoices on a big Burroughs accounting machine. The woman shrugged and looked a little less hospitable and spoke to Jeanie. She turned and looked at me, first a green-eyed speculation, and then recognition. She turned her machine off and came over to the fence, angling so that I had to drift over toward the corner, and we ended up at the maximum distance from the other two women.

Delicate little features, face wide across the far-set eyes, fat little mouth over the pointed chin. "Your name is McGee, huh?"

The piped music, which always seems to be Montovani in places like that, made our conversation private. I nodded. She made a hand gesture and said, "Those old crows got ears that come to points, believe me. Dori said a big tall guy, kind of battered here and there, with a lot of tan and real pale gray eyes. But she didn't say how tall and how big. I could tell from her voice she's turned on about you. She called me after Fred was gone, like seven this morning, and she sounded a little plotzed. She was scared I'd be sore she'd told you about me. She said you're okay, so if it says that in her book it says it in mine. I like to dropped my teeth when she says fourteen gals. I would have said ten at the most, the very most." She looked over her shoulder at the wall clock. "I can switch lunch hours with the girl over there on the register. She hates going at eleven-thirty. That's ten minutes. We can't talk so good here. I can feel Mr. Frandel looking at me through that glass right now, boring a hole in the back of my head with his eyes. Look, you mind buying something? It helps. Then I'll be coming out that door there into the back parking at eleven thirty."

I joined the browsers and came upon something I had been wanting to add to the tools aboard the *Flush*: a compact, light-weight electric screwdriver, variable speed, reverse, a goodly batch of interchangeable heads, all in a tiny aluminum case for $26.95. No reason why Lennie shouldn't buy his bird dog a little present for the boat. The only flaw in the rig was that some idiot, through cynicism or indifference, had specified steel pins in the aluminum hinges and a steel latch on the case.

So by the time I paid and got out of there, Mrs. Jeanie Dahl was standing in the shade leaning against the building, ankles crossed, elbow propped in the palm of her hand, cigarette down by a third. She smiled and pushed herself away from the wall and followed me to the convertible. I turned the air high and, when we turned onto the highway, I ran the power windows back up.

"Where do we go?" I asked.

"Right down there where the sign is on the right. Bernie's. There's kind of a crazy grove behind it and you can take stuff out there. I'd like a cheeseburger and a vanilla shake."

I carried our food in a cardboard box out to cement tables and benches in the shade of big Australian pines. We were the only customers in the grove. The other five tables were empty. A pair of Florida jays flew down and landed on the end of the table, hopped cautiously toward us. She held her hand out, arm flat on the table, crumb in her palm. The bolder of the pair, after much inspection, grabbed it and flew to the nearest table to eat it. She continued to feed them as we ate and talked.

"I think he had some kind of protection, sure. But he didn't say anything real definite, right out like. More like saying to me a couple of times there wasn't a thing to worry about, because I live with my mother and my kid, and I said to Lew a couple of times that my mother would make my life hell on earth, and my lousy ex still wants the kid and it could be a chance for him to get Davie away from me, I mean if there was some kind or raid or something like that."

"So if somebody was in with him, it would be logical for that somebody to pick it up where Lew left off, if Lew is dead."

She wiped her vanilla mustache off on the paper napkin. "McGee, I was thinking I wouldn't exactly be eager to go along with Lew on anything if he shows up again. I mean having him be a deputy makes it one kind of thing, and having him be out on bail, waiting for a trial in circuit court is something else. You know? Maybe if he lost his protection, they might want to charge him with this other thing, too. And if I got a subpoena, believe me, I think I'd go out of my mind. I guess the best thing to do is sort of keep my fool head down for a while. If nothing happens, maybe in a couple of weeks or so I can set up a date with a local man I just so happen to know, and I've got the idea it could turn out to be a permanent kind of a thing, and he's so turned on about me, I ought to be able to get a regular allowance, if he isn't too chicken to try to set us up a place right here instead of going way off somewhere. I don't want to lose the stuff I bought on time, like the color TV. My mother and Davie would be lost if we had to go back to that crummy little black-and-white Sears. Look, what is it you want to know, anyway? She said you'd probably give me back my picture like you did hers. It's better it shouldn't be floating around if something happened to Lew."

"I'm puzzled about how he operated. Certainly he wasn't contacted out at that ranch, or at the Department. He must have had some other base of operation."

"Why would he have to? I don't know about how it was when he started it, but by the time I got in, it was on account of one fellow telling another fellow who to get in touch with. Then Lew would meet the fellow someplace, like at the Adventurer bar in the afternoon and size him up and if he looked all right, or there were two or three and they looked okay, he'd tell them the rules, all night only, and no heavy drinking beforehand, and cash on the line in advance. Then they'd pick out who they liked and Lew would phone and say where and when and who to ask for, and if you couldn't make it, the guy made another pick. He tried to steer away from any gal having any regulars. He said that could turn into trouble. There was some locals, not many, and that was pretty much set up for out of town someplace. The next day or a day later, Lew would get the money to me. It was . . . easier, I guess, not to have to take the money from your date yourself. And it was more like a date that way, even though you'd know and the guy would know it was paid for ahead. What you were supposed to do was tell Lew if you got any kind of a bad time, like a fellow getting mean and slapping you around, or having a friend show up for a spare piece. Then Lew would take the guy off the list for good. I don't think I'd want to be set up by any-body else unless they kept it under control like Lew did. But lately he was getting careless, like the guys weren't such a nice class of peo-ple, and he took longer coming around with my share so twice I had to remind him. And the last time I saw him, a month ago anyway, he called the house about eight at night and told me walk down to the corner and meet him. So I did and he picked me up in a police car and drove out into the country like a maniac and wouldn't tell me what it was all about. It started to rain and he took off to some crazy little shacky place at the end of nowhere and took me in there and liked to ruin my clothes yanking me out of them, and he shoved me onto a cruddy old bed and he was so rough it scared me, and it wasn't ten minutes, I swear, before I was back in that car, sniveling, scared to death of the way he was driving. He let me out at the corner in the rain, and thank God my mother was too hooked on the television to take a look at me when I came in and went to my room."

"Where was this shack?"

She looked startled. "Hey, that was sort of what you were asking before, wasn't it?"

"Sort of. Was it locked?"

"With a padlock, yes. It was just one room, a pine shack with a crooked old floor, set up on blocks instead of pilings. It had elec-tricity. I remember I saw a hot plate on some packing cases by the wall. There was a little narrow hall to a back door, with a little room with a john and a sink off one side of it, and a storeroom like off the other side."

"Where was it?"

"It was dark and raining and I couldn't find it again in a thousand years. I know we started out Cattleman's Road because I remember wondering if we were going to his place, but it didn't seem likely because he said that if I ever called him there ever, he'd spill my teeth all over the floor. And he would, too."

"You went a long way out Cattleman's Road?"

"A long way. Miles and miles and at a hundred and something miles an hour. Then he turned left, skidding on the corner like a racing driver. We must have been out of the county, or almost. Then he turned right and the road was so narrow the bushes were rubbing on the sides of the car. It went around a lot of curves and the lights shone on the shack and big trees around it and on the rain falling down hard. I asked him where we were and what he wanted. But he . . . I was going to say he didn't tell me anything, but he did say something that didn't make any sense. I can't remember."

"Please try."

"It was something crazy. He said it was his birthday present. I don't know whether he meant me or the house. Then he was running me through the rain to the door, pulling me by the wrist, and mud was slopping up on the backs of my legs and my hair was getting soaked, and I had begun to wonder if the crazy bastard had taken me out there to kill me. I think part of my crying all the way home was relief."

"Did he say anything else?"

"No. Oh, when he reached across me and opened the door to let me out on the corner, I started to get out and he grabbed me by the shoulder and pulled me back. He dug his fingers into my shoulder so hard I had marks for a week. He said I didn't remember where I'd been, and I didn't want to tell anybody about being anywhere with him or he'd give me a face that that would turn my kid's stomach. I wanted to laugh. I didn't know where the hell I *had* been."

She looked at her face in her handbag mirror and told me how this year she was going to get a really good tan. She said she had better be getting back to work. She asked where the picture was. She studied it and started to tear it, then instead put it in her purse, snapped the clasp.

I drove her back and before she got out she said, "Dori told me to tell you maybe she'll be in touch. Look, she's a crazy wonderful kid and she's bored out of her skull. Fred is a nice guy. It's been too long since she's had any kind of fun. You'd be doing her a favor, and you shouldn't miss out on it anyway, because she's a really fabulous lay, and she loves it. It isn't a sales pitch, honey. It's a freebie, because she likes you a lot."

"And she's bored."

"I told her they should have a kid, but they keep taking tests and nothing happens. Freddie works hard, but, Jesus, if you tell him a joke, you gotta spend a half hour explaining to him where he should have laughed. Anyway, she's maybe my best friend, so don't get turned off because she's a little on the chubby side, okay?"

"And if you remember anything more about the place, call me at—"

"I know where you are. Thanks for the lunch, McGee."

"You're most welcome."

"And the picture. Say, I didn't get to see the others, dammit. No time now. Maybe I'd know some she didn't."

"I'll get back to you."

"You *do* that! Bye now." Knowing I was watching her, she wagged her little pink skirt all the way to the door, turned as she tugged at it, and blew me a small kiss with her pocketbook hand.

I wrote mental ads as I drove into town: Girls, do you want extra pocket money? Have you ever thought of part-time hustling to supplement your income? Just a relatively few hours a month in pleasant surroundings. Opportunities to travel. Tax-free income. Must be between twenty and thirty, amiable, reasonably pretty and well built, and able to devote time and effort to your second occupation. Do you like people? Are you truly interested in meeting new people of means? Earn as you learn.

It would not be such a nifty little sideline for Jeanie and Dori and company if one of the syndicate operations moved into Cypress City and took over Arnstead's list and picked what looked useful enough and moved them out and put them on the circuit, broke them to total obedience. I remembered the time long ago when Miguel and I forced our way into the circus in Juarez one night, thinking to find the Australian with Miguel's money among the spectators. Four soft paste-white women of indefinite years under the blue spotlights, sweating with the effort of working their circus routines with the black, the dwarf, the burro, and each other. We brought it to a halt when Miguel hit the room lights, knife ready. No Australian among the eight men and three women spectators. As Miguel made his eloquent apologies to the cold-eyed management, easing their indignation with a gift of pesos, one of the performers, a dead-eyed woman with a curved knife scar from forehead to corner of the mouth, which had nicked the eye and turned it milky, padded over to me, her sweat coppery-sharp in the stifling room and said, "Mister, didn't you used to live in Dayton, Ohio? Weren't you a young kid selling cars for the Buick agency in Dayton, Ohio?"

I had time to tell her no. Sorry, no, lady. Then the room lights went off and the dwarf stung her across the rear with his little whip and she yelped and leaped and then went tumbling back onto the mattresses under the blue spots, tumbling back into the interrupted performance. We left, and found the Australian a week later.

It has always bothered me that I could just as easily have said yes.

sixteen

I went to the office of the county clerk and put on my most affable and folksy manner and asked if they had any alphabetical list of the taxpayers on the *ad-valorem* tax roles. They sent me to the assessor's office, and a girl there sent me to the central records department, where they sent me back to the clerk's office. Finally I settled for a look at the big book of aerials of the entire county, and by using the line drawing on the front as a guide, I was able to find the pages covering the nothern half of Cattleman's Road to the Wagner County line.

I found three places where a northbound car could turn left. Each seemed to have quite a few places where a car could then turn right onto private land. Each photograph had a transparent overlay bound into the book with property owner's names, and the number of the book of deeds and the page in the book which covered the property.

Hullinger, Reiter, Rench, Dowd, Albritton, Eggert, Alderman, Jenkins, Hyatt, McCroan, Featherman. Lots of Featherman land and lots of Hullinger land.

So on the second aerial of the last road I found on the overlay an irregular oblong, far smaller than the surrounding parcels, and it said: "Arnstead—3.12 acres. Book 23, page 1109."

I could make out the faint track of entrance drive, and part of the shape of a roof hidden by the pines. I measured the scale and found that the entrance was almost exactly two miles from the turn at Cattleman's Road.

The spectacled girl showed me where Book 23 was. I found the old quit-claim deed to Lewis B. Arnstead, a minor child, from his father, for the sum of one dollar and other valuable considerations.

Often when you are the most hopeful, nothing works. Then you try a long shot and come up with it.

Before I left I used a pay phone and tried Betsy and got my dime back.

There was no breeze and the sun of early afternoon was hazy and hot. As I passed Cora Arnstead's place, I saw the black horse standing in the shade near the pond, grazing. The geese were asleep on the grass by the pond, one sentinel sitting with his head high. The stunted cattle were at the far end of the pasture.

I had no trouble finding the turn, nor finding the driveway two miles west of the turn. The brush touched the sides of the white car. An armadillo stared me to a stop, then went trundling off into the thicket.

It was, as Jeanie Dahl had called it, a shack. Old black cypress siding on a hard-pine frame, with a tar-paper roof, gray-white with age, patched here and there with black tar. Holes in the window screens. Curtains yellowed by age. The stout padlock on the door hasp had been broken. I pushed the door open and went into the sickening oven-heat of the interior. It smelled as if lions lived there. The old swaybacked bed was out from the wall, mattress slashed in a half dozen places, soiled old sheets and blankets on the floor. Interior wallboard had been pried loose. Sections of the flooring had been ripped up. Chunks of the Celotex ceiling had been torn down.

Somebody had gone through it with utmost thoroughness, and had given the same attention to the toilet room and the storeroom. I saw some places which I thought at first could have been overlooked. But then I found the hiding place someone else had found first. It was the hearth in the shallow brick fireplace. It was of fire brick resting on a cement slab. Brush the ashes away and take out the fire bricks on the left-hand side, and the top of a mail-order cylindrical safe was exposed. A hole had been chipped and drilled down into the poured concrete, and the safe let down into it and cemented in. The dial had been prybarred off and then the prybar had been inserted in the hole behind the dial, and the cheap hinges had torn loose. The top was in the fireplace. The interior of the safe, about the dimension of two number-ten tins end to end, was empty.

I sat on my heels and looked at the heap of black charred fragments of paper on the right side of the hearth. Photographic paper burns in a distinctive way and leaves a recognizable kind of ash. With a splinter from the torn floor I carefully shifted the pieces of ash. There were some small fragments of a different kind of paper which had not burned completely. They were apparently sheets from a notebook, torn, but then burned in small packets so that the outside sheets were blackened but the inside ones were merely brittle and yellowed. Fragments of names, portions of addresses, dates, amounts. I could not find matching bits from any one page, but found enough to conclude that it was a customer list, with the girl indicated by initials. DLA, LF, DS, BD, LP, LF, HA.

The ledger accounts and advertising and probably the insurance documents of a very small business enterprise. Insurance in the form of confessions, photographs, letters. Cottage industry, bankrupt due to unforeseen circumstances. Proprietor found himself in a hole.

Suddenly I had enough of the oppressive heat, the lion-cage stench, dusty cobwebs, dead bugs, and old ashes. I stood up and started out toward the relative coolness of outdoors, and saw on the wall a cheap gaudy electric clock of the type which makes a sudden appearance in cut-rate drugstores at Christmastime. Dangling cord, unplugged. Small gilt face with a radiating array of black metal spikes.

I moved back and found the position of the lens. The peanut can ashtray was on the floor near the corner. Yes, the table had been there, the end of the bed there, Lilo Perris standing there, her head in the way of the clock face.

Confirmation of partnership. The chunky, brawny little sunbrown girl with all the contradictions in her face, who worked as Arnstead's enforcer, so suited to the occasional chore that even after a year and a half, the photograph of her could turn Mrs. Freddie Severiss cold-pale and sweaty, her throat bunching to swallow the sudden bile.

Then I went out, my shirt sweat-pasted to my back, out of the plundered lion cage into the dusty dooryard, into that midday silence when the birds and insects are still, with no breeze to hiss through the pines, or make rain-sounds in the fronds of palmetto.

I walked around the edge of the area, footsteps silenced by the brown cushion of old needles. A track led off to the side, portions of old car tracks in dried mud. I walked twenty feet down that shaded place, and was about to turn back when the angle of the sun made a single bright silvery glint through a line of brush.

So I went further, and saw it, the plastic sunflower growing in alien country. Circled the brush and found the tan VW, sitting there with the brute endearing patience of all small ugly machines. She was not in it.

She was forty feet from it, standing there against the trunk of a tall old pine, her knees slightly bent. When she had tossed the skirt and blouse on the bed and taken her shower, she had put on lime-colored slacks and a tailored lemon-gold shirt.

This was another of the games that Betsy played. Add rose to blue and the color can be a strange and memorable lavender. They had taken the ends of the length of galvanized fence wire, and twisted them together on the far side of the big tree, tightened them enough with pliers. She had stood erect then, perhaps. But later as the wire bit ever deeper into her throat, she sagged, the knees bending. Bulging clown-face in a long lavender look, eyes popping, vein-broken and yellowed, fat black tongue thrusting from the lips in permanent grimace. A game. Fright mask to tease the children. Look at me. Do I scare you? Just a little? I really don't like this game very much, dear. I've dirtied my pretty slacks and I've begun to smell frightful, and the steak I promised is still in the freezer, the wine cooling. But I was delayed. By a game I don't like very much.

I found myself over by the little tan car, my eyes smarting, and I saw my fist in slow motion move six inches, jolt against the side window in back, saw the radiating cracks from the point of impact. Looked at my fist, saw how quickly the flesh was puffing. Idiot woman. Silly, sentimental, pushover broad, trading a tumble amid her gift-shoppe decor for the sound of the ancient wornout words— love, fate, kismet, eternity, meaningfulness, affection.

Pull back, McGee. You are grown up, you hope. And you spread bad luck where'er you go. Somebody gave her the final game to play, and maybe it was quicker than it looks. And why don't you look at that shovel and that hole and start thinking logically, and keep yourself from looking at her, and breathe through your mouth when you are near her.

Old long-handled shovel, rusty and with a dull edge. It leaned against the same tree. I saw where the grave had been started too close to the tree, and there had been too many roots. So the shoveler had moved over to the side and had dug out an area five feet long and a yard wide, and about two and a half feet deep at one end and eighteen inches at the other. Not a good shoveler. The dirt removed had not been piled neatly and handily, but had been thrown too far. Hasty, frantic shoveling. Wear yourself out too quickly. Perhaps trying to finish before having to be someplace, or trying to finish in the last of the daylight. Then, perhaps, reconsideration. What's the big rush? She's not going anywhere and nobody is coming here. Don't move the car yet. Come back and tuck her down into the loam and stomp it flat and spread the needles. Then the risk of moving the car is less.

Whatever you remembered, Betsy Kapp, whatever you tried to check out, it was the wrong thing. And there was no director to step in and stop the drama. Did you come here, or did you go to someone who brought you here?

"What a crazy day," she had said. "What a weird kind of a day."

I studied the moist bottom of the unfinished grave. A lot of footprints in the deeper end. Size ten probably. Broad. Maybe a D. Small crosswise corrugations, like on the composition soles of work shoes, but worn away in the center, under the ball of the foot. A triangular nick out of the heel of the right shoe, on the outside toward the back, half an inch long.

I walked back to the shack area, back to my car. I fixed the front door precisely as it had been. I reviewed everything I had done. The only evidence that someone had been here was the star cracks in the side window of the VW, and I could not undo that. It might not be noticed or, if noticed, someone might think they had not happened to see it earlier. It went with the scalloped edges of the fenders, the dinged bumpers.

Run breathless to the Man and say, "Sher'f, my God, I found her and she's stone dead, plain and pure murdered to death"?

And get patted on the head and reminded I am a civilian, and be told that I would probably find out in due course what happened.

I was going to stop playing it their way. They had this big poker table working, and they had let me take the empty chair, provided I played my cards face up on the table and played by their rules. If I was naughty, they would deal me out of the next hand.

No more earnest efforts to please. No more defensive play. No more letting the house man deal. As of now, it was intensely personal, time to kick over the table, scatter the chips, break out my own deck, deal my own game—without explaining the rules.

The handle they use on you is your wistful need to pick up your life again right where it was interrupted, to be allowed to go in peace. When you decide that you do not give a damn about your own continuity, then you can even win a hand, and sometimes you can break the house.

I went roaring out of there, and on the way south on Cattleman's Road I found myself bumping the heel of my sore hand against the rim of the wheel, and humming a tuneless hymn of anticipation.

"Sorry to keep calling you up like this, Sheriff, but I tried Betsy's phone again just now and didn't get an answer. Have you found out anything?"

"Nothing yet. But we put out an all points hold on the car."

"I was thinking about her cat. Okay if I go over there and feed it and let it out in that fenced yard awhile?"

"You can get in?"

"Sure. I've still got that key I told you about."

"No objection, Mr. McGee. I heard you were in the courthouse looking up some property. What was that all about?"

"It was just a wild idea that didn't work out."

"It might be better if you just have some patience. Our investigations are proceeding."

"It must be quite a work load, Sheriff."

"How so?"

"Murder of Frank Baither. Disappearance of Lew Arnstead. Disappearance of Betsy Kapp. I'd heard this was a quiet country."

"It has been, and it will be again. Incidentally, I questioned my chief deputy about the incident with Mrs. Kapp. His version differs in certain particulars, but there was enough substance for me to give him an additional warning. I wouldn't want to lose him. He is a very valuable man, and the department is shorthanded."

"I think I better stay away from Billy."

"Until he has a chance to calm down. Yes."

"Well, thanks, Sheriff. I'll be in touch."

Had Raoul been a little kid, he would have been standing crosslegged and moaning. When I opened the door he went at a humpbacked lope to a grassy corner, squatted and with a dreamy distant stare, emptied the inflated feline bladder. He came strolling back into the kitchen, stared into his empty dish and said, "Raoul?" I opened the cupboards until I found his canned glop, whined one open on the electric machine, tapped it into his dish. He ate a few hungry gobbles, then looked up and walked out of the kitchen. I followed him into the living room and into the bedroom. He looked in the bathroom and turned around and came out again, saying, "Raoul?"

"Not here, furry friend. And she won't be."

He sat down and began to wash. When in doubt, wash. I opened the lower left drawer of the dressing table and took the weapon out. Still loaded. Untouched. In Florida you can have one in the house, or in your car, but not on the person. I thought it would be nice to have it in the Buick. I poked around until I found a small, brightly-colored, rubberized beach bag with a draw string. I dumped a dozen extra rounds into the bag and put the revolver in carefully, making certain that I knew its exact position in the opaque bag. I placed the bag on the passenger seat, toward my side, making it look entirely casual, yet so placed that my hand would fall on the grip naturally and without strain or obvious effort.

Before I locked up, I asked the cat what the hell I was going to do with him. He seemed to have an amber-eyed confidence that I was going to make every effort to maintain him in the comfort to which he had become accustomed . . . and to let him out oftener.

I remembered the Shell Ridge Road turnoff from the long night walk I had taken with Meyer. It was not far from the south line of the County, slanting off to the right, southwest.

Rural mailboxes. Small frame houses on fill, with the wet marsh behind them, some cypress and live oak hammocks. All of them were on the right side of the road. The left side was fenced wetlands, posted at the proper legal intervals, the wire and posts new. Hounds and banty chickens and little kids and swamp buggies and campers. White dust behind me off the crushed white shell of the limestone road.

Read the signs on the boxes. Stane. Murrity. Floyd, Garrison. Perris.

Perris was a one-story block house painted a pale, water-stained green, with a roof of white asbestos shingles. There was a gnarled and handsome oak in the front yard. There had been white board fencing, but it was rotting away. There had been river gravel in the drive, but most of it had rain-washed away. Some dead trucks and cars sat out to the side of the house, hip deep in the raw green grasses of spring. There were parts of other dead vehicles strewn around. There was a big frame building behind the house, with both overhead doors up, so that I could see into it as I turned into the drive, see a litter of workbenches and hoists and tools. A dainty little baby blue Opel with a savage little snout was parked under the spreading shade of the live oak out in front, its slanting windshield spattered with the grease of the exploding bugs of high-speed travel. When I parked beside the slab porch and turned the engine off, I could hear the muttering hum of a big air-conditioning compressor at the side of the house, and a tinny resonance of the sheet metal housing.

It was three-fifteen when I rang the doorbell. I waited and as I started to ring it again, Lilo Perris pulled it open and looked out through the screen. She wore what I think is called a jump dress, a kind of mini-dress which is shorts rather than a skirt at the bottom. It was a vivid orange, deepening her tan, whitening teeth, bringing out the healthy blue-whites of her eyes. There was a little flicker in those eyes as she looked at me, then glanced beyond me and saw the white convertible out there. No alarm, no surprise. Just a little click of recognition, identification.

At first she was just a girl with a blunt little face, twenty-two or -three. Brawny little chunk of a girl. Then came the extraordinary impact of a total, driving sexuality. I could remember only two other women who had exuded that degree of psychic musk at close range —one was a successful film actress who could not act and had no need to, the other a woman who, before her thirtieth year had married and divorced three fortunes, cutting herself an ample slice of each. It was arrogance and availability. It was posture and look that said, "Here it is, baby, if you're man enough, and I don't think you are, because nobody has been man enough yet." But not that kind of presentation alone. Two other things with it. A total health, the kind of health you see in show dogs and race horses. Glossy pelt, glistening eyes, blood-pink membranes, with pulse and respiration infinitely slow with the body at rest, preparing it for explosive demands. In addition, a perfection of detail, the natural eyelashes like little curved and clipped bits of enameled black wire. No dentist would have defied reality by making teeth that perfect.

"If you were selling something, man, nobody wants to buy if you get the house heated up." Deeper voice than expected, but without huskiness. A clear, flexible contralto.

"So ask me in, Lilo."

She came out and yanked the door shut and let the screen slap shut. She went down the single porch step and across the front yard, certain I would follow her. She picked up a sandspur on the tough sole of her bare right foot, and hardly breaking stride, licked her fingertips, brought the knee high and plucked it off. I saw the velvety bunch and flex of muscles in her brown back as she did so. The jump dress had a deep V back.

In the oak shade she turned and braced an orange haunch against the front fender-curve of the Opel and said, "I'm kind of a car freak. I like to fly this thing, but there's a shimmy up front over eighty and that bastard Henry can't find it. I told him he finds it or I strap him to the goddam hood and wind it up and let him see for himself."

And that was the last ingredient, a flavor of total and dangerous unpredictability. One could never feel at ease with her unless she had been welded into a steel collar, and there was a short length of chain fastened to a heavy eyebolt in a strong wall. And even then you'd take care to see that there was nothing within her reach that she could use to hit with or slice with, or throw. It was the same feeling as the time the pretty lady came aboard *The Busted Flush* with her ocelot, unsnapped his chain, and told him to stay on the yellow couch. He did, and watched every move I made, with pale-green eyes that never blinked, with an occasional ripple of muscles in back and flank. He seemed to smile at me, as if telling me that we both knew he could rip my throat open before I could say "Pretty kitty." It made us very aware of each other in a feral way. If she wanted to strap Henry to the hood of the Opel, she would do so. And if she wanted to wind it way up and then bang the brakes to see how far ahead of her down the highway she could propel Henry, she would do that, too.

I could not use her unless I could appraise her well enough to find strengths and weaknesses. She was so unlike what I had expected, I had to discard all plans, including the wild one of getting her out somewhere where I could thump her unconscious and let her wake up wired to a tree facing the horror of Betsy Kapp. One cannot make any impression on an ocelot by showing it a dead ocelot.

"Nice little car," I said.

"The name is McSomething. Somebody told me."

"McGee."

"McGee, what you are doing is boring me. Can you think of anything to build this up a little? Maybe you get your kick out of memorizing me or something."

"It's like this, Lilo. Hyzer said stay around. So I was killing time until he said leave. But maybe there are some things lying around that could be interesting."

"Depends on what freaks you, Mac."

"The lush life, and so it is always a question of financing it, isn't it?"

"You want to cut yourself in on how I've got it made, living here on my big estate, with all the swimming pools and the billiard room and all that?"

"Maybe it's just that you have talents you're not getting the maximum return from. You made one hell of an impression on Doris Severiss."

A sharp look of renewed interest. A merry, hearty, crinkly laugh. "Now how *about* you!"

"You could go around drifting and dreaming, girl, and never get loose from this big estate of yours. Lew Arnstead was making a dollar."

"Maybe your idea of a dollar, not mine, Mac. Lew had a nickel-dime way of thinking. He had some ass on call, and he shook some people down here and there, but it was too big a risk for what he was taking out of it. I told him. I told him forty times, honest. I told him he oughta contact somebody in the big time and wholesale those pigs of his for cash and have somebody come and get them before he got in a mess and Hyzer threw him out."

"And you'd know all about that?"

"A few years back, Mac, I used to go on trips with a friend. You keep your ears open, you learn how things are."

Not at all a dull-minded girl. A shrewdness about her that was impressive.

"But didn't you take on some risk when you helped him straighten out Mrs. Severiss?"

She made a face. "I was stupid. I get bored and I do stupid things and get in trouble. I shouldna. He was telling me his problems and I said let me handle it, and he said go ahead. Just that once with her and once with his schoolteacher, what's her name. Geraldine Kimmey. She got herself in a bind by groping some little kid, and then after Lew dated her up three or four times, she wanted to bluff her way off the list, so I had her sing me a lot of soprano where nobody could hear the high notes." A sudden, merry, ingratiating smile. "A shrink could have a picnic checking me out. When I get all edgy and uptight and mean-acting, making somebody scream and sweat works just like a charm. The better they yell, the more warm and friendly I feel toward them. I like to fell in love with Geraldine. It's like I was helping them get past something, or over something. I wonder sometimes if it's got anything to do with being so strong.

"You look healthy enough."

"It's more than that. I'm some kind of freak. Wanta see?"

"Sure."

She looked into the blue car and reached in and took out a beach towel and shook the sand out of it. She went to the front bumper and used the towel to avoid the bumper edge cutting into her hands. She braced herself, back to the bumper, torso erect, knees flexed, shifted her grip and her stance, then took a deep breath, let it out then snatched up the front end of the car, stood with her knees locked, holding it. Under the thin layer of fat beneath the skin, a female attribute, the sculptured muscles bulged in thighs, calves, shoulders, and arms. Thick cords bulged in her throat as her face slowly darkened. She turned her head slowly and smiled at me a strangely provocative and knowing smile. Then she lowered it quickly. She wiped the sudden sweat from her arms, throat, and face. I had felt an unexpectedly savage surge of absolutely simple and immediate sexual desire for her, a brute impulse to fell her where she stood and mount her. And she knew it, and had deliberately caused it. There is a perverse streak in all of us, an urgency to experience the unusual. She was totally feminine, and sometime, somewhere, she had discovered that a demonstration of the unusual power of her body would provoke the male. Such physical strength is a rarity, a kind of genetic aberration which could be a throwback to prehistory, to a primitive construction of muscle fiber quite dissimilar to our own. It is more common in men than in women, is quite often coupled with a low order of intelligence which leads to the sideshow career of bending horseshoes, driving spikes barehanded, and folding coins with thumb and forefinger.

She tossed the towel into the car and said, "I can put most men down arm wrassling. Not very girly-girl, huh?"

"You seem to be all girl, Lilo. I had the idea you were probably on Lew's list."

"Peddling it? Hell, no. I'm not on anybody's list. Lew was on my list, you could say. No matter what anybody says, it's a short list, Mac. With Lew it was sometimes, when he had hung around so long looking like a hound dog it got on my nerves, or when there was something I thought he knew that he wasn't planning to tell me. He always told me."

"Past tense."

"Dead, isn't he?"

"What makes you think so?"

"Because he isn't hanging around me, Mac. And that's the only thing that would keep him away. And because he was going bad fast. He was popping those pills like candy and they were scrambling his brains. He was seeing things, hearing voices, forgetting what he did last, and no idea of what he'd do next. So I guess somebody had to kill him before he spoiled somebody else's fun and games. Somebody tucked him into a swamp. What kind of games are you trying to play with me, Mac?"

"I've been interested in you since last Thursday night when I came within an inch and a half of killing you."

"Me? What the hell are you talking about?"

"The only reason I can come up with why you ran in front of my car was because there was somebody out there in the night you wanted to have see you. But you cut it too close."

Three seconds of silence, then the jolly grin again, and a wink. "I sure did, friend. What happened, my foot slipped coming up that bank, but I thought I could still make it. Then all those headlights were close enough to touch. I felt the breeze from that fender on my bare tail. I didn't mean to put you in the canal though. Sorry. Sure, I wanted somebody to see me. I wanted somebody to see that it was a girl not a man, because they were after Frank Baither."

"Who?"

"Somebody who wanted to kill him and did. Frank was the first and the only real man I ever did know. Some kid stuff before I met him, but after that nobody touched me but Frank, until they jailed him and then sent him up north. He's the one I went on trips with. We were gone four months when I was sixteen one time, and he made thirty thousand dollars and we spent twenty of it."

"What did he knock over?"

"He and two other guys took a casino in Biloxi for ninety on a three-way split. No, it was a hundred, because I remember he had to give ten to the cop who set it up for Frank because the casino was shorting the cop on the insurance money they were paying. Then we went out to California because there was a payroll thing Frank wanted to look at. He decided he didn't like it, and later some other people tried it and one got killed and the other two ended up in Q."

"Who came to kill Frank last Thursday?"

"Two men who'd been in on something Frank never told me about. He said their names were Hutchason and Orville. He said they thought he'd given them a short count on a split. The way it happened, I was practically living there from the time he got back, because he had a lot to catch up on. He heard something outside and woke me up and got his gun and told me to go on home, sneak as far as the road and go like hell. One of them followed me, or both of them. I thought they would think it was Frank and shoot me. So I ran across in front of your car so they'd see me. I went on home. It's only about three and a half miles from here, about. I went back early in the morning and saw the county cars and found out they'd killed him. I just . . . just didn't think anybody could ever kill Frank. You know, I didn't think you'd have a good enough look at me for long enough to remember me."

"If the sheriff knew there'd been a girl there with Baither, wouldn't he know it had been you?"

"He might think on it, but Mister Norm doesn't fuss with me much."

A back country silence, standing in shade. She stood against the big trunk of the tree, one knee flexed, bare foot against the rough gray bark. She idly scratched the rounded top of her brown thigh, and I could hear in the silence the whisper of her nails against the skin. The animal hunger she had awakened with that odd display of strength had not died away. She caught and held my eye and read it, and built it back again with but a slight arching of her back, softening of her mouth.

"Could be," she whispered. "It just could be."

"Think so?"

"Like part of whatever game we're playing. Saying one thing, holding other things back. We can go someplace, try us out. You'd be thinking I'd say more. I'd be thinking you might say more about what you know, or think you know. That would come after the edge was off. I'm not like this often, Mr. Mac. Could be more than you can take on?"

"I manage to totter around."

She said, "I got to go in a minute, see if that damn Nulia has got the old lady cleaned up right this time. Last time she got through the room still stank, and I had to whop her old black ass and make her do it over right."

She grinned, shoved herself away from the tree, and thumped me on the biceps with a small hard brown fist, a considerable blow, and ran to the house, fleet as a young boy.

seventeen

She was in the house over ten minutes. She came out and beckoned to me and headed toward my car. By the time I got to it she had jacked the driver's seat forward and turned the key on. I got in the passenger seat and put the rubber beach bag on the floor.

"Easier than giving directions," she said. "I don't want to drive mine until Henry gets that shimmy out of it. Okay with you?"

"Sure."

"Pretty bag belong to a nice lady?" She backed out onto the unpaved road, and headed southwest.

"Friendly lady name of Jeanie Dahl."

"Mmmm. That's where you found out about me and Dori Severiss."

"And Lew's sideline."

She was driving more conservatively than I had expected. "Thought you were getting the scoop from ol' Betsy Kapp, knowing you wasted no time moving in on those giant titties. Never knew just how much Lew talked to her. Never could figure out how they got together in the first place. He had a funny soft spot for that fool woman. I told him once he ought to sign her onto his little team. Even offered to go convince her, but he told me if I ever went near her, he'd club my head right down between my knees, and I think he meant it."

I saw the sign indicating we were leaving Cypress County. "Hyzer asked me to stay in his jurisdiction."

"Right now, mister, does that mean a hell of a lot to you?"

"I wouldn't say that it does."

"We aren't going to be out of it long, honey. Right turn coming up, before we come out onto the Trail, and it swings back into Cypress County. Car rides nice."

"Seems to. Where are we going?"

"A place a friend of mine lent me when he went in the Navy. It's real private."

And it was. It was a fairly new aluminum house trailer of average size, set on a cement-block foundation on a small cypress hammock in marshy grassland. Limestone fill had been trucked in to make a small causeway between an old logging road and the hammock. A flock of white egrets went dipping and winging away through the cypress and hanging gray moss when she parked by the trailer.

She squatted and reached up and behind a place where a block had been left out for ventilation purposes, and pulled out the keys. She went over and unlocked a small cement-block pumphouse and tripped a switch that started a husky gasoline generator.

"Now we've got air conditioning and, in a little while, ice cubes, Mac, honey."

"Can I object to Mac?"

"You can ask for anything your evil heart desires, man."

"Travis or Trav or McGee."

"So I settle for McGee."

"You do that."

She unlocked the trailer and stepped up into it. "Hey, let's open this thing up until the air conditioning starts doing something."

We opened the windows. It was tidy inside. It had the compact flavor of a good cabin cruiser, with ample stowage. She checked to make certain there was water in the ice-cube trays. She turned on a little red radio and prowled the dial until she found some heavy rock and turned it up far enough to drown out the sound of the generator and the whine of the refrigerator and the busy whackety-thud of the compressor on the air conditioner.

She reached around herself and undid the few inches of zipper that reached from the V back to the base of her spine, and said, "Can you think of anything special we're waiting on, McGee?" She shrugged it forward off her shoulders, lowered it and stepped out of it and flipped it aside. I noted with a remote objectivity that her breasts were a slight quarter-tone lighter than the rest of her, and that the bikini band around her hips was as white as in the photograph.

She was as totally at home in her naked hide as any animal. She moved without either coyness or boldness, walked over to the bunk bed, knee-walked toward the wall, rolled over onto her back. "As any jackass can plainly see, I am all the way ready. Whyn't you close the other windows, but let's leave this here one open the way it is? You're sure in some terrible rush, huh? Gun shy, McGee?"

I closed the windows with all deliberate speed. It had to be a setup. Though Meyer might try to argue the point, young girls do not make a habit of suddenly propositioning me, driving me off to a hideaway, peeling off their clothes, rolling onto their backs, and breathing hard.

But just how was I being set up? Strong as she was, I couldn't see her doing much bare-handed damage to me. If there was a weapon, where was it? Down behind the mattress? There were no cupboards she could reach. As I unbuttoned my shirt, I noticed that the two little hooks which held the aluminum screen in the window were undone.

Set up. Phone call from the house. Lots of noise. She had opened that window, so she had unhooked the screen. She had moved over to the far side of the bunk bed, under the window. We were expecting a visitor. Maybe he had arrived and was squatting under the window, awaiting the sounds of festivity. She was certainly powerful enough to hold me or anyone motionless long enough, and perfectly positioned.

She was obviously in a state of sexual excitement, her face slack, eyes blurring. She was rolling her hips slowly from side to side, and her breasts were swollen, nipples thrusting, belly muscles twitching and rippling.

"Come on," she said in a petulant smothered tone. "Come on!"

So I fumbled with buttons long enough for her to roll up and crawl toward me, reaching to help, and when she was positioned correctly I thought of the way Betsy's face looked, and I hit Lilo Perris as hard as I have ever hit anyone, and as perfectly. I reached up as though getting my hands free of the shirt buttons, then I dropped my hand. It traveled about eight inches before it hit her on the left side of the chin, and kept going another foot and a half after it knocked her mouth open. Sensing a reluctance to hit a female, I had told myself to hit through the target and beyond, not hit at it.

When you hit at something, you pull it. When you hit someone in the nose, you try to smash an imaginary nose on a person standing directly behind him. That gets the back into it.

She dropped immediately and bonelessly, face down, head hanging over the side of the bed, one arm dangling, legs splayed in frog posture. I put my fingertips against the pulse in her throat and it was fast but strong.

Now, honey, we get ready for visitors. Try the cupboards. Nothing. Nothing. Hmm, an extension cord. Box of Kleenex. Nothing in the next one. There now! Nice fat roll of black plastic electrician's tape.

Roll you over in the clover. Feel the jaw, shift it about a little. No looseness. No gritty sound of bone edges. Didn't even chip a pretty tooth. Beginning to puff and darken right there on the button, though. Thumb the mouth full of tissue, and draw a black X with tape across it. Bring your arms in front of you, and hold your elbows so they touch, and wind the tape around and around. A nice binding just above the elbow, another around the forearms, a third around the wrists, Now clasp the loose hands together and . . . around and around like this. An awkward attitude of prayer, dear girl. Up with the knees, close together. One binding just above the knees, one just below, and one around the ankles. Now, my muscular darling, we roll you up into a ball, into fetal position, and we put the extension cord around your legs under your knees, thread it up between your upper arms and breasts, and we tie it right here, at the nape of your neck, just firmly enough. Comfy? Special treatment for a very strong girl.

Radio blasting away. Sound protection works both ways. Stay down, so you won't be seen by anybody looking in the windows, McGee. Careful with the door. Bit by bit. Nothing. Step down. Strategic window on the other side. Ease around the end. Nothing. Now up to the last corner, lie flat, stick head around the corner made of block.

And by God, what do you know, there is broad, brown Henry Perris, master mechanic, wife-stealer, and Sunday pronger of the stepdaughter, standing very tense, squatting below the window next to a handy pile of block. What has good old Henry got in his hand? Why, he has what looks like a short section of hoe handle with a short sharp piece of metal sticking out of the end of it. Head bent in attitude of listening. Fingertips against the aluminum love nest. What are you waiting for, Henry? A signal? Why, of course, how logical. In extremis, the lady yells to the unwary chap in the saddle, "Now! Now!" And good old Henry stands on the blocks and lifts the screen out and leans in the window and sticks that sharp piece of metal right into the back of lover boy's head, right where the base of the skull fastens onto the neck, and for a lady who gets her jollies out of hurting people, if her timing is right, that must, indeed, be a memorable thrill. Same thrill as the lady spider devouring the mate while they are still coupled.

One might, in fact, suspect that Hutchason and Orville both met this same fate in this same place at these same hands, because there was no time to set up anything so complex in the time she had on the phone.

I eased back and stood up. Insight is perhaps what pops to the surface of the mind after subterranean processes of logic have taken place. If Perris and Lilo were two of the team of five who took the money truck, then Frank Baither went to Raiford knowing they would stay right in the area, waiting for the division after he got out. And if Hutch or Orville showed up, they could not make Henry or Lilo tell them something they did not know. And it would be the assigned chore of Henry and Lilo to quietly take them out of the scene. Baither would certainly know that Lilo was, by inclination, a competent executioner. Unless Frank were out of reach, she could have no chance to get them off guard, to get close enough. And then, of course, the lie to Frank when he came back. They never showed up. Maybe something happened to them. They never showed up, Frank.

Then the dead men had been used to decoy Frank Baither. To send him clattering around in the night in the old pickup, so that they were in position for him when he came back.

Out of the delusion of their own irresistible male charm, Hutch and Orville, one at a time, had clambered so eagerly onto the deathbed, coupled with the strong brown spider. I realized that had I not found Betsy's letter to Lew, had I not seen the sweat and pallor on Dori Severiss's face when she told me of Lilo, I could have been less on guard. I could have bought her rationalization about it. "You'd be thinking I'd say more."

No problem to phone Henry at the station. And he could scoot west on the Trail, turn onto the far end of Shell Ridge Road, be there before we got there. She had driven slowly. He could drive beyond the little causeway to the hammock, tuck his car away, come back under the cover of the noise of generator and rock radio.

I had revealed too much to her. But maybe it did not have to be very much, if she was that twisted. "It's like I was helping them get past something or over something." Helping them get over the problem of living, of breathing. And Dori saying, ". . . smiling at me and giggling and calling me love names and saying how much fun it would be to really kill me."

Thoughts roaring through the mind like a train racketing through a tunnel, while another part of my mind flipped through the possible ways of taking Henry Perris. I did not know how well he would move. I knew he could be as powerful as he looked. And I knew he had a useful weapon in his hand.

Estimate the triangle. Henry was fifteen feet from me. The white convertible was parked twenty feet in back of Henry, and perhaps thirty feet from me. Burst out in a full run and I could almost be at the car before he could react. She had turned it around and parked it heading out. Driver door was on this side. Beach bag on the floor on the far side.

So run around the hood, yank door open, pick up bag, find shape of gun through the fabric, and come up with it with a very good chance of taking one step to the side and firing across the hood through the fabric. If he was too close, there'd be no time for shoulder or thigh. If he was far enough away, one into the ground at his feet might do it.

One and a two and a three and go, McGee. Don't lose your stride by looking at him. Not until you round the hood. Now look. And he is down off the blocks, and he is yanking the bright rubberized beach bag open in fumbling haste, and you should think a little better, McGee. Your thinking is spotty. You work one thing out and get overcome with your goddam brilliance, and forget that she parked the car in a blind spot, where it could not be seen from any window of the trailer, and so he had to use that angle as his approach, and it would be natural to check the car, heft the bag, finger the distinctive shape, bring it along.

All the shots are going to do out here is startle the egrets and puzzle the brown girl, if she is awake yet. And unless you get smart very fast, they are going to make some very final and very ugly holes in a fellow you have often felt kindly toward over the years.

Fact: It is not accurate at any long range. Take a quick look into the car. Fact: The keys are gone. Fact: He has the gun out of the bag. Fact: It is too damned long a run for cover, if you want to get into that cypress. Probability: If you stay by the car, he will angle out to the front or rear, stay fifteen feet from it, and pot you in perfect safety.

I dropped and looked under the car. Coming at the predicted angle toward the rear end of the car. Not running. Better if he was running. Plodding along. Patience and good nerves.

Find place with best clearance under the thing. Okay. Onto the back. Pull yourself along under it like a cat playing under a sofa. Out the other side, roll up onto the feet and into full speed for the first few steps, then sacrifice speed for that crouching zigzag, like long ago, when they'd put the old tires on the practice field. Absolutely ice-cold target area in the middle of the spine. Corner of the trailer apparently receding into the distance. Not coming close very fast. Bam. No impact. That thing would hit you like a small sledge. Bam. And you are around the corner, skittering, skidding, the comedy runner, sliding to a bulge-eyed frantic stop, yanking the door open, plunging into the trailer, falling to hands and knees, spinning, yanking the door shut, taking the wheezing breaths, feeling the tremble in the knees.

The red radio is hollering about "a little help from my friends." Sidle to a window and try to spot him. Sudden silence. Music chopped off. Dying wheeze of the air conditioning, fading whir of fan. Methodical fellow. Taking his time and thinking it out. Avoiding mistakes.

I crept to the galley area, opened logical drawers, found a flimsy carving knife, a dull paring knife, four rust-flecked oyster knives, steel blade and handle, rounded tip. Tried one. It balanced precisely at the juncture of handle and blade. Each was forged out of a single piece of mediocre steel. One in the right hand, handle outward, blade flat against the underside of the thumb and the heel of the thumb. Provided a little amusement that time I spent holed up with Miguel in the Sierras. He had the single throwing knife. Tree target. Basic lessons. Always the same motion, a long forearm snap. Always the same force. Let it slide away from the thumb, naturally. Useful only at reasonably exact distances. Make a half turn and chunks home at fifteen feet. Hold the handle end and get a full turn at thirty feet. Hold the blade and get a turn and a half at forty-five. Got arm-weary throwing it and foot-weary trudging up to yank it out of the tree and going back to the mark. I had the other three oyster knives by the handle in my left hand. Miguel said a man who tries for the target at thirty feet, when it is an important target, is frivolous. Fifteen feet is so much more certain. At the slow rate of spin, it will be blade first from twelve to eighteen feet, enough to slash at the outer limits of the range. At ten feet or twenty it will strike flat. Do not try to adjust. Throw always for the right-angle impact at fifteen feet.

A rattle of small stones under the nearby footstep, beyond the aluminum. "McGee?" Hoarse voice. No urgency. Calm and reasonable. "Want to do some dickerin', McGee?"

I backed away from the side of the window, then leaned a little forward, cupped my hand to confuse the point of origin of my voice. "What are you selling, Henry?"

He was selling gunshot wounds. Not bam this time. More like braing. Hole at chest height a foot in from the window edge and an exit hole high on the far side. I thudded both feet on the carpeted flooring and moaned and backed away.

"No good, you tricky bastard. I heard it go whining off, tumbling. Couldn't have touched you. What did you do to her?"

Lilo answered. She squalled behind the packed wad of tissue. A sound of pure animal anger, muffled, like a cat in the bottom of a laundry hamper.

"Tied and gagged, eh?" Henry said. "That would take some doing. That I would like to see. I really would. Getting warm enough for you in there?"

No point in answering him.

"I've figured out something, McGee. I think what I'll do is go around and turn off the bottle gas for the stove at the tank and cut the tubing and shove the end back into the hole and turn the gas on again. Good idea?"

Yes, it was a splendid idea. Simple and effective. After a while he could figure some way of igniting it, if I didn't come choking and stumbling out. It was such a good idea, that it did not seem logical that he would stand around and chat about it. He would go do it. So there was a factor that kept him from doing it. And that was most probably the serious effect it would have on the health of Miss Perris.

I moved back to the galley, put the knives down, and in one surge slid the small refrigerator out into the middle of the work space and crouched behind it.

"Henry, at the very first whiff of propane, I am going to take one of these dull kitchen knives and saw that throat open on your little pal. You had better believe it."

"Now why should that make any difference to me?"

"I wouldn't know. The abiding love of a stepfather for a high-spirited girl, maybe. It's the only thing you left open that I could try, Henry."

"Go ahead and cut away." Just a little too much indifference.

"Henry, you could try to smoke me out. Or you could get a piece of rope or cable and fasten it low on one side of this thing, throw it across the roof, hook it to the Buick, and roll this thing over. Let's see now. You've got a car here. You could swing the Buick around and get a good start and just run the hell into this hunk of aluminum. But if I smell smoke, Henry. Or feel movement. Or hear the Buick. Or hear anything else I can't understand, I am going to start sawing."

In the long silence Lillian made muted bleating noises, and even tethered as she was, managed to snap and flex enough muscles to bounce herself around on the bunk bed.

"She tied up good? Can't get loose?"

"Guaranteed," I said. I moved as quietly as I could, over to the bunk bed and sat close to her, and put the oyster knives on a shelf above the foot of the bed, blades outward. "Matter of fact, Henry, I'm sitting so close to her that if you try any more trick shooting, you can just as easily get her as me."

I looked down at her. She was on her left side in her curled position, her feet toward me. She looked at me with a ferocity that was an almost physical impact. Then her muscles bulged and her eyes closed as she strained to stretch or break the tough tape. I could hear little poppings and cracklings of joints and sinews. Then she let her breath out and relaxed, snuffling hard. I reached and gave her a friendly caress along the flank, a little pat on the brown haunch. She snapped into the air like a shrimp on a dock, eyes maniacal.

"We can work this out, McGee," he called.

"Now just how do we do that, Henry?"

"The thing you want to do most is stay alive."

"I guess I'd give that the number one priority."

"I could trade some time, maybe. I don't know how much time I'd need with her, or how much time I'd need after I get through with her. If I back off, far enough, and get the car keys to you, you could get away from here. But there'd be the problem of you going straight to a phone and messing me up."

"And you can't take my word."

"I wouldn't think so."

"And I can't take yours, Henry. Stalemate."

"What?"

"It's a chess term. Neither player has any way to win."

"Oh. By God, I sure messed up when I tried the idea of using that envelope. I guess I was edgey. I thought you were some dumb-dumb who'd look good to Mister Norm. Lilo told me it was a bad idea, but I told her to do it anyway."

"You left the envelope in the phone book in the booth when you went to deliver the Olds, eh? Then she picked it up and took it to Baither's place."

"I guess you just fixed it so there's no way I can leave you go now, McGee. Sure. Lew let her into Frank's house to see where it happened. Gave her a chance to drop the envelope when Lew wasn't looking. All she had to do was promise Lew a quick piece. Lew wasn't so hooked on it, he'd have chopped up his old mother and sold her for cat food for a chance to get into Lilo's pants. She kept that boy on short rations."

Lilo was trying to tell me something with her eyes. Pleading. Working her mouth around. I leaned and got an edge of the tape with my thumbnail and ripped the X off her mouth. She tongued the spitty mass of Kleenex out and swallowed several times.

She said in a low voice, "I know where a lot of money is. He wants to make me tell him. If you kill him, I'll tell you. We can take it all and go away."

"Killing is something I charge high for."

"Your end would be four hundred and fifty thousand. Right down the middle. No tricks. I wanted to leave him out because he's stupid. You're not. I need somebody like you to help me with it."

"No tricks."

She smiled her happy smile, her pretty and disarming urchin grin. "No tricks, honey. Ever."

"So tell me right now where it is. You know. Give me a motivation."

"Afterward. I promise. Get this tape off, huh?"

Henry shouted from a new position outside the trailer, "Having a little talk, are you? She trying to sell you something, McGee?"

"She's trying to sell me you, Henry."

I saw her face contort, and I put my finger to my lips before she could join the conversation. I reached and heeled her jaw shut and put the old X of tape back on, tore some more strips and sealed her off, and once again she tried the bonds, in a convulsion so violent it seemed possible she might break bones in the effort.

"You know what she is?" Henry called.

"I've got a pretty good idea."

"What she was doing to Frank kept making me sick to my stomach, McGee. I was over at the window, gagging, when he finally told her, his voice so weak I couldn't hear it. She had that ice pick into his heart before I could take half a step. She wanted to make sure he wouldn't say it twice. You want to trust her?"

"I don't want to trust either one of you."

Again he had changed his position. He was moving quietly. "It's that word you said before. Stalemate?"

He was back near the pile of block under the window above the bunk bed. I could guess the chance he was thinking of taking. Crouch on the block then come erect and fire through the screen. The window was three feet square, and the bottom sill was about twenty inches above the level of the bed. I debated the idea of backing off and then taking a dive out the window. The unhooked screen would swing out. But I would have to hit it hard enough to carry all the way through, to get my legs high enough to clear the sill. I would overshoot him and land sprawling and rolling away from him, giving him the perfect shot, because he would have time to recover from surprise before I could reverse direction and get back to him. If I waited until his silhouette popped up in the window, I'd give him a wing shot.

The last thing he would expect would be for me to come back outside where he had the considerable edge. I slipped my shoes off and leaned closer to the window. "Henry, if you are thinking of taking a pot shot through the window, I've got her right in front of me. Think it over."

I gathered my four oyster knives and went toward the door as quickly and as quietly as I could. He would think it over for a few seconds, and realize his best move would be to suddenly yank the screen off and stand up and cover me and the girl at close range. He could come in over the sill and have it all his own way, because he could get so close I couldn't use her for cover. She was too small.

Out the door and down, and quickly around the front of the thing. Heard the tiny clatter of the falling screen as I rounded the last corner. Henry leaning in the window, fifteen feet away. Miguel's voice from long ago, speaking inside my head. "The elbow, *amigo*, should point toward the target, and it should not move until after the release. At the release the arm is straight, then it moves down so the hand ends up to the rear of the right calf of the leg. Throw strong, but never hurry it. The left foot is ahead of the right, both knees bent. The knife is close to the right ear before the throw. The wrist, it is locked. It does not move. The aim is to the center of the body. If it is an armed man, finish the throw with a dive to the ground, and then roll to the right, if it is a right-handed man, because he must then swing the gun to fire across his body, which is more difficult, no?"

So, squinting in the dazzle of sunlight against bright aluminum, I threw strong, and plucked the second blade from my left hand and threw strong again, and dived forward and rolled hard to the right, found the third blade as I came up, heard the close-range shot, felt the sting of gravel against my thigh, knew as I released the third that I had hurried it too much and was off target. Nearly dropped the fourth, fumbling for it, snapped it back into position, and held it there as Henry in a crooked crouch showed me his white grin, fired directly down into the ground, and tumbled off the block, lifting his arm to break the fall. He rolled onto his back and over onto his face, an arm pinned under him. Both legs quivered and kicked and leaped about, like a dog asleep in a dream of running. Then he flattened against the packed earth in that unmistakable stillness, that death-look which changes the clothes into something stuffed with cold ground meat.

I had a sudden chill which chattered my teeth. I approached him. His arm was flexed, hand over his head. Right hand and gun were somewhere under him. The first one had to be the one socketed into the left armpit, hitting when he was still leaning in the window. Another lay on the ground by the blocks, unstained. A third was hanging by the tip from a long groove it had sliced in the aluminum side, under the window. There wasn't much blood on the coveralls near the protruding steel handle. It had to have done a mortal damage in there, in the arteries above the heart.

"So a knife is ugly, Travees? I know. And a gun is ugly and death is ugly. Sometimes there is only a knife to use. And the difference is the knowing how to do it. We are here for a time. So? Why not learn from one who knows, to pass the time?"

Thank you, Miguel. Thanks for the lessons. Without them both of us would be dead, instead of only you. Sleep well.

eighteen

I went back into the increasing temperature of the trailer. She had wormed herself around so she could watch the door, sweating so heavily in the heat she looked oiled. I could see the momentary astonishment in the lift of black brows. She had no reason to believe the shots had not gone into me.

And if I could walk in, the stepdaddy had to be dead. The upper half of her face changed, showing that she was trying to smile under the black tape. If I took it off, she would tell me that all is well, lover. We bury Henry in the marsh. Half the money is yours. We'll be a great team.

I sat on the corner of the bed and looked at her. Making someone dead is a game for the unimaginative, for someone who cannot ever really believe they, too, can die. The curse of empathy is to see yourself in every death, and to see the child hidden in the body of every corpse. The local box score was sick-making. Hutch, Orville, Baither, Lew Arnstead, Betsy Kapp, Henry Perris. Might as well add Linda Featherman. Meyer came close to being on the list.

I don't know what she read in my face, but it took the smile-try away. Her eyes turned watchful. Glossy black hair was sweat-matted, and droplets slid down her cheeks, her ribs and breasts and belly, darkening the faded blue spread.

I got up and opened the other windows so some breeze could

come through. Her eyes followed me. I stopped by the bed and said, "Somebody will come after you, Lillian."

Violent negative shake of the head. Grunting attempts at speech. She doubled further, grinding her mouth against her round knees, trying to wipe the tape off.

I took a last long look at her. "I wouldn't want to hear anything you could say. I wouldn't want the whole score, if you were part of the deal. Or double the score."

I put the screen back on and went inside and hooked it. I made sure the other screens were all hooked. I locked the trailer and put the keys in my pocket, sat on the low step outside and tied my shoes. I had to touch Henry's body to get the keys to the Buick.

After a quarter mile I rolled the windows up and turned the air on full, aiming the outlets at me. My shirt was unbuttoned, and the chill air dried my sweaty chest. I found my way out to Shell Ridge Road, and turned back on it, heading northeast.

When I came to the Perris place, I turned in and went to the door. An elderly woman, tall and stringy, opened the door and looked at me without expression. She was saffron-brown, the racial mix of Seminole and black in her face.

"Are you Nulia?"

"Yem."

"Miss Perris asked me to stop and tell you that she won't be back tonight, and neither will Mr. Perris."

"Fixing to go on home now, back to keer for my own. No way I can stay on. She *know* that."

I found one of Lennie Sibelius's fifty-dollar bills, damp with my exertions. I handed it to her and said, "Please stay on and look after Mrs. Perris, Nulia."

She looked at it and would not let herself be impressed. "Some bad thing going on, cap'n?"

"You could say that."

"I pray to the Lord ever living day of my lifetime for the devil to come-a-crawlin' up out of hell, huffin' fire and stompin' his clove hoofsies, and claim his own, and snatch her back down to the black pit and the eternal fire." She put the fifty in her apron pocket. "I'll stay take keer, but working for you, cap'n, not her, til you come tell me stop. Much obliged."

Twenty after five by the bank clock when I got to the center of town. Temperature: ninety-two degrees.

Parked beyond the patrol cars. Went inside. Business as usual.

One of the brisk ones behind the high counter said that the sheriff was busy. I said I wanted to see him right now. It did not sound like my own voice. He looked at me and read something in my face that made him go into a point like a good bird dog.

A few minutes later he took me to Hyzer's office and stood behind me. I said, "I want to tell you some things. You ought to have your tape rolling. I would like to have King Sturnevan here to listen to it."

"He's off duty."

"Can you call him in?"

Hyzer found a number on a list under the glass on his desk, dialed it, and in the silence I could hear the burr of the rings at the other end. He hung up after the eighth. "Will Billy Cable do?"

I thought it over. It had to be one or the other of them. It couldn't be both. I nodded. Hyzer told the desk man to tell communications to call Billy in.

I sat in a chair six feet from the desk and waited. Sheriff Norman Hyzer continued with his desk work, in faultless concentration. In seven minutes by the wall clock, Billy Cable knocked and came in. He looked at me with hard-faced antagonism.

"Can you have him sit over there beside the desk, so I can watch his face, Sheriff?"

"What kind of shit is this?" Billy said.

"Sit over here, Cable," Hyzer ordered. "The tape is on, McGee."

"Sheriff, did you ever hear how one of the planets, one way way out from the sun, was discovered? Nobody had ever seen it because not enough light hit it, and they didn't know it was there and didn't know where to look."

"You called me in off patrol to listen to—?"

"Keep your mouth shut, Billy."

"They measured the pattern of orbit of all the other planets, and they found out that the pattern wasn't quite right, that there had to be some gravitational attraction they hadn't found yet. So they worked up the math and figured out where to look, and found it. I know the patterns aren't right. I can't make them fit. So somebody else has to be in this. Somebody has exerted force and pressure to distort the patterns, Sheriff."

"What sort of things have impressed you as being . . . a divergence from the norm, Mr. McGee."

"You diverge a little, Sheriff. You have this great air of efficiency and high moral rectitude. People seem to believe that you know everything that goes on in your county. Yet you let one of your deputies run a call-girl operation right under your nose, using his badge to muscle them into the operation."

"Sher'f, do you want me to—"

"You are going to listen to this with your mouth shut, Cable, if I have to have you bound and gagged."

"Yes, sir."

Hyzer was looking at me attentively. I said, "You also took the risk of demoralizing your own troops, Sheriff, by letting Arnstead get away with acts which would have gotten another deputy tossed out. When you finally did bring charges against him and threw him out, it surprised him."

"Go on, please."

"And I cannot understand your appraisal of Lilo Perris. There are enough people in this county who know that she is a sick, vicious, twisted, dangerous, rotten animal so that somehow some of the information should have filtered back to you. You did a nice job of reconstructing the money-truck job as being Baither's project. You must have known the previous relationship between Baither and the Perris girl. She would be the logical one to have played the part of the young waitress in a blonde wig. But you either have a blind spot, or you want to sell others that blind spot by calling her just a healthy, high-spirited young lady. So that either puts you into the middle of the scene, Sheriff, or it means that somebody has a kind of leverage they can use on you which can prevent you from doing the kind of job you pretend to do."

"She may have foolishly placed herself in a position where—"

"Sheriff! Here is a letter I have been carrying around with me. I had it hidden in the car. Betsy Kapp wrote it a few months ago to Lew Arnstead. As a practicing student of human nature, I think you will agree that it has that perfect ring of truth. It illustrates one of those . . . positions she foolishly placed herself in." I leaned and flipped it onto the desk, saying, "I suppose you could bring in Roddy Barramore and get a confirmation."

He read it to himself, and it made the skull-shape show through the flesh and skin. His face seemed to shrink and dwindle. He cleared his throat and, in a flat voice, read it into the record. I could see that it cost him, but I could not understand why.

He said, "When Mrs. Kapp is located, I will want to get further confirmation from her that she wrote this letter."

"Mrs. Kapp was wired to a tree sometime Sunday evening. The wire was around her throat, and she is very very dead."

Hyzer picked his hat up and stood up. "You'll take us there right now."

"When I'm through. A little delay won't make a damned bit of difference to her."

After a long hesitation he sat down. "Where did you get this letter?"

"I found one of Lew's little hidey-holes." I reached into the front of my shirt and heard Billy's hand slap at his holster, and I quickly pulled out the packet of pictures. I tossed them onto the desk. "Arnstead's sample case. Arnstead's Rent-a-Broad. I know who some of them are. Lilo Perris, for example. Geraldine Kimmey. Linda Featherman."

Billy hitched his chair closer, leaning to peer at the photographs as Hyzer examined them.

"Jesus H. Christ!" Billy said.

I said, "Don't act as if you never knew he was in the business, Billy."

"Hell, I knew he had some hustlers working. But Miss Kimmey! And the Featherman girl? Hell, no!"

"Sheriff, Betsy Kapp's body is not far from the place where Lew Arnstead had his number-one storage place. Somebody tore the place up and found his barrel safe under the fire brick on the hearth and tore it open and had a bonfire. I think that's where he hid the items that gave him the most leverage over the women. Special pictures, written confessions, assignment lists, date, time, price, and place. So somebody very interested in removing all evidence regarding some specific girl could have gone there and burned the records on all of them, and taken the money he kept there. They could have known or suspected Lew was dead, and wanted to keep somebody else from picking up where he left off. Or they could have thought he was still living, and wanted to put him out of business, or get one specific girl off the hook. Or maybe they didn't want anybody to ever be able to prove that one of Mister Norm's deputies had been running a string of women."

"Lots of possibilities, Mr. McGee."

"Try another one, too. Lew and Betsy Kapp had a special relationship that was different from the setup he had with his other women. He could have told her about that place, and she could have gone there at the wrong time, when somebody was cleaning it out."

"Shall we go now?"

"After some more possibilities and some things I know are true, Sheriff. Five people on the truck job. Baither, Perris, Hutch, Orville, and Lilo. Hutch and Orville came into the area, probably quite a while back. I think I know where you should look for the bodies. About the envelope. Lilo got into the Baither house before she let Lew take her into the pump house. The previous night she worked on Baither until he told her where to find the money. Henry was there. But it had made him sick and he had walked away from it and didn't hear it. So she put the ice pick into Baither so he wouldn't tell it twice."

Hyzer folded his hands and rested them on the edge of the desk and sat with his eyes closed.

The phone rang. He picked it up. "Sheriff Hyzer. Yes, King. Go ahead. What! All right. Go back there and stay there. We'll be along."

He hung up and pinched the bridge of his nose, eyes closed, scowling. At last he looked at me and said, "McGee, as long as we're putting the cards face up, I'll tell you that Sturnevan wasn't off duty. I got permission to let him work in the county to the south of us. I'm the only one who knows that. The call I made to his home was just some misdirection. I had him put a beeper on Henry Perris's Rambler and hook up the directional equipment in his own private car. He just phoned in to say Perris got away from him, and he had to spend a lot of time cruising back roads until he found the one that would finally take him in the right direction to locate the car. He found Perris and the girl. They're dead."

I hadn't worried about fingerprints, or the tire prints of the Buick. And Nulia would talk about her fifty dollars. "The girl was all right when I left the trailer," I said. "But Henry wasn't. He was dead. I killed him. I came here from there."

Cop eyes. Suddenly you are on the other side of an invisible fence, and they stare across the fence at you, like a rancher would stare at a sick steer.

"I left the gun under him. He fell on it. Henry was very determined to kill me. I threw an oyster knife into him. I'll reenact it at the scene."

Hyzer stood up and said to Billy, "Make sure he's clean and we'll bring him along. Have Wallace and Townsend follow with their gear. Make sure they bring the floodlights. I'll radio Doc on our way down there."

Back over the same roads, riding in the same cage where I had ridden with Meyer, in the same faint stink of illness and despair. The second car was close behind us when we pulled up to the trailer. There was a big sunset beginning to take shape, tinting the aluminum trailer a golden orange.

They got out and left me in the cage. King was standing by an old green-and-white Dodge sedan, in much the same off-duty uniform he had worn when I met him at the Adventurer, cigar in the corner of his mouth. They talked for a little while and then Billy came back and let me out.

"From the beginning," Hyzer snapped. "A short version. No oratory. We can fill in the details later."

So I gave them the bones of it, including where the gun came from, how he had nearly gotten me out by my car, how I had gone inside and gotten out again, and where I had stood, and the condition of the girl when I left her.

They took me in for a look at her. She was still trussed up. She was on her side on the rug beside the bunk bed. The rug was soaked. There was a blue plastic bucket on its side on the rug near her head. The tape had been pulled off her mouth. Her hair was soaked. Her face was dark under the tan, a strange color. The light was going fast. Eyes half open. Foam caked in the corner of her mouth.

"Somebody held her head in that bucket," Billy said, "pulling it out to give her a chance to talk and shoving it in again when she wouldn't. So finally she did and McGee shoved her head back into the bucket and held it there until she drowned for sure, then let go of her. She fell over on her side just like that and he walked out."

"Billy," I said, "you are a hundred-and-ten-percent jackass."

"Sher'f," he said, "you think he would have said anything at all about this if King hadn't called in when he did? You know damn well he wouldn't."

Hyzer did not answer. He kept staring at the body of the girl.

King said, "You don't make good sense, Billy. Why would he come in at all? No, sir. I say somebody come here after he left and before I could find my way to where that damn needle kept pointing."

There were too many big men in that trailer. It was overcrowded. The girl lay dead at our feet. I felt faint.

Hyzer pushed by us and we followed him out. The doctor arrived, the ambulance following him in. By then they had to hold lights on the bodies, but they were short examinations. No enigma as to the cause of death.

"On the man," he said, "it got just deep enough to slit the arch of the aorta, I'd say. Death in eight to ten seconds. Visible petechical hemorrhages in the girl's eyes and characteristic darkening of the skin. Death by drowning or suffocation. Need the time pinned down? I took the temperatures. At least one hour, possibly two."

"There's another one for you," Hyzer said.

"Another one! What the hell is going on?"

"I'll get in touch later."

They had taken the pictures for the record. I watched them slide the two meat baskets into the ambulance and take off into the dusk at leisurely pace. No hurry anymore.

I walked over to where Hyzer stood and said, "On my way back I stopped at the Perris place and gave the woman there some money to stay with Mrs. Perris. I told her the girl and Mr. Perris wouldn't be back tonight. I thought the girl would be in custody. I didn't know she'd be dead."

He looked at me. "What?"

"I said I stopped and gave . . ."

"Yes. Yes, I heard you. Cable, Sturnevan, stay here and help them finish up. Billy, you ride back in with King. No. Have King show you where Perris's car is and you bring that in. I'll take McGee back with me. Come on." As we approached the car, he said, "You can ride in the front."

"Thank you."

He drove badly. The car wandered and he would slow down and speed up for no reason.

I saw in the reach of headlights the blue Opel under the big tree, and then he swung into the driveway and stopped.

"Come on," he said and I followed him to the doorway of the lighted house.

Nulia opened it and said, with a pleasure that surprised me, "Evenin', Sher'f Hyzer. Evenin'! Y'all keer to come in the house?"

I followed him in. "How is she tonight, Nulia?"

"Well, you know. Nothing much changes."

"I think the best thing to do is tell her right away. They're both dead, Nulia. Henry and Lillian."

She held her clenched hands against her chest and bowed her head, closed her eyes, lips moving silently. "Amen," she said. "Best she should know. What in the world will happen to her now?"

"I'll see that she gets care. McGee, you wait here."

He went through the living room with assured step and into a hallway.

Nulia said, "Sher'f comes to see Miz Wanda sometimes. Calls me to my own place, asks me to call him when I'm sure they's both out for a spell. She like a ball of soft bread dough. Cain't move one finger. Sure needs a heap of keer. For talking, she blink her eye. One time for yes, two times for no. Closes them entire when she don't want to talk anymore."

He was in there fifteen minutes. His face looked weary when he came out. "She taken it okay you think, Sher'f?"

"I guess so."

"Shouldn't want to cry no eyes out for them two, her or anybody else. I'm all fixed to stay here the night. My eldest brang me what I need."

I went out and got in with him and he drove better. He slowed down and put a spotlight on the side of the road, then made a careful turn over a short private bridge over the drainage canal and drove into a yard.

"Baither place?" I asked.

He said it was, turned off the lights and motor and got out. He leaned against the door on the driver's side as if suddenly taken ill.

"You all right, Norman?"

"He had two weeks before he set himself up for my jail and his guilty plea and Raiford. He could reasonably figure on two, three, or four years, because he was going to go after a perfect record up there. He did all the little maintenance chores necessary when you are going to leave a house vacant in this climate through the hot seasons, through the chance of hurricane. I used to come out here and try to think like Frank Baither. I think he set up a meet to make the split, set it up far enough from here so he bought the time to tuck it all away. It was bulky, you know. I got the track deposit list. Twenty-three thousand in ones, for example. They're counted by weight. Ninety-nine bills on the scale or a hundred and one, and the pointer swings way off center. Automatic banding. A hundred and fifty-one five in fives. Three hundred seventy-three eight in tens. One hundred eighty-eight three in twenties. Ninety-six thousand in fifties. Eighty-eight thousand in hundreds. Nine hundred and twenty thousand six hundred dollars. Take just the tens. Over thirty-seven thousand pieces of paper. Two hundred and forty pounds or so. The whole thing could go into six heavy suitcases."

"How did they get it back here?"

"Just a guess. Al Storey remembers that about that time Henry Perris found some winch trouble on the big wrecker, and drove it to his place to work on it over the weekend. So he would have covered the name on the cab doors with a fake name, changed the plates. When the money-truck crew passed out, he put the hook on it and took it to the rendezvous point where the other car or cars were waiting. After they broke it open, they probably offloaded the money into Baither's car, and he and Lillian drove back here with it, taking a different route than Henry did, bringing the truck back. They could have talked the other two into moving out quickly, into going into Miami and setting up an alibi. We'll meet at the X motel at Jacksonville or wherever. The two pickup specialists would buy it, because Baither had the reputation for never crossing anyone, and for good planning. But he never had one that big before, one big enough to set him up for life. No more risk. So he crossed them, and left Henry and Lillian to take care of the other two when they came around. Frank Baither was making a business investment in setting himself up for Raiford. It took suspicion off him, if anybody ever decided the money-truck job looked like his handiwork. And his insurance was that he was the only one who knew where he hid it. I don't think it mattered to him who killed off who. I think the money is here somewhere. Clean and safe and dry. But I haven't been able to find it."

I whacked at the mosquitoes humming around my ears, and scratched the chigger bites on my thighs that I'd picked up on the night walk with Meyer.

Silence. "But I guess it doesn't matter. It's all over for me here. I'll wind it up. Billy can operate it until they appoint somebody to take over until election."

"Why?"

"It's all turning sour in some strange way. I don't mean in a personal way. I knew in the back of my mind that I was wrong. I kept my eyes shut about . . . a personal matter, and told myself I would do such a total and dedicated job in every other way that it wouldn't matter. But it doesn't work that way. The scales don't measure the way they should. One little thing in one side weighs more than . . . everything else in the other side."

A fractional moon rode above the dark line of treetops. I could not risk saying anything. He was talking to himself. Yet he was at the same time making a rare offer of friendship. He was asking for help of some kind. A man proud, thoughtful, and troubled.

"It isn't just that I slaved over that tape playback and weeded out almost every trace of the accent of the people I grew up with. And it isn't that I realized and acceped the fact that I have a better mind than I thought I had when I was the high-school muscle man. Those things can isolate a man from his beginnings. But there is something else in the air. The faces of the young ones and the look in the eyes of the old ones. The guidelines are blurred. Are cops pigs? If I operate within a system where juvenile court cannot touch rich kids, where the innocent—meaning those presumed innocent because they have not yet been tried—are jailed with the guilty when they can't raise bail, where judicial wisdom is conditioned by friendship and influence, where there are two kinds of law, one for blacks and one for whites; then if I go by the book, I am a kind of Judas goat, and if I bend the rules to improve—on my terms—the structure of local law, I am running my own little police state. I'd better get out of it because I can't live with either solution."

"Not with a little rule-bending here and there?"

"Like I bent rules for Lilo Perris? And Lew Arnstead?"

"That gravitational influence I was talking about?"

"Do you know what it is? You go around making guesses."

"She was your daughter. She knew it and Lew knew it."

"Is it *that* damned obvious!" he said, his voice breaking.

"Only to a man who mentioned her name to Johnny Hatch, and who was told by Nulia you visit Wanda from time to time."

It was a shabby, ordinary little story, and he felt compelled to tell it in detail, a way of punishing himself. Wanda had been married to Johnny Hatch over a year. She was bored and restless and full of vitality. Norman Hyzer had come home for Easter vacation from college, engaged but not yet married. The Hyzer backyard and the Hatch backyard had a common rear property line, though they were on different streets. She'd asked him to help her dig up a small tree and move it, asked him into her house to clean up afterward, kidded him, teased him, challenged him, and seduced him. Though aching with guilt, he had found himself unable to stay away from her during the brief vacation. Later he could take a more objective view of it and see how easily she had engineered it, and how little it had meant to her.

But when he came back with his wife and baby daughter after his people were dead, to clean out the house of personal things and ready it for sale, she had come casually in through the back of the house to tell him that he had a very pretty little three-year-old daughter by her, named Lillian. She told him the date of birth and asked him to figure it out for himself. There was a baby boy, Ronnie she said, definitely Johnny's. But Lillian was his seed.

And they had made love that afternoon on a mattress on the floor in the upstairs hallway, and again the next morning, and had either still been making love or had finished at about the same time his wife and daughter were crushed to death by the fleeing car.

It was classic Biblical guilt and retribution, sin and punishment. He had come back and had become sheriff. He learned one aspect of Johnny and Wanda's divorce that was not public knowledge. Johnny's attorney showed the judge, in chambers, medical evidence that a man of Johnny's blood type could not have fathered a child with Lillian's blood type when the mother had Wanda's blood type. But there was enough evidence against her without that.

"She was the only person in the world of my blood," Hyzer said. "She was . . . maybe a symbol of the little girl who died. It's easy to close your eyes and ears, to say she could not be warped and rotten. Wicked, in the classical meaning of the word. Bend the rules. Let her off with a reprimand. Because she would have that mocking look her mother had. She knew, and knew I wouldn't acknowledge her. Arnstead found out four years ago. He picked Wanda up for drunk, and out of all the babbling and mumbling and weeping he heard something and got her sobered up enough to tell the rest of it, and got her to write it down before she was sober enough to realize he was using her."

Arnstead let him know what he knew, not in a confrontation, but in little hints. Wanda had become fat and coarse and loud, and Hyzer had already let the girl off too easily too many times. A sheriff who is snickered at, loses authority, and elections.

"Balancing it out doesn't work," he said. "Lew didn't push it too hard or too obviously, so I told myself he wasn't doing any actual harm, maybe even some good. I told myself that his girls would be hustling anyway, so it was better to have them kept in line."

"Then he went too far?"

"Beating a prisoner. Neglect of duty. Culmination of months of little things. So I had to. It was go down one way or go down the other way, and in the end you make a choice."

"Now I know why you were so anxious to nail us for the Baither thing."

He thought it over. "Yes. A suspicion in the back of my mind I couldn't consciously admit to myself, and you and Meyer were the way out. That's proof enough I better close it out and move along. Bend the rules and you start bending your own judgment, too."

"Without finding out who killed Lilo?"

"That's part of closing it out. After Wanda had the first stroke, when she could get around, she came to see me. The left side of her face looked dead. She made me promise to look after Lillian, keep her out of trouble. I promised. That was part of it, too, I guess. Then, a little while ago, after I told her, I wanted to know how she felt. Brutal damned question. I asked her if she was sorry Lilo was dead. She blinked her eyes twice. Same answer for Henry. That letter you showed me . . . Even mother-love couldn't live through that."

I had to make a guess that he wanted some kind of an answer. "You have a couple of incurable hang-ups, Norman. One is an old-timey hang-up on decency. The other hang-up is thinking too much, trying to separate cause and effect and locate where the guilt is. You are not with the scene, man. Guilt only happens to people who get caught. Sex is a handshake. Man has poisoned himself and he's on the way out, so pick up all the bread you can in any way you can. Enjoy."

"Sure, McGee. Sell yourself first."

"I keep trying, but I haven't been able to get into the spirit of the thing somehow. I keep going back to this role-playing of mine, you know, with the white horse and the maiden fair and the grail and the dragons and all that crap."

One flat and mirthless grunt of laughter from Sheriff Hyzer.

I said, "I do not want to be sickly sentimental, and I know that it is pagan barbarism to venerate the empty flesh when the spirit is long gone, but I think of Betsy out there in the night wired to that goddam tree, and how her face looks, and I keep thinking of how careful she was to look . . . nice. That's the only word. Nice."

He opened the car door. "Show me. I can call the people in from there."

nineteen

He had a big bright camp-light in the trunk of the cruiser. We walked slowly, and he kept the light on the ground so that we could avoid destroying any foot tracks or tire tracks.

I had trouble orienting myself at night. The tan Volkswagen would have been a big help had it been there. But it was gone. And Betsy was gone and the shovel was gone. In the grove we could walk around freely because the soft springy mat of brown needles of many seasons would not hold a print.

"Are you sure?" he asked.

"That's the third time. I am very damned sure, yes. Please stop asking. All right. One of these trees in this area, and it was about the same size around the trunk as that one."

It was Hyzer who spotted a silky lemon-gold thread clinging to the bark of a tree of the proper size, about four feet off the ground. Then in close inspection under the bright beam, I found a couple of blond hairs caught in the bark. That gave me enough orientation to show him where the half-dug grave had been.

I knelt near him and held the light while he carefully brushed away the blanket of pine needles, brushed down to the ground where it had been freshly, moistly stamped flat, leaving the same sole marks I had seen in the dirt in the half grave.

He grunted and began, just as carefully, to brush the needles back over it. "What are you doing?" I asked.

"I'll take the risk of assuming Mrs. Kapp is buried right here. Will your . . . sentimentality get in the way of leaving her here for a while?"

"No. It was the tree part that got to me. This is endurable. What do you have in mind?"

"Knowing something that somebody doesn't know you know is a useful thing in this line of work. Sometimes you don't know in advance how you'll use it. I'll come out alone tomorrow and take a cast of the shoe prints and any tire prints I can find. Let's take a look inside that shack now."

Whoever had come back to the unfinished business of burying her, had done a halfway job of tidying the shack. He had scattered the ashes, put the broken lid back on the barrel safe and covered it with the fire brick. I showed Hyzer the safe.

On the way back into town I told him, without telling him too much, exactly how eager I was for all kinds of publicity and press coverage.

Deputy Billy Cable had drafted an official release and he was holding it for Hyzer's approval. Hyzer sat at his desk and read it and said, "Billy, go and make certain every mouth is closed and stays closed, and then come back here."

Billy was back before Hyzer finished changing the release. Finally Hyzer handed it to him, saying, "Get it typed up again and get somebody to take it on over to Mr. Goss."

Billy read it and looked dismayed. "But . . ."

"What's wrong?"

"You've got it person or persons unknown, and this son of bitch McGee *confessed* he kilt Henry Perris."

"He thought he did, Billy," Hyzer said soothingly. "It was an honest mistake. Could you really believe a man could throw an oyster knife that deep into Henry's armpit from almost twenty feet?"

"Well, I heard him tell how . . ."

"The way I reconstruct it, it is a heavy piece of metal and it struck Perris on the skull and knocked him out. After McGee left to come here and report it, the next person along saw the opportunity and picked up the knife and thrust it into the unconscious man."

"If that's the way you want it."

"That's the way I want it."

"And you took out the part about Mrs. Kapp."

"Mr. McGee took me to the place where he thought he saw her, but he was apparently mistaken."

"I don't want to upset you, Sher'f, but shouldn't your chief deputy know what the hell is—"

"Come back here after you send that off and I'll tell you."

When the door shut, I said, "Many thanks."

"I'll try to stick with that, McGee. But if somebody goes on trial for killing Lillian, I'm not going to turn over a doctored file to the State's attorney for grand jury indictment. You'll have to go back into the picture, and with that weapon he had to stab you with, and with the photographs of the holes in the trailer, you should be able to satisfy the court that it was self-defense. I will testify that you made immediate confession, but that I kept it quiet for the sake of not giving the killer too much free information. Raise your right hand."

It had a lot of golden ornamentation and an eagle and three shades of colored enamel, red, white, and blue. It said that I had finally finked out all the way, and was a sworn deputy sheriff of Cypress County, Florida, with all the rights and privileges pertaining thereto. There was a wallet card with the sheriff's signature and mine. And I pinned the badge inside the wallet and practiced flipping it open a few times, thinking of how Meyer would laugh himself into hiccups.

Billy Cable came in as I made the final practice flip, and tucked the wallet away. His eyes bulged.

"Norm!" he wailed. "I mean, Sheriff. Him? After all!"

The whip cracked, and Cable came to sudden attention. Hyzer said, "You are the best officer I have, Cable. And in ninety-five percent of your duty assignments you are superior. In the remaining five percent you turn into a vain, stupid, inept man, causing me more trouble than you are worth. Do you know what this flaw is?"

"I . . . ah . . . no, sir!"

"I request you to make a guess, then."

"I guess . . . well, sometimes I maybe let my own personal feelings; . . . Sir, a man can't be a machine!"

"Cable, off duty you will let your feelings and your emotions and your prejudices slop all over your personal landscape. You can roll and wallow in them. On duty, on *my* time, you will be a machine. Is that absolutely clear?"

"Yes, sir." It was a very small "yes, sir." Cable was swaying. Only the most effective chewing can make a grown man sway.

"Temporary Deputy McGee will be privately assigned by me, and will not be subject to your authority or control in any way, nor will you make any mention of his status. Now go and shake his hand and welcome him to this department."

Cable came over. His eyes looked slightly glassy and his palm was damp. "Deputy . . . glad to . . . hope you enjoy your . . ."

"Thanks, Billy The name is Trav."

"Now you can both sit down," Hyzer said "We will discuss McGee's theory of gravitation, and the identification of unknown influences. Billy, I made out a schedule of . . . recent events. I checked out the duty cards and duty reports, and I have placed your approximate location and activities in the right-hand column. I see no chance of your having been involved directly in any way."

"For God's sake, Sheriff! If you think I—"

"Didn't we just have a little discussion about emotion?"

". . . Sorry, sir."

"This is a guide, merely to show you how I want a special project handled. You are the sample. I want you to run these six deputies through the same thing, without letting anyone know what you are checking out. I want you to make certain that the deputy cards and duty reports are correct as to the hours involved."

"Somebody in the family?" Billy asked.

"McGee thought it had to be either you or me. It isn't either of us. So let's be certain it isn't *any* of us."

For one precarious moment, full of fellowship and conscious of the ornate badge of authority, I wanted to give them the full report on Lew Arnstead, so it could be added to Hyzer's list of unusual events. Sure, and good old Betsy would swear to every word of it as being the truth. I would bounce about three times right on the place where now the badge rested, and hear the steel door clang.

Hyzer stared with raised eyebrows at Cable until suddenly Cable came to with a start and hopped up and hurried out of the office.

"And that leaves us," said Mister Norm, "with two more places to go. Or three. Lew Arnstead. Mrs. Kapp could have guessed where he would be, could have known about that hideaway shack, gone out there, and found him closing the store, picking up the money, getting ready to move."

"And forgot where the safe was?"

"Or tore the place up after he killed Mrs. Kapp to make it look like a stranger. Relocked the safe and tore the door off."

"Was he that subtle?"

"Any police officer learns what other police officers look for and how they make their judgments. Acquired subtlety, call it. He knew that Lillian had tricked him and left that envelope of yours in the Baither place. So he goes after her. And he finds her."

"You said three possibilities?"

"Somebody trying to either get a woman free and clear of Arnstead for good, or get even for what happened to the woman."

"Featherman?"

"A possibility. Maybe Mrs. Kapp arrived and found someone there, and Arnstead was there, dead. He could be under those pine needles too."

"The black jeep hidden on Betsy's street doesn't fit that one."

"Or the first one, either. Unless we get too fancy, and jam pieces into the puzzle whether they fit or not. Lew abandoned the jeep there to cause confusion. Or somebody picked him up right there and took him out to his shack."

"Or, Sheriff, Henry and Lillian killed him because they couldn't risk you finding out who engineered leaving that envelope. Maybe Henry and Lillian knew about that shack and they had to make sure Arnstead hadn't hidden anything out there that could tie them into Baither's death. And Betsy walked into that scene."

"That was my third guess," he said. "Save the best until last."

"Lillian knew about the shack. That photograph of her in that batch in your desk drawer was taken out there. Remember that clock on the wall?"

He took them out, found hers and studied it. "Very good, Deputy. Observant."

"When you find yourself in a sling, it's time to start thinking clearly or start running."

He put the pictures back, slammed the drawer hard. "Around and around and around," he said. "The mythological animal that grabs its own tail and starts eating and disappears down its own throat."

"A fifth man in on the money-truck job? Or maybe Henry and Lillian nailed either Hutch or Orville, but not both."

"We're going further and further into the mist," he said. "So we haul it back to specifics. Mrs. Kapp's car might tell us something. There are hundreds of little tracks across that scrubland up there. Tomorrow I call in a chopper for an air search. The biggest specific is the plausible assumption Lillian told someone what she learned from Frank Baither. That bucket technique is efficient. She would probably try some lies. So the technique is to keep at it until you get the same answer time and again."

"Do you have any idea how powerful she was?"

"Yes. I saw one demonstration. I see your point. Either one strong person or two people to handle her like that, even taped up."

"I'd buy two."

Then he told me my assignment. We checked the inventory of confiscated weapons, and I settled for a Ruger standard carbine in .44 Magnum, with a five-round capacity, four in a front tube and one in the chamber. I'd had one aboard *The Busted Flush* for a time and had used it on shark coming after the hooked billfish, until one day I had decided that the shark was doing his thing, and it was bloody and disrespectful to kill an honest scavenger just because he happened to come into the ball park when you are trying to win. From that day on, the rule when fishing from the *Muñequita*, after towing it to billfish country behind the *Flush*, was that the lookout would yell out when he saw the first fin, and you would release the billfish then and there instead of later, at the side of the boat. We do not bring dead meat home and hang it high for the tourists to say *Aaah* over. We take a picture of the good ones as somebody leans down to clip off the leader wire. The stainless hook corrodes out of the marlin, tuna, or sailfish jaw in days, leaving him free to go take the dangling bait of the commercial long-liners, fight his heart away against the resistance of the buoys, and, after the shark have browsed this free lunch leave his jaw or his whole head on the hook for the deckhands to haul up and toss away on the pickup round.

So I knew it would fire five 240-grain slugs as fast as I could pull the trigger, bust each one right through a seven-inch pine tree, and had a reasonable accuracy for a weapon a yard long overall, weighing less than six pounds.

They had grabbed it off a poacher. Norm Hyzer approved of the choice and gave me a handful of jacketed factory loads. After he explained what I was to do, I asked if I could have another few pieces of equipment. So he drove me to the shopping center and pointed out the hardware store that stayed open late. I bought my junk, and then hit the supermarket and provisioned myself for a forty-eight-hour vigil. Hyzer said he would check me out of the White Ibis after he dropped me off, and put my gear in the rental car and shut it up in his own garage, well out of sight.

It was ten-thirty when he dropped me off at the Baither place, wished me luck, and drove off.

It took longer than usual for my vision to adjust to the night. Priority one was slathering myself with repellent before a couple dozen of the more muscular hummers got together and lifted me up and wedged me into a tree to consume at their leisure.

I checked out the pump house by leaving the flashlight on inside, closing the door, and waiting again for night vision to see how much light came out. It was pretty good. A narrow crack above the knob, and a wider gap at the bottom. I could fix those on the inside by cutting some strips from one of the old blankets inside.

It took over an hour to set it up the way I wanted it. I had bought enough wire so I could take the long way through the brush from the pump house to the old wooden bridge. I turned out my flashlight each time I heard a car coming. In time I located an old gray warped plank with the right gap underneath and enough give to it. I taped my little brass terminals from a dismembered flashlight to the warped underside and to the supporting timber. I brought the buzzer along the road and put it down close enough to hear it from the bridge. There was no way to walk across or drive across without closing the circuit.

For somebody who, for some reason, wanted to come in from another direction, I used the primitive old black thread and rattle-can device. Closed the pump house door, turned on the flashlight, covered the cracks, made and wolfed a pair of thick sandwiches, drank a quart of the almost-cool water. Stretched out on the narrow cot to find the place to prop the weapon where my hand would find it with no fumbling, no loss of time.

Turned the light out, opened the door, stretched out on the cot again. I invited sleep by willing the relaxation of neck and shoulders. Deputy McGee on duty. It is to laugh. Or cry.

And I let myself down into that dark turbulence knowing I would find there the dusty-looking eyes of Arnstead, and Betsy playing her lavender game with stomach-turning grimace, and a flat steel handle sticking straight out of a twill armpit, and the foam caked into the corner of the dead mouth of the mad young girl.

twenty

At first light I got up and checked my warning system, took my thread and tin cans down and stowed them under the cot. Later, at sunup, I prowled the area, locating logical access so I could do a better job of hooking up the dangle-cans at nightfall.

I found a way of wedging the pump-house door so it would appear to be locked if anybody tried it. Hyzer did not want the seals broken on the doors to the Baither house. I found a window catch I could slip, and climbed in over the sill. The wide white tape still dangled from the armchair where Baither had died, and under the chair and in front of it were the crusted black places on the brown rush rug where his blood had dried.

I found a shady thicket with a good view of the terrain and settled in, carbine beside me. There was a nostalgia about it. Not the warm kind, with the misted eye and the sad smile. The other kind, that sucks the belly muscles in, and gives you access to the old automatic habits of survival, such as holding half a breath from time to time while you listen to bird sounds and bug sounds, waiting for them to stop in some unseen area. Listening for some little clink or jingle of equipment, or oiled snick of weaponry being readied. Nostrils widen and you snuff the faint movement of the breeze, for taint of alien sweat. You move a little bit from time to time because if you remain still, muscles can lock and when you must move, it might be necessary to move quick as a lizard, or take the hammer blow of unexpected automatic weapon.

At eleven the bridge boards rattled and an old white Mustang came in, packed with kids: two bleached boys in the bucket seats, three limber, noisy, bikinied young girls sitting high on the downfolded top. The driver swung it around the old red pickup so spiritedly, one of the girls nearly fell off. The girl in the middle grabbed her. They stopped and I could hear them clearly from my sun-dappled thicket.

"Tommy! You bassar, you like to kee-yul me, doon that crazy kind of drivin'."

"Not ef you land on your haid, Bunny Lee."

They piled out and went to the house and circled it, peering in every window. I heard the girls saying how spooky it was. They were all telling each other what happened to Frank Baither.

"Let's bust in and get a good look," one of the boys said.

"Hell with that," the other said. "Ol' Hyzer has got it sealed. You maybe want him on your ass? Not me."

"Come on," the first one said. "Look at old Norma Jean here. She's dead set on getting in there and making out with me in old Baither's sack."

"That's grass talking, goddam you Tommy!" a girl said.

The girls were slapping at their bare legs and shoulders. One of them said, "Get me out of here, you guys. I'm about to get et up. There's nothing here. Let's go bug old Dolores."

They ran for the car, piled in and charged out, shrilling the tires when they hit the paved road.

I took another tour. There was a crude patio off the other side of Baither's house, about twelve feet square, three steps down from a sealed door to the living room. It had a low wall around it of block painted pale blue. There were some planting pots with dead sticks coming out of the baked dirt inside. The patio area was paved with solid cement block a little larger than shoeboxes. They had been laid on tamped earth with sand poured between the cracks and watered down. It had been a sloppy job. The rainy season had washed the foundation uneven. Weeds grew out of the cracks. An old redwood chair, bleached gray, with a broken arm, crouched in a corner. Some blocks were missing.

I sat for a little while on the low wall, being scolded by a blue jay. I was thinking of Betsy Kapp in her grave up near the other end of Cypress County. And something in the back of my mind was looking at more immediate things, and finally sent the message upstairs that it seemed odd that some of the blocks looked paler and newer than others.

So I squatted and lifted one out and turned it over and replaced it and had the answer. Hyzer had directed a thorough search. So the blocks had been taken up and they had done some digging, or some probing with sharpened reinforcing rod, and had then replaced the patio floor. They had not taken the time or trouble to replace them all the same side up as they had been before. So the ones which went back in upside down looked a little newer. They had not had as much time to weather.

In fact, they had not even taken the trouble to put them all back. Four were missing from the far corner.

Everyone has their own fund of small idiotic compulsions. There are people who have to have their papers perfectly aligned with the edge of the desk. There are picture straighteners, and compulsive cleaners of ashtrays. I am a jigsaw freak. If I find myself in a room where there is a partially completed jigsaw puzzle, I find myself circling, then hovering, then finding the piece that goes here and the piece that goes there. Small triumphs. I cannot stand the sight of a fishrod rack that will hold five rods and has only four rods in the clips. I go through life fitting objects into their obvious and proper places.

So while thoughts moved away from the scene, back to the trailer this time, Henry circling it, I went scuffing through the rank grass and weeds, back and forth, around and around the three sides of the patio, moving further away from it, hunting for the block that would satisfy my moronic sense of order and fitness.

I woke up about forty feet out from the patio. No block. Irritation. What the hell did they do with it?

Pause for thought. Okay. So they searched the patio. Took up all the block. Piled it out to the side probably, but close. No need to tote it an inch further than necessary. Very probably they had piled it on the broad low wall.

So maybe there hadn't been quite enough block to pave the patio in the first place, and I was looking for something that didn't exist.

I went over to the corner and gave it close inspection. No, dammit. You could see the oblong depressions in the dirt underneath. And here was where one of the vine weeds had been torn when they had been lifted out. Green at the root end, and brown beyond the tear.

I straightened up and stood with my mouth hanging open. I stood in a comic strip, with a big light bulb suspended in space over my head.

I heard Lennie Sibelius, in that resonant and flexible voice, ". . . medium height with a bull neck and very broad thick shoulders. As a kid he had worked for his uncle who operated a little yard making cement block, and he had carried enough tons of mix and tons of finished block to give him that muscular overdevelopment."

My light bulb faded and dimmed. Hold it a minute, temporary deputy. Wouldn't a brand new patio completed during Frank's two weeks before he went to jail stand out like one very large and very inflamed thumb? And this block looks old. Maybe twenty years old.

But Baither had that old truck and he could take the original block far away and dump it. And he could add stain and dirt to the next mix. I yanked a block out and put it on its side on top of the wall. I yanked a second block out and slammed it down on the first one. It bounced off and nearly landed on my instep. The second smash broke a corner off. The third blow broke it open like a walnut. The meat inside the shell was the right size and shape. It had to be skinned. I got down to two banded packets of ten-dollar bills. Two thousand racetrack dollars. It had been wrapped in heavy plastic, tightly taped, then dipped in paraffin. From then on the process could be easily guessed. Pour a layer in the bottom of the greased wooden mold. When it started to set up, put the package on it, well centered, and finish the pour.

One hell of a lot of work, Mr. Baither. Two weeks of it. Off somewhere, probably, where you wouldn't be disturbed. Truck it in and lay it down, trying to make it look as beat as the original block, chipping it, scarring it. You could have added a little rock salt to the mix to get the right pitted effect. You must have been tired, fellow, when you finally got shoved into a cell.

I never would have found it or thought of it had not those four been missing, and had I not seen from the broken weed that they had been taken recently. Somebody would have been in a sweat to make certain that the water treatment had gotten the truth out of Lilo Perris. So they had nipped in and grabbed samples last evening, before Hyzer posted me here.

Dilemma. Turn the whole thing over to Hyzer right now. He had said, "Unless you get a visitor, don't call me and blow the cover. I'll get in touch with you."

Explicit. Follow orders. But first take certain steps which are part precaution, part ugly surprise.

I found a rusty old pickax behind the pump house. I soon learned the force required to pop the blocks open without gouging the cash. I stacked the waxed oblongs on the broad wall. There were one astonishing number of blocks in a twelve-by-twelve space, and I found only seven which were solid all the way through.

I improvised a Santa sack out of a frayed old army blanket from the pump house. I made it in five heavy loads, and I didn't finish the job until four-thirty. I crawled into my thicket, aching and winded and incomparably smug. Some very sneaky thoughts came sidling into my mind. With a little applied intelligence a man ought to be able to tie himself up impressively, and give himself a good thump on the head . . . "My God, Sheriff, he must have gotten behind me somehow, I never got a look at him."

It would figure out to about twenty years of splendid living. Untraceable. With nobody with an ugly disposition coming looking for it, and you. Maybe.

I remembered Meyer telling me that if I ever scored very very big, I had the natural tendency to turn into a one-hundred-percent bum. "And when you lose that last one percent," he said, "I might find you dreary. Sporadic monetary anxiety becomes you. It keeps you polite."

When the sun was very low, I began to make my preparations for the night. I was near the pump house when the buzzer sounded, and as a wind had come up I could not tell whether it had been a vehicle or a footstep which had done it. I ducked around behind the pump house, and heard the car, looked around and saw the green sedan with the blue flashers on the roof.

So I came out, carbine in hand, a tired and honest man ready and willing to make his honest report to his honest temporary boss man. But it was King Sturnevan who pulled his bulk out from behind the wheel and watched me approach, his back to the round golden sun.

"King," I said, "I hope you're delivering groceries and a cold beer."

"If I'd thought of it, pally, I'd of done just that."

"Then suppose you go tell Mister Norm it would be very nice if he would bring one hot sandwich and one cold beer to the recruit."

"Tell him and duck?"

"Seriously, I have to see him. I want him to get on out here as soon as he can. Would you call in, please?"

"Sure thing." He got into the car again. He fiddled with the transmitter, spoke into the hand mike. "Nine to CCSD, come in. Nine calling CCSD, come in." Nothing. He tried a couple more times, then got out, saying, "I told Red this damned set has got something loose on it. Sometimes it works, sometimes it's like dead."

"There's a window I can slip, and I think the phone in there is working. I'm not supposed to call in. Why don't you use it and just say to him that . . . you want to show him something at the Baither place."

"You got something to show him? You find something, McGee?"

"Yes and no. Look, King. I'm reporting direct. You know how it is."

"Hell, I know you're reporting direct. He just said I could stop by and see how you're making out. So whyn't you tell me and I can run back in and give him a direct report, and keep it off the air and off the phone?"

I wanted to think it over, and I eased over to lean against the side of the car. But he got in the way, a little clumsy on his feet. But he had moved very well in his little shower-room demonstration.

So I said, "Okay, King. That's probably the best way. I'll tell you the whole thing. But let's sit in the car. Okay?"

"It's too hard for me to get in and out of that little tin bucket. They make cars too small for guys my size."

"Okay. You stand outside and I'll get in the car."

And when he was still in the way, I knew. And I jumped back a good ten feet from him and put the muzzle of the carbine in direct line with his belly.

"What's with you, buddy boy? You some kind of flip?"

"Put the right hand on top of the head, slowly. Now!"

"Dammit, you're acting like . . ."

The holstered weapon was on the belt threaded through his pant loops. "Now undo the belt buckle with the left hand. Now the top button. Unzip and let them fall."

"But . . ."

"King, you better believe me, I will blow a hole right through the middle of you."

He let the pants drop, and I had him pull them off and move away from them, away from the car, so I could circle and, holding the gun on him, look into the car. I didn't see it at first, and if he had been more casual, maybe I never would have noticed it. He had pulled the mike jack out of the radio panel. The mike was on the dash hook, the connector cord hanging straight down.

"I nearly handed it to you," I said.

"You better start making sense soon. This is King. This is the guy on your side, pally." He really looked upset and distressed. He wore blue boxer shorts. His legs were massive and white and hairless. It made me think of something else. I had him unlace a shoe, take it off, and back away from it. I advanced as he backed up. I picked it up and held it toward the light and saw the serrations across the bottom, the place at the ball of the foot worn smooth.

I took a deep breath and let it out slowly, and took the slight tension off the trigger. "You nearly had it right then, King. It was close."

"Somebody better lock you up before you hurt somebody, boy."

"How are you at grave-digging?"

"Now you wouldn't ask a fella big as me to dig his own hole."

"You don't work very hard, King. Got any fresh blisters?"

He looked involuntarily at his right hand, and, like a little kid, put it behind him. "Worked in my garden lately."

"What did you plant in your garden? A dead lady?"

"For God's *sake*, McGee!"

"And spread the pine needles back neat. But we brushed them away very carefully, and this shoe is going to match the mold Hyzer took. You didn't have any trouble following Henry's car. You hung back and saw me leave and went right in. Held her head in the bucket. You're big enough and strong enough."

"You shove it under the skin, or take it right in a vein?"

"King, I am not going to risk messing around with you. You are too good. Now turn around very slowly. I am going to wrap you up, and when your place is searched, they are going to come up with some chunks of broken cement and some wax and some plastic and some cash money."

It was my intent to get close enough to chunk him in the back of the skull with the butt of the carbine, then cuff him to his own steering post, once I drove the car close enough.

He didn't turn around. "You want to be a boy scout, McGee, go ahead and put one right through the middle. You were close before, you said. Go ahead."

"Why Betsy?"

"Good question. Why not?"

Again I had to consciously ease back on the trigger finger so that it rested lightly.

He said, "She came to check Lew's place about the time I was getting the lid off that cheap safe. She decided I'd killed Lew. She didn't say it. But she showed it. I thought I'd set the two of you up nice. I wanted to know what happened to Lew's body, and after I started digging the hole, she told me. So I twisted the wire tight and I had to leave then to go on duty."

"Why Lew?"

"I thought maybe he found out from Lilo where Frank hid the money. I knew he had some money stashed. I had a good idea where. It was peanuts. Eleven thousand. And a bunch of rotten things. Rotten letters and rotten dirty pictures. I had to burn those. They weren't decent. Linda Featherman treated me right. She spoke to me like a human being, not a fat old box-fighter turned cop. Lew gave me the wink after she was dead, and I knew he meant she was one of his women, and I decided to kill him. I investigated an accident she was in. She treated me fine. Just fine."

"You've been lucky, King. Because basically you are one very dumb guy."

"Do you *know* how much money I shoulda had? Do you *know* the kind of payoff I would have had if I hadn't had bad hands and bad managers, and didn't cut easy. I had everything else going for me. I would have had one million bucks anyway, pally. Right now. I had everything else. Speed, punch, instinct."

"So the money is yours by rights."

"I would have had more even."

I realized he had somehow managed to get too close. As I started to move back, he bounded in low, banging the barrel aside with a forearm, and swinging a big left into my ribs, low on the right side. I felt them go, felt myself float back and down and heels over head, light as thistledown. Felt myself plucked up and saw him in the red glow, bounding and shuffling, moving in. Saw a fist come afloating, and felt my stomach being smashed loose, saw the sky spin, fell again, and felt cold metal under my lips.

"Come on, pally," he said in a wheedling tone, far away. "Upsy daisy. Dance with the old King a little."

Hand found the metal. It was so much fun for him his way, but he'd lost me. Finger found the trigger guard. I had been broken in half in the middle and the two halves were at least a yard apart. I rocked the right half onto its back, bringing the carbine up, and pulled the trigger as fast as I could, but the little joltings of the weapon came at least five minutes apart. A shark sank in a red-sun-sea, and the red rolled over me, and the further I sank, the darker it got.

twenty-one

On a very fine day in May, Meyer brought Miss Agnes around to the door of the Lauderdale hospital, and the cheery Gray Lady wheel-chaired me down the short ramp and out to the curb. Meyer came around and I pulled myself up, stepped on that obsolete convenience known as a running board, and sat on the seat and swung my legs in.

I thanked the lady and she told me not to hurry back. Miss Agnes looked better than I had ever seen her. Ron had hand-rubbed so many coats of blue that you could see down into the surface.

"She running good?" I asked Meyer.

"Aside from driving like an armored lorry, fine."

The whole world looked bright and new and far too brilliant in every color and outline. A couple of weeks inside can do it. My clothes felt strange. And they were a little large for me.

"Nice to be out," I said.

"For a while there, nobody thought you would be."

I knew that. I had lost quite a few days in there somewhere. The doctor absolutely refused to believe that that damage had been done by two blows from the human fist. He said the muscle cover was tough and hard enough to withstand a blow like that. He said I shouldn't have had three crushed ribs, a rupture of the external oblique muscle, liver hemorrhages, and a perforation from a piece of rib bone in the bottom of the left lung. That's what brought on the pneumonia that they couldn't seem to find the right antibiotic for. I had been in shape, but not in shape for the ring.

"Forget about the trial," Meyer said.

"What do you mean? What happened?"

"Sturnevan died this morning. He was coming along fine. The smashed hip was all wired together and seemed to be healing in good shape. Hyzer phoned me. Said to tell you. He said they told him it was a massive coronary occlusion."

"We should both have died, lain there on the ground eight feet apart and quietly bled to death. But those kids came back to break into the house. Meyer, my friend, our luck doesn't run so good in Cypress County."

"I have no pressing need to return. Oh, and Hyzer said your check will be coming through in another few days. Two and a half percent of the total amount recovered. Something under twenty-two thousand."

"Nobody's luck ran very good in Cypress County."

"Nine hundred and twenty thousand is maybe an unlucky number. Your hands get sweaty and you become accident prone."

"Meyer, did they locate any bodies near that trailer?"

"I told you they did. Ten days ago I told you. You looked like you were listening."

"Who?"

"They don't know. They'd been there too long. A tall body and a shorter body, both male, both with a round puncture hole in the base of the skull. I told you that, too."

"Don't get surly about it. Does it hurt to tell me twice?"

"I'm thinking of the other things I told you I'll have to tell you twice."

"There'll be time enough. We aren't going anywhere. Did I happen to do any talking when I wasn't tracking very well?"

"A certain amount."

"Anything interesting?"

"It was all very dull stuff. You know, the usual run of delirium. Sex and violence. Nothing original."

"Thanks. That light is red."

"Even if I hadn't seen it, I would have seen it when you sucked air through your teeth, McGee. Telling me out loud also is superfluous. I might get angry and run into somebody."

"You're driving. So drive. I'll leave you alone."

"A blessing."

"Did you get anybody for the job, Meyer?"

"If I didn't, wouldn't I get stuck with it myself? Yes, I found a woman to cook and clean. An ugly one. A little bit hard of hearing. In your condition I did you a favor and found an ugly one that reads little books of inspirational poems in her spare time."

"You're too good to me, Meyer."

"Wrong preposition. For."

"The light is green, Meyer."

"Do I do this to you when you're driving? Do I complain when you go running into canals?"

"No. But you keep bringing it up."

So soon we went under the pedestrian bridge and turned left and Meyer eased Miss Agnes into a slot reasonably near the entrance to F dock.

"You want to ride on one of the delivery carts?"

"Let's walk. Slow."

So we walked along to F-18, and there were yelps from far boats, and sounds of welcome from nearby ones. And unkind comment. Are you McGee's father, mister? Meyer, who's the clean skinny old man? McGee, where's your tan? Fall into the oatmeal? Let me give you the address of my ex-husband's tailor, darling.

Have fun, people. All I want to do is get aboard and lie down.

So as I tottered across my little boarding ramp, holding carefully onto the safety cable, I noticed that my houseboat looked almost as good as my ancient Rolls pickup. It gleamed and glistened. It looked so good, it embarrassed me. Why couldn't I maintain it like that?

"Meyer, who is the compulsive polisher?"

"That deaf woman has a lot of extra energy. She asks me what next, and one day I said she could clean the outside of the boat, too."

Meyer helped me into the lounge and down the corridor past the galley into the master stateroom. The bed was crisply made up and turned down. I undressed and got in, and Meyer said I would probably feel better if I had my usual, a nice knock of the Plymouth over ice, and I told him he was a nice man. I heard him tinkling around out there.

The tinkling approached and I put my hand out and opened my eyes, saying, "Meyer, where is . . ."

And Heidi Geis Trumbill put the drink in my hand and laughed aloud in her pleasure at my surprise. She was still the most elegantly textured pussycat of them all, a little older now, not a pound heavier, with more of the awareness of living in her eyes, more of the taste of times and places in the look of her mouth. Elegance, freshly tanned, leaning her perfume close to kiss me quickly and softly on the lips, and then sitting down on the side of the bed, looking at me misty-eyed.

"McGee, you idiot, are you crying?"

"It's weakness, love. This water runs from the eye. Means little. Or a lot. Take your pick. But *now!* The last time I saw you was . . ."

"When I got in the car with the luggage and left you standing there, dear. St. Croix. I looked back. you looked so dejected. And my heart was breaking and breaking."

"You went to find your own life, find that right guy, have fat babies I think you said. Well?"

"I found him, but somebody else had found him first. It was a long bad scene, dear, and I cut away from it six months ago. I've been painting like a madwoman. My show sold out."

"What are you doing here?"

"Don't you know? I'm ugly and hard of hearing and I will read inspirational poems aloud to you."

"Did you clean up this crock boat?"

"Look at my poor hands, dear. Look at my nails!"

"Seriously, how come . . ."

"Travis, darling, a long time ago—maybe not so awfully long ago really, but it does seem way back—I told Meyer that you had picked up all the pieces of me and put me together, and that if you were ever in need of the same he was to find me, through my gallery, and let me know and if I did not happen to have any compound fractures, I would come to you on a dead run. I got here a week ago yesterday."

"So that's why Meyer has looked so bland and smug and mysterious. Why didn't you come to the hospital?"

"Hate them, darling. Sorry. Wasn't this better?"

"This is as good as anything can get. My God, you look lovely. You are something way out else, Heidi."

"Do you need putting together?"

"Haven't you noticed me?"

"Oh hell, I don't mean looking like sudden death. That's a body thing. I mean putting together."

I looked at her and knew that I did. "Something was going wrong and it went further wrong. I don't know. I lost it, somehow, without knowing what I lost. Some kind of . . . sense of light and motion and purpose. I went ragged around the edges and bleak in the middle. The world seems to be coarsening, and me with it. Everything that happens takes away, and less flows back. And I respond less, and in the wrong way. I still amuse myself but there's some contempt in it now. I don't know . . . I don't know. . . ."

"Darling, there's that water from the eye syndrome again."

"Sorry."

"There's nothing so really wrong with you, you know. It's second adolescence."

"Is that it?"

"Of course, Travis, darling. I had delayed adolescence. Remember your absolutely dreadful analogy of comparing me to that old yellow Packard you bought when you were a child, and finally got running so beautifully?"

"Indeed I do."

"In your ravings you let Meyer know you had promised the cruising month of June aboard this fine houseboat to a lady who, for reasons he wouldn't tell me, won't be able to make it. You may tell me or not, as you wish. But I am substituting."

"That is very good thinking, Heidi."

"The cure for my delayed adolescence was a grown-up man. And I think a grown-up woman can cure a recurrence of adolescence, don't you?"

"Shock treatment, eh?"

"McGee, I am a very grown-up woman, far more so than that grim day we said goody-by on that lovely island."

"I think you are. Yes. I would say so."

She looked at me and I suddenly knew exactly what Mona Lisa was thinking about. It was exactly the same smile, though on a face far more to my liking.

"I think, dear, that it is going to be absolutely essential for the health of both of us, and the sanity too, if you will kindly get a lot of lovely sleep, and eat the rich marvelous foods I am going to cook for you, and exercise a little more each day, and take the sun and. . ."

"I guess it's pretty essential. Yes, indeedy."

"Because we are going to further places on our cruise, darling, than anybody has ever reached before on a boat this slow in one single lovely month."

I finished the drink. She took the glass. She told me later that I fell asleep smiling, and that Raoul, the cat, joined me later, curling into a warm nest against my waist.

Bright Orange
for the Shroud

to Roger, Beauregard, Geoffrey, Marilyn, Chloe, Francis, Trampas and Knees

one

Another season was ending. The mid-May sun had a tropic sting against my bare shoulders. Sweat ran into my eyes. I had discovered an ugly little pocket of dry rot in the windshield corner of the panel of the topside controls on my houseboat, and after trying not to think about it for a week, I had dug out the tools, picked up some pieces of prime mahogany, and excised the area of infection with a saber saw.

Cutting and sanding the new pieces to fit was a finicky chore. Sawdust stuck to my sweaty chest and arms. I was sustained by an awareness of the cool dark bottles of Dos Equis beer in the stainless steel box below, and by the anticipation of trudging from Bahia Mar over to the public beach where a mild wind from the east was capping the deep blue swells with white.

Also I was sustained by the determination that this would be a slob summer for McGee. It wouldn't be a gaudy summer. There wasn't enough bread for that. But a careful husbanding of funds would see me through, leaving the emergency fund untapped, ready to finance some kind of an operation in the fall.

I needed a slob summer. The machine was abused. Softness at the waist. Tremor of the hands. Bad tastes in the morning. A heaviness of muscle and bone, a tendency to sigh. Each time you wonder, Can you get it back? The good toughness and bounce and tirelessness, the weight down to a rawhide two oh five, a nasty tendency to sing during the morning shower, the conviction each day will contain wondrous things?

And I wanted it to be a loner summer. There'd been too much damned yat-a-ta-yak, fervid conversations, midnight plots, and dirty little violences for which I had been all too unprepared. The pink weal six inches below my armpit was a reminder of luck. If my foot hadn't slipped exactly when it did. . . .

A knife blade grating along a rib bone is a sound so ugly and so personal it can come right into your sleep and wake you up ten nights running.

I got a good fit on the biggest piece, drilled it, and was setting the long bronze screws home when I heard a tentative and hollow call from dockside.

"Trav? Hey, Trav? Hey, McGee?"

I turned and walked to the aft end of my sun deck and looked down at the dock. A tall, frail, sallow-looking fellow in a wrinkled tan suit too large for him stared up at me with an anxious little smile that came and went—a mendicant smile such as dogs wear in the countries where they kick dogs.

"How are you, Trav?" he said.

And just as I was about to ask him who he was, I realized, with considerable shock, that it was Arthur Wilkinson, dreadfully changed.

"Hello, Arthur."

"Can I . . . may I come aboard?"

"Certainly. Why ask?"

The gangplank chain was down. He came across, stepped onto the afterdeck, tottered, tried to smile up at me, grabbed at emptiness and collapsed onto the teak deck with a knobbly thud. I got down there in two jumps, rolled him over. He'd abraded the unhealthy flesh under one eye in the fall. I felt the pulse in his throat. It was slow and steady. Two fat teen-age girls came and stared from the dock, snickering. See the funny drunk, like on television.

I opened the aft door to the lounge, gathered Arthur up and toted him in. It was like picking up a sack of feather-dry two-by-fours. He smelled stale. I took him all the way through and put him down on the bed in the guest stateroom. The air conditioning was chill against my bare sweat. I felt Arthur's head. He didn't seem to have a fever. I had never seen a man so changed by one year of life.

His mouth worked, and he opened his eyes and tried to sit up. I pushed him back. "You sick, Arthur?"

"Just weak, I guess. I guess I just fainted. I'm sorry. I don't want to be . . ."

"A burden? A nuisance? Skip the social graces, Arthur."

I guess you always look for a little spirit, a little glint of the fang on even the most humble dog in town.

"I'm very polite," he said listlessly. "You know that, Trav. A very polite man." He looked away. "Even . . . even when he was killing me, I think I was probably very, very polite."

He faded away then, like a puff of steam, quickly gone, his eyes not quite closed. I put my fingertips against the side of his throat—the pulse was still there.

As I was wondering just what the hell to do next, he came floating back up, frowned at me. "I can't cope with people like that. She must have known that. Right from the start she must have known about me."

"Who tried to kill you?"

"I guess it really doesn't matter very much. If it hadn't been him, it would have been the next one, or the one after that. Let me rest a little while and then I'll go. There wasn't any point in coming to you. I should have known that too."

Suddenly I recognized a part of that stale smell about him. It was a little bit like freshly baked bread, but not as pleasant. It's the distinctive smell of starvation, the effluvium of the sweat ducts when the body has begun to feed on itself.

"Shut up, Arthur. When did you eat last?"

"I'm not real sure. I think . . . I don't know."

"Stay where you are," I told him. I went to my stainless steel galley, looked in a locker, picked out a tin of clear, rich British broth, poured it into a pan and turned the burner on high. As it heated I looked in on him again. He gave me that reappearing nervous smile. He had a facial tic. His eyes filled with tears, and I went back to the broth. I poured it into a mug, hesitated, then tapped the liquor locker and added a fair jolt of Irish whiskey.

After I helped him get propped up, I saw he could hold it all right in both hands and sip it.

"Good."

"Take it slow, Arthur. I'll be right back."

I sluiced the sawdust and sweat off in a fast shower in the huge stall the original owner had built aboard *The Busted Flush*, put on denims and a T-shirt and checked him again. The mug was empty. He was slightly flushed. I opened the promised bottle of beer and went back in and sat on the foot of the bed.

"What the hell have you done to yourself, Arthur?"

His voice blurred. "Too much, maybe."

"Maybe I asked it the wrong way. What has Wilma done to you?"

Again the tears of weakness. "Oh Christ, Trav, I . . ."

"We'll go into it later, boy. You get out of the clothes and into a hot shower. Then you eat some eggs. Then you sleep. Okay?"

"I don't want to be a . . ."

"Arthur, you could begin to bore me. Shut up."

After he was asleep, I took a good look at his arms. Big H could pull a man down quickly. No needle marks. But it didn't have to mean anything. Only the eyedropper group, the ones who pick the big vein open with a pin, acquire scars. Any tidy soul with a decent hypo and enough sense to use an alcohol swab afterward can go unmarked indefinitely, as any urban cop can tell you. He was still a little grimy. It was going to take more than one shower, or two. The beard stubble didn't help either. I checked through his clothes. They had been cheap originally. The labels were from Naples, Florida. He had a flat cigarette package with three one-inch butts carefully stowed therein. He had a match folder from Red's Diner in Homestead. He had two pennies and some lint. I rolled his shoes up in the clothing, carried the bundle out at arm's length and dropped it into the trash bin on the dock. Then washed my hands.

The sun was going down. I went topside. The cockpit cocktail hour, with music and girl-laughter from neighbor cruisers. As I drove the remaining screws home without working up a sweat, I kept thinking of Arthur Wilkinson as I had seen him last, over a year ago.

A big fellow, big as I am, but not the same physical type. Slow, awkward, uncoordinated—a mild and rather pedantic guy. I could remember coming across a few of the same breed way back in high school basketball days. Coaches would hustle them on the basis of size alone. They were very earnest, but they had no balance. You could catch them just right with the hip and they would go blundering and crashing off the court. For them, high school was the final experience in any body-contact sport.

Arthur Wilkinson had been a member of the group for a few

months. I met him when he was trying to decide whether or not to invest some money in a marina enterprise. He was going around, talking earnestly to boat people. He surveyed me at drinking time, and stayed, and came back other times—came back once too often, perhaps, that time somebody had brought Wilma around.

He had told me about himself. Upstate New York boy. Little Falls. Department-store family. Got a degree from Hamilton College. Went to work in the store. Became engaged to a doctor's daughter. Didn't particularly like or dislike the department-store trade. Future all lined out, nailed down. Then it all fell apart, one piece at a time, beginning with the death of his widower father, then his girl marrying another guy, until, restless, irritable, unhappy, he had sold out his controlling interest to a chain, liquidated other properties and headed for Florida.

He got along fine with the group. He was amiable and very decent. We felt protective about him. He had been schooled for survival in Little Falls, and might indeed have been formidably adapted to that environment, but away from it there was something displaced about him. He was perfectly frank about his problem. He had left, after taxes, almost a quarter of a million dollars. It was in good solid securities, bringing in, after personal income taxes, nearly nine thousand a year. But he felt it shameful to squat on it. He wanted to move it around, put some work with it, make it produce. Some of the genes of his great granddaddy kept prodding him.

The group changes; the flavor remains the same. When he was in the pack, he was the gatherer of driftwood for the beach picnics, the one who drove drunks home, the one who didn't forget the beer, the understanding listener who gets girl-tears on his beach coat, the pigeon good for the small loan, the patsy who comes calling and ends up painting the fence. All groups seem to have one. He had a fair complexion, blushed readily. He always looked scrubbed. He laughed at all the jokes, nearly always at the right place, even though he had heard them before. In short, a very nice guy, that Arthur Wilkinson. Part of the group, but nobody got really close to him. He had that little streak of reserve, of keeping the ultimate secrets. Liquor might have unlocked him except for one thing. When he took one over his limit, he fell smilingly, placidly, irrevocably asleep. And smiled in his sleep.

I could remember that for a little while Arthur and Chookie McCall had something going. She had just finished a dancing engagement at the Bahama Room at the Mile O'Beach. She's big, beautifully proportioned, vastly healthy, a dynamo brunette with a stern and striking face. Chook had fought with Frank Durkin and he had taken off and she was rebounding, and certainly Arthur was a better deal than Frank. Without a dime, Arthur would have been worth nine Frank Durkins. Why do so many great gals latch onto a Frank Durkin to mess up their lives? When she got a three-week gig up at Daytona Beach perhaps Arthur could have gone with her, but he didn't make the right moves. Then Wilma Ferner moved in when Chook was away. . . .

There are a lot more Arthur Wilkinsons in the world than there are Wilma Ferners. And this Wilma was a classic example of the type. Little, but with a bone structure so delicate she made a hundred and five pounds look like a lush abundance. Fine white-blond hair always in that initial state of disarray which creates the urge to mess it up completely. Husky theatrical voice which covered about two octaves in what was, for her, normal conversation. Lots of anecdotes, in which she played every part, face as mobile as a clown's, making lots of gestures, flinging herself around, the gestures seemingly awkward at times until one noticed that they kept that ripe little body in a constant state of animation and display, a project given a continuous assist by her wardrobe. There were little traces of accent in her normal speech, when she wasn't imitating someone, but it seemed to vary from day to day. Hold a small clear wineglass of Harvey's Bristol Milk up to the light and it is pretty close to the color of her eyes. And, once you got past all the crinkling and sparkling and winking, her eyes had just about as much expression as still wine.

She came in on a big Huckins out of Savannah, amid boat guests in various conditions of disrepair, much of the damage evidently being accomplished by people beating people in the face with their fists. She moved into a hotel room ashore, in the Yankee Clipper, and after the cruiser took off without her, she somehow managed to affix herself to our group, saying that the lovely people on the Huckins were going to pick her up on their way back from Nassau, and she had begged off because she could not *endure* Nassau one more *stinking* time.

In that venerable and useful show-biz expression, she was always on. The gals seemed to have an instinctive wariness of her. The men were intrigued. She claimed to have been born in Calcutta, mentioned the tragic death of a father in the Australian diplomatic service, mentioned directly and obliquely her own careers as set designer in Italy, fashion coordinator in Brussels, photographer's model in Johannesburg, society and fashion editor on a newspaper in Cairo, private secretary to the wife of one of the presidents of Guatemala. As she cooed, twisted, bounced, exclaimed, imitated, chuckled, I must admit that I had a few moments of very steamy curiosity. But there were too many warning flags up. The pointed nails curved too extremely over the soft tips of the little fingers. The poses and pauses were too carefully timed. And there was just a bit too much efferves-cence and charm. Perhaps if she had come along a few years earlier —before I had seen and learned all kinds of con, before I had found some of the sicknesses no clinic can identify . . .

So we wondered who would nail it. Or vice versa. She was carrying a weapon at port arms, waiting for a target of opportunity.

I remember a very late night when I sat alone with my hairy econ-omist friend named Meyer in the cockpit of his small cruiser which he christened *The John Maynard Keynes*, after a beach time when Wilma had been so totally on she had sparkled like the moonlit surf.

"Wonder how old she is?" I asked idly.

"My friend, I have kept meticulous track of all pertinent inci-dents. To have done what she claims to have done, she is somewhere between one hundred and five and one hundred and seven. I added five more years tonight."

"Psychopathic liar, Meyer?"

"An inexact science uses inexact terms. I spit on parlor expertise, Travis."

"Sure. I have one suspicion, though. There is so much merchan-dise in the showcase there's nothing left back in the storeroom."

"I wouldn't gamble on that either."

"What the hell would you gamble on, Meyer?"

"A man with no trace of the feminine in him, with no duality at all, is a man without tenderness, sympathy, gentleness, kindness, responsiveness. He is brute-mean, a hammer, a fist. McGee, what is a woman with no trace of the masculine in her makeup?"

"Mmm. Merciless in a different way?"

"You show promise, McGee. The empathy of kindness is a result of the duality, not of the feminine trace. Our strange friend, the Ala-bama Tiger, is maneuvering the lady just right. And she resents it. He moves in with a forked stick, and he'll pin her head to the ground and then pick her up in such a way she can't get her fangs into him. Maybe women are the only things in the world he knows so well."

I told Meyer he was crazy, that anybody could see that the Alabama Tiger and Wilma Ferner had disliked each other on sight. Meyer wouldn't argue it. On the adjoining deck, in a big rich Wheeler, the Alabama Tiger maintains what is by now the longest floating house party in the world. He is a huge, sloppy guy, once a murderous All-American tackle, who later made a pot of money and decided to spend it on boats, booze and broads. He stays blandly, cheerfully tight during all waking hours. He has a face like crude stone sculpture, carved into a mild grin. In forty seconds he can make you feel as if you are the most interesting person he has ever met, and you will feel as if you never met anyone more understanding. He could charm tenement landlords, post-office employees, circus dwarfs and tax assessors.

When Wilma finally took aim, Arthur Wilkinson was the hapless target, and there was not one damn thing any of us could do about it. He had less chance than a lovely wench when the Goths came to town. His eyes glazed over. A broad fatuous grin was permanently in place. She was at his elbow, steering him, to keep him from walking into immovable objects. He thought her june-bug cute, delicate and dear, infinitely valuable. He felt humble to be so favored, to be awarded this rare prize. Any hint that the june-bug might be a scorpion didn't offend him. He just couldn't hear what was said to him. He laughed, thinking it some kind of a joke. After the minimum waiting time, they were married late one afternoon at the courthouse, and left in a new white Pontiac convertible, the back seat stacked with her matched luggage, her smile as brilliant as a brand-new vermin trap ordered from Herter's catalogue. I had kissed the dear little cheek of the june-bug bride. She'd smelled soapy clean. She called me a dear boy. My present was a six-pack—Metaxa, Fundador, Plymouth gin, Chivas Regal, Old Crow and Piper Heidsieck '59. For the expendable marriage, you give the expendable gift. She left a message for the yacht that wouldn't be back to pick her up. And I knew the two of them would not come back to Lauderdale as long as she was in command. She had sensed the appraisal of the group, and would require a more gullible environment.

Three days after they left, we all knew something was wrong with the Alabama Tiger. Instead of his benign and placid condition of mild alcoholic euphoria, he swung between morose sobriety and wild, reckless, dangerous drunks. The permanent house party began to dwindle. It was Meyer who dug the reason out of him after finding the Tiger sitting lumpily on the beach at dawn with a loaded .38 tucked inside his shirt. And because he wanted a little help in keeping an eye on him, Meyer told me the story.

Wilma had secretly invited the Tiger over to headquarters at the hotel one morning. With a deftness, Meyer said, more common in the Far East than in our less ancient cultures, she had quickly learned how to turn him on and off, as if he were a construction kit she had wired herself. Then, with a dreadful control, she had taken him right to the edge and hung him up there, incapable of either release or retreat.

"In his own deathless words," Meyer said, "whooflin' and shakin' like an ol' hawg hung on the charger wires. He honestly began to believe it was going to kill him. He could feel his heart beginning to burst. And she was laughing at him, he said, her face like a spook. Then suddenly, without release or warning, he felt dead. He heard her singing in her shower. After she was dressed, she kissed him on the forehead, patted his cheek and left. He thought of killing her as she bent over to kiss him, but even that seemed too unimportant for the effort involved. Suddenly he had become an old man. She had accepted the tension between them, the contest of wills, and had taken a little time out to whip him before leaving. It might interest you, McGee, to know that it happened last Thursday morning."

"She had married Arthur Thursday afternoon.

"There could be a little heart damage," Meyer said. "There certainly seems to be plenty of emotional damage."

Monday night, late, I walked over to the Tiger's big flush-deck Wheeler and from fifty feet away I decided, with that sense of loss you have when a legend ends, that the oldest permanent floating house party in the world had finally ended. One small light glowed. But from twenty feet I picked up the tempo of Hawaiian music on his recordplayer system, turned very low. Approaching, I made out a girl-shape in the glow of dock lights, dancing alone slowly on the after deck under the striped canvas canopy, highlights glinting on the glass in her hand as she turned.

She saw me and angled her dance toward the rail, and I saw that it was one of the Ching sisters, Mary Li or Mary Lo, the identical twins who sing-and-dance at the Roundabout, closed Mondays. She was involved in a variant of the dance forms of her native Hawaii. It is impossible to tell the twins apart. Almost impossible. I had heard that Mary Lo is distinguished by a tiny vivid gemlike tattoo of a goodluck ladybug, but so intimately located that by the time one encounters it, any thought of choice has long since been obviated.

Her hair swayed dark and heavy as she turned, and her smile was white in duskiness. "Hey you, McGee," she said in a low tone. "Long as one little thing keeps swinging, Poppa Tiger's bash is still alive. You haul aboard, make yourself a cup there."

As I made my drink she said, "We running a fox roster, man, the chicks who swung good here, keeping him braced up."

"How is he making it, Mary?"

"Now he smiled some tonight, and he cried just a little time because he said he was done for good and all, but a little time back my sister came topside all tuckered and said he made out, and now they sacked out like death itself, and this here is the party, McGee man, down to just me. And now you, but Frannie coming by after she gets off work at two, bringing that bongo cat, and I say things pick up from here, pick up good. A swinger boat, with booze like a convention, you got to brace the management when he's down."

"The only reason, Mary?"

She stopped her dance eye to eye, a handspan away.

"Like that dirty-mind cop wants to close us down, Poppa Tiger goes way upstairs and has the clout to mend his ways. Like our nephew needed the school letter that time, Poppa Tiger writes pretty. I just want to keep the free booze coming, man, and tap that locker full of prime beef, and get the boat kicks."

"I knew better. I thought it would be nice to hear you say it, Mary."

"Brace up this dead drink for me, on the house. It's fat vodka, one cube and a smitch from the little cranberry-juice can."

"Gah."

"Don't drink it, just make it."

We had some drinks, and I watched her dance, and we had some laughs because the old bear was on the mend. Frannie brought along some other kids from the club she was working. And as unexpected by-product of celebration, I learned beyond any chance of confusion that the night dancer had been Mary Lo. Selections from the Tiger pack are not my usual type, as it tends to be too casual and mechanical for the ornamented romanticism of the McGee, who always wants a scarf in token to tie to the crest of the cut-rate helmet, wants the soul-torn glance, the tremors of the heart, the sense—or the illusion—of both choice and importance. But Mary Lo left no bad taste. She made it like a game for kids, chuckling and crooning her pleasures, and it did indeed pleasantly blur the use Wilma made of the same game. After they have strangled the king with boiling wine, it is therapeutic to get a little tipsy on a more palatable brand.

two

Arthur fell back into my life on that Tuesday afternoon. Acquaintance rather than friend. The dividing line is communication, I think. A friend is someone to whom you can say any jackass thing that enters your mind. With acquaintances, you are forever aware of their slightly unreal image of you, and to keep them content, you edit yourself to fit. Many marriages are between acquaintances. You can be with a person for three hours of your life and have a friend. Another one will remain an acquaintance for thirty years.

While he slept I dug into the more remote lockers in the bow section until I found the small ragged suitcase I remembered. Girl-bought clothes for a version of McGee of long ago, when I hid out and they hunted me, and I was afraid the stink of my rotting leg would clue them in. Killed the two of them while in delirium. No memory of how she got me to the hospital. Heard later how she managed to keep them from taking the leg off. Now there is that crooked pale arroyo, long down the right thigh, deep into muscle tissue. Function unimpaired. But a chancy time, deep there in fevers, seeing the pearly gleam of the gates, talking to the dead brother, sometimes looking up out of a well at the professional faces bending over the bed.

These were the clothes she brought me, the clothes in which I was wheeled out into the vivid unreal world, clothes in which I first tottered about, ten feet tall and two inches wide, certain that if I fell off the crutches I would break like a glass stork. They would fit Arthur nicely in his dwindled condition and were only slightly musty from long storage. In a housewifely mood, I hung them out to air, thinking of the money the dead ones had stolen, quite legally, from the dead brother and how, quite illegally, the girl and I had stolen it back, cut it down the middle.

While Arthur slept, I wondered how the hell to get rid of him. That was the extent of my Christian charity. I could accept being an aid station but not a convalescent clinic. I went over the composition of the group as Arthur had known it, looking for a substitute pigeon. I had my slob summer all planned. Immediately after the dry-rot surgery and a few other maintenance matters, I wanted to take *The Busted Flush* down to Dinner Key, get her hauled and get the bottom scraped and painted, and then chug at my stately 6+ knots —with a six-hundred-mile range on the two 58-hp Hercules Diesels— over to the Bahamas on a dead-calm day. The 52-foot barge-type houseboat can take pretty rough weather if forced to, but she rolls so badly she tends to bust up the little servomechanisms aboard which make life lush. I had been mentally composing a guest list, limited to those random salty souls who can get away, hold their liquor, endure sunshine, make good talk, swim the reefs, navigate, handle the lines, slay food fish and appreciate the therapeutic value of silence. It is the McGee version of being a loner—merely having some people about to whom you don't have to constantly react. Arthur did not fit that specification closely enough.

When darkness came I took the aired clothes below and put them on a chair in the guest stateroom. He was snoring in a muted way. I closed his door, fixed myself a Plymouth gin on the rocks, closed the lounge curtains, looked up Chookie McCall's number. No answer. I hadn't seen her or heard anything about her in two months. I tried Hal, the bartender at the Mile O'Beach who keeps good track of our gypsy contingent of entertainers. Hal said she'd been working at Bernie's East up to May first, when they closed the Brimstone Room, and as far as he knew all she was doing was a Saturday-morning one-hour show of dance instruction on KLAK-TV. But he had it on good authority she was all set to regroup her six-pack and open back at the Mile O'Beach in the Bahama Room come November 15th.

"Hal, is Frank Durkin back yet?"

"Back yet! Don't sit on your hands until he gets back. Dint you hear what they got him on?"

"Only that he took a fall."

"It was assault with intent to kill, or felonious assault or whatever the hell they call it. Three to five up in Raiford, and you can bet Frankie will get smart-ass with those screws up there and they will keep him for the five. Chook goes up to see him once a month. She'll be making a lot of trips. All that woman could find something better, McGee, and you know it. She don't get any younger."

"Younger? Hell, she's only twenty-five at the most."

"Ten years in the entertainment business, and thirty when they turn Frankie Durkin loose. It adds up, Trav. If I was trying to locate her tonight, I think maybe Muriel Hess would be a good bet. She's in the book. They've been working together on material for when she starts up here in the fall."

I thanked him and tried the number. Chook was there. "What's on your mind, stranger?"

"Buying a steak for the dancing girl."

"Plural?"

"Not if you can help it."

There was a long palm-over-the-mouthpiece silence, and then she said, "What kind of a place, Trav?"

"The Open Range?"

"Yum! I'll have to go back to my place and change. How about coming over for a drink? Forty minutes?"

I shaved and changed, and left a note for Arthur in case he woke up. Because of all the boat errands, I had Miss Agnes parked nearby, my electric-blue Rolls pickup truck, an amateur conversion accomplished by some desperate idiot during her checkered past. She is not yet old enough to vote. But almost. She started with a touch, and I went along the beach to where Miss McCall lives in the back end of a motel so elderly it has long since been converted from transient to permanent residence. She's in what used to be two units. Wrapped in a robe, smelling of steam and soap, she gave me a sisterly kiss, told me to fix her a bourbon and water. I handed it in to her.

In a reasonably short time she came out in high heels and a pale green-gray dress. "McGee, I think I say yes because how many guys I go out with can I wear heels with?" She inspected me. "You're too heavy."

"Thanks. I feel too heavy."

"Are you going to do anything about it?"

"I've started."

"With booze in your hand?"

"I'm starting a little slow, but I'm one of those who lose it with exercise. Not enough lately. But a lot more coming up. Chook, you are *not* too heavy."

"Because I work at it *all* the time."

She was indeed something. All that woman, as Hal had said. Five ten, maybe 136 pounds, maybe 39-25-39, and every inch glossy, firm, pneumatic—intensely alive, perfectly conditioned as are only the dedicated professional dancers, circus flyers, tumblers, and combat rangers. Close up you can hear their motors humming. Heartbeat in repose is in the fifties. Lung capacity extraordinary. Whites of the eyes a blue white.

Not a pretty woman. Features too vital and heavy. Brows heavy. Hair harsh and black and glossy, like a racing mare. Indian-black eyes, bold nose, big broad mouth. A handsome, striking human being. When she was five years old they had started her on ballet. When she was twelve she had grown too big to be accepted in any company. When she was fifteen, claiming nineteen, she was in the chorus of a Broadway musical.

While I freshened the drinks she told me that she was working out with Muriel, a New Nations theme, researching the music and rhythms. She said it would give them some exotic stuff and some darling costumes and some sexy choreography. We sat to finish the drink. She said Wassener, the new manager, was considering a no-bra policy for the little troupe next season, and was sounding out the authorities to see how bad a beef he might get. She said she hoped it wouldn't work out, as it would mean either canceling out two good girls she already had lined up, or talking them into wax jobs. "Posing and blackouts and that stuff," she said, "it's a different thing. You just keep your chin up and you arch your back a little and tighten your shoulders back, but I've been trying to tell Mr. Wassener dancing is something else. My God, a time step in fast tempo, and all of a sudden it could look like a comedy routine, you know what I mean. If he thinks it'll draw, what he should get is a couple of big dumb ponies and just let them stand upstage on pedestals maybe, in baby spots and turn slow."

After I agreed, there was a last-inch-of-the-drink silence, and I knew I had to say something about Frank Durkin. Like being forced to discuss ointment with somebody with an incurable skin rash.

"Sorry to hear Frank took such a long count."

She sprang to her feet and gave me a look Custer must have gotten very tired of before they chopped him up. "It wasn't *fair*, goddam it! The guy was being very smart-ass, and Frankie didn't owe him any fifty dollars. It was a mistake. When he followed him out into the parking lot, all Frankie was going to do was scare him. But he jumped the wrong way and Frankie ran over him. What they did, Travis, believe me, they judged him on the other times he's been in trouble. And that's unconstitutional, isn't it? Isn't it?"

"I don't know."

"He has that terrible temper. Right in court he tried to get his hands on the judge. Believe me, he's his own worst enemy. But this isn't fair at all."

What could anyone tell her? To forget him? She'd swing from the floor and loosen your teeth. The only times she ever tried to forget him was after their savage quarrels. She was a very fine woman, and Frankie Durkin was no damned good. Sponged off her. Kept her on the hook with promises of marriage. Fancied himself crafty and managed to outsmart himself in most deals. Then cursed his luck. I would have said his luck was excellent—because he would have long since been caged or fried as a murderer if, in several known instances, he'd achieved his heart's desire. I saw him in his fury once. His pale blue eyes turned white as milk. His underprivileged face went slack as taffy. And, grunting with each breath, he began to try to kill a friend of mine. Could have made it if they'd been alone. As he wasn't worth breaking any hand bones on, I took the billy I kill toothy fish with and bounced it off his skull. After three lumps he was still trying to crawl toward Mack's throat, but the fourth one pacified him. When he woke up he seemed unfocused, like a man after a hard fever. And had no hard feelings at all.

"How is he taking it?"

"Real hard, Trav. He keeps telling me he can't stand it, he's got to do something." She sighed. "But there's nothing he can do. Maybe . . . when he gets out, he'll be ready to settle down. Let's get out of here."

Miss Agnes drifted us silently over to the mainland, to the Open Range, a place disfigured by mass-production Texas folk art, steer horns, branding irons, saddle hardware, coiled lariats and bullwhips. But the booths are deep and padded, the lights low, the steaks prime and huge. Chook ordered hers so raw I was grateful for the low candlepower of the booth lamp. I invested some additional ditch-

Arthur money in a bottle of Burgundy. I have seen Chook under other circumstances do the social-eating routine. But with me she could follow her inclination and eat in the busy, dedicated, appreciative silence of a farmhand or roustabout, chugging her way deftly through tossed, baked and extra rare, and at last leaning back from the emptiness to give me an absent, dreamy smile and stifle a generous belch.

Judging I was at the exact moment, I said, "Small favor?"

"Anything at all, Trav darling."

"I'm cutting you in on a lame duck who showed up. In bad, bad shape. It would be sort of for old time's sake for you."

"Who?"

"Arthur Wilkinson."

I thought I saw a momentary softness in her eyes before they turned fierce. She leaned forward. "I tell you what I am not. I am not a trash basket. I am no place you can dump the leavings from that pig."

"Put your wheels down, Chookie. Who's the most naïve little chick in your troupe?"

"Huh? Well . . . Mary Lou King."

"She engaged?"

"Sort of. What is this, anyway?"

"Now suppose say . . . Rock Hudson came barreling in at her, all guns blazing. What would Mary Lou do?"

Chook giggled. "Gawd, she'd roll over like a dead bug."

"I'm under a handicap. I never did find out what status you reached with Arthur. He'd never volunteer that sort of information, as you well know. It was my guess it got pretty humid."

She studied her nails. "When Frankie took off that time, he busted my place up before he went. Everything. He even tore up my scrapbooks. He said I'd never lay eyes on him again as long as I lived. And I don't even know what it was we were fighting about. Okay, so I needed a gentle guy. Not for sex. I'm not cold—maybe I'm more the other way than I should be, but, hell, I can always put on old music and dig out old routines and a practice uniform, work hard for a few hours and sleep like a baby." She gave me a quick dark glance. "I guess I should be honest. Mostly it was to have somebody close, but that's no reason to knock the other part of it. And maybe I was trying to use him to tear loose from Frankie. At first I told him all my lousy troubles. And we took some walks. And then after one walk we ended up in my bed. And if I'd left it entirely up to Arthur, we wouldn't have. I had to make it easy for him without letting him catch on to what I was doing. You know me, Trav. I'm not a pig. I suppose . . . if I taught third grade in Webster Falls, I wouldn't last too long. But in the business I'm in . . . I'm thought square. You know?"

"I know."

For just an instant I had a feeling of waste and loss. There was so much shrewdness, native intelligence, perception there. The awareness of self, undistorted, a virtue growing ever more rare in our times. It made you wonder what this creature of such vast vitality could have become if she had taken some other direction with her life. Too many of the good ones aren't being used up all the way.

But a little personal resonance got to me. Because I'd never found the right way of using myself up. So I had settled for a variation of the lush life, bumming along the golden strand until funds sagged too low, then venturing forth to clip the clip artists, wresting the stolen meat—legally stolen usually—out of the bandit jowls, then splitting the salvage down the middle with the victim—who, without the services of McGee, would have had to settle for nothing, which, as I have often pointed out, is considerably less than half.

It isn't a very respectable dedication. So just say it's a living. Sometimes I get a very faint echo of the knight-errant psychosis. And try to make more out of it than is there. But everybody's hall closet is full of lances and shields and other tourney gear. The guy who sells you insurance gets singed by his own secret kind of dragon breath. And his own Maid Marian yoo-hoos him back to the castle tower.

Maybe, somewhere along the line, I could have gone the other route. But you get a taste for the hunt. You keep wondering how close the next one is going to get to you. And you have to see. And nothing can slow the reflexes like the weight of mortgages, withholding, connubial contentment, estate program, regular checkups and puttering around your own lawn.

But now they are phasing out the hunters. Within this big complex culture, full of diodes, paper clips, account numbers, they are earnestly boarding up the holes, sealing the conduits, installing bugs and alarms in every corridor. In a few years there'll be no room left for the likes of McGee. They'll grab him, carry him away and adjust him to reality, and put him to work at something useful in one of the little cubicles in the giant structure.

So who are you to think of a fuller life for Miss Chookie McCall?

"Could it have worked out with Arthur?" I asked her.

She shrugged those strong shoulders. "He's almost five years older, but he seemed kind of like a kid. I don't know. So considerate and so . . . grateful. He was getting to be a better lover. It was like, at first, getting him to think things were his idea. Trav, honest to God, what was I supposed to do? Ask him to please come to Jacksonville with, me? I mean there's pride too. He wanted to. But he thought it wouldn't be right. I wanted him there. Maybe it was like putting up a wall, a little at a time, shutting out the hurt from Frankie. Maybe we could have made the wall thick enough and tall enough. Maybe not. Maybe when Frankie came back, it would have been the same for me, Arthur or no Arthur. Frankie crooks his finger and I crawl to him. I won't ever know, will I, because Arthur didn't go up to Jax with me, and so we didn't have that three weeks and we didn't have the four months back here before Frankie came back, broke and sick and mean as a basket of snakes. I came back and Wilma had Arthur skinned and nailed to the bar, and the son of a bitch shook hands with me as if he couldn't remember my name. Pride still counts with me. I am not going to be a damned rescue mission, Trav. Believe me. Go look for a little mother somewhere else. He made his lousy choice."

"Okay. I see your point. But just stop by the boat and take a look at him."

"No! You don't get clever with me. Once in Akron the dressing room was alive with mice, and I set a trap. All it did was maim one little bastard, and three weeks later, after I got him back on his feet, I turned him loose. He'd lick peanut butter off my fingertip. Trav, I wouldn't go anywhere near Arthur."

three

When I got back to *The Busted Flush* with Chook, Arthur Wilkinson was as I had left him, the note still there. I put on the overhead light. I heard her suck air. Her strong cool fingers clamped on my hand. I looked at her thoughtful profile, saw her tanned forehead knotted into a frown, white teeth indenting her lower lip. I turned the light off and turned her, and we went back to the lounge, two closed doors between us and Arthur.

"You should get a doctor to look at him!" she said indignantly.

"Maybe. Later on. No fever. He passed out, as I told you, but he said he just felt faint. Malnutrition is my guess."

"Maybe you got a license to practice? Trav, he looks so horrible! Like a skull, like he was dying instead of sleeping. How do you know?"

"That he's sleeping? What else?"

"But what could have happened to him?"

"Chook, that was a very nice guy, and I don't think he had the survival drive you and I have. He's the victim type. Wilma was his mousetrap, and nobody cared if he got maimed. No peanut butter. We had one in Korea. A big gentle kid fresh out of the Hill School. Everybody from my platoon sergeant on down tried to get the green off him before he got nailed. But one rainy afternoon he got suckered by the fake screaming we'd gotten used to, and he went to help and got stitched throat to groin with a machine pistol. I heard about it and went over as they were sticking the litter onto a jeep. He died right then, and the look on his face was not pain or anger or regret. He just looked very puzzled, as if he was trying to fit this little incident into what he'd been taught at home and couldn't quite make it. It's the way some earnest people take a practical joke."

"Shouldn't we see if Arthur is really all right?"

"Let him get his sleep. Fix you a stinger?"

"I don't know. No. I mean yes. I'm going to take another look at him."

Five minutes later I tiptoed into the companionway beyond the head. The guest stateroom door was closed. I heard the tone of her voice, not the words. Gentleness. He coughed and answered her and coughed again.

Back in the lounge I locked the big tuner into WAEZ-FM, and fed it into the smaller speakers at low volume, too low to drive my big AR-3's. I stretched out on the curve of the big yellow couch, took small bites of the gin stinger, listened to a string quartet fit together the Chinese puzzle pieces of some ice-cold Bach, and smiled a fatuous egg-sucking smile at my prime solution to the Arthur problem.

In about twenty minutes she joined me, eyes red, smile shy, walking with less assurance than her custom. She sat on the end of the couch beyond my feet and said, "I fixed him some warm milk and he went right to sleep again."

"That's nice."

"I guess it's just being exhausted and half starved and heartsick, Trav."

"That was my guess."

"The poor dumb bastard."

"Outclassed."

I got her stinger out of the freezer and brought it to her. She sipped it. "There isn't anything else you can do, of course," she said.

"Beg your pardon?"

She looked at me and opened her eyes very wide. "Get it back, of course. They cleaned him clean. That's why he came to you."

I got up and went over to the tuner and killed Mr. Bach. I stood in front of Chook. "Now just one minute there, woman. Hold it. There's no . . ."

"For God's sake, stop looking as if you're going to bray like a wounded moose, McGee. We talked about you once."

"Make some sense."

"He wondered about you. You know. What you *do*. So I sort of told him."

"You sort of told him."

"Just how you step in when people get the wrong end of the stick, and you keep half of what you can recover. McGee, why in the world do you think he came right to you! Could anything be more obvious? Why do you think that poor whipped creature crawled across the state and fell on your doorstep? You can't *possibly* turn him down."

"I can give it a very good try, honey."

Silence. She finished the drink. She clacked the empty glass down. She came up off the couch, moved close, stood tall, fixed me with a poisonous stare, upslanted, fists on hips. "Did I do you a favor coming here?" she said in almost a whisper. "Do you owe me for that, and for one or two other small things I could name? Do you want me to go after them myself? I will, you know. I'm calling you on this one, you big ugly lazy jerk. They smashed him. They gutted him. And there's no other place he can turn." Giving emphasis to each word by rapping my chest with a hard knuckle, she said, "You-are-going-to-help-that-man."

"Now listen . . ."

"And I want a piece of the action, Travis."

"I have no intention of . . ."

"The first thing we have to do is get him on his feet, and pry every living piece of information out of him."

"How about that weekly television thing you . . ."

"I'm two tapes ahead, and I can go down there and do three more in one day. Trav, they didn't leave him a *dime!* It was some kind of land-development thing. Over near Naples."

"Maybe by fall . . ."

"Travis!"

By the following Saturday afternoon *The Busted Flush* was swinging on two hooks in Florida Bay, two miles off Candle Key, all larders stocked, five hundred gallons in the fresh water tanks. With alterations from time to time, I've tried to make the old barge-type houseboat ever more independent of shoreside services. Except when home at Bahia Mar, I like to avoid the boat basin togetherness. Under one hatch I have a whole area paved with husky batteries, enough of them so that I can stay at anchor and draw on them for four days before they begin to get a little feeble. When they're down, I can use them to start up an electric trickle-feed generator which can bring them back up in six hours. If I ever get careless enough to run them all the way down, I can break out the big 10 kw gasoline generator and use it to get the electric one started. At anchor I switch everything over to 32 V. I can't run the air conditioning off the batteries, but I can run it off the gas generator. Then it is a decision as to which will be the most annoying, the heat or the noise.

The sun was heading for Hawaii. Just enough breeze for a pattycake sound against the hull. I was stretched out on the sun deck. A line of pelicans creaked by, beating and coasting, heading home to the rookery. What I had learned so far from Arthur didn't sound promising. But I comforted myself with thinking that while we were getting him in shape, I was doing myself some promised good. I was on cheese, meat and salad. No booze. No cigarettes. Just one big old pot pipe packed with Black Watch for the sunset hour. Due any time now.

Every muscle felt stretched, bruised and sore. We'd anchored at midmorning. I'd spent a couple of hours in mask and fins, knocking and gouging some of the grass beards and corruption off the hull. After lunch I'd lain on the sun deck with my toes hooked under the rail and done about ten sets of situps. Chook had caught me at it and talked me into some of the exercises she prescribed for her dance group. One exercise was a bitch. She could do it effortlessly. You lift your left leg, grab the ankle with your right hand, and play one-legged jump rope with it, over and back. Then switch hands and ankles and jump on the other leg. After that we swam. I could win the sprints. In our distance events, she had a nasty habit of slowly drawing even and then slowly pulling away, and an even nastier habit of smiling placidly at me while I wheezed and gasped.

I heard a sound and turned my head and saw her climb the ladderway to the sun deck. She looked concerned. She sat cross-legged beside me. In that old faded pink suit, dark hair in a salty tangle, no makeup, she looked magnificent.

"He feels kind of weak and dizzy," she said. "I think I let him get too much sun. It can sap your strength. I gave him a salt tablet, and it's making him nauseated."

"Want me to go take a look at him?"

"Not right now. He's trying to doze off. Gee, he's so damn grateful for every little thing. And it broke my heart, the way he looked in trunks, so scrawny and pathetic."

"He eats many lunches like today, it won't last long."

She inspected a pink scratch on a ripe brown calf. "Trav? How are you going to go about it? What are you going to try to do?"

"I wouldn't have the slightest idea."

"How long are we going to stay here?"

"Until he has the guts to want to go back, Chook."

"But why should he *have* to? I mean if he dreads it so."

"Because, dear girl, he is my reference library. He doesn't know what very small thing might turn out to be very important, so he doesn't think of it or mention it. Then when it's about to go off in my face, he can tell me where the fuse is, which is something he can't do from a hundred miles away."

She looked at me speculatively. "He wants to give up the whole idea."

"Okay. Sure."

"*Damn* you!"

"Sweetie, you can take a good and gentle horse, and you can start using a chain on it. Maybe you turn it into a killer. And maybe you break it right down to nothing, to a trembling hunk of meat. Then can you ever turn it back into a horse? Depends on the blood line. Sometimes you don't want the victim along. Sometime, like this time, you have the hunch you'll need him. I won't go into this without him. So he has to forget the chain. You're along to turn him back into a horse, Chook. You've got to prop him up. I don't want you in on any of the rest of it."

"Why not?"

"It sounds just a little too dirty so far."

"And I have just walked out the convent gates in my little white pinafore. Come *on*, Trav!"

"Miss McCall, the most dangerous animal in the world is not the professional killer. It's the amateur. When they sense that somebody is taking back what they went to so much effort to acquire, that's when they get violent. The essentially dishonest man is capable of truly murderous indignation. In this instance, the bitch will be looking on, heightening the performance, looking for blood. I don't think she'll relish losing."

I sensed mischief as she studied me. "I guess any man would find her pretty exciting."

"Hell, it's exciting to be pushed out a window. Or run over."

"And you didn't have the least little urge, darling? She did sort of have an eye on you."

"The scorpion is a very cute little brown bug, the way she plods along with that tail curled over her back. She's a living fossil, you know, unchanged in millions of years. It's imaginable that some bug-lover might want to pick one up and stroke her scaly little back."

Big brown girl in scanty pink, in Zen-pose on my splendid vinyl imitation of teak. It is real teak on the aft deck below, partially justi-fying such trickery. Staring dubiously at me. "Men aren't that bright about those."

"Arthur wasn't."

"And what have *you* got? Radar?"

"Alarm systems. Bachelor devices to detect poisonous types. One good way is to watch how the other women react. You and the others, when Wilma Ferner was around, all your mouths got a little tight, and you were very polite to her. And you made no girl talk at all with her. No clothes talk. No date talk. No guided trips to the biff. No girl secrets. Just the way, honey, a woman should be damned wary of a man other men have no use for."

That was a little careless, and too close to home. Frankie gives most men the warm sweet urge to hit him heavily in the mouth. Chook's dark eyes became remote. "If the breeze dies it could get buggy here."

"The long-range forecast says we'll get more wind instead of less." I rose smartly to my feet. If I'd been alone, perhaps I would have crawled moaning to the sun deck rail and hauled myself up. Vanity is a miracle drug. I could count on three or four more days of tor-ment before, I hoped, the limberness would come back, along with the hardened belly and lost pounds and unjangled nerves.

As I stretched and yawned, Chookie said, "Hey!" and came to me and in a very gingerly way touched, with one fingertip, the pink weal below my left armpit. "I didn't notice that. It's new, huh?"

"Aw, it's just a scratch."

"Knife?"

"Yup."

She swallowed and looked ill. "The idea of knives, it makes my stomach turn over. And it makes me think of Mary Lo Ching."

While I'd been away on this last one, the one that gave me the funds for a slob summer, an animal had gotten to Mary Lo with a knife. The twins had been working in Miami Beach, in March. They got him in a few hours by rounding up known sex offenders. They'd thought this one harmless. He'd been tucked away a few times for short falls. Peeping, indecent exposure. His profession was fry cook.

All the time he was working himself up to a big one, and Mary Lo had been in just the wrong place at the wrong time. He hadn't been selective. Just the first one he could get to. They didn't count the wounds. They just said "more than fifty."

The psychiatrists call it a sickness. The cops call it a hell of a problem. The sociologists call it a product of our culture, our puritanical tendency to consider sex a delicious nastiness. Some of them escalate to the big violence. Others stay with a small kick, peering into bedrooms. You can't give a man life for that, nor even constructive psychiatric help during a short sentence. He cuts brush on the county gang, tormented by the other prisoners, driven further into his private madness. Then he comes out and cuts up Mary Lo, and at once everybody is an expert on how he should have been handled by the authorities, up to and including gelding the very first time he committed a nuisance in a public park.

"Anybody know anything about Mary Li?" I asked.

"Just that she went back to Hawaii." Chook stepped back a pace and looked at me from ears to heels as if examining one of the metal sculptures in the garden of the Museum of Modern Art. She shook her head sadly and said, "McGee, I swear, I never really noticed before how many times you've been torn up."

"This one here happened when I was three. My big brother threw a hammer up into a tree to knock some apples down. The hammer came down too."

"Do you *like* being in a crazy kind of business that gets you so close to being killed?"

"I don't like to hurt. Every little nick makes me that much more careful. Maybe I'll get so careful I'll have to find some other line of work."

"Seriously?"

"Seriously. Miners get silicosis. Doctors get coronaries. Bankers get ulcers. Politicians get strokes. Remember about the alligators? Honey, if *nothing* happened to people, we'd all be ass-deep in people."

"And I should see what happened to the other guys. Okay, you can't be serious." She marched off, and went down the ladderway like a . . . a dancer going down a ladderway.

I could be serious in that particular area, but not on her terms. I'd had enough stitches to make a quilt, and had enjoyed not one of them at all, at all. And most floor nurses have a top-sergeant syndrome. I went below and packed the promised pipe. Chook was in the stainless steel galley, banging pots. I went through to the guest stateroom where I had quartered myself. Chook had made that decision while we were provisioning the boat, when she brought her gear aboard. She had declared flatly that she wasn't going to mouse around. All three of us knew she'd slept with Arthur before his marriage, and the huge bed in the master stateroom—the bed that had been there when I'd won the boat—gave her a better chance to keep watch over him, and if he wanted to make something of it, then she was willing to be compliant on the basis of therapy, affection, old time's sake, morale—call it whatever the hell you feel like calling it, McGee.

I had told her I avoided putting names on things whenever possible, and I transferred my personal gear and went back to the hot greasy chore of smoothing out the port engine which, after too much idleness, was running hesitantly, fading when I gave it more throttle, complaining that it wanted its jets cleaned.

By midevening, Arthur Wilkinson felt better. It was a soft night. We sat in three deck chairs on the afterdeck, facing the long path of silver moonlight on the black water.

I overpowered his reluctance and made him go over some of the stuff he had already told me, interrupting him with questions to see if I could unlock other parts of his memory.

"Like I told you, Trav, I had the idea we were going to go farther away, maybe the southwest, but after we stayed overnight in Naples, she said maybe it would be nice to rent a beach house for a while. Because it was April we could probably find something nice. What she found was nice, all right. Isolated, and a big stretch of private beach, and a pool. It was seven hundred a month, plus utilities. That included the man who came twice a week to take care of the grounds, but then there was another two hundred and fifty for the woman who came in about noon every day but Sunday."

"Name?"

"What? Oh . . . Mildred. Mildred Mooney. Fifty, I'd guess. Heavy. She had a car and did the marketing and cooking and housework. She'd serve dinner and then leave and do the dishes when she came the next day. So it came to maybe twelve hundred a month for operating expenses. And about that much again for Wilma. Hairdresser and dressmaker, cosmetics, mail orders to Saks, Bonwit's, places like that. Masseuse, a special wine she likes. And shoes. God, the shoes! So say in round figures there's twenty-five hundred a month going out, which would be thirty thousand a year, three times what was coming in. After wedding expenses, and trading for the convertible, I had five thousand cash aside from the securities, but it was melting away so fast it scared me. I estimated it would be gone before the end of June."

"You tried to make her understand?"

"Of course. Wilma would stare at me as if I was talking Urdu. She couldn't seem to comprehend. It made me feel cheap and small-minded. She said it wasn't any great problem. In a little while I could start looking around and find something where I could make all the money we'd ever need. I was worried—but it was all kind of indistinct. The only thing that really seemed to count was just . . . having her. In the beginning, it was so damned . . . wonderful."

"But it changed?"

"Yes. But I don't want to talk about that."

"Later?"

"Maybe. I don't know. It all turned into something . . . quite different. I don't want to try to explain it."

"If I left?" Chook said.

"No. Thanks, but that wouldn't make any difference."

"Get on with it then. When was the first contact with the land-syndicate people?"

"Late May. She'd gone walking down the beach in the late afternoon, and she came back with Calvin Stebber. Some kid had hooked a shark and he was fighting it and beaching it with people watching him. That's how she got in casual conversation with Stebber, and it turned out they knew a lot of the same people, so she brought him back for a drink. Short and heavy and very tan. Always smiling. I'd say he wasn't much over forty, but he looked older. And he seemed . . . important. They jabbered away about people I've read about. Onassis, Niarchos, people like that. He was very vague about what he was doing. He just said that he'd come down to work out a small project, but it was dragging on a lot longer than he'd estimated. He seemed . . . fond of Wilma. He wished us happiness.

"After he left, Wilma got quite excited. She told me that Calvin Stebber was enormously rich and went around making very successful investments in all kinds of things. She said that if we played our cards right, maybe he would let us in on whatever he was doing, and certainly the very least we could expect would be four times our money back, because he was never interested in smaller returns. To tell the truth, it seemed to me like a good way out, if she could swing it. With four times the capital I'd have enough income to keep her the way she wanted to live. Stebber was staying aboard a yacht at the Cutlass Yacht Club, and when he left he asked us to stop by for drinks the next day.

"The yacht was absolutely huge, maybe a hundred feet long, some kind of a converted naval vessel, I think."

"Name and registry?"

"*The Buccaneer*, out of Tampa, Florida. He said friends had loaned it to him. That's when I met the other three men in the syndicate."

I had to slow Arthur down so that I could get the other three men nailed down, made into separate and distinct people in my mind.

G. Harrison Gisik. The old one. The sick one. Tall and frail and old and quiet. Bad color. Moved slowly and with apparent great effort. From Montreal.

Like Stebber, G. Harrison Gisik had no woman with him. The other two each had one. The other two were each local.

Crane Watts. Local attorney. Dark, good-looking, friendly. And unremarkable. He came equipped with wife. Vivian. Called Viv. Dark, sturdy, pretty—scored by sun and wind—an athlete. Tennis, sailing, golf, riding. She was, Arthur thought, a lady.

Boone Waxwell. The other local. From a local swamp, possibly. Sizable. Rough and hard and loud. An accent from way back in the mangroves. Black curly hair. Pale, pale blue eyes. Sallowy face. Boone Waxwell, known as Boo. And he came equipped with a non-wife, a redhead of exceptional mammary dimension. Dilly Starr. As loud as good ol' Boo, and, as soon as she got tight, slightly more obscene. And she got tight quickly.

"So okay," I said. "The four members of the syndicate. Stebber, Gisik, Crane, Waxwell. And Stebber the only one living aboard. A party, with Boo and his broad making all you nicer folks a little edgy. So?"

"We sat around and had drinks. There was a man aboard who made drinks and passed things, a Cuban maybe. Mario, they called him. When Calvin Stebber had a chance, when Dilly was in the head and Boo had gone ashore to buy cigars, he explained to us that sometimes, in deals, you weren't able to pick your associates on the basis of their social graces. 'Waxwell is the key to this project,' he said."

"How soon did they let you in on it?" I asked him.

"Not right away. It was about two weeks. Wilma kept after him, and she kept telling me that he said there wasn't a chance, that there wasn't really enough to go around as it was. But she didn't give up hope. Finally one morning he phoned me from the yacht and asked me to stop by alone. He was alone too. He said I had a very persistent wife. Persistence alone wouldn't have been enough. But this deal had dragged on so long that one of the principals had backed out. He said he felt obligated to offer it to other associates, but as long as I was on the scene and because he was so fond of Wilma, he had talked Mr. Gisik into agreeing to let me in, with certain stipulations."

"Is that when he explained the deal to you?"

"Just in broad outline, Trav, not in detail. We were in the main lounge, and he spread the maps out on the chart table. What he called the Kippler Tract was marked off and tinted. Sixty-one thousand acres. It was a strange shape, beginning north of Marco and getting wider over east of Everglades City, and going practically to the Dade County line. The syndicate was negotiating the option of it on a two-year basis at thirty dollars an acre against a purchase price of a hundred and twenty an acre. As soon as they had a firm option, he and another group were setting up a development corporation to buy the tract from the syndicate for three hundred and eighty dollars an acre. It meant that, after taking off syndicate overhead and operating expenses, the members would end up with five dollars for every dollar invested in the option—which would come to one million eight hundred and thirty thousand just for the option. He showed me the prospectus of what Deltona was doing at Marco Island, where the Collier interests along with Canadian money were planning a community of thirty thousand people. He said his staff had investigated every aspect of the plan, projected growth, water resources and so on, and if we could just get the option, it couldn't miss.

"Then he told me that he was in for seven hundred thousand, Gisik for four hundred thousand, a New York associate for five hundred thousand. The remaining two hundred and thirty thousand was represented by Crane Watts and Boo Waxwell, one hundred even by Watts. He said those small pieces were a nuisance, but it was essential to have a bright young lawyer on the scene, and that Boo Waxwell was the one with the close association with the Kippler heirs and able, if anybody was, to talk them into the deal. The New York associate had bowed out and there was five hundred thousand open. He said my five hundred thousand would become three million, a net return of one million nine after taxes, and my investment back.

"I said I'd like one hundred thousand worth, and he looked at me as if I was a dog on the street and he rolled up the maps saying he hadn't realized he was wasting his time as well as mine, and thanks for stopping by. Wilma was furious. She said I'd blown the whole thing. She said she'd talk to Calvin Stebber again and see if there was any chance at all of his taking me in on the basis of two hundred thousand. I said it didn't seem smart to gamble the whole thing, and she said it wasn't a gamble."

"Then he let you in."

"Reluctantly. I sent an airmail special to my brokerage house to sell at current market and airmail me a certified check for two hundred thousand. We met on the yacht. I signed the syndicate agreement, and it was witnessed and notarized. It gave me 9 and 15/100 shares in the syndicate."

"And you didn't have a lawyer of your own check it out."

"Travis . . . you can't understand how it was. They seemed so important. They were doing me a favor to let me in. Without Wilma, they would never have let me in. It was my chance to afford her. And from the moment I'd messed the deal up when I had the first chance, Wilma wouldn't let me near her. She'd hardly speak to me. She moved to a different bedroom in the beach house. And . . . they said it was a standard agreement. It was about six pages, single-spaced, on legal-size paper, and I had to sign four copies. Wilma stood with her hand on my shoulder as I signed, and gave me a big kiss when it was over."

"Stebber left soon after that?"

"A day or two later. About then Boo Waxwell began to hang around. He'd drop in without warning. It was obvious to me that he was attracted to Wilma. And she seemed too friendly toward him. When I complained to her, she said Calvin Stebber had said we had to be friendly to him. I tried to find out from Waxwell how things were going, but he'd just laugh and tell me not to sweat."

"When did they ask for more?"

"On August first I got a letter from Crane Watts. It referred to paragraph something, subparagraph something, and asked for my check in the amount of thirty-three thousand three hundred and thirty-three dollars and thirty-four cents at my earliest convenience. I was shocked. I dug out my copy and looked at the paragraph. It said that members of the syndicate could be assessed on the basis of participation to cover additional expenses. I went to see him right away. He wasn't as friendly as before. I hadn't seen his office before. It was north of the city on the Tamiami Trail, and it was just a cubicle in a roadside real-estate office. He acted as if I was taking up valuable time. He said that negotiations had progressed to the point where the Kippler heirs had decided they wanted thirty-five dollars' option money per acre, which meant the syndicate members had to come up with an additional three hundred and five thousand dollars, and simple mathematics showed that 9.15 percent of that was what he had requested by letter.

"I said that I didn't think I could make it, and that I guessed I'd just have to accept a proportional reduction of my share of the venture. He gave me a funny look and said he could understand my request, but if I had examined the subparagraph immediately following, certainly I'd realize it couldn't be done. I hadn't brought it. He got out an office copy and showed me the paragraph. It said, in effect, that if any participant failed to meet approved assessments, his share of the venture was forfeit, and would be divided among the remaining members in proportion to the interest they held at the time. He said it was perfectly legal, and the document had been signed, notarized and recorded.

"I went back to the beach house and it took me quite a while to get it through Wilma's head. Finally she understood that unless I came up with the additional money, we'd lose the two hundred thousand. She said it wasn't fair. She said she would phone Calvin Stebber and get it all straightened out. I don't know where she finally located him. She didn't want me in the room. She said I made her nervous. After she talked to him, she came out and told me that he'd said his hands were tied. If he made any special arrangement for me, the others would raise hell. She said she'd asked him if he'd buy my share out, but he said his cash position at the moment was too low even to consider it at that time. He recommended raising the money, saying it was undoubtedly the last assessment, and he was certain the deal would go through any day. Wilma was agitated for a long time, but finally we sat down and tried to work it all out. I had, at current market, about fifty-eight thousand left in just two stocks. Standard Oil of New Jersey and Continental Can. I was going to have to sell something anyway to meet current expenses, as we had five hundred in the bank and three thousand in unpaid bills. I left twenty thousand in stocks, paid Crane Watts and the bills and put three thousand in the checking account.

"On September first the option price went up to forty dollars an acre, and they asked for exactly the same amount again. By then I had four hundred in the bank and the twenty thousand. But I knew we *had* to raise it. I'd taken the agreement to another lawyer by then. He said it was ironclad, and only a damn fool would have signed such a thing. That was the time Wilma really cooperated. I thought that she was really beginning to understand the value of money. We sat down together and put everything into the pot. The rest of my stock, the car, my cameras, her furs and jewels. She went over to Miami and sold her stuff. We were just able to get it all together, with about four hundred dollars over. We paid off, and gave up the beach house and moved to a cheap motel room five or six blocks north of the intersection of Fifth Avenue and the Trail, the Citrus Blossom it was called. We cooked on a grill in the room.

"She kept asking what in the world we'd ever do if they asked for more. And she'd cry. It was her idea that I should make up a list of old friends who might come in on a good thing. She kept after me. I didn't want to do it. Finally I had a list of thirty-two reasonably successful people who might be willing to trust me. She rewrote my letter several times, making it sound like the greatest opportunity in the world, and we made up thirty-two originals on the motel typewriter and sent them off, asking for a minimum of one thousand each, and any amount up to ten thousand they might want to put in. Then we waited. There were sixteen replies. Eight of them said they were sorry. Eight sent money. Four of them sent a thousand each. Two sent five hundred. One sent a hundred dollars and one sent fifty dollars. Fifty-one hundred and fifty that we put in the joint account. No letters came in the next week. I sent signed notes to the eight friends as I had promised in the original letter. Then I got a call at the motel from Crane Watts. Calvin Stebber was staying at the Three Crowns in Sarasota, and he wanted us to come up and see him. Watts said it might be good news. Wilma had such a headache she said I better go alone. We had no car. I took a Trailways bus to Sarasota and got there at five o'clock, and at the desk they told me Mr. Stebber had checked out but he had left a message for a Mr. Wilkinson. I identified myself and they gave it to me. It merely said that it looked as if it might be another six months or so before the deal would go through, and probably before the time was up there would be another assessment, just a small one, for operating expenses. My share would probably not be over eight or ten thousand.

"I just sat there. I couldn't seem to think clearly. I took a bus back. I didn't get to the motel until a little after midnight. My key wouldn't work. I hammered on the door. Wilma didn't answer. I went to the office and the owner came to the door after I'd rung the night bell a long time. He said the lock had been changed and he hadn't been paid for two weeks, and he was holding onto my clothes and luggage until I paid up. I said there was some mistake, that my wife had paid him. He said she hadn't. I asked where she was, and he said that in the middle of the afternoon he'd seen her and some man carrying suitcases out to a car and driving away, and it made him think we were going to beat him out of the rent, so he had put my stuff in storage and changed the lock. He hadn't noticed the car particularly, just that it was a pale-colored car with Florida plates. She hadn't left any message for me. I walked around the rest of the night. When the bank opened I found out she'd cleaned out the account the previous morning, when I thought she'd gone grocery-shopping and came home with that headache."

Toward the end of it his voice had grown dull and listless. Chook stirred and sighed. A gust of the freshening breeze swung the boat, and some predatory night bird went by, honking with anguish.

"But you found her again, later on," I said, to get him started.

"I'm pretty tired."

Chook reached and patted him. "You go to bed, honey. Want me to fix you anything?"

"No thanks," he murmured. He got up with an effort and went below, saying goodnight to us as the screened door hissed shut.

"Poor wounded bastard," Chook said in a half whisper.

"It was a very thorough job. They got everything except the clothes he had on. They even milked old friendships."

"He hasn't much resistance yet. Or much spirit."

"Both of those are up to you."

"Sure, but try to make it a little easier on him, Trav, huh?"

"She took off in late September. It's late May, Chook. The trail is eight months cold. Where are they, and how much do they have left? And just how smart are they? One thing seems obvious. Wilma was the bird dog. Rope a live one and bring him to Naples. Remember, she got booted off that cruiser out of Savannah. I think there was one on there a little too shrewd for her, so she took a long look at what we had around here. And picked Arthur. Marriage can lull suspicion, and she used sex as a whip, and when she had him completely tamed and sufficiently worried about money, she contacted Stebber to tell him the pigeon was ready for the pot. It was a professional job, honey. They made him ache to get in on it. They made him so eager he'd have signed his own death warrant without reading it."

"Was it all legal?"

"I don't know. At least legal enough so that you'd probably have a three-year court fight to prove it wasn't, and then it would be only a civil action to recover the funds. He can't finance that. He couldn't finance two cups of coffee."

"Can you do anything?"

"I could try. If you can prop him up a little, I can try."

She stood up and came over and gave me a quick hug, a kiss beside the eye, and told me I was a treasure. Long after she left, the treasure lifted a few score aches and sorenesses and went to bed.

four

Late Sunday afternoon, up on the sun deck, I got the rest of the account from Arthur Wilkinson. Chook had him heavily oiled against additional burn. She was using the sun-deck rail as a torture rack, and I was pleased to turn so that I could not see her. I had taken so much punishment all day, it hurt to watch her. But over Arthur's recital I could sometimes hear her little gasps of effort, a creak of a joint strained to the maximum, and even that was mildly upsetting.

Arthur had gotten absolutely no satisfaction from the young lawyer. He had offered to sell Watts his syndicate shares for twenty-five thousand. Crane Watts said he wasn't interested. Next, in a kind of bemused desperation, he had tried to find Boone Waxwell, had learned that Waxwell had a place at Goodland on Marco Island. With the last of the small amount of money he had taken on the Sarasota trip, he had taken a bus to the turnoff to Marco, had hitched a ride to the island bridge, and then had walked to Goodland. At a gas station they told him how to find Waxwell's cottage. He got there at sunset. It was an isolated place at the end of a dirt road, more shack than cottage. A pale gray sedan was parked in the yard. Country music was so loud over the radio they didn't hear him on the porch, and when he looked through the screen he saw Wilma sprawled naked, tousled and asleep on a couch, and with a particular vividness he remembered her pale blond head resting on a souvenir pillow from Rock City. Boo Waxwell, in underwear shorts, sat slumped by the little radio, bottle on the floor between his feet, trying to play guitar chords along with the radio music. He saw Arthur and grinned at him, and came grinning to the screen door, opened it and pushed Arthur back, asking him what the hell he wanted. Arthur said he wanted to speak to Wilma. Waxwell said there wasn't much point in that on account of Wilma had gotten herself a temporary divorce, country-style.

Wilma had then appeared in the doorway beside Waxwell, light of the sunset against her face, a small and delicate face puffy with sleep and satiation, eyes drained empty by bed and bottle, nestling in soiled housecoat into the hard curve of Boo Waxwell's arm, looking out at him with a placid and almost bovine indifference, outlined in that end-of-day glow against the room darkening behind her.

He said it was strange how vivid the little things were, the precise design in faded blue of an eagle clutching a bomb, wavering as the muscles of Waxwell's upper arm shifted under the tattooed hide. The irregular deep rose shade of a suck-mark on the side of Wilma's delicate throat. And tiny rainbow glintings from the diamonds of the watch on her wrist—the watch she had claimed she sold in Miami.

Then he knew that it had all been lies, all of it, with nothing left to believe. Like an anguished, oversized child, he had rushed at Waxwell to destroy him, had landed no blow, had been pummeled back, wedged into a corner of porch post and railing, felt all the grinding blows into gut and groin and, over Waxwell's diligent shoulder, had seen the woman small in the doorway, hugging herself and watching, underlip sagging away from the even teeth. Then the railing gave way and he fell backward into the yard. He got up at once and slowly walked back the way he had come, hunched, both forearms clamped across his belly. He had the feeling that it was the only thing holding him together. His legs felt feathery, floating him along with no effort. Somewhere along the dirt road from the cottage he had fallen. He could not get up. He felt as if something was shifting and flowing inside him, the life moving warmly out of him. He would have slept, except for mosquitoes so thick he breathed them in, snuffing them from his nose, blowing them from his lips. He squirmed to a tree and pulled himself upright and went on, trying all the time to straighten himself up a little more. By the time he got to the bridge he was almost straight. There was a pink glow left in the west. He began the long walk back to the trail and for a time he was all right, and then he began falling. He said it was very strange. He would find himself way out by the center line, and then when he went over to the shoulder, a dark bush would seem to leap up at him and he would land heavily, gasping.

An old pickup truck stopped as he was trying to get up, and they came and put a bright flashlight beam on him, and from far away he heard a man and woman discussing in casual nasal tones how drunk he was and from what.

Summoning the last of energy, he said very distinctly, "I'm not drunk. I've been beaten."

"Whar you want we should take you, mister?" the man asked.

"I've got no place to go."

When things came back into focus, he was between the man and the woman on the front seat of the pickup. They took him home. East on the Trail to the turnoff to Everglades City, through Everglades and across the causeway to Chokoloskee Island, and over to the far shore, where these people named Sam and Leafy Dunning lived with their five kids in a trailer and attached cottage and prefab garage. He learned later they had spent a picnic day over on Marco Beach, and when they had picked him up, the five kids and the picnic gear and beach gear were in the bed of the old pickup.

Sam Dunning, in season, operated a charter boat out of the Rod and Gun Club over at Everglades City. It was out of season, and he was netting commercial with a partner, even shares, using an old bay skiff.

For three days Arthur could hobble about like an old man. All he could keep down were the soups she fixed for him. He slept a great deal, sensing it was in part an aftermath of the beating, and partly the emotional exhaustion of what had happened to him. He slept by day in a string hammock in the side yard, and by night on a mattress in the garage, waking often to find the children staring solemnly at him.

Leafy borrowed old clothes from a neighbor, big enough to fit him, while she washed and cleaned and mended what he'd been wearing. He thought that it was the fourth day before she asked him any questions at all, came out into the yard when he was walking around in the afternoon, feeling a little steadier on his feet. There were pieces of old car and pieces of marine engine in the yard, coarse grass half hiding them. He sat in the shade of the live oak tree on an overturned dinghy, and Leafy leaned against the trunk, arms folded, head tilted, a wiry, faded, bright-eyed woman in khaki pants and a blue work shirt, visibly pregnant.

"Who did beat on you, Arthur?"

"Boone Waxwell."

"All them Waxwells are pure mean as moccasin snakes. You got folks to go to someplace?"

"No."

"What kind of work you do mostly?"

"Well . . . in a store."

"Get yourself fired?"

"I quit."

"Clothes you had on were right good. Messed up, but good. And you talk nice, like you had good schooling, and you eat polite. Sam and me, we looked in your clothes, but you got no papers at all."

"There should be a wallet, with a license and cards and so on."

"And maybe a thousand dollars? If you had one, Arthur, you spilled it out falling all over that road. What we got to know, Sam and me, is if the police got some interest in you, because they can go hard on folks giving anybody house room."

"I'm not wanted for anything. Not for questioning or anything else."

She studied him and nodded to herself. "All right, then. What you got to have, I guess, is some kind of work to get some money to be on your way, and you can stay on here till you got it, paying me board when you start drawing pay. I guess there's some men got it in them to just roam. That's all right for kids, Arthur, but a grown man, it turns into something different, and without a steady woman you can grow old into a bum. You think on that some."

Sam had found him work on the maintenance crew readying the Rod and Gun Club for the season opening. He sent in the bureaucratic forms necessary to reassemble the paper affirmations of his identity, a replacement driver's license, a duplicate social security card. When he was laid off at the Club, he found a job as common labor on a development housing project over near the airport.

Sam Dunning partitioned a small corner of the garage, and Leafy fixed it up with a cot, chair, lamp and packing-box storage disguised by a piece of cotton drapery material thumbtacked to the top edge. He paid her twelve dollars a week for room and meals, after long earnest bargaining. She wanted ten. He wanted to give fifteen.

There on the sun deck, in a thoughtful voice, Arthur told us that it was a strange time in his life. He had never done manual labor. Until he acquired a few basic skills, the foreman came close to firing him several times for innate clumsiness. The skills pleased him—

rough carpentry without owl eyes surrounding the nail heads, learning when the cement mix was the right consistency, learning how to trundle a wheelbarrow along a springy plank. He said it was as if he had turned half of himself off, settling into routine, speaking when spoken to, sitting with the Dunning kids when Sam and Leafy went out on Saturday nights. On days off he helped Sam with boat maintenance, and sometimes crewed for him on a charter. He felt as if he was in hiding from every familiar thing, and, in the process, becoming someone else. He spent almost nothing and accumulated money, without counting it. He could lie on his cot and keep his mind empty. When it would veer toward Wilma or toward the lost money, he would catch it quickly, return it to the comforting grayness, feeling only a swoop of dizziness at the narrowness of the escape. Sometimes he awoke from sleep to sense erotic dream-memories of Wilma fading quickly, leaving only some of the tastes of her on his mouth, textures of her on his hands.

Leafy had her child in January, her third boy. His present to her was an automatic washing machine, a used one in good condition. He and Sam got it tied into the water line and wired the day before Sam brought her home. She was ecstatic. Her attitude toward him warmed perceptibly, and soon, in the most obvious ways, she began to try to make a match between Arthur and a seventeen-year-old girl down the road named Christine Canfield. Christine had run off to Crystal River with a stone-crab fisherman and had come home alone at Christmas, slightly pregnant. She was the youngest of three daughters, the older two married and moved away, one to Fort Myers, the other to Homestead. Christine was a placid, pleasant, slow-moving child who smiled often and laughed readily. She was husky, brown-blond, pretty in a childlike way.

"Nobody's in the place Cobb Canfield put up for his Lucy before Tommy got the good job in Fort Myers. You could fix it up right nice," Leafy said.

"Listen, she's only seventeen years old!"

"She's carrying proof she's a woman, and it hardly shows yet. She likes you fine, Arthur. She's healthy and she's a worker, and they're good stock. And she got the wild run out of her, and Cobb'd be so grateful to get it worked out, he'd do you good, believe me. Christine'd make you a good steady woman, not like some her age on the island."

"I should have told you before, Leafy. I'm married."

Her eyes narrowed as she accepted this new problem. "You plan on taking up again with your wife, Arthur?"

"No."

"She got cause to come looking for you?"

"No."

She nodded to herself. "The law doesn't pay it no mind unless somebody comes along to make a fuss. You just keep your mouth shut about that wife. Cobb is too proud to let her set up any common-law thing with you, so all you have to do is keep your mouth shut and marry her, and who does that hurt? Nobody, and does you both good, and gives that bush kitten she's carrying a daddy. Christine, she can make a garden bear the year round, and with a snitch hook she's good as you'll ever see, and it don't make for bad living having a young wife grateful to you."

Chook completed her series of tortures and came and sat by us, breathing deeply, brown body gleaming with perspiration, hair damp. "Surprised we ever saw you again, Arthur."

"Maybe you wouldn't have. I thought about it. She was as trusting and affectionate as a dog you bring in out of the rain. I could have stayed right there the rest of my life. But I kept remembering eight friends who had believed in me. Somehow that was worse than my money being gone, the way theirs went with it. I couldn't hide from that the rest of my life. And the pressure from Leafy and Christine merely made me more aware of it. So I told them I had something personal to take care of, and I'd be back as soon as I could, maybe in a few weeks. That was two months ago. I went back to Naples thinking I could try to recover enough just to pay back my friends."

He had gone to the Citrus Blossom Motel and found that his possessions had long since been sold, leaving a deficit of nine dollars on the room. He paid it out of the seven hundred he'd saved. He found another room. He bought the clothing I'd thrown in the dockside trash can. He went to see Crane Watts. Watts got the file out. There had been one additional assessment. When attempts to contact Mr. Wilkinson had failed, his participation was eliminated according to the terms of the agreement. As they had been unable to acquire an option of the Kippler Tract after lengthy negotiations, the syndicate had been dissolved and all monies remaining in the account had been divided on the basis of final participation. Arthur had demanded the addresses of Stebber and Gisik, and Watts had said that if he wished to write them, the letters could be sent to

Watts' office for forwarding. Arthur told Watts, with some heat, that he felt he had been defrauded, and he was damned well going to stir up all the trouble he could for them, and if they wanted to settle, to avoid investigation, he would sign an unconditional release in return for a ten-thousand-dollar refund. Watts, Arthur told us, looked unkempt in beard stubble, soiled sports shirt and bourbon breath at eleven o'clock that morning. Heartened by Watts' lack of assurance, Arthur had lied to him, saying that his attorney was preparing a detailed complaint to be filed with the Attorney General of the State of Florida, with a certified copy to the Bar Association. Watts, angered, said it was nonsense. There had been no illegality.

Arthur gave his temporary address, and said that somebody better get in touch with him, and damned soon, and bring the money.

He got a phone call at five that evening. A girl with a brisk voice said she was phoning at Crane Watts' request, to say that Calvin Stebber would like to have a drink with Mr. Wilkinson at the Piccadilly Pub on Fifth Avenue at six and discuss Mr. Wilkinson's problem.

Arthur was prompt. The taproom was luxurious and exceedingly dark. He sat on a stool at the padded bar, and when his eyes had adjusted, he searched the long bar and nearby tables and did not see Smiling Calvin. Soon a young woman appeared at his elbow, a trim and tailored girl, severe and pretty, who said she was Miss Brown, sent by Mr. Stebber who would be a little late, and would he come over to the table. He carried his drink over. Miss Brown parried his questions about Stebber with secretarial skill. She took microsips of a dry sherry. He was paged, went to the phone, found that it was a mistake. Someone wanted a Mr. Wilkerson, sales representative for Florida Builders Supply. Back at the table, suddenly the room tilted and he sprawled over against Miss Brown. She giggled at him. Then, in foggy memory, Miss Brown and a man in a red coat were helping him out to Miss Brown's car. He woke up in another county, in Palm County, in the drunk tank, without funds or identification, sick, weak and with a blinding headache. In the afternoon a sheriff's deputy, with a massive indifference, told him the score. He'd been picked up, stumbling around on a public beach, stinking and incoherent, brought in and booked as John Doe. They had a film strip of him. Standard procedure. He could plead guilty and take a thirty-day knock right now, or plead not guilty and go loose on two hundred dollars' bail and wait for circuit court which would be about forty days from now. And he could make one call.

He could have called Leafy. Or Christine. He elected the thirty days for himself. After four days of lockup, he signed up for road work as the lesser of two evils, swung the brush hook in lazy tempo under the tolerant guards, always turned his face away from the glitter of the tourist cars staring their way by, wore road-gang twill too small for him. Out of tension, or despair, or aftereffects of whatever Miss Brown had dolloped his drink with, or the greasy texture of the rice and beans, he could keep little on his stomach. Road-gang work gave him a fifty cents a day credit. He bought milk and white bread, and sometimes he kept it down and sometimes he didn't. Sun and effort dizzied him.

One bush to be chopped was Stebber, and the next was Watts, then G. Harrison Gisik, Boo Waxwell, Wilma, Miss Brown. As he began to fit the issue work clothes, in afternoon delirium he recalled what Chook had told him about me. And he knew that he'd be a fool to try anything else on his own. Maybe a fool to even ask for help. They gave him back his clothes and let him go, with a dollar thirty left from his work credit. He tried to hitch his way across the peninsula, but something was wrong, somehow, with the way he looked. They would slow down, some of them, then change their minds, roar on into the pavement mirages. Sudden rains soaked him. He bought sandwiches, had to abandon them after the first bite. He got a few short rides, found dry corners to sleep in, remembered very little of the last few days of it, then had the vivid memory of coming aboard *The Busted Flush*, and the deck swinging up at him, slapping him in the face as he tried to fend it off . . .

"Just enough to pay my friends back," he said. "I understand you take the expenses off the top and divide what else you can recover. If it wasn't for them, I'd give up, Trav. Maybe it's hopeless anyway. I had all that money, and now it's all unreal, as if I never really had it. My great-grandfather barged a load of fabrics, furniture and hardware up from New York, rented a warehouse and sold the goods for enough to pay off the loan on the first load and buy a second free and clear. That's where the money started. Eighteen fifty-one. By nineteen hundred there was a great deal of money. My father wasn't good with money. It dwindled. I thought I was better. I thought I could make it grow. God!"

Chook reached and gave his oily shoulder an affectionate, comforting pat. "Some very smart people get terribly cheated, Arthur. And usually it happens far from home."

"I just . . . don't want to go back there," he said. "I dream that

I'm there and I'm dead. I see myself dead on the sidewalk and people walking around me as they go by, nodding as if they knew all along."

Chook took my wrist and turned it to look at my watch. "Time for you to choke down another eggnog, Arthur old buddy. Nicely spiked to give you a big appetite for dinner."

After she left, Arthur said, "I guess the biggest part of the expense is feeding me."

I laughed more than it was worth. After all, it was his first mild joke. Sign of improvement. Other signs too. Stubble shaved clean. Hair neatly cropped by Chookie McCall, an unexpected talent. Sun burning away the pasty look. Pounds coming back. And Chook had him on some mild exercises, just enough to begin to restore muscle tone.

She came up with his eggnog and a list. Perishables were dwindling. Eggs, milk, butter, lettuce. Candle Key had a Handy-Dandy-Open-Nights-and-Sunday. The wind would make easy sailing in the dink. The little limey outboard runs like a gold watch. My shoulders felt as if they were webbed with hot wires. So, with an excess of character, I left sail and motor behind, climbed down into the dink, and headed across the two miles of bay, rowing with the miniature oars.

Coming back against the wind was almost as much fun as migraine, and it didn't help a bit to have the wind die the instant I clambered aboard and made the dinghy fast. Chook came and took the groceries. As she did so, and with a dull red sun sitting on the horizon line, we were invaded by an advance guard of seven billion salt-marsh mosquitoes. They are a strange kind. They don't bite, but some ancestral memory tells them they should get in position to bite. They are large and black and fly slowly, and when you wipe a dozen off your arm, they leave black streaks like soot. They are inept at the mosquito profession, but come in such numbers they can rattle the most easygoing disposition. As you breathe them in, you find yourself asking in desperation—But what do they *want?*

Chook and Arthur had showered and changed, and it was immediately obvious they had somehow made each other totally unhappy. Arthur was leaden and remote. Chook was brisk and remote. All they would exchange were the most formal politenesses. I showered amid the fading scent of Chook's perfumed soap, in that absurd mirrored stall, big enough, almost, for a Volkswagen garage. It is a grotesque waste of space in a fifty-two-foot houseboat, even with a twenty-one-foot beam, almost as much of a waste as the semisunken pale blue tub, seven feet long and four feet wide. I imagine that the elderly Palm Beach party who lost the vessel to me over the poker table needed such visual stimulations to do right by his Brazilian mistress.

In response to the unexplained drearies of my boat guests I had a vicious attack of the jollies, regaling them with anecdote, absurdity and one-sided repartee, much like a solitary game of handball. Once in a while they would pull their lips away from their teeth and go heh-heh-heh. And then politely pass each other something that was within easy reach of everyone in the small booth adjoining the galley.

I judged it a favorable development. People were choosing up new sides. Chook and I had been united in caring for the sick. Now any relationship, even a rancorous one, which shut me out was proof that he was not entirely defeated. She had to pump some spirit into him or my chances of any salvage were frail indeed. And maybe this was a start.

five

On Monday we pulled the hooks and droned in stately fashion down to a new anchorage off Long Key, charging the batteries and getting beyond the range of the sooty mosquitoes which were restricting us to the below-decks areas. During the swimming that followed, I was heartened by a small triumph. The long contest was around a distant marker and back to the boarding ladder. Halfway back she pulled even and moved a half length ahead. I knew from the pain in my side that in another hundred yards I would begin to wallow and roll and lose the stroke. Suddenly the reserves were there—missing so long it was like welcoming an old friend. It was as if a third lung had suddenly opened up. I settled into it until I was certain, then upped the tempo and went on by her in a long sprint finish, was clinging to the ladder when she arrived, and feeling less like a beached blowfish than on other days.

"Well, now!" she gasped, looking startled and owlish.

"You had to let me win one of these."

"The hell I did! I was busting a gut trying to keep up." She snapped her head back and gave me the first grin I had seen since rowing back with the groceries.

"Come with me," I said, and swam slowly away from the *Flush*, rolled and floated and, looking back, saw Arthur busy at the chore I had given him, putting new lacing in a section of the nylon fabric that is lashed to the rail around the sun deck. Chook made a surface dive and came up beside me, and blew like a porpoise.

"I could put you two in the shower stall," I said. "What you do, you each take a corner of a silk handkerchief in your teeth, left hands tied behind you, six-inch knife in the right hand."

"Skip it, McGee."

"It's just that the way you two go around chuckling and laughing, it gets on my nerves. I keep wondering what could make two people so hilarious."

"Maybe you could guess. I'm a big girl. I'm a big healthy girl. And I'm leading a very healthy life. I'm sleeping with him, in that half-acre bed of yours. And that's the precise word, McGee. Sleeping. Just that. So I thought maybe he was well enough, and it was going to take you a long time to get back with the groceries. I showered first, and got into a sexy little thing made of black cobwebs, and dabbed a little Tigress here and there and yonder, and spread myself out like picturesque, with my girlish heart going bump bump bump. It's not as if it had never happened with him before. And the son of a bitch acted as if I'd solicited him on a street corner. He was offended, for God's sake. He made me feel sleazy."

"Maybe you're putting the wrong interpretation on it."

"There comes a point when I stop being understanding, friend. And that was it. It's his move. And unless he makes one, there's an invisible wall right down the middle of that bed. It's made of ice cubes. All he'll get from me is some practical nursing care."

In the night I was awakened by the creak of the lines as the *Flush* was trying to go around on the tide change, swinging further each time until pushed back by the breeze. I always rig two bow hooks in such a way that she shifts her weight from hook to hook when she changes end for end. As this was the first night at the new anchorage, I wanted to check and see that she wasn't working loose with all the swinging, and that she would swing the way I had guessed. As a rule of thumb they will always swing with the bow toward the nearest shallows. But the wind can make a difference, and there can be a tide current you didn't read.

So, as the easiest way out, I went forward and up through the hatch. I pulled the line she was still on and found it firm. I have a reflector plate under my riding light, and it keeps the decks in relative shadow, but just enough gets past the plate so you can check lines when your eyes are used to the darkness. From the relation of the way she was swinging to the lights along the keys, I could tell she was going to go around the right way. I decided to wait until she was around and then check the other anchor line. I had a lot of scope, big Danforths and a good bottom, so it was a thousand to one I was fine. But there are a lot of dead sailors who took things for granted. On a boat things go bad in sets of threes. When you pull a hook and then go hustle to get the wheels turning, something will short out on you so that you go drifting, dead in the water. And that is the time when, without lights, you drift right out into the ship channel, see running lights a city block apart coming down at you, run to get your big flashlight, fumble it and drop it over the side. A boat is something that never has just one thing wrong with it.

As I sat on the corner of the bow hatch, waiting, I felt a little faraway thud. I felt it through the soles of my bare feet, wondered what the hell, then realized it was the dink tied astern, swinging in the wind, nudging mother. I padded back along the side deck, put another line on its little stern cleat and snubbed it up against the two fenders hanging over the transom. I'd gone aft on the port side, and went forward on the starboard side, and came suddenly on a pale ghost that nearly made me leap over the rail. It startled her too, and then she made a miserable snorting sound and came into my arms for comfort. She had on a skimpy white hip-length nightie. She clung, snorting again. Her body heat was high, her breath hot and humid. She had that flat-sweet unmistakable scent of female sexual effort. Her nipples were hard as little pebbles against my bare chest.

"Oh God, God!" she whispered. "He can't do it. He tried and tried and tried. I helped and helped and helped. Then he was no damn good at all, and he started crying, and I had to get out of there. Oh God, Trav, my nerves are shot, shot, shot."

"Steady, girl."

"That damn bitch might just as well have cut them off," she said, and sobbed again, and got the hiccups. She hicked and gasped and ground her face into my throat, held me in an iron grip, and, with each hick, gave me a little thud with those powerful hips. I was not unresponsive. Hell, a bronze statue three thousand years old would have made its reaction as evident to her as I did.

"God, darling—hic—be a dear—hic—and take me off—hic—the hook."

"And you know it wouldn't stop there, and wouldn't that do Arthur a lot of good, though? Wouldn't that brighten his hours, improve his morale?"

"But you—hic—want me, darling. Please—hic—"

"Okay, Chook."

"Bless you!" she said. "I love you so. Hic."

"I'll help you out," I said. I bent to get one arm behind her knees. She went loose, thinking, perhaps, I was going to tote her topsides to the sun pads on the upper deck. I swung her up and out and over the rail and let go.

Shriek. Ka-swash. Then some coughing, and then some strident and bitter abuse from the dark water. I strolled back to the boarding ladder, bent and gave her a hand, hauled her up onto the after deck and told her to stay right there. I brought her a towel and a terry robe.

"After *all!*" she said in a cold and level voice. "Really!"

"Your language is improving."

As she belted the robe, she said, "You're all bastard, aren't you?"

"Listen. Did it or did it not cure the hiccups?"

Suddenly we were laughing, and in laughing we were friends again, and went topsides to the big padded bench at the topside controls. I went and checked the anchor line, came back with cigarettes for her, a pipe for me. The running light dimmed the stars, but not entirely.

"You were absolutely right, of course," she said. "And let me believe, damn it, that it cost you something too."

"More than I care to think about."

"So maybe failure finished him off. We don't know that. But I damn well do know that I would have moved into your bed for the duration of the voyage, captain, and that certainly would finish him."

"Like that little knife they use when the matador hasn't been able to kill with the sword. Some stocky little guy, like a butcher, moves in and gives it to old bull right behind the ears. And he goes down as if he'd been dropped off a roof."

"Then those damned mules pull him all the way around the ring instead of right on offstage. Why do they have to do that?"

"A tribute, maybe."

"Trav, how in the *world* am I going to act toward Arthur tomorrow? He felt so . . . wretched about everything."

"Open and obvious affection, Chook. All the little pats and smiles and kisses. Little hugs. Just as if it *had* worked."

"But why in the world should . . . Oh, I think I get it. No penalty for failure. Encouragement to try again. No social disgrace. But if it ends up the same way, I don't think I can endure it. Oh hell, I suppose I can always run out and jump overboard, screaming."

"And hiccuping."

"Honestly, and you have to believe me, I never got in such a state before in my life. It's something about a boat, I guess. And the phase of the moon. And Frankie gone for years. And feeling . . . so *damned* sorry for Arthur. And, of course, being so bloody awful healthy. Poor lamb. He was *so* apologetic and crushed. Well, thanks for practically nothing, McGee. Night."

I made the pipe last. I sat up there, bare feet braced on the wheel spokes, and wondered why Chook should bring out the martyr in me. Twice now, with her, I had gone so noble it semisickened me. And such a glorious package. But was she? Maybe she was a little too much. She created a certain awe in the standard-issue male. I had noted that fewer passes were made at her than she had a right to expect. All that robust, glowing, powerful vitality might actually have given me a subconscious block, a hidden suspicion that I might, in the long run, be unable to cope—an alarming prospect for male vanity, of which I was certain I had my share. When these dreary suspicions threatened to spoil a pretty night, I went forward, back down through the hatch and into my spartan bed.

Too restless to go to sleep quickly, I found another reason, perhaps just as ego-damaging, why I could resist intimate involvement with Chook. Except for her inexplicable bondage to Frank Durkin, she was uncommonly staunch and stable. Though shrewd, diligent and perceptive, she did not have any of those inner contradictions, complexities and vulnerabilities that are born of self-doubt. She was all of a piece, confident of her total survival, and—in that sense—utterly wholesome. Maybe I could be stirred only by the wounded ducklings. Maybe I could respond best to the cripples I cut out of the flock, the ones who, by contrast, could give me a sense of inner strength and unity. And a whole woman might, conversely, serve to give me a less fictional image of the inner McGee, showing the fracture lines and the clumsy ways I had pasted myself back together, and too many tricks with mirrors. When you have learned control over your own dear little neuroses, you can have empathy with the ones who are shaking themselves apart, and get your jollies out of teaching them how to dampen the vibrations. But a sound and solid one can only make you aware of how frequently precarious your acquired controls can become. It could be that this wariness of the sound ones and the true ones was one of the hidden reasons why I had to be a roamer, a salvage expert, a gregarious loner, a seeker of a thousand tarnished grails, finding too many excuses for all the dragons along the way.

This kind of emotional introspection, this self-fondling, is strange medicine. A little bit, now and again, can accrete a small quotient of wisdom. But, like nitroglycerin for the weakened heart, too much of it at one time can blow your head off.

Maybe it was all a lot simpler than that. Physical attraction was strong, but without emotional attraction. Once begun, we would go the long route, and at the end of it there would be absolutely nothing, very probably not even the friendship. And that was good enough to warrant a knowing abstention.

Tuesday Chook seemed to be overdoing the whole routine. The response was perhaps as noticeable as she would have gotten from petting a dead dog. Pats and squeezes, kind words and quick kisses, and special little treats from the galley. Arthur seemed too deep in humble apathy to notice or care. But from time to time I saw him stare toward her with a mildly baffled expression. She laid it on so thick, I felt more comfortable at long range. I gave myself the most rigorous day yet. There is one which can match anything they thought up during the Inquisition.

Sit. Hook feet under something solid. Lace fingers behind neck. Lean slowly back until shoulders are approximately ten to twelve inches off the deck. Stop right there. And stay there until the sweat bursts and every muscle is jumping, and then stay there a little while longer, then come slowly, slowly back up to the sitting position. Another: one-legged deep knee bends, taking about two seconds to go down and two seconds to come back up. Continue until body weight seems to approximate seventeen tons.

Alternate ten-minute rest periods with fifty-minute workouts all day long, then soak in a tub so hot you have to get into it by inches, then eat twenty ounces of rare beef, a peck of salad, stretch out topsides and look at the stars, and blunder off to bed.

I was awake for a little while in the first gray of the false dawn and heard the lovers. It was a sound so faint it was not actually a sound, more a rhythm sensed. It is a bed rhythm, strangely akin to a heartbeat, though softer. Whum-fa, whum-fa, whum-fa. As eternal, clinical, inevitable as the slow gallop of the heart itself. And as basic to the race, reaching from percale back to the pallet of dried grasses in the cave corner. A sound clean and true, a nastiness only to all those unfortunates who carry through their narrow days their own little hidden pools of nastiness, ready to spill it upon anything so real it frightens them.

Heard even in its most shoddy context, as through the papery walls of a convention motel, this life-beat could be diminished not to evil but to a kind of pathos, because then it was an attempt at affirmation between strangers, a way to try to stop all the clocks, a way to try to say: I live.

The billions upon billions of lives which have come and gone, and that small fraction now walking the world, came of this life-pulse, and to deny it dignity would be to diminish the blood and need and purpose of the race, make us all bawdy clowns, thrusting and bumping away in a ludicrous heat, shamed by our own instinct.

Hearing them, I felt placidly avuncular. Enjoy. Find that one time that has no shred of self or loneliness. Seal it so that from now on McGee is the third wheel, all interrelationships solidly structured from now on. Celebrate the nowness of it, and subside into affections.

The almost inaudible pulse hastened, then slowed, and ended. I heard the far-off drone of a marine engine, fading into the distance, a commercial fisherman perhaps, heading for the grounds off East Cape. Ripples slapped the hull. What assurances, gratitudes, immediate memories were the lovers entwined whispering to each other? Did they listen to the slowing of their hearts? Were there little catches at the end of those long breaths that were deep as sighs? Was it beautiful for you too, darling?

When I awoke again it was with the sense of total well-being I had been aiming for. The pounds were gone. A few slight areas of muscle soreness were not enough to diminish that good feeling of resiliency and vitality.

The body, once you are old enough to stop taking it for granted, becomes like a separate entity. The way it will endure neglect makes you feel guilty. Having survived trauma, and being still willing to carry you around after healing itself, it deserves better. Cherishing it and toughening it are acts of appeasement for past omissions.

In my line of work, neglect was especially asinine. Like being a front-line type with a rusty rifle, or a neurosurgeon with a hangover. One half-step, or one-twentieth-of-a-second lag in reaction time can make the difference. Any violent necessity is usually the result of something having gone wrong, a probable error of judgment. But the probability is always there.

Now, with just minor versions of the total torture of the days past, it would hold its edge.

My shower serenade did not stir the drowsy lovers, nor did the banging of pots. After breakfast I broke out a small spinning rod, rigged it with a yellow jig, installed sail, rudder and centerboard on the dinghy, and went off to circle the edge of distant grass flats. I released a couple of small jacks, one weakfish, and then, just as I was coming about, hooked into a stranger, a stray pompano who didn't belong in that kind of area. He ran better than three pounds, and I had him split, buttered, and on foil under the broiler as the lovers came fumbling, blinking and yawning out into the daylight. Call the pompano a sacrifice on a special altar. They claimed nothing had ever tasted as good. They finished him, every crumb, while I stood smirking like a kindly old aunt in a TV commercial.

All her actions toward him that Wednesday were precisely as on the day before. But without the Charge Nurse flavor. She had a doe-eyed glow, a lazy smugness. The gestures were returned in kind. I was the outsider. Arthur had his chin up, for a change. And he risked a few of his mild, strained jokes—rewarded with girlish howls of glee. I tried to keep out of their way. But at times *The Busted Flush* can seem small. In midafternoon I invented an errand at Long Key, a replacement filter, and with an identical expression of repressed anticipation on their faces, they waved to me as I went putting off toward Long Key.

Friday morning I put the essential question to him. I brought the anchors in, and he helped me spread the lines at the bow to dry before stowing them. In the early gray, so silent and eerie it gave one a tendency to whisper, the *Flush* floated dead in the water at the high-tide change, with the mist magnifying the sun image in the east to a gigantic ball, suitable to a science-fiction movie.

Arthur was beginning to look fit. Scrawny, but fit.

"What about it?" I asked him.

Squatting, he stared at me. "About it?"

"You ready to help me go after the loot, Arthur?"

He stood up. "I . . . guess I'm ready now."

I made an appraisal. He wasn't the same fellow who'd been a part of our ever-changing group better than a year ago. He looked almost the same, though thinner. I guess it was the eyes. Before, he had been able to watch you with the same pleasant fixity of stare of a family beagle. Now the eyes came up, then fell away, came back, shifted away.

"Listen, Arthur. The attitude is not anger, nor indignation, nor hate. No heroics. No punishments. We go in cold and shrewd and savvy. And you stay out of contact. You are my intelligence officer. I bring you pieces of it and we work out how they fit. But if I need you for any contact, I want to know you'll do it exactly as I say, whether you understand or agree. I want to know you won't let it shake you up."

"Trav . . . all I can do is promise to try."

"How do you feel about it?"

He tried to smile. "Butterflies."

"You can have butterflies, but you've got to have an operational attitude too. We're going to steal meat out from under the tiger's paw. We'll divert the animal's attention. We'll keep Chook out of it. And it starts right now."

He moistened his lips and swallowed. "Where are we going?"

"On a hunch, I'm going to start at Marco."

six

I took the *Flush* up to Flamingo, through Whitewater Bay, and out the mouth of the Shark River into the Gulf of Mexico. The Gulf was flat calm, so I took her about six miles out, figured the course to take me just outside Cape Romano, and set the reliable old Metal Marine. It began turning the wheel back and forth in fussy little movements of a few inches at a time. I checked it to see that it was holding. Sun came hot through the slight overcast, and in the greasy calm the only breeze was from our stodgy cruising speed. At noon I got the marine forecast from the Miami Marine Operator. Fair for the next twenty-four hours, winds slight and variable. A tropical disturbance centered below the Yucatan Straits, moving north-northeast at five to six knots.

Chookie brought lunch topside. They both seemed subdued. I realized uncertainty was bothering them. You have to have an instinct about how much briefing the troops should have. Too little is as unsettling as too much.

"What we're up against," I said, "is the big con. It's a quasi-legal variation of one of the little cons, the finding the wallet routine."

"What does that mean?" Chook asked.

"Once they select a mark, the operator drops a wallet, a fat one, where he'll spot it. The accomplice gets to it a fraction of a second ahead of the mark. They move into an alley. The accomplice counts the money, and the mark sees that there is, say nine hundred dollars. Then the operator moves in, a very plausible guy. An acquaintance of the accomplice, but the accomplice very respectfully calls him mister. Says he found it, alone. Operator takes the mark's side, proclaims they both found it and should share equally. Accomplice agrees, grudgingly. No name or identification in wallet. Operator says the honest thing to do is watch the want ads for one week. If nothing appears, then it is theirs to split. Gets a brown envelope, seals wallet inside with tape, accomplice and mark initial the tape as a form of seal. Okay, who is to hold it? After argument, it is decided the mark can hold it, provided he gives the accomplice three hundred dollars to hang onto as a proof of good faith. Operator holds the envelope until mark can return with the three hundred. Addresses are exchanged. Mark watches want ads for a week, gleefully tears envelope open, finds ratty old wallet stuffed with newspaper. The switch was made while they waited for him to come back with the three hundred. Or, when the mark is smarter, they make the switch right in front of him, let him carry the envelope, and go to the bank with him. These things always depend on human greed. This option con, Arthur, was a more sophisticated version of the same tired old thing, with Stebber as the operator, Wilma as the roper, Gisik, Waxwell and Watts as accomplices. When they make a hit, they go to ground. But as this one was quasi-legal, some of them had to stay out in the open—Watts and Waxwell. I suspect they got small pieces. So what we have to do is put out some bait."

Chook scowled at me. "To get Stebber and Gisik out in the open? You don't look like a mark, Trav. And if you run into Wilma, she knows you."

"I have somebody all roped, and I need some competent help to pick him clean."

"Who?" Arthur asked blankly.

"We'll have to invent him. But if I have to produce him, we should have somebody in mind, somebody who could run over here at short notice and put on a good act."

"And you do have somebody in mind, don't you?" Chook said accusingly.

"You ever run into Roger Bliss?"

She didn't know him. I told them about Roger. Except for an unfortunate taint of honesty, he could have become one of the great confidence men of our times. After a fine-arts education, he had gone to Italy to study and paint. There he had gotten in with the movie crowd and had been put to work doing character bits. He was a natural mimic. He'd learned he'd never make it as a painter. And, in time, the movie thing bored him. Now he owned a small expensive sales gallery in Hollywood, Florida, had nurtured a profitable list of art patrons, lived well, was often restless, particularly during the slack season, and had helped me a couple of times in the past, when I needed someone who could be, on request, a convincing psychiatrist, Air Force colonel, college dean or Oklahoma wildcatter. He had a wicked ability of being absolutely plausible, down to the smallest mannerism and detail of dress. I would make sure he was available, just in case. And think up a cover story which would make Stebber and company salivate freely.

So we cruised up the flank of the Everglades, past the misted shoreline of the Ten Thousand Mangrove Islands. It is dark, strange country, one of the few places left which man has not been able to mess up. The great river of grass starts up near Okeechobee, the widest shallowest river on the continent, and flows south. The hammocks of oak, cabbage palm, fifty other varieties of trees are the quaking islands in the thirty-mile width of the saw-grass river. On the broad moist banks are the silent stands of cypress. Where the tides seep up into the river, at the northernmost limits of brackishness, the dwarf mangrove starts. The Ten Thousand Islands comprise the vast steamy tidal basin where the river enters the Gulf and Florida Bay.

Man, forever stubborn, has made but a few small dents in this eternal silence. Perimeter outposts—Everglades, Marco, Flamingo, Chokoloskee. But he has never thrived. There is rich soil there, rich enough so that a hundred years ago tomatoes grown in the Everglades were bringing twenty-four dollars a case in New York during the winter season. But hurricanes thrash through, pushing salt tides that take years to leach out of the poisoned soil. The fevers, the bugs, the storms, the isolation—these things have always broken the spirits of all but the toughest, the kind of human who can describe the peak of the mosquito season as the time when you can swing a one-pint jar and catch a quart of them.

The tough Calusa Indians were there at the time Christ was born, building storm-shelter islands out of the shells of the oysters and clams they ate, leaving a staggering enough tonnage of shells by the time the Spaniards totally eliminated them that miles and miles of the first rude roads into the edges of the Glades were paved with those shells.

This is the land of the great enduring myth of the Seminole. They were a ragtag ethnic jumble, driven all the way down from Georgia and the Carolinas, until finally after the forced resettlement of most of them in the southwest, there were not two hundred and fifty left —scattered, hiding, demoralized—not worth any further military effort. For fifty years their numbers remained about the same. Then slowly they reestablished a new culture composed of remembered fragments of many old ones, speaking pidgin versions of old tongues. They had even begun to acquire a kind of plaintive dignity, but then the white man pushed the Tamiami Trail across the Glades from Naples to Miami, eliminating them as a tribe, turning them into roadside merchants of such a vast gypsy cynicism that of all the artifacts they manufacture and sell to the tourists—not one bears any relation to their customs, habits, or prior way of life. They are the carnival Indians, degraded by commerce, curious heirs to the big colorful lie that they were never whipped, never made a truce. They are the comedy Indians who, never having used tom-toms in their history, never having used the tomahawks or bows and arrows like the Plains Indians, now make vast quantities of each and sell them to people from Ohio.

Now, of course, having failed in every attempt to subdue the Glades by frontal attack, we are slowly killing it off by tapping the River of Grass. In the questionable name of progress, the state in its vast wisdom lets every two-bit developer divert the flow into the draglined canals that give him "waterfront" lots to sell. As far north as Corkscrew Swamp, virgin stands of ancient bald cypress are dying. All the area north of Copeland has been logged out, and will never come back. As the Glades dry, the big fires come with increasing frequency. The ecology is changing, with egret colonies dwindling, mullet getting scarce, mangrove dying of new diseases born of dryness.

But it will take a long time to kill it. And years from now foolish men will still be able to kill themselves off within miles of help, hopelessly lost among islands which all look exactly alike. It is a black land, and like every wilderness in the world, it punishes quickly when a mistake is made, quickly and with a casual, savage indifference.

I studied the chart and picked a spot. I went beyond Marco Pass to a wide pass named Hurricane Pass. The channel was easy to read from the topside controls. The *Flush* draws four feet and is heavily skegged to protect the shafts and wheels. Roy Cannon Island, deserted, lies just inside the pass. It was low tide as we came in just before sunset. The pass is so wide, Roy Cannon has a sand beach. I edged a little north to get the protection of the headland which forms the north edge of the pass. At dead slow I ran the bow into the beach sand. With Chook and Arthur helping, we put out all four anchors, the two bow ones well up on the beach, wedged into the skeletal whiteness of mangrove killed by the sand which had built up, probably after Hurricane Donna had widened the pass. I carried the stern hooks out into water neck deep, wedged them in, stomped them firm. She would rest well there, lifting free with the incoming tide, settling back at the low. I'd topped off the fuel and water at Flamingo. We swam as the sun went down, and then clouds of mosquitoes, shrill with hunger, drove us belowdecks to break out the bombs and drop the ones that had come in with us. It was such a hot and airless night, I started the generator and put the air conditioning on. After dinner, over coffee, I took Arthur through the best physical descriptions of the four men that he could manage, particularly Stebber and Gisik. I wanted to be certain to know them if the names were changed.

Saturday morning early I saddled up the dinghy and, taking Chook with me, droned south inside the islands to Marco Village. We achieved invisibility. There is an easy way to do it along that coast. I wore khaki pants, a white T-shirt, a baseball hat with a long bill, dark glasses. She wore white denim stretch pants, a blue halter, dark glasses, and a little pot-shaped straw hat some female had left aboard, embroidered in red yarn across the front—Drink Up. We brought along a tackle box, two rods and a red beer cooler.

Marco Village saddened me. The bulldozers and draglines had gotten to it since my last visit. The ratty picturesque old dock was gone, as was the ancient general store and a lot of the old weather-beaten two-story houses which had looked as though they had been moved down from Indiana farmland. They had endured a half century of hurricanes, but little marks on a developer's plat had erased them so completely there was not even a trace of the old foundations.

But even the scurry of multimillion-dollar development slows to a sleepy pace in the island heat of late May. Loafers identified us instantly by type as we tied up and clambered out of the dinghy, and from then on their total bemused attention was on the fruitful flexible weight encased in the white stretch denim, with Chook quite comfortably aware of admiration and speculation. I asked my question, and we got one bad lead and then a better one, and finally found a sallow, thoughtful young man who took us to where his boat sat lashed to a trailer. Sixteen foot, heavy-duty fiberglass hull, with a forty-horse Evinrude bolted to the reinforced transom. Twin tanks. All required gear.

"I don't know about a week," he said. "Figured on using it some myself. I'd have to get"—he wiped his mouth, stared into the distance—"a hundred dollars, mister?"

"Seventy-five. I buy gas."

"I got fourteen hundred dollars in it, mister."

"Seventy-five right now, and if I only keep it three days, it's still seventy-five."

He made a responsible show of studying my driver's license, giving sidelong glances at Chook's scanty halter, and got very helpful and cheery when he had the seventy-five in hand, describing places where we could hook into big snook and baby tarpon. He put it in the water for us. Boldly lettered on the white fiberglass, in pink, and for some obscure reason in Old English calligraphy, was the name *Ratfink.* We took off sedately, towing the dinghy astern, dock loafers watching us out of sight. Arthur was waiting on the beach when we returned. Without the burdens of Chook and the dinghy, I took *Ratfink* out into open water and found I had made a good guess on the hull design. It was very fast and stable, and when I came smashing back through my own wake, I found it was a dry boat.

Another can of gas aboard would give it all the high-speed range I'd need. It had one of the new control rigs, shift and throttle on the same handy lever. The cable control gave it a quick steering ratio. I taped a piece of white cloth over the too-memorable name, and with some black electrician's tape I made an alteration in the registration number, turning a six into an eight and a one into a seven. It would stand inspection from ten feet away.

I changed to slacks and a sports shirt, stowed a light jacket and tie in the locker under the forward deck, told them to be good kids and took off up the inside route to Naples, an estimated twelve miles away, less than a half hour in my jazzy craft.

I found an adequate little marina just short of the highway bridge on the southeast side of Naples. I filled the tanks, bought an extra five-gallon can, had it filled with the right gas and oil mix and stowed it aboard. I said I might be leaving it there off and on for a week. The man said a dollar a day. And how about leaving a car here, I asked, when I'm out in the boat? Right over there next to the building, where that pickup is, it'll be okay there, no charge. I paid him a week on the dockage, and after he had shown me where to put it and wandered away, I tied it up in such a way that though the lines were firm, I could free them with one yank, shove off bow first, hit the starter button and be on my way. This was one of the elemental precautions. Never go in until you are damned well sure how you are going to get out. There are few roads in the Glades country, but more waterways than have ever been counted. With the jacket over my arm, I went up to Route 41 and walked across the highway bridge and down the other side of the bayou to the Fish House Restaurant. It was clean and quiet. The decor was seashells stuck into cement on the pillars, beams and ceiling. Tourists had pried out a lot of the ones within reach. I found they served a clam chowder with character. It would cure debility, angry the blood and turn a girl scout troop into a baritone choir.

I didn't bother phoning Crane Watts' office. His residence was on Clematis Drive. A maid announced it as The Watts Resydense and told me, "They's at the Club." And when I asked if it was the Cutlass Yacht Club, she said, "Nome, they plays tennis at the Royal Palm Bath Club."

I looked up car rentals, phoned one and was told they couldn't deliver. Just one man on duty. I took a cab to the place the other side of town. I signed up for a dark green Chev, four door, with air conditioning. The attendant told me to go about another mile north and then look for the Bath Club sign on a road to the left, turn and go about a half mile. I couldn't miss it. I didn't.

I found a parking place in the lot. The huge pool, behind woven fencing, was a gabbling, shrieking, belly-whomping mass of kids. They had a crescent of private beach dotted with bright umbrellas and oiled brown flesh, prone and supine. Despite the early-afternoon heat, their dozen asphalt courts beyond the pool area were all full. You could see at a glance it was very proper tennis. Everyone raced about in spotless white, sweating and banging hell out of the ball, calling out Love, Add, Out and Nice Shot.

The clubhouse was a flaking Moorish pastry onto which had been pasted a big wing in supermarket modern. I wandered in and found a bulletin board in a corridor. They are always useful. The bulletin board was folksier than the tennis. There was a mimeographed copy of the last club bulletin tacked to it. Seems that on May tenth the Taylors had given a big farewell bash for Frank and Mandy Hopson, before they left on their dream trip, three whole months in Spain. Crane and Viv Watts were listed among the guests. I found a phone booth and book, but it gave me no clue as to good old Frank's occupation, if any. I roamed until I found a door labeled Office. I knocked and pushed it open. A thin girl was alone in there, typing. She had a pert look, a large toothy smile.

"May I help you, sir?"

"Sorry to bother you. I just got to town today. I called Mr. Frank Hopson at his home but I couldn't get an answer. I remember him speaking of this place, and I thought maybe Frank and Mandy might be out here."

She made a sad mouth. "Oh, dear! They went away on a long trip."

"Don't tell me they finally made it to Spain. Son of a gun."

"They were as excited about it as a pair of little kids, believe me, Mr. . . ."

"McGee. Travis McGee. They've been after me for years to come over and see them. Well . . . that's the way it goes. At least I got a look at the club."

She hesitated for some additional inspection. I am conspicuously large, and I have a permanent deepwater tan, and I would not look out of place on a construction crew. But the slacks and shirt and jacket were top grade and she knew it. And I smiled at her like John Wayne admiring a speckled calf.

"Well, I think we can do better than that for any friend of the Hopsons," she said, making her decision. "How long will you be in town?"

"Maybe a week. On business."

"Mr. and Mrs. Hopson would certainly want you to use the club." She winked. "In fact, I *distinctly* remember Mr. Hopson saying that you should have a guest card if you ever appeared while they were gone." She pulled the sheets out of her typewriter, ran a card in and filled it out. I gave her the Bahia Mar box number. She signed the club manager's name, put her initials under it, and handed it to me with a little flourish. "These are good for two weeks, Mr. McGee. You can sign and be billed directly. The only restriction is that you can't bring guests here. Except your wife, of course."

"Unmarried. How about just one lady? One at a time."

"No one could object to that. Please don't be shy about mingling and introducing yourself. You'll find all the members very friendly, particularly toward any friend of Mr. Hopson. And please put the card number on the chits you sign. Tonight we're having an outdoor steak roast, buffet style. If you want to stay for it—it's really very good—I can take your reservation."

"Might as well. Thanks. You've been very kind, Miss . . ."

"Benedict. Francie Benedict." The smile opened her up back to the wisdom teeth. "I do wish I could show you where everything is, but I do have to finish this."

"I'll just wander around."

"You can rent swim trunks from Albie in the men's locker room."

She was typing again as I pulled the office door shut. I found a dark, cool quiet bar in the Moorish part. The sedentary types were there and, in the adjoining cardroom, several grim tables of male bridge. I stood at an empty expanse of mahogany bar. The bartender approached with one eyebrow shoved up in cautious, supercilious interrogation. I whipped out my card, and his smile of acceptance would have looked more plausible if he'd been outfitted with those stainless steel teeth the Russians have developed. After he served my Plymouth gin on ice, the clot of members down the bar motioned to him. He leaned across the bar. There was a whispered question and answer; they looked me over and got back into their argument.

A pudgy chap with a statesman's face and careful coiffure of white locks said in liquor-slurred tones, "But you got to face facts, Roy. The fact remains, we got the evidence right in front of us, the decay of the nashal moral fiber, mob rule in the streets, violence, punks killing decen' people. Am I right or am I right?"

I could imagine the same tired concept being stated in a thousand private clubs across the country on this May afternoon. They see the result, but they are blind to the cause of it. Forty million more Americans than we had in 1950. If one person in fifty has a tendency toward murderous violence, then we've got eight hundred thousand more of them now. And density alone affects the frequency with which mobs form. The intelligence of a mob can be determined by dividing the lowest IQ present by the number of people in the mob. Life gets cheaper. Cops, on a per capita basis, get fewer. And the imponderables of the bomb, of automation, of accelerating social change create a kind of urban despair that wants to break loose and crack heads. All the barroom sociologists were orating about national fiber while, every minute and every hour, the most incredible population explosion in history was rendering their views, their judgments, even their very lives more obsolete.

They should hark to the locust. When there is only a density of X per acre, he is a plain old grasshopper, munching circumspectly, content with his home ground. Raise it to 2X and an actual physical change begins to occur. His color changes, his jaw gets bigger, and the wing muscles begin to grow. At 3X they take off in great hungry clouds, each cloud a single herd instinct, chomping everything bare in its path. There is no decline in the moral fiber of the grasshopper. There is just a mass pressure canceling out all individual decisions.

"Am I not right, sir?" demanded the pundit, making a stately turn to include me. I had not heard the more recent statements.

"Absolutely," I said. "Right on the button."

I was roped into the group, met the mellowed and important gentlemen, heard fond words about good old Frank Hopson, and discovered, fortuitously, that Frank was a realtor. "But with his holdings, he doesn't have to work at it much. It's mostly management and rental stuff on what he owns. Poor bastard, he's a land merchant, and he can't take a capital gains on anything, so he just doesn't sell it off."

One of them said, not to me, "I heard that for a while there, young Crane Watts was trying to work something out for Frank, some deal whereby he could put everything in one package, real-estate business and all, give up his license and retire and sell all his holdings to an outside corporation and take his capital gains."

A man beside me lowered his voice and said, "He'd be a fool to let Watts work on anything."

"It was some time ago," another said in the same low tone, and they stared toward the cardroom. I spotted the one who most clearly matched Arthur's description. He was playing bridge at the farthest table, slumped, peering slack-jawed at his holding. He selected a card slowly, raised it high, whacked it down with a wolf yelp of laughter, then hunched forward, glowering, as the opposition gathered the trick in.

"I don't know how he can afford that game."

"He seems to get it somewhere when he needs it."

"She's such a *damned* fine girl."

"Sure is."

I detached myself and went wandering to the courts looking for that damned fine girl, Vivian Watts. A kid resting between sets pointed her out to me. She was in a singles match against an agile blonde boy of about nineteen, almost ten years her junior, I would guess. It was the only court with an interested gallery. She was of the same physical type as Chook, not as tall. She was dark and tanned, sturdily built but lithe. And, like Chook, she had that hawk-look of strong features, prominent nose, heavy brows. As with all natural athletes, she had an economy of motion which created its own grace. She wore a little pleated white tennis skirt, white sleeveless blouse, white band on her dark hair. Her brown and solid legs had a good spring, bringing her back into a balanced readiness after each stroke, the way a good boxer moves.

It was easy to see the shape of the match. The boy was a scrambler, going after everything, returning shots it didn't seem plausible he could reach, lobbing them high enough to give him time to get back for the smash, and preventing her from coming up to the net to put them away. She tried a cross-court volley and put it just outside.

"Broke her service again," a bald little man beside me said. He was as brown and knotty as walnuts.

"How does it stand?"

"Six-three to Viv, then seven-five to Dave. Now's he's got her nine-eight."

He had a big serve and she waited well back, handled it firmly, moved to center court and drove his ground stroke right back at his ankles. He aced her, on his next serve. Then on the next serve he tried to come to the net and she made a beautiful passing shot. Her return of his next serve floated and he let it go out by six inches. He took the advantage on another service ace. At match point, she again tried the passing shot as he moved up quickly, but the ball slapped the tape and, to the accompaniment of a concerted partisan groan, fell into her court.

She went to the net and, smiling, tucked her racket under her left arm and held out her right hand to the boy in a quick, firm congratulatory handshake. The smile was the first change of expression I had seen. Her tennis was poker face, with no girlish grimaces of despair when things went wrong.

They moved off the court as other players moved on, and I drifted along with them, over toward tables in the shade. The boy went off, apparently to get her something to drink. When I moved near enough, she looked up at me with an expression of inquiry, and I saw that her eyes were a very deep blue instead of the brown I had expected.

"Just wanted to say that was very good tennis to watch, Mrs. Watts."

"Thank you. Last year I could take Dave. Next year I won't take a set. Do I know you?"

"Frank and Mandy Hopson fixed up a guest card for me. I'm just in town for a short time. Travis McGee, Mrs. Watts. East coast."

The boy brought drinks, a Coke for himself and iced tea for Viv Watts. She introduced him. Dave Sablett. He seemed a little stiff-necked about her asking me to join them. He had a proprietary air toward her, to which she seemed quite oblivious. She was still breathing deeply, her hair damp with sweat. We chatted for a little while. They were signed up for mixed doubles beginning in a few moments. They were the club's mixed-doubles champions.

I watched the match begin and it was clear after two points they were going to take it readily. So I went back inside to see, perhaps, at closer range, the other half of this happy marriage.

seven

In the Saturday dusk I got a drink from the outside bar and moved out of the throng. In a few minutes Viv Watts came over to where I was standing. She had on a yellow summer cotton, a new mouth. Her manner and expression were tense.

"Maybe *you'll* tell me what happened in there, Mr. McGee."

"Nothing important. I guess your husband got a little abusive and his partner quit. So he was getting ugly about having no chance to get even. Nobody wanted to partner him. It was turning into a scene, so I . . . sat in."

"How much did you lose?"

"Not enough to matter, Mrs. Watts. When I found out what the stakes were, I said it was too rich for my blood. Three cents a point can be murder. I said I'd go for a half cent, and your husband said he'd pick up the slack."

She looked away with a slightly sick expression. "Five and a half cents a point. Dear God!"

"He wasn't in any shape to play. Oh, he wasn't leading out of turn or forgetting the bid. Nothing like that. He just got too optimistic."

"What did you lose?"

"It doesn't matter."

"I insist!"

"Twenty-one dollars. But really . . ."

She bit her lip, unsnapped her white purse and dug into it. I put my hand on her wrist, stopping her. "I really won't take it."

She gave up, saying, "I really wish you would. Did he go home?"

"No. After he settled up he didn't feel very well. He's in that small lounge off the card room . . . resting."

She frowned. "Maybe I should take him home."

"He's sacked out. So he's just as well off there, isn't he?"

She stared beyond me at nothing, her eyes bleak. "He just seems to be getting wor . . ." She caught herself, gave me an awkward glance. A man going sour puts an attractive wife in a strange bind. Still tied to him by what remains of her security, and by all the weight of the sentimentalities and warmths remembered, she is aware of her own vulnerability and, more importantly, aware of how other men might well be appraising that vulnerability, hoping to use it. Feeling the weight of interest and speculation on the part of friends and neighbors, and sensing that she is moving ever closer to disaster, she feels obligated to be more circumspect. Because this, too, is a kind of loyalty. She wants, when it is over, to find no way to blame herself.

"Get you a drink?" I said.

"Please. Scotch and water, please. Tall and weak."

As I brought it to her I saw young Dave Sablett talking to her and saw her quite obviously send him away. He looked back at me, surly and indignant.

"Mr. McGee . . ."

"Trav."

"All right. Trav, do you think he might make a fuss if I tried to take him home now?"

"He well might, Vivian."

She looked startled. "That makes me feel strange. *Vivian*. Vivi when I was little, and Viv now. Vivian when my mother was really cross with me. Vivian on official papers. But it's all right. Maybe I'd like to be called that by someone. It could . . . remind me I have to be a grownup these days."

"None of my business, of course. But is something really wrong with him? Health? Business?"

"I don't know. He just . . . changed."

"Recently?"

"I couldn't say just when it started. A year ago anyway. Trav, I just can't stay here and . . . be calm and social and charming, damn it. Not knowing they're watching me and saying poor Viv. He prom-

ised it would be different this time. But if he refuses to come home
. . . it could be worse."

"I could bring him along without a fuss."

She chewed her lip. "He might respond better to you. But I don't
want to spoil your evening."

"I'm here only because I couldn't think of anything else to do."

"Well . . . if you wouldn't mind."

She showed me where I could bring him out the side door to the
far end of the parking lot. The sun was gone, the steak grills cherry
red, orange flames flickering atop the Polynesian pedestals in the
cookout area, music resonant over the outdoor speakers. We brought
both cars around and I parked behind hers, a small white Mercedes
with dented fenders. I told her to wait and start up after I put him
in my car, and I would follow her home.

I shook Crane Watts up out of the murks of sleep, and he came
up thrashing and whining with irritation. "Lemme lone! Chrissake!"
He focused on me, the uncertain peer of the still drunk. "You, partner. Cheap half a cent bassar, and you were no damn help at all. I
needed you like a head cold, partner what's-is-name. Gimme anything better than clowns and I can take that pair."

"You're going home, Crane."

"Hell you say! You being boyscout for that bitch? Screw you, sa-
maritan. I'm staying. I'm going to have a ball."

I plucked him up off the couch and caught the fist he threw at
me, opened it quickly, regrasped it in an effective come-along, a hold
which leaves the index and little finger free, and press the middle
two fingers against the palm of the captive hand. Crane Watts, face
convulsed, drew his other fist back, and I gave him a good taste of a
pain sufficiently exquisite to bypass the alcohol. His face went blank
and sweaty and the blood drained out of it. He made a small squeak
and lowered the poised fist.

"Is there some trouble here?" a nervous voice asked, and I turned
and saw a club employee in the doorway.

"No trouble. I was just getting ready to take Mr. Watts home."

I cued Watts with a little pressure. "Just going home," he said in
a grassy whisper, and with a strange imitation of a reassuring smile.
The employee hesitated, said good night and went away.

Crane Watts made a very cautious attempt to pull his hand free
and found that it added to the pain. He walked out very carefully beside me, quite erect, taking small dutiful steps, not wavering a bit. A
Nassau police official had showed me that hold. Improperly applied,

it snaps the bones or dislocates the knuckles. In correct adjustment, it pulls the nerves of the two middle fingers against the knuckle bones in a way that you can hit ten on the dolorometer. Nine is the peak for childbirth and migraine, and all but the most stoic faint at some point between nine and ten. You watch their color, their sweat and the focus of their eyes to keep it below the fainting point. And it is a quiet thing. Small pain makes people roar and bellow. The excruciating ones reduce them to an almost supersonic squeak. Also, intense pain is one way to induce a sudden sobriety. By the time I opened the car door for him, I knew he would be no further trouble. I pushed him in and went around and got behind the wheel, started up and followed the Mercedes.

"Jesus," he groaned, hugging his hand against his belly.

"It'll throb for ten minutes or so, and then it will be all right."

"It goes all the way up into the back of my neck, fella. Is it some kind of judo?"

"Something like that."

After a few minutes he slowly straightened up. "Beginning to go away, like you said."

"Sorry I had to do it, Crane. I promised your wife I'd get you home."

"Maybe I didn't give you a hell of a lot of choice. Or her." I felt him staring at me as we passed street lights. "What's your name again?"

"Travis McGee. Friend of Frank Hopson. Over here from the east coast on business."

"Look at that! She turns without any kind of signal at all."

"Maybe she's got a lot on her mind."

"Sure. Like how to get more overspin on her backhand. Don't let her sucker you, McGee. That's an ice-cold bitch. She's slowing for the driveway. It's on the left there."

It was a broad driveway and one of those long low Florida block-houses with a tile roof, a double carport and, beyond any doubt, a big screened cage off the rear, with or without pool. Awning windows, glass doors on aluminum tracks, a heat-pump system—you could guess it all before you saw it, even to a couple of citrus trees and cocoanut palms out back. Terrazzo floors, planting areas in the screened cage and a computerized kitchen. But even at night I saw other clues, a front lawn scruffy and sunbrowned, a dead tree at the corner of the house, a driveway sign saying The Watts which was turned, bent and leaning from someone clipping it on the way in.

I parked in the drive, behind her car. He got out at once, advancing to meet her as she walked back toward my car.

"Congratulations, sweetie baby," he said. "Now you got proof I spoiled your evening. See how early it is? Now you can suffer."

She planted her feet, squared her shoulders. "There might be one member left who would trust you to write up a simple will or even search a title, dearest. So let's protect all that charming innocent faith as long as we can, shall we? Come on in the house before you fall down." She turned toward me. "I'd offer you a drink, but I guess you've had about all anyone would want of this, Trav."

"I might come in for a few minutes, if it's all right. I would like to ask Crane about something. Something maybe he could help me with."

"Him?" she said, loading the word with enough contempt for a month.

"Loyalty, loyalty," Crane mumbled.

We went into the house. She turned lights on. She kept turning lights on, even to the outside floods in and beyond the screened cage, rolling the glass doors open, and, with a gaiety very close to hysteria, she said, "And this is our happy mortgaged nest, Mr. McGee. You may note a few scars and stains. Little domestic spats, Mr. McGee. And did you see that the pool is empty? Poor little pool. It's a heavy upkeep item to operate a pool, more than you'd think. And we don't care to run the air conditioning this summer. You wouldn't believe the bills. But you know, I do have my little indulgences. My tennis, and my once-a-week cleaning woman for some Saturday scrubbing, in case we entertain on a Saturday night, but there aren't many people left we could invite, really. But, you see, I pay for the tennis and the cleaning woman. I have this lovely little trust fund, a whole hundred and twenty-one dollars a month. Don't you think wives should have an income of their own, Mr. McGee?"

She gave me a brilliant smile, sobbed suddenly, whirled and ran, her hands over her face. She went out of sight down a corridor and a door closed behind her.

Mumbling almost inaudibly, Crane Watts took a bottle from a bar corner and headed for the kitchen. As he passed me, I lifted it out of his hand.

"I need that!"

"Not if we're going to talk. If we're going to talk, you need a shower and you need some coffee, before and after the shower."

"Talk about what?"

"Maybe how you can help me make some money."

He wiped his face slowly with his hand, stopped and looked at me with one skeptical eye between his fingers. "Mean it?" I nodded. He sighed. "Okay. Hang around. Make coffee, if you can find the stuff."

I found powdered coffee. I made a strong mug of it and took it toward the sound of the shower. The bathroom door was ajar. I put it on the counter top next to the sink, yelled to him that it was there, and went back to the living room. Houses where love is dead or dying acquire a transient look. Somewhere there are people who, though they do not know it yet, are going to move in.

He came wandering in, mug in his hand, hair damp, wearing a blue bathrobe. He sat wearily, sipped the coffee, stared at me. His color was not good. There were dark stains under his eyes. He had a drinker's puffiness, not far advanced, but enough to alert the observant and the wary. But the mists had lifted.

"Why me?" he asked. "That's the best question I can ask."

"I could need a hungry lawyer."

"You found him. Maybe I'm not as hungry as I have to be. I won't know, will I, until you tell me."

"I'm doing a favor for a man. For a fee. He trusts my judgment and my knowledge of Florida land values. He just came into a very big piece of money. He wants to put half of it in securities and half in land. A broker is working up a portfolio for him. I'm . . . hunting around."

"You an agent?"

"No. If I could locate something good, a very promising investment, something in the eight- or nine-hundred-thousand range, he'll give me ten thousand finder's fee. He's interested in raw land."

"And you need a lawyer to check out something quietly?"

"Not exactly. I found a couple of very clean deals, one near Arcadia and the other up the coast, south of Cedar Keys. Each is worth the finder's fee."

"So where does a hungry lawyer fit?"

I stood up. "Let's adjourn to the office."

Looking bewildered, he followed me to the bathroom. I turned the cold water in the shower on full, then leaned on the counter top. He understood quickly enough. "You're more careful than you have to be, McGee."

"I always am." He leaned against the counter top beside me, and we spoke over the roar of the shower. "Ten thousand seems smaller every day, Watts. If a deal could get more complex, maybe a little more would rub off. Like if something could be picked up and held and resold. You might have more ideas about that kind of thing than I would."

"Why should you think so?"

"From some bar talk today I got the idea you pulled off something pretty cute."

"Oh, it was cute all right," he said angrily. "It was even legal. But all I got was peanuts, comparatively speaking. It wasn't anything I set up. This lousy town. Other lawyers get a little tricky and everybody says how smart they are. You know what I got? A whispering campaign. I'm down to a practice that just about pays the light bill."

"Maybe you could try it again, and cut yourself a bigger piece. Legally, of course."

"Maybe your guy is too shrewd for it. The one they cleaned was truly stupid."

"My guy is no giant, and he's never held a job in his life. You said *they* cleaned. Who?"

"Some out-of-town operators."

"Would we need them?"

He frowned, tugged his lip. "It wouldn't hurt at all to bring one of them in on it. He's damned good." He straightened up. "You're acting as if we're going to try it, and you don't know a damn thing about it."

"All I want to know is that there's no ten years in Raiford afterwards."

"Nothing like that. It's all legal, believe me."

"How does it work?"

"Your guy has to go along with certain things. Like being willing to be in on a land-syndicate operation. And your guy should be off balance a little. They used a woman on the last one."

"Is she still around?"

"Not that I know of. Why?"

"It could work with my man too."

"Listen. You said he trusts you. The way this thing works, it isn't halfway. It has to clean him completely, or it doesn't work. Would that bother you?"

"Not on his account. But it makes me a little nervous. We're talking about close to two million dollars, Watts."

"With family lawyers riding herd on it, maybe?"

"No. How does it work? Make it simple. I'm not a lawyer."

"You make your man believe the syndicate is going after one hell of a big piece of land. Everybody puts money into the syndicate trust account, on a share basis. The trustee is one of the syndicate. In this case it would be that man I told you about. The sucker thinks everybody is putting in cash. But, by separate letter of agreement, the trustee agrees to accept demand notes from the other partners, in view of their long association and so forth. There's a clause in the syndicate agreement permitting additional assessments. Every time one comes along, the sucker comes up with cash and the others turn over promissory notes for their assessment. Another clause in the agreement says that if anyone can't meet an assessment, they are dealt out, and their share is divided pro rata among the other partners. Another clause says that if it is decided the operation is not feasible, the syndicate will be disbanded and the funds in the trust account divided among the partners pro rata. So you just assess him until he's dry, cancel him out with due notice, and a little while later close up shop and divide the pie. You have to keep him thinking that the whole thing is right on the verge of turning into a big fat gold mine."

"And you got a piece of that pie?"

"Hardly. I got a twenty-five-hundred-dollar fee and a five-thousand bonus. I was promised ten, but after it was over there was no way I could blow the whistle on them without putting myself in a sling, and they knew it."

"What did they take the man for?"

"About two hundred and thirty thousand. When it was too late, he went to another lawyer. That's how the news got all over town."

"But you can still afford to lose five hundred dollars in a bridge game?"

He put his head in his hands. "Cut it out, will you?"

"Could you rig the same kind of operation again, for my man?"

"I don't know. It's a lot bigger. I don't know how good my nerve is. I'd have to bring that other man in on it. Maybe he wouldn't want to come in alone. Maybe he'd want to use the same people as before. They'd cut themselves big pieces."

"So how could we defend ourselves against being left the small end?"

He shook his head. "I've got a headache, McGee. There are ways. You work this thing out in the open. We could set up the trust account so it would require three signatures for any withdrawal, and with our promissory notes being as good as the others, we could get in for any percentage we could dicker for."

"He's my man. What if we go for half between us, forty percent for me and ten for you? And let them cut the rest up any way they want, just so they swing it."

"But wouldn't he know you can't come up with that kind of cash? I think it would have to . . ."

The bathroom door opened and Vivian stared in at us. "What the hell are you doing?"

"I'm getting rich, sweetheart. Close the door. As you leave."

I got a duplicate of the look she gave him. She yanked the door shut.

"One other thing, Watts. I suppose you have to set up a fictitious piece of property."

"Oh, no. That would classify it as fraud. We dealt with the executor of the Kippler tract, sixty-one thousand acres. We made legitimate option offers."

"So where are you if he said okay, let's deal?"

"He couldn't. It's all tied up by the terms of the will. But how could we know that if he didn't tell us?"

"And he didn't?"

"No. He wrote nice letters. Seriously considering your last offer. Must discuss it with the heirs and the tax attorneys and so on. They went in the file, in case anybody ever had to see the file. And he kept demanding a higher option offer."

"Which required assessments. So he was coached?"

"Of course. And he got a nice little gift afterward. Hell, McGee, the whole file on this thing is clean as a whistle."

"Could we use the same tract again?"

"Well . . . not on option terms. Too much money involved this time. Maybe on a purchase basis. With a good chance of resale if we could pick it up right, say at two hundred an acre. Twelve million. Then your man comes in for, one-twelfth . . . something along that line, where it would leave enough plausible spread to assess him out of the picture. You see, you have to know just about the absolute total the sucker can come up with. Once hooked big, then they have to keep throwing more in because they think it's the only way they can protect themselves. The beauty of it is that when it's over, they are picked so clean there's hardly any chance at all of them coming up with any civil action to recover, and it's a little too clean to make it attractive to any lawyer to tackle on a contingency basis. What's your man's name?"

"We'll have to think about this and talk about it later. What's the name of your expert?"

"He might be busy with something else. You'll get in touch?"

"Soon."

"In the meantime, just for the hell of it, and it can't do any harm, call your man and act excited and tell him you think there's a chance you can get him into something that will double his money in a year. Is he interested in doubling his money?"

"He wants to be nationally known as a wheeler and dealer."

"What line of work *are* you in?"

"Salvage and demolition."

"On your own?"

"Without overhead. Whenever the right kind of job comes along, I bid it in, rent the equipment, subcontract everything I can, come out with a low-profit percentage that's big enough to live well until the next chance opens up."

He nodded. "Very smart. Very nice. So why all this sudden larceny, friend?"

"I wasn't the low bidder the last few times, and the operating capital is getting a little too puny."

"How can I contact you, McGee?"

"I'm staying with friends. I'll be in touch."

I did not see Vivian when I left. And I could well imagine how Crane Watts would feel the next morning when he remembered the conversation. The man suddenly and artificially sobered has a period of fraudulent lucidity. He thinks he is under control, but the cerebral cortex is still partially stunned, all caution compromised. Attempts at slyness are childlike and obvious. The business of the shower had reassured him. If I was that careful to drown out any listening devices, then, hell, I had to be okay.

In the sober morning it would have a dreadful flavor to him, and he would be aghast not only at all he had told me, but at the memory of even contemplating the same sort of thing with so much money involved. He'd know it was too big for that same kind of operation.

But he was hungry. His seams were splitting and the sawdust was leaking. I wondered if he was bright enough to realize that under that seedy look of failure was an old-time conscience, prodding him into self-punishment. Such as playing losing bridge for high stakes.

Now I had things to go on, pieces to pry loose. The solo operator is often invulnerable. But group operations are weak as the weakest thief in the team. An equation applies. The weakest is usually the one who gets the smallest end of the take. And knows the least. But because of the quasi legality of this operation, Crane Watts had useful information. The big con often needs a plausible local front man. I could guess how Arthur's money had probably been split. A hundred thousand to Stebber, fifty to Wilma, fifty to G. Harrison Gisik, the balance to Watts, Waxwell, the Kippler executor and operation expenses. The role of Boone Waxwell troubled me a little. Beating Arthur so severely had been stupid. But maybe they felt they needed an enforcer. For whom? Watts wasn't likely to get out of line. Perhaps there'd been a germ of truth in their story to Arthur, that Waxwell was essential to negotiations on the Kippler tract. That could mean control of the executor. And where was the coldly efficient Miss Brown? And would that cheap redhead with the improbable name—Dilly Starr—know anything useful if she could be found?

I drove slowly toward the center of the very rich and pleasant little city of Naples, wondering how good old Frank was enjoying Spain.

eight

When I walked into the big drugstore on Fifth Avenue in Naples, I was slightly surprised to see that it was not yet nine o'clock. There were some rowdy teen-agers at one of the counter sections, and I sat as far from them as possible. I like them fine in smaller units. But when they socialize, showing off for each other, they sadden me. The boys punch and shove, and repeat each comment in their raw uncertain baritone over and over until finally they have milked the last giggle from their soft little girls with their big, spreading, TV butts. And they keep making their quick cool appraisals of the environment to make certain they have a properly disapproving audience of squares. And have you noticed how many fat kids there are lately? And the drugstore comedians are usually the rejects. The good ones, as in any year, are taut, brown, earnest and have many other things to do, and can even—unthinkably—endure being alone. This little fat-pack was nearing the end of their school year and, predictably, would slob around all summer, with a few of them impregnating each other. They would dutifully copy the outlook and mannerisms of their momentary idols. Some of them would check out this summer as a bloody stain on a bridge approach. The survivors, ten years hence, would wonder how come their luck was turning so bad, why life wasn't giving them any kind of break at all.

I had coffee and a sandwich, and went to a booth to check the thin Naples phonebook. Mrs. Mildred Mooney was listed. Seventeen Twenty-first Avenue. After the fifth ring she answered in a listless voice, said she was Mrs. Mooney.

"I wondered if I could stop by and talk to you about something. my name is McGee."

"I guess not. Not tonight. I was supposed to baby-sit and I got one of my sick headaches and I had to get somebody else, and I already gone to bed, mister."

"At least I can tell you what it's about, I'm trying to help a man you worked for. He needs help. Arthur Wilkinson. You might have some information I could use, Mrs. Mooney."

"He's a *real* nice man. He was real good to me. He had some terrible bad luck, losing all his money like that, so sudden and all. But I don't see how I could help."

"I won't take up much of your time."

After a long silence she said, "Well, I can't seem to get to sleep anyhow."

"I'll be along in a few minutes then."

She sat in a corner chair in the small living room of her efficiency apartment, sat in the dimness of a single small lamp burning in the opposite corner. Dumpy woman with a worn face and bushy gray hair, wearing a quilted wine-colored robe.

"When I'm like this," she said, "it's like bright light was needles sticking into my eyes. It comes on me about three or four times a year, and then I'm just no good for anything until it goes away. I got regular people, and I can get enough work to keep me going. Working at that big beach house last year was more than I like to take on. It was good pay for around here, and just the two of them, but she didn't lift a finger. And I lost a lot of regular people taking steady work like that, and it took so long to get my regular people it seems like I ended up about even, except for working harder. Oh, I don't mind work, but when they come and go you have to look out for yourself so you have something coming in steady. But I want to tell you right now, I make it my rule not to talk about my people. You start that and the first thing you know it gets around, then they don't want you. Land, the things I seen, I could fill a book, and you better believe it."

"I wouldn't want to ask you to talk about any of your regular people, Mrs. Mooney. I want you to consider something that maybe you never thought of. I want you to think back, and see if it would make any sense to you to believe that Wilma was a part of a conspiracy to defraud Arthur Wilkinson of his money."

"But wasn't she his wife like they said?"

"They went through a ceremony. Maybe she wasn't free to marry. Maybe it was just one of the ways of setting him up, to make it easier to take his money."

She made several little clicking sounds with her tongue. After a thoughtful silence she said, "I came close to quitting a lot of times out there, believe me, and stayed on account of him. She was a pretty little thing, and real lively, but I'd say older than maybe he knew. She sure did spend an awful lot of time on her face and hair. You know one thing she would do I never did hear of before? She would *sandpaper* her face, and that's God's truth, take little strokes to get it raw almost and then put on white goo and some kind of mask and lay down for an hour. She was loving to him, most of the time, nice enough to me when he was close, but with me and her alone, I was just a piece of furniture. She didn't see me, and if I said anything she didn't hear me. She'd turn on me sometimes, just as mean as a wasp, eyes all narrowed down. Not hot angry, but cold as can be. I don't have to take that from anybody. But he was a nice nice man. I tell you, the way she used him was wicked. She had him waiting on her hand and foot, something she wanted that was closer to her than him, he had to go get it and bring it to her. He brushed her hair, that real pale thin kind of hair, a hundred strokes, putting a little bitty dab of some kind of perfume oil on the soft brush every ten strokes, with her whining if he lost count. She had him oil her head to foot for going in the sun, and another sickening thing, I tell you, she had him run her little electrical razor, shaving the fuzz off her pretty legs, then she'd feel to see if he did it good, tell him where he missed, and pat him when he finished. My husband Mr. Mooney, God rest his soul, was a *man*, and no woman ever lived could have turned him into a lady's maid like she done with Mr. Wilkinson. I felt so sorry for that poor man. I don't know, Mr. McGee, I thought it was just bad judgment, him investing in something that turned out bad for him. But I guess she was the kind out for herself and no regard for anybody else."

"So let's say she was setting him up for Mr. Stebber to cheat him. Would that fit?"

"Mr. Stebber seemed like a real gentleman, the kind that thanks you nicely for any little thing. A smily man. And you could tell he was a real big man, successful and all. She knew him from some-place. Then there was that tall sick-looking man with the funny name."

"Gisik."

"He didn't have much to say at any time. He acted as if he was busy thinking about important things happening far away. I guess if Mr. Wilkinson got cheated, then young Crane Watts must have got the same dose. They say he's going downhill something terrible, drinking and gambling and his practice going down to nothing, and probably they'll lose the house, so it's a blessing there's no children. It's children get hurt the worst in a thing like that. They don't un-derstand. They're not regular people of mine, or ever were, so it isn't like I'm saying anything nearly everybody doesn't know al-ready."

"I understand."

"There was one hanging around they called Boo. From out of the swamps around here, from the way he talked. Low-class man, I'd say. And if anybody was robbing anybody, I'd say he was the one. And if she was in on it, I'd say she was in on it with that Boo fellow."

"Why do you say that?"

"I guess because he kept dropping in." I sensed reservations.

"There must have been something else."

"I'd rather not say."

"Any little thing might help."

"It . . . it isn't a decent kind of talk, and I don't want you think-ing the wrong thing of me for staying on where that kind of thing was going on. It's not I'm an old maid. I was married twelve years to Mr. Mooney, God rest his soul, and had three dear babies who died, every one of them, breaking my heart every time, and breaking it for good when Mr. Mooney passed away in such terrible pain it was a blessing when it ended. What happened, it was an afternoon not long before they had to give up the house, and Mrs. Wilkinson and that Boo fellow were out by the pool, side by side in those tip-back chairs, her keeping her face turned up to the sunshine. The mister had gone into town for some reason, and I just happened to look out the utility room window where I was sorting laundry. I was looking at them sideways, sort of, her in a naked little white suit, the bottom part like a little narrow band with fringe on it. And I just happened to see him reach over slow and put . . . put his hand down into her lap. It came into my mind that she was sleeping and she'd wake up fighting mad. But she didn't move. You know how you want to stop looking at something and you're kind of froze? When she did move . . . it was just to make things a little bit easier for him, her face still turned up for the sun and her eyes closed. When she did that, I stopped looking, and I worked like a crazy woman, throwing those clothes around, getting them all mixed up so I had to sort them all out again, spilling soap all over when I got them in the machine. When I heard the sploshing around I looked out, and by then they were in the pool, laughing around. I knew then and there that the mister had a wicked wife, and I made my plans to give notice the end of the month, but before I could tell them, they told me they were giving up the beach house. That Boo man was around there a lot, and by then, those last weeks, Mr. Stebber and the sick one had gone away, back to Tampa I guess."

"Tampa?" I said it so loudly I startled her.

"Well, of course, it being where he lives."

"How are you sure of that?"

"Because I'm a real good cook. Mr. Mooney, God rest him, said I was the best he ever knew of. And that man loved to eat. I don't measure things. I just put things together and they *seem* right. I did restaurant work once, but I hated it. There you have to measure everything because you have to make so much. I'm not lying when I say there've been visitors down here offered me more money than I'd care to mention to go back north with them. Mr. Stebber is one of those who lives for eating. You can tell it. Mostly it's fat happy men like him. They shut their eyes when they take the first taste, and they make a little moan and smile all over themselves. He came out there to the kitchen at that beach house and said it was just between the two of us, and when the Wilkinsons didn't need me any more, I should come to Tampa to cook for him. He said I'd have no heavy housework, and my own room and bath with color television. He said he was away a lot and when he was away it would be like a vacation for me. He said that I'd never have to cook for more than seven or eight at the most, and that wouldn't be often. He said he had a great big apartment in one of those cooperative places, looking out over Tampa Bay, with a colored woman that came in by the day to do the heavy housework.

"Well, I told him that I just couldn't ever bring myself to move that far away from Mr. Mooney's grave. The three babies lived a little while, every one, long enough to have their names given to them. Mary Alice and Mary Catherine and Michael Francis, marked on the stones. There isn't a Sunday no matter how I might feel or how the weather is, I don't go out and neaten up the plot and set there and feel close to the only family I ever had.

"He said again that it was just between us, and if I changed my mind later on, then I could call him up, but the number wasn't in the book, and he gave it to me and told me not to lose it. But on that very next Sunday out there it seemed to me that Mr. Mooney somehow knew I was carrying that number in my pocketbook, so I took it out then and there and tore it up and let the wind blow it away. Are you sure it wasn't just maybe the missus and that Boo fellow cheated the mister?"

"They were all in on it, Mrs. Mooney."

"I do declare. You never can tell, can you? And they cheated that Mr. Watts too?"

"I think that's a very accurate statement."

"I can't think of anything else that would help."

"Do you know a redheaded girl named Dilly Starr?"

"I can't say as I do. I guess a person would remember a name like that."

"Or a Miss Brown, possibly Mr. Stebber's secretary?"

"Her neither," she said. "Is Mr. Wilkinson all right?"

"He's fine."

"Kindly give him my regards when you see him. He's a *nice* person. I suppose *she* ran off. Well, that's good riddance. I guess he couldn't help himself with her. When she was mad at him, she'd treat him like she treated me all the time, like a piece of furniture, wouldn't let him anywheres near her, and when he did exactly like she wanted, then she was . . . after him all the time. A woman shouldn't use *that* to break a man's spirit. That part of it is a wife's duty." She shook her head and clucked. "That little woman had him so he didn't know what end was up or what time of day it was. It makes a man a living fool."

When I thanked her for giving me the time, she said, "I'm glad you came by, Mr. McGee. It took my mind off the way I feel, and maybe I can drop off to sleep now. I hope the mister gets his money back."

At ten thirty I stopped at a gas station and picked up a road map to refresh my memory about distances in that sparsely settled area. I was wondering about taking the thirty- or forty-minute drive to Marco Island and seeing if I could locate Waxwell, but I didn't have any sound ideas about the approach. The radio news, announcing thunderstorms moving in from the Gulf, estimated to hit the area about midnight, made up my mind for me. I went to the marina, parked and locked the green Chev, and took a cautious fifty minutes driving the *Ratfink* home through unfamiliar waters.

The lovers had the lights out and the *Flush* buttoned up. I unlocked the after door to the lounge and went in and put some lights on. In a few minutes Chook came aft, into the lounge, black hair a-tangle, pulling and settling a flowered shift down on her hearty hips, squinting through the light at me.

"The thunder woke me up," she said. "Then I heard you."

"And didn't know it was me, and came blundering out. Without the pistol."

She sprawled into a chair, yawned, combed her hair back with her fingers. "So those things spook me, Trav. And it isn't going to get that rough anyway."

"I'm so glad to hear the reassurances of a qualified expert."

"Are you serious?"

"If somebody put neat little holes in our three heads, took the *Flush* out into that pass, headed her west, set the pilot, opened the sea cocks, dived overboard and swam back, then they could stop being nervous about a quarter of a million dollars. Some people just as alive as you, dear girl, implausible though that may seem, were probably killed today somewhere in the world for the price of a bowl of rice. If I come aboard at night again, and there's no gun in your pretty paw, I'm going to welt you pretty good, enough to keep you on your feet for a few days."

"Man enough?"

"Try me."

She made a face. "Okay. I'm sorry." She jumped at the next white flash of lightning, and the rain came with the thunder, roaring against the deck overhead, hissing into the baywaters around us.

"Have a happy day?" I asked.

"Nice, Trav. Nice."

"How is he?"

She gave me a wicked grin. "I think if you hung him by his heels in a barrel of ice water, he might start to wake up a little."

"Don't overdo a good thing, girl."

"And does that happen to be any of your damned business?"

"Don't flare up at me. It's a reasonable suggestion. You've got ten times his vitality. If I have to use him, I don't want some damned zombie."

"You won't have. You'll have a man. Something you wouldn't have had before. Who set you up to know everything about everything, you silly bastard? It's up to him every time. He deals every hand. So who's pushing him into more than he can handle? I want him to strut a little. To take charge. With her, you know what he got? When the cupboard was locked, nothing. Other times, she took charge. Until there just wasn't any response possible, and then she'd tell him he was a damned poor excuse for a man. That was poisonous, Trav. Poisonous. Merciless. Any woman can accept more than any one man can give. It's a question of mechanics. She can make him feel inadequate, and once she gets him really worrying about whether he can or he can't, then more often he can't.

"I tell the poor guy he's too much, that he's ruining me. Here is a great triumph. We were walking on the beach there, making dumb jokes. All of a sudden he gave me a great wallop across the fanny with the flat of his hand, laughed like a maniac, and ran like a kid with me chasing him and cursing him, just because, you see, all of a sudden he felt good. It made me want to cry. That sweet guy, he's a sexual convalescent. I don't demand. I take it as it comes and fake it when it doesn't, because right at this stage he has to feel that he's terrific. And another thing, that's the same for man or woman. When it's good, it doesn't drag you down. It refreshes. When it's a bad thing between people, bad in their heads and bad in their hearts, maybe hating a little, that's when it makes you drag around afterward, feeling sour and old. This way, you have a little nap, you wake up starved, you go around humming and whistling. So don't give me this quack about zombies, Trav. Maybe I'm being a damn fool. I don't know. I don't love him. He just isn't . . . quick enough, maybe, the way he thinks, and we don't really laugh the same way at the same things. But I am terribly terribly fond of him. He's so decent. Now it's like watching a kid grow up. Maybe it's penance for me. I've bitched up some guys, sometimes meaning to, sometimes not."

She gave me a rueful smile and shook her head. "Oh, hell. I sound as if I was making such a big fat sacrifice, huh? Yes sir, old girl, it's a terrible chore, isn't it? Such dull work. McGee, if you've earned one of those beautiful Mexican beers for yourself, I'll open one for each of us. And you can tell me your adventures. Believe me, we *did* worry about you."

"Every minute. Get the beers."

As she came back with them, the rain moved on away from us as quickly as it had come, making the night silence more intense. She listened intently, her face still, as I recounted events, facts and the resultant guesses.

She shook her head. "That club part. You've got a lot of gall, you know that?"

"People take you at the value you put on yourself. That makes it easy for them. All you do is blend in. Accept the customs of every new tribe. And you try not to say too much because then you sound as if you were selling something. And you might contradict yourself. Sweetie, everybody in this wide world is so constantly, continuously concerned with the impact he's making, he just doesn't have the time to wonder too much about the next guy."

She frowned. "You want to move fast, and find out as much as you can in a hurry. Right?"

"Right."

"Then I think this Boone Waxwell might be more up my alley."

"You have just one job, and you're doing it nicely."

"Do you want to be efficient? Or protective?"

"Both, Chook."

"But you've got no approach to Waxwell."

"I didn't until this moment."

"Like what?"

"The simplest thing in the world. Crane Watts happened to mention him. Watts said Waxwell might know where to locate the woman they'd used last time."

"But if he does, that's no good. Wilma knows you."

"I have a feeling he won't take me at face value."

"He'll get in touch with Watts, won't he?"

"And raise hell. Hell conditioned by the idea that maybe there's another pigeon to be plucked. Anyway, it never works to line it all out ahead of time. It's better to stay loose. And go in any direction that looks good."

"Tomorrow?"

"I'll run over to Goodland in the reliable *Ratfink*. Alone."

nine

In the milky early mist of Sunday morning, the Gulf was placid, so I went out the pass. I looked back as *The Busted Flush* dwindled, looking smaller and smaller against the beach, blurring into the mist. Her lines are not lovely. She is a burly lady, and she waddles. But she has, on some intensely festive occasions, slept more than I bothered to count. In fact, I have a treasured memory of one leisurely trip up the Intercoastal—destination, a big birthday binge for an old friend at his place at Fernandina Beach. On the third morning out I came across a sandy little girl up on the bow, sunning herself in a cute little suit, painting her toenails, whistling with great precision a series of riffs I recognized as a Ruby Braff improvisation. She had a great figure, and an ugly charming buggy little face, and I had never seen her before in my life. She looked up at me in pert inquiry and asked who in the world happened to own this darling boat, because she had just decided to buy it.

There was a crowd aboard again. A crowd of two, and I had left Chook to brief Arthur when he got out of the shower.

I turned south, running a half mile offshore, watching the day brighten as the mist began to burn off. I again had the clothes and gear of the fisherman and almost became one when I saw an acre of water being slashed white ahead of me and, further offshore, birds working over it. I ran at it, killed the motor at the point where momentum drifted me to the outer fringe of the activity. I peered down into the green and saw, a few feet below the surface, a combat squad of big bonita wheeling to hit back into the bait school. School bonita run all of a size, and allowing for the magnification of the water, and my momentary glimpse of them, they had to be upwards of six pounds. All they would do would be tear up my light spinning gear on the chance of boating something inedible. They are the great underrated game fish of the Gulf coast. On light gear, a six-pound bonita is the equal of a twenty-pound king mackerel. There is one thing they all do. Work them, with great effort, close to the boat, and they give you one goggle-eyed stare, turn and go off in a run every bit as swift and muscular as the first one. And they will keep doing that until, on light tackle, they die in the water. It seems a poor reward for that much heart in any living thing, particularly when the meat is too black, bloody, oily and strong to make edible. Bonefish quit. Barracuda dog it. Tarpon are docile once they begin to show their belly in the slow rolls of exhaustion. But the only way you can catch a live bonita is to use gear hefty enough to horse him home before he can kill himself.

I continued south, past Big Marco Pass, and put on dark glasses against the increasing glare. I have ample pigment in my hide, but a short supply in the iris. Pale eyes are a handicap in the tropics. I passed what was Collier City once upon a time, then cut inside around Caxambas. The dozers were working even on a Sunday morning, orange beetles making expensive home sites upon the dizzy heights of the tallest land south of Immokalee—bluffs all of fifty and sixty feet above sea level. I checked my chart, went around the indicated islands, and came in view of the mild and quiet clutter of Goodland: houses, trailers, cottages, shacks spread without plan along the protected inner shore, beyond a narrow beach of dark sand and rock and shell.

I cut to idle and went pooting in toward a rickety gas dock. Beyond it was an improvised boatyard with so many pieces of elderly hull scattered around the area, it looked as if they had spent years trying to build a boat by trial and error and hadn't made it yet.

I tied up. The pumps were padlocked. A gnarled old party sat mending a gill net with hands like mangrove roots. "Do any good?" he asked.

"All I saw was bonita outside. Didn't mess with them."

He looked at the sky, spat. "Won't be much now till near sundown. Big snook come in right under this here dock last night, popping loud as a man slapping his hands. Joe Bradley, he got one upwards of eighteen pound."

"That's a good snook."

"If'n you don't know how it used to be around these parts. You want gas? Stecker don't unlock till ten Sundays."

"There's a man here I was told to look up. Will my gear be okay if I leave it right there?"

"Sure. Who you looking for?"

"A man named Waxwell."

He grunted, pulled a knot tight, spat again. "There's Waxwells spread all the way from here to Forty Mile Bend. There's Waxwells in Everglades City, Copeland, Ochopee and, far as I know, a couple way up to La Belle. When they breed it's always boy babies, and they breed frequent."

"Boone Waxwell?"

His grin was broad, showing more gum than teeth. "Now that one is a Goodland Waxwell, and he could be to his place, which isn't too likely of a Sunday morning, and if he is at his place they's a good chance he got a ladyfriend visiting, and if he's there and he don't, it's still a time of day he could get mean about anybody coming to visit. Come to think on it, there isn't anything he won't get mean about, one time or another."

"I won't let him hurt my feelings."

"You look of a size to temper him down some. But be careful on one thing, or size won't do you no good atall. What he does, he comes smiling up, nice as pie, gets close enough and kicks a man's kneecap off, then settles down to stomping him good. A few times he's done it so good, he's had to go way back into the Park until things quieted down. A couple times everybody thought we'd be rid of him for a few years, but the most it ever turned out was ninety days the county give him. He prowls four counties in that fancy car he's got now, but around here he keeps to hisself, and that suits everybody just fine."

"I'm grateful to you. How do I find his place?"

"Go out to the hardtop and go down that way to the end where it curves around to come back on itself, and on the curve two dirt roads slant off, and this is the one furthest from the shoreline, and he's maybe a mile back there, little more than a mile and a half all told. Only place on that road."

I didn't see the cottage until I came around the last bend in the shell road, and then it was visible between the trees, a hundred and fifty feet away. Once it had been yellow with white trim, but now most of it was weathered gray, the boards warped and pulping loose. The shingled roof was swaybacked, the yard overgrown. But a shiny television antenna glinted high above it, outlined against the blue sky. A mockingbird sat atop it, rocking with effort as he created melodic patterns. A big Land Rover, new but caked with dried mud, was parked by a shed at the side. A large, handsome lapstrake in-board launch sat strapped on a heavy-duty boat trailer. Parked at an angle, and almost against the rungs of the sagging porch, was a white Lincoln Continental four-door convertible, top up, the current model, dusty, with a rear fender bashed, taillights broken on that side. The collection of hardware was as if a very large child had been giving himself a happy Christmas. The closer I got, the more signs of neglect I saw. I went and looked into the skiff. It was loaded with extras, including one of the better brands of transistorized ship-to-shore radio units. But birds had dappled the royal blue plastic of the seats, and there was enough dirty rainwater aboard to fill the bilge and be visible above the floorboards.

I couldn't imagine Boo Waxwell having much of a credit rating. So I could estimate at least twenty-five thousand dollars' worth of toys in his yard. And guess there would be more in the house. Kids with lots of toys neglect them.

The mockingbird yelled and insects shrilled, underlining the morning silence. I broke it up by facing the front door from thirty feet away, and yelling, "Waxwell! Yo! Boone Waxwell!"

In a few moments I heard some thumping around inside, saw a vague face through a dingy window. Then the door opened and a man came out onto the porch. He wore dirty khaki pants. He was barefoot, bare to the waist. Glossy black curly hair, dense black mat of hair on his chest. Blue eyes. Sallow face. Tattoo as Arthur had described it. But Arthur's description hadn't caught the essence of the man. Perhaps because Arthur wouldn't know what to call it. Waxwell had good wads of muscle on his shoulders. His waist had thickened and was beginning to soften. In posture, expression, impact, he had that stud look, that curiously theatrical blend of brutality and irony. Bogart, Mitchum, Gable, Flynn—the same flavor was there, a seedy, indolent brutality, a wisdom of the flesh. Women, sensing exactly what he was and knowing how casually they would be used, would yet accept him, saying yes on a basis so primitive they could neither identify it nor resist it.

He carried a shotgun as one might carry a pistol, barrel pointing at the porch boards a few feet ahead of his bare toes.

"Who the hell are you, buster boy?"

"I want to have a little talk with you, Waxwell."

"Now int that right fine?" He lifted the muzzle slightly. "Git on off my land or I'll blow a foot off you and tote you off."

And unless I could come up with something to attract his attention, that was just as far as I was going to get. You have to take your chances without much time to think. I knew he could check. But somehow I could not imagine Waxwell being very close to the lawyer. Or trusting him. Or trusting anyone.

"Crane Watts said maybe you could help me out, Boo."

He stared at me with a mild, faked astonishment. "Now int he some lawyer fella over to Naples?"

"Oh, come off it, for crissake! I'm trying to line something up, and maybe there's some room for you too, like the last time. The same kind of help. You understand. But this time, maybe nobody takes any of the money back to Tampa. We can use you, and we can use the same woman, I think. Watts said you'd know how to get in touch with her."

Earnest bewilderment, "Mought be some other Waxwell you want. You makin no sense to me noways, buster boy. You stay right where you are, and I come back out and we talk on it some."

He went into the house. I heard him talking to someone, then heard a faint female response. He came back smiling, buttoning his shirt, shoes on, and a straw hat in cowboy shape stuck on the back of his curly head. He had indeed a merry smile, and he stuck his hand out when he was six feet from me. As I took it, I saw the first flick of what the old man had warned me about, and I jumped to the side. The unexpected miss swung his heavy right shoe as high as a chorus-girl kick, and at its apex, I chopped down across his throat with my left forearm, driving him down to hit the ground on his shoulders with a mighty, bone-rattling thud.

He stared up at me in purest astonishment, and then he began to laugh. It was an infectious laugh, full of delight. "Man, man," he gasped, "you as rough and quick as the business end of an alligator gar. Taught ol Boo a Sunday-school lesson." He started to get up, and his face twisted. He groaned. "Think you bust somethin. Hep me up." He put his hand up. I took it. He swung his heels up into my belly and kicked me back over his head, and I had enough sense, at least, not to hang on and let the leverage slam me into the ground. I hit rolling, and kept rolling, and even so his heel stomped the ground an inch from my ear before I rolled under his trailered boat. As I straightened up on the far side, he came running at me around the stern of the boat. He was a very cat-quick and deadly fellow, and he bulled me back against the lapstrake hull, screwed his heels into the ground, and began throwing big hooks with each fist, just as fast as he could swing. When they do that, it is best to try to ride it out. It is better than being bold and catching one. My defensive attitude gave him confidence. And, at best, I do not impress. I am a rawboned gangler, with a look of elbows and awkwardness. But the left shoulder is curled comfortingly around the jaw, and the right forearm stays high enough. And the best way to catch the rhythm is to keep an unfocused stare on the other man's belly. Then you can roll and ride with it, and still be prepared to turn a thigh into the optimistic knee. He hammered away at my arms, elbows, shoulders, and my swaying crouch kept me within easy range. He got in one dandy under the short ribs, and one over the left ear that rang woodland bells. He matched each effort with a hard explosive snuff, and finally as they began to come in with less snap and at a slower pace, he seemed to realize he was doing very little damage. So he tried to change his style from alley to club fighter, moving back a little, trying the unfamiliar jab, hoping to cross with the right. But I took him down a little alley of my own. Queensberry, even when it is by way of Graziano, is bad on the knuckle bones. And that is what makes the TV gladiators so hilarious. Just one of those wild smacks in the jawbones would have the hero nestling his splintered paw between his thighs, and making little damp cries of anguish. So, half turning, crouching, I slumped a little to make him think he'd worn me down. It suckered him into pulling in again. I came down hard on his instep and, with my hands locked, brought my right elbow up under his chops. In a continuation of the same motion, unlocking my hands, I turned toward him, whipping him across the eyes with an open backhand. Unexpected agonies in expected places in very rapid sequence can give a man the demoralizing feeling he has stumbled into a milling machine. I thumbed him in the throat socket, gave him a homemade thunderclap with an open slap on the ear, hooked him deeply just under the belt buckle—the only traditional blow in my brief routine—and as he bent, I clapped onto his wrist, turned it up between his shoulder blades and ran him two steps into the side of the boat. His head boomed it like a jungle drum and he dropped loose, made an instinctive effort to come up, then went loose again and stayed down, sleepy cheek on the damp earth by a trailer wheel.

As I fingered tender areas, appraising damage and feeling pleasantly loose and limber and fit, I heard high heels on the porch. I turned and saw a girl put a giant white purse and a white cardigan on the top step, then come across the scruffy dooryard, tilting along on the high heels of soiled white shoes. She wore a sheer pale yellow blouse, her bra visible through it, and a tight green skirt in a very vivid and unpleasant shade. She looked like a recruit from that drugstore group. Fifteen, I imagined. Certainly not over sixteen. Still padded with baby fat. Wide soft spread of hips, premature heft of breasts, little fat roll around the top of the waist-tight skirt. A round dumpling face, child-pretty, and a puffy little mouth, freshly reddened. She stared steadily at Waxwell as she approached, and she continued combing her flaxen hair with a bright red comb, guiding the strokes with her other hand. She stopped close to me, looking down at him. Her child-skin was so incredibly fine that even at close range in the morning light I could see no texture or grain. I could hear the whispery crackle as she pulled the comb down through that straight, healthy, blond hair.

"Done me a favor if'n you kilt him," she said in a thin childish voice.

"There he is. Finish the job." Still combing, shifting to the other side, she looked up at me, head tilted. I had expected girl-eyes as vulnerable as the rest of her. These hazel eyes were old and cold, and with a little twist of recognition I remembered the wise old eyes of the urchins of Pusan, the eyes which remained unchanged by the appealing, begging, belly-empty smiles they gave the G.I.'s.

"Could might do just that sometime," she said. "Or somebody will. Onliest way I could get stopped from coming on over here. Hah! He jus three month from me Pa's age. But you don't kill off Waxwells. It comes out the other way around."

Boone Waxwell grunted and slowly worked himself into a sitting position, head between his knees, hands tenderly holding the top of his head. He peered up at us through lashes I had not noticed before, dense and black and girlishly long.

"Look, I'm going to be going along now, hear?" the girl said.

"So you go long, Cindy." She stared down at him, shrugged, started back toward her purse and sweater.

She stopped halfway and called back to me. "Mister, he'll be thinkin on some way to bust you up when you least expeck."

"Ain't goin to work on this old boy. Get on home, girl," he said.

Waxwell pulled himself up, leaning against the boat. He shook his head, put a finger in his ear and wiggled it. "You deefed me up on this side, like a little waterfall inside. And husked up my voice box. Some kind of that judo?"

"The home study course from Monkey Ward, Boo."

Cindy creaked the shed door open and went in and wheeled out a red-and-white Vespa scooter. She rested it on the brace, opened the package box, put her big purse and sweater inside, took out a white scarf and carefully turbaned her hair. She did not look toward us. She took the white shoes off and put them in the compartment. She jacked down on the starter and, with it running in neutral, tucked the brace up, hitched the green skirt halfway up the heavy white meat of her thighs, pushed it off and slid aboard, shifting into forward. She wobbled a little, then straightened as it increased its snoring sound, and went off through the sunshine down the shell road, the drone hanging in the air after she was gone, then fading out.

"Little young for you, isn't she?"

"The man says they big enough, they old enough. I give her the loan of that scooter bug. Cindy, she's my nearby girl this year. A nearby girl is when it's too damn much trouble to go after anything else. She lives just over this end of Marco Village. I can swing by that shacky old place and give a long, a short and a long on the car horn, and have me time to come back home here and get settled down, and then I hear that scooter bug like a hornet coming through the night, and she says she won't never again come when I honk for her, but ever time she comes on in pantin and blowin like she run the whole way stead of ridin."

"Why don't her folks stop her?"

He gave me that warm engaging grin, and a broad wink. "Maybe ten years ago it was, Cindy's daddy, Clete Ingerfeldt, him and me had a little talk about Clete's missus, and I pure liked to whip the ass clear off him. He got such a strong memory of it, I even say hello to him his chin gets all spitty. I tell you, fat stuff got the hang of it a lot better than her old lady ever did." He gave me a stare of amazed innocence. "You come way out here to find out about my love life?"

"I came out here to talk about making some money. Like the money you made off Arthur Wilkinson."

"Now I don't recall we made a dime. If that deal went through, we were fixing to make out good. But all we ever got back was the money we put in, less the expense money that come off the top."

"All of a sudden, Boo, your diction improves."

He grinned. "Sometimes I had to go away for a spell. Got me exposed to the high-and-mighty. Got me some college women to learn me."

"If you give me another chance, I'll learn you too. It's a promise. If you get tricky one more time, I'm going to give you a strong memory like you gave Cindy's father. You're going to totter around like a very old man for a very long time."

He studied me carefully. "Lord God, you got a size on you. I shoulda looked more careful to start. From those wrists, you'll go twenty pound more than I guessed. First time I been whipped in four years. But I ain't Clete Ingerfeldt. You could bust half the bones I got, and I'd put my mind on mending up and coming after you, and you better remember it, and knowing I couldn't take you even, I'd take you any ways seems safe, take you way up Lostman's River and stuff you under the red mangrove roots for crab food, and it wouldn't be the first time I took care of some little problem that way." There was no bluff in it. It was an absolutely cold and factual statement.

"Then I'll put it another way, Boo. If you try something, and it doesn't work, I'll make sure you never get well enough to even get in and out of a boat."

I watched him, saw the flicker of appraisal in his blue eyes, half hooded by those long lashes. He hooked his thumbs over his belt. Then, with that flashing speed which can come only from long and intensive practice, he snapped his brass belt buckle loose, yanked it free, exposing the bright limber blade holstered within the belt leather. The wrist snap came before I could hope to reach him. The blade chunked into the damp earth an inch from the outside of my left shoe, driving so deeply that only the brass buckle showed, as if balanced on end. He leaned against the boat with a lazy grin. I bent, put a finger in the buckle, pulled the blade free, wiped the earth from it between thumb and finger. The hilt was weighted to give it a midway balance point. I handed it to him. He fed it back into the scabbard, clinched the belt.

"What's the message that get through to you, friend?" he asked.

"That I can stop watching you, because you'd just as soon talk about money."

"Let's get on in the house. I'm dry as a sandy beach for sure."

He had more toys in the house. A big rack of new sporting arms, small rust spots beginning to fleck the bluing. Color television. Expensive camping and fishing gear stacked carelessly in corners. In the kitchen he had a hotel-size refrigerator, its new enamel dappled with dark finger marks, its innards stacked full of premium beer. I saw cases of very good liquor in a kitchen corner.

Everything not new was battered and squalid. I looked in the door of the tiny bedroom. The double bed was a rumpled tangle of soiled sheets marked in a leopard pattern. They looked like silk. The pattern seemed apt. The bdroom had the pungent odors of a predator's cage, a cell for the cat carnivore.

We drank beer in silence and then he said in grotesque hostlike apology, "I was fixin to keep fat stuff out here to hoe this place out today, but it slipped clean right out of my mind. I guess it'll be until after exam week fore she can get to it. I don't want to mess up her schooling."

I sat on a chair with a broken arm. "Haven't they ever heard of statutory rape around here?"

"First somebody has to complain, friend. What the hell *is* your name?" I told him. He repeated it aloud. "You in some line of work?"

"Whatever happens to come along."

"That's the best kind they is, McGee. But sometimes you work with somebody who like to mess things up because they get jumpy for no reason at all. Then you don't want to work with them again. And maybe they do damn-fool things like sending somebody around who could maybe be the law."

"Crane Watts," I said. "Great guy. If the law asked him for a match, he'd fink out. It makes me wonder about you, Boo baby. But maybe you went along because it was close enough to legal. Watts filled me in. I can use some of his ideas, but not him. Not to help me with *my* pigeon. A fatter one than Wilkinson. And it is not going to be split so many ways. From what Watts said, the take from Wilkinson had to be split between him, you, Stebber, Gisik, Wilma and the executor of the Kippler estate. I was hunting up a hungry lawyer, and found him. But I need a *smart* hungry one."

He wiped his mouth, and he looked very uneasy. "That dumb bastard talks awful quick, don't he?"

"You and me, Boo. We know the ways to make them talk quick. I got interested. He got pretty jumpy."

"Like to watchem jump," he said dreamily.

"When he got scared sober, he tried to deny the whole thing. Maybe I like that assessment bit, to keep it legal. But maybe hit-and-run would be easier all around. Either way I need the woman. The way I understand it, the woman works with Stebber. But do you think she'd come in on something without bringing him in?"

"How in hell should I know about that, buster boy?"

"How in hell should I know until I ask, Waxwell!"

"What did Watts say?"

"Before I got around to that he'd started to do so much lying I couldn't sort it out."

"I say it wouldn't hurt to have Cal Stebber. That fat happy little son of a bitch could sell snowflakes in hell. He makes it go smooth. But you get Watts, and you don't get Stebber or the woman. Or Boo Waxwell. He was a one-time thing. I got only one more little piece of business with lawyer boy, and that's all. You see that Viv? She look at ol Boo like he's a spitty place on the sidewalk. I got it in my mind to take care of that. I had other things going then, and no time to line her up. She's got next to no man a-tall, and it's sure a waste. She's all solid woman, and when ol Boo gets her steadied into it one of these days, she'll come on like an ol walkin-beam pump machine with no place to turn her off. I got that one marked in my mind, because any fool can see she sure ain't gettin what she come after so far." He winked. "And she was just a little *too* snotty to ol Boo, which is always a good sign ever time. They get like that when they get little ideas in their pretty little heads, making them skitty."

I sensed it was a diversion, but could not imagine why.

"But to get back to it, Waxwell. Is the woman as good as Watts seems to think?"

He shrugged, went out after more beer, came back and, as he handed me mine, said, "She had Arthur clamped down like one of those little hairy dogs rich women tote around. She married him legal. Always does, Cal Stebber said. Gets herself Alabama divorces. Make no money claim and it goes through quick and easy. Married up with maybe eleven of them, and her and Stebber and Gisik, one way or another, picked ever one clean. Averages out maybe one a year. Maybe she don't hit it off so good with your man. She's no kid anymore."

"Where can I find her?"

He stared blankly at me. "Why ask me?"

"Why not? Watts told me that after you cleaned Wilkinson, you and Wilma shacked up right here."

He looked around at the room as though seeing it for the first time. "Here? Why would he say a thing like that?"

"Because Wilkinson told him how it was, months later, when he showed up demanding money. Wilkinson was sent on a wild-goose chase up to Sarasota. When he came back to the motel, Wilma had cleared out. Wilkinson told Watts he found you and Wilma here, and you beat him up."

Waxwell threw his head back and guffawed, slapped his knee. "Oh, that! Goddam! He sure did come around here. Drunk or sick, God knows. I had me a little friend here, waitress that come over from Miami to see me. Little bit of a woman no bigger than Wilma, silvery-color hair like Wilma. About sundown and the light not too good. That fool Arthur got it in his head she was Wilma for sure. Maybe out of his head from losing the money and her taking off. Hard to say. I had to bust him up a little and run him off the place."

He shook his head, stopped smiling, looked earnestly at me. "Mind you, I'm not saying I wouldn't want to a had Wilma here a while. I did give it a little try. But I struck out swinging on three pitches, man. Hurt my pride some, but it wasn't the first time I missed and won't be the last, and a man has to face it there's some you can't get to. With her, it was all business. She didn't see no point in just for the fun of it. Cold, maybe. I don't know. Or maybe no money, no kicks. Way I figure it, while Arthur was riding that bus up to Sarasota, she was long gone on her way to Miami with her end of the loot, and from there God knows where, someplace where she could live good until the money got small enough so she had to start on suckering the next one for them to squeeze dry."

I used a long drink from the bottle to make certain my face didn't show anything. The momentary diversion, and then the strange earnestness. The house and yard full of toys. Mildred Mooney could not have invented that rancid little scene by the beach-house pool. Nor could Arthur have invented the telling detail of the little diamond watch he thought Wilma had peddled. Conversely, Waxwell could not have known of being seen by Mrs. Mooney, nor of Arthur's instant recognition of the diamond wristwatch. What could he have been worth in the Wilkinson swindle? Five thousand? Ten at the very top. Maybe twenty-five thousand. And it wouldn't buy many new toys. I had a sudden and vivid image of that small, delicate, pampered face, wavery under the black slow run of water, of fine silver hair strung into the current flow, of shadowy pits, half seen, where sherry eyes had been.

"So Stebber would be the one for me to ask, I guess," I said.

"Most likely to know. By now maybe they got a new one going for them."

"So if I have to work through Stebber, then he's in on it. And my end is smaller."

"McGee, what got it in your head you got to have one particular broad, just because she did good on the last one? I could pick you one right out of the air. Thinking on one right now. Little ol gal way up in Clewiston, wasting her talent. Doing waitress work. Had her teaching license, but lost it for all time. Dresses good. Acts like a lady. Pretty face but built only a little better'n fair. Sugar sweet, and a born thief. But I swear and garntee, she get any plain ordinary fella into bed just one time, from then on he can have trouble remembering his own name or how to count to ten. And that's all you need, isn't it? That's how Wilma set them up for Stebber."

"I better think the whole thing over, Boo."

"It's Rike Jefferson over to Everglades, executor on the Kippler land, writing any damn letter they tell me to tell him. He married the youngest Kippler girl, how come he got that job, and she's years dead. I yell frog one time and Rike jumps till his heart gives out. Down in Homestead is Sam Jimper, a lawyer man crooked as a ball of baby snakes, but knowing I was behind you with my eye on him, he'd sooner french-kiss a gator than try to get cute two ways. I'm telling you the way to do is you forget Watts and Stebber and all them, and let me get Melly on down here and you look her over, and give her a trial run if you don't believe me. She won't take as big an end of it as you'd have to give Wilma. But I get a good cut because you need me to set it up, because without a genuine big piece of land, all recorded and setting there to look at, you've got no way to give a man an itch to double his money, so as to show off for his cute new little schoolteacher wife. And I tell you, Sam Jimper's got an office paneled in black cypress big enough for a ball game, nothing like that closet Watts has got. I say you give Melly five hundred dollars for front and just turn her and aim her at your man, married already or not, he's got as much chance as a key lime pie in a school yard."

"Don't tell me how to run it, Boo. Don't tell me who I'm going to use. Maybe I don't need some nut who tries to kick my knee off before he knows who I am or what I want. I have to think this out. I don't want it messed up. It's the biggest piece of money I'll ever get hold of. Right now I'm going to let things sit for a while. Maybe you make sense. I don't know. If I decide you do, you'll hear from me."

"What if'n I think of something else that'd help?"

"Tell me when I get in touch."

"An if you don't?"

"Stop leaning on me, Boo."

He chuckled. "So you got to go talk it over with somebody. Look like you got a partner."

"What's that to you?"

He stood up. "Nothing. Not one damn ol little thing, buddy boy. None of my business. Maybe you're just the errand boy, talking big. Come back. Don't come back. Ol Boo's gettin' along sweet and fine. Leave off your car down the road?"

"Left a boat in Goodland and walked in."

"Drive you in."

"Don't bother."

"Got to go see somebody anyways. Come on."

It was going sour. I could sense it. We went in the Lincoln. The abused engine was ragged, and he took the curves of the narrow road in careless skids, spattering shell into the ditches. After coming to a noisy, smoking stop at Stecker's Boatyard, he got out with me and strolled out to the dock, talking slurred, amiable nothings. The old man was gone. The pumps were unlocked, but I did not want to spend extra time within range of that blue-eyed stare. I gave it full throttle and at the end of the long white-water curve away from Goodland, I looked back and saw him standing motionless on the dock, watching me, thumbs hooked onto that lethal belt.

It had been all right, and then it had gone subtly wrong in a way I couldn't explain. I had the feeling it had been a near thing getting away from him at all. Something had changed him—some factor of doubt, some special alertness. A twig snapping, maybe, in the tangly backwoods of his mind, bringing the head up, ears cocked, eyes narrow. I now knew it was all going to move quickly, and I could no longer set the pace. I had done my little prying and poking. The avalanche had started its first grumblings. Then comes the time to try to outrun it.

ten

After exposure to Boone Waxwell, the look of Chook and Arthur on the early afternoon beach had the flavor of a great innocence. She was hovering around him, cheering him on with shrill yips. He was braced against an impressive bend in one of the big boat rods. When I beached the *Ratfink* near the *Flush,* she hollered to me to come tell them what Arthur was fighting.

I trotted down to where they were. I saw a slow massive boil about a hundred yards out. Arthur, grunting, was trying to horse it enough to get some line back.

She held her fingers about eight inches apart. "A shiny little fish I caught, but we think he was dead after Arthur threw him out there a couple of times.

Arthur gave me a strained grin. He and his quarry were in stasis. I waded in and felt the taut line, then felt that slow distinctive stroke, a kind of ponderous convulsion.

"Shark," I said. "Sand shark or a nurse shark, probably. Longer odds on a hammerhead."

"My God!" Chookie cried. "We've been *swimming* in there!"

"Heavens above!" I said. "And sometimes a bat will fly into a house and bite somebody. Or a raccoon will charge, snarling, into a supermarket. Sweetie, the sharks are there *all* the time. Just don't swim when the water is all roiled and dirty."

"What'll I do?" Arthur asked in a strained voice.

"Depends if you want him."

"My God, I don't want him."

"Then set the drag tight, aim the tip at him, and back away from the water."

He did. After five strenuous steps, the nine-thread line popped, out by the leader swivel. As he reeled in, there was another boil, farther out, as the shark went off to think things out.

"Sharks have no bones," I announced. "Just gristle. They have rows of hinged teeth that straighten up as they open their mouths. They shed teeth from the front row and the other rows move forward. About one third the body weight is liver. The tiny spikes on their hides are tipped with enamel of the same composition as tooth enamel. Their brains are little nubs on the front ends of their spinal cords. They have no intelligence anyone has ever been able to test. They are a roving, senseless, prehistoric appetite, as unchanged as the scorpion, cockroach and other of nature's improvisations which had good survival value. A wounded shark being eaten by his chums will continue to eat anything within reach, even hunks of himself which might happen by. End of lesson."

"Gah," said Chookie. "And thanks a lot."

"Oh, two more items. There is no effective shark repellent. And they do not have to roll to bite. They can lunge up and chomp head on, but when they bite down, then they roll to tear the meat loose. Now, children, we go into conference, critical variety. Everybody into the main lounge."

When they were seated and expectant, I said, "I learned that it wasn't Wilma you saw with Boone Waxwell, Arthur. It was a girl who looked a little like her."

Arthur's jaw dropped. "But I was certain it. . . . Oh, come *on!* I know it was Wilma. Or an identical twin. And I saw her watch. She told me once it was a custom design. I couldn't mistake it. No, that was Wilma, even to the way she was asleep in there, her posture."

"I agree. It was Wilma. And ol Boo went to great lengths to prove it wasn't. It seems it is very important to him to establish that Wilma was never there."

"But why?"

"Because that's where he killed her. And took over her share. And used it to buy himself lots of pretty toys he doesn't take very good care of."

"Killed Wilma," Arthur said in a sick voice. He swallowed. "Such a . . . such a tiny woman."

"And it's a good guess she was your legal spouse, Arthur. She'd been working with Stebber for years. Maybe he had a little stable of Wilmas. Legal marriage makes it neater, and divorce is no great problem. You might have been husband number eleven. Marriage enlarges the areas wherein the pigeon can be plucked."

"What a charmer," Chookie said softly. "Lady spiders eat their mates for dessert. I read about one real smart kind of little boy spider. He doesn't come courting until he's caught a juicy bug. Then while she's enjoying the gift, he's off and away like a flash."

"A quarter of a million dollars is a juicy bug," Arthur said.

"Made her rates pretty high," Chook said tartly. "Trav, my God, how did you figure this out?"

"I didn't. It just seems like what must have happened." And I gave them a condensed but uncensored report. His little knife trick made Chook gasp. I got paper and wrote down the names he had mentioned before they slipped out of my mind. I gave the most weight, detail and careful choice of words to the feeling I had right at the end.

"So here it is. This is his country. I'll bet he knows every boat for fifty miles around. He's not going to take me at face value. He's going to feel uneasy until he finds where I'm holed up. By now it's certain that there are people at Marco who know where we're anchored, know there's two men and a woman aboard. The more he learns, the less he's going to like the smell of it. And he's the type to make his moves and to do his thinking later. Cute as we've been, we've left a clear trail."

"So we rub it out and pick a new base," Chook said.

"Right. And then we think up some good safe way to decoy ol Boo, so I can have enough time to take that rat nest of his apart."

"What do you mean?" Chook asked.

"This is a recovery operation, isn't it? I doubt he's spent it all. He wouldn't bank it. It's in some hidey-hole. And not an obvious one. He's devious, not in any reasoned way, but by instinct. He has that bluff, battered soldier-of-fortune look, and a ton of ironic charm in that grin, and he makes me think that under other circumstances he'd be the man I'd want to go ashore with in a strange port where there would be good booze and a chance of trouble. But that would be wrong. The essence of him is feline, and not house kitty. A bigger predator. I wonder how many people he's conned with that swampy folk talk which isn't even very consistent. It's a good cover. His way of life is a predator way of life, a cat-habit. He has his home range, most of four counties to roar around in that abused Lincoln, whipping the other males so ruthlessly nobody challenges him, bringing prey back to the den, protecting the den violently and instinctively, and ready at any time to fade back into the Glades. I'm saying all this because I don't want us to make the mistake of assuming he will respond predictably to any action of ours. Something that might send another man hustling to a faraway place might make Boo Waxwell run a little way and circle back. And, when he came so damned close to stomping me, I realized it has been a long time since I have seen anyone move that fast."

"Trav?" Chookie said in a strange and subdued tone.

"What, dear?"

"Maybe . . . maybe he is *you*, gone bad. Maybe that's what he smelled. Maybe that's why you can handle him."

My immediate instinct was to get blazing mad, tell her it was a rotten analogy. It was a response the head-feelers would call significant.

"Maybe I'm being dumb or something," Arthur said. "If this man is all that dangerous, and you're pretty sure he . . . killed Wilma, well then I'd think there would be things the police could find out. I mean, maybe an identification of the gray car he had when he took her from the motel while I was gone. Maybe he went with her to the bank when she cleaned out that joint account, before I left on the bus. I could swear I saw her at Waxwell's cottage. Maybe somebody else saw her there, or when he drove her in through the village. I mean wouldn't we be better off if he was in jail?"

"Arthur, it is very nice to believe in an orderly society. By and large, all the counties of Florida have pretty good law officers. Some are excellent. But the law isn't growing even half as fast as the population. So it is selective. From their point of veiw, how excited could they get over the possibility of a transient woman of dubious character getting herself killed well over six months ago, a woman who was never reported missing. Collier Cousty will have some deputies who know the score in the Marco Island area, and much as they might itch to put Boo away for keeps, they'd know their chances of finding a body if he was able to take it into the islands and rivers and swamps and hide it. Now after Boo beat you so badly and those nice people who found you on the highway took you in, you must have had some idea of getting the law after Boone Waxwell. Did they give you an opinion?"

"They said to forget it. They said nothing would happen, and it could make trouble for them. They said there were Waxwells all over, and a lot of them were decent quiet people, but there were a lot of wild ones like Boone, and if they wanted to take it out on Sam Dunning, sheltering somebody trying to make trouble, his nets would get cup up and his charter boat could catch fire and nobody would know who did it. The best thing to do, they said, was keep your head down. Trav, I ought to see those good people. I went off and said I'd come back soon. And they haven't heard a word . . . it isn't right."

"Another thing, Arthur," I said. "If you made the complaint about Boo, remember it would be coming from a man who recently chopped brush on a Palm County work gang. A man with no funds and no employment. When there isn't enough law to go around, it has to work on a status system. And suppose you *did* get them to take Boone Waxwell in. They'd seal his cave, and maybe they would come across whatever he has left, if anything. Then it would be out of reach for keeps." I looked at Chookie. She sat with chin on fist, scowling. "You're getting good grades so far," I said. "What else should we do?"

"I would think that if Wilma was alive she would have been in touch with Calvin Stebber, and if she's dead, he'd be wondering about her. It would be a way to make sure. After all, this Boo Waxwell could maybe have gotten money somewhere else. And maybe Wilma told him to lie about her being there."

"And," I said, "Stebber might be the one to decoy Boo away from his cave." I stood up. "It's gone past the point where we need an imitation pigeon."

"How about the money of mine that Mr. Stebber has?" Arthur asked.

"I want to get a chance at it. So now let's unhook this beast and get out of here."

We brought the bow anchors aboard, worked the *Flush* out by hauling on the stern anchor lines. When we coasted close enough they pulled free. I hoisted the dinghy up by the stern davits and made it fast, as, under dead slow speed, Arthur took us out through the wide entrance of Hurricane Pass. We towed the *Ratfink* astern, motor tilted up and covered with a tarp. When we were clear and headed north up the Gulf, I put it up to cruising speed and went aft and adjusted the length of the tow line until the *Ratfink* was riding steadily at the right point of our wake. The bright afternoon was turning greasy, sky hazing, big swells building from the southwest, a following sea that began to give the old lady a nasty motion and made it impossible to use the automatic pilot. The little solenoids are stupid about a following sea. They can't anticipate. So you have to use the old-timey procedure of swinging the wheel just as they begin to lift your back corner, then swinging it back hard the other way when the bow comes up. You labor for long seconds apparently dead in the water, and then you tilt and go like a big train. Chook brought sandwiches to the topside controls, and I sent Arthur to dig out the bible on coastal accommodations.

The Palm City Marina, thirty miles north of Naples, had the sound of what I wanted. And from the way the weather was building, it was far enough. We'd begun to get enough wind to pull the tops off the long swells and the sun was gone in haze, the water changing from cobalt to gray-green. The *Flush* heaved and waddled along, setting up a lot of below-decks creaking, clinking, clanking and thumping, and about every tenth swell the port wheel would lift out and cavitate, giving us a shuddering vibration. At least I never had to slow her down. Her cruising speed was what other boats slow down to when the seas build. When the driving rain came, I sent them down to take over on the sheltered controls. As soon as I felt the wheel being taken, I pulled the lever that freed it, put a loop over a spoke, snapped the big tarp down over the topside panel and throttles and padded below, soaked through.

They had the wipers going, were peering earnestly into the rain curtain, and Arthur was misjudging the seas enough to bounce pans off their galley hooks. They let me take over with an obvious relief. Soon, as the heavy rain flattened the swells, she began to ride much easier.

"They put those little signs in boats," Chook said with a nervous laugh. "Oh Lord, thy sea is so vast and my boat is so small. Trav, you don't have any funny signs around."

"And no funny flags to hoist. I almost fell for one little brass plaque, though. It said that marriages performed by the captain of this vessel are valid only for the duration of the voyage. Arthur, go see how the *Ratfink* rides. Chook, go make coffee. Busy yourselves. Stop peering over my shoulders. Then check all ports to see if rain or sea is coming in. Stow any loose gear you come across. Then, as a pagan rite I recommend—after you've brought me the mug of coffee —you people get bars of soap, go aft and strip down and try that warm hard rain out on the afterdeck."

After an hour, as I had anticipated, the wind direction had shifted to the west. I made an estimate of my position along the line I had penciled on the chart, put an X at that spot, then changed to a more westerly course so I could take it as a quartering sea on the port bow rather than rocking along in the trough. She steadied, and I put it into automatic pilot, read the compass course, figured the deviation and drew a new line on my chart. According to my computations, another eighty minutes would put us at a point offshore from Palm City where we would turn and run on in. The rain was coming down harder than before, and with less wind. I prowled, looking for my companions of the storm. The clues were obvious. The closed door to the master stateroom. And, in the main lounge on the rug, a damp blue bath towel. It made me remember a line from a story of long ago, written, I think, by John Collier, about when the kid finds the foot, still wearing sock and shoe, on the landing of the staircase leading to the attic. "Like a morsel left by a hasty cat." So make this a towel left by a hasty morsel. Hard warm rain, soap, giggles and the tossing and pitching of a small boat are aphrodisiacs vastly underrated. I eeled up through the forward hatch with my soap so I could keep a watch ahead. It was a cool abundance of water, sudsing as only rainwater can. I had a few discernible bruises on my arms where Boo's fists had sledged, and a round one on the short ribs. When I took a deep breath there was a twinge there, sign that the blow had probably ripped a little of the cartilage between the ribs. Fatuously I admired the new flatness of the belly, and the absence of the small saddlebags over the hip bones. Narcissus in the rain. I dropped back below, redogged the hatch, toweled in a hurry, hopped into dry clothes and trotted back to the wheelhouse, peering through the windshield arcs for the collision course you always anticipate when a bunch of little gears are steering your boat.

Chookie, in a crisp white dress, black hair pinned high, came bearing a tray with three cocktails and a bowl of peanuts, Arthur bringing up the rear. They were elaborately conversational. Rain made a dandy shower. A little chilly but real stimulating. Then both rushed in to find a safer word than stimulating, and managed merely to underline it, giving Arthur such a steaming red face he turned away to stare out the side ports saying, My, it certainly is coming down, isn't it?

And, my, it certainly was still coming down when we got to my estimated destination. It always seems a waste when all that nice useful rain whishes down into the salty sea. I pulled it back until we barely had seaway, and turned on the little whirling red bulb of the depth finder. The Gulf has such a constant slope, the bottom is a good location guide. We had twenty-one feet under the hull, twenty-five total, and if other things were right, that would put us three and a half miles off Palm City, according to the depths on the chart. I looked up the frequency of a commercial radio station in Palm City, with a tower almost in line with the harbor. When I had picked it up on AM, a baseball play-by-play, I changed our heading to zero degrees and rotated the direction-finder loop until I had a good null. I was about a sea mile short of my estimated point. I put it on the new course, again with a following sea, and we waddled and rocked on in until the sea buoy appeared out of the murk, giving me a course on the chart for the channel between the keys. Inside, we were in flat water, and it was no trick finding the private markers for the marina channel.

It was, as I had hoped, loaded with big cruisers. Two air-horn blasts brought a kid out of the dock house wearing a plastic raincoat with hood. He directed us with hand signals and ran around to the slip. I worked it around and backed it in, went forward in a hurry and got a loop on a piling and around a cleat and snubbed us down. In fifteen minutes we were all set, lines, fenders and spring lines in place, gangplank onto the dock, all identified and signed in. And the rain was slacking off.

I was damp, but not enough to change again. Chook distributed dividends from the shaker and said, "Okay. I bite. Why here?"

"Multiple reasons. If you want to hide a particular apple, the best thing you can do is wire it onto an apple tree. Lots of these big lunkers around us are in wet storage for the summer. We're one face in the crowd. We're not far from Fort Myers, where they have air service to Tampa. We're a half hour by car from Naples, a little better than an hour from Marco. If he finds out we anchored off by our lonesome once, he'd expect us to do it again. And if he does find us, and if he does have any violent ideas, it's a damned poor place for him to get away with them. Also, it would reassure Stebber if it turns out I can fix up a meeting here."

Arthur said, "I think it was across that causeway over there, over on the beach on that key where they found me stumbling around. Should . . . should I sort of stay out of sight?"

Chook said to me, black brows raised in query, "With your fishing hat and those fly-boy dark glasses?"

"See no reason why you should," I said.

Chook leaned to pat Arthur on the knee. "You have a dear face and I love you, but darling, forgive me, you aren't terribly memorable."

"I guess one of us is enough," he said, making one of his rare little jokes, waiting then with no confidence anyone would laugh.

I got the evening weather news. As I had expected, the wind was swinging around into the north, and by dawn they expected it to be out of the east at three to five knots, clear weather, occasional afternoon thunderstorms. It meant that by early morning, with the *Ratfink* bailed and fueled, I could make a good fast run close inshore down to the little marina in Naples, tie it up there at that handy and useful location, then take the rented car back to Palm City. The evening was laundered bright, the air fresh, and Chook declined a chance for a dinner ashore, saying she had a serious attack of the domestics, a rabid urge to cook. After dinner, while the two of them were policing the galley, I took the little battery-operated Mirandette tape recorder into the stateroom I was using and closed the door. For some reason, I cannot perform the feat with people listening, and sometimes I cannot perform it at all. The little machine has astonishingly good fidelity, considering its size.

Try, playback, erase. Try, playback, erase. I learned that to get Waxwell's tone quality I had to pitch my voice higher, and put a harder and more resonant edge on it. The slurs and elisions were easier to manage, along with that slight singsong cadence of the swamplands. When I got a reasonably satisfying result, I left it on the tape.

I went up on the sun deck for the long slow evening pipe. When one is down to this mild reward for abstinence, there is only one way to cheat. I found an oversized pot in the pipe drawer, a massive Wilke Sisters product, and nearly sprained my thumb packing Black Watch into it. We all sat up there in the warm night, marina lights sparkling on the water, traffic moving across the distant causeway. They sat together, about ten feet from me, off to my right. They rustled a little now and then. And whispered. And several times she made a furry and almost inaudible chuckle, as sensuous as a slow light stroke of fingernails. It began to make me so edgy I was grateful when they said their early, husky good nights. I think it was becoming a little more for her than she estimated. I hoped it would get big enough to pry her loose from Frankie Durkin. But any kind of future for Chook and Arthur would depend on my making a pretty solid recovery for him. If she had to support him, or share the job of supporting the two of them, it wouldn't work out so well. It would make him restive. And this was her time to have kids. And it wouldn't mix well with her strenuous brand of professional dancing. She had the body for kids, the heart for them, the need for them, and love enough for a baker's dozen.

So if you don't recover enough, do you need to clip a full fifty percent of it, McGee?

Next there will be a choir of a thousand violins playing I Love You Truly. Or, perhaps, Paddlin' Maudlin Home.

Back in my empty lonely nest, I turned the recorder on, and with the larynx memory of how I did it before, became Boo Waxwell giving a sour little talk on the joys of love and marriage. Then I played the tape from the beginning. The part I had previously approved sounded just about the same as the new addition. That meant I had it nailed well enough to risk it.

eleven

It was a little after nine in the morning when I tied up the *Ratfink* as before in the little marina. I went over into town in the green sedan, ordered drugstore coffee, and, as it was cooling, shut myself in the phone booth and called Crane Watts' office number.

He answered directly, sounding remarkably crisp and impressive and reliable. "Crane Watts speaking."

"Watts, this Boo Waxwell. How about you give me that number for Cal Stebber in Tampa. Caint lay my han on it."

"Now I don't know as I'm authorized to . . ."

"Lawyer boy, I git it fast, or in five minutes I'm right there, whippin yo foolish ass down to the bone."

"Well . . . hold the line a moment, Waxwell."

I had a pencil ready. I took down the number he gave me—613-1878.

"Address?" I asked.

"All I've ever had is a box number."

"Nev mind. Lawyer boy, I plain don't like the way you give that McGee the whole story."

"Don't you think you made that plain enough last night, Waxwell? I told you then and I'm telling you now that I didn't tell him half the things he claims I told him."

"Too dog-drunk to know what you told him."

"I'm doing my level best to get a line on him, and as soon as I learn anything useful, I'll get in touch with you. But I don't know why you're upset about it. It was a perfectly legal business arrangement. Another thing, Waxwell, I don't want you ever coming to my house again, like last night. You upset my wife, the way you acted. See me here if you have to see me at all, but I'm telling you now, I'm no more anxious to have any future association with you than you are with me. Is that quite clear?"

"Think I'll come by anyways and bounce you some."

"Now *wait* a minute!"

"Talk sweet to ol Boo."

"Well . . . maybe I did sound a little irritable. But you see, Viv knew nothing about . . . that business arrangement. You said too much in front of her. She cross-examined me half the night before I could get her quieted down. And she still isn't satisfied. I'd just rather you wouldn't come to the house again. Okay?"

"I swear, lawyer boy, I never will. Never again. Less something comes up all of a sudden."

"Please, just listen to reas . . ."

I hung up, sweating lightly, and went back to my coffee. Boone Waxwell had wasted very little time getting to the only man who might know anything about me. And had charged that man with digging up information. Watts could get my Bahia Mar box number from the club records. That wouldn't be much help. But there was a new factor. Waxwell did not seem like a patient man. Perhaps no later than this afternoon he would be phoning Watts to find out what he'd learned. And he would be very intrigued to know it was his second call of the day, and interested to know that he had asked for Stebber's unlisted number earlier. He would work that out in short order.

I aimed the Chev north up 41 through light traffic, keeping a watch front and rear for State Police, who object violently to any speed approaching three numbers. I pulled into a marina parking space at Palm City at ten o'clock. The *Flush* was locked. A note on the rug inside the rear door to the lounge said they'd gone grocery-shopping. I went hunting and found them in a Food Fair two blocks away, Arthur trundling the basket, Chook mousing along, picking out things, wearing that glazed look of supermarket autohypnosis. Eleven minutes after I located them, I had a protesting Arthur locked aboard with instructions to stay put and out of sight, and I was backing out of the parking space with Chook beside me, hitching at her skirt and buttoning the top buttons of her blouse.

If the feeder flight out of Fort Myers hadn't been ten minutes later coming in from Palm Beach, we would have just missed. And I had been too busy driving to do more than fragmentary briefing. I bought two round-trip tickets to Tampa. With stops at Sarasota and St. Pete, the ETA was twenty past noon.

Once aboard, I gave it to her in more detail. "But with just a phone number?" she asked.

"And a little jump. And a prayer for luck. And the name of a yacht."

"Golly, suppose you worked all this hard at something legitimate, McGee. No telling how big you might be."

"A state senator, even."

"Wow!" She checked in her mirror and fixed her mouth. "What good am I going to be to you?"

"I'll figure that out as we go along."

At Tampa International, with Chook standing outside the booth looking serious, I tried the number. As I was just about to give up and try again, a cool, careful, precise female voice said, "Yes?"

"I would like to speak to Mr. Calvin Stebber."

"What number were you calling, sir?"

"Six one three-one eight seven eight."

"I am sorry. There is no Calvin Stebber here, sir."

"Miss, I suppose that it's one of the oldest code situations in the world. You always ask for the number to be repeated, and the party calling is supposed to change one digit. But I don't happen to have the code."

"I haven't the faintest idea what you're talking about, sir."

"No doubt. I am going to call you back at exactly quarter to one, twelve minutes from now, and in the meantime you tell Mr. Stebber that somebody is going to call who knows something about Wilma Ferner, Wilma Wilkinson, take your choice."

She hesitated a half breath too long before saying, "I am terribly sorry that all this means absolutely nothing to me, sir. You've made a mistake, really."

She was very good. So good the hesitation seemed to lose significance.

I tried it again at the promised time.

"Yes?"

"Is Mr. Stebber interested in Wilma? This is me again."

"Actually, you know, I shouldn't be so childish as to let this non-sense fascinate me, whoever you are. I suppose it's because I am having a dull and boring day. Do you think that could be it?"

"Nonsense fascinates lots of people."

"You *do* have rather a nice voice. You know, if you aren't too busy for nonsense, you could break up my afternoon with more of it. Why don't you mystify me again, say, at three fifteen?"

"It will be my pleasure. I'll be the one with the red rose in his teeth."

"And I shall be wearing a girlish smirk. Good-bye, sir."

I stepped out of the booth. "What are you grinning at?" Chook demanded.

"The good ones are always a pleasure. She couldn't contact Stebber so quickly. But without giving away one damn thing, she lined me up to call back at three fifteen. Then if Stebber is interested, they open a door. If not, she gives me the girlish chitchat, and I hang up never really knowing for sure. Very nice."

She pulled herself taller. "It means you're outclassed, doesn't it, sweetie? Stebber has this terribly keen girl, and you're making do with a big dull dancer."

"Oh for God's sake, why should a little impersonal admiration raise your hackles?"

"Feed me," she said. "All women are at war all the time, and when I've got hunger pains, it shows a little more."

We went to the upper level, where she ate like a timber wolf, but with more evidences of pleasure than any wolf would exhibit. There was so much of her, and it was so aesthetically assembled, so vivid, so a-churn with vitality, that she faded the people for ten tables around to frail flickering monochromatic images, like a late, late movie from a fringe station. She provided me, in certain measure, with a cloak of invisibility.——Okay, fella, but describe the guy she was *with*.—— Just a guy. Big, I think. I mean, hell, I don't think I really looked at him, lieutenant.

She sipped coffee and smiled, sighed, smiled again.

"You look like a happy woman, Miss McCall." I reached across the table and touched her with a fingertip right between and a little above those thick black brows. "There were two lines here."

"Gone now? Son of a gun. Gee, Trav, I don't know. I talk. I talk my fool head off. There in the dark with him holding me, mostly. Things I've never told anyone. He listens and he remembers. I skip around, back and forth through my dumb life. I guess I'm trying to understand. I'm talking to myself at the same time, about Frankie, about how my mother made me ashamed of growing too big to fit into her dream, about running off and getting married at fifteen and annulled at sixteen, knocking around, and then buckling down and *really* working hard and making it and saving money so I could go back in style and knock their eye out. I knew just how it would be, Trav. I would wear that mink cape into that house and my mother and my grandmother would stare, and then I would let them know I hadn't gotten it the way they were thinking, and show them the scrapbook. Nineteen years old. God!

"There were strangers in the house, Trav. An impatient woman, and kids running all over the place. My grandmother had been dead over a year, and my mother was in the county home. Premature senility. She thought I was her sister, and she begged me to get her out of there. I got her into another place. A bill and a half a week for a year and a half, Trav, and then she had one big stroke instead of continuous little ones, and she died without ever *knowing*. Arthur asked me how I really know that. Maybe she had some lucid spell when she knew and was proud." Her eyes swam and she shook her head. "Okay. He's good for me. Like my head was full of little knots. I talk and talk and talk, and he says something, and a little knot loosens." She scowled. "The thing about Frankie, when he finds out something bugs you, a long time later he'll say something that'll make it bug you more. I explained that to Arthur. He says maybe that's why I need Frankie, so he can punish me and I don't have to punish myself.

"Trav, you really have to give Arthur *something* to do. I can only hoist him up so far. You treat him like a tanglefoot kid, and when I make him into a man it doesn't hold. It doesn't last. Maybe, Trav, that's a more important part than the money. He talks about those jobs at Everglades. Wistful, sort of. When he ran the store it was all kind of set. The buyers knew what to buy for that city. And he had good display and advertising people, and the merchandising was kind of all established before he got into it. But he said if you can put up rough studding and it stands true and the foreman comes around and says okay, then you think people are going to live there for years, and winds won't blow it down. I can't say it like he does. But you see, except for the store, which was all set anyway, everything he ever did got bitched up. Everything except those crummy little jobs. If you trust him to do something, he'll trust himself more."

So I promised I would, and I told her we had time, before three fifteen, to get a little better set. I bought a newsstand map of Tampa and I rented a pale gray Galaxie. They are turning Tampa into the customary nothing. It used to be memorable as one of the grubbiest and most infuriating traffic mazes south of the Chelsea area of Boston. Now they are ramming the monster highways through it, and one day soon it will become merely a momentary dinginess. They've opened up the center of the city into a more spacious characterlessness, and, more and more, they are converting Ybor City into fake New Orleans. In some remote year the historians will record that Twentieth Century America attempted the astonishing blunder of changing its culture to fit automobiles instead of people, putting a skin of concrete and asphalt over millions of acres of arable land, rotting the hearts of their cities, so encouraging the proliferation of murderous, high-speed junk that when finally the invention of the Transporlon rendered the auto obsolete, it took twenty years and half a trillion dollars to obliterate the ugliness of all the years of madness, and rebuild the supercities in a manner to dignify the human instead of his toys.

I left Chook in the car and went into the reference section of the library and looked up the *Buccaneer* in Lloyd's Register of Yachts. There were a slew of them, and I found the one registered out of Tampa that was a hundred and eighteen feet long, a converted Coast Guard cutter, owned by Foam-Flex Industries. I phoned them and was shunted up through the pyramid to the Vice President in Charge of Sales and Promotion, a Mr. Fowler, with a little trace of Vermont in his speech.

"On anything like that," he said, "you'd have to check with Mr. Robinelli at the Gibson Yards, where we keep her. The way it works, we set up an advance schedule for executive use of the vessel, and empower Mr. Robinelli to charter her when such charters will not interfere with company plans in any way. These charters, and I wish there were more of them, help with maintenance, dockage, insurance and payroll of the permanent crew. I don't have a copy of the advance schedule handy, but I could have someone get it. I happen to know she is at the yard right now. If you . . ."

I told him not to bother, and that I would check with Mr. Robinelli. I looked up the address of the yard, and went back to the car and found it on the city map. There was enough time to go check it out. It was over in the big busy commercial harbor, where a dozen freighters were loading and off-loading, where industrial smog hung low and heavy in the heat, where the air stank of chemicals and where, in that manufactured haze, some huge piles of sulphur gleamed a vivid and improbable yellow. I parked by the office of the Gibson Yards, and I could see the *Buccaneer* at a dockside mooring. Two men in khakis were working topsides. She had a lot of bright-work, and I did not envy anyone the housekeeping chore of sluicing the local grime off her every day.

Robinelli was chunky and brusque, a three-telephone, four-clip-board, five-fountain-pen man, a trotting fellow with no time for small talk. I represented myself as spokesman for a group interested in chartering the *Buccaneer* for a cruise to Yucatan, say twenty days. Ten in the party. Would she be available any time soon? At what rate?

He jumped into his desk chair and scribbled on a pad. "Call it an even three thousand. Includes food, steward service. Crew of four. Bring your own booze. Everything else laid on." He spoke more loudly, with a whipcrack in his voice, and a thin woman with a limp came at a halting half trot to hand him a clipboard. He snapped through the top pages. "She's open as of July 10th for thirty-two days. Have to know by June 30th the latest. Certified check in full two days before departure. No charter passengers sixty-five or older. Insurance provision. Cruises at fourteen knots. Sixteen hundred mile range. Radar, salt-water conversion unit, draws nine feet, seven pas-senger staterooms, three heads with tub and shower. Antiroll fins. Go look at it." He scribbled a note, handed it to me. "Let me know. In writing."

I took Chook down to the dock with me. A husky kid with a blunt indifferent face, big freckled biceps, a khaki shirt tailored to fit as tightly as his young hide looked at the note, said the captain had gone ashore for the day and we were welcome to look around. We took a quick tour. The conversion was well done. She had become luxury transportation without losing her businesslike flavor.

Topside again, I said, "Thanks." Stuck my head in the engine room. "Solid old lunkers," I said. "With that big slow stroke, they should live forever. But in the conversion, didn't they put in a different precombustion system?" I had read the dirt under his nails accurately. Pleased alertness washed away the air of indifference, and in about four minutes he told me more than I cared to know about the brute diesels in the *Buck*.

"I heard about her from a friend of mine who had her on charter. Cal Stebber."

"Who?"

"A very important man. Short, heavy, very friendly. He was on her last summer in Naples. He was down there on a land deal."

"Oh, *him!* Yeah, Nice guy. But it wasn't a charter, exactly. We had a three-week layover at that Cutlass Yacht Club on account of one job ended there, and we had to pick the next bunch up there, so Mr. Stebber made a deal with Captain Andy to stay aboard for a while. Sort of a dock-side charter. Captain Andy got hell from Robinelli. Hell, if he hadn't turned in the money, Robinelli wouldn't have known a damn thing about it. I think it was fifty a day they settled for. And the deal was that Mr. Stebber had some people he wanted to look real good for, so we were briefed to say, if anybody asked us, friends had loaned it to Mr. Stebber."

"I know Cal lives right here in Tampa, and I had his unlisted number and didn't bring it. Forgot his address. One of those cooperative apartments on Tampa Bay. You wouldn't have it aboard, would you?"

"Golly, I don't think so. He got on and he got off at Naples, and we were tied up the whole time. He paid cash. There wouldn't be any reason to . . ." He stopped and tugged his ear, looking into space. "Wait a minute. There was something. Yeah. Bruno found it when he was sweeping up after Mr. Stebber left. One cuff link under something. Solid gold with some kind of gray-looking jewel in it. Captain Andy had that phone number, or got it somehow, and when we got back to Tampa he got hold of Mr. Stebber and . . ." He turned to face forward, and yelled, "Hey, Bruno. Here a minute."

Bruno, lanky and unprepossessing, came shambling aft, wiping soapy hands on his thighs, staring with great glinteyed approval at Miss McCall.

"Say Bru, you remember the guy you took that gold cuff link back to last year?"

"Give me twenty bucks, man. I remember pretty good."

"Where was it you had to go?"

"West Shore Boulevard, below Gandy Bridge, like near McDill. Some number, I don't remember. Pretty nice place, man."

"Could you tell this man something so he can find it?"

"Don't lean or I come up empty. Give me room to think. It had a number, and it had a name. Pale-color building, and like four buildings hooked together, him in the one closest to the water, top floor. Maybe seventh floor, eighth floor. Anyhow, the top one. Something about the name, it didn't make sense. I got it! West Harbour. Even spelled wrong. Oh-you-are instead of oh-are. And no harbor there, man, no matter how you spell it. Docks and a half-ass breakwater and more little sailboats than they had little cruisers, but nothing I'd call a harbor."

As we headed away from there, Chook said, "Half the time I don't know what's on your mind. I have to just stand there, looking relaxed. It's a weird way to come up with his address, McGee."

"There are probably other ways. Maybe not too many, if he's quiet and careful. People leave tracks. You don't know where they left them. If you range back and forth across territory where you know they've been, then you have a better chance of blundering across something. You just saw good luck. I've had a lot of bad days too. If Stebber wants to play, or if he doesn't want to play, either way I'm glad to know where he is. I think we'll call him right from there."

It was almost three thirty by the time I located West Harbour. It was rich and tasteful, the grounds spacious and landscaped, the architecture styled to avoid a cold and institutional look, without severe geometry or mathematical spacing. The main entrance drive split into three separate drives—delivery, guests and residents. I left Chook in the car, the keys in the ignition.

"I am going to be out of there by four thirty or sooner. I won't send word. If I want to take longer, I'll come down and tell you myself. So at four thirty, you drive right out of here, stop at the first pay phone you can find, tip the police, anonymously, that something very strange is going on at the Stebber apartment, West Harbour, the tower nearest the waterfront, top floor. And then find your way back to the airport. Turn this car in. Here's your airplane ticket. If I don't show for the seven o'clock plane, get on it anyway. Take the other car back to the marina. Here are the other car keys. Check Arthur off the boat, lock it up, go check into a motel. Make it . . . Mr. and Mrs. Arthur McCall. Tomorrow morning, find the Chamber of Commerce. They all have visitors' books. Sign in under that name, with the motel address, including the unit number. Get it?"

"I got it."

"Need money?"

"No. I've got enough."

I used a pay booth in the West Harbour lobby to phone Stebber's unlisted number. "Yes?" the same voice said, in the same cool modulation.

"Me again, smirking girl. A little off schedule."

"The gentleman you were asking about before, sir, would be happy to meet you at the bar at the Tampa Terrace Hotel at five o'clock."

"Couldn't he see me now, as long as I'm right here?"

"Here?"

"At West Harbour, dear. In the lobby."

"Would you please hold the line a moment, sir."

It was a very long moment. She came back and said, "You may come up, sir. Do you know the apartment number?"

"I know where it is, but not the number."

"Four dash eight A. Four is the tower, eight is the floor."

I took the walk to the tower nearest the water. The path had a screen of shrubbery. There were curves, stairs up and stairs down, little public courts with benches and some curious cement statuary. The lobby of Tower Four was spacious and empty. You can equate expense with the space they are willing to waste. Two small self-service elevators. At eight the door hissed open and I walked into a small foyer, indirectly lighted. B on the right; A on the left. I pressed a stainless steel button. There was a three-inch circle of mirror set into the door. I winked at it.

The girl beind the voice opened the door and said, "Do come in, sir."

"I did not get a really good look at her until she had led me through a short entrance hallway and down two carpeted steps into a large living room, where she turned and smiled her greeting again. She was medium height, and very slender. She wore pants carefully tailored to her slenderness, of a white fabric worked with gold thread in ornate and delicate design. With it she wore a sort of short coolie coat of the same fabric, and three-quarter sleeves and a wide stiffened collar which stood up in the back and swooped down around her shoulders, making a theatrical frame for a slender, pale, classic, beautiful face. Her hair, a very dark and rich chestnut brown, was combed smooth and straight, falling to frame her face, soft parentheses, to chin level, with copper glints where daylight touched it. But the eyes were the best of her. Crystal mint, that clear perfect green of childhood Christmas, the green you see after the first few licks have melted the sugar frost. In walk and smile and gesture she had all the mannered elegance of a high-fashion model. In most women who have that trick, it is an irritating artifice. Look, look, look at gorgeous incomparable me! But she managed, somehow, to mock herself at the same time, so the effect was of elegance shared. It said: Having it, I might as well use it.

"I'll tell him you're here. It would be nice to tell him a name, wouldn't it?"

"Travis McGee. You have a name too."

"Debra."

"And never never Debbie."

"Never indeed. Excuse me." She swayed off, closed a heavy door softly behind her. And for the first time the room came into focus. Probably thirty by fifty. Twelve-foot ceiling. Window wall with a spectacular view of the bay, terrace beyond it with a low wall, chinky redwood furniture. An almost transparent drapery had been pulled across to reduce the afternoon glare, and there was a heavier drapery racked at the side of it. Giant fireplace faced with coquina rock. Deep blue carpeting. Low furniture, in leather and pale wood. Bookcases. Wall shelves, built in, with a collection of blue Danish glassware, and another, glassed in, with a collection of the little clay figures of Pre-Columbian Latin America. The cooled air was in slight movement, scented very faintly with pine.

It was a very still room, a place where you could listen to the beating of your heart. And it seemed to lack identity, as though it might be a room where executives waited to be called into the board meeting beyound the dark and heavy door.

After long minutes the door opened and Calvin Stebber came smiling into the room. Debra two paces behind him and, in her flat white sandals with gold thongs, maybe an inch taller. He marched up to me and stared up at me, smiling, and I could feel the impact of his superb projection of warmth, interest, kindliness, importance. You could be this man's lifelong friend after ten minutes, and marvel that he found you interesting enough to spend a piece of his busy life on you. It was the basic working tool of the top-grade confidence man.

"Well now, Mr. McGee, I do respect Debra's instinct, and I must say that she was correct. You have not the faintest odor of the law. You do not look irrational, and you do not look a fool. So do sit down, young man, and we will have our little chat. Sit there, please, where you won't get the glare in your eyes."

He wore a dark green blazer, gray flannel trousers, a yellow ascot. He looked ruddy and fit, chubby and wholesome as he smiled across at me.

"And," he said, "our little telltale in the foyer had advised us you are not carrying some lethal hunk of metal. Cigar, Mr. McGee?"

"No thank you, Mr. Stebber."

"Please, Debra," he said. She went to a table, took a fat foil-wrapped cigar from a humidor, peeled it and, frowning in pretty concentration, clipped the ends carefully with a little gold gadget. She lit a kitchen match, waited until the flame was right, then lit the cigar, revolving it slowly, getting a perfect light. She took it to him, her every move theatrically elegant, and this time all elegance was directed at him, and without irony, more as if it was her obligation to herself and to him to be as consciously lovely as she could manage to be. A gift for Calvin.

"Thank you, dear. Before we begin, Harris phoned up here about your companion, Mr. McGee, and I suggested he bring her up."

"It might be a pretty good trick."

"Harris can be very persuasive." A buzzer sounded. "There they are. Do let her in, dear. And tell Harris to bring the car around at five."

I did not get a look at Harris, but Chook told me later he was so much beef in a gray chauffeur's uniform, he would make me look shrunken and puny. She said he had plucked her out of the car the way she would lift a kitten out of a shoe box. I realized later that the long wait when I had phoned upstairs was to give Debra time to alert Harris on another phone, possibly a house line to the service area.

Chook came into the room thin-lipped with fury, rubbing her upper arm. "Trav, what the hell is going on!" she demanded. "That big clown lamed me. And *you*, fat little man, I suppose you're the chief thief."

Stebber scurried over to her, great concern on his face. He took her hand in both of his and said, "My dear child, the last thing I wanted was to have Harris hurt you or anger you or frighten you, really. I merely thought it rude to have you waiting down there in the car in the hot sun. But seeing what a striking creature you are, my dear, it's doubly a pleasure to have you here. Come over and sit with me here on the couch. There! Now what is your name?"

"But I . . . Look, I only . . . Well . . . Barbara Jean McCall." It was a measure of his charm that I have never known her name until that moment. She made no attempt to pull her hand away. She looked bedazzled. I glanced at Debra and she gave me a wise, measured wink. "Chookie, people call me. Chook sometimes I . . . I'm a professional dancer."

"Chookie, my dear, with all that grace and vitality and presence, I can't imagine you being anything else. I bet you're *very* good!" He released her hand, gave her an approving little pat on the arm, turned and looked up over his shoulder at Debra, leaning against the back of the couch and said, "Debra, dear, say hello to Chookie McCall, and then you might fix us all a drink."

"Hello, dear. I'm tremendous with daiquiris if anyone cares."

"Well . . . sure. Thanks," Chook said. I nodded agreement.

"Four coming up swiftly," Debra said, and Chook did not take her eyes off the willowy grace of Debra until a door swung shut behind her.

"Spectacular creature, isn't she?" Stebber said. "And, in her own way, quite natural and unspoiled. Now let's get to it, Mr. McGee. You used a name over the phone. A password. And you show a certain amount of resource and ingenuity. But, of course, we have a problem. We don't know each other. Or trust each other. What is your occupation?"

"Semiretired. Sometimes I help a friend solve a little problem. It isn't anything you need an office for. Or a license."

"And this handsome young woman is helping you help a friend?"

"Something like that. But when a friend gets caught in a big con, it isn't easy. Old grifters like you keep the action safe and almost on the level. Maybe you even pay taxes on the take. And you train your ropers and shills and let them take the risks. I suppose you're so used to living nice, Stebber, you don't want to risk taking any kind of a fall. How badly do you want to avoid a fuss? When I know that I know how much pressure I've got." I kept it very casual.

He stared at me for long alert seconds. "Certainly not bunko," he said. "Wrong type, completely. Could you have been with it?"

"Not with it. Close to it a few times. Helping friends."

Chook said irritably, "What's going *on?*"

Debra reappeared, bringing four golden-pale daiquiris on a teak-and-pewter tray. I said, "Cal Stebber's in the bait business, honey. He gets the hungry ones, and they get hauled aboard and gutted."

Debra made a face at me as I took my drink from the tray.

"What a dreadful way to say it. Really! You must have made some very bad investments, Mr. McGee."

"Debra, dear," Stebber said. "Have we given up waiting for our cues?" It was said with loving patience, and with an almost genuine warmth. But the girl's color changed, the tray dipped, the glasses slid an inch before she regained control. She made an almost inaudible murmur of apology. Discipline was rigid on this team.

After one imitation sip, I put my drink aside. Debra sat graceful and subdued on the arm of the couch. Stalemate. I decided I'd better gamble on my knowledge of the type. Perhaps, twenty years ago, he could have taken chances. Now his life would seem shorter to him. If I had no information he wanted, I wouldn't have gotten into the apartment. Now he was regretting even that. And I could say with almost total certainty that my chance of prying any of Arthur's money out of this one was zero. I had to give him some confidence. And I thought I might have the name that would do it.

"Know the Moaner, Cal?" I asked him.

He looked startled. "My God, I haven't thought of Benny in years. Is he still alive?"

"Yes. Retired. Lives with his son-in-law in Nashville. Phone is under the name of T. D. Notta. You could say hello."

"He knows you?"

"It isn't a real warm friendship."

He excused himself and left the room. Chook said, *"Somebody could give me a scorecard."*

"When the Moaner was young and spry, back, they say, in Stanley Steamer days, he got his start in Philadelphia, diving into the front end of slow-moving cars. He'd bounce off and roll away and moan like to break your heart. His partner wore a cop suit and came running up and spilled the fake blood on the Moaner when he bent over him to take a look at him. He worked up from there. Fake masterpieces, they say. And he worked the ships. Ran bucket shops, telephone swindles. All the long-time grifters know each other." Debra made a sound of amusement. Her morale was returning. But when I tried to pump her, she was both silent and amused.

When Stebber returned he had shed large hunks of his public personality. "The old bastard sounds pretty shaky, McGee. He doesn't like you. One of the last scores he made, a little one, you got it back before he could get out of range."

"For a friend."

"He says you don't holler cop. He says . . . Debra, dear, why don't you take Miss McCall to your room and make girl-talk?"

When Chook looked at me in query I nodded approval. They left. As the door closed, Stebber said, "Benny says you can get cute.

And he says it isn't a good idea to send anybody after you. He said you made two good boys as sorry as could be. He said don't try to figure you for a mark in any direction. And you're pretty much a loner. But if you say you'll deal, you'll deal."

"So you want to know what I've got and what I want."

"I know Wilma didn't send you. She's not damn fool enough to think of making a deal to come back in. And she would have given you the phone code. It's a simple number switch, based on what day of the week it is. Seven digits in the phone number. Seven days in the week. When she asks the caller to repeat the number, you just add one to whatever digit represents that day. You would have said seven one three-one eight seven eight."

"And having told me, to show how much you trust me, you'll change the code as soon as you can."

"You hurt me, my boy."

"The secretarial type who fed Arthur the knockout at the Piccadilly Pub. Could have been Debra, I suppose."

"You have a good eye. Few men could see how severe and plain she can make herself look. And how is poor Arthur?"

"Insolvent."

"It had to be him, of course. Wilma's most recent venture. Your Miss McCall. She has a special interest in Arthur?"

"You could put it that way."

He awarded me a sad, sweet, knowing man-of-the-world smile. "Odd, isn't it, how those very vital and alive ones are attracted to such shadowy, indistinct men. Poor Arthur. Not much sport there. Like shooting a bird in a cage."

"You must have felt sorry for him, Stebber. Or you would have taken his last dime."

"Wilma had her way. No pity, no mercy. He was just another symbol of what she has to keep killing, over and over."

"That's one of the shticks of the half-educated, this bite-sized psychiatry, Stebber. You do it pretty well."

Ruddiness deepened and then faded. It was nice to mark him a little in an area where he least expected it. "But we aren't progressing, McGee. We want information from each other. And the magic word is Wilma."

"For a top operator in the big con, which you seem to pretend to be, Stebber, you put together a damned shaky team. Crane Watts and Boone Waxwell are weak links."

"I know. Also Rike Jefferson, the executor. Weakness and unpredictability. But it was a . . . sentimental flaw. I couldn't take the time to set it up more soundly. Harry couldn't spare the time. Mr. Gisik. An old associate. A valued friend. He died six weeks ago in New Orleans after heart surgery, God rest his soul. As this venture was . . . reasonably legal, I took the risk of operating with weak people. But they were paid what they were worth. Your being here is, I suppose, one of the penalties of a clumsy operation. But let me assure you, Travis McGee, clumsiness stops out there beyond the main gate."

"I think there's another penalty too."

"Yes?"

"I think Wilma is dead."

It hit him very solidly. He reverted to that mask face which can be acquired only in prison or in the military. It shows nothing, asks nothing. He stood up slowly, paced to the window and back. "I've thought so too," he said. "Without quite admitting it. Let me put it this way. She was with me for fifteen years. And it is not an emotional loss. It's the end of . . . an effective professional relationship."

"Fifteen *years!*"

"She was nineteen when we found her. I had a steady partner at the time. Muscle. I went in for more active gaffs at that time. Southern California. She was in a place that catered to movie money. In little frocks and jumpers and pinafores. Alice in Wonderland haircut, face scrubbed, talking in a thin little lisp, doll in the crook of her arm, bubblegum in her little jaw, she could pass for eleven or twelve. There's a steady demand at good rates for that sort of thing. But they couldn't control her. She kept going on the gouge on her own. Greedy and reckless and merciless. We took her off their hands. She responded to discipline when she found we weren't at all squeamish about it. We improved her diction and cleaned up her vocabulary. We put her in full makeup, high-fashion clothes, and worked the class lounges and hotels. She had a good natural eye for a mark. After the fun and games, the gaff was to hit the mark in broad daylight on his grounds—home or office—the three of us, Wilma as a scared, bawling fourteen-year-old saying she truly loved the scared clown, my muscle as her murderously inclined father, me as an officer of the juvenile court, with her faked birth certificate in hand. The way out we'd finally give him was for him to spring for two or more years in a private institution for her, with the fee adjusted to how we had checked him out before the visit. You want to see real horror, you should have seen their faces when we laid the gaff on them. When we were home free, my God how she would laugh! A laugh to chill the blood. She learned fast. She was a quick study. She read a lot, remembered a lot. And lied a lot about herself. I think she even believed most of it."

He sat in silence on the couch, almost unaware of me. He was a dumpy, tired little thief dressed for a costume party.

"I gave up the rough lines. She became a partner. She'd cruise on her own, rope them, bring them back within range, set them up, clean them out, divorce them. Had she been more merciful I think she would have been a poisoner. Mercilessness can be a flaw. And believing your own lies. And she had another flaw too. She could never get any sexual satisfaction from the marks. After the scores she'd almost invariably find some brute stud, usually ignorant, rough, dirty and potentially dangerous. But she always kept the whip hand, drove them hard, walked out when she was ready." He sighed, stirred, pumped himself back up to full con-artist scale, aimed personality at me like a two-mile flashlight.

"McGee, do I do all the talking?"

"I think she must have been carrying her share in cash. And was killed a few days after she left the motel in Naples while Arthur was off on his bus trip. I'd guess the playmate who killed her has spent at least twenty-five thousand. Cars, a boat, guns, toys. I'm helping my friend Arthur. If I could come up with a good way of making a recovery from you, I'd give it a try. I take expenses off the top and keep half the net salvage. So moving in on her playmate could be full of ugly surprises, and if I knew how much she was carrying on her, I'd know if there was a balance worth the risk."

"And if I give you the figure?"

"Then I'd have to figure out whether to tell you who and where. And if you're lying. Suppose she was carrying just twenty-five. So you tell me a hundred so I will go prodding and maybe get jammed up in a way that will keep me from ever coming back with some cute idea for you. Or maybe I eliminate the playmate, which would satisfy you up for the way he cooked your future plans for Wilma. Or suppose she was carrying a hundred and you tell me it was twenty-five. I say who and where and you send muscle after it."

He pondered it. "Stalemate again. I see your point. There's no way I can get you to take my word that the very last thing I would do these days is go after a hijacked take, or send anyone. Risks alarm me, Travis McGee. I have too much to lose. You could check something out. I own twenty percent of the West Harbour Development

Corporation. And some other things here and there. Muscle is seldom combined with wits. You seem to be a striking exception. Someone gets killed and the muscle gets tricked into a state's evidence revelation, and the middleman I would use implicates me. No thanks. Besides, Debra and I are negotiating a score as big as the one Arthur contributed. By falsifying records, bribing minor officials, making some careful changes in old group pictures—school and church—and with the help of some brown contact lenses, some minor changes in hair and skin texture, we have given Debra an iron-clad identity as a mulatto, as a pale-skinned girl who actually did disappear at fourteen. The curious revelation has come as a horrid shock to her young husband of four months, and an even worse shock to her wealthy father-in-law, the ex-governor of a southern state, a fevered segregationist, a man with political ambitions. The positive rabbit test—also faked—is bringing things to a climax. The fat settlement is for divorce, abortion and total silence. There was a real chance they might solve it by having her killed. But Debra is not squeamish. Actually, she takes too many chances. Very good family. She was risk-hunting when I found her. Jumping out of airplanes, racing overpowered little boats and automobiles, skin-diving alone and too deep, potting at cape buffalo with a handgun. She's incredibly quick and strong. Now she has found something, finally, which satisfies her. The hunt. Along with the constant and very real danger of displeasing me.

"McGee, all I can ask you to do is accept my story of what happened. There was a hundred and thirty-five thousand left in that trustee account for the syndicate in the Naples bank. I arranged in advance for them to have cash available. It is not difficult in Florida where cash is used so often in real estate closings. The day Arthur came up to meet me, my man Harris drove me to Naples. I closed out the account at noon, kept five thousand for incidental expenses and took the balance to that grisly motel room and gave it to Wilma. She was almost packed. We had arranged she would return to Tampa in the car with me in time to catch a Nassau flight. I had her ticket. The money represented the final take for both of us. I gave her the prepared deposit slip for my share. Bahamian banks have a pleasant policy of never divulging information on an account unless the depositor appears in person and signs a specific authorization. She said she'd made other arrangements, that someone was going to drive her to Miami and she would fly over from there. I made mild objections."

"And you let her fly off with all that money?"

"She liked money. Without me, she'd have a lot less to spend. We were together fifteen years. Taking cash into the islands is easy. She was shrewd and tough. And far from retirement."

"So, as I said at first, maybe you're fattening the figure."

He called Debra in. I gave them no chance for signals, made her face me with her slender back toward him. She verified the details and the amount, asked no questions, left without a word when he told her to go.

I could have gathered up Chookie and left. I doubted he'd have tried anything. But there was an implied obligation. And if he did indeed come after what Boo might have left, it could turn into a diversion I might be able to use.

"Boo Waxwell picked her up at the motel. Arthur went to Waxwell's place at Goodland and found her there. Boo beat him badly. I jounced Crane Watts around first. I used his name to open Waxwell up. I invented the yarn that Arthur had gone to Watts and told him he'd seen Wilma at Waxwell's. I said I was trying to set up a similar kind of operation to the way you cleaned Arthur out, and needed the woman. He claimed, wide-eyed, it was a little ol waitress friend from Miami. But Arthur remembers Wilma wearing the watch he thought she'd sold in Miami. He wouldn't invent that. And, of course, he has all his new toys."

Stebber nodded slowly. "Her usual type. A little more complex, probably. Whenever she tamed them, that finished it for her. I tried to keep him away from Arthur's beach house while we were still building the con. Hard man to control. Yes. Of course. It fits. She wouldn't have waved the money at him. He smelled it somehow."

Debra knocked and appeared with a blue extension phone. "Crane Watts," she said. "Do you want to take it in here, darling?"

"Or take it at all? Please." She stooped lithely, plugged it into a baseboard jack receptacle, brought it to him and drifted out.

In full heat and radiance he said, "How *nice* to hear from you, Crane, my boy! . . . Start from the beginning. Slow down, boy . . . Yes . . . I see . . . Please, no assumptions. Confine yourself to the facts."

Watts talked for a long time without interruption. Stebber made a sad face at me. Finally he said, "That's enough. *Do* pull yourself together. No person named McGee or named anything else has tried to contact me on that matter. Why should you think in terms of an official investigation? As a lawyer you must know it was a legal business matter. This McGee is probably some sharpshooter who found

out Arthur had lost some money in an unwise investment and is trying to shake some of it loose. Tell Waxwell too that neither of you
should be so agitated. Please don't phone me again. I retained you
for legal work. It's finished. So is our association."

He listened for a short time and said, "The status of your career
could not mean less to me, Watts. Please don't bother me again."

As he returned the phone to the cradle I could hear the frantic
tiny buzzing of Crane's agitated voice. Frowning, Stebber said,
"Strange that Waxwell should be so eager to bully my phone number out of Watts. He says he gave him the number but not the
code—as if he expected congratulations. I would think, if your guess
is right, I'd be the last person he'd . . ."

Changing the pitch and resonance of my voice, I said, "Ol Boo
make that lawyer boy itchy."

It astounded and delighted him out of all proportion to the ac-
complishment. Patience and a good tape recorder can make a respectable mimic out of anyone.

"Maybe some day we could find a project to our mutual advantage," he said.

"I can think of one right now. Decoy Waxwell up here and keep
him here for one full day and I send you ten percent of all we
recover."

"No thanks. I don't think the man is entirely sane. And he goes by
hunch. I wouldn't risk it. Decoy him with a woman, McGee. The
McCall girl could keep him occupied long enough."

"Let's say she's squeamish, Stebber. Loan me Debra for the same
cut. Ten percent."

"I wouldn't consider it for one . . ." He stopped suddenly. His shy
glance was more obscene than any wink or leer could have been. "If
you could have her back in three days. And . . . if you could leave
Miss McCall here with me. As a guarantee of good faith."

"How bulky would the money be?"

"New hundreds in Federal Reserve wrappers. Thirteen packets,
one hundred bills thick. Perhaps not quite enough to fill a fair-sized
shoe box. You didn't answer my question about Miss . . . Chookie."

"Given a choice, given time to think, I imagine she'd pick Boo
Waxwell."

"Why give her a choice, dear boy? You'd find Debra charming
company. And I can assure you few men make the impact on her
you've already made. And when you get Miss Chookie McCall back
you'd find her quite anxious to be agreeable, and not at all conten-

tious. Truly effective disciplines, McGee, leave the loveliness untouched and the soul just an interesting bit queasy and apprehensive. It's a superimposed useful anxiety."

"Speaking for Miss McCall, no thanks."

"Some day, perhaps," he said and went and called the girls. They came walking slowly back into the big room, and I saw Chook wearing an odd expression, Debra looking secretively amused.

They both walked us out to the elevator, all charm and assurance, convincing us we were lovely people who had stopped in for a lovely drink. As the elevator door closed, my final look at them showed their gracious smiles, the smiles of an elegant couple, tastefully appointed, mannerly. And virulent as coral snakes.

Chook stayed lost in her silence and did not explode until we were a half mile away. "Girl-talk! *Girl*-talk! Do you know what that skinny bitch was doing? She was trying to . . . to *recruit* me. Like a goddam Marine poster. See the world. Learn a trade. Retire in your prime."

"Recruit you as what?"

"She didn't say right out. She inspected me like a side of meat and said I was prime. Too bad I was wasting myself in such hard work for so little money. Damn it, I make *good* money. Men, she said, the right kind of men, could get so expensively intrigued with a big, dark, fierce-looking girl like me. And that man, Trav. He made me feel weak and silly and young, and he made me feel anxious to make him like me. At first. But at the end there, I was thinking how nice it would be to squash him like a bug. They scare me, Trav. In a way I don't think I've been scared since I was a kid, when my grandmother got me so worked up about white slavers, if I saw two men standing on a street corner, I'd cross the street so they couldn't jab me with a needle and sell me to the Arabs. Trav, if we have to have anything to do with those people, something really awful might happen. My God, Trav, you should see the clothes she's got. Furs and originals and nine drawers of undies and a shoe rack, I swear to God, with a hundred pair of shoes at least. And all the time she was kind of laughing at me inside, as if I was a dumb oaf of a girl, a nudnik. What *happened*, Travis?"

"In short form, he confirms the hunch Waxwell killed her. She was carrying her share and his of Arthur's money. She was to put his end in a Nassau bank account. A hundred and thirty thousand dollars. I think he already had taken a fat slice of the rest of it. Everybody else had been paid off. But he writes her off and the money off.

He wants no part of it. He says. Maybe I believe him. I don't know. He might send somebody down. We have to play it that way."

"A hundred and thirty thousand!" she exclaimed.

"Less what old Boo has blown. Rough guess, eighty-five or ninety left."

"But that's good, isn't it? Isn't that better than anything you expected?"

"Putting my hands on any part of it, Chook, is going to be better than I expected. And I haven't done that yet."

twelve

It was after nine at night when I parked at the marina and we went aboard *The Busted Flush*. No light showed. I had the irrational hunch that something had gone wrong. Maybe I had been exposed to too much calculated deviousness for one day. But as I flicked the lounge lights on, there was Arthur slouched on the big yellow couch. He had a tall glass in his hand, dark enough for iced coffee. He gave us a big crooked glassy grin, hoisted the glass in such an enthusiastic salute of welcome that a dollop of it leaped out and splashed his shirt.

"Warra sharra numun!" he said.

Chook stood over him, fists on her hips. "Oh, boy! You've done it real good, huh?"

"Shawara dummen huzzer," he said, in pleased explanation.

She took the glass out of his hand, sniffed it, set it aside. She turned to me. "As you remember, it doesn't take much. The poor silly. It was such a strain to be shut up here all this time." She took his wrist, braced herself. "Upsy-daisy, darling."

She got him up, but with a wide, loving grin, he enfolded her in big arms and, utterly slack, bore her over and down with a mighty thud of their combined weights. Chook worked free and stood up, rubbing a bruised haunch. Arthur, still smiling, cheek resting on his forearm, emitted a low buzzing snore.

"At least," she said, "it's not what I'm used to. A happy drunk."

Between us we stood him up, draped him soddenly over my shoulder. I dumped him into the big bed. "Thanks, Trav. I'll manage from here," she said, and began to unbutton his shirt, looking up from the task to give me a slightly rueful smile. "Rich warm memories of Frankie Durkin," she said. "But there the trick was to keep from getting a split mouth or a fat eye before he folded."

Up on the sun deck I heard the sound of the shower, and a little while later she came climbing up into the night warmth in her robe, bringing two beers.

"Rockaby baby," she said. "Tomorrow he'll be a disaster area." She sat beside me. "And what now, captain?"

"Confusion. I was thinking that, at the right distance, in the right garments, you might pass as Vivian Watts, tennis player. And if Viv left a message for ol Boo to join her in assignation at some far place, it might intrigue him. But it won't fit together. The odds are she despises Waxwell and he knows it. Then it struck me that she could properly blame Waxwell for her husband's downhill slide. And she might leap at the chance to give him a bruise if there was a chance of a piece of money to square all overdue accounts and have enough left over to move along to a place where Crane Watts could start all over again. That means sounding her out. Quietly and soon. But with something specific. That's as far as I've gotten."

"Hmm. And Waxwell would think it fishy if she made a play. But he does have . . . a certain interest in her?"

"Avid."

"What if he found out somehow that she had left her husband and gone off someplace alone to think things out, all alone in some hideaway place, away from people. A place hard to get to. She wouldn't be there, of course, but it would take him a long time to get there and find out and get back."

"And when he got back and found out he'd been cleaned out, who would he go after first, Chook? That isn't a happy thought."

"See what you mean. But what if she and her husband got all set to take off, so then you could give them some of the money and they'd be gone before he got back?"

"And if I can't find the money?"

"Then he wouldn't have much to be sore about, would he?"

"And she could say that she started off and changed her mind and came back to her husband. If he asks. You have a talent for this, Miss Chookie."

"Thanks a lot. Trav, I don't see how you *can* expect to find it, even if you had a whole day."

"I have an idea about that. Remember the story of Bluebeard?"

"What's that supposed to mean?"

"I'll tell you if it works."

"And you have to think of a place she might be likely to go. And some way of getting the word to Boone Waxwell. And you have to talk her into it in the first place."

"I think she's desperate. I think she's ready to try anything. And she would be the logical one to ask about a place she might go. Meanwhile, playing it by ear, we've got ourselves located on the wrong square on this board maybe. Maybe not. Hell, I guess not. With the car, and with the little boat at Naples, maybe right on the edge of the board is the best square to occupy."

"And you'll use Arthur somehow, dear? Some safe way?"

"I promise."

She patted my arm. "Thank you very much. Do men's work. Leave the lady home to give tearful thanks at the safe return."

"I can't take him with me tomorrow. Or you. Not for the morning mission."

"What is it?"

"I want to see if the Bluebeard idea is any good before I take the Viv idea any further."

Tuesday morning at nine thirty, from a gas station a quarter mile from the junior high school, I phoned the administration office and asked to speak to Cindy Ingerfeldt. A woman with a tart, skeptical voice said, "This is the next to the last day of exams. I can check to see if she is taking an examination or if she is in a study period, but I shall have to know who you are and the purpose of the call."

"The name is Hooper, ma'am. Field investigator for State Beverage Control. I'll have to ask you to keep that confidential. The girl could have some useful information. Could you give me a rundown on her, what kind of a kid she is?"

"I . . . I don't imagine you'll find her cooperative. Cindy is quite mature for her age. A very indifferent student. She's just marking time here, as so many of them are. I take it her home life is not too pleasant. She's not a popular child. She keeps to herself. She's tidy about her person, and would be really quite pretty if she lost some weight. Mr. Hooper, if you want to interrogate the child, you could come here and I could turn over a private office to you."

"I'd rather not do it that way, ma'am. Word could get back to some pretty rough people. I wouldn't want to cause her that kind of trouble. That's why I ask you kindly to keep this to yourself."

"Oh, dear. Is the child . . . involved in anything?"

"Nothing like that, ma'am. You know, if you really want to cooperate, rather than me trying to get anything out of her over the phone, I'd appreciate it if you could just make some reason to send her down the road to the Texaco station. I won't take much of her time, and send her right back."

"Well . . . let me check her schedule." About a full minute later, as I stared through the booth glass at the distant building and the ranks of yellow buses behind it, she came back on the line and said in a conspiratorial way, "She'll finish her history test at ten. I think the most inconspicuous way would be for me to go and see her in person as she comes out, and I will send her along then. Will that be all right?"

"Just fine, and I certainly do appreciate your cooperation."

At a few minutes before ten, I moved the car, parked it fifty yards closer to the school, aimed in the direction of the gas station. At a few minutes after ten I saw her in the rear-vision mirror, trudging along toward me, both arms hugging a stack of books to her bosom. She wore a green striped cotton blouse, salmon-colored pants that ended halfway between knee and ankle, white sneakers. When she was near enough, I reached over and swung the door open, saying, "Good morning, Cindy."

She stared at me, came slowly toward the car, stopped a few feet away. "Oh. You, huh." She appraised me with those wise old eyes. "What's on your mind?"

"Get in."

"Lissen, if Sunday give you any ideas, forget it. I don't know you, I'm not in the mood, and I got enough problems, mister."

"I want to fix ol Boo's wagon, Cindy. And he'll never know you were involved in any way. I just want to ask some questions. Get in and we'll drive around and I'll drop you off right here in fifteen minutes."

"What makes you think I should want to mess Boo up someways?"

"Let's just say you could be doing your father a favor."

She pursed her small mouth, gave a half shrug and climbed in. She plunked her books on the seat between us and said, "No driving around. Go like I tell you."

Her directions were terse and lucid. They took us three blocks over, two blocks to the left, and into a sheltered grove with picnic tables and fireplaces, willows thick around a pond. When I turned the engine off she sighed, undid a button of her blouse, poked two fingers into her bra, squirmed slightly, and pulled out a wilted cigarette and a kitchen match. She popped the match a-flame with a deft thumbnail, drew deeply, exhaled a long gray plume that bounced off the inside of the windshield.

"How'd you get old Mossbutt to leave me loose?"

"I said it was official. Beverage Control investigation. When you go back she'll want to know. Tell her Mr. Hooper said not to talk about it to anybody."

"That's your name?"

"No."

"Is it official?"

"What do you think, Cindy?"

"Prolly not."

"You're right. Sunday you gave me the impression you wish Waxwell was out of your life. Was that an act?"

"I don't know. Guess not. If he wasn't so damn mean. And not so old. Don't take me no place. Miami, he keeps saying. Sure. I should live so long. The way it goes, shit, I've gotta make some kind of move myself, because I hang around, it's going to be the same, no matter what. A bunch of the kids, they got a chance to bus up and work tobacco in Connecticut this summer. Working hard and being far away, I could get over being so hooked, maybe. Goddam mean old man, he is."

The last drag drew the fire line down close to her thumb. She snapped the butt out the window, holding her breath, then exhaled, openmouthed. She turned toward me and rested her plump cheek on the seat back. "What d'ya wanna know?"

"Do you know Boo murdered a woman out there at his place last year?"

She hooded her eyes, examined a thumbnail, nibbled the corner of it. "Friend a yours?"

"No. Just the opposite. It didn't seem to surprise you."

"I guess I had the feeling something happened. She a midget or something?"

"That's a funny question."

"There was some black lace panties I tried to get on. I'm fat but not that fat. I busted them trying. When I asked too many times he popped me on top of the head with his fist so hard I got sick an heaved up."

"She was a very small woman. I understand he makes you work around the place."

"Oh, Christ, I don't mind that. He lives like a hog. It's just he won't let me keep ahead of it. He lets it go, then it's twice as much work."

"Is he always there when you're cleaning up?"

"When I'm there, he's there. What he says, I ever come around when he's gone, or come without him calling me he's got something special he's saving for a big surprise. I'm not fixing to get any surprise from him for sure."

"All right, when you are cleaning the place, is there any particular part of the house he won't let you touch?"

"Huh? I don't get it."

"As if something could be hidden in the house?"

"Huh? No. Nothing like that. But I sure God stay clear of the grove there back of the shed. One time, back in March I think, it got hot unexpected like. He'd come by and give me a blast on the horn pretty late. At like three in the morning, him asleep and snoring by then, I was there smelling some stinking fish he'd forgot about and left on the porch maybe since that noon. Redfish. They turn fast when it's hot. It got my stomach rolling over finally, so I up and pull my dress on and go out and pick them up by the stringer, get a shovel from the shed and go off back into the grove to bury them, holding my breath mostly. I hardly dug half a hole and he come at me, running flat out, grunting, that belt knife of his winking in the moonlight, charging bare-ass crazy right at me. Me, I take off through the grove and hear him hit a root or something and go down hard. Then he's coming on again, yelling he's going to kill me, and I'm yelling I was burying his stinking fish before the stink made me snap my lunch.

"Then he was quiet, so I snuck in a circle and see him back in the open part of the grove, finishing digging the hole. He dabbed the fish in and covered them over, then he hollers for me to come on in, saying it was okay, he was just having a funny dream and he woke up. Hell he did. A long time after he went back in the house I get the nerve fin'ly to sneak back in, and the way I got grabbed sudden in the dark from behind, it like to kill me. But what he wanted to do was just horse around. You know. Laughing and tickling. And he got me all turned on prakly before I got over being scared. And I tell you one thing, I never seen any shovel anywhere around his place since. But he isn't so dumb he'd bury that dwarf woman onto his own place. Not with a couple million acres of glades close by, where he could put a little dead woman back in there so far and so deep, the whole army and navy couldn't find her in a hundred years. Why, he could just float her into a gator pool and them gators would wedge her down into the mud bottom for ripenin and have her et'n to nothing in a couple weeks. Maybe they can catch him *killin* somebody, but they'll never get him for it afterwards. I'll tell you one more thing for sure. If'n you mess him up good, and he knows who done it, you're best off leaving him dead your own self. That's the thing about that tobacco work. I get maybe up past Georgia someplace and the bus stops and there he is, leanin on that white Lincoln grinnin, and I pick up my suitcase off'n the rack and get off that bus, because that's all there'd be to do. And he knows it."

On one of her notebook sheets I drew a crude sketch of the cottage and shed and road, and she made an X where she had started digging, and drew in some lopsided circles to indicate where the trees were standing.

As I let her off, she looked at me for a moment, eyes squinty and her lips sucked in. "I'd hate for you to say I told you this stuff."

"Cindy, you're fifteen years old, and you're going to get out of this mess and in another couple of years you won't remember much about it."

There was a bleak amusement in her woman's eyes. "I'm three weeks from sixteen, and it'll keep right on going on until Boo gets tired of it, and there won't be a day in my life I don't remember some part of it or other."

I drove into Naples, on the alert for Land Rovers and white Lincoln convertibles. I found a hardware store several blocks along Fifth Avenue, parked in their side lot, bought two spades and a pick and put them in the trunk. Then I thought of another device that might be useful, a variation of the way plumbers search for buried pipes. I bought a four-foot length of quarter-inch steel reinforcing rod, and one of those rubber-headed mallets they use for body and fender work. Naples was drowsy in the heat of the off-season, prenoon sun. I phoned Crane Watts' office number, and hung up when he said hello. Next I phoned his home number. It did not answer. I tried the club and asked if Mrs. Watts was on the courts. In a few moments they said she was, and should they call her to the phone. I said never mind.

When I arrived at the club the parking lot was nearly empty. There were a few people down on the beach, one couple in the pool. As I walked toward the courts I saw only two were in use, one where two scrawny elderly gentlemen were playing vicious pat-ball, and, several courts away, the brown, lithe, sturdy Mrs. Watts in a practice session. The man was apparently the club pro, very brown, balding, thickening. He moved well, but she had him pretty well lathered up. There were a couple of dozen balls near the court. He was feeding her backhand, ignoring the returns, bouncing each ball, then stroking it to her left with good speed and overspin. She moved, gauged, planted herself, pivoted, the ball ponging solidly off the gut, moved to await the next one. The waistband of her tennis skirt was visibly damp with sweat.

It seemed, for her, a strange and intense ritual, a curious sublimation of tension and combat. Her face was stern and expressionless. She glanced at me twice and then ignored me. Gave no greeting.

Finally as he turned to pick up three more balls she said, "That'll do for now, Timmy."

He took a handkerchief from his pocket and nopped his face. "Righto, Miz Watts. I make it three hours. Okay?"

"Anything you say."

As Timmy was collecting the balls in a mesh sack, she walked to the side-court bench, mopped her face and throat with a towel, stared at me with cold speculation as I approached.

"Pretty warm for it, Vivian."

"Mr. McGee, you made an excellent first impression on me the other night. But the second one was more lasting."

"And things might not have been what they seemed."

She took her time unsnapping the golf glove on her right hand, peeling it off. She prodded and examined the pads at the base of her fingers. "I do not think I am interested in any nuances of legality, Mr. McGee, any justification of any cute tricky little things you want to involve my husband in." As she spoke, she was slipping her rackets into their braces, tightening down the thumb screws. "He is not . . . the kind of man for that kind of thing. I don't know why he's trying to be something he isn't. It's tearing him apart. Why don't you just leave us alone?"

As she gathered up her gear, I picked the words that would, I hoped, pry open a closed mind. "Vivian, I wouldn't ask your husband's advice on a parking ticket, believe me."

She straightened up, those very dark blue eyes becoming round with surprise and indignation. "Crane is a *very* good attorney!"

"Maybe he was. Once upon a time. Not now."

"Who *are* you? What do you *want?*"

"I want to form a little mutual-aid society with you, Vivian. You need help and I need help."

"Is this . . . help I'm supposed to get, is it just for me or for Crane too?"

"Both of you."

"Of course. I get him to do some nasty little piece of crooked work for you, and it will make us gloriously rich and happy."

"No. He did his nasty little piece of crooked work last year, and it didn't do either of you any good."

She began to walk slowly, thoughtfully, off toward the distant entrance to the women's locker room, and I walked beside her. She had been laboring in the sun for three hours. Under the faded cosmetic and deodorant scents of a fastidious woman was an animal pungency of work-sweat, a sharpness not unpleasant, the effluvium of ballet schools and practice halls.

"What I can offer, if things can be worked out, is a long-odds chance and a suggestion. I think he's whipped himself here. I think you're both whipped. If you had some cash, right now, you should settle up what you owe around here and get out. Try it again in a new place. What is he? Thirty-one? There's time. But maybe he's lost you along the way, and you're not interested."

Under the shade of big pines the path narrowed and I dropped behind her. Her back was straight and strong, and the round of her sturdy hips, in tempo with the smooth brown muscular flex of her calves, gave the tennis skirt a limber sway. She stopped suddenly and turned around to face me. Her mouth, free of the tautness of disapproval, was softened and younger. "He hasn't lost me. But don't play games. Don't play cruel games, Travis. I don't know what's been going on. He says he got into something and he didn't know it was a bad thing until too late."

Sometimes you have to aim right between the eyes. "He knew from the start. He knew it was fraud, with a nice little sugar coating of legality. They paid him well, and he helped them screw a man named Arthur Wilkinson out of a quarter of a million dollars. It got around, Vivian. Who'd trust him now? He's terrified that somebody is going to wipe off the pretty icing and expose the fraud. He consorted with con artists and trash like Boone Waxwell, went into it with his eyes open for the sake of what he thought was going to be twelve thousand five. But he doesn't have the nerve to be a good thief. He began to shake apart. They kissed him off with seven thousand five, knowing he didn't have the nerve to get hard-nosed about it. And if he keeps dithering around, spilling his guts to strangers like me, maybe they'll get so tired of him they'll send somebody around to put a gun in his hand when he's passed out, and stick the barrel in his ear."

She wobbled on those good legs, and her color went sick under the tan. She moved off the path and sat, quite heavily, on a cement and cypress bench, staring blindly through the shade toward the bright sea. Her mouth trembled. I sat beside her, watching that unhappy profile.

"I . . . I guess I knew that he knew. Sunday night, after Waxwell left, he swore on his word of honor Waxwell had been lying, trying to needle us by all those little hints that Crane had been in on something all along."

She turned and looked at me in a pleading way, her color getting better, and said, "What makes him so *weak*?"

"Maybe what's left of your good opinion of him is the only thing he has left, Vivian. Would you still want to try to save it?"

"His best friend at Stetson, his roommate, wanted Crane to quit here and go in with him in practice in Orlando. He might still . . . I don't know. And I don't know about me even. I think if I could get him straightened out again, then it would be time to decide about me."

"If what I want to ask you to do works out, I want you and your husband to be ready to leave any moment, to get ready so you can leave. Arrange the big things later, like getting rid of the house and so on."

"Right now our equity in that might buy one day's groceries," she said bitterly. "One way or another, I can make him do it."

"How much would it take to clean up your bills here and give the two of you say a month or six weeks a good long way from here, in some hideout? Don't look so skeptical. You wouldn't be hiding from the law. It would be a chance to get him dried out. And then he might begin to make more sense to himself—and you."

"My father left me a cabin on a couple of acres of ridge land near Brevard, North Carolina. On Slick Rock Mountain. It's so lovely up there. You can look out across ridge after ridge, all gray-blue in the distance. Wood fires on summer nights." Her mouth twisted. "We honeymooned there, several thousand lifetimes ago. How much to settle up here? I don't know. He's been so secretive. Maybe we owe more than I know. I'd think three or four thousand dollars. But there might be other debts."

"And getting started in Orlando later on. Call it ten."

"Ten thousand dollars! What could I do that would be worth ten thousand dollars to anyone? Who do I have to kill?"

"You have to be bait, Vivian. To lure Boone Waxwell out of his cave and keep him out for as long as you can, a full day minimum, more if we can manage it."

Those good shoulders moved slowly up. She locked her hands, closed her eyes and shuddered. "That man. God, he makes my flesh crawl. The few times I've ever seen him, he's never taken his eyes off me. And he acts as if he and I have some special secret we share. All those little smirks and chuckles and winks, and the way he struts around me, puffing his chest and rolling his shoulders, laughing with a little snorting sound, like a stallion. And he puts double meanings in everything he says to me. Honestly, I freeze completely. He makes me feel naked and sick. That pelt of hair sticking out of the top of those ghastly shirts, and all that black hair on the backs of his hands and fingers, and that sort of . . . oily intimacy in his voice, it all makes my stomach turn over. Travis, if what you have in mind involves his . . . even touching me in any way, no. Not for ten thousand dollars, not for ten thousand dollars a minute." She tilted her head, looking at me in a puzzled way. "It isn't because I'm . . . prissy or anything. No other man has affected me that way. I am certainly not . . . unresponsive." And again, the wryness around her mouth. "Of course I haven't been able to check that in some time. When one becomes a very infrequent convenience for a drunk, an accommodation, the opportunity for any kind of response is very goddam rare."

A dime of sunlight came through the pine branches overhead, glowed against the firm and graceful forearm, showing the pattern of fine golden hair against the dark skin. She shook her head. "It's like nightmares when you're a kid. I think that if Boone Waxwell ever . . . got me, I might walk around afterwards and look just the same, but my heart would be dead as a stone forever. Oh, I guess I'd make nifty bait all right. He did everything but paw the ground Sunday night."

"The point is to make him think you have gone to a place where he can get at you. A far place, that'll take him a long time to get to. And a long time to get back when he finds it was a trick, and when he gets back, both of you will be gone. But you can't let your husband in on it. Because in his present condition, Waxwell can spread him open like a road map. We have to make Crane believe you *have* gone to a specific place, and somehow give Waxwell the idea of prying it out of him."

"Then you can get the money, while he's gone off after me."

"I had the idea you'd be just this quick and bright, Vivian."

"The money . . . Crane helped steal?"

"A good part of it."

"But then it's still stolen money, isn't it?"

"Not when, this time, you get it with the blessing of the man they took it from."

"The man you're working for?"

"In a sense. Arthur Wilkinson. And I think he should tell you in person that he approves the arrangement. You think of how we can best set it up, this decoy operation. Maybe Arthur and I can meet you tonight."

"I could have some specific plan by then, I think, Travis. You could come to the house at eleven."

"What about your husband?"

"The big suspense in my life every evening is whether he'll pass out in his big leather chair or totter to bed first. I try to cut down the intake. I make his drinks, on demand. It is a delicate problem. If I make them too weak, he comes blundering out into the kitchen and snarls at me and puts another big slug in the glass. He stares at television and doesn't see a thing or remember a thing. It's no problem, really. Tonight I'll make them strong, and frequent. And by eleven you could march a fife and drum corps through without him missing a snore. When he passes out, I'll put the light on over the front door." She took a very deep breath, let it out in a sigh. "Maybe it *can* work. Maybe people can go back and start the race a second time."

Back aboard the *Flush* I was in time for lunch only because Chook had delayed it until there was an improved chance of Arthur's keeping it down. He was wan and humble, reeking of guilt, his eyes sliding away from any direct glance.

"All these empty boats around us," he said. "I don't know. I kept hearing things. A little creak or a thump, after it got dark. Each time I *knew* he was sneaking aboard. And I knew what he has to do, Trav. He has to get rid of everybody who can link him with Wilma. And I *saw* her there. I went back and forth in the lounge in the dark, with the loaded gun, and I'd peer out the windows and see things, see some shadow duck across an open space over there, coming closer. I felt I could empty the gun right into him and he'd come right on at me, laughing. He certainly found out the name and description of this boat, and I just *knew* he'd hunted until he'd found it. Then I thought a drink would give me some confidence. And one didn't. But the second one worked so good, I thought three would be even better. Hell, I can't even remember what I *did* with the gun. We hunted all over. Chook found it. In a corner up against a locker. I must have dropped it and kicked it. I'm a lot of help to everybody."

Chook stepped from the galley to the dining booth and glowered down at him. She wore pale blue stretch pants that rode low on her hips, and a red bikini top so narrow that only a perfect adjustment, which she attained but seldom, kept the umber nipple areas entirely covered. Half leaning over the booth in that cramped area, in the glow of sun off the water shining through the ports, it seemed an almost overpowering amount of bare girl.

"Why don't you go sit in the garden and eat worms, lover?" she demanded. "Your self-pity rends my girlish heart. You got drunk, a condition so rare you can find it only in medical books. God's *sake*, Arthur!"

"I got terrified."

"That man beat you within an inch of your life, with Wilma watching it and enjoying it, and if that railing hadn't broken, maybe he would have killed you. Do you think a thing like that shouldn't leave a mark?" She hissed with exasperation. "Since when is it a sin to be scared? Am I going to move out of your bed because you can get frightened? Are people going to spit on you on the street? Drop this *boy scout* bit. Every day in every way, nine out of ten people in this big fat world are scared pissless. You have some obligation to be different? Even the mighty McGee isn't immune, believe me. God's *sake*, Arthur!"

She strode back into the galley area, made a vicious banging of copper pots.

"Wow," Arthur said in a low tone of awe.

"She's right," I said. "And tonight you get another chance to get a little jumpy, Arthur. You and I are going calling."

His throat slid up and down in a large, dry swallow. He put his shoulders back. "Fine!" he said heartily. "Just fine! Looking forward to it."

Chook appeared with a big scarred pewter plate for each of us, banged them down. "Huevos rancheros," she said. "There's enough chili in those eggs, lover, and enough heat in that sausage to give your stomach something brand new to think about." She brought her own plate and slid in beside him. "Ours are merely hot, my lamb. Yours is volcanic. And choke it down or you'll wear it like a hat. It's an old home remedy for the squeams."

Arthur made it. It was a noble effort. It gave him tears, the snuffles and the sweats, and frequent glares of astonished agony before snatching at the soothing blandness of buttered bread.

"You briefed him?" I asked her when we'd finished.

"On the whole thing, at least when he wasn't clattering off to go whoops."

"Cut it out, Chookie!" Arthur said firmly. "Enough is enough. Let's drop it for good." He stared her in the eye.

Suddenly she grinned, nodded, patted his arm. "Welcome back to the human race."

"Glad to be aboard," he said politely.

"Wilma's background too?" I asked.

"It's so strange," Arthur said. "I never knew her at all, did I? I realized something odd today. I can see her very vividly, the way she stood and sat and walked. But in every memory, she's turned away from me. I can't bring her face back at all. I can remember the color of her eyes, but I can't see them. So now somebody I never knew is dead. And . . . she was married to somebody I didn't know very well. I see two strangers living in that beach house. Does that make any sense?"

"It does to me," Chook said. "Trav, please, what happens tonight? Until you're both back safe, I'll be half out of my mind. Please tell me."

thirteen

It was very close to eleven when I turned the dark green sedan onto Clematis Drive. The other houses were dark. There were more vacant lots than houses. As I approached the Watts home I saw that the light over the front door was not on. And so I touched the gas pedal again and started by, saying to Arthur, "I guess lawyer boy is still semiconscious."

Quite a few lights were on in the house. And just as I passed it, I saw, in the darkness of the side lawn beyond the carport, something that made me give a little sound of surprise.

"What's the matter?" Arthur said in a strained voice.

"Good ol Boo's white Lincoln tucked nearly out of sight at the side there. Top down. See it?"

"Yes, I see it. My God. We better go back, don't you think?"

I did not answer him. I turned left onto the next street, and after the first few houses there was nothing but the emptiness of development land, where asphalt turned into damp dirt with deep ruts. I backed and filled and got the car turned around, and on the last swing I turned the lights off, proceeded slowly by faint watery moonlight. I bumped it up over curbing and tucked it into the shadows of a clump of cabbage palm. In the silence a slight wind rattled the fronds, making a rain sound.

"What are you going to do?" he asked. There was a tremor in his voice.

"Take a look. Both the Watts cars are there. I'll cut across and come out behind the house. That's it, over there. The lighted one. You wait for me right here."

"And what if you g-get into trouble, Trav?"

"I'll either come back on the double, or I won't. Then, if I don't, if you think you can handle it, get as close as you can and see what you can see. Don't take any chances. Use your judgment. Here." I took the pistol out of my jacket pocket and shoved it into his hands. Morale builder. I had to turn my frail reed into something stauncher, just in case. Even at the expense of making me feel naked.

"I don't like this," he said. He was not alone in that appraisal.

"If it turns very very sour, go and get Chook and get out of the area fast. Use this car and drive all night, right up to Tallahassee. In the morning get hold of a man in the State Attorney General's office. Remember this name. Vokeler. Truman Vokeler." He repeated it after me. "Don't talk to anyone else. If he's away, demand he be sent for. And you and Chook level with him. Everything. He'll take it from there. Trust him."

"Why don't we just . . ."

I got out of the car and closed the door. I walked fifty feet into the field, stopped and waited until I had enough night vision to pick up the contour of the ground and keep from falling over palmetto and small bushes. I kept the vision by not looking directly at the house lights. Brush was thick beyond their rear property line and I moved toward a gap and came upon a woven cedar fence, low enough to step over. Once in the back yard, I stopped in the shadows, examining the house, refreshing my memory of the layout. Kitchen windows were lighted. Light from the living room shone out into the cage, on plantings and shadowy terrace furniture. I could hear no sound. There was an odd flickering light which puzzled me. After moving a little way to the side, I could see through the cage and into the living room. Crane Watts was slumped in a big green-leather wing chair, legs sprawled on a hassock, head toppled to the side. I could detect no sound or movement in any part of the house, nor see any other person.

I moved around toward the carport side, crouched and ran to the side of the convertible, waited there, resting on one knee, listening. I came up cautiously and looked into the empty car, then leaned and felt cautiously. The keys weren't in it. I went to the rear, crouched and felt the nearest tail pipe. There was just a slight residual heat. Recalling how he drove it, I could guess it had been there some time. I moved close to the house and around the corner and along the front of it, ready to flatten myself among the unkempt plantings should a car come down the street. The awning windows across the front of the living room were almost wide open. I crouched below them, cautiously. I saw Crane Watts from another angle. All I could see of him was the sprawl of legs on the hassock, one hand dangling. The chair faced the television set. It accounted for the flickering light. The sound was completely off. A handsome Negro girl was singing. The camera had moved in for a close-up, the white teeth, tremolo of tongue, effortful throat, vast enunciations of the lips. All in a total silence, total until I heard a faint buzzing snore from the man in the green chair, and another.

I ducked down and continued across the front to the far corner. As I went around the corner I saw the long shadow I cast and knew that I was outlined against the single street light on the other side of Clematis Drive, and knew it would be a Very Good Thing to get back where I had been. Out of darkness ahead came a sound. *Thop.* And with it a whisper of air movement touching the right side of my throat, and immediately thereafter the workmanlike chud of lead into a palm trunk a hundred yards behind me.

They would say, when Whitey Ford made that incredible motion to nip the base runner off first, that the man was caught leaning. The man was leaning one way, and realized what was happening, and yearned to go the other way, but he had to overcome the inertia of himself before he could move back. I was off balance. I yearned for the safety I had left. Either it was a cheap silencer he was using, or a home-made one, or a good one used too many times. Good ones go *thuff.* Not *thop.* I did not review all my past life in a microsecond. I was too busy changing balance and direction, and thinking, How stupid, how idiotic, how . . . Arthur-like. I did not hear the next *thop.* I heard only the monstrous tearing blast as the slug tore the whole top left side of my head off with such finality, the world ended in whiteness without even any residual sense of falling.

. . . my head was in a fish bag, in a fetid closure of stink, laced with engine oil. My hand was way off, around a corner, down another street, utterly indifferent to the master's demands. So if you won't come, I told it, wiggle a finger. I wiggled a finger. No problem, boss. Try the other hand. The right hand. The good one. But that is im-possible, en-tirely. Cleaved I am, from crown to crotch, the right half discarded, wound fitted with plexiglass so they can see all the moving parts in there, all the little visceral pumps and pulses.

The rebel hand floated up and came drifting, unseen, all the way back, caught upon something, pushed, and the fish bag was gone and I lay in a black fresh wash of air, made one little hitch, another, looked at two moons riding, two half moons absolutely identical. Well now. That *is* unusual. Each star had a twin, both in the same relationship as were the twin moons. I struggled with some massive concept of duality, something which, could I but grasp it and put it into coherency, would alter the whole future of mankind. But some nagging little temporal worry kept trying to intrude. A graveyard slab was over me, tilting. Actually two of them, one merging into the other. I stared and the slab became two white leathery backs of a front seat, merged in the same way, and by painful deduction I established that I was on the rear floor of a car. And suddenly it was Boone Waxwell's car, and I was dead. Caught leaning. I got my hand up there to find out how I died. It felt very bad up there, and very tall. All caked and torn meat. Stickiness and miscellany which could not be me. I tried to find the other half of myself. The hand, more docile and obedient, went a-searching. It found dull dead meat, and I thought someone was tucked in there with me. But when I prodded it and squeezed it, there was some deep and muffled ten- derness announcing itself as my right arm. My efforts brought the edge of the stinking tarp flapping down over my face once more, and I pushed it down and away. Dead was one thing. Becoming crab food was a further unpleasantness. The fellow was certainly casual about it. Kill me, dump me in his car, throw a tarp over me, take care of the body when he found the time. But if the body happened to be gone . . .

Reaching up, I found the release on the rear door. It clicked and I shoved with my good leg. I slid over the sill a little, forcing the door open. I pushed again and again until my shoulders were over the sill, but my head hung down. I got the good hand under the back of my head, pulled it up, shoved again and slid out until my shoulders were on turf, hips still up on the sill. Two more shoves and my hips fell onto the ground. Then I could push against the outside of the car with the good leg. The dead leg followed me out. Rolling over was a major feat, requiring careful planning, proper shifting of dead parts into positions where leverage would work. Twice I got up to the balance point and the third time I flopped over.

Rested, then with the help of my hand, got my head up to take a look. Two of everything. Far things were doubled. Close things were two things merged, blurred into each other. Blinking did no good. I was between his convertible and the side of the carport. I had begun to wonder if I might not be entirely dead. The raw scrubby land out back would be . . . *that* way. Worry about the fence when I got to it. If I got to it. Go that way. Get to back corner of carport, turn left. Go along back wall of carport and house. Come to cage. Turn right. Go along edge of cage and then straight out across yard.

In a little while I found the only possible method of locomotion. Roll onto the dead side, stay propped up by pressure of left hand against ground. Bring left knee up as far as I could get it. Use leg as brace and reach as far ahead as possible with left hand. Dig fingers into soil. Then pull with hand, and push with edge of left shoe, and slide on the dead side. Not quite as dead. It had begun to tingle in a very unpleasant way. Pins and needles. But it wouldn't respond to command. I estimated that five or six good efforts took me my own length. I awarded myself a brief rest at the end of each McGee-length. Four rests brought me to the carport corner. Four more rests and I seemed to be halfway to the cage. It seemed to me that a long time had passed since he had shot me in the head. There seemed to be only one light in the house. I felt I was rustling the half-dead leaves of the plantings too loudly. At least I was in moon-shade on the back side of the house.

I stopped for an earned rest, face down in moist grass. I was ordering a dead-hand finger to wiggle when, directly over me, in a voice that was half a hard resonance and half a husky whisper, with a dreadful, intimate jocularity, Boone Waxwell said, "Gone play dead now, hey?"

I waited to feel the cool fat end of that silencer against the nape of my neck.

"You answer ol Boo now, hear?" he said in that same wheedling, jolly imitation of affection. "Gone play dead? Little ol country-club pussycat gone try that little game that didn work the other times neither?"

And suddenly it was all clarified by the thin, faint, weary sound of Vivian's voice. I could not hear the words. It was utter hopelessness. I turned my head slowly and looked up at the side of the house.

Even with the irritating double vision I could see what the situation was. Sliding glass bedroom doors were open. The screening was not eighteen inches from my face, and the terrazzo floor level perhaps eight inches above ground level. In faint illumination through a half-open door to the hallway, I could see the bottom corner of a bed, possibly twelve inches from the other side of the screen.

My impulse was to scramble away like a crippled bug before he looked out and saw me. Realization of the situation was like smelling salts, pushing the mists out of my mind, bringing me from stubborn dreamy labor of escape up to a vividness of alarm, awareness of life. At the edge of panic I heard, distinctly, a rustle, slow shift of weight, sigh, whispery sound of flesh stroked. And if I could hear them so distinctly, it was only wild luck he had not heard my labored squirming.

"Now why'd I want to go away, pretty pussycat?" he asked in mock astonishment. "What for I'd do that when we ain't even half finished off?"

Again her begging, toneless plaint, her tired whining.

"Pore little dead pussycat, thinks she's all wore down. Ol Boo, he knows better. Such a sweet piece you are now. And you do so fine, so real fine."

I heard an aimless shifting, rustling, small thud of elbow against wall or headboard, a sudden huff of exhalation, a silence. Then he said, in the voice people use to play games with small children. "What's this! And this here? How in the worl can this be a-happenin to a pore dead pussycat? It beats all!"

There was a small thrashing, a silence, a whine, another silence.

In a voice suddenly tightened and gritty with effort, he said, "Now how this for you?"

There was a scampering rustle, a loud whimper, a restraining clap of hand onto flesh. And a silence longer than before.

"AAAAAAA," she said. And again. "AAAAAAA." It was not a sound of pain or of pleasure, of fright, of want, or of denial. It was simply the sound of sensation, purified, dehumanized, so vivid that I could visualize her head thrown back, eyes wide blind staring, mouth wide and crooked.

And the random and meaningless sounds of motion began a cyclic repetition steadying into a slow heavy beat.

Across that beat, in a rhythmic counterpoint, she cried "OGodO-GodOGod!" in a voice of that same clarity and formality and impersonality I had heard her use to call Love and Ad and Game and Let.

"Stay with it," he gasped.

And, released from my unwilling voyeurism by the sounds of them, I went hunching and scrabbling along, turning away from the house, heading out across the open yard, aching to get out of earshot of what they had built to, away from that furnace-gasping, whumpety-rumpety, plunging, wall-banging, flesh-clapping prolonged crescendo of the prewearied flesh, crawling and hitching, weeping inwardly sick weak tears for the plundered wife, wondering how in God's name I'd ever had the benign stupidity to formulate the jackass theory that the sounds of love could never be sickening. This was as pretty as the raw sound of a throat being cut. Or the sound of the great caged carnivore at feeding time.

The hurt on the dead side was beyond pins and needles. Though the surface felt numbed, each pressure brought a dead aching pain, as though I had been burned. I felt as if each grunt of effort was tearing the inner lining of my throat. Finally, reaching, I stubbed my outstretched fingers against the fence. I hitched closer to it, reached up and got my hand around the top edge of it. I rested there, breathing hard. Distance had faded the sounds of them, losing those sounds in bug-shrilling, frond-clatter, mockingbirds, a dog barking two streets away. The little fence was improbably high. I had an arm ten feet long, thin as a pencil reaching up and up to take a weak grasp on the roof edge of a building, and any idea I could hoist myself up and over was absurdly optimistic. From the mortgaged house came the finishing cry of the tennis player, a tearing hypersonic howl like a gut-shot coyote. Her eyes were a very dark blue, and with suncoin on the tawny forearm, she had closed her eyes and shuddered at the thought of any Waxwell touch. I borrowed from her cry the energy of desperation, pulled myself up and up, hooked my chin over the bruising wood, and got just enough response from the dead arm to swing it up and over, fence edge biting into armpit. I writhed and pushed and worked, hung there with the edge across my belly, reached and found a tough curl of root, pulled, tumbled, rolled onto my back on the slight slope beyond the fence.

So die right here, McGee. Cheat the bastard out of that much. But maybe, with a light, he can follow you. Torn and flattened grass. Wetness that could mean you leave blood. Maybe it's as obvious as the sheen a snail leaves on a sidewalk. And Boo would act with the same jolly and intensely personal manner, giving death the same intimacy as assault. Now what's ol Boo found hisself here? My, my, my.

I tried the dead arm and it came up slowly, as remote from me as those coin games where you look through glass and work the claw to pick prizes out of the bin of candy. It steadied, outlined against the double images of the stars. I put the good hand up and took hold of it. No feeling in the skin, like taking a stranger's hand. But when I squeezed it a bone ached, announcing identity.

So scrabble on, this time getting a partial use of it, a slight helpful leverage of elbow. Then, when next I rested, I heard a clumsy thrashing and stumbling coming toward me. I felt more irritation than alarm. A damn-fool way to go busting and blundering through the night. It came on and was going to pass me, ten feet away, and I saw it, the shape and posture of the doubled silhouette familiar.

"Arrar," I said in a voice I'd never heard before. It stopped him. There was something loose and sloppy and wrong about the right side of my mouth. I firmed it up with effort. "Arthur."

"Trav?" he said in a nervous whisper. "Is that you?"

"No. It's just one of us gophers."

He felt his way to me. "I . . . I thought you were dead."

"You . . . could be right. Gemme *outa* here!"

He couldn't carry me. It was not the kind of terrain to drag people across. We got me up, with fumbling clumsiness, dead arm across his shoulders, his left arm around my waist, dead leg dangling and thumping along between us like a sack of putty. It was damned high up there. Like standing on the edge of a roof. And he kept coming close to losing me when we'd get off balance. He would brace and heave and I would manage a little hop on the good leg. Several weeks later, we came upon the car. During the final fifty feet I had been able to swing the dead leg forward, sense the ground under it, lock the knee and lurch forward on it. He fumbled me into the passenger side of the front seat. I slumped, resting my head on the seat back. He went around and opened the door and got halfway in and stopped. The courtesy light shone down on me. I rolled my head and looked at him. The double image slowly merged into one and then separated again. Double or single, he wore a look of horror.

"My God!" he said in a thin high voice. "My God!"

"Get in and close the door. He shot me in the head." I had to speak slowly to make the right half of my mouth behave. "It isn't supposed to make it pretty."

He piled in, anxiety making him breathe hard, fumbling with the ignition, saying, "I got to get you to a doctor . . . a doctor . . ."

"Hold it. Got to think."

"But . . ."

"Hold it! How much time's gone by?"

"Since you . . . it's quarter of two."

"Took you long enough."

"Trav, please try to understand. I . . . I went after you a long time ago, when you didn't come back. I sneaked over there, like you said. I got into the side yard, behind a tree, looking at the house. I couldn't hear anything. I didn't know what to do. And all of a sudden he came around the side of the house, in sort of a springy little trot, grunting with effort and he . . . he had you over his shoulder. He passed the light from a window. Your . . . arms and head were dangling and bouncing all loose and dead. And . . . he trotted right to the car and stopped short and gave a heave and you . . . you fell into the car, in back. He didn't open a door or anything. You made such . . . such a thud, such a dead thud. He stood there for a little while and I heard him humming to himself. He opened the trunk and got a blanket or something out of there and leaned into the car, apparently covering you up. Then he went back into the house. Lights started going out. I heard a woman sobbing like her heart was breaking. And I . . . couldn't make myself look at you. I crept away. Please understand. I got far enough to run, and ran back to the car, and started up to Palm City to get Chookie like you said. I went very fast, and then I went slower and slower. I pulled off the road. I wanted to come back. I tried. I couldn't. Then I went all the way to the marina, but I stopped outside the gates. I'd have to tell her what happened. I'd say it was the only thing I could have done. But it wasn't. She'd know that. I couldn't face her. I couldn't come back. I wanted to just run away. I turned around and came back, and it took me a long time to make myself get out of the car and . . . come looking for you. The only way I could do it was telling myself he was gone, he'd driven away with you. Trav . . . is he gone?"

"He's still there."

"How did you . . . get to where I found you?"

"I crawled. Arthur, you came back. Hang onto that. It can be worth something to you. You came back."

"Why is he still there?"

"I . . . I guess it's the hospitality. Shut up. I'm trying to think."

"But maybe . . . we're waiting too long," he said. "I should put you in the hospital and call the police."

"You have a very conventional approach. But shut up."

When I had it worked out, I had him drive east on the Trail into the empty night land of cypress, billboards and roadside drainage ditches. With no traffic from either direction, I got the automatic pistol. I had to keep my right hand folded around it with my left hand, and give the trigger finger a little help. I emptied it into the wilderness. On the way back to the hospital, I coached him carefully.

He parked near the emergency entrance. He helped me walk in. Double vision had become infrequent. The life in the dead arm and leg felt closer to the surface. Now they felt as if I had a thick leather glove on the arm, fitting firmly to the armpit, and a similar stocking on the leg. It was a trim little hospital, and they were doing a big business. The staff was trotting around. Fresh blood dappled white nylon. Doctors and relatives were arriving. Somebody in the treatment room kept screaming until suddenly it stopped, too suddenly. A woman sat weeping in a chair in the corridor next to the check-in desk, a red-eyed man clumsily patting her shoulder. Arthur made ineffectual attempts to attract attention. I got a few absent glances from staff people until finally a harried burly nurse hastened by me, skidded to a stop, came back and stared at me, lips compressed with concern. She got me over to a chair, down to a level where she could look at my head.

"Gunshot," she said.

"Yes indeed," I said.

"It's all we need," she said. She grabbed an orderly, told him to get me bedded down in Trauma Room C right away. I was there five minutes with Arthur standing by before a young, squat, redheaded doctor came swiftly in, followed by a tall, narrow, pock-marked nurse. He pulled the light down, hunched himself over my head. His fingers felt like busy mice, wearing cleats.

"How long ago?" he asked Arthur.

"Three hours, approximately," I said. He seemed a little startled to get the answer from me.

"How do you feel right now?" he asked me.

"Shot."

"We're not in the mood for smart-ass remarks around here tonight. Seven local young people were in a car that didn't make a curve north of here about three quarters of an hour ago. We lost one on the way in, another here, and we're trying like hell to keep from losing two more. We'll appreciate cooperation."

"Sorry. I feel mentally alert, doctor. I'm not in pain. When I first regained consciousness, I had double vision, and no feeling or control in the whole right side of my body. The symptoms have been diminishing steadily, but my right side feels . . . leaden, as if every muscle had been strained."

"Why has it been so long, and how did you get so messed up?"

"I was alone. I had to crawl to where I'd be noticed."

"Who shot you?"

"I did. It was an accident. A very stupid accident. That gentleman has the gun."

"Outside the city?"

"Yes."

"We'll get a deputy over to make out a report. It's required."

He turned the overhead light out, shone a pencil beam into each eye, taking his time. The nurse took pulse and blood pressure, and I gave my name and address. Redhead went out and came back with an older doctor. He looked me over, and they went over into the corner and I heard some of the words they feed Ben Casey. One is practically a television cliché. Subdural hematoma.

The older doctor left. Redhead came back and said, "You seem to have your luck with you, Mr. McGee. The slug hit right at the hairline at such an angle it grooved the skull but didn't penetrate, traveled about a full inch under the scalp, and then probably tumbling after impact, tore free. A sharp blow on the so-called funnybone can numb the hand. The left hemisphere of the brain controls the motor nerves and sensory nerves of the right half of the body. We feel that a shock of that severity could well have stunned and deadened the synapses on that side, the nerve functions, the ability to originate and transmit orders to the right side of your body. Sensation and control are returning so rapidly, we feel you should be back to normal feeling and use in a day or so. I see no clinical evidence of concussion, but there could be a rupture of small blood vessels in the impact area, and slow bleeding. So we'll keep you here a few days for observation. Now the nurse will clean the wound and prep you for a little stitching." He got a hypo, held it up to the light. "This is just to deaden the area to save you discomfort."

He pricked me twice in the scalp and once in the left temple area and went away. The nurse tested, and when I could not feel her touch, she cleaned and shaved the area. She went and summoned the redhead. I could hear, inside my head, the sound as he pulled the stitches through. When he drew them tight, I could feel the pull in my left cheek and temple. When the cleaning had started, Arthur had gone into the hall. Not until the antiseptic dressing was in place did he come back in, looking queasy.

Then they rolled me down the corridor to what seemed to be a combination treatment room and storage room. Bright lights were on. The deputy got up when I was wheeled in. He was elderly, florid, heavy and asthmatic, and he licked his indelible pencil after every few words he wrote on the form in his clipboard. I swung my legs over the side of the wheeled stretcher and sat up. There was a mild wave of dizziness, a momentary recurrence of double vision, and that was all. He put the clipboard on the foot of the stretcher and hunched over it.

"Got the name off the records. Let's see identification, McGee." He took my driver's license and copied the number on his form. For local address, I gave him the name and registration number of my houseboat and told him where it was docked.

"Scalp wound, self-inflicted," he said.

"Accidentally self-inflicted, Deputy."

"Weapon?"

Arthur handed it over. He took it with the familiarity of the expert, pulled the slide back and locked it back, checked chamber and clip, sniffed the muzzle, then pushed the clip ejector. It doesn't work. I've been meaning to have a gunsmith fix it. You have to pry it before it comes loose.

He fiddled with it and said, "Jammed in there."

"That's how come I got shot, Deputy."

"You carry this around on your person?"

"No, sir. I'd have to have a permit to do that. I keep it in the car or on the boat. What happened, I had it in the car, and I wanted to get that clip out. I thought it would be safer to empty it first. So I drove off the Trail down a little road, away from any houses, and fired it until it seemed empty. I didn't count the shots. Then, let me take it a minute, I sat down on the doorsill of the car where I could see by the dome light what I was doing. Like a damn fool I held it this way to get the slide back. My hand was sweaty, and I guess there was a misfire on the last one in the chamber. But it fired when it got a second chance. Next thing I knew, I woke up on the ground beside the car. When I felt able, I decided the best thing to do was try to crawl back to the main highway. It numbed my whole right side. But that's going away now. You see, Deputy, my friend here was making a long-distance call from a roadside phone booth. He was having trouble getting it through. I got bored. I thought I'd just get off the highway, empty the pistol and get the clip out of it. It had been on my mind. I told him I'd be back in a few minutes. When I didn't come back, he thought I'd gone down a side road and got stuck in the mud. He looked and looked, after he got through phoning. I guess it was the third road where he found me, almost all the way back out to the highway."

"Third road," Arthur said. "So I walked in and got the car and brought him right here. I thought he was dying."

"He don't look dead. But them kids out there do." He bounced the pistol on his broad tough hand, handed it to Arthur and said, "See he gets it fixed, mister." He left.

I slid off the stretcher. Arthur started toward me to help me and I waved him back. In cautious balance I plodded slowly around the little room. I had to pivot and swing my hip to get that leaden leg forward, but with the knee locked it took my weight.

My lightweight jacket was a ruin, dirt, rips, and grass stain, slacks not quite as bad, but bad enough. I balanced and took the jacket off, checked the pockets, tossed it to Arthur and pointed to a porcelain can with a lid worked by a foot pedal. He balled it up and stuffed it in. A blank doorway led, as I hoped, into a little washroom. With the dull clumsy help of the reluctant right hand and arm, I got the mud off my face and hands, the dark scabs of dried blood off the left side and the back of my neck. I used a damp towel to scrub down the right side of the slacks, the side I had dragged. I studied myself in the mirror. I didn't look like a disaster case. I looked as if I had been rolled in a waterfront alley. The dressing was too conspicuous.

"They'll clean you up when they put you to bed."

"Hat," I said. "Go right when you go out this door and find another way out of here. I tossed the hat on the shelf behind the back seat of the car. And get back to me with it the same way you get out. And fast."

"Listen, I won't do it! You *can't* leave. It's dangerous!"

"So are home-canned vegetables. Get the hat."

I sat on a white stool and waited. Merry McGee, the valiant quipster, with a hole in his head and the horrid conviction it *was* bleeding in there. My precious, valuable, irreplaceable head. Under the bullet groove would be some little white needles of splintered bone, sticking down into the gray jelly where everything was stored, all those memories unique to me.

A fat nurse opened the door and said, "Mr. McGee? Come along."

"I was told to wait here until they check something out."

"Tests can be taken in the ward, sir."

"Something about radiology."

She frowned. "Seems odd. I better go find out what's up."

She bustled away. When I saw Arthur in the doorway, I heaved myself up and got out of there in my curious hitching gait, putting the baseball cap on as I went down the hall. I did my very best walking as we passed a woman at a desk near the main entrance. I waited in shadow by the curb, leaning against a tree. Arthur brought the car around, something he should have thought to do when he got the hat. I didn't remark on it. He was managing better than I could have hoped.

"Clematis Drive," I said as he got behind the wheel.

"But how can you . . ."

"Arthur, my friend, you will be orderly and agreeable and stop twitching. I want you near me. I want you to stay near me. Because I am highly nervous. And if I stop making sense, or my speech goes bad, or my leg and arm get worse again, you hurry me back there so they can saw a little round hole in my head. Otherwise, just take on trust the strange idea I might know what I'm doing, because I'm too pooped to argue. Just drive. And pray my hunch is wrong. What time is it?"

"Five something. Chook will be . . ."

"She'll sweat it out."

As we turned onto Clematis, I looked over and saw the first paleness in the east. The dark trees and houses had begun to acquire third dimensions as the first candlepower of Wednesday touched them. The Watts house was lighted up again, almost completely. The big white convertible was gone.

"Turn into the drive . . . No, keep going, and put it in the driveway of the next house. Hurricane shutters are on. It's empty for the summer. Turn out the lights before you turn in."

As we started back down the sidewalk, I said, "If anything comes, car or bike or pedestrian, either way, help me hustle into the brush and flatten out."

"Okay, Trav. Sure."

Nothing came. We went around the side of the house. Waxwell had taken off with typical flair, wheels digging deep gouges in the soft lawn.

I tried the outside screen door of the cage. It was latched on the inside. As I wondered whether it was worth trying to call her I smelled, adrift in the predawn stillness, a faint stench of fecal matter. I turned to Arthur and said, "When we're in the house, don't touch a thing unless I tell you. Stay away from the windows in the front of the house. Squat low if you hear a car."

Bracing myself against the frame, I put a knee through the screen, ripping it. I reached through, unlatched it and, when we were inside, smeared the metal handle where I had touched it, with the palm of my hand. The odor was stronger in the living room. The television set emitted a constant cold light, the random snow pattern after broadcasting is over. The odor was much stronger. Crane Watts had slid down between chair and hassock, half sitting, head canted back on the chair seat. His face was unnaturally fat, his eyes bugging wide, pushed out by pressure behind them. It was a moment or two before I found the point of entry, the charred ear hole. And I knew. I knew exactly what else I would find in the silence of that house. The husband had slept through too much. Too many empty evenings slack in the chair, while the wife's heart grew more hopeless. But when Boo came in, came at her, she would have cried out to the husband. Many times, perhaps, before she knew it was too late, and he was too far gone and would sleep through every endless lift and stroke, every new and demanding invasion, every cuff and slap, every jolly instruction, every rough boosting and shifting of her into new postures for his pleasure. So, having slept, husband, sleep longer yet. Forever. I wondered if she remembered who had said a nonsense thing about a pistol barrel in the ear. And, accustomed only to the antiseptic violence of television and the movies, I imagined that the sudden ugliness had shocked her. After such a small tug at the trigger. The huge terminal spasm had flounced him off the chair, opened his bowels. And hydrostatic pressure had bloated his face to an unrecognizable idiocy. I even knew what she would instinctively cry at such ghastliness. "I'm sorry! I'm sorry!" It would end her autohypnosis, the trance state of the amateur murderer, and leave her no choice at all but to do what I knew I would find.

I heard the dry gagging behind me and saw Arthur with his back to the body, hunched over, hands to his mouth. I bumped him away, saying, "Stop it! Not in here, you damn fool!"

With a struggle he gained control. I sent him to wait out in the screened cage. I hobbled into the kitchen and, with my thumbnail, turned the lights off. It's what they so often do in the night. Maybe some forlorn fading desire to keep the darkness back. But if they could turn on all the lights in the world, it wouldn't help them. I knew where I'd most probably find her. She was in the empty tub and had slid almost flat, head over on her shoulder. She wore a floor-length orange housecoat, with white collar and cuffs, buttoned neatly and completely from throat to hem. It had been a good vibrant color for her swarthy handsomeness. She had fixed her hair, made up her mouth. The dark stain between her breasts and slightly to the left was teacup size, irregular, with one small area of wet sheen remaining. I bent and put the back of my hand against her calm forehead, but there was no warmth. The weapon, a .22-caliber Colt Woodsman with a long target barrel, lay against her belly, the butt under her right wrist. She was barefoot. Though she had fixed herself up for dying, there were marks she could not conceal, swollen lips, blue bruise on the cheek, long scratch on the throat—marks of that long hard use.

I sat on the edge of the tub. Dishonor before death. And more effective with that popgun than she would ever know. Two shots, even with the barrel against the target, seldom kill two people. Her death was not as messy as her husband's. Heart wounds give a tidier result. To prove a guess, I went to the shower stall. The soap was moist. There were water droplets on the shower walls. A big damp yellow towel had been put neatly on a rack. So, after she had heard Boone Waxwell drive off, she had dragged herself out of bed and plodded in and taken a shower, probably just as hot as she could endure it, scubbing herself mercilessly. Dry off. Go take the pretty housecoat from the closet and put it on. Sit at your dressing table, and fix your hair and your bruised mouth. The mind is numb. Get up and walk through the house, room to room, turning on the lights. Stop and look at the snoring husband. Breadwinner, mate, protector. Pace some more. Reach deep for the rationalizations. Women have been raped before. It hasn't killed them. There is a legal answer. Let the police handle it. Turn him in.

"Now let me get this straight, Mrs. Watts. Waxwell was there from ten something last night until two or three this morning? And you claim that during that time you were repeatedly raped, during that whole time your husband was sound asleep in front of the television set? And Waxwell was a client of your husband? And you had met him before? And he left his car parked at your house, a very conspicuous car, all that time?"

So she paces and tries to think clearly, and she knows that if she does nothing, Waxwell will be back. Next week or next month, he will be back, again and again, as he promised he would.

And that brings her to the thing she has been trying so desperately to force out of her mind. Had he taken her quickly, she could have merely endured him, been a helpless vessel for him. But he was so damned sly and knowing, so crafty and so patient that each time, even the last time, he had awakened the traitor body, so that while the soul watched, the body gasped and strained to hungry climax, to dirty joy, grasping powerfully.

So she would pace and stop to look at the husband who had let that hunger in her grow so big she could betray herself. And then

• • •

I found the note on her dressing table. Her personal stationery, monogrammed. A downhill scrawl with an eye-shadow pencil. "God forgive me. There was no other choice left. My darling was asleep and felt nothing. Sincerely, Vivian Harney Watts."

On the other side of the room beyond the plundered bed, the lowest drawer of his chest of drawers was open. Cartridges a-spill from a red-and-green cardboard box. Extra clip. Little kit with gun oil and collapsible cleaning rod. The shells were medium longs, hollow-point. So, with luck, the one she used on herself might not have gone through her to chip or stain the tub. I went back in and cupped the nape of her neck and pulled her up far enough to see. The back of the orange housecoat was unmarked. I made my gimpy hitching way out to the screened cage.

"She's dead too. I have some things to do. I'll try to make it fast."

"D-do you need help?"

I told him no. I went back and looked for signs of Waxwell. He would not go without leaving some trace. Like a god, he would mark the boundaries of the new area he had claimed. But I found nothing, decided I needed nothing. First, on a table by the bedroom door, I made a little pile of things to take away. The note, the gun, the other things from the drawer that belonged with the gun. By the time I had gotten her half out of the tub, I wished I could depend on Arthur to help me with this sort of grisly problem. She was a very solid woman. She had not begun to stiffen. Death gave her a more ponderous weight. Finally I was on my feet with her in my arms. Her dead forehead lolled over to rest against the side of my chin. Carefully bracing the bad leg, and willing the bad arm to carry its share, I hobbled into the bedroom with her. I put her on the bed. Out across the back yard the morning was a pearl pale shade of gray. I closed the draperies. She was on her back on the bed. I grasped the hem of the housecoat and with one hard wrench tore it open to the waist. Fabric ripped, and the small white buttons rattled off the walls and ceiling. I tucked the bottom of the housecoat up under her, pulled it up around her waist. She lay in dead abandon. On the white of her hips and upper thighs were the myriad blue bruises left by Waxwell's strong fingers. Begging silent forgiveness, I thoroughly tousled the black hair and, with my thumb, smeared the fresh lipstick on her dead mouth. She had gotten all prettied up to die. In the bedroom lights I could see little segments of dark blue iris where the lids were not quite closed. Sorry I ruined the housecoat. Sorry they'll see you like this, Vivian. But you'll like the way it works out. I promise you, honey. They'll pretty you up again for burying. But not in orange. That's a color to be alive in. To be in love in. To smile in. They won't bury you in it.

I tipped the dressing-table bench over. Using a tissue, I picked up a jar of face cream and cracked the dressing-table mirror. I turned the other lights out, left just one of the twin lamps on the dressing table on, and shoved the shade crooked so that it shone toward her, making highlights and deep shadows on the tumble of dead woman.

I crammed the stuff from the table into my pockets. I left one light on in the living room, a corner lamp with an opaque shade. Day was beginning to weaken the lights. With my thumbnail I turned the sound control on the television until the hiss of nonbroadcast was loud. We left. I saw no one on the way to the car, or when Arthur drove us back up Clematis Drive.

"What did you do?" he asked.

"She didn't live long enough to have her chance to decoy him off his place. I've given her a chance to do it dead."

On the north edge of town, up the Trail, I had him pull over and park near a phone booth near the curbing, at a gas station showing only a night light. I had one dime in change. Just enough.

The sergeant answered by giving his name.

I pitched my voice lower than usual. "Look, you want to do me a favor, you write down a license number, okay?"

"Give me your name, please."

"I shoulda phoned you hours ago. Look, I can't sleep. Maybe it's nothing. But the thing is, I don't want to get mixed up in anything. I don't want to get involved, see?"

"If you'd tell me where you're calling from."

"Knock it off, Sergeant. Write down the number, hey?"

"All right. License number what?"

I gave it to him and said, "A white Lincoln convertible with the top down, this year's maybe. The other two cars, I figure they *belong* there, see?"

"Belong where?"

"At this house I'm telling you about. The Lincoln was on the lawn over to the side. Listen, I'm just passing through and I don't want to get involved in anything. When I get a little buzz on, I got to walk to clear my head, okay? So I went over and found some damn back street. I looked at the street sign later. Clematis Street, or Drive, I think. Yeah, it was Drive. I parked and started walking. You know, you walk around a couple of blocks, you feel better in the morning. Right?"

"Mister, will you get to it?"

"What do you think I'm doing? It was hours ago. Maybe around three sometime. I didn't check close. Okay, from this house comes this sound of a broad screaming. Honest to God, my blood runs cold. I'm right in front of the house. Then I hear a kind of sharp crack, not like a shot but sort of like a shot, and the scream stopped like her throat got cut. Maybe the crack was her old man giving it to her across the chops. What I did, I turned around and headed back to my car, and I make a mental note of the license number. You can tell the house because of the other two cars, one is a little light-color Mercedes and the other is a tan Plymouth. Tan or gray. So maybe you should check it, I don't know. I just got a feeling about it somehow."

"And can you give me your name?"

"John Doe, Joe Citizen, Jesus, Sergeant, I just don't want to get mixed up in anything. I don't know the house number. I couldn't see it. But it's not what you'd call a mile long, that street."

I hung up and got back into the sedan.

"Now can we go back?"

"Yes. Keep the speed down."

fourteen

Chook woke me at twenty minutes before noon, as I had asked. She sat on the side of the bed. I hitched myself up, flexed my right hand. Arthur appeared in the doorway, stood there watching me.

"How is it now?" Arthur asked.

"Better. It just feels asleep. The leg too. The hand feels weak."

"She's been coming in every half hour at least to see if you looked all right," Arthur said.

"And you don't look so great," she said.

"I feel as if I'd been hung up by the heels and beaten with ball bats."

"Head ache?" she asked.

I fingered the dressing, lightly. "It's not an ache. It's a one-inch drill bit. It makes a quarter turn every time my heart beats. How about the gun?"

"It was too rough to go outside in the dinghy," Arthur said earnestly. "I got as far as the middle of the pass and dropped it there. Okay?"

"That's just fine, Arthur."

Chook said, "I guess . . . you didn't know you were going to walk into anything so rough." I interpreted the appeal in her eyes.

"Damned glad I took you with me, Arthur. Chook, between us we managed."

"I was nearly out of my mind! Trav, I'm still scared. I mean now there's no way to prove she did it, is there?"

"Waxwell killed them both. He didn't pull the trigger. He killed them. And if his slug had hit a sixteenth of an inch lower . . . Wish I could have seen the bastard when he looked into the back end of that car. Nothing will go wrong, Chook. They'll find enough to prove he was in the house. There's a busted screen to show how he got in. And he isn't a pillar of any community. How has the news been?"

"Like you thought, so far."

I shooed them out, got into my robe and joined them in the lounge. I found I could manage an inconspicuous gait, if I kept it slow and stately. I put the big set on AM and cut the volume when a noontime used-car commercial over the Palm City station blasted us.

Their local news announcer had the usual airedale yap and the usual difficulty with long words. "This morning state, county and other law enforcement officials are cooperating in a massive manhunt for Boone Waxwell of Goodland on Marco Island, wanted for questioning in connection with the rape murder of housewife Vivian Watts of Naples and the murder of Crane Watts, her husband, a young Naples attorney. Based on an anonymous tip from a passerby who heard screams and what could have been a shot emanating from the thirty-thousand-dollar home on a quiet residential street in Naples in the small hours of the morning, city police investigated at dawn and found Mr. Watts in the living room, dead of a small-caliber bullet wound in the head, and Mrs. Watts in the bedroom, the scene of a violent struggle, shot through the heart. The anonymous tipster gave police the tag number and description of a car he saw parked in the side yard at the time of the shot he heard, and the car has been identified as belonging to Boone Waxwell, Everglades fishing guide, who for some years has been living alone in a cottage over a mile west of the village of Goodland.

"When County police arrived at the Waxwell cottage this morning, they found the car reported as having been at the scene of the crime. Goodland residents state that Waxwell had another vehicle, an English Land Rover, as well as an inboard launch on a trailer. The truck and boat trailer are missing, and a thorough search of all waterfront areas is now under way. Goodland residents say Waxwell kept to himself and did not welcome visitors. They said he seemed to have ample funds, but could not account for how he had acquired them. Waxwell is about thirty-seven or thirty-eight years old, five foot eleven, about a hundred and ninety pounds, blue eyes, black curly hair, very powerful, and believed to be armed and dangerous. On forcing entrance to his cottage, police found quantities of arms and ammunition. He had been in difficulty before for minor acts of violence, and has successfully fled on two other occasions to avoid prosecution, returning after those who filed the charges had dropped them.

"The preliminary medical opinion, pending a more detailed examination, is that Mrs. Watts, an attractive twenty-eight-year-old brunette, was criminally assaulted prior to her death. Waxwell apparently gained entry by forcing a screened door which opened onto the patio in the rear of the house. Time of death is estimated for husband and wife as occurring between two and four A.M. today. Mrs. Watts will be remembered as one of the finer amateur tennis players on the lower west coast. A close friend of the family, not identified by police as yet, hearing of the double murder, reported that on Monday Mrs. Watts had complained about her husband being annoyed by Boone Waxwell over some business matter. It is reported that Crane Watts was the attorney for a land-syndicate operation in which Waxwell had a minor interest.

"Authorities, fearing that Waxwell may have gone back into the wilderness areas of the Ten Thousand Islands, plan to organize an air search using the facilities of the Coast Guard, the National Park Service and the Civil Air Patrol. It is believed that . . . Here is a flash which has just come in. The English truck and the boat trailer have just been found pulled off into deep brush near Caxambas, adjacent to a shelving beach often used by local fishermen for the launching of trailered boats. The effort to hide the vehicle and trailer seems to indicate that Waxwell sought to conceal his avenue of escape. This station will issue further bulletins as received.

"And now to other local news. The Fort Myers Chamber of Commerce today issued a statement regarding . . ."

I snapped it off. "I wish they'd got him," Chook said.

"They will," I said. "And he won't have the money with him. He's not that much of a damn fool."

They both looked puzzled. "But it would take him only five minutes to dig it up and take it along," Arthur said.

"Think of the timing. He thought I was dead. He risked stashing me in the car while he spent three hours with the woman. My guess is he tricked or scared her into saying I was coming by at eleven. Then he tied her up or locked her up while he played games with me. If she heard those sounds, she wouldn't have recognized them as shots. He wouldn't have told her he killed me. His style would have been to tell her he'd scared me off, probably. Okay, so he found the body gone. Either I woke up and got the hell out of there, or somebody took the body away. Whoever took it away hadn't called the police. Or at least hadn't had time. I think he would want to clear out until he could figure out what was going on. If I was dead, who could prove he did it? I think he was too sure of himself with the woman to think for a moment she'd charge him with assault. In fact, she'd be more likely to swear he was never there at all. If he got back to his cottage by three o'clock, which I think is a good guess—good enough for our purposes—he would be feeling easier in his mind every minute. After all, the woman had obviously enjoyed it. The husband had slept through it. He would have checked the three o'clock radio news. All quiet. So why would he complicate his life by carting all that money around with him? If he was picked up, how would he explain it? He thought then he would be coming back to his shack. It was better off in the ground. He'd take some with him, not enough to be awkward. By first light he could be way back in Big Lostman's Bend country, setting up camp on some hammock back there. I saw the radio rig on that boat. It's a big one, including an AM band. So what does he find out when it's too late to go back for the money? Boone Waxwell is wanted for rape and murder. So we get to the money first. They'll have the area sealed and staked out. So we run a bluff. If we find fresh holes in the ground I will be one very astonished McGee."

"Bluff?" Chookie said uncertainly.

"Arthur looks very reliable and respectable. And I know he's got the nerve for it." Arthur flushed with pleasure. "So we do a little shopping first. I mean you two do. I'll make out the list."

There seemed to be an unusual number of cars and people in Goodland when we drove slowly through at two thirty, and we were stared at with open curiosity. There was an official car parked at the entrance to the shell road that led to Waxwell's place. Two men squatted on their heels in the shade. One sauntered out and held up his hand to stop us. He was a dusty little lizardlike man in bleached khakis. He strolled back and stared in curiously. Chookie, secretarially severe in white blouse, black skirt, horn-rimmed glasses, hair pulled back into a bun, was driving. She rolled the window down and said, "This is the way to the Waxwell place, is it not?"

"But you can't go in there, lady."

Arthur rolled the rear window down. I was in the back seat beside him. "What seems to be the trouble, officer?"

He took his time looking us over. "No trouble. You can't go in."

"Officer, we're working on a very tight timetable. We're advance technical staff for network television. The generator truck and the mobile unit will be along within the hour. I'm sure they've cleared everything. We have to mark locations, block out camera angles and placement. I'd like to get it done before they get here."

"The shack is sealed, mister."

"I don't have to get into the shack. That's up to the lighting people. That's their problem. We're setting up the outdoor shots and interviews, officer. And we'll lay some cable so it'll be all ready for them to hook on."

Arthur was very earnest and patient. He wore my bright blue linen jacket, white shirt, black knit tie. I yawned and turned a little more to make doubly certain the man would see the CBS over the breast pocket of my work shirt. Mailbox letters from the five-and-ten, backed with stickum. Gold. I hoped he had noticed the same letters on the big toolbox off the boat, resting on the floor beside my feet.

I said, "Hell, Mr. Murphy, let 'em sweat it when they get here."

"I don't like your attitude, Robinson. They depend on us to do a job."

"I was told no kind of reporters at all," the dusty deputy said.

"We are *not* reporters, sir!" Arthur said indignantly. "We're technicians."

"And you don't want to git into the shack?"

"We wouldn't have time if we wanted to," Arthur said, and looked at his watch. My watch. A gift I never wear. It tells the day, month, phase of the moon, and what time it is in Tokyo and Berlin. It makes me restless to look at it.

"Well, go on ahead then, and you tell Bernie down there that Charlie says it's okay."

Bernie was on the front steps, and he came out with a shotgun in the crook of his arm. He had one of those moon faces which cannot look authoritative. And when he found out Charlie said we were okay, he was delighted to be so close to the mysterious functioning of something he watched every day of his life. Too delighted. The gold letters and the reel of cable were symbols of godhead, and his smile was pendulous and permanent. We could not sustain the myth of locating proper areas to ground the equipment with Bernie hovering over every move. Chookie took him away from the play, notebook in hand, easing him back to the porch to get his expert opinion on who would be the best people to interview, and who had known Waxwell the longest, and what other interesting places were there in the area where the mobile unit could be set up.

I'd had them pick up another length of rod, and Arthur had sharpened both of them with a file from the ship's tool supply. I picked two likely spots, and with Bernie out of sight, we each began an orderly search pattern, working out from the initial probe, an expanding checkerboard pattern, six inches between the deep slow stabs into the moist earth of the open area in the grove.

"Trav!" Arthur said after about twelve minutes. I took him a spade. It was eighteen inches down, a super-king-size special-bargain glass jar that had once held Yuban powdered coffee and now held three packets of curled new bills. The jar went into the car trunk, tucked back behind the spare. I moved to the border of his area. Six feet from the first find I struck something that felt metallic at about the same depth. Prince Albert tobacco can that had once held a pound and now held three more curled packets. Put it with the jar. Fill the holes. I checked my watch. We worked as fast as we could. I could not move well yet. Arthur was faster. We covered a continuously expanding area. When the total elapsed time was forty minutes, I said, "Knock it off."

"But there could be . . ."

"And there might not be. And we want to get out with what we've got. Move!"

As planned, he sank a rod deep, and I taped a cable to the exposed stub. We put the other rod down ten feet away, ran cable from it back toward the cottage, and I wired the two ends into the impressive heavy-duty receptacle they had picked up in a hardware store.

We drove out. Chook, eyes on the narrow road, said, "I knew the time was running out. You didn't get anything, did you?"

"Not what we expected. Just a token. Sixty thousand."

She hauled the car back from the brink of a damp ditch. She stopped at the entrance. Arthur rolled the window down. "We're all set, thanks," he called. "We're going to go out now and check with Project Control, officer. These things change very rapidly, depending on the news breaks. At least, if they do decide to use that location, it's all set for them. I personally appreciate your cooperation."

"Glad to help out, mister."

"If there's a change of plan, don't worry about the gear we left there. It shouldn't be in anyone's way, and somebody will be through later to pick it up."

Out on the main road off the island, heading toward the Trail, Arthur began to giggle. And it became infectious. And soon we were all roaring and howling, with, for Chook and Arthur, a potential edge of hysteria in it. Gasping, we told Arthur Wilkinson he was superb. He was big media, through and through.

"Next let's try a bank job," Chook said. And we were off again.

In the interest of avoiding any unfortunate coincidence, we turned north on 951 before we reached Naples, then west on 846 to come out at Naples Park Beach eight miles north of the city.

Once aboard the *Flush*, and with the amount verified, and the cash locked into the safe up forward, I felt the nervous tension easing in my neck and shoulders. A good man with the right tools could probably peel that box open in an hour. But once upon a time I invited a qualified expert to see if he could locate the safe without ripping out any interior trim. After four hours of delving, rapping, tapping, measuring, he said there was no safe aboard and he damn well didn't appreciate that kind of practical joke.

At quarter after five, the three of us sat, drink in hand, in the lounge. We were trying to sustain the mood of celebration, but it was dying fast, the jokes forced, the grins too transient.

"I suppose," Arthur said, "that if you look at it one way, if what they did was legal enough, then we've stolen the money."

"Hijacked is a better word," I told him. "And if your marriage was legal, and if she's dead, then the money is her estate."

"And some of it is Stebber's."

"Which he has no interest in claiming."

"For goodness' sake, Arthur," Chook said. "Don't split hairs. Trav, how does it work out for Arthur? What will he have left?"

I got pencil and paper from the desk drawer. As I wrote, I explained the figures. "Sixty thousand less about nine hundred expenses is fifty-nine, one. From that we will deduct that fifty-one hundred and fifty you borrowed from friends."

"But that isn't fair to you!" he said.

"Shut up. Half the balance of fifty-three thousand nine fifty is . . .

twenty-six thousand nine seventy-five to you, Arthur. Or a little bit better than a ten percent recovery on what they took you for."

"You are certainly in a lovely line of work," Chookie said with a small dash of malice.

"What's *wrong* with you, woman?" Arthur demanded with unexpected heat. "Without Travis I wouldn't have gotten dime one back. What's he supposed to do? Take a chance of getting killed for . . . for a per diem arrangement?"

"I'm sorry, darling. I didn't mean it," she said, looking startled.

"And if we recovered nothing, then he'd get nothing. He'd be out what he's spent."

"I told you I'm sorry."

"That's what trips up thieves every time," I said. "They start quarreling over the split. Arthur, why don't you take your end of it, your lousy little recovery, and buy a lot and build a house?"

"Huh?"

"Get a construction loan. Get Chook to help on layout and decoration. Do every possible part of it you can manage by yourself. Put it up and sell it and build another."

He looked at me in a startled way, and then with a growing enthusiasm. "Hey!" he said. "Hey, now! You know, that might be just . . ."

"Gentlemen," Chook said, "don't let me interrupt anyone's career, but I think I would be a very much happier girl if we got the hell out of here. The weather report was good. We can run at night, can't we? I don't want to seem frail and foolish, but I would just feel better to be . . . out of touch."

"Let's humor the lady," I said.

"To make me really happy, gentlemen, let's make it a nonstop flight all the way home."

"One stop at Marco," I said. "To tell that kid where to pick up his *Ratfink*, and give him transportation money to go get it."

"And another stop," Arthur said, "if nobody minds too much. I mean Sam and Leafy Dunning were very good to me. Too good for me to just write a letter and say everything is fine. And . . . they saw me when I was so whipped by everything . . . I'd like to have them see me . . . the way I should be. I want to see if Christine is getting along all right. And maybe see some of those men I worked with. I don't know if they'd take it, but I'd like to give the Dunnings some of that money. They need a lot of things. Maybe just a thousand dollars. And . . ."

"And what, dear?" Chook asked.

"My carpenter tools are there. I had to buy them out of my pay. I guess it isn't even forty dollars' worth, but I'd like to have them. I *used* them. And they might be good luck if I . . . try to build a house."

fifteen

On Thursday at high noon, on the last and most beautiful day of May, we turned into the marked channel leading through the islands to Everglades City. Pavilion Key was south of us. I had checked the charts and decided we would do best staying with the official channel, entering the Barron River where it flows into Chokoloskee Bay, going a little way up the river to tie up at the big long Rod and Gun Club dock. I could have wiggled my way down Chokoloskee Bay to Chokoloskee Island, but it would have had to be high tide going and coming. And it was just as simple for Arthur to find some way to get across the causeway to Chokoloskee.

I stood at the topside controls, chugging the *Flush* along the channel between the Park islands. Down on the bow deck, Chook sat on the hatch wearing little red shorts and a sleeveless knit candy-stripe top. Arthur stood in an old threadbare pair of my khaki shorts, pointing out places to her, probably telling her of things that had happened when he had crewed for Sam Dunning on his charter boat. The slow diesel grind of the *Flush* obscured their words. I saw the animation on their faces, the shapes of laughter.

Arthur, though still too thin, was looking better. The months of labor in this area had built muscle tissue which malnourishment had reduced to stringiness. Now muscle was building smoothly again, rippling under the pink-tan hide of his back when he pointed.

Chook had put him on isometrics, and I had come across him a few times, braced in a doorway like Samson trying to bring the temple down, trembling from head to foot, face contorted. It embarrassed him to be caught at it, but the results were showing—the results of that, and the limbering exercises she gave him, and the huge calorie intake she was forcing on him.

And, then, after the straight shot across the bay, we came into the Barron River, into the smooth green-brown flow of it, with the old frame houses of the mainland shore off to port, clumps of cocoanut palm standing tall, skiffs tied handy. On the right, with its thousand feet of concrete dock, running along the river bank, was the Rod and Gun Club, first the long two-storied, citified motel wing, then the high screened pool area that connected it to the old frame part, then the cottages beyond. Four presidents of the United States have hidden out here, finding a rustic privacy and some of the best fishing in the hemisphere. Giant poinciana trees were in bloom, many of them reaching heavy branches low over the water, breezes dropping the flaming petals into the smooth flow of tide and current, and a gigantic mahogany tree shaded the main entrance to the old part, the steps and the porch.

A stubby, sturdy, white charter boat was tied up there, a man hosing her down, probably after a half-day charter. A boy knelt nearby on the cement dock, cleaning three impressive snook. I saw a tarpon that would go about ninety pounds hanging on the club rack.

I decided to put it ahead of the old white cruiser. Arthur, in the bow, readied a line. At dead slow the engine noise was reduced so I could hear voices forward. As we passed the fishing boat, the man with the hose looked over and said, "Well now, hydee, Arthur!"

"How you, Jimbo?"

"Fine, fine. You crewin on that there?"

"Seen Sam?"

"Busted his foot up some. Hoist slipped and the engine out of his skiff fell on it. He's over home mendin."

"Sorry to hear it."

When I balanced forward motion and downstream current, Arthur jumped to the dock with a line and I waved him on to the piling I wanted. With it fast, I cut off the engines and the flow swung the stern in. I put on a stern line and spring line. Chook asked about fenders, and I saw that the rub rail would rest well against the pilings and told her not to bother.

We had lunch in the old paneled dining room, under the glassy stare of wall-mounted fish. Just a few tables were occupied. The season was dwindling with the club a month from closing until fall. We had hot monster stone-crab claws with melted butter. Arthur introduced us to the waitresses, and as they served us efficiently, they filled Arthur in on all local news and gossip, including the latest rumors on the manhunt for Boone Waxwell.

A Coast Guard chopper had made a tentative report about seeing a glimpse of a boat answering the description, about thirty miles south of us a little way up the Clark River from Ponce de Leon Bay, just as it disappeared under overhanging trees. A fast patrol launch had been sent to investigate.

The opinion was that years ago a man could hide out from the law almost indefinitely in all that cruel silent maze of swamp and hammock, creek, river and island, but not now. Not if they really wanted him. The choppers and the patrol boats and the radio net would inevitably narrow the search area and they would go in and get Waxwell. Probably not alive, considering what he was like and what he had done. They were saying that his best bet would be to get as far in as his boat would take him, sink the boat in the black water, and try to make it sixty miles across that incredible morass, heading northwest, keeping to cover, and come out maybe way over in the Westwood Lakes area. A Boone Waxwell might manage that, but three miles a day might be all even he could manage, so it could be three weeks before he came out the other side, if he didn't founder in bottomless black gunk between hammocks, if he could keep the mosquitoes and stinging flies from swelling his eyes shut, if he didn't get fever, if he kept out of the jaws of gators, moccasins and other venomous species of water snake, if he could tote or trap the food he'd need to see him through, if he could avoid the swamp buggies and air boats they'd be sending in on search patterns.

There was one detail I had overlooked, and from the lobby I phoned the hospital in Naples and got the cashier. She said with considerable severity that I had left AMA, Against Medical Advice, and it had been so noted on my record. She gave me the total amount of the fee, including use of emergency-room space, tests, the four X-rays and the repair job. I said I would put a check in the mail, and she softened enough to tell me that I would be foolish to avoid seeing a doctor. The wound should be examined, dressing changed, stitches removed in due course.

After making the call, I found Chook out on the porch, and she said that Arthur had borrowed a car and had gone off to see the

Dunnings. We went to the boat and she changed to white slacks. We anointed ourselves on all exposed areas with Off and walked around the town. The original Collier, having made his fortune in advertising placards in streetcars in the north, had come down and created Everglades City by keeping a huge dredge working around the clock for over a year, building it up out of the swamplands. It served as a survey base and construction base for the building of the Tamiami Trail across the Glades to Miami. It had been a company town until finally, not long ago, the Collier interests had moved out. So there was an empty bank, an abandoned hospital, an abandoned headquarters, an unused railroad station, the rails long since torn up, the ties rotted away. But it was coming back now, with the big boom going on at Marco, with the Miami population pressure moving ever westward, keyed by the land speculators.

My leg could take only so much of it. At four o'clock we were back aboard. I took a shower. Showers created an eerie effect on the desensitized skin of my arm and leg, as if they were wrapped in cellophane which dulled the needles of the hard spray. I wore Chook's shower cap to keep the dressing dry. After the shower I took a nap. Chook woke me a little after six to say Arthur wasn't back and she was getting concerned about him.

"Maybe it's taking him a long time to get them to take that crisp new thousand."

"I wanted to get out of here, Trav."

"We'll get out. The weather is still holding. The days are long. I'd like a little light to get through the channel, and then it doesn't matter. A south southeast course after we're clear, and when we pick up the lights of Key West off the starboard bow, we'll pick us an anchorage, or, maybe better, I'll lug it way down so that by dawn we'll be about right to pick up the channel markers to go up Florida Bay. Stand watches."

"I just feel as if we ought to get going."

Arthur came trotting along the dock at seven, carrying his wooden box of carpenter tools, grinning and cheerful, apologetic about taking so long. He said he had a terrible time about the money, particularly with Sam, but when he had finally put it on the basis of the kids, Leafy had argued his way. It was finally decided they'd put it in the bank and consider it Arthur's money and touch it only in case of emergency, and then consider it a loan. He said that Christine was placidly, healthily, happily and obviously pregnant, and she'd found a nice boy from Copeland who was going to marry her, much to Leafy's satisfaction.

As we chugged across the bay toward the channel through the islands, toward the last burnt orange sunset line, the first stars were visible. Chook, with a holiday gaiety, had changed to what she called her clown pants, stretch pants that fitted tight as her healthy hide, patterned in huge diamonds of black, white and orange, very high-waisted, and with it a white silk blouse with long full sleeves. She moved in dance steps, brought the helmsman a lusty drink, lucked onto a Key West station doing the best efforts of the big bands of yesteryear, and turned it loud. Between her dancing, her happy jokes, her bawdy parodies of the lyrics she happened to know, she would bustle below and take a few pokes at what she promised would be a gourmet adventure. She turned us into a party boat.

We were in the winding and sometimes narrow channel between the mangrove islands when I heard a curious sound which I thought came from one of my engines, as if something had caused it to rev up. I checked the panel and saw that the rpm's were normal. Chook and Arthur were below. The loud music had masked the sound I had heard.

But I heard Chook's scream. And just as I did, I saw something out of the tail of my right eye and turned and saw, in the deceptive dusk light, the empty white boat moving astern of us, turning slowly as we passed it. The boat I had seen on the trailer in Boone Waxwell's yard.

There is damned little you can do in a narrow channel. I yanked the twin levers into reverse, gave the engines one hard burst to pull the *Flush* dead in the water, and put the shift levers in neutral. The only thing that immediately came to hand was the fishkiller, a billy club near the wheel. I forgot the damned leg. When I hit the lower deck it crumpled and spilled me. I scrabbled up and went in the after door to the lounge, into the full blast of the music. Lights were on in the lounge. Mr. Goodman was doing Sing, Sing, Sing, the long one with all that drum. Tableau. Arthur stood in the posture of a man with severe belly cramps, staring at Chookie McCall standing in the corridor just beyond the other doorway, Boone grinning over her white silk shoulder. One arm was pulled behind her. She looked scared and angry. She tried to twist away. Boone's arm went up, metal in the hand picking up a gleam from the galley brightness beyond him. It came down with wicked force on the crown of her dark head, and I saw her face go blank as she fell forward, falling heavily face down, with no attempt to break the fall, landing half in and half out of the lounge. With one bare foot he tentatively prodded her buttocks. The flesh under her circus pants moved with an absolute looseness, a primitive and effective test of total unconsciousness. When faking or semiconscious, those muscles will inevitably tighten.

Arthur, with a groan audible over the drum solo, charged right toward the muzzle of the revolver Boone had clubbed her with. Boone merely squatted and put the muzzle against the back of Chook's head and grinned up at him. Arthur skidded to a clumsy, flailing halt and backed away. Waxwell shifted the revolver to his left hand, put his right hand to his belt, deftly unsheathed the narrow limber blade. He moved forward a little, picked her head up by the hair, put his right hand with the blade under her throat and let the head fall, forehead thumping the rug. Arthur backed further. Waxwell aimed the gun at my belly and made an unmistakable gesture of command. I tossed the fish club onto the yellow couch.

"Cut the music off!" Waxwell yelled.

I turned it off. The only sound in the silence was the idling rumble of the diesels.

"McGee, you want your bilges to pump pink for the next three month, nobody gets cute. Right now we got things to do. McGee, you get on up topside and keep this barge off'n the stubs, and ease on back to my boat, very gentle. If you can transmit from topside, I'll hear your power generator whine, and I'll slice this gullet here wide open. Arthur, boy, you get you a boathook and fish up the bowline and make it fast when we come up on it, hear? Now *move!*"

It did not do me a bit of good to realize how he had managed it. He'd been tucked back into some little bayou under overhanging mangrove, had let us move by in the narrow channel, all lights and music, and then had come out and come up on us in a fast curve from astern, up to the starboard side, amidships, making the roaring sound I had heard, had cut his engine, jumped and grabbed the rail, come in through the doorway onto the side deck to take Chook unawares in the galley, gun in his hand.

We were in a turning drift toward a channel island, and I eased it away from trouble, put one engine in forward and the other in reverse to bring it cautiously around within its own length. I needed no special warning to watch for stubs. Tide currents undercut the old islands. Mangrove and water oak settle deep and die, and the above-water parts weather away. But the underwater segment hardens, usually one blunt-tipped portion of the main trunk, curving down to where the hard dead roots still anchor it. It will give when you run into one, spring back and maybe slide along the hull. But if the angle is right they will punch a hole through one inch of mahogany.

I brought the *Flush* around, then scanned my spotlight across the water and picked up the white boat.

"Get it at the port stern," I called to Arthur. When we were on it, I heard it bump the hull once, and looked back and saw him get the line, stoop and bend it around a transom cleat.

"Now you go on just like before," Waxwell bawled to me from below. "Only dead slow. You see any traffic, you sing out. Keep it in mind, ol buster boy. I can as well ditch the three of you and run it myself, so be real good. Arthur, hike your tired ass in here and bring me a bucketa cold water for fancy-pants."

Arthur went below. I kept to the channel, barely maintaining steerage way. I thought of fifty splendid ideas, and maybe half of them would work and all of them would leave Chook shrunken, bleached and dead. In my great cleverness, I had left him with nothing to lose.

As we came out of the channel, moving out toward the sea buoy, and as the first swells began to lift us, I heard voices aft, turned and saw the three of them back there. Chook stood in a listless slump, hands lashed behind her, head bowed, dark hair spilling forward. Waxwell held her with a companionable hand on her shoulder, upright knife clamped under his thumb. I watched Arthur, at Waxwell's instruction, bring the white boat close, refasten it, clamber over and drop into it and hand up a bulky duffle bag, a rifle, a wooden box, apparently heavy. We were past the sea buoy and out into deep water. At Waxwell's orders, Arthur freed the smaller stern anchor, lifted it high overhead and smashed it down into the bottom of the towed boat. He retrieved it by the anchor line, smashed it down twice more. By then Waxwell's boat was visibly settling, and putting enough drag on that stern corner so that I had to turn the wheel to compensate. When the gunnels were almost awash, he had Arthur free the line. He yelled up to me to put the spotlight on it. When it was fifty feet astern, it showed a final gleam of white and went down.

"Give it a south-southwest heading, McGee," he yelled. "Put it up to cruising, put it on pilot, and get on down here."

He sat on the couch beside Chook. He lounged. She had to sit erect, hands behind her, and she kept her head down, chin on her chest. He put us in front of him, a dozen feet away, on straight chairs, with the request to keep our hands on our knees.

He looked at us and shook his head. "Couldn b'lieve my ol eyes. Had to figure to take me a boat. Holed up where I figure the best chance to get me a good one, rough up some of them power-squadron types, get em on the way out from Everglades with the best chance of full tanks, teach em to do exactly like ol Boo wants. And by God here comes this *Busted Flush* I heard about in Marco from when you were anchored over off Roy Cannon Island, folks that rented Arlie Mission's outboard, the one you come to Goodland in with the name covered over. One teeny little son of a bitch of a world. My, my."

He beamed. "Now would you look at ol Arthur there. I plain give him the cold sweats. You know, I heard them Dunnings tooken you in, and you were workin around that part. No need to come look you up, I figured. I needed just one time to put ol Boo's mark on you. Never did think you'd get sassy again."

"Did you kill Wilma?" Arthur asked.

But Waxwell was studying me. "You're more surprise than this broad-ass barge, friend McGee. I'd a swore you were drippin loose brains when I toted you to the car." He chuckled. "Give me a real turn findin you gone. But I figgered it out."

"Congratulations."

"It had to be that fat little son of a gun, Cal Stebber. A smart one. He would have had somebody along on account of Arthur here wouldn't be any use to anybody. Come took you outen the car to take you to get patched up. It was you got him worked up about me, McGee, lettin him know whereat Wilma was seen last. So I figger after I drove off, he went on in and shot them two dead, phoned in my license, knowing he could lay it onto me and it would be safer the law takes care of me than him trying it. With me on the run, maybe he even figgers to get aholt of the cash money Wilma was toten, but I have the idea it'll stay where it is till I'm ready to go back for it. That fat little fella messed me up for sure. And kilt off one of the best ol pieces a man could hope to find, afore I even got her broke in real good. But there come ol Boo's luck like always, bringin him one on the same style, oney bigger and younger, hey, pussycat?"

Lazily he touched the blade point to her upper arm near the shoulder. She gave a little jump, but made no sound. The fabric was pulled tight where he had touched. A bright red dot appeared where he had touched.

"You did kill Wilma," Arthur said.

Waxwell gave him a pained look. "Now Boo isn't one to waste somethin that fine. Little tiny bit of a gal, but I tell you, she was just about as much as ol Boo could handle. What happened, Arthur boy, she liked thangs real rough, and I guess it was the second night after you were there, we boozed up pretty good and it went wrong somehow, caught her wrong some way, and wrenched up her back, real bad. She couldn't even get up onto her feet come mornin. And my, how she talked mean, like she was the queen and I was some bum. I was supposed to lift her gentle into the car and tear-ass off to a hospital. But I felt right sickly, said I'd get around to it sooner or later. Never did hear such a dirty mouth on a woman, the thangs she called me. And she wouldn't be still, even when I asked her nice. So I went over there and, just to give her the idea, with my thumb and finger I give her one little quick pinch in her little throat. She looked up at me and her eyes begin to bug out and her face gets dark red. Her little chest was pumpin, tryin to suck air in. I must have bust somethin. She waved her arms, flapped around a little, shoved her tongue out and next thang you know, she's dead as a mullet, her face all purpled out. Arthur, I sure didn't mean to do it like it happened, but after I been through her stuff, I found enough cash money, had I knowed it was there to start, I'd done it more on purpose. She's up the Chatham River, boy, down in the deep end of Chevelier Bay, her and her pretties sunk down with cement block, wired real good, even that little diamond watch down there with her, because enough money can make a man afford to be smart."

"Half smart," I said.

He looked at me with mild disapproval. "I tried to like you, boy, and I just couldn't work it out."

"You bought a lot of fancy gear with that money, Boo. It makes people wonder where you got it. And bought a scooter for poor fat little Cindy. That attracts attention. You tried to make me swallow a clumsy lie about a girl who looked like Wilma. You got nervous about me and went flailing around, getting Crane Watts all rattled. Hell, man, you didn't even get rid of all Wilma's stuff. How about the black lace pants Cindy tried to get into and couldn't?"

"I din find them until . . . you're all mouth, McGee. Cindy told you that, hah? What else she talk about?"

"Everything she could think of."

"I'm going to get back to her some day. And real good. Enough talkin. I got to look this boat over. Arthur, you go find me some pliers and some wahr. Move, boy!"

When Arthur came back with them and went slowly toward Boone, even I could tell he was going to make a play. I gathered myself to do what I could, feeling no optimism. There was a clumsy rush, a fleshy smack, and before I was halfway up, Arthur was tottering back to turn and fall heavily. I sat down again. Arthur sat up, his eyes dazed and his mouth bloody.

Boone lifted Chook's heavy dark hair out of the way, took the top of her ear between thumb and finger and laid the knife blade against her temple. Without any trace of anger he said, "Just one more time, one more little bitty thing, and I slice off this pretty little piece of meat and make her hand it to you, lover boy."

Arthur got slowly to his feet. "Now you pick up that wahr and pliers and wahr McGee's ankles together, and when he lies down and puts his arms around that table leg that's bolted fast to the deck there, you wahr his wrists good."

In a little while we were neighbors, Arthur and I, tightly and efficiently wired to the adjoining legs of the heavy wall table, and Waxwell had gone off to make a tour of inspection of the *Flush*, pushing Chook ahead of him speaking to her with that same heavy, insinuating jocularity I had heard him use on Vivian Watts, saying, "That's right, that's fine. You just go along there, pussycat, and ol Boo'll stay right with you. My, my, you a big sweet piece of girl for sure." His voice faded as they went past the galley and staterooms toward the bow.

"My *God*, my *God!*" Arthur moaned.

"Steady down. Aside from one damn-fool play, you're doing fine."

"But she acts half alive."

"She's still dazed. That was a hell of a rap. He did it very neatly, Arthur, getting aboard. We have to just hope he's smart enough to know he needs us."

"What for?" he demanded bitterly.

"If he doesn't know, I'll tell him. They'll check all boats leaving the Everglades area. He'll have to have us handy to get us a clearance, while he keeps us in line by staying out of sight with a knife at her throat. So we wait for a chance, one that we can make work."

"He'll never give us one. Never."

"Let me take the lead. Try to be ready all the time. Your job is

Chook. She's his leverage. The minute I make a move, your job is get her away from him. A flying tackle, anything."

They came back to the lounge, Boone chuckling to himself. "You got this thang as prettied up as a Tallahassee whorehouse, McGee. This big old gal says her name is Chookie. Now ain't that one hell of a name? Come on, darlin. We're goin to see what she's like topsides."

After they went out, I said to Arthur, "Act as if that last punch broke you down completely. You're whipped. It will make him less wary thinking he only has me to watch."

"But, my God, Trav, if he . . . if he leaves us right here like this and takes Chook back there and . . ."

"There won't be one damned thing you can do about it, I can do about it or she can do about it. It will happen, and be over and done, and we'll still have exactly the same problem."

"I couldn't stand that."

I did not answer him. I felt a change in movement of the boat and knew he was at the topside controls. He added rpm to both engines. They were out of sync at the new throttle setting. In a few moments he smoothed them out. I identified the clunk as he put it back into automatic pilot.

He brought Chookie back into the lounge. "Sure can't turn much knots in this tub. But she's fueled up and got a good range. I figured the heading to the Marquesas Keys, McGee."

"Congratulations."

"How it's goin to work, we're goin to cut between Key West and the Marquesas, then make like we were headin along the keys to come on up to Miami. But what we're goin to do, we're goin to cut it real real wide outside the keys, and come dark tomorrow night, we douse all runnin lights and run for Cuba as fast as this here bucket will go. Time them Cuban patrol boats intercept us, the only folks aboard will be a poor simple ol backwoodsy guide and his real quiet lovin girlfriend, both running from the capitalists. If you both behave nice, I'm goin to set you loose in that little dinghy halfway to Cuba. If you make me one piece of trouble, you get to go swimmin with an anchor. Clear?"

"Yes, sir. Mr. Waxwell sir."

"Now if I was half smart, like you claim, McGee, I'd just run this sweet thang back into that big bed and settle my nerves down a little. But she feels poorly and it would play pure hell if somebody run up to check us over. So once we pass a check, there's time to wahr you on up again, hoe this beard down, rench off the swamp water in that fancy shower and bed this pretty thang down."

I could turn my head and look up at them. Boone turned her, snipped the scrap of nylon line from her wrists with a flick of the knife blade, scabbarded the blade and snapped the false buckle into place. He turned her around and she stood staring dully down at her wrists, rubbing them. He took the revolver from the waistband of his pants where it had been snugged against a softness of belly.

"Now you gone be a sweet pussycat. You see this here? You gone go hot up some food for ol Boo. He's gone loose these boys for a time, and you play any games, he goes eenymeenyminey, and whichever one it comes out, ol Boo blows his kneebones to pebbles."

She gave no sign of hearing or understanding. His right hand flickered, cracked her cheek so hard it took her a quarter turn around, making her take a long step to catch her balance. He pulled her back by the arm and said, "I getten through to you, gal?"

"Please, please," she said in a wan little voice.

"Sure hope you got more life in you on your back, pussycat, than you got on your feet." He fondled her roughly and casually, breast and belly, flank and hip, while she stood flatfooted, enduring it like a mare at an auction. He pushed her toward the galley. She took two jolting steps to catch her balance, and then walked on slowly, not looking back. She could have been, I thought, in a sleep-walking concussive state, or it could be her own game of possum. If the former, it might deaden things for her. If she was being clever, I had to be alert for the opening she wanted to give me.

When Boone bent over Arthur with the cutting pliers, I tried a little idea of my own. "Better do me first, Boo."

"Why?"

"I've got the reserve batteries on charge, and there's no regulator on that bank. It's past time to change back. I go by an estimate of time. It could burn them out. So if you set me loose first, then you can take me forward so I can switch them over."

"Now why you fret about batteries that ain't hardly yours anymore?"

"It's rigged so the lights feed off the bank being charged, Boo, and if the lights went out all of a sudden, you might get nervous with that gun."

"That's being right bright there, buster boy."

He released me and, when we went forward, gathered up Chook

from the galley and brought her along to prevent her going to the lounge and releasing Arthur. He wasn't going to make any obvious mistakes. As I went forward, ahead of the gun, I was trying desperately to figure out a problem in compass compensation. The compass that controlled the automatic pilot was set well forward, away from any chance bulk of metal which could put it off, cased in a wooden box in a sort of flat shelf area forward of the forward bilge hatch. I wanted to change the automatic pilot direction from southwest to southeast. Okay, so I had to move magnetic north . . . to the left. And with north behind us that meant I had to put my hunk of metal . . . this side of the compass box and to the left. And it had to be a guess. If I pulled it off too radically, Waxwell would feel the change when we corrected onto the new course. And too small a change would do us no good. And there was nothing down in that hatch that had anything to do with batteries. But I kept a big wrench down there, in a side rack, one too big for the toolbox. And there was a switch down there, obsolete but never removed. It had run a separate forward bilge pump before I had put the three of them on the same control. I had to move fast, and in the dark. I yanked the hatch up, told him to hold it, and dropped down. I got the wrench on the first grab and slid it onto the shelf, behind the purposeless switch and changed the blade from up to down. I waited a few moments, pushed the wrench closer to the compass.

"Climb on up out of there, McGee!"

"All done," I said cheerfully. I jumped up and sat on the edge of the hatch, feet dangling, casually examined my knuckle as if I had barked it.

"Come on!" he said impatiently. As I turned to climb out, I found the wrench handle with the side of my foot and pushed it further toward the compass box. I sensed the course change then, stumbled on the edge of the hatch, fell clumsily to create a diversion. He moved cat-quick out of reach, letting the hatch slam, keeping the gun on me.

"Foot's asleep from that wire, Boo," I said apologetically.

"Get on back to your chair, boy."

Back in the lounge, as if in answer to a prayer, I heard a beginning patter of light rain on the deck above. I doubted Waxwell had the training to use the navigation aids aboard to figure a position, but I knew damned well that he could take one glance at the stars and know the heading was way off.

Arthur and I sat on the straight chairs. Waxwell instructed us in how to act if we were intercepted by launch or float plane. He would be below, with the girl tied and a knife at her throat. And if we were boarded, he estimated he had a good chance of taking them.

"Was that the gun you had the silencer on?" I asked him.

"Damn mail-order thang," he said. "Too loud. Tried it one more time once I got home that night and it pure blew all to hell."

Chook came shuffling listlessly in with sandwiches and coffee for him. He took the tray on his lap, sat her at his left, held the knife in his left hand close to her ribs, put the gun on the couch at his right, kept his eyes on us as he wolfed the sandwiches. I tried to get some clue or signal from Chook. She sat dull-faced, hands slack in her lap, staring at the floor. The diesels were roaring at high cruise, setting up little sympathetic vibrations, rattlings and jinglings. The Gulf was as flat calm as I've ever seen it, and the gentle rain continued. I knew that sooner or later he would go up top and check the control panel and the compass direction. I knew I had altered it, but I had no way of telling how much. I wanted to delay him. I looked at my watch and saw to my surprise it was nearly ten o'clock.

As he put his empty coffee mug down I said, "Want to hear on the radio how they're about to catch you?"

"Let's have a good laugh, sure thing."

I went over and spun the dial on AM, brought in Key West, and was pleased to hear them give national news first, ten minutes of it. Boo sent Chook to bring him more hot coffee.

"And on the local scene, the big hunt for Everglades killer Boone Waxwell has shifted abruptly to a new area tonight. Just as authorities were beginning to fear that Waxwell had slipped out of the net in the Clark River area, two small boys, skiff fishing in the islands west of Chokoloskee Bay, returned home to Everglades City at dusk to report seeing a suspicious-acting man in a boat that tallies with the description of Waxwell's boat in which he made his escape from the Caxambas area."

"Swore them little bastards din spot me," Boo said.

"Based on the boys' account of details not released previously, authorities are convinced they saw the fugitive, and all efforts are now being concentrated on sealing the area and conducting a massive search beginning at dawn."

"Well, I just *did* get out of there in time now," Waxwell said.

"But they'll have our name and description from the Rod and Gun," I told him, "and I'll bet you they're trying to raise us on all bands right now. They'll start an air search for us at dawn, Boo baby."

With furrowed brow he held his hand out for the coffee. Chook came slowly toward him, dragging her feet, the mug steaming. She reached as though to put it in his hand, then hurled the contents at his face. He could have seen it only out of the corner of his eye, but quick as she was, he was quicker, reminding me of the way he had almost gotten to me to stomp me before I rolled under his boat. He got his face and eyes out of the way, but a dollop of the boiling brew hit him across the throat and shoulder. With bull-roar, he was up off that couch, knife in the left hand, pistol in the right. By then I was in midair, launched at his knees. As he spun away from me, he took a flashing slice at Chook, and she evaded it only by the speed of a dancer's reflexes, jumping back, curving her body, sucking her belly away from the very end of the blade. I rolled up onto my heels, squatting. Arthur was trying to edge around behind him, a heavy pottery ashtray poised.

Boo backed away, put the gun on Chook. "In the belly," he said tightly. "That's where the bitch gets it. Lay that down gentle, Arthur boy. Back away, McGee."

I knew from his eyes we were not going to have another chance. Not now.

And then there was a funny hollow thump from up forward, and then a horrible smashing, thudding, grinding, ripping noise, with the bow going up, canting, slowing so abruptly we were all staggered. She is not a fast old lady, but she has thirty-eight tons of momentum. To a boat owner, a noise like that is like hearing the heart torn out of you, and it froze me in place. And Arthur, still staggering, hurled the ashtray at Boone Waxwell. Sensing something coming, Boone whirled to fire. Arthur confessed later he had hoped to hit Boone in the head. The broad dimension of the ashtray hit the hand and the pistol as Boone was swinging it around. The heavy pottery broke into a dozen fragments and the pistol went spinning toward Chook's feet. She pounced on it and came up with it, holding it in both hands straight out in front of her, eyes squinched, head turned slightly away from the expected explosion. It made one hell of a *bam* in the enclosed space. Boone tried to run to get behind Arthur, but ran right into the chair I threw at him. Another wild *bam* from the pistol in the hands of the very earnest brunette convinced him, and he ran out onto the afterdeck. The poor old diesels were still laboring, trying to shove the *Flush* all the way up onto the island. He scurried to the port side and swarmed up the ladderway to the sun deck. I started after him and Chook yelled to me to look out. She braced herself on the tilt of deck and fired up at him. Maybe Waxwell thought to go forward and jump off onto the mangrove island. But the determined girl apparently convinced him he should take to the water. The forward twenty feet of the *Flush* was wedged up into the mangrove tangle. When he ran across the sun deck, I ran across the afterdeck, nearly knocking Arthur overboard.

I got around the corner in time to see him make his leap into the black water, a dozen feet short of the mangrove roots. He jumped high and wide to clear the narrow side deck, jumped feet first like a kid going off a high board. He hit just where the bright galley lights shone out the port, silvering the water. You expect a great splash. He stopped with a horrid abruptness, the waterline still a few inches below his belt. He remained right there, oddly erect, silent, head thrown back, cords standing out in his neck. I thought he had wedged himself into a shallow mud bottom. But then I saw he seemed to be moving back and forth, a strange sway like a man on a treetop. He reached down to himself, putting his hands under the water, and he made a ghastly sound, like someone trying to yell in a whisper. He turned his head slowly and looked toward the three of us. He held his right hand out toward us, opened his mouth wide and made the same eerie sound once more. Then he bowed slowly to us, lay over gently, face down. Something seemed to nudge at him from below, nudge him and shove him free, and as he floated toward darkness, slowly there reappeared, with a slowness that told of the length of it that went down through black water to the dead root system, just an inch or so showing above water, the dark rotted end of the stub, four or five inches thick, upon which he had burst himself and impaled himself.

Chook was clinging to Arthur and crying as though her heart had broken.

Her arms went around his neck, and the gun slipped from her slack fingers, put a little dent in my rail before plopping into the sea. I sent them inside, got a light and the longest boathook, went to the starboard deck, hooked him most gingerly by the back of his shirt collar, towed him forward and hung him against the small dark shoots of the new mangrove sprouting at the waterline. Only then did I remember my laboring engines and run to turn them off before they burned out. Arthur sat in the lounge in the big chair, Chook in his lap, all arms wrapped tightly and all eyes closed, making no sound and no movement. I crawled the bilge with the big flashlight, looking for some little hole the size of a motorcycle sidecar. Probably some seams were sprung, but she looked sound. Surprisingly sound.

When I went back through, Arthur asked me if he could help. I took him aft and we sounded all around the stern area with boathooks and found there was plenty of water back there. I sent him forward in the bilge with a light and a little emergency horn on a compressed air can to give me a blast if broken mangrove trunks started to come in.

I tried to back it straight off. I got about a yard with full throttle, thought things over, then tried one forward and one in reverse to swing the stern. It swung, with an unpleasant crackling sound from up forward. I had noticed that the compass put us on a dead easterly heading at the time we hit. It'd gotten more change than I'd hoped for. Figuring time, we couldn't be very far south of Pavilion Key, maybe halfway down to the Chatham River. I backed, gained a little more, swung it the other way, backed again. After the fourth swing, she suddenly came all the way off, making very ugly noises.

I backed clear, turned her, put her on pilot on a due west heading, and at very meager rpms, went scrambling down to the bilges to see how she was. And she was, astonishingly, bone-dry sound. Apparently the hull shape had just pushed that springy mangrove aside.

I located our position with the radio loop, close enough for my purposes. I remembered the wrench and got it away from the pilot compass before I ran us aground again.

A Coast Guard chopper circled us a half hour after dawn, making that distinctive whappling noise. He hung off the stern while we all beamed and waved at him, and finally, after he had done everything but throw his hand phone at us, I gave a great gesture of comprehension and ran to my set. He moved a half mile away so I could hear and came in on the Coast Guard frequency. I was astonished we'd been so close to a maniac like Waxwell, yes indeed. Wow. It makes you think. When we broke off, he gave himself a little treat. He came over and took a long appreciative look at Chook. She had come out in a little flimsy shorty nightgown to wave at the pretty helicopter, and the flyer and his buddy up there swung craftily around to put the rising sun behind her. But the instant he was gone, we stopped grinning like maniacs.

"Is it right, Trav," she said. "All those people hunting and hunting?"

"The tide was an hour past high when I snagged him onto the shore. There aren't any branches over him. They ought to find him soon."

I put her on radio watch, monitoring the Coast Guard frequency. At quarter of eight she came up to tell us they had the body and a positive identification. She looked wan and dreary, and we sent her back to bed. But before she went, she gave Arthur a rib-cracking hug, stared into his eyes with her head cocked, and said, "I just thought I'd tell you something. Frankie would not have done what you did. For me. For anyone. Except Frankie."

After she sacked out, we went through Waxwell's gear. We deep-sixed it, rifle and all. Except something we found in the box under his dehydrated rations. Carefully folded into Saran wrap. Ninety-one brand new hundred-dollar bills in serial sequence.

Chook came up for air at three in the afternoon, all soft and blurred and dreamy.

"What do we do," she said, "anchor for four or five or six days, like on the way over, huh?"

"Okay," they said, simultaneously, and it was at that moment I decided the unexpected nine thousand was a wedding present, if my hunch paid off.

sixteen

My hunch paid off, on the Fourth of July, with perhaps the only beach-picnic reception of the season serving hamburgers and champagne to about two hundred types, from beach bums to a state senator, from waitresses to a legitimate, by blood, baroness.

And on the afternoon of July fifth as I was once again making the motions of assembling the delayed cruise over to the islands, a merry voice called me up from the engine room and there, at my gangplank, slender and graceful as a young birch tree, dressed in a pale high-fashion gray, five matched pieces of luggage standing beside her, cabdriver hovering in the background, stood Miss Debra Brown, Calvin Stebber's disciplined cigar lighter and daiquiri mixer, her crystal-mint eyes alight with mischief and promise.

"It's all right, driver," she said.

He turned to go and I said, "Hold it, driver."

"But darling," she said, "you don't understand. There was this contest, three words or less, how and where and with whom would you most like to spend your vacation, and you *won*, darling McGee. And here I am!"

I slowly wiped my hands on the greasy rag I had brought up from below. "So Uncle Cal got it in his head I got a very nice piece of Wilma's bundle, and you've cooked up something that might work."

She pouted. "Darling, I hardly blame you. After all. But really, I have just been terribly terribly mopey ever since you visited us. You genuinely intrigued me, dear. And this is a very seldom thing with Debra, believe me. Poor Calvin, he finally got so weary of all my little sighs and hints that he told me to come over and get it out of my system before I came down with the vapors or something. I swear to you, dear McGee, this is an entirely personal affair, and has nothing whatever to do with . . . my professional career."

It was a temptation. She was a convincing elegance. Headwaiters would unhook the velvet rope and bow you in. Elegance with the faintest oversweet odor of decay. Perhaps for any man there can be something very heady about a woman totally amoral, totally without mercy, shame or softness.

But I had to remember her, too vividly, lighting Stebber's cigar.

"Sweetie," I said, "you are a penny from heaven. And you probably know lots and lots of tricks. But every one would remind me that you are a pro, from Wilma's old stable of club fighters. Call me a sentimentalist. The bloom is too far off the rose, sweetie. I'd probably keep leaving money on the bureau. You better peddle it. Thanks but no thanks."

The lips curled back and her face went so tight, I saw what a pretty and delicate little skull she'd make, picked clean, as Wilma's now was, in the dark bottom of Chevelier Bay. Without a word she whirled and went off toward the distant cab. The driver looked at me as if I'd lost my mind. He managed three bags on the first trip, and came after the others at a trot, looking whipped with a salty lash.

I don't know what it is that makes that difference. I don't know now, and maybe I never will. Maybe the people who fit have some forlorn fancy about perfecting themselves in their own image, about living up to some damned thing always a little out of reach. But you try. You reach and slip and fall and get up, and you reach some more.

I went below, slapped a wrench on a nut, put my back into it, and took the hide off the top of three knuckles. I sat down there in the hot gloom like a big petulant baby, sucking on my knuckles, remembering the shape and sway of her in gray, walking away, and thinking some of the blackest thoughts I own.